O'TKAN KUNLAR
(BYGONE DAYS)

O'TKAN KUNLAR (BYGONE DAYS)

BY

ABDULLAH QODIRIY

TRANSLATED BY

MARK REESE

EDITED BY

UMIDA HASHIMOVA AND
UMIDA KHIKMATILLAEVA

Library of Congress Control Number: 2019914747

Copyright: 2018, Number TXu002087519 O'tkan Kunlar, Bygone Days, Nashville TN

ISBN: 978-0578467290

Published by Muloqot Cultural Engagement Program

https://theuzbekmodernist.com/

Back cover photo: Abdullah Qodiriy (from the Qodiriy family's private collection, used by kind permission)

Translator: Mark E. Reese

English editor: Anne McPeak with Sal Robinson and Alexandria Laureys

Uzbek editors: Umida Hashimova and Umida Khikmatillaeva

Front cover artwork: Gulzor Sultanova

Cover design and interior layout: Andrew Staniland

This book would not be possible without the generous support of:

MR. FARID MAQSUDI

MR. FARHOD INOGAMBAEV

MR. ROBERT BUZAN

and

AMAKI, MR. EDWARD RICORD

IN MEMORIAM

God takes the best of us first and it is to them that I dedicate this book:

David Oleg Reese, beloved son of Mark and Yelena Reese. Thomas Sandve, beloved son of Bill and Rahima Sandve. Umar Siddiqov son of Otabek and Khurshida Siddiqov. Sakina Hunsicker, beloved daughter of David and Mamura Hunsicker. Abdullaziz Muhammadkarimov, father, patron, and selfless supporter of Uzbek culture. Henry Janiszewski father, husband, friend and bon vivant. Sonja Kwis Hendrick the teacher who showed me the way. This last March, we lost Nortoji Imamova—wife, mother of many, source of strength.

Professor Ilse Cirtautas of the University of Washington passed over the summer. Her incalculable contributions to Turkic Languages and Literatures is without peer. She will be sorely missed.

CONTENTS

Foreword to *O'tkan Kunlar*   1

Introduction   3

Acknowledgments   11

About the Translation   15

Volume One

From The Author   23

Chapter 1 *(Otabek, Son Of Yusufbek Hajji)*   24

Chapter 2 *(A Young Man Suitable For The Khan's Daughter)*   32

Chapter 3 *(Bek In Love)*   40

Chapter 4 *(He Does Not Like The Weather In Margilan)*   43

Chapter 5 *(If Only I Had This Kind Of Son-in-Law)*   46

Chapter 6 *(Bloody Clouds Over Tashkent)*   53

Chapter 7 *(Responsibility)*   56

Chapter 8 *(Congratulations!)*   61

Chapter 9 *(Welcoming)*   67

Chapter 10 *(Toi, Kizlar Majlisi)*   71

Chapter 11 *(An Unexpected Happiness)*   78

Chapter 12 *(Slander)* 83

Chapter 13 *(Jail)* 88

Chapter 14 *(Seeking Help From Tashkent)* 97

Chapter 15 *(Tashkent Under Siege)* 99

Chapter 16 *(Azizbek)* 102

Chapter 17 *(Yusufbek Hajji)* 107

Chapter 18 *(Announcement)* 111

Chapter 19 *(The Verdict)* 116

Chapter 20 *(Languishing For Freedom)* 124

Chapter 21 *(Revolution)* 128

Chapter 22 *(One Poor Miserable Wretch)* 133

Chapter 23 *(Musulmanqul)* 139

Volume Two

Uzr 151

Chapter 1 *(The Aspirations Of Parents)* 152

Chapter 2 *(Will You Not Forget Me?)* 162

Chapter 3 *(The Sash Of Mad The Gourd)* 176

Chapter 4 *(The Hindu Jodugar)* 181

Chapter 5 *(Treachery)* 192

Chapter 6 *(Burning With Fever)* 200

Chapter 7 *(Qutidor Expels Otabek From His Doors)* 209

Chapter 8 *(Happiness And Unhappiness)* 217

Chapter 9 *(What To Do For One Who Cannot Forget)* 232

Chapter 10 *(Who Cries The Most Among Us; Or, In The Grip Of Suffering)* 236

Chapter 11 *(Navo; Or, Melody Of The Novel)* 242

Chapter 12 *(Horrifying News And A Terrible Night)* 247

Chapter 13 *(An Unsmiling Happiness)* 251

Chapter 14 *(On The Trail Of The Enemy)* 263

Chapter 15 *(Monday Night)* 273

Chapter 16 *(Recognising Himself)* 278

Chapter 17 *(The Sympathetic Murderer)* 284

Volume Three

Chapter 1 *(Musulmanqul's Tyranny Finds Its End)* 299

Chapter 2 *(Dark Days)* 312

Chapter 3 *(The Massacre Of The Qipchaqs)* 319

Chapter 4 *(It Is Impossible To Hide The Moon With An Apron; Or, Murder Will Out)* 327

Chapter 5 *(The Letter)* 331

Chapter 6 *(Capricious Uzbek Oyim; Zainab's Sorrow)* 334

Chapter 7 *(Meeting Of The In-Laws)*   342

Chapter 8 *(Underlying Hostility)*   347

Chapter 9 *(Hajji Shakes The Hem Of His Robe; In Which He Renounces Worldly Affairs)*   353

Chapter 10 *(Hasan Ali's Trick)*   356

Chapter 11 *(Kumush's Word Game)*   362

Chapter 12 *(A Kundosh Will Always Be A Kundosh)*   369

Chapter 13 *(We Will See Each Other In Better Times)*   382

Chapter 14 *(Khushroi Bibi And Zainab)*   392

Chapter 15 *(She Comes To Her Senses)*   397

Chapter 16 *(Her Delivery Date Nears)*   402

From The Author   418

Endnotes   421

Bibliography   487

Reference Materials   493

Special Thanks For Contributions   494

FOREWORD TO *O'TKAN KUNLAR*

A Universal Melody That Chooses No Time Nor Place

The venerable Uzbek people originally occupied a vast area ranging from Siberia in the north to Turkistan and Afghanistan in the south. It is well documented in historical and literary sources that we engaged for centuries in a cross-fertilization of economic, cultural and scientific knowledge that moved forward the march of humanity. Unfortunately, either through the vicissitudes of time or through human indifference, since the 1920s artificial boundaries have dampened that give-and- take. This is particularly true in the region of Turkistan where barriers between the peoples of Uzbekistan and Afghanistan persist to this day.

And as with our own disjointed and divided lands, I wonder then how to best create closer ties between Uzbekistan and America? Ten centuries ago our countryman Abu Rahan Beruni in his Codex Masudicus exhibited great prescience in discovering the Earth's circumference, thus theorizing the existence of the Americas: "We propose a land exists beyond our own known world." One thousand years later we find ourselves arriving full circle from Al Beruni's prophecy through relations between Uzbekistan and the United States—and in the spirit of his work we should see a literary and cultural exchange.

We Uzbeks especially need to familiarize our own community of creatives engaged in literary endeavors with the full landscape of American literary production—not only well-known writers such as William Faulkner or Langston Hughes, but also contemporary ones such as Margaret Atwood. On their end, I believe that it would not be a great stretch of imagination to add Abdullah Qodiriy to that canon of writers. As you read his novel *O'tkan Kunlar*, decide for yourselves if our hero Otabek would be as at home on the streets of New York as he was in Tashkent and Margilan. What about the humanitarian spirit of Yusufbek Hajji with his flowing white beard rendering aid to the suffering in

1

Washington, D.C. or in Oxford, Mississippi? Isn't Uzbek Oyim with her sharp tongue standing as mistress over her domestic domains someone you might know? Or, would it defy credulity to imagine the same strength of spirit in our Uzbek women exhibited through Kumush in your own American cities and small towns?

Those who appear to us in the novel are not just literary constructs solely concerned with Uzbek identity, but also universal symbols imbued with the same spirit of America. We must recognize that those esteemed and beloved characters that form our novel's narrative also exhibit the same sense of dignity and achievement characteristic of Americans. Our mutual values of what is good and true should persist, forever instilled in each other's culture. I believe that Mark Reese's loving translation of Abdullah Qodiriy's novel *O'tkan Kunlar* into English has achieved that end.

Literature forms the foundation of a people, of a homeland through its timeless draw upon a universal consciousness. It gives purpose and enlightens the soul through the melody of the human heart. That melody gives form to humanity, if we will only listen. In that thread I believe that if the message of the novel *O'tkan Kunlar* were to make its way into the hearts and minds of readers in America and around the world, even a small precious sliver, it will become a part of them and lift them up, making content the spirit of my grandfather Abdullah Qodiriy in his place of rest.

With great respect and affection,

— Khondamir Qodiry (October, 2019)

INTRODUCTION

Og'rinqning tuzalasi kelsa, emchi o'z oyog'i bilan kelur. (Chagatai)
Og'riqning tuzalgisi kelsa, emchi o'z oyog'i bilan keladi. (Modern Uzbek)
If pain desires succor, the healer will arrive soon to render aid.
— *O'tkan Kunlar*

Abdullah Qodiriy wrote his classic origin story of the Uzbek people, *O'tkan Kunlar*, at a time of great tragedy and triumph when the cultural landscape of Central Asia grappled with the countervailing forces of reform and modernity. He was born on April 10, 1894 and died during Joseph Stalin's Great Terror on October 4, 1938. Qodiriy belonged to a short-lived phenomenon of Central Asian intellectuals known as the Jadid movement which are now largely lost to general western readerships. Hailing from what is now the Republic of Uzbekistan, the Jadids represented a generation born in Turkistan—an area that comprised most of the Former Soviet Central Asian Republics, Northern Afghanistan and Xinjiang. Their lives straddled Tsarist rule, the Bolshevik Revolution and the delimitation of borders that created the Central Asian Soviet Socialist Republics in 1924. Qodiriy's world witnessed great promise through the rise of ideologies that were poised to disrupt the socio-cultural makeup of societies on a global scale. Advances in technology gave impetus to forms of expression that helped solidify national identities. By the time of the publication of *O'tkan Kunlar* in 1926, Central Asians witnessed revolution, famine, civil war and ethnic violence not just as distant global events but as a part of their daily lives.

Central Asia before Russian conquest could be described as the classic ecumenical society of the Turco-Persian-Arab-Indo world. The Jadids' overall political agenda represented that of many colonized peoples at the time—reform, modernity, self-rule. Drawing upon their rich Central Asian heritage in order to recast disparate, nascent ethnic identities into a form suitable to their idea of a nation state was central to their agenda. Their weapons were the products of the Enlightenment: the printing press, the

3

journal, the novel, the play, the implementation of agrarian and medical reform.

A great deal about the Jadids has filled academic papers both in Uzbekistan and the West. Debate continues regarding the exact nature of the movement: Where did they lie on the spectrum from Avant Garde to traditionalist? Were they dedicated Communists, or Muslims, or both? Did they seek reform within the framework of Islamic Law? A compelling body of evidence shows that the Jadids were not the only reform minded individuals in Turkistan at the time, but that the Khanates and Emirate too attempted internal reforms in the face of a globalized world. Perhaps the especially diverse ethnic makeup of the Qoqan Khanate, where the novel is set, forced the ruling Shahrukhid dynasty to constantly accommodate and balance the interests of the various contending factions within their court. This style of leadership had a profound influence on attempts at self-rule post-Bolshevik Revolution, as seen through the short-lived Qoqan Autonomous Republic whose multi-ethnic makeup selected a Kazakh as their first leader.

With *O'tkan Kunlar* then, we not only gain insight into the Qoqan Khanate twenty years before the Russian conquest of Tashkent. We also witness an indictment of the political, economic, and cultural shifts that wracked early 20th century Turkistan. Qodiriy in his novel uses the tropes of Memory and Loss to warn his readers not just of the death of the ecumenical world typical to the Central Asia of his youth; he foretold what the dissolution of his hopes and dreams for reform held for their own lives– we will have our world dictated to us, we will forever pine for the lost hope of self-rule.

Many of the issues that Central Asians faced in the early part of the century have eerie parallels to our own period Post-9/11: What is the role of Islam in society or government? What is the role of women in Islam? How should we counteract corruption? What defines a marriage? How will we define ourselves? How will we define ot hers? In Qodiriy's case especially, in doing so, how do we maintain our humanity?

Abdullah Qodiriy came from a family of simple means. Through his own force of intellect, he managed to achieve both a Madrassa and modern education, most notably through the Russian model. Comfortable in Turkic, Persian, Arabic, and

Russian, Qodiriy began his career as a scribe for a Tashkent merchant but found his way to the Briusov Institute to study journalism in Moscow by 1924.

His two main novels, *O'tkan Kunlar*, or *Bygone Days*, and *Mehrobdan Chayon*, or *The Scorpion from the Mihrab*, set the standard for Uzbek prose and provided the benchmark for aspiring Uzbek authors. *O'tkan Kunlar*, written between 1920 and 1926, was initially printed as a serial in the journal *Inqilab*, or *Revolution*, before being consolidated into one text. His plays, such as *The Pederast*, depicted the moral degradation of Central Asian society, in this case through the trials and tribulations of a Bacha, or dancing boy. The appeal of theater to Qodiriy and his colleagues (the writer Cholpan rendered Shakespeare's Othello into Uzbek) was the ability to reach a largely illiterate society through a well-established oral tradition—much of the dialogue in *O'tkan Kunlar* seems formulaic as if meant for theatrical performances.

A salient characteristic of all of Qodiriy's work is that he drew upon the lives of all strata of Central Asian society to render his prose into a language evocative, humorous, and often dripping with irony and sarcasm. His readership recognized his writing as their own colorful linguistic cacophony that meant everyday life in Turkistan: Old, dying Chagatai usages, the language of Babur and Navoi, slowly made way for modern Uzbek. The once permeable line between Turkic and Persianate languages solidified along national lines—hence the complicated relationship between their offspring Kazakh, Kyrgyz, Uzbek and Tajik. The colonial reality of Russian with its promises of upward social mobility and a reorganized society became an irresistible pull.

The Turkic literary language Chagatai was seen as the natural progenitor of the Uzbek language for purposes of reform. Persian is for literature and the court, Arabic for the law, and Turkic for war was a time worn adage that harkened back to Alisher Navoi's period. The Jadids 400 hundred years later were forced again to argue that Uzbek was perfectly capable of handling the demands of modernity—a debate still ongoing today. The transition from Chagatai to modern Uzbek is a complex discussion delving deep into the bowels of linguistic inquiry. The quote sited at the beginning of the introduction is a small sample of the orthographic and grammatical changes that took place to reform the old into the new. We should know, however, that the Jadids were central to the effort to create a modern idiom suited for the demands of their day.

After the publication of *O'tkan Kunlar* to great acclaim, Qodiriy found himself in jail for deploying his characteristic wit against Akmal Ikramov, the First Secretary of the Central Committee of the Communist Party of Uzbekistan, in the journal *Mushtum, The Fist*, where Qodiriy served as Editor. Upon release Abdullah Qodiriy refrained from working in the press but continued to translate. He is well known for having rendered Nikolai Gogol's *Marriage* and Anton Chekhov's *The Cherry Orchard* into Uzbek. Both plays were controversial for their period and closely mirrored Qodiriy's own agenda of depicting the benefits and pitfalls of social reform. Throughout the 1930s he continued to write and eventually became a delegate to the Uzbek Soviet Socialist Republic's (UzSSR) Writer's Union—an organization established in 1934 meant to consolidate disparate literary groups and modulate writing along Soviet ideological lines. Interestingly a year before the establishment of the Writer's Union was published for the first time in a Latin script, Yana Alif, rendered from the original Arabic script, Yana Imla. Shortly thereafter Qodiriy's work was vilified as nationalistic and antagonistic to Soviet rule and he was again arrested in December 1937, and executed in October of 1938. *O'tkan Kunlar* was subsequently banned and illegal to own. Such is the emotional dissonance of Abdullah Qodiriy's work and life that he was the first of those murdered in 1938 to be rehabilitated in 1956.

In 1958 his novel was republished in Cyrillic, albeit heavily censored. Almost every Uzbek of that generation can remember the time they were first allowed to own a copy of the novel. After Uzbekistan's independence the Jadids received wide acceptance as the progenitors of artistic expression and martyrs for their fierce convictions in championing reform. Indeed, Qodiriy's prose holds such weight that many Uzbek dictionaries today use phrases from *O'tkan Kunlar* as the basis to explain colloquialisms and obscure usages no longer extent in modern Uzbek.

The narrative of the novel follows Qodiry's hero Otabek through the political and cultural landscape of Turkistan twenty years before Russian conquest. Otabek is the son of Yusufbek Hajji who is a local notable and member of the Ulama in Tashkent. We find Otabek at a caravanserai in Margilan, a town in the eastern region of Uzbekistan, with the Azan, or Muslim call to prayer, sounding throughout the night sky. The Azan sets the daily rhythm of life in the Muslim world, but it is also uttered upon the birth of a child as an affirmation of faith. So begins the life-cycle of Qodiriy's Turkistan and the overall tone of the novel.

Otabek in this initial chapter is pining for the woman he glimpsed on the banks of a stream while performing ablution. That woman, Kumush, is destined to be his bride not through a traditionally arranged marriage but as an act of love—much to the ire of the groom's mother Uzbek Oyim. What follows is a voyage through a world in decline beset by the avarice and corruption of the denizens of the Qoqan Khanate. Qodiriy gifts us with the street life of Turkistan with its chai khanas, shrines and mendicants. We also gain insight into the corruption undermining the court of Khudayar Khan. Matters of good governance, marriage reform, the role of Islam in society, the rights of women, and ethnic tensions between sedentary and nomadic peoples depicted in 1845 as the reason for Central Asia's conquest held as much truth in Qodiriy's own epoch as they did then. Even today the current President of Uzbekistan in his struggle to reform Uzbek society references the novel, especially regarding Kundashlik, or polygamy, as an unassailable literary foundation for his policies.

Indeed, the author's most biting criticisms in the novel point toward the moral turpitude within his own society. The enemies on the horizon that both Otabek and Yusufbek Hajji warn against, i.e. the Russians, are depicted as a force of nature abstract and not yet fully realized. As the novel reaches its denouement the reader can discern the bitterness felt by the author toward his own failed venture of self-rule. Fittingly, as with all life cycles in the Muslim world, the novel ends with the Jannazah, or burial, of our hero Otabek in Tashkent.

Abdullah Qodiriy holds a sacred place in the collective memory of Uzbeks. He bore witness and gave voice to the creation of a world increasingly unfamiliar to his generation, more homogenized, more artificial. In many ways his personal narrative reflected the fates of millions like him who suffered, with great bitterness, from the broken promises of the early 20th century to rewrite society. Yet, Abdullah Qodiriy represents at times an inconvenient hero to the Uzbek people. His life was not that of a distant 15th century ruler, but one within the relatively recent memory of Uzbeks one generation removed from his murder—making his work immediate and relevant to their own circumstances. The very question of Reform infers imperfection. No matter what the issues are that ail a society, whether through external or internal causes, Reform demands that the society in question engages in acts of self-reflection.

So, Qodiriy for many years in post-Independent Uzbekistan did not receive the acknowledgement he deserved. His work was spoken of but in hushed, reverent tones. Dissertations and conference papers were written surrounding his work, but often relegated to a few specialists in Uzbek academia, not constituting a national discourse. His image was often fetishized both in Uzbekistan and the West, but his ideas were never publicly recognized.

Thus, I believe Uzbekistan suffers from a profound crisis of context. With such a rich world heritage, everyone from Europe to the vast landmass of Asia can lay claim to it as their own. One could say, however, that Abdullah Qodiriy's memory and message consciously or unconsciously for years formed the underlining strata of Uzbek identity that the citizens of the republic most desired. When someone in Tashkent lays flowers at a statue of Amir Timur that individual also renders homage to those who died attempting to preserve his memory. When one reads poetry under the shadow of Alisher Navoi's monument, a stone's throw from Uzbekistan's parliament building, they complete the circle that the people of Turkistan began in the early 20th century—a modern state based upon their distinct Turkic heritage, one made on their own terms. Perhaps through the death of Abdullah Qodiriy and his cohort, Uzbeks came to understand that the pain of memory and loss fills the space between surrendering your old world for a new one.

Yet, that new world is now one of their own making. Two years ago, I was invited for the first time in many years to attend a function at the Embassy of Uzbekistan in Washington DC. Ambassador Javlon Vakhabov that week had his diplomatic credentials recognized and the embassy prepared an event to celebrate. What immediately struck me was how un-Soviet the event was. The exuberance of the youth attending was palpable—something I had not seen since the early 1990s. Uzbeks in their 30's and 40's with educations in the West and in positions of responsibility mingled and laughed, excited for the future. Most of the crowd would have had memories of the Soviet period during their early childhood, but it was their parents' historical and cultural reference point. The majority of those attending had their whole lives ahead of them. They knew they were the future leadership of Uzbekistan. As the ambassador delivered his speech, people beamed with pride. I shared in that moment as well. A good portion of my youth was spent handing out exchange applications, starting NGOs, teaching, and, most of all, learning in Uzbekistan, not to mention starting a family. I felt that those around me 20 plus years prior could have been my students and they all turned out well.

That night you could sense a fragile moment of hope for reform in the air. It would demand from those who would pick up the mantle of change to engage in visceral acts of reckoning and reconciliation. It was clear that crowd was up to the challenge. Perhaps it is through the lens of Abdullah Qodiriy's *O'tkan Kunlar* that we can step forward, lend a hand, and have our children measure our success.

*****

Adeeb Khalid, *The Politics of Muslim Cultural Reform, Jadidism in Central Asia* (Berkeley: University of California Press, 1998)

Paul Georg Geiss, *Pre-Tsarist and Tsarist Central Asia* (London: Routledge, 2003): 44–45.

Paolo Sartori, *Moving Beyond Modernism: Rethinking Cultural Change in Muslim Eurasia (19th-20th Centuries)*, Journal of the Economic and Social History of the Orient 59/1-2 (2016)

Devin DeWeese, *It was a Dark and Stagnant Night ('til the Jadids Brought the Light): Clichés, Biases, and False Dichotomies in the Intellectual History of Central Asia*, Journal of the Economic and Social History of the Orient 59/1-2 (2016)

Edward A. Allworth, *The Modern Uzbeks* (Stanford, CA: Hoover Institution Press, 1990)

Scott Levi, *The Rise and Fall of the Khoqand Khanate, Central Asia in the Global Age, 1709–1876* (Pittsburgh, PA: University of Pittsburgh Press, 2017)

Special thanks to Dr. Bahodir Karim—the genuine scholar of Abdullah Qodiriy: Dr. Баходир Карим «Ӯткан кунлар»га кайтиб...Чоп этилган07.02.2016МуаллифZiyouz.uz

ACKNOWLEDGEMENTS

September 2019 will mark the 25th year of my involvement with Uzbekistan. This present translation represents the culmination of a voyage to understand a complex and misunderstood part of the world that has continued to enrich my life. I have met many heroes during this period that have aided me not just with the translation but with the rich and varied life I have been fortunate to live. I owe my gratitude and love to the following:

President Shavkat Mirziyoyev for awarding me the Presidential Order of Dostlik. The Republic of Uzbekistan's Ministry of Foreign Affairs—most notably Ambassador Javlon Vakhabov, Mr. Akhror Burkhanov, and Mr. Rakhmatulla Nazarov.

The United States Peace Corps, Uzbekistan—you are all in my heart. The city of Qoqan for showing me your world.

Lola, Zoya, Munira as my first Uzbek language instructors in 1994. Mirv Ali Ismailov, Larissa Aganjanova, and the staff of the US Peace Corps office in Tashkent for looking over my shoulder. Hajji Bobo and the Badghisi family for their long friendship and feeding me on the road to Termez. Galina Gennadivina, Victor Victorvich Bichkov, the students and staff of Maktab 23, the "Jewish Mahalla" on Oktiyabrskaya, most notably Ibrahimjon, Olmoshon and Saparjon and their families for taking in someone far from home. Ibrahimjon and Saparjon for showing me the grace and beauty of Muslim life in Qoqan, an example of a faith in its purist form. Hakimjon Muhammadeav of Marifat Maktab for his depth of wisdom and love of the Uzbek and English languages. David Abramson for his years of work, truly one of Qoqan's originals.

Professors Cirtautas, Waugh, Karimi-Hakkak, Wheeler, Kuru, and Williams for all their lessons, knowledge and mentorship. Jipar Dushembaeva and her family for showing me Naryn. Ilse for her standards, Karimi-Hakkak for love of the written word, Brannon for all his vast knowledge of religion—I have always carried your lessons with me. Professors Devin DeWeese and Bakhtiyar Babajanov for their advice over the years and phenomenal scholarship.

Al-Bukhari Institute, Tashkent Islam University, Academy of Sciences Department of History, Al-Beruni Institute, Sharq Shunoslik Institute, the University of Washington, the Bureau for Educational and Cultural Affairs, especially Heather Grant and David Hunsicker, the true Turkshunos, for allowing me to establish the grant. Alisher Abidjanov, Umida Khikmatillaeva, and Otabek Saddiqov for carrying on the torch. Umida Khikmatillaeva and Umida Hashimova for their constant support and insight during this long effort. Gulnisa Nazarova and her family for their Uighur language lessons, milliy taom, and warmth of friendship. Christopher Runyan for being the pirate. Qahramon and Kamollidin and the gentlemen of Abu Qassim Madrassa for their artistry. Abdullaziz Muhammadkarimov who stood apart in his kindness and selflessness. The Khidoyatov and Umarov families for offering me assistance when I needed it most. The crowd at Cassandra's—Bob, Bill, Roza, Mark, Ivana, Diego etc. for listening to my ruminations of Uzbek literature.

The translators, interpreters, cultural advisors of Operation Enduring Freedom—for all you did even if no one will remember. The men and women of WWLR and KBR for the strangest ride I've ever had. Rosie for your leadership and honor. Roza for getting me the job. Joe Guido for your friendship and shared pain—any colleague who can talk Betty Friedan in a war zone deserves my enduring respect. Melvin Brown and Mike Zinke for having my back. Lily Taheri for your father's book of Hafez. The folks in Tampa for listening to my tales of Uzbekistan. Kiran Pervez for years of critique and collaboration.

To the midshipmen and military personnel of the United States Naval Academy: you are the best of us. To the faculty of the Department of Political Science for the profound lessons you imparted and your support during a tragic moment in my life. Rae Jean Goodman, Priscilla Zotti, John Freymann, Steve Wrage, Ambassador John Limbert and Parveneh Khonim, for all your compassion.

Many midshipmen crossed my path, but: McKlain, McCreary, Elledge, O'Keefe, Cameron, Kissin, Jan, Scully, Zotti, Bonsall, Atwill, Laureys, Mestre, Davids, Prather, Sandoval, Bentley, Riley, Lodge and the many others who traveled with me, who attended lectures, who took my Central Asian Politics and FP130 course, and comforted Yelena and I during our loss. Sam Oatjudge as Godfather to Michael. Emily Elledge and Polly Kissin for your singular kindness. Julia Beth Grimm and Gary Bloesl for your genuine friendship and shared burdens.

In the Turco-Persian-Arabo-Indo world, if I can extend that term out, there is a concept of Adab—how one comports oneself, decency, kindness. It is also the root for the word Adabiyot, or literature. In a harsh world, kindness is the greatest act of heroism one can exhibit. There are those whose bravery, dedication, and love toward Uzbekistan made this book possible. They stepped forward to help me when it was not advantageous to them, other than their singular service to a higher cause, Uzbek literature: Farid Maqsudi for your trust. Farhod Inogambaev for your leadership. Mis Amigos Kamilla and Nodir Zakirov, Mirjahon Turdiev, the Feminist, the truth-talker, and the servant to those in need. Navbahor Imamova for her patience, strength and profound wisdom. Behzod Elamonov, you are the future. Zulkhumor Mirzaeyeva for your sacrifice—you w ere the first to interview me and it cost you dearly. Munira Nurova for the bravery of your work. Kamilla Sultanova for your energy and support. To Umid Gafurov, Shakhnoza Karimbabaeva, Christopher Fort, Nasrulla Nigmatullaev, Iskandar Madgaziyev, Jabbor Ishonkulov for all your support. Feruza Rashidova of UzTea for your hospitality and leadership. Saida Rashidova for your vision. Filip Noubel of Global Voices for your life well-lived and helping me develop my ideas. Ulughbek of Kokand Silkroad, Azizbek and Khusnaddin for helping me during my trip and general kindness. Alim Anarkulov for the great video! Nigora Umarova for her article in Jahon Adobiyot. Anora Saddiqova from UzA for her interview. Ibrat Jumaboyev for my very first interview at BBC and your friendship. Gavkhar Saidazizov for the book and your confidence. Jennifer Murtazashvilli for being a truth talker. Hamid Ismailov for all your support and your tireless pioneering of Uzbek literature. For Anne McPeak, Sal Robinson, and Alexandria Laureys for their editing skills! Edith Grossman for her knowledge of translation. Gulzor Sultanova for your artistry and grace in creating the book cover. Andrew Staniland for his eagle-eyes.

To the Qodiriy family: without the writings of Abdullah Qodiriy our world would be a dimmer place. The strength of your name a nd the kindness and hospitality you have me shown during my struggle to make this book a reality has given me the strength to persist. I hope this translation does not betray your confidence.

To my dear wife Yelena for your love and depth of patience as I pursued this obsession. To my sons David and Michael—you are the blood of my heart and my greatest achievement. Mom, Dad, Sheryl, David, Ed, Tom, Kayla and Meghan, Erin, Alex and Ethan many thanks for your love and patience as I traveled to the other side of the world. To Oleg, Tatyana, Kapitalina and Mathias— all my love.

The Four Horsemen of Litchfield Park, Arizona, brothers for life.

ABOUT THE TRANSLATION

Translation should be a derivative Art. Grammar and usage represent guideposts to the translator who attempts to transfer the author's voice and cultural milieu to a reader often on the other side of the globe. No two translators will ever agree on a final rendering of a text—nor should they if the end result is to be a meaningful contribution to literature. Turkic languages present many challenges in attempting to render them into a European language. Sentences tends to run on taking a long circuitous journey to their destination, if one is even sought. Idiomatic phrases lose their depth when translated into their English equivalents. The renowned Turkish language translator Maureen Freely best describes the Turkish author Orhan Pamuk as engaging in a narrative trance through his writing. In that vein I tried to render the *O'tkan Kunlar* into a language that is accessible to a general readership, or someone attempting to learn English, yet give Qodiriy's audience a sense of the unique culture that made up his world.

The text is full of old Chagatai usages that were finally erased with the development of modern Uzbek. Persian phraseology is employed by Abdullah Qodiriy as he attempts to capture what Devin DeWeese called the 'multi-valent' society of Turkistan before the delimitation of borders. The novel is so rich in opaque idiomatic expressions that almost no one in Uzbekistan completely agrees upon their meaning. The inherent challenges of translating Qodiriy's prose into English is further undermined with a dearth of source material in English to aid the translator. One often has to rely upon anecdotal information as original materials are often guarded jealously by those engaged in literary production in Uzbekistan. Finally, I followed the original formatting of the novel in all its incongruities so the reader gets a sense of a writer engaged in a pioneering work.

Inevitably the translator must retell the tale in a language familiar to his or her target audience yet strike the balance of remaining true to the author's voice. As with Freely, I agree that western readers are often coddled with clumsy attempts to bring

Turkic phrases etc. into a western idiom. Those efforts often fail and reduce the original to a two- dimensional extraction. In that vein I wanted to preserve the title of the novel in its original— *O'tkan Kunlar*—out of respect for the sacrifices made by the author and my love of the Uzbek language. To know the name of something in its original form in my view is the greatest way to render it homage.

Also, it's time for the world to learn some Uzbek. The same policy applies towards key terms in the novel. They are recognized from Turkey to India, and now even Whole Foods markets. Naan is naan, not bread. Naan is a product of the soul and we must know it as such. The same applies to my endnotes. They are meant for the reader, if they so choose, to learn more about the complex historical, cultural and linguistic landscape of Qodiriy's period, as interpreted by me over a twenty-five-year period.

What I hope for most with this version of Abdullah Qodiriy's *O'tkan Kunlar* is that it begins a dialog outside the normal channels available since 1991. I hope that it inspires a greater movement towards collaboration with the wonderful people of Uzbekistan. Perhaps travelers will read the book while touring the country and find greater context to what they see. If young translators in Uzbekistan are inspired to attempt their own works of creative endeavor, I will consider this all a success.

All the victories in this novel belong to the people of Uzbekistan; all the defeats are mine.

O'TKAN KUNLAR
(BYGONE DAYS)

VOLUME ONE

FROM THE AUTHOR

Since it seems we have set foot in a new era, fine, we should follow the spirit of this new age and its innovative forms of expression and, just as with those who wrote *dastans*, we should renew our creative impulse through the novel and the short story— and in that vein, I am also driven by a sense of obligation to familiarize our people with the Tahirs and Zuhras, the four dervishes, the Farhads and Shirins, and the Bahram Gurs of our time.

As such, I have had a strong desire to experiment with our era's means of capturing the creative impulse, namely the novel, and in so doing, I have fulfilled my goal by producing *O'tkan Kunlar*. One could say that people can only further advance their skills through slow, methodical development and through meeting their shortcomings face to face at the outset of their endeavor. My wish has been to put this aphorism to test and not shrink in fear from my many failures and setbacks, which are often attached to one so overly enthusiastic.

They say that history will teach us the mistakes of the past. With that in mind I have drawn upon the darkest and filthiest days of our history, not so long ago, mind you, that being the epoch of the khans.

— Abdullah Qodiry (Julqulboi)

1

OTABEK, SON OF YUSUFBEK HAJJI

It was the year 1264 of the Hijra,[1] the seventeenth day of Dalv, a winter day. The sun descended into the horizon as darkness set in, and one could hear the call to prayer resonating in clear tones throughout the still evening air...

Built to face the southeastern gate of the city, a well-known caravanserai teemed with merchants hailing from Tashkent, Samarqand, and Bukhara, all of whom were settling in for the night. These traders, finally free of the day's burdens, had just returned to their small cells and were preoccupied with the cooking of supper. Compared to the still daylight hours, a lively atmosphere permeated the caravanserai: it was as if the rooftops themselves were lifted to the sky by the raucous banter and the merchants' roaring laughter.

At the far end of the main yard, a room stood apart from the others through its singular beauty: while the other rooms bore only felt rugs, this room displayed deep-red carpets; while others laid their heads on cotton quilts, here the owner slept among silk and *adras*[2] bedding; while the other living quarters reeked of the soot of blackened lamps, this small room was lit with a single brilliant candle; and while the other tenants displayed a carefree and facetious nature, the occupant of this room appeared to be cast from another material altogether: He was a young man of thoughtful mien whose downy moustache had just recently emerged. An imposing build lent him gravitas, and he had a light-skinned, handsome face with dark brows and pensive eyes that seemed perpetually lost in thought.

We must not linger too long on frivolous worldly concerns, yet the young man's room drew one's attention not only through the finery so lavishly laid out in it, but also because the room itself seemed to mirror the thoughtful quality of its inhabitant. The man we describe is Otabek, son of Yusufbek Hajji; a man born from a line of well-respected Tashkent notables.

On this particular evening two men entered through the main gate of the caravanserai, one of them inquiring from a local denizen:

"Has a man who goes by the name of Otabek stopped here?"

The man motioned toward Otabek's door in response. Taking their cue, the travelers made their way in the direction of the room we described a moment ago.

The first of the two associates had a small frame and a round face that bore a newly matured beard. He might have been entering his twenty-fifth year, barely a man; he went by the name Rahmat. He was the son of Ziyo Shohichi, a notable well known as one of Margilan's[3] cultivated elite. The second man was about thirty-five years old, gangly, with a swarthy, pockmarked face, beady, stone-gray eyes, and a tangled beard; he gave off a vague sort of unseemliness difficult to pinpoint but nevertheless present. Even though he possessed considerable means, his notoriety grew not from his wealth but more from the carnal aspects of his nature—he was a well-known womanizer. In fact, nobody would recognize him from his name alone. When people gossiped behind Hamidboi's back, they added the epithet "the womanizer."[4]

Hamid had never met Otabek. Since he was Ziyo Shohichi's brother-in-law, he had felt compelled to accompany Rahmat on this trip, fulfilling his duties as an uncle.

When the two entered the small room, Otabek greeted both as welcome guests.

"We are sorry, dear Bek," Rahmat apologized, "we regret inconveniencing you." Otabek appeared unperturbed by the disruption and motioned for them to sit in the place of honor.[5]

"You do not bother me in the least bit; on the contrary, you lighten my heart with this unexpected visit. This is my first time here. I have no friends or relatives in Margilan, and my unfamiliarity with the city and inclination toward reclusiveness has driven me to distraction."

An older man entered the room, greeting the guests with salaams as he did so. The man, known as Hasan Ali, was approximately sixty years old, with a long, solemn, pallid face, a pronounced forehead, and a long snow-white beard. He had round

25

black eyes, and though the whites were yellowed with age, they seemed to pierce through all artifice.

Though the feathery down of his beard attested to years well spent, one would never have been able to guess that he was of advanced age. His youthful vigor and ageless complexion did not betray his years. After reciting the Fatiha[6] for the guests sitting around the coal *sandal stove*,[7] Otabek asked Hasan Ali, "Are you well, Father?"[8]

"Thank God," said Hasan Ali. "The coal smoke made me a bit queasy.

I am much better now."

"If you would do something for us..."

"What is your command, my son?" Hasan Ali asked Otabek.

"Thank you, Father. I would be grateful if you would prepare us some tea."

"Fine, my Bek,"[9] Hasan Ali replied, leaving the room to complete this request.

After once again conveying their heartfelt greetings and good wishes,[10] Rahmat asked Otabek, "What is your relation to that gentleman, Bek- aka?"[11]

Otabek looked at the door, hesitating before answering Rahmat's question. With Hasan Ali a safe distance from the room, he spoke quietly so as to not offend him.

"He is our slave."[12]

Hamid was surprised by Otabek's explanation.

"Your slave?"

"That's correct."

In Hasan Ali's youth, Otabek's grandfather had bought him for fifteen pieces of gold from a Turkmen slave trader who abducted people from Iran. Hasan Ali had been a slave in Otabek's household for approximately fifty years. Over the years he had earned a place as an honored member of the family. He exhibited great devotion to his owner Yusufbek Hajji,[13] but even more so to his master's son Otabek. In his care for Otabek, he was the personification of duty and devotion; one could see that they held each other in high regard by their camaraderie and mutual affection. Although when he had turned thirty the family had procured a wife for Hasan Ali as due reward for his devotion, he had yet to sire a child who survived infancy. As solace, Hasan Ali was loyal to Otabek as only a father could be toward his son. He wished only one thing in return.

"After my death, if Otabek recites the Quran on behalf of my soul, commemorating the fact that at one time there lived a man named Hasan Ali Ota,[14] that would be all I need to rest my bones in peace."

It could be said of him that he was an *Oq Kungli Odam* who humbly beseeched Otabek to fulfill his final wishes and in turn received assurances that they would be fulfilled.[15]

Once the tale of Hasan Ali's origins had been relayed to the group, Rahmat asked Otabek, "What did you bring from Tashkent, Bek-aka?"

"Just some trifles: fabric, leather boots, and a few pots."

"Margilani fabric and leather boots sell quickly in the bazaar," commented Hamid.

Otabek leaned forward with a pair of scissors and intently trimmed the wick of the candle so that it would burn brighter.[16]

At that moment a palpable uneasiness descended upon the guests, stealing from them the initial joy of meeting and causing them to cast furtive glances at their host.

An intractable silence persisted upon each attempt to move the conversation along, and, as each failure mounted, a pregnant pause ensued, compounding everyone's mutual embarrassment. Rahmat sought to move the discussion forward by prodding the others.

"How do you find Margilan? Do you like it?" he asked.

Otabek fidgeted and hesitated to answer the straightforward question.

"How to put it... as a matter of fact, I like Margilan...[17] Indeed, Margilan is the best city in all of Turkistan[18] for silk weavers and such," Otabek answered.

Hamid and Rahmat looked at each other: had that been an attempt to brush off the question? Sensing that they might have been offended, Otabek seemed to snicker at his own clumsy, half-hearted reply and explained, "From the moment I arrived, Margilan began to wear on my nerves. Perhaps it is because I have no friends here... I immediately felt like an outsider... Presently, Margilan pleases me because I have dear visitors such as yourselves..."

"Please forgive me, Bek-aka," said Rahmat. "I heard just today of your arrival in Margilan from my father. If I had known sooner, I certainly would not have left you to your own devices or allowed you to sink into boredom like a stranger."

"Truly?"

"Yes, that's the proper thing to do in this situation. When my father goes to Tashkent, he immediately heads to your house, but you stopped at this caravanserai instead. No one would blame us for taking insult."

"You are right to be offended," conceded Otabek. "But first, finding your home was a challenge; second, the camel drivers were appointed to this serai, leaving me no choice but to follow."

"That is no excuse for your remaining aloof..." said Rahmat.

Hasan Ali entered with a teapot, spread out the tablecloth, and offered a basin so that the men could wash their hands.[19] With the time-honored exchange of compliments, inquiries as to one another's health, whether they found themselves too bored, how life treated them, and various other sundry pleasantries, the hosts began the custom of attending to their guests' needs.

Hamid absentmindedly mopped up *shinni*[20] with a piece of bread and asked, "How old are you, Bek?"

Before Otabek could even move his lips from the cup, Hasan Ali answered for him.

"If God grants him life in this Year of the Monkey,[21] Bek will turn twenty-four."

"I have reached my twenty-fourth, but truly I am not sure exactly how old I am."

"You are twenty-four, Bek," Hasan Ali insisted.

Hamid continued his line of questioning: "Are you married?"

"No."

Hasan Ali, unsatisfied with this abrupt answer, broke in on Otabek's behalf once again. "We wished to find a girl for the bek, because, first of all, he is destined for matrimony, it is the natural course of things; but previously he resisted the idea, so we could not plan a wedding for him until now. The honorable Hajji's hope is to arrange a marriage for Otabek upon journey's end."

"My thoughts lead me to believe that there is nothing in the world more disastrous than marriage," said Rahmat, turning to Otabek. "After marriage, if your wife's character is suitable, all is well. Otherwise, it is the most painful ordeal anyone can undergo in this world."

Otabek seemed to warm to Rahmat's view. "No doubt your words carry some truth," he said, "but we must add that although the woman must be suitable to the man, the man must also be suitable to the woman."[22]

"As far as I am concerned, from a man's perspective, I don't think we need to take into account whether a man suits a woman's tastes," said Hamid a bit abruptly. "For a woman, just having a husband is in itself sufficient; as my nephew states, if the woman suits the man, that is the only consideration that matters."

Rahmat turned his head and flashed an ironic smile at Otabek. Otabek's expression paid Rahmat in kind as he then looked at Hamid with a great deal of skepticism.

"Within the institution of marriage, freedom of choice belongs solely to our parents," said Rahmat. "It falls to our parents to marry us off. They are unconcerned with whether their selection of a bride pleases the son or not. If the parents find the bride pleasing, that is enough. It is unseemly for the daughter or the son to say no to their parents; it is against our Shariyat.[23] Let's say I married in order to please my parents, but my wife is in keeping with my parents' tastes, not mine; and, as you have said, maybe I am also unsuitable for my wife... you have a point, Bek-aka."

Otabek listened attentively to Rahmat's views and turned to Hamid as if to say, What will you say to that?

"Nephew," said Hamid, looking at Rahmat. "First, of course your marriage is for your parents; it is not your place to take offense at your parents' decision. If your first wife is not suitable, take another one that suits your tastes—have two wives. If this does not work, take a third. Complaining that one's wife is not to one's taste and whining aloud to everyone is unmanly."

Rahmat again smiled knowingly at Otabek, replying, "When you take another wife, your suffering will be only greater. What good will that bring?" he asked. "It is fitting to pass through life devoted to one wife. I seem to recall... aren't you yourself one of those men with two wives? In your house, hostilities are an everyday affair and shake the roof; no peace can be had, not even for a minute."

"For a stripling such as yourself, of course, even one woman is too much," said Hamid, sniggering. "What do you mean, I am tormented by too many women? If blood falls in drops from the horse whip, you can enjoy life among even a hundred women. I am not tired, the fires of conflict and strife are inconsequential to me, and presently I am even entertaining the idea of making room for a third woman in my household!"

"You have no peers in this regard, Uncle..."

Hamid beamed proudly at Otabek as if offering a challenge. As for Otabek, he only sat, bemused by the colorful exchange. Hasan Ali made his exit again to prepare the plov[24] and Otabek poured the guests more tea once Hamid's screed came to an end. Upon Hamid's final word, the debate cooled. The three of them stared off in different directions, deep in some hidden recesses of their minds, pondering some unseen issues. Moments passed lost in contemplation, until Rahmat asked his uncle, "Have you heard whether Mirza Karim-aka has given his daughter's hand in marriage to a suitor?"

For some reason known only to Hamid, this casual gossipy question transformed his face, ruining it. He set his jaw, as if preparing to confront the unwelcome topic, which perhaps threatened some hidden, tender hope. He sought to dismiss the subject, muttering under his breath, "I haven't heard a thing. It's probably just rumors, probably nothing has happened."

Rahmat, attempting to keep the conversation from falling into a lull again, declared to Otabek, "There's a girl in Margilan... Such a beauty! I think she has no equal; in all our city, I have seen no beauty to rival her own."

Hamid glared at his nephew and affected calm as he attempted to mask the signs of a gnawing obsession. Oblivious to his uncle's demeanor, Rahmat blundered on. "In our city there is a merchant, Mirza Karimboi. She is his daughter. Maybe you are familiar with Mirza Karimboi—he used to work in the bazaar as a tax collector when he was in Tashkent?"

"No, I don't know him."

Hamid's countenance now appeared stricken, as if he were losing his patience. Nevertheless, Rahmat continued. "His house is situated on the corner of the shoe market. He is very wealthy, and he is well known among Tashkent's elite—because of that, your father may know him."

"Perhaps," said Otabek, seized by an involuntary shiver as if chilled by an unseen draft. His face shifted from its usual calm to a strange, slight swaying from side to side. Rahmat seemed oblivious to the onset of Otabek's nervous condition, but Hamid noticed the subtle change, discreetly following every move of Otabek's face, every change in posture that seemed to betray some secret torment. It was difficult to discern whether Hamid's notation of the seemingly inconsequential ripples of emotion coming from Otabek revealed some unknown design. Perhaps it was just an innocent curiosity. They lapsed into another unfortunate silence.

"Now, when will you be our guest, Bek-aka?" Rahmat's question shook Otabek from his trance.

"When time permits, God willing."

"No, Bek-aka," said Rahmat. "You must arrange a day. We came here with the express purpose of extending an invitation to you."

"Calm down... what is the hurry?"

"There is nothing to worry about. If you agree, we intend to move you from this serai to our home. Let us agree on a day suitable for you to be our guest. My father is eager to sit with you and talk about the situation in Tashkent."

"It is inconvenient for me to leave this serai at this moment," said Otabek, "but I am ready to visit your father anytime."

"Fine, Bek-aka. Can you name a time to visit?"

"As you know, in the evenings, I am free. At the same time, I would never refuse your father's hospitality, nor his convenience."

"Fine," said Rahmat. "I would like to ask one more question: Would you be offended if people unfamiliar to you attended our gathering? But I would like to add that they would be our closest associates, such as Mirza Karim..."

Otabek flushed a shade darker at this last request but quickly recovered his composure. "To me it makes no difference."

After the plov was finished, the guests said their farewells and parted ways.

2

A Young Man Suitable For The Khan's Daughter

Otabek's eyes passed again and again over the two strangers greeting him—clearly showing wariness about their intentions... Ziyo Shohichi noticed his apprehension and introduced them to Otabek: "Naturally, you are unacquainted with these gentlemen," he said. "Let me introduce one of your father's closest friends, Mirza Karim Qutidor,[25] as well as Akram Hajji, a merchant from Andijon." Mirza Karim Qutidor appeared to be about forty-five years old, with strong brows and dark eyes; he was well dressed and had a handsome face. Akram Hajji was roughly fifty-five years of age.

Otabek again regarded Mirza Karim.

"Thank you for introducing me to my father's closest friend, taksir," he said, showing his deference toward Mirza Karim and Akram Hajji. "My father also entrusted me with paying his compliments to his dearest friend..."

"Thank you, we wish you health and very much appreciate your greetings," they replied.

Ziyo Shohichi's household was hosting the party. Those attending were Hamid, Rahmat, and Hasan Ali, as well as the individuals just introduced—and all were assembled in Otabek's honor. After their introduction, Otabek's and Qutidor's eyes met. Qutidor attempted to ask Otabek something, but Akram Hajji and Ziyo Shohichi continued to ramble, cutting him off.

When their eyes met a third time, Qutidor smiled and asked, "Do you remember me?"

Otabek, giving him his attention, answered, "No, Amaki."[26]

"How old are you?"

"Twenty-four years old."

Qutidor seemed to be engaged in some sort of reckoning. "Perhaps you cannot remember me," he said. "You were a five- or six-year-old boy when I lived in Tashkent... It seems like yesterday I was last in Tashkent and a guest in your house... But really, more than fifteen years have passed since then, and you have become a young man... Life seems to have shot past like an arrow."

"You have been to our house?"

"I have been a guest on many occasions," said Qutidor, "when your grandfather was still with us."

Leaning into the edge of the conversation taking place next to him,

Hasan Ali put in a few words: "His Honor came to our house many times to visit. You were very young, Bek," he said. "Your uncle would occasionally take you with him to the serai."

Otabek gave Qutidor a shy smile.

"I regret not being able to recall your visits," he said.

Qutidor wanted to brush away his embarrassment, but Akram Hajji cut him off, asking, "Your father, Hajji Akamiz,[27] what work is he doing these days?"

Otabek said, "He is the adviser to the bek of Tashkent."

"Azizbek[28] is still the mayor of Tashkent these days?"

"Yes, he is."

"Betrayer Bek, be gone! Aziz the Bacha!"[29] scoffed Hamid, whose broad grin, aimed at Akram Hajji, seemed to insinuate some sordid knowledge. "Muslim Cho'loq's gatherings have recently reached a most lascivious level because of Azizbek's incessant pursuit of cavorting with the *bachas*." he guffawed, beaming proudly at all those gathered as if he had arrived at some earth-shattering revelation, some profound truth. As for those witnessing the strange, indecorous, even illicit display by Hamid, it only produced an exchange of raised brows.

Several moments passed among the circle of men as they attempted to gather their thoughts, until finally Akram Hajji broke the spell, asking, "I've heard that your hakim of Tashkent is quite the tyrant. Is that true?"

"Absolutely true," said Otabek. "The population tires of Aziz's oppression."

Otabek's unvarnished answer struck not only Akram Hajji dumb, but all those present. To speak so boldly and openly about Azizbek's abusive rule was inconceivable, especially considering Azizbek was his father's own master.

All of Ferghana[30] knew of Azizbek's reputation as one of the most despotic and coldhearted leaders in all of Turkistan, a ruler who governed the population of Tashkent[31] with a heavy-handed and chillingly brutal authority. However, the underlying purpose of Akram Hajji's line of questioning was to determine the loyalties of his dearest friend's son. He was not disappointed by the thoughtfulness of his response. He looked wonderingly at Otabek, but he nevertheless maintained his distance, since Otabek's honesty could be nothing more than a cynical ruse to conceal some deeper motive not yet revealed.

"Your father is Azizbek's adviser," said Akram Hajji. "Why can't he exert some influence over Azizbek and guide him away from his present course?"[32]

"Alas, Amak," said Otabek, smiling. "You seem to have misjudged the importance of my father's rank. As for our laws, it is impossible to enact them when the leadership undermines them by passing extralegal, cruel judgments. Even if my father is considered Azizbek's closest confidant and adviser, his is just a title with no power; Azizbek only heeds my father's advice on superficial matters. I will give you an example, something that happened recently. During a Friday gathering, a man praised Azizbek. Another man confronted this supporter, retorting, 'Why do you praise Aziz, a man whose sole experience is that of a bacha?'

"A spy eavesdropping on the debate went to Azizbek and informed him of the contents of the discussion. The next day, Azizbek summoned these two men. He assigned to the man who had praised him an important position and sentenced the other to death. When my father, present during the sentencing, appealed for leniency regarding the condemned man's fate, Aziz shouted to the executioner, 'Dispatch the condemned man immediately!' When my father again appealed for leniency on the man's behalf, Azizbek joked that 'Maybe we should send Hajji to this man's same fate.' So, you see how he is valued?"

"Then why don't people petition or protest against this sort of behavior?"

"Ask me how many complaints we have submitted already..." said Otabek. "In addition to those filed by the victims of Azizbek's oppression, we have sent ten complaints... but what can we do if Azizbek's master is many times more disheartening? One point I must bring to light: Recently Azizbek has begun to ignore Qoqan's orders and decrees. All our complaints are based on the hope that

34

Azizbek will acquiesce to Qoqan's power, but it could be that Qoqan is turning a blind eye to our petitions for redress. All the same, though the people of Tashkent are fed up with Azizbek's oppression, they do not know where to go to seek justice."

With Yusufbek Hajji's impossible position clarified for everyone, especially Akram Hajji, nobody continued the line of questioning. Since the guests had been invited to share a meal, the dinner table was then prepared for them. Ziyo Shohichi and Rahmat urged on the guests' appetites by encouraging them to take more—Oling, Olinglar!33—yet Otabek ate very little and sat seemingly lost in a daydream. The yet undiscovered reasons for his distraction persisted throughout the meal and remain worthy of our further observation.

While in his meditative state, his eyes unconsciously fell on Qutidor. As soon as his eyes met those of Qutidor, he looked away, picking up something from the tablecloth he had no intention of eating... While the other attendees did not notice Otabek's condition, Hamid continued to watch his every shift in mood...

"What cities have you gone to for your business, Bek?" Qutidor asked.

"I have seen many cities in our country," said the bek. "And I have traveled to the city of Shamai as well."34

"Indeed! You have even been to the city of Shamai?" said Ziyo Shohichi in wonder.

"I went this past year. My visit was most unseasonable, and I endured many hardships."

"You are a true tradesman," said Qutidor. "Even at our age we have not seen our own major cities, yet you have already seen Shamai."

" 'Those who walk are a river; those who sit are a reed mat,' " said Akram Hajji.

Few in Turkistan had ever traded in Russian cities. Otabek, who had actually been to a foreign country, had a unique perspective among the men in the room. Qutidor and Ziyo Shohichi, who had heard all sorts of fantastic tales about Russians, were very interested to investigate the truth of those rumors from Otabek and asked him to give his impressions of Shamai. Otabek relayed his memories of the city. His audience sat fascinated by

Otabek's clear articulation of Russia's political, economic, and social development.

"Before going to Shamai, I thought that all government systems were like ours," stated Otabek, "but my travels there changed this opinion. My experiences deeply affected my beliefs about life, transforming me. When I saw the Russian government's policies, I realized that our leadership's approach and tenets are frivolous, as if we are playing at governance. I cannot imagine what will happen to our situation if our government continues with this current anarchy... When I was in Shamai, I thought that if I had wings, I would fly to my motherland, I would descend directly upon the khan's palace and implement each and every one of Russia's governmental policies.[35] The khan would take heed of my proclamations, writing decrees benefiting all levels of society, ruling by enlightened Russian ideas. In one month I would see my people on the same level as the Russians. But when I returned to my homeland, my dreams and aspirations showed themselves to be mere fantasy. No one would listen to me. Even when there were people who were willing to listen, they would retort, 'Will the khans listen to your dreams, and will the beks even carry them out?' With this simple question they shattered my dreams. At first I could not fathom that they actually believed their own words, but later I found that they spoke the truth. Indeed, who will listen to the prayers of the dead baring their soul to the living? Will those already buried in a cemetery listen to calls for help? Who will listen?"

The group was held in rapture by Otabek's impressions, listening in disbelief to ideas and views they had never before encountered. These "Fathers of Turkistan,"[36] who had never even considered such a course for their motherland, fervently latched onto Otabek's vision of a future that rose deep from within his pure heart and was clearly expressed with the most sublime intentions.

"If we had a khan like Umar Khan,"[37] said Qutidor, "we would overtake those Russians."

Ziyo Shohichi disagreed: "We find ourselves in this situation because of our own behavior."

Not wanting to be left out, Hamid added, "God gave the unbelievers wealth and power."

"In my opinion, maybe the Russians' superior position comes from their solidarity," said Otabek. "We regress more every day, and the reason for this is our infighting.[38] I think, to put it another way, Uncle Ziyo's ideas are particularly poignant. No one among us appreciates the dangerous implications of our present condition. It is just the opposite: There are those who spoil the peace and create conflict. The roots of this conflict and disorder have spread, and each time this tragedy only destroys simple people. Think, for example, of the Qora Chopan and the Qipchaqs.[39]

"Consider this: What benefit do we gain from this conflict, and what do the Qipchaqs really achieve? It is those same leaders I mentioned previously who benefit politically from scattering the seeds of hostility among common people. Who would have thought that the unscrupulous man in this situation is Musulmanqul?[40] What did he ever do for his homeland other than cause bloodshed?

"Without any justification, Musulmanqul invented divisions among us only because of a personal grudge. He provoked a conflict and, for no reason, killed his in-law, Sher Ali,[41] and in turn allowed innocent Murad Khan[42] to be martyred. He then did away with Tashkent's mayor, Salimsoqbek[43]—who was as harmless as a lamb—and elevated a despot like Azizbek to power, Azizbek who then declared himself ming boshi.[44] Impetuous Khudayar Khan,[45] a mere child, became khan through Musulmanqul's backing. Throughout this entire period, he rode on the shoulders of the population. At first, could anyone have blamed Musulmanqul if he undertook these actions ostensibly with the good intentions of destroying oppression and bringing peace to the homeland?

"But in fact, control of Tashkent was delivered to the savage Azizbek by Musulmanqul's own hand. If Musulmanqul is truly a member of the human race—and I have my doubts—it is hard to imagine how a human can give birth to such a savage. Until we shake off the bonds of leaders who secure power through violent means, salvation will never be delivered. Only by eliminating those who harbor ill will toward the people and replacing them with leaders who seek justice and goodness, only in this way will we find our road to redemption."

Otabek continued to expound on innovative and unprecedented ideas to the men at the gathering, all of whom sat in amazement, staring at him with their mouths open... Indeed,

Otabek's ideas about the reasons and consequences of the constant infighting in his land rang true. His ideas gave to those present a means to discover and clarify their own feelings on the subject; he expressed in the open what they had always kept to themselves and never dared to voice aloud.

Otabek went to take ablution.

"He is indeed his father's son," said Ziyo Shohichi, looking at his guests.

"Let him live long and faithful to the call of his heart," said Akram Hajji. "The boy is vastly more intelligent than other boys. If it were in my power to appoint rulers, I would make him a khan... Where did he graduate from?"

Overjoyed by these compliments and unable to contain himself, Hasan Ali replied, "He was one of the leading students at the Beklarbegi Madrassa,[46] but after three years, upon his father's request, he went into trading."

"Allah has bestowed many blessings on the boy," said Qutidor.

They all praised Otabek to the skies, but Hamid remained silent and appeared irritated. Qutidor's questions about Otabek's marital status— and what they had revealed—made Hamidboi especially nervous, and he struggled to maintain the appearance of nonchalance...

But he could only suffer so much through Hasan Ali's insipid responses to these queries, his infernal blathering regarding the bek's unnatural indifference to the fairer sex, not to mention his myopic obsession with his charge's apprehensions about marriage, before he finally lost his patience.

"Maybe the bek believes he is worthy even of the hand of the khan's daughter," he said sarcastically. "People of his sort make girls suffer even if they do finally marry..."

Hamidboi's unprovoked impudence defied all bounds of civility, so Hasan Ali was justified in losing restraint.

"I do not know if fate intends that he marry the khan's daughter," he said, throwing a sardonic grin in Hamid's direction. "However, if the khan accepts him as his son-in-law, he is more than suitable. Even to me, a mere slave bought with gold, he has never once uttered a rude word, so a girl born free should not expect to suffer from this boy. In my view, he is far from the type of person who beats his wife, who marries again and again, and who oppresses women as if they were animals. He is far from that type of person, my brother Mullah Hamid."[47]

We the readers will remember that Hasan Ali heard from Hamid's own mouth that he whipped his wives. Hasan Ali's rejoinder shamed Hamid in front of the others, and he was unable to muster a word in his own defense. Ziyo Shohichi, embarrassed by this turn in the conversation, looked to Hamidboi as if to say, So you got outdone? Then he turned to Hasan Ali and said, "Sorry, Father, our Hamidboi was created for the sole purpose of offending others with the most egregious remarks."

Qutidor came to Hasan Ali's defense: "Your words are true, Father. Otabek is suitable for a khan's daughter."

These words were meant as balm to Hasan Ali's injury, leaving Hamid with no room to continue this war. Hamid's eyes to fell to the ground in mock shame, yet he continued to aim a malicious grin at Hasan Ali.

After the plov, Hamid was the first to make his farewells, and he was soon followed by the others as they spread out to their homes. Since Otabek's way took him on the same road as Qutidor, Otabek joined him. As they neared Qutidor's house, Qutidor said to Otabek, "We expect you to be our guest the day after tomorrow. Are we agreed?"

"Agreed, Amak."

"We are the corner door... Maybe you will be our guest tonight?"

"Thank you, goodbye. Go in health," Otabek replied, neither accepting nor rejecting the invitation.

At last they bid each other farewell.

At that very moment, a shadow crept out from around the corner, wrapped in a *chopan*.[48] This shadow had been covertly observing their conversation, and now it faded away back into the darkness, moving in the direction of the other guests.

3

BEK IN LOVE

The serai already known to us slept peacefully as midnight descended. With a few turns of the key, Hasan Ali undid the lock to their room, entered, lit a candle, and waited for Otabek while spreading out his bedding. Yet, strangely, Otabek remained outside for some time and even when the door to their cell finally opened, Otabek still lingered in the doorway. He was deep in thought and oblivious to everything around him. Yet the door remained ajar as the welcoming candle burned bright and his mattress waited for him.

"I prepared your place for you, Bek."

Barely stirred from his reverie by Hasan Ali's intrusion, Otabek practically sleepwalked into the room, dropping down at the edge of his bed. Hasan Ali waited for the bek to change out of his clothes, since he wanted to take the now fully glowing candle to his own room. However, Otabek continued to sit on his bedding, his mind deep in some trance. To Hasan Ali's watchful eyes, Otabek's demeanor had changed over the past few days, with a strange mood lingering and controlling his every move. This state of affairs alarmed Hasan Ali. The bek seemed to have forgotten that he was among the living, taking no heed of people's presence, as if preoccupied by some other interest. Hasan Ali had observed his melancholy from its initial glimmer to the present moment. At last, Hasan Ali became impatient with Otabek's impenetrable dark mood.

"Do you have anything else for me to do?"

Otabek looked up at Hasan Ali's face, not comprehending the question; his eyes were fixed at some point in the distance. His vacant stare only increased Hasan Ali's anxiety. Hasan Ali did not understand Otabek's condition. Otabek suddenly straightened, aware of the depth of his detachment at last, like a sleepwalker suddenly waking.

"Why aren't you in bed yet?" he asked.

"Do you have anything else for me to do?" Hasan repeated.

40

"What work could I have for you at this hour? You may go and take the candle with you."

Hasan Ali lifted the candleholder and made his way toward his room. His quarters were next to Otabek's in order to protect their goods— fabric, footwear, and sundry other items were piled high on the floor. Hasan Ali spread out his things, silently saying to himself, "*Tavba.*"[49]

Even if a faint awareness of Otabek's mood swings had flickered at the edges of his consciousness, until now, he had not realized the severity of his present melancholy. His descent into a sort of torpor forced Hasan Ali to mull over a myriad reasons for the declining stability of his master's son. Sitting on his bed, lost in thought, twisting his long white beard around his right hand, he considered the possibilities: "Maybe it's financial troubles. He did not eat much at Ziyo Shohichi's house, maybe it's some foreign ailment... could he be sick..." Yet he arrived at no conclusion. Otabek was conscientious about his finances; he never hid them from Hasan Ali. And he would hear complaints from Otabek if he had taken ill.

A multitude of potential disasters spiraled in his mind, obscuring any hope for an explanation or a solution; at last he stood and extinguished the candle that shone in its niche. In the ensuing darkness, he knew neither right nor left, only the pitch black. Feeling his way toward his door, he eased it open as silently as he could and stuck out his head to look about the serai.

Confident no one was around, he crept outside in his soft leather boots and approached Otabek's room, looking around the compound to make sure he was still alone.

Only the sound of horses chewing on hay in their stables and the crow of distant roosters disturbed the tranquility of the slumbering encampment. Hasan Ali lay down beneath the small window of Otabek's room, listening in on its occupant. He heard nothing. Three or four minutes of stillness led Hasan Ali to believe nothing was amiss. As he began to stand up, a heavy sigh broke from the room—"Ouf!"

Hasan Ali shot straight up, pricking his ears, eyes widening and darting about as the strange sigh from Otabek's room echoed in his head. He could only conclude that Otabek was ill. Determined to aid the bek, he grasped the door handle. He was about to open the door and rush to Otabek's bedside, but he stilled his hand—doubting now whether Otabek was indeed ill. At last, he left off debating whether or not he should disturb Otabek's peace and returned to his quarters. But his concern for Otabek increased tenfold. Though he disrobed and lay down to sleep, he could not close his eyes. He pored over the various symptoms of the bek's illness. Before their travels, Yusufbek Hajji had commanded him, "My son is young. Throughout your lifetime, you have experienced the hot and cold of the world. You are also my confidant. Your duty is to mind my son's every step." Otabek's mother, Uzbek Oyim,[50] had entreated him with tears in her eyes, saying, "I entrust Otabek to you, and I entrust you to God." These enjoinders rang in his ears. His sleeplessness persisted. Wearing only a long shirt, Hasan Ali again put on his robe, left his room, and resumed his position outside Otabek's small window, standing guard under it.

A cold snap came on that night, with a bitter wind blowing from all four points, wracking Hasan Ali's body as he sat, half-naked and shivering, by the doorway in the arms of the cold. Yet he managed to brush it aside by surrendering his body to its severity and sending his good thoughts to Otabek's room. He continued to eavesdrop on the room for a long time. Eventually he took a long breath and moved his head away from the crack in the door. Otabek's steady breathing had satisfied his fears. Although he felt immediate danger to his charge had been averted, he remained still. He remained still and sat there, quivering in the cold. Some time passed before Hasan Ali finally calmed down and began to wish for his warm bed. At that moment, he heard from the interior of the room a sleepy voice: "Black eyes, brows like bent bows."

"What?" Hasan Ali exclaimed, again putting his ear to the cracked door. Now his entire body became as one ear as he lost himself entirely and focused all his attention on the inside of the room. A few moments passed and then the same voice, talking in its sleep: "Face is like a moon, smiling up at me, and then running, startled... off..."

Hasan Ali now knew what he couldn't discern the first time; in this second instance, he had discovered the root of the matter. Hasan Ali decided that further observation would be unnecessary. He got up and went back to his room, shaking his head. "Bek is in love."

42

He put his robe on his bed; he lay down under his blankets and asked, from deep within his heart, "Really, truly, is he in love?" Whose daughter could he have met in the course of five or six days in this unfamiliar city? Where could he have met her? Even as he drifted off to sleep, Hasan Ali continued thinking: With whom could he have fallen in love? So wholeheartedly, haunted by her even in his dreams? Thinking about it in terms of Otabek's previous disinterest in women, he could not believe that Bek was in love. But on the other hand, there were those words from Bek's own lips, "Face is like a moon, smiling up at me, and then running, startled," repeating themselves over and over. There could be no other interpretation of Otabek's melancholia in the past few days than the rapture of love! Hasan Ali debated both sides of the dilemma with himself, weighing the different aspects. Though he couldn't believe it, the words "smiling up at me... running, startled" still reverberated in his ears.

As night turned to morning, his sleepy brain could not resolve this puzzle and, as he drifted off to sleep, he decided that tomorrow he would test Otabek to verify that he was, in fact, in love.

4

HE DOES NOT LIKE THE WEATHER IN MARGILAN

The morning tea was prepared by Hasan Ali's own hands. Otabek sat silently while Hasan Ali took note of his mood. The silence between them lingered for some time as they drank their cups of tea. Finally, Hasan Ali surveyed a sullen Otabek several times over.

"It seems to me that you have been despondent these past few days."

Otabek looked at his interlocutor and made a gesture of confirmation. "I don't know," he said, stopping for a moment. "You must be feeling my depression as well. I don't know... Maybe it is Margilan's weather, perhaps it does not suit my temperament."

"It is just as you say," replied Hasan Ali. "The weather of Margilan is horrible. My mood has swung back and forth over the past couple of days. If we don't leave Margilan soon, I think something bad will happen to me."

Hasan Ali fixed his eyes on Otabek. If last night's sleep talking had raised Hasan Ali's suspicions, then he was certain that mentioning an imminent departure would reveal the truth of the matter.

Otabek sensed a dead-end street. Completely hemmed in, he made no response at first.

"We will return," he said after thinking for a while. "Then again, our negotiations for the price of our goods have been unsuccessful. Customers have asked for prices that are too low. For that reason, maybe we will stay for several days longer... I don't know..."

Hasan Ali's test was a success, and he restrained a laugh when met with Otabek's evasion. A tense silence rose between them. Hasan Ali hesitated over whether to speak directly to the issue or leave it alone. He considered himself a trusted confidant and a worthy steward of his ward's secrets, and so he decided at last to speak openly with Otabek.

"My son, Otabek..."

"Please, speak freely."

"What do I mean to you?"

Otabek did not understand his intent and looked at Hasan Ali with questioning eyes. "You?" he said, smiling. "Though you are not my father, you are a man who has loved me with nothing but the most dedicated paternal love. You have always been a faithful and kind presence—hence you are my spiritual, moral father."

"Bravo! My son," said Hasan Ali, "your answer was as I thought it would be. Now I will ask you this: As a slave who is faithful to you, who is, according to you, your spiritual father, would I wish any harm on my son? What do you say to this?"

Otabek, surprised by this unanticipated question, responded, "Although I do not understand your intentions, Father, I will answer. Until now not only myself, but my entire family has considered you a paternal soul guiding us all, because you wish us only goodness and nothing else."

Hasan Ali did not change his tack. "Maybe it was this way before, but now, especially you..."

"Especially me? Please be frank."

"Your trust in me seems exhausted. I would like to know what transgression I have committed against you."

"You speak most strangely," said Otabek, alarmed. "What sort of ill omen do you see in me that would make you think I no longer trust you? There is no need for us to bandy about meaningless words. I rely on your tender mentorship and presence. I believe that my secrets will be kept as if in a mother's womb when I tell them to you. You must believe this, Father."

"But your tongue and your heart are saying different things, my son."

Growing impatient with Hasan Ali's steady rebuttals, Otabek said, "You are mistaken, my father."

"I am not mistaken. On the contrary, I am confident that I am in the right."

"Prove that my tongue and heart are at odds."

Offended, Hasan Ali raised his ponderous brows. "You are keeping some private matter from me."

"You mean I am hiding a secret from you?"

"Yes, you are, my son," said Hasan Ali. "If your declarations are sincere, if you believe me trustworthy, please don't conceal your concerns from me."

Otabek, deflated, scoffed and shook his head, yet he reverted to his former agitation. "Do you think I have a secret?"

"You do."

"Be so kind as to tell me about your discovery."

Hasan Ali raised a cup to his mouth, sipped some tea, and revealed his thoughts. "Since our arrival in Margilan, you have been in a strange mood," he said. "Though you brush this off as 'the bad weather of Margilan,' I have found out otherwise."

Otabek felt compelled to turn his face away from Hasan Ali, who stared hard at him. It was as if this all-seeing old man could decipher all his private thoughts from only the slightest degrees of change in his facial expressions. Feeling Hasan Ali's eagle eye upon him, he scratched his forehead. "Fine, continue."

"If you hide your secrets from me..." Hasan Ali said, fully satisfied now and certain of his discovery. "Very well, maybe you

45

have a right to hide them, but are you going to achieve anything from concealing them in this way?"

Otabek blushed and looked at the ground as if he had committed an egregious sin. As if the embodiment of mercy, Hasan Ali's sonorous, patrician voice broke into Otabek's thoughts and took the unbearable weight off his back

"Nothing is unbearable, my son," he said. "True love is a gem of the heart that very few men receive in their lifetime; at the same time, in most cases, it visits many evils upon a man. Even though it is hard to endure, please do not obsess over your love, it is best forgotten. Do not dwell too long..."

At these words, Otabek raised his head and looked into Hasan Ali's eyes. He took a deep breath and looked at the ground again, as if he wished to follow Hasan Ali's advice. "It is impossible to forget; I haven't the willpower."

A long silence intervened. Both were lost in thought. Hasan Ali had the habit of chewing his beard when he was concentrating on something. Now he was busy twirling his beard as he bit the tips of his moustache.

After much consideration, he resolved to find a way to conclude this lingering issue at a later date. Meanwhile, the feverous tension that wracked Otabek made its return.

5

IF ONLY I HAD THIS KIND OF SON-IN-LAW

"The house situated on the corner of the shoe market..." By now the reader is familiar with the master of this house. Broken down, mottled with handprints, rickety after years of labor, the main gate screeches and moans as if calling for help; in short, if we tried to classify this long-suffering gate, we might put it in the "ancient as history itself" category. After three or four steps through the opening, we are immediately beset with the terrors of Bukhara's dungeons,[51] only finding relief from the light filtering in at the end of a dark corridor—and the hope of an exit. Avoiding a tumble by feeling our way, one shaky step at a time, through the dark prison passage, we happen upon the bank of a flowing stream that meanders through a stone courtyard, and, sighing in relief, we are finally delivered to freedom. It is at this point that we notice a beautiful house with a veranda built on the east side of the enclosure, with its facade facing west; though today it is nothing to boast about, during its heyday the building was considered an example of great architectural refinement and taste. No one is present in the yard or the encompassing building, and so it can be assumed that these initial living spaces are detached from the main abode and function as guest rooms. Small cells with padlocks on their doors stand along the west and east walls. We can surmise that they are intended to store goods—a sure sign that the owner is a man of means. The southern section of the yard is the back wall of the store and is obscured by overgrown cherry trees.

Now we say our farewells to the outer enclosure, move around the Mehmon Khana,[52] and enter the Ich Kari,[53] or inner courtyard, of the complex. The connecting passageway leading to the interior is as dark as the previous one since it is enclosed on all sides. If we turn right at the end of the corridor, we will reach the stables; if we take an immediate left, we will arrive in the main area with an opening as grand as the first one. The four sides of the enclosure are surrounded with buildings serving different functions. The two sides of the main building, the centerpiece, are flanked by large wings that form separate living spaces. Blue, green, and white ornamental tiles juxtaposed with carved wood panels redolent with geometric and floral designs embellish the front veranda, which is supported by four wooden pillars in the center and two pillars on each side, giving the whole architectural piece a sense of balance. In the middle of the pillared veranda sits a man on a raised platform in the place of honor facing the door, wearing an otter jacket lined with black velvet. He sits before a sandal covered with multicolored atlas[54] blankets.

A second introduction for this person is unnecessary, because this man is already familiar to the reader as Mirza Karim Qutidor. On either side of the sandal, a woman reposes. One is wearing a long dress of khan atlas[55] inside a sleeveless silk robe. Over these items hangs a loose white silk scarf. She is about thirty-five, beautiful, and slim. She has a face that personifies kindness as well as modest deference to her husband, without any sign of artifice. She is Qutidor's wife—Oftob Oyim.

As for the second woman, she is an elderly lady of about seventy years, the mother of Oftob Oyim—Oysha Bibi. Near a stone stove sits a woman busy boiling water for tea. She is a tad rougher than the rest and is about forty-five years old. As for her, she is the family servant— Toibeka. For now, we leave our introductions to these ladies and enter the room through a small door that also acts as a window, to the left of the veranda. In the center of this room we see a girl sitting on silk blankets. While lazing on feather pillows, she seems distracted. Perhaps the cold has made her lethargic, or maybe reasons not yet revealed to us hint at a young woman pining away.

Her dusky locks, arrayed carelessly over the pillow, her jet-black eyes under thick curly eyelashes, fixed on one spot as if having a vision... black brows... two thin brows arched, quivering... her face like a full moon, pearly white, slightly blushing, as if embarrassed by someone's presence... recounting the moment, considering it all... At the very moment when her delicate hands twist the blanket, she touches her beauty mark, then takes her head from the pillow and sits up.

Her yellow silk dress cups her petite, well-formed breasts as they heave and fall. After sitting up, she shakes her head, grinning innocently. This movement makes her locks spill over her face—disheveled, as if meant to break your heart. This belle, the very picture of a maiden angel, is the daughter of Qutidor—Kumush Bibi.

For several days, she had complained of a headache and spots in front of her eyes, perhaps the result of catching a cold. Her mother did not wake her from her deep slumber, not wanting her to overexert herself—not even for prayers.

But now Kumush Bibi rose, dressed, and left her room. She washed her face with warm water prepared by Toibeka, returned to her room, dried her face, and went out to the veranda. Greeting those sitting on the platform, she sat near her father.

Qutidor studied his daughter and asked, "Are you well, my daughter?"

"No, dear Father, I still have a headache."

Qutidor put his hand on his daughter's forehead.

"Oh, Kumush! You still have a fever," he said. "You need to take care of yourself, Daughter, wrap yourself up in a thick comforter. If you sweat it out you will brighten up, my dear." He then asked Toibeka to freshenKumush's tea with warm milk.

Oftob Oyim seconded her husband's observation. "She still has a fever; her face is flushed and puffy."

With her weak voice, Oysha Bovi suddenly interrupted their conversation. "Especially last night, you don't know, but she frightened me to death. She was delirious, speaking all sorts of feverish words..."

Kumush Bibi shot a glance at her grandmother.

"This all is because of the fever," said Qutidor. "Today I will consult a *tabib*.[56] My sweet daughter, please drink some tea," he said and again looked her over. After finishing his tea and breakfast, Qutidor recited the Fatiha and rose. To Kumush he said, "Keep in mind I have invited guests today." And then turning to Oftob Oyim: "Please send a servant to tidy the Mehmon Khana. Prepare those newly sewn *korpacha*;[57] let her cover the sandal with them. Lay out the big carpet. Is there any fruit for the table?"

"Yes, there is."

"That's good. In a little while, I will send you to get meat to make us some varaqi."[58]

From the mention of *varaqi*, Oftob Oyim realized this would not be an ordinary guest.

"Who is the guest?"

"You have never met him. He is a young man from Tashkent. There will be three or four other friends as well. Is everything understood?"

"I understand, I understand."

Kumush Bibi paid no heed to her father's instructions. Upon Qutidor's departure for work, Oftob Oyim sent Toibeka to the guesthouse to do chores while she began to prepare the dough. Kumush Bibi seemed gripped by an inexplicable malaise whose origins evaded diagnosis; whether she was consumed by a secret obsession or just suffering from a strong headache, she was impenetrable, like a flower whose tender petals cling to each other in the cold night, refusing to reveal its secrets. Her grandmother attempted to make her laugh with stories and anecdotes, yet she remained still and distant, giving only a half-hearted smile.

Kumush remained in this state for about an hour before finally standing up, sliding her delicate feet into shoes recently purchased for her by her father, and making her way over to her mother, busy in the kitchen with her duties.

As Kumush passed from her seventeenth to her eighteenth year, she was taking on her mother's height and had bloomed into a fuller frame, coming into her own as a woman. She helped a little bit with her mother's duties and then went back outside. Looking out from the veranda, she watched Toibeka, who was preparing the rug in the guest room, but soon gave up on this distraction and leaned against the middle column.

This moving about eased some of her pain—her heart broke free of its burden, and her dark eyes brightened. Her swollen face returned to its natural grace and composure, losing its puffiness. She leaned her weight against the pillar, arched black eyebrows quivering as she gazed at the entryway for some time, then descended the steps from the raised enclosure and moved toward the passage that led to the stream bed.

The stream flowed under a workshop, with part of it twisting three or four steps through the yard into the open air before again disappearing under the bridge house. Kumush Bibi found a pleasant spot near the exposed stream, jumped to the other bank, and sat down. Her eyes gazed wistfully at the water's surface. The exuberant stream purled past as the small waves lapped upward, reaching out to her as if demonstrating their reverence, worshipping her. The water slowly whirled around in circles, spellbound by her enchantments, then rippled farther out into larger rings—where her reflection only made her charms more apparent to her devotee—then slowly passed under the bridge. She stared at the endless flow of water, finally reaching out, cupping her hands, and wetting her face. A couple of drops kissed her, dripping back into the whirling pools below. As they fell it seemed as if the water held a mystical vitality, a whole life of its own.

The stream's ardor reached a crescendo as she passed the water over her face two or three more times. The depths took on a life of their own, as if portending an evil conspiracy hatching deep within, brooding in the cold blackness, a plot to destroy the beauty of her reflection, a harbinger of peril and doom. She washed water cupped in her hands over her pearly white teeth, rinsing them two or three times, then abruptly left the stream bank.

Recovering some of her lightheartedness, she returned through the passageway, and her lithesome frame gained a spring in its step. Oysha saw her and was happy about the change she detected. "Are you feeling better now, Daughter?"

"Thanks to God, I am."

"Don't do anything for now, Daughter. Get some rest."

Short winter days meant that one could barely accomplish anything before sundown. This day darkened like the others, almost without a word. Half an hour after the sun dropped from the silvery, overcast sky, the guests arrived. Qutidor solemnly welcomed them with the openheartedness that was in his nature. Toibeka moved quickly between the male and female rooms, serving refreshments, changing the tablecloth, and handing tea to the guests. After she had finished serving, Toibeka sat down near Oftob Oyim and ate her cold food.

"Who were the guests? Did you recognize them?" Oftob Oyim asked.

"You have not lived until you have seen the youngest guest," said Toibeka, quickly chewing her plov on the left side of her mouth while talking out the right side. "So handsome, so intelligent, so clever, sitting in the seat of honor... it seems that he is not yet twenty years old, his moustache is just now growing. He is a worthy son-in-law for us," she said, laughing, and looked at Kumush Bibi. On hearing this description, Oftob Oyim also laughed and glanced at her daughter.

"Oh dear, Kumush Bibi," she said, "did you hear that? Toibeka has already found a husband for you, but all you know how to do is complain about a headache." Kumush Bibi's slight smile allowed them to glimpse her pearl-white teeth through her ruby lips, yet nothing but cold sarcasm surfaced. "As if your ultimate duty was only to find a husband for me."

Toibeka ignored Kumush Bibi's sarcasm. "My sister, you still don't know," she said. "You should take a look at that young man. You will be left saying 'vai, vai, vai'[59] At my age, I could only hope to have him as a husband," she said, bursting out with laughter.

Kumush Bibi quickly turned her face from Toibeka, who continued, "Marry as soon as you can. I wish I could marry. I am

51

not worth even one of his hairs. But you would equal him. Equal with equal, type with type, dung in its very own bag! Ha ha ha!"

At other times Kumush enjoyed these kinds of jokes from Toibeka, but now they displeased her. Feigning anger, she left for her room. Oftob Oyim considered the guest and his visit to be a momentary distraction—as if he were nothing more than a Bacha providing some diversion... so she gave this exchange no second thought.

"Aunty, could you please check if they need anything?" said Oftob Oyim to Toibeka. "Maybe they need tea."

Quickly swallowing a last taste of her food, Toibeka went outside. After a short while, she returned to their spot on the veranda, quaking in her shoes as if she had seen a ghost.

"God damn it, I nearly died from fright."

Ticking away at her beads on her prayer rug, Oysha Bibi only gave Toibeka a distant look and continued on with her prayers. Oftob Oyim smiled indulgently and asked, as she sat down near the sandal, "What happened? What gave you such a fright?"

Taking deep breaths to calm herself, Toibeka sat down under the column. "I took a tablecloth outside into the yard in order to freshen it. Suddenly, out of nowhere, I discovered someone concealed under the cherry tree. I gave a shout from the shock. It seemed to me he was spying on the guests!"

"Who was it?"

"I couldn't recognize him in the darkness. He looked like Hamidboi the Black. Maybe it was him or maybe it was someone else. God knows, he scurried into the undergrowth and fled..."

After they had seen off the guests and while Qutidor disrobed, Oftob Oyim asked, "Beautiful boy this, intelligent boy that... Toibeka crowed on about him. Who was he?"

"Our guest," said Qutidor, "the son of my close friend from Tashkent, Yusufbek Hajji."

"Is he worthy of Toibeka's boasts?"

"Yes!" said Qutidor, perking up a bit. "May God bless everyone with such a son."

Laughing, unable to control herself, Oftob Oyim told Qutidor what Toibeka had said to Kumush and what her reaction had been. Even Qutidor could not resist laughing.

"Her ravings are well founded. May we be blessed with a son-in-law like that."

6

BLOODY CLOUDS OVER TASHKENT

While the previous events were transpiring, disturbing news arrived in Margilan:

Tashkent's Hakim Azizbek had incited a rebellion against the khan of Qoqan. He had murdered the major divan beks tasked by the khan with collecting Haraj and Zakat[60] taxes. The next day the rumors took an even more dramatic turn: "Musulmanqul deployed five thousand soldiers under the command of Nur Muhammad Qushbegi to Tashkent!"[61]

The populace greeted the news with their characteristic quietude, even a studied indifference. No one was surprised, not seeing anything extraordinary in these events. And their reaction was justified, since they had witnessed these sorts of political rivalries play out all too regularly. They thought, if not today, then another day, one of their Buzukboshi[62] or one of the privileged Oftobboshi,[63] anyone, it didn't matter who, one of their beks would rise to power through this sort of infighting. But we cannot include Otabek among the ignorant; he could not remain indifferent to the rumors, nor remain calm. On hearing these reports, he lost his appetite. He could see with his eyes wide open, with perfect clarity, the terrible consequences, the great calamitous events that would result from the anarchy to come. He foresaw his people, his nation of Muslims, teetering on the edge of a cliff, below it a bottomless abyss, on the verge of falling terribly downward, and when he heard the news, he thought, Protect us, dear God.[64] He was stunned, lost in himself, and his past grievances toward the state of his homeland returned: "Unable to separate right from wrong, citizens are thirsty to drink one another's blood, all for the benefit of a group of ambitious despots with dark visions of the future!"

As Otabek sat, despondent, lost in thought, Hasan Ali entered the room with a letter in his hand. Handing it to Otabek, he said, "It is from Tashkent. Maybe it is from your father." Otabek opened the letter. It was written on paper in thick pencil strokes.[65] It read:

By the name of the creator... Let it be known and clear to the light of our eye, power of our loins, fruit of our life, our son Mullah Otabek.[66]

Thank God, we, your supplicant father, gentle mother, and close friends, under the protection of Allah, are in good health and praying for the light of our eyes, day and night continuously, with hopes and wishes. In blessed times, at a happier hour, let God bless the hour that we all meet again, amen! Next, we want to say that we thanked God when we received your letter regarding your safe arrival in Margilan.

You might want news of the situation in Tashkent, but perhaps you have already heard it all in Margilan. Here, Azizbek, with the support of unknown forces, rebelled against Qoqan, killing the beks from the khanate who came here for tax collection and hanging them from the gate of the orda.[67] I think Qoqan is preparing an answer to these actions. Today we heard from Kerovchi[68] that Nur Muhammad Qushbegi was sent to Tashkent with five thousand soldiers. What is the fate of the nation, my son? Today the people vowed their loyalty to Azizbek. The savage Azizbek's bloody sword struck keenly the heads of many people. Sons, fathers, mothers, brothers were all sacrificed. Their wracked bodies were left out to rot in the open, yet nevertheless the nation promised fidelity; they swore to defend Azizbek until the last drip of their blood. Under the orders of Azizbek, all the people of Tashkent were gathered in front of the orda—there were mullahs, intellectuals, all levels of our city's society. Standing in the guard tower, Azizbek greeted the people. The people, honored to see Azizbek, cried out with tears in their eyes upon hearing his greetings. My son, since you can distinguish between white and black, read carefully what I am about to write.

Displaying two bodies hung from the orda gate, Azizbek asked the people, "Dear citizens, do you see these two found guilty? Why has this verdict fallen upon them? Why was it visited upon them in this manner?"

The people replied, "We don't know, master!"

Azizbek answered his own question: "Here are the bodies of two bastards, soldiers of Musulman the Lame, leaders of the Qipchaqs[69] and the enemies of all Qora Chopans![70] I executed them as revenge on behalf of my Black Robe citizens, to bless the martyred spirits of your Black Robe brothers who died by the hands of the Qipchaqs. Are not my actions justified, my people?"

The people answered, "They are just, it is justice! You defended us, Taksir.[71] All Qipchaqs should likewise be punished!"

Azizbek now explained his true purpose: "Why would I perform this act of goodwill on your behalf, the Qora Chopan? Without a doubt, I will be persecuted by the Qipchaqs. They want to expel me from Tashkent, even kill me! What say you to this?"

The people shouted to the heavens the following answer: "We will give up our souls to the last drop of blood! The Qipchaqs will not dare to touch a hair on you while we are alive!"

Azizbek thanked the people and opened up his heart's deepest wounds: "Thank you, my citizens! I have heard the Qipchaqs are advancing under the direction of Nur Muhammad Qushbegi against Tashkent. Do we prepare to meet their attack or not, my people?"

People: "Of course, of course, we must prepare, our master! If you allow us, we will begin restoration of the fortress's defenses today."

"Thank you, my people! As long as I have your support at my back, I have no worries."

"As long as you are safe and at peace, we will not give way to the Qipchaqs. Bless us in the restoration of the fortresses, our master."

Azizbek delivered his blessings, and the people started to prepare for battle.

My son, one doesn't know whether to cry or laugh at the people's fate. However, bloody clouds have appeared over Tashkent. Only God knows how this will resolve itself. Most importantly, there is one thing I need to remind you of: please be cautious in discussing politics. Remember the past victims who have been killed for the same miserable reasons. Only God knows what we deliberate in our souls. In Ferghana they may consider me Azizbek's ally and will consider you the son of a traitor— consider these matters carefully and mind your step! In these days of ill will, our lives are in danger— you must not forget this! I must add, do not come to Tashkent until matters settle. After Tashkent calms, if I am safe, I will send news to you. Here all your closest friends remain in good health.

Written in Tashkent on the 27th of Dalv 1847.[72]

When he finished the letter, Otabek read it again, clarifying some points. Reaching the description of the events involving Azizbek, he burst out, with uncontrolled hatred, "You fox!"

"Do not come to Tashkent until matters settle!" Upon rereading this phrase, he said quietly to himself, smiling at the prospect of delaying his return home, "If that is the case, let it never settle, let there never be peace!"

7

RESPONSIBILITY

Communiqués were arriving in Qoqan daily, and fifteen days had passed since soldiers from Quqan Khanate had laid siege to Tashkent, yet no word arrived on whether Tashkent had been retaken.

The day before, the only news on people's lips was that "Nur Muhammad Qushbegi has been wounded, fifteen hundred of Qoqan's soldiers have been killed." It seemed that Azizbek was not so easily subdued.

Upon hearing of the unfolding tragedy in Tashkent, Otabek became more pensive; his worries about his hometown mingled with his lovesickness, only compounding the pain. He detached

56

himself from the world, not emerging from his room, speaking a word to no one. Day by day, he buried himself deeper and deeper in his living quarters.

We resume our tale with Hasan Ali who, upon taking morning tea, burned to execute the plan he had hatched the day before. Marked changes in Otabek's demeanor—a sallow face, reclusiveness, deep melancholy, to name a few—alarmed Hasan Ali and compelled him to move from observation to action as an agent on Otabek's behalf. At any rate, from the moment he had discovered that the reason for Otabek's mental decline was a hidden love, Hasan Ali had not let him far from his sight. Who is the beloved; whose daughter is she? Is it possible to do something? He turned these dilemmas over in his mind, leaning against the wall and weighing his options. He thought of Otabek's youth, the fragility of youth, hesitating before speaking to the bek.

"Otabek is young. Young love is flighty like the wings of a bird; here today, gone tomorrow. Perhaps they will forget it today or tomorrow." This was the shape of his thoughts.

Finally, Otabek's increasingly obsessive behavior and daily shifts in mood compelled Hasan Ali to abandon his current plan, forcing him to seek out other methods. Although the logical course of action seemed obvious, he nevertheless hesitated, considering a hundred other options, which propagated a thousand more variants, but finding no cure for Otabek's pain, he finally settled on a course of action, saying to himself, Let's see whether my steps will be blessed. That very day, after finishing dinner, Hasan Ali went to his room, changed into his evening clothes, and then entered Otabek's room. Otabek was reading *The Baburnama*.[73]

So as to not reveal his true intent, Hasan Ali asked Otabek whether he needed anything more from him: "Do you need me, Bek? I want to go to the bathhouse."

Without taking his eyes from his book, Otabek answered, "I have nothing else for you. You may go."

Hasan Ali departed just as nightfall descended. A dusky haze hung in the air, enveloping him, as a frigid wind blew from all four directions. Small, random speckles of fresh snow whirled in tight spirals, encouraging people to flee to the warmth of their homes.

Usually the mud reached waist-deep during the day, threatening to suck pedestrians into the warm morass, but now the mass of sludge had frozen under a new blanket of snow, creating a path and easy passage if one made their way through the firm clods of earth that dotted the area.

In contrast to this grim tableau, the "crunch, crunch" of stepping on the patches of snow produced a melodic counterpoint to the horrific mire underfoot. Though stores were closed for the day, teahouses hummed at capacity. Men stoked the flames in the central hearths, kindling fires, while others coerced bachas into lascivious roles, posing for the patrons as their very own khans or khan's daughter. Among those who favored khans were young mullahnamos,[74] who were scattered among the customers in grandiose turbans, as well as men in their seventies... Long winter nights make for crowded teahouses.

There were customers seeking pleasure by drinking tea tenderly prepared by bachas, all the while reveling in their beauty and praising Allah's name and omnipotence for creating these delicate chimeras that for just a moment cast aside the ruse to reveal not the face of a woman but that of a young boy.

Hasan Ali arrived at Ziyo Shohichi's residence, made his way into the yard reserved for the male quarters, and looked toward a closed window of the Mehmon Khana. The light cast through its window into the yard indicated someone was at home. A candle shone through a crack in the door as he approached and announced that a caller had arrived at no ordinary house, but, rather, to a home of heavenly radiance.[75] Hasan Ali straightened his clothing and entered the dwelling. Ziyo Shohichi was praying unattended in the guesthouse. Hasan Ali, relieved to find him alone, waited for him to finish. Ziyo Shohichi performed Namos[76] according to the prescribed movements and rotated left and right on the prayer rug while softly repeating to himself, "Asalam-Ala-Kum." He raised a hand in blessing as he said the final words of the prayer. After exchanging greetings, Ziyo Shohichi said: "Come in, Father! Are you at peace?"

"Thank you, everything is fine."

They sat warming themselves at the *tancha*.[77] An uncomfortable moment of silence hung between them as they struggled to find words. Ziyo Shohichi's eyes prompted Hasan Ali, as if to ask, What is the purpose of your visit?

"Don't be alarmed, Bey-aka, I came out of an 'obligation.'"

"Did Otabek send you?"

"No, I came on my own accord, Bey-aka."[78]

Again, Ziyo Shohichi did not understand. As Otabek's slave, it was a bit out of place for Hasan Ali to pay a visit to Ziyo Shohichi's house, not to mention unusual to have intimate discussions with slaves who arrive to discuss matters of "obligation." Puzzled, he finally asked, "Your obligation?"

Hasan Ali grinned slightly. "If I tell you my 'obligation,' you won't believe me."

"All right, well?"

"As you know," continued Hasan Ali, "we came to Margilan about twenty-five days ago, almost one month. Since our arrival, Otabek has been very ill."

Ziyo Shohichi was surprised.

"Has he been sick? He seemed to be in good health..."

"You are right," said Hasan Ali. "For many days the nature of his sickness remained obscure even to me."

"All right, what kind of sickness does he have?"

"Love."

"Love?"

"Love!" repeated Hasan Ali. "During these past twenty-five days, he has lost track of everything. You would not believe it. I worried over him for many nights until I discovered the truth."

"Do you know who his beloved is?"

"I do. It is Qutidor's daughter."

"Yes, yes... Indeed, indeed!" Ziyo Shohichi exclaimed, losing his train of thought for a moment. After a little while, he asked, "Do you know this for sure?"

"I know it for certain."

"Did he tell you?"

"He did not actually tell me. He only alluded to it."

"Where did Otabek see this girl?"

"Unfortunately, I don't know."

In light of the now obvious reasons for Hasan Ali's late visit, Ziyo Shohichi asked, "Now what do you propose?"

"The main purpose for my visit was this very issue," said Hasan Ali. "To see if you could provide any insight or means to resolve this matter... perhaps we can then act accordingly. In short, I put myself in your hands."

Ziyo Shohichi sat thinking. He said "Interesting" a few times and put some snuff under his tongue. Meanwhile Hasan Ali relayed the events surrounding Otabek's finding love.

"A very delicate issue," said Ziyo Shohichi at the conclusion of the account. "If Otabek gets married in Margilan, will Yusufbek Hajji be offended?"

"Long live Bey-aka! Your slave has thought long and hard about this. If he is offended by our actions, how could we avoid it if we were forced by circumstances to act in this manner? But I am also weighing the other side of this issue: Do you think Qutidor will agree to a marriage?"

Ziyo-aka again mulled it over, scratching his head.

"As you have mentioned, this is a very delicate issue," he said. "I know that Qutidor has a favorable opinion of Otabek, but there is the problem of distance... What if he says, 'I will not give my daughter to a foreigner'?[79] Who knows... ?"

"In my opinion, we, at any rate, should ask for Qutidor's consent to our proposal," said Hasan Ali. "If he agrees, all is well. If not, we deliver his decision to Otabek; after that, maybe his heart will cool."

These words were well received by Ziyo-aka.

"In that case, what do you think, when should we go to Qutidor?"

"It's up to you."

Ziyo-aka thought for a while and then a smile came over his face. "We will go now," he said. "Let us perform the job of matchmaker at least once in our lives."

When Ziyo-aka rose to get dressed, Hasan Ali asked him, "Do you think it's all right for me to go with you, or should you go alone?"

Ziyo-aka waved his hand. "There is no harm if you come too," he said.

8

CONGRATULATIONS!

Ziyo Shohichi's broad, toothy grin gave Qutidor pause: to what did he owe the pleasure of this unannounced visit?

"Leave off with building your fire and prepare the tablecloth for your newly arrived *sovchi!*"[80] Ziyo Shohichi's zeal forced Qutidor to leave the smoldering branches in the fire and go order tea.

Upon Qutidor's exit, Hasan Ali murmured half-aloud, "If fate would only bless us in this matter."

"If God wills it, all will be well. We will not consider him human if he doesn't accept such a man of quality for his son-in-law," said Ziyo Shohichi firmly.

Qutidor returned. Ziyo-aka and Hasan Ali exchanged meaningful glances. Qutidor expected an explanation to emerge from Ziyo-aka's mouth, since an unexpected guest of his stature augured a weighty matter... An interminable silence persisted, compelling Qutidor to resort to pleasantries with Hasan Ali: "Is Bek all right?"

In this moment, Ziyo-aka perceived his opening to state his intent in the most diplomatic manner possible. Gesturing to Hasan Ali to hold his tongue, he answered, "The reason for our abrupt appearance is—well, one could say Otabek's health demands it."

Qutidor did not catch the insinuations beneath this bumbling, asking again, "Is Otabek in good health?"

"Until now Otabek has been in good health," said Ziyo Shohichi, weighing each word, "but it appears Bek's future health is in your hands."

Again, not comprehending his intent, Qutidor looked with surprise at his guests. "I don't understand..."

"I mean Otabek has been in good health until now," said Ziyo-aka again. "But his future health is in your hands."

"In my hands?"

"By your will."

"The health of a young man of Otabek's quality is the concern of every wise man," said Qutidor, surprised. "But what you say is interesting, that one man's health is determined by another man's will."

Ziyo-aka didn't change his expression; his persistence betrayed some other purpose.

"Don't be surprised, my friend," he said. "Bek's future health is indeed subject to your will. This is not some game or play at words. It is true."

Suddenly Qutidor divined about whom and what the matter concerned—and as a result, he broke into a cold sweat. Ziyo-aka smoothed the tablecloth laid out by Toibeka and broke some bread into pieces. He then offered a piece of bread each to Hasan Ali and Qutidor, and let his words flow freely.[81]

"Love is such a precious pearl, fated for very few people," he began. "The son of your closest friend, Yusufbek Hajji, for several days has lamented some hidden pain. His servant, truly Otabek's spiritual father, Hasan Ota, has been searching for a cure to his secret agony.[82] But as for Bek, he veils his sickness, revealing it to no one. Ever faithful to his master, Hasan Ali observed him closely one night, and the truth of Bek's torment came to light.

" 'Observance of the Shariyat confers no shame,' they tell me, my friend. Though this wisdom rings hard on our ears, I recall it for good reasons: One day, the wind of fate blows and raises the veil of someone's daughter sitting under the curtain of innocence and, at the same time, reveals that innocent girl to Otabek. At that moment, real, true love was born in Bek's heart toward her."

Adding some words on his own behalf, Ziyo Shohichi let the words sink in as Qutidor sat flustered. Qutidor was not alone in his troubles—the sovchi also shared in his disquiet. All three understood the gravity and delicateness of the situation; an agreement was suspended in their thoughtful silence. Though the purpose of their visit was as clear as day, for some reason Qutidor pretended to not understand: "And whose daughter is this?" he asked.

Ziyo Shohichi replied, "Your beloved daughter."

Qutidor bowed his head, looking sheepishly toward his feet—perhaps embarrassed now by his own naivety. An impenetrable chasm rose up between the three of them as Qutidor emanated a glacial calm—he was stubborn and not forthcoming with his feelings on the matter, further compounding everyone's unease. Ziyo-aka was forced to break the impasse: "Our visit gives you a son worth the world and, if God wills, on our return we will present to Otabek a companion who is the very ideal of innocence—the best wife imaginable in the world."

Ziyo's insurmountable argument made Hasan Ali's heart flutter in anticipation of an agreement. At any moment he would hear consent or refusal from Qutidor's mouth—would he acquiesce or not? As for Qutidor, he remained dumbstruck, unsure how to respond to these two people waiting impatiently for an answer, shifting their weight from side to side.

"I would count myself the happiest of fathers if Otabek honored us as our son-in-law," said Qutidor finally. "But the decision is not entirely in my hands. My wife, who nourished my daughter on her own milk, her feelings must also be taken into consideration. Not consulting with her on this matter would be the greatest insult. If you don't mind, I would like to speak with her first."

Qutidor showed undeniable sincerity and devotion to his wife in his reasoning, and the two sovchi could feel their blood quicken as they gained new hope for success.

"This is not horse trading; this is dealing with our beloved children's lives, my friend. Consult with your wife. Tell her what you know about Otabek and his father, and after careful deliberation, give us an answer."

After these words, Qutidor left the Mehmon Khana, entering the Ich Kari. Kumush lay asleep. Toibeka snored in the small alcove near the kitchen, loud enough to shake the whole room. Opening the door, Qutidor said to Oftob Oyim, who was sitting and waiting for him, "Take a candle and follow me."

The room, lavishly decorated, was fit for a museum. There was an array of richly colored silks and atlas-covered blankets stored in recessed shelves along with piles of feather pillows; there were rows of fine Chinese tableware, ornate cups of delicate porcelain, as well as teapots, plates, and pitchers; and the walls were covered with swords, shields, helmets, daggers, and sabres in silver filigreed sheaths. An assortment of men and women's clothing, draped or folded, lined the walls; there were chokmon[83] coats and travel robes as well as vibrant red carpets and silk blankets. One's eyes were dazzled by the display of wealth.

Qutidor smiled at Oftob Oyim, who waited eagerly for his words. "Wife, do you know about the matchmakers outside?"

Oftob Oyim showed no surprise upon hearing the word sovchi from her husband. Over the past two or three years their house had been crowded daily with groups of people seeking to make an engagement. She dismissed these newly arrived matchmakers as one of these groups.

"God bless them! Who are they?" Qutidor smiled again.

"They are Ziyo Shohichi and another person unknown to you."

Oftob Oyim noticed that today's go-betweens had affected Qutidor positively, and she sensed genuine excitement in her husband's voice and mannerisms.

"On whose behalf did they come?"

"Do you remember we received a young trader from Tashkent as a guest about fifteen days ago?"

"I remember the young man who Toibeka crowed about."

"May you live long, wife!" said Qutidor. "They came on behalf of that young man."

Oftob Oyim became alarmed, protesting to her husband, "But he is a foreigner!"

Seeing Oftob Oyim's panic, Qutidor scratched his forehead and said in a hopeless voice, "I also had the same concern. Other than that, he is a perfect match, possessing all the qualities we desire in a son-in-law."

Oftob Oyim epitomized the quintessential wife who respected above all the will and wishes of her husband—honoring and worshipping his whole being. Therefore, as an obedient wife—and even though she did not in fact agree with her husband about the betrothal— it was Otabek she chose to rail against, calling him a *musafir*. She sought to invent even the most obscure and outrageous shortcomings in Otabek—traits so egregious and irrefutable that Qutidor's heart would have no choice but to grow cold toward this favorite.

"Whose son is that young man? Do you know his father?"

Oftob Oyim's question damaged her efforts to undermine the enemy. Qutidor spoke highly of Yusufbek Hajji's personality and his current social standing, as well as Yusufbek Hajji's regard for

Qutidor himself, all in great detail. Finally, he added, "It is impossible to criticize this young man's family background. To be honest, the generation this young man belongs to is rather more advanced than our own."

Now Oftob Oyim took a different tack: "Is he married or not?"

"He is not married. I learned this from his servant at one of our gatherings."

"How old is he?"

"No more than twenty-five, but no less than twenty-two."

"Why does he want to be our son-in-law? Couldn't he find a girl from Tashkent?"

"Even if there are many girls available, they say he finds them unsuitable," said Qutidor, shyly lowering his voice to sooth her doubts.

Oftob Oyim found no way to counter her husband's inclination to accept the offer. By all accounts, the young man was an ideal match and fulfilled the aspirations they had for their daughter perfectly, but deep in her heart, first and foremost, he was a foreigner. The realization that, after so many years of looking for a suitable son-in-law, they might suddenly hand their daughter over to a stranger from Tashkent left Oftob Oyim despondent. She felt slighted by being presented with a foreigner; it was most difficult for her to swallow.

"So, what do you say, wife?"

Oftob Oyim feared protesting too openly as her husband might become upset, but in her heart, she was dead set against marriage to a foreigner.

"I can't oppose someone you have found suitable and hinder your wishes," she said, after thinking awhile. "You are the father, after all, and you have more of a right to choose a son-in-law than I do. Of course, I can't believe that you would give your only daughter, the apple of your eye, to such a dissolute stranger. From the point of view of the head of the household's right to choose, I have grounds for dispute, but my main issue is that the groom is from Tashkent; he will take your daughter with him to his home city and separate us from our only child... I don't know about you, but I can't stand this kind of separation... I think you did not think carefully about this side of the problem, my dear."

"You are right, my wife," said Qutidor, after duly considering her views. "But it seems like fate, or maybe something else. For some reason, I admire this young man. I'm not sure what you think of my idea, but let's not overthink the issue and let's give the matchmakers the following answer: that they must not take Kumush from Margilan, she must remain with us. If they accept our condition, we will have not just a daughter, but two children. If they do not agree, then they will have themselves to blame. What do you think about this, my wife?"

"But what about the fact that he is a foreigner?"

"We will not countenance any reproaches as to our choice in a son-in- law; we only seek a genuinely honorable man for her. If people spread rumors about our daughter marrying a 'foreigner,' so be it."

From the very outset of the conversation, Oftob Oyim had understood her husband's wishes. And so she answered grudgingly, "It's up to you." Receiving the answer he had hoped for, Qutidor went out to the matchmakers and announced the conditions. On behalf of Otabek, Ziyo-aka accepted his stipulation and congratulated Qutidor on gaining a son-in-law of Otabek's quality. And so they ended "The Matchmakers' Unexpected Visit" without unnecessary ceremony but with a binding agreement of betrothal. After praying for the two youngsters to love one another and to produce many children, the matchmakers were given gilded robes. Hasan Ali, beside himself, thanked Qutidor over and over, showering him with blessings.

"Congratulations on your new robes."

"To you too: Congratulations on your new son."

"You are most welcome," said Qutidor, from the heart. "May all your wishes come true."

9

Hasan Ali grew delirious from the night's great fortune, and his old eyes drooped from fatigue. He counted the ways to present the pending betrothal to Bek, dreaming about how he would welcome the news. He felt in his heart that Otabek's whole view of life and the world would change for the better. A vision danced before his eyes of Otabek revitalized by his announcement; the same man who sequestered himself alone in his room for weeks would now walk through the streets, through the bazaars, to Qutidor's house, happy and excited.

After entertaining these thoughts, his eyes grew even wearier and once again he saw Otabek before him, exclaiming, "Father, I will never forget what good deeds you have done for me" and thanking him profusely.

Hasan Ali woke a second time from his fantastic musings and began to think: "Poor wretch, you must be mooning over your beloved. Perhaps you are suffering from a headache, lying there breathless, not knowing whom to call to soothe your complaints. Your hopes have been cut short because you think you have no allies. Worry not, my young master. Your father Hasan Ali has not forsaken you in this matter. Tonight will be the end of your sad evenings and the beginning of nights filled with light and poetry, my dear master."

Yet again Hasan Ali was easing into sleep as images swam before his eyes, images of Otabek and a charming, beautiful girl— both of them smiling at Hasan Ali as if they were saying, "You are our true father." Still sleepless, Hasan Ali muttered to himself, "I am turning sixty-four and could not have children. I will leave this world without progeny. Why shouldn't Otabek be my son, and his wife my daughter, with their children running after me, calling me Grandpa? When I lie under the earth, forgotten by the world, it would be enough if they remembered me with the kind words 'There once was a time when we had a grandfather named Hasan Ali.' "

The night had long since turned into morning, yet he could not keep himself from imagining Otabek's happiness. These thoughts kept him from sleep. The time had come to deliver Otabek into a life of contentment.

After tea, Hasan Ali left his room, went to their common area, and sat down in front of Bek with a package under his arm. Hasan Ali wanted to weed out his melancholia, plant seeds of hope, and water them with affection.

"Now, congratulations," he said.

Otabek looked at Hasan Ali, confused. Smiling, Hasan Ali took out from under his arm a gilded robe, placing it on the sandal.

"What sort of robe is this?" asked Bek.

"Congratulations, I said."

"Congratulations for what?"

"Congratulations on your pure and beloved fiancée, not to mention a father-in-law of the likes of Qutidor. Hasan Ali now has a daughter- in-law."

A striking transformation overtook Otabek: he was struck dumb, and his eyes widened, bulging out of their sockets. Sitting contorted in an unnatural pose and greatly agitated, he asked, "What do you mean by these words?"

"Do not question the good news I have brought you. Just believe what I say," said Hasan Ali, laughing. "Ziyo Shohichi and I decided to marry you to the daughter of Qutidor and carried out our decision last night. I mean simply that I engaged you to the daughter of Qutidor."

Losing control, Otabek asked quickly, "To which of his daughters did you betroth me?"

"To the one and only daughter of Qutidor," said Hasan Ali. "Don't worry. Ziyo Shohichi said that Qutidor will visit after tea. We are going to finalize the details of the wedding with him."

It was hard to discern whether Otabek was happy or upset. He showed no sign of either refusing or accepting this engagement...

Kumush encountered an extraordinary situation as if she had just awoken from a dream: it seemed everybody had had the same vision of a wedding the night before. They were all talking about buying new feather pillows and were even discussing at length the groom's clothing. Oftob Oyim was ordering her husband to buy a new gold belt for the groom... There is no other way to say it than

"Good heavens! Who is the groom Oftob Oyim refers to so openly? Whose daughter is going to be married? Are there other daughters besides Kumush Bibi?" They only have one daughter... therefore Kumush is going to be married.

All these discussions defied comprehension.

"Who is going to be married?" she asked everyone.

"Kumush."

"Does Kumush like her groom or not? Is it necessary to know her opinion or not?"[84]

"It is not necessary to discuss this with her."

"Why?"

"It is tradition! Kumush must be married to a man suitable to her parents," declared Toibeka.

After Toibeka's explanation, Kumush found out about the groom. "Listen to me, my lady," said Toibeka, laughing. "Don't ignore your aunt Toibeka. She has miraculous powers. If your aunt takes something to her heart, the angels will at once command 'Amen.' The other day I told you about a young guest. You became upset. From this day forward, you are engaged to that same man. Now because of that you must bless and trust me with your secrets!"

On hearing this news, Kumush's black eyes filled, drenching her eyelashes with tears.

"Don't cry, my mistress," said Toibeka. "We know the source of these tears. Where men laugh from happiness, girls like you cry. You are crying from joy... I also cried when I became engaged, but in my heart I waited impatiently for the wedding day..."

"My patience is finished, Aunt!" said Kumush. "Do not say another word."

"I will say no more," said Toibeka, "but I will say this truthfully: Oh, if only you had seen that groom. You would truly know, my lady, how handsome and clever he is. Your stars are closely aligned. You are perfect for each other."

Kumush could not stand it anymore and cried out in a pained voice, "Ah, don't say another word. I will die!"

Hearing Kumush's angry shouts, Oftob Oyim and her mother, Oysha Bibi, ran out of the house.

"What happened? What's the matter?"

Kumush covered her head under the blanket of the sandal and lay down. Toibeka, fearing a sticky predicament with the ladies of the household, told them, "I was only describing her future husband. She became angry with me."

Oftob Oyim berated Toibeka, "You are an imbecile. You embarrassed Kumush! Nobody will punish you if you leave well enough alone. Go do your work!"

The older women interpreted Kumush's tears as simple shyness and went back into their room, rummaging again through the contents of a chest and continuing with their wedding preparations. Kumush lay still for several moments, her head under the blanket and her eyes wide open. Then, finally, she got up and went over to the men's part of the yard. Her eyes were red and her eyelids swollen after a long cry; her face was puffy. But these changes didn't lessen her charms, or her grace; on the contrary, they made her ten times more beautiful. She sat down at the edge of the veranda, putting her face in her right hand, and lost herself in her private thoughts—long minutes spent remembering, contemplating, dreaming. She finally freed her hand from her face, eagerly taking a breath, and as if waiting for somebody, glanced around...

"The bank of the stream, the mystical bank of the stream..."

Her tears fell freely and her delicate legs tiptoed toward the water's edge. When she reached the embankment, she jumped to a dry patch, crouching down in a place that will soon be known to us. Taking some water in her hands, she washed her face and slowly looked toward the passage, then back at the water. Nobody knew Kumush's pain, nobody could know what she dreamed about, only this stream knew her secrets... The spirit of the water was speaking to her, was listening to her heart, but nobody but Kumush could know their private deliberations. She washed the pearls from her eyes with the transcendental water, not once, but again and again. Her emotions soothed, redness leaving her eyes, she walked slowly back inside the Ich Kari.

10

TOI, KIZLAR MAJLISI[85]

The male guests were celebrating in the male half of the outer courtyard of Qutidor's house while the female guests filled the Ich Kari. Honored with a lavish meal of *suyuq osh*[86] and rich halva and fresh *nishaldah*,[87] all were shown every courtesy.

The constant interplay of instruments resonated from the outer yard; the *dutars, tamburs, rababs,* and *nays*[88] were accompanied by the most renowned singers of the city; they watered the world around them with the ever-flowing spring of their songs, caressing the ears of the guests. The wedding brimmed with joyous spirits, reaching a crescendo...

In the Ich Kari, where the women were making merry, a clamor of revelry and a racket commingled: if we were to use a mother's witticism, we'd say "There are more guests than sand in the desert; therefore, disorder reigns." Wives crowded all the rooms and the entire Ich Kari. Some were eating cups of plov, halva, and other delicacies right in the yard. Someone else was busy calming crying children, attempting to put them to sleep. Other women were singing a wedding song and yelling "Yor-yor!"[89] at the top of their lungs, while yet others laughed raucously, ruining the tranquility of the world. The tumult reached to the seventh heaven.

Amid all this exuberance, Oftob Oyim seemed lost in thought, consumed with low spirits, her face a shade paler than usual. Perhaps she had become tired of the guests, perhaps she was distracted for some other reason; we have seen her behave strangely before, especially while engaged in the event's preparations. Yet, telltale signs, such as instead of going into a guest room for a guest's belongings, she went into a storage area, were manifest to all. To the men and women who had come to congratulate her on the betrothal, she simply replied with a furtive "Thank you."

Standing in the doorway of the granary, Oftob Oyim called to someone among the wives. Seeing the middle-aged woman she summoned, perhaps fifty years of age, walk toward her, leaving behind a gaggle of ladies who were joking among themselves, their sides splitting in laughter, Oftob retreated into the granary. Once the other lady entered, Oftob Oyim quickly closed the door so that it was open just a crack, her face bearing an expression of deep grief...

"Why do you look so miserable, Oftob Oyim?" asked the woman, looking into her sad eyes.

Taking a deep breath, Oftob Oyim peeked through the door and said in a small voice, "If they shone a light into my innermost soul, they would find a great hollowness inside me, my sister." Tears welled up in her eyes.

"Why?"

"Because of my daughter..."

"What happened to your daughter?"

"Today is the seventh day of the engagement, and she has been crying day and night, shedding rivers of tears. When I ask her why she is so upset, she tries to hold back the torrent, yet in the end cries even harder. Today's tears were the worst of them all. No matter how much we pleaded or tried to console her, we could barely get her to the bathhouse."

The woman, surprised at Oftob Oyim's description, asked, displaying the appropriate gravitas toward the situation, "What on earth? Maybe your groom is ugly?"

"I haven't seen him myself," said Oftob Oyim. "But according to those who have, he is very handsome. I have heard that he is a clever young man. Kumush's father regards him highly; he himself chose him as the groom."

"Does Kumush know anything about him?"

"She does," said Oftob Oyim. "We all brag about the groom to her, but our praises aggravate her further, causing her to wail even more."

All kidding aside, the woman now saw the seriousness of the situation, yet an answer to the bride's distress eluded her. Attempting to console Oftob Oyim, she told stories from past weddings where brides-to-be wept before their nuptials, only to become intimate partners to their grooms afterward.

"Don't worry, Oftob Oyim," she said. "If your groom is so singularly handsome, we will soon see your daughter cling to him like a flowering vine."

"Oh, sister," said Oftob Oyim hopelessly. "My heart is not in it."

"Let it go. Believe me! Oftob, how many crying girls I have seen who, upon leaving their wedding beds, have become even more enamored than the young men; your daughter is one of those cases! Don't worry, Oftob!"

"Let it be so."

"It will be so," the woman cackled. "Wait, what will you give me if your daughter changes as I said?"

"A head-to-toe ensemble[90]."

"Remember your word, Oftob. If God wills it, we will see her entwined like a morning glory around her husband. Go and greet your guests with good cheer."

With that, the women left the granary and moved among the others.

A bridal shower is a congregation as redolent as a bed of flowers; such slender tulips, such vibrant parrots, and such beautiful turtledoves! A garden redolent of delicious flowers abounded in the house of Kumush's uncle.

Approximately thirty or forty girls were assembled together in the residence. The purpose of their gathering: to convey into the sublime sisterhood of wives, the world of the feminine, one of their most beautiful, most charming maidens as she blossoms into a woman. The exuberant shepherdesses wore their most elegant dresses, sparkling with precious stones. If you managed to infiltrate the four walls of this paradise, if your eyes were but once to pass over the conclave of beauties, from that moment on, without a doubt, you would be lost forever to another plane of existence, your mind transported in ecstasy. "This flower's charm... No, the other one surpasses that one! Which one shall I choose? That one must be best of all!" In this manner, your composure would abandon you, you would be unable to decide; people would mock you, a disgraced fool for all the world to see.

Indeed, the members of the convocation surpassed each other—all precious spirits, beautiful as Pari.[91] All of the heavenly host perform as the bridal shower's poets, dancers, artists, and musicians. Only Kumush remained absent, not back from the bathhouse. Because of that the celebration had not yet begun. Even if it had, it would have lacked the proper enthusiasm as the guest of honor had not yet arrived. Everybody was confident that Kumush's presence would animate the festivities—they were all impatient to begin.

At last one of the women exclaimed, "They are coming!" All the girls crowded at the room's small window, looking out into the yard. Kumush entered with only her two yangas.[92] If only Otabek could have witnessed this moment! If only he would come and see his beloved returning from the bathhouse... the souls who loved her at that moment would beg her to put them out of their misery, to shoot an arrow into their own wounded hearts. Her tender innocence would be that same arrow, piercing his heart with desire.

A white silk scarf covered her head. She wore a white silk dress under a fur coat embroidered with silver thread; wrapped around her neck, a beaver-fur collar kissed her chin; black braids[93] cascaded like silken rivulets; her fresh face blushed... The yangas handed Kumush over to the girls standing in the yard:

"Ladies, we present Kumush to you! Lighten her mood, maidens!"

Two or three girls ran out into the yard, removing the paranji[94] from Kumush and leading her to the house. After they had transferred Kumush to her attendants, the yangas made their retreat. The clearing was empty of men and women, only the girls remained. With the celebrants leading her by the hand, Kumush entered the room, filling it with her fragrance. The young ladies greeted Kumush with various good wishes: "How are you? Congratulations on your bridal robes."[95]

Kumush's murmur barely echoed above the din. "May they bring happiness."

She sat in the place of honor. Her female attendants encircled the room—a sudden hush descended upon them. All the eyes looking toward Kumush expectantly were suddenly overcome with gloom. What were they sad about? What concerns harried the girls? Can we ever truly know the impenetrable inner hearts of maidens?

The girls sat around the room like a wreath of flowers; serene faces lost in thought lent them a charming allure, multiplying their beauty a hundredfold. If we were forced to single out one flower from the arrangement as the most beautiful, our previous distraction would not apply—without hesitation, we would choose Kumush.

She stood out as a solitary rose among tulips, a full moon among stars. Yet the stillness persisted.

At every gathering, there are those who perform the duties of a master of ceremonies, those who enliven a dead celebration. This gathering was no exception. Gulsin Bibi could not contain her frustration about the low spirits among the attendees. She broke the silence, bursting with the words, "Why have we gathered here? Why are we sitting here, sadly looking at the ground? Did we come here for a funeral?"

Khanum Bibi joined Gulsin: "Don't think too hard, friends. We all have the same fate. Stand up, Sevara! Make a fire in the yard and heat your *childirma*.[96] Anorgul, pick up your dutar. Kumush, do not sit there and brood, lighten up. Tomorrow you will regret your heavy heart." Khanum Bibi's words made the party burst out laughing. Even Kumush begrudgingly gave her a slight smile, and pearly white teeth peered briefly from beneath her ruby lips.

At this, a spontaneous jubilance transformed the room. Dutar in hand, Anorgul played the song "Ortaklar,"[97] giving form to the unspoken words of the girls' hearts. Not waiting for the other girls to dance, Khanum Bibi jumped up from her seat and started to move to the music. When the childirma and the strings of the dutar worked in unison, the party became even livelier. Hands started to clap; the dancing became lively. Finally, after all the doors of the room were closed and candles lit on the shelves, the mood of the party reached its crescendo. The candlelight flickering in the wind highlighted the young women in their ecstatic state. The celebration brought to mind the fairies from the story "*Alif wa Laylah.*"[98] The dutar player began the song "*Ifor*"[99] as the childirma again gently joined in. Gulsin Bibi's delicate dance steps now responded to the music. The dutar's notes tugged at the heart's strings, while the childirma quickened its pace. The bridal shower became lively, engaging all the senses. Stepping softly, Gulsin Bibi circled the room, becoming one with the rhythm of the dance and threatening to cause the men of the world to tremble with their whole beings.

You would be mistaken, however, if you thought that Kumush Bibi was interested in the festivities or enjoying them along with the others. Even though she was physically present at the gathering, her thoughts traveled elsewhere: her eyes watched the girls dancing, but her dreams had flown to some other land. If one divined the true underlying mood of the spectacle, one understood that Kumush's joyous celebration was in fact reminiscent of a funeral...

After two hours of revelry, the attendees became tired and stopped dancing. Gulsin and Khanum Bibi now sat down together and started singing quietly while someone strummed the dutar. Gulsin was the first to sing, and her clear voice tinkled like a light bell as she sang "Yigilarman."[100]

"Friends, when I touch the strings of the dutar, my soul will cry for my love,[101] painfully I recall my beloved."

Khanum Bibi added her voice, repeating the stanza. The different melodies and voices accentuated each other, transforming the listeners down to the very blood in their veins, elevating humanity to great heights. Startled from her mournful reverie, Kumush sat up suddenly and shuddered, looking around at the girls.

The singers went on to the second verse:

Though I only glimpsed him for a moment, he captured my soul.
I have never beheld a man more handsome.
Upon seeing you, I stored your image in my heart.
You stole my heart, yet I would never see my beloved again.

Struck with the power of these lines, Kumush's eyes filled with tears. The singers passed to the third verse:

If only I could see my beloved again, I would devote to him all that is sacred in me.

Fourthly:

76

Is the beloved who has tormented me aware that I suffer day and night?

Kumush was losing her poise... Fifthly:

Tell me, friends, truthfully, how long can I be apart from my beloved?

Lastly:

My patience has left, my temperance has left... all has left me. I will break my dutar on the earth.

Nobody listened to the last verse because Kumush was crying, leaning on the girl next to her. Everyone grew alarmed and their eyes and ears were fixed on her.

"What has happened, Kumush?"

"Why are you crying, Kumush opa?"[102]

"Is something hurting? Are you in pain?"

Kumush opened her eyes, lifting her head off the shoulder of her friend, and looked around at everyone, her eyes moist with tears. Gaining her wits again, she quickly took a handkerchief from her pocket and dried her tears.

"Why were you crying?" asked Gulsin.

Kumush forced herself to smile at Gulsin Bibi. "Just—it's nothing..." she said.

"Oh poor, poor thing, but damn you, Kumush! If I had a husband like that I would fly to the sky in joy!" said Gulsin Bibi, feigning annoyance.

The girls laughed heartily at Gulsin's words. In light of Kumush's despondency, they sought to lighten her heart and distract her. They stopped the other amusements and moved on to the most interesting game of the bridal shower: *lapar*.[103] Gulsin played the role of groom while Khanum Bibi took Kumush's part, and as the two exchanged double entendres, the crowd fell into sidesplitting laughter. No matter how they tried to amuse Kumush, however, it was not enough. Kumush would not reveal her pearly teeth. She sat alone, buried deep in sorrow. Girls were served plov and sweets from the *toikhana*.[104] After the girls had finished eating, the yangas entered and asked permission to take Kumush. The celebration's attendants, feigning defiance, joked with them, saying, "We will not surrender Kumush Bibi to you." Kumush even believed her friends' protests for a moment and, while leaving the room with the yangas, she looked to the girls as if pleading for help. But they were leaving one by one, having ferried their friend into a new world, a world of wives.

11

AN UNEXPECTED HAPPINESS[105]

It was difficult to get Kumush to agree.[106] The mullah repeated the question six or seven times: "Will you, Kumush Bibi, the daughter of Mirza Karim, give your authority to Muhammad Rahim, son of Yuldosh, your uncle, to offer your hand in marriage to Otabek, son of Yusufbek Hajji, a devout Muslim from Tashkent? Do you agree to this?" She finally acquiesced, though only after her yangas pressured her to accept.

At around five in the evening, all the wedding attendants were waiting impatiently in Qutidor's house, watching for the groom to arrive. Plovs, sumptuous dishes, and other various lavish foodstuffs had been prepared for the groom. At last, at about five-thirty, Otabek appeared, accompanied by Rahmat's friends, between twenty or thirty young men.

He was dressed beautifully. Resting on his head was a silver silk Chalma turban,[107] and on his shoulders hung soft marten furs lined with a coarse-spun fabric. He wore garments ordered especially from Shamai, a sky-blue cloth tunic with matching trousers. His feet displayed supple leather boots and around his slim waist was a silk sash made by the masterful hands of Kumush Bibi.[108]

His face was red and his mouth bore a pained smile. His nervous eyes searched about in different directions for someone. Though they had finished eating their plov, the people of the *mahalla*[109] continued sitting, eyeing the groom, nudging and whispering to each other. "Good, good, he is a worthy groom, both bride and groom are equal to each other," they observed appraisingly, "like an apple and a pomegranate." From among the throngs of wives sitting on the roof waiting for the groom,[110] Oftob Oyim's older sister quickly descended to her, whispering: "Oftob, quickly, burn some *isiriq*[111] to protect him from the evil eye." Qutidor stood at the gate, arms crossed across his chest, receiving the guests and stealing glances at his son-in-law—secretly smiling to himself. On the veranda of the main guest room, Ziyo Shohichi sat, his white beard on display, along with a respected imam, severe in bearing, while Hasan Ali, Kumush's representative, and several other persons also sat in the same area. The groom and his attendants approached the imam to discuss the issue of *mahr*.[112] The negotiations were conducted between Ziyo Shohichi, who represented Otabek, and Muhammad Rahim, Kumush's representative. After a long discussion, they agreed upon the following amounts for the mahr: "Three hundred gold coins, a house with a large walled yard in Margilan, which will be purchased after the wedding, with all promises witnessed, a milk cow, and household items..."

Otabek willingly agreed to these terms. The mullah enthusiastically began to read the Khutba.[113] Making his recitation in Farsi, he delivered a prayer on behalf of Allah and his prophet through the Salawat,[114] and, after additional finely worded Khutbas, he stopped at the critical point: "Do you, Otabek, son of Yusufbek Hajji, accept as a legitimate wife, according to the tenets of Shariyat, Kumush, the daughter of Mirza Karim?" This question was also delivered in Farsi,[115] piercing Otabek's heart through with euphoria. He struggled to hold back an exuberant smile. Otabek thought to himself, What sort of question is this? Do I accept? Of course, I accept!

Though he had planned to respond from the very outset by crying out, "With great pleasure, of course I accept!" he suddenly felt ashamed at the idea of appearing desperate to Kumush's guests, who could whisper "Look how impatient he is!" so he held back an immediate response. The mullah began again. "Do you, Otabek..." Though a groom should only reply on the third attempt—according to tradition—Otabek could not restrain himself.

He became suddenly fearful that instead of a pleasant resolution at the third query, the tradition would be reversed and they would declare, "He does not want to marry Kumush." He burst out, exclaiming, "I accept!"

Praising God with the words *"Al-hamdulillahi, Al-hamdulillahi,"*[116] the mullah completed the Nikah ceremony. The wedding attendants prayed on behalf of the bride and groom. Everyone raised their hands in prayer. Even the wives on the roof helped out by joining in prayer and offering an "Amen." The groom's men took him to the guest room. The wedding celebrations began in earnest.

Otabek's impatience with the interminably long, drawn-out feast grew minute by minute.

Finally, toward the evening, they recited the evening Khuftan prayers.[117] The extravagant meals had been eaten, the tables cleared, tablecloths removed. In reality, the events only lasted an hour and a half, but for Otabek even one minute seemed like many years of suffering. Finally the yangas asked the groom if he was ready to be escorted to the next stage. After a heartfelt recitation of the Fatiha, they asked that he and his wife have a long life filled with love, and they brought Otabek into the Ich Kari.

Hasan Ali was waiting in the veranda of Bek's guest rooms. "Congratulations on your marriage!"

"Thank you."

Hasan Ali scrutinized Otabek's appearance from head to toe. Then, with fatherly love and tears in his eyes, he patted him on the back, said a brief prayer, and gestured him to enter. Otabek walked toward to yangas. He felt as if he were caught in a dream: What is this? Is this a dream or reality? Is this truly happening?

Now, dear reader, we enter the Ich Kari.[118] On the way to Kumush's room, wives and children waited for the groom, forming a reception line. Some of the wives held candles in their hands. The room intended for the groom had been decorated with wedding gifts. Most of the household staff, who were mentioned above in the description of Qutidor's house, assembled themselves near Kumush's room. Not only were there different elaborate embroideries, all hand-stitched by the women, but a big chandelier hung from the ceiling, with candles lined up in rows of thirty, giving the room an unearthly glow. Kumush stood dressed in the white clothing that we saw earlier during the bridal shower...

Her beauty was an ethereal vision graced with the various shades of white, blue, and yellow of the room... Glistening tears dropped from her eyes; she ignored the advice from the yangas, as urgent whispers crept in from outside: The groom is coming! Upon hearing this news, her eyes again swelled with tears, and her expression changed into a visage resolute yet resigned to a life of sadness. Leaving Kumush in this state, the yangas hastened out of the room as the groom appeared. Otabek stood in front of the women, who crowded him from all directions. Following him, Oftob Oyim's sister fanned smoldering wild rue to protect the proceedings from the evil eye. The wives, holding the candles, gave Otabek a final inspection and saw him off.

The groom at last reached the room. His face blushed red from shyness as if he could not hide his shame. At this point, the door opened and the yangas welcomed him into the room.

"Come in, Bek."

Otabek's heart beat so loudly that perhaps even the yangas could hear it. After beckoning Otabek to enter, they went out and closed the door, leaving just a crack so they could still see in. Kumush stood in the center of the room, teasing the edges of her scarf, not looking up at the newcomer. Suddenly, a strange hand softly clutched her delicate hands, busy with fraying the soft silk: "Darling."

Startled by the intrusive hand, Kumush tried to resist with a "Don't touch me!" then retreated, freeing her hand from Otabek's grasp.

In a frightened and shaky voice, Bek asked her, "Why do you pull away? Why don't you look at me?" She had not looked at him, nor did she wish to. But because of his persistence, she relented and glanced up at her groom, giving him a reproachful look... She insisted on this defiance for some time. At last, realizing his identity, she moved nearer to Otabek.

"Are you him?"

"Yes, I am him," said Bek.

They stole furtive glances at each other.

Taking a deep breath, Kumush said, "I don't believe my eyes."

Gazing at her wide eyed, Otabek said, "Me neither."

At that moment, their lips met of their own free will... Small delicate hands touched his shoulders, strong hands grasped under her arms. Kumush looked at Otabek for a long time and said, "What an unexpected happiness," and then she laughed in a mercurial, silvery voice, following the spirit of her name. This laughter was heard even in the outer yard. The cracked door quickly closed. Taking Otabek's hand, Kumush led him to the platform prepared in the middle of the room.

"If I had known that it was you, I would have welcomed you in another way," she said.

"You thought it was someone else?"

"Not just thought, I did not even dare dream it could be you," she said and laughed again. But when they neared the platform and Otabek stopped to place a gold ring on Kumush's slender finger, she became embarrassed and looked at the ground.

"I didn't prepare anything for you."

"You feel bad about not preparing something? Don't feel bad. It is fine," said Bek. "Will you refuse me if I ask you for something?"

"I will not refuse."

Pointing to the black beauty mark above Kumush's upper lip, he said, "If you let me kiss that spot, it would be the greatest gift you could have prepared for me." Kumush blushed crimson.

Let us now step back in time to another moment in our story.

On the second day of his visit to Margilan, Otabek was in the boot bazaar. As the Asr prayers neared their end, he asked for water to make an ablution from one of the storekeepers. The clear stream that ran along the street was at the very bottom of an embankment, making it difficult to retrieve water from it. The storekeeper showed him a suitable place to purify himself, saying, "If you go in through the gate, in that corner you will find a shallow area used for ablutions."

Following these directions, Otabek happened to enter into the area of Qutidor's yard relegated to males. At that moment his eyes fell upon an angel coming out of one of their guest rooms to perform some task. Kumush too could not take her eyes off the handsome young man who had stopped at the bank of the stream already known to us. Unable to resist each other's gaze, they could not tear themselves away for many moments. Finally succumbing

82

to bashfulness, she relented and turned away gracefully, running into a dark corridor that led into the Ich Kari. With this movement, the forty small braids[119] covering her back swayed from side to side. Moving quickly out of sight, Kumush once again cast a glance back at the young man, gracing him with a light smile. With upturned lips, she gave him the gift of a "Farewell." Kumush disappeared, but Otabek stood still for several moments, as if held fast in the earth's grip. At last he blinked, and though he continued to daydream about the mysterious angel whom he had encountered for a fleeting moment, reality finally imposed itself... He sat down near the stream to draw some water to wash with, yet his eyes still glanced toward the passage that hid the mystery. But the maiden did not reappear. He went ahead and performed his ablutions but, even as he stood and dried his hands and feet, he remained rooted to the spot, his eyes fixed on the far bank. Perhaps she had bound Otabek through invisible means, some unseen snare, and she was watching her prisoner from some remote corner.

Otabek waited too long and ended up missing the prayers; finally, he summoned the willpower to leave Qutidor's yard. A love story was born from that moment, one now quite familiar to the readers, only growing stronger day by day. This explains Kumush's simple question, "Are you him?" Kumush's dream had come to life, and this first innocent love brought two young hearts together.

12

SLANDER

"Today is the seventh day since their wedding. Otabek married Qutidor's daughter."

Hamidboi heard the news on his return from Qoqan. While contemplating the various terrible means and methods of revenge that gave rise to a sinister demeanor worthy of his mood, the phrase "he married Qutidor's daughter" echoed in his ears.

His arrival from Qoqan meant a great calamity for his two wives, both of whom were beaten for no apparent reason. They avoided him out of fear for their well-being. Understandably, both *kundosh*[120] dreaded setting foot in the same room with him, loathing his awful visage. Hiding in the dark corners of the yard, disgusted by his behavior, the two women were united in wishing for his death. "If he had died in Qoqan and his corpse had been eaten by dogs, he would not have our pity," they whispered.

Deep in thought, he considered his next step. In that moment a predatory brutality could be discerned in him. His posture showed that he would soon prey upon an innocent. He contemplated evil, seeking the right course of action to accomplish his wicked designs. A malignant sneer then appeared. Snapping his fingers, having finally made a decision, Hamid leaped up, snatching his dirty turban from a peg on the wall, and left the room. Giving some instructions to the foreman and workers in his outer yard, he walked through the great gate and onto the street. Clumsily winding his turban around his head while walking, he struggled to get the turban just right as he traversed the narrow streets. He finally made it to the western side of the city—to the neighborhood of beks.

At the edge of the beks' district, located near the great south gate, two soldiers with swords and rifles were talking to each other. An individual already familiar to us approached them and asked, "Is the bek at home?"

Since he was rudely intruding upon their conversation, one of the men gave him a hostile glare. The second one pointed his rifle at a house, answering, "Go!"

He passed through the gate into an enormous yard where approximately fifteen armed men were sitting in a circle, heating themselves at a fire that was devouring a tree stump. He walked toward the guard standing at attention in front of the main doors of the house. He requested an audience with the qorboshi,[121] asking for permission to enter the veranda. He was led in by the sergeant at arms.

The qorboshi, a man between forty and fifty years of age, had a blue turban wrapped around his head, a heavy O'ratepa robe bound with a silver belt around his waist, and a silver sword in a sheath on his knees. His naturally dark complexion was yellowed by years of using *koknar* or *tiryak*.[122] He sat, carefully reading an order.

The qorboshi absentmindedly acknowledged the visitor's greeting and in a colorless voice, asked, "What are you doing here?"

"Taksir, I have a complaint to register."

The sergeant at arms left the visitor and went to stand alone near the door, his fist clenched at his chest out of respect.

"What kind of complaint do you have?"

"Your Honor, if you would permit me to sit?"

"Very well, sit."

The applicant moved forward, half-bowed, and kneeled on the faded, tattered carpet in front of the qorboshi. Putting the folded order in his robe, the qorboshi looked at the visitor with disdain.

"Where are you from?"

"Taksir, I am from here—from Margilan."

"What is your name?"

"Taksir, Hamidboi."

"What is your profession?"

"I am a master weaver," he said, attempting to be vague.

"Good enough. Tell me your complaint."

Affecting a dramatic voice, Hamid delivered his complaint. "To our honored father-in-law of the khan, Shah-an-Shah,[123] even under the just rule of Musulmanqul Bahadur.[124] The Qora Chopan do not wish to lay down their arms quietly. The people of Tashkent remain in opposition to his rule, planning insurrection against our elder brothers the Qipchaqs. They desire self-rule and are condemning the country to anarchy. Until now we thought that these rebels were led only by Azizbek and his chief adviser, Yusufbek Hajji, in Tashkent. But their seeds of rebellion have spread into Margilan as well."

The qorboshi's eyes widened. "What are you saying? Who are the rebels in Margilan?"

"One of them is the son of Yusufbek Hajji, an agitator from Tashkent by the name of Otabek who is now staying in Margilan. The second is his coconspirator and father-in-law, Mirza Karim Qutidor."

"Are they indeed?"

"It is so, Your Honor."

"Where did you learn this information?"

"Not long ago, I was at one of their meetings, Your Honor."

"All right, all right, what sort of meeting?"

"Many things were said at the rendezvous, Taksir," said Hamid. "Otabek, who was the head of the gathering, told us of the Qipchaqs' oppression and hegemony, and how under the mandate of seizing power from the Qipchaqs in Tashkent, Azizbek and his father started an underground movement. He told us that Margilan must also follow their path, and participants at the meeting, especially Mirza Karim, supported this plan. If we do not prevent this plot, disaster looms for the future of our lands and governance, Taksir."

"In whose house did the meeting take place?"

This was an unexpected question. It made him lose his composure. If he named the meeting place, his brother-in-law and cousin Rahmat would also be incriminated and he would have cut off his feet with his own ax. He was confused, and he began to stall. His confusion delayed his response, which came at last: "I don't remember the place of the meeting, Your Honor."

To this suspected dissembling, the qorboshi shouted angrily: "Don't remember?"

Hamid became more flustered and said in a weak voice, "Even if I could remember it, I can't tell you the location."

"Ah, you can't tell me the location?" the qorboshi said, laughing angrily at him. "If you do not tell me immediately, you will be thrown into the pit reserved for traitors."

"I am sorry. Spare me, Taksir."

The qorboshi growled like an animal. "No excuses!"

Hamid reverted to his last resort; he started to dig in his pocket and, with great difficulty, took out his purse. Taking out about ten gold coins without counting them, he handed them to the qorboshi.

"Taksir, I have a small gift for you."

The moment Hamid began rummaging through his pocket, a calmness came over the qorboshi. Taking the gold coins and placing them in his pockets, his voice returned to its former stateliness, and his words were suddenly polite.

"So, as you say, it was in a hidden location, Hamidboi."

"Taksir..."

86

"So, they planned insurrection as well?"

"Taksir... If we do not act decisively, we risk utter destruction."

"Of course we are going to punish these insurgents... I will now go to the beks[125]... and give a report. We will catch these cowardly traitors before this evening is over," said the Qorboshi. Hamid's countenance eased. As the qorboshi really began listening to him, the joy of revenge and the hope for resultant paradise played in Hamid's eyes. How easily the qorboshi had swallowed his bait.

Taking from the shelf a reed pen and an inkwell, the qorboshi placed them in front of Hamidboi. Preparing to write, he asked, "Could you tell me in full, Hamidboi, who were the conspirators?"

"One of them was the son of Yusufbek Hajji from Tashkent, Otabek."

"Yes, yes! So you've said, the son of Yusufbek Hajji. So those cowards are going to sink Margilan into a sea of blood? And the second?"

"Mirza Karim from Margilan, who recently married his daughter to Otabek."

"A bastard will find another bastard, even in the dark... And the third?"

"Hasan Ali, the slave of Otabek."

"The fourth?"

Thinking for some time, Hamid answered, "I do not know whether he was in Margilan or not: Akram Hajji from Andijon."

The qorboshi wrote.

"The size of the conspiracy is considerable. Who else?"

"Nobody else, Taksir," said Hamid, adding, "if Otabek and Mirza Karim are caught, the head of the snake will be crushed. As for the others, they are not major conspirators, Your Honor."

Finishing his report, the qorboshi put the document in his robe. "Now this will be settled. Tomorrow morning you will hear of the scandal." Standing up from his place, Hamid bowed, thanked the qorboshi, and took his leave.

13

JAIL

An orda[126] used to stand near the city walls in the district of Yormazar[127] but now acres of orchards with apple, apricot, pear, and mulberry trees have been cultivated in that area.

The defensive walls, whose battlements displayed an intricately carved floral design, reached a height of eight meters and were buttressed with mud-brick parapets, while the arch of the main gatehouse was flanked on both sides by guard posts, each containing a pair of young men wearing *Galcha* robes[128] and fur caps on their heads. Swords swung on their leather belts as they lazed against their rifles. Dusk had just fallen as someone inside slammed shut the front gates that had been left ajar, binding them with a great chain that made a loud clang. Now that it is impossible for us to gain entry, let us walk around the perimeter of the structure...

If we walk two hundred paces to the left, the wall extending out from the gatehouse ends abruptly in a corner. The one tower built especially in this section of the battlements is now empty of soldiers. From here I think we will continue farther south along an empty stretch of the fortifications as we take another four hundred paces, moving along the southeast edge of the ramparts to yet another unfortified tower. If a man were to look out from this vantage point, he would see the far southwest section of the complex. Traveling around the four points of the enclosure, we will measure out a total of sixteen hundred paces, and we will find ourselves again at the familiar gate on the western side.

By now night has fallen and it is impossible for us to recognize the face of the man standing next to us. The guards we noted at the main gate remain standing, still as statues, in the dark.

Hearing the echo of horse hooves in the city streets, one of the guards questioned his mate.

"Is that the sound of hooves?"

The second guard looked toward the road. "There are three horsemen coming."

"Who rides at this late hour?"

"No one else but the qorboshi would arrive at this time. Maybe it is he."

Indeed, the qorboshi arrived with his two adjuncts, dismounted from his horse while handing the reins to the soldiers, and gave the guards an order: "Tell them to open the gate."

The night sentries were informed, and the qorboshi entered as they opened the main gate. Since we have already reckoned the perimeter of the structure, we can now estimate its internal dimensions. A north- facing curtain wall divided the orda into two sections. The largest section of the yard was intended for the hakim's[129] family; the outside yard was bare of structures on the south, east, and western walls. On the north face, a substantial keep stood behind the inner gate, measuring forty meters by twenty meters; it was crenellated and had fifteen windows. On one side of the edifice, fifty soldiers gathered around a fire. The scullery, the stables, and the toilets were located near the detachment of soldiers.

The qorboshi stopped near the gatekeeper and asked, "Is the bek present?"

Forcing the gate shut, the gatekeeper answered, "I don't know, Taksir."

The lamplighter, making his nightly rounds of the castle, set fire to a large torch, which lit up the inner courtyards. Upon entering, the qorboshi moved directly to the right of the gate. The quality of the houses announced to the traveler that this was the best district in the whole quarter, as great skill had been demonstrated by the artisans who constructed the buildings. Passing the first sentry of the watch who was standing near the entrance, the qorboshi navigated through their guard niche—a small room carved out from the walls and plastered with stucco—and entered a small anteroom. Then he passed through the second door and entered the great hall.

The hall's decorations displayed great refinement and delicate craftsmanship. Candlelight from fifty chandeliers illuminated the walls, which were gilded with a celestial array of silver filigree, blues, reds, white alabasters, pinks, yellows, and blacks, creating a whole universe within the space of the hall. A large carpet on the floor woven with a luxurious tulip design charmed the viewer into believing that he lay in a bed of flowers. At the center of the hall of honor, sitting on a silk blanket placed right across the main entrance, near small gold-filigreed doors, was a pleasant, richly dressed young man of approximately fifteen years of age in a red velvet robe. He was eating plov.

Entering through the doors, the qorboshi smiled at the young man.

"Ah, Ahmadjon, it is good that you are here."

Ahmad did not move from his place.

"I am always here. Help yourself to plov."

"Thank you. Is Qushbegi in?"

"He is in," said Ahmad. "I am stuffed with plov. Help yourself, eat!"

"In that case, please pass it to me with your blessed hand."

Ahmad eagerly scooped up a large handful of plov, reaching out to the qorboshi. The qorboshi leaned forward and ate directly from Ahmad's palm, as if devouring him... a few moments passed in this manner. The central door of the hall opened and a middle-aged man appeared. He had a full face with ponderous, bushy brows standing watch over heavy-lidded cynical eyes, and a sparse beard; he stood at average height and wore a gold brocade robe with a sword hanging from his waist. Ahmad and the qorboshi immediately stood up and bowed—it was clear that this person held a high position. The man approached briskly, sat on the silk blanket, and began speaking concisely.

"How are you, Xoliqbek? Are your lands peaceful? Take a seat, please."

"Thank God they are under the benevolent shadow of your state," said the qorboshi, paying homage nervously by clenching his hands and kneeling at Qushbegi's feet. Taking the empty dish wrapped in a tablecloth, Ahmad exited through the door from which Qushbegi had entered.

"Nothing about the thieves from yesterday? Did you catch them?"

"Under the shadow of your state, one of the thieves has been caught. I think soon the other shall be caught, with your help."

"Is there other news?"

90

The qorboshi lent his face some gravity. "Under the auspices of your power, I think I have discovered a lair of conspirators who pose an immediate threat to our rule."

Taking his sword, which until then had hung casually by his side, Qushbegi placed it on his knees.

"What sort of conspirators?" he asked coldly.

"A cabal of insurgents, Taksir," said the qorboshi. "Who could pose a greater threat to our rule than the Black Robes of Tashkent?"

Qushbegi's back straightened a little, his eyes widening. "Well?"

"As you well know, the leaders—none other than Azizbek and Yusufbek Hajji—continue to incite rebellion in Tashkent. Unsatisfied with a local rebellion, they plan to bring destruction to Margilan, as they have sent their trusted man here. For their designs, they have found a local leader."

"Do you know him?"

"I recognize his name, Taksir," said the qorboshi in a proud tone. "He is the son of Yusufbek Hajji and is in league with several conspirators from our beloved Margilan."

"The son of Yusufbek Hajji?"

"Your Honor, his name is Otabek."

Qushbegi's eyes lit up and his forehead furrowed as he tugged at his beard with his left hand and evaluated this information. This news excited him. It seemed to him above suspicion, and it made even more sense considering the fact that Yusufbek Hajji was well known as one of the leaders of the rebellion so it was logical that he would send his son to Margilan to create an uprising.

"Where is he staying?"

"In the house of a local citizen named Mirza Karim Qutidor."

"What kind of relationship does he have with Mirza Karim?"

"Bless you, Your Honor," said the qorboshi. "The closest person to Otabek whom we have found in Margilan is this Qutidor. Several days ago, he gave his daughter's hand in marriage to Otabek, making him his son-in-law. We are told that Otabek discusses all his plans with him."

"Who has gathered around them?"

Removing his report from his robe, the qorboshi passed it to Qushbegi. "All the conspirators we presently know of are documented here."

As soon as he finished reading the report, Qushbegi ordered the qorboshi to immediately arrest those who were listed in it. Paying his respects again, the qorboshi left. Qushbegi read the report again and sank deep into thought.

Uttaboi Qushbegi[130] had just returned from the orda at the very moment the qorboshi entered, paying his obeisance.

"I brought most of them, Your Honor, but I could not find two of them."

Qushbegi asked with impatience, "What about Otabek?"

The qorboshi answered triumphantly, "Caught, My Honor! Qutidor as well."

"Bring them in."

Qushbegi appeared visibly relieved as the qorboshi exited, giving orders to those in the outside hallway. Upon his return, he bowed and asked Qushbegi again for permission to sit. After gaining his acquiescence, he took his place. Otabek and Qutidor, between two armed escorts, came through the door and paid obeisance to the bek, who ordered the soldiers to leave and quietly called on the accused to approach...

While Otabek seemed dazed, almost detached from the world, Qutidor shook in fear and his face was pale and feverish. Together the men crouched in front of Qushbegi. Qushbegi focused on Otabek, looking down at his submissive figure. Qushbegi began interrogating him: "Are you the one they call Otabek?"

"Yes, Taksir."

"Are you the son of Yusufbek Hajji from Tashkent?"

"Yes, Taksir."

"Are you staying in Margilan?"

"Yes, Taksir."

"Have you been long in Margilan?"

"Approximately forty days."

"What is the purpose of your visit to Margilan?"

"Business, Taksir."

"Are you alone?"

"Another person accompanied me."

Qushbegi glanced at the list in his hand and continued: "Who is Hasan Ali?"

Otabek's confusion turned to suspicion, but he continued with his answers, attempting to appear casual.

"He is our servant. He accompanied me from Tashkent."

"Where is Hasan Ali at present?"

"In Margilan."

"Is he staying with you?"

"No, he isn't. He is taking care of our belongings at the caravansary. We have some goods stored there."

"Who is this person with you now?"

"My father-in-law."

"For how long has he been your father-in-law?"

"Today is the eighth day."

"Were you married before?"

"No."

"Being from Tashkent, for what reason did you marry someone from Margilan?"

Uncomfortable at this line of questioning, Otabek hesitated. As if Otabek's discomfort had revealed the truth of the matter, Qushbegi demanded, "Answer me!"

"Fate, Your Honor."

Qushbegi thought for a while and then asked, "Who else in Margilan do you know?"

"Besides three or four persons, I don't know anyone in Margilan."

"Perhaps you know Akram Hajji?"

"Yes, I know him. We attended several meetings together."

"Where is your friend Akram Hajji at present?"

"I don't know, Your Honor," Otabek replied and looked at his father- in-law as if turning to him for an answer.

Qutidor responded, "Most likely Akram Hajji is in Andijon at present."

"All right, Otabek, you answer this time: Where did the meetings attended by Akram Hajji take place?"

Finally sensing the purpose of these questions, Otabek gained control of the inquiry.

"Our first meeting, approximately a month ago, took place in the house of Ziyo-aka, and the second one, at my father-in-law's," he said, indicating Qutidor. "These meetings were attended by Akram Hajji as well."

"During the meeting at Ziyo-aka's house, who was there?"

"Ourselves and Ziyo Shohichi," he said and, after considering the question for a little while, he added, "Ziyo-aka's son, Rahmat, Akram Hajji, and Hasan Ali. As well as another person named Hamid."

On hearing the name Hamid, the qorboshi gestured in confirmation.

Qushbegi nodded in reply and continued.

"Who participated in the second meeting?"

"The persons I have just mentioned were at the second meeting as well. Only Hamid was absent."

"How many days did you say your visit to Margilan has lasted?"

"Approximately forty days."

"Well," said Qushbegi. "tell me, for what purpose did you remain in Margilan for a whole forty days?"

"It is well known that Tashkent is under a blockade. It would be unwise to return there at this time."

"Since you yourself are a Black Robe," said Qushbegi, grinning sarcastically. "Have you become afraid of your Qipchaq brothers?"

"I do not understand your joke," Otabek scoffed. He spoke as if addressing a commoner. Not so much in his choice of words, but his response dripped with sarcasm, and as a result Qutidor slouched in fear, his stomach churning with butterflies. To speak, even if truthfully, in such an impertinent manner was tantamount to a death sentence. Although Uttaboi held the reputation of being one of the great hakims of the day, he still held the traditional values of a ruler... The Hakim blustered at Otabek's words.

"Have you forgotten that your father, Yusufbek Hajji, is the enemy of the Qipchaqs? Have you inherited your father's prejudices? Have the prejudices of your father also been passed onto you?"

"Who is the enemy of the Qipchaqs? Against whom does my father instigate treachery? For the love of God, speak plainly, Taksir! Otherwise, I am going to burst!"

"Do not feign ignorance of these matters," said Qushbegi. "Who is your father's agent? Why were you sent to Margilan? What are you scheming with Qutidor? We have documented proof of your treachery. You plan to incite your brothers in Margilan against Qipchaq rule. We are well aware of all your plans."

Otabek and Qutidor could only manage to gasp "Oh my god!"

Otabek's neck constricted and his face turned blue; Qutidor just sat quivering. Otabek struggled to gather his composure.

"Someone has slandered us, Your Honor," he said. "Do you really believe my father is the enemy of the Qipchaqs? And that I traveled to Margilan in order to foment a rebellion here?"

"We do not think, we know. We also understand the motivation behind Qutidor giving his daughter's hand in marriage to you in order to make you his son-in-law." Qutidor remained stock still as if frozen in a picture. Otabek could barely control his emotions.

Qushbegi, along with the qorboshi, persecuted the two men as if they had already been proven guilty; they perceived every movement as an admission of guilt. After three or four minutes of silence, Otabek began, "You have judged us as insurgents, as dissidents. Whether your judgments of us are true or not, I believe further inquiry will reveal the truth. I am not flattering you out of fear of being under your sword, but because you are a representative of the government, someone who is well known as a conscientious man, I will reiterate my father's and my own view:

"We do not support either the Qipchaqs or the Tashkent Black Robe alliance. We feel that neither faction is more suited than the other to control the government. Therefore, to offer up the future of the people of Turkistan to one of these groups would be like giving lambs to wolves.

"If we were to reveal the true motives within the hearts of those contending for power on either side of the contest, we would see one faction who seek to rob the people solely in pursuit of financial gain; whereas the other desires only beautiful wives and a luxurious life. Those participants in the conflict only see these two pursuits but not the third pursuit, the highest, that of creating peace and prosperity for the people. This sacred endeavor is absent.

"Taksir, in our view, we seek, perhaps not through actions, but through a greater vision, that third and higher purpose for the people. So far, this greater purpose lives only in our dreams. Your

Honor, we support those who have dreams of the third, greater purpose. The reason for my father's proximity to Azizbek is not because he supports either the Qipchaqs or the Black Robes, but instead to serve his higher goal, to bring his convictions to life. It is a tragedy that my father's hopes that Azizbek will serve a greater good have come to naught: recently, for the sake of his dark wishes, Azizbek has turned his face from the khan of Qoqan and because of this has caused the blood of many innocent people to be shed. Believe me or not, it is your will, but I am deeply ashamed to be accused of such a petty slander. I say this in accordance with my conscience, Your Honor!"

After Otabek concluded his self-defense, Qushbegi became perplexed. His mind could not get around the contradiction that Otabek was the son of Yusufbek Hajji, and Yusufbek Hajji was the aide and spiritual leader of Azizbek. He decided, on the other hand, that Otabek's passionate rebuttal was well argued and could not be discounted, though it might be a calculated defense. At last, he resolved to investigate this matter thoroughly and not come to a hasty conclusion.

"Regardless, it is apparent you are a person with many predatory designs," Qushbegi stated. "For that reason you must stay in prison until we get to the root of the matter."

Speechless, Otabek remained stock still, his mouth gaping wide open. Qutidor looked at his son-in-law, as if to say, "Is there no way out?" Qushbegi waved his hand, dismissing the prisoners. The soldiers stepped forward and escorted the presumed guilty parties to prison.

"Tomorrow, bring the conspirators who hosted illegal gatherings in their homes along with the other attendees who are still at large!" Given Qushbegi's final order, the qorboshi exited with his leave.

14

SEEKING HELP FROM TASHKENT

For Kumush, who had possessed the blessings of unexpected happiness for eight whole days, this new turn of events created an unexpected disaster. As for Hasan Ali, still exultant over Bek's marriage to his "beloved," this calamity was no small tragedy. To add insult to injury, Oftob Oyim remained overcome; the mother who had just given away her only daughter—the very white and black of her eyes[131]—to the groom, and had been joyous over seeing them inseparable, was now inconsolable at the fact that not only her son-in-law, but also her own husband had been thrown into the abyss. Prisoners to their heavy thoughts, they were still in disbelief over the sudden events. Kumush lamented the future of her unexpected happiness. She did not even know whether they would be reunited again. Hasan Ali, whose worries had just eased because of Otabek's marital union, found himself vexed to yet again be in a bind. Oftob Oyim, increasingly depressed, crawled inside herself.

Kumush and Oftob Oyim shed endless tears as their only consolation against this disaster. The men's arrest placed a full burden onto Hasan Ali's shoulders. With no one to assist her in gaining her husband and father's freedom, Kumush's tearful eyes pleaded with Hasan Ali, as if saying, What should we do? Qutidor had no other male relatives to fall back on, and the only possible support on Oftob Oyim's side of the family was Kumush's uncle Ahmad Bek, who was known as a "devotee"[132] and lived between Qoqan and Khujand,[133] which made seeking his assistance impractical.

Therefore, since he was the only person faithful to Kumush and her mother, Hasan Ali took the burden on his shoulders.[134] In your native land, where you grew up, you always have your brothers or friends. Even in the worst of times you can at least receive moral or material assistance from them. But our Hasan Ali was not in Tashkent. He was in Margilan. He was a foreigner in a city where few knew him. At first Hasan Ali had high hopes for help from Ziyo Shohichi and his son Rahmat. He knew that he had no one else to render aid. Unfortunately, those hopes were soon dashed. Ziyo-aka and Rahmat were imprisoned, and Hasan Ali himself was pursued by the authorities. Hasan Ali and Kumush's desperation and fear multiplied. He had escaped imprisonment with Otabek and Qutidor only because he had been staying at the caravanserai. After the qorboshi's soldiers began their search for Hasan Ali, Kumush's and Oftob Oyim's hope for their loved ones' imminent release began to seem in vain. At first, Hasan Ali wanted to give himself up and share in the other prisoners' fate and, if fate would have it, in their release. Kumush and her mother would not permit this: "Your freedom might be useful to the prisoners," they said. Hasan Ali found their reasoning sound, but his worries doubled. He lived every minute in fear of being discovered. He hid from the qorboshi's soldiers, changing his hiding place several times a day.

Hasan Ali lost his appetite, and he could no longer sleep at night. He asked himself constantly, Why were Otabek and Qutidor arrested? What were they accused of? Is there something I do not know about Otabek? He also considered the fact that he knew of all of Otabek's dealings but was unsure about Qutidor—Could Otabek be taking the blame for some dirty business of Qutidor's? This disaster reminded him of the adage "The time of your death is not decided by fate but assigned by the bloodthirstiness of your rulers, the 'brotherhood of beks.' " At this moment of clarity, he could only shake his head and sigh.

For five days no one knew why Otabek and Qutidor had been imprisoned. During this period, Hasan Ali could not do anything on behalf of the prisoners in Margilan; saving his own life from the efforts of the qorboshi's soldiers proved a big enough challenge.

Finally, he reversed his decision to remain in Margilan and instead planned to flee to Tashkent. The current state of affairs remained, but reports arrived that the Army of Qoqan were still blockading Tashkent. Hasan Ali was informed that entering the besieged city would place him in great peril. Nevertheless, he felt he had to leave for Tashkent because it was the only place that could offer him the possibility of assistance. Arriving at this decision, he consulted with Kumush Bibi and Oftob Oyim. Unfortunately, they could offer him no guidance. All they could do

98

was weep over his plan. Hasan Ali could only try to reason with them, saying, "It seems we can find no solution here. I must go to Tashkent to seek assistance."

Kumush countered in a faltering voice, "If you couldn't find a solution in Margilan, how will you find one in Tashkent?"

"We have to try, my daughter. Maybe your father-in-law, or perhaps someone else, can find a solution to this mess," said Hasan Ali.

"What will happen to us, if the oppressors..." said Kumush, unable to finish her thought. She burst out crying. Forcing back his own tears, Hasan Ali calmed Kumush Bibi.

"Do not give in to dark thoughts, my daughter," he said, trying to console her. "Qushbegi is better than most hakims. If God wills, they will be freed from prison before I return from Tashkent."

That very night he prepared for the road. For his trip to Tashkent they chose Qutidor's fleetest dun Saman Yo'rg'a[135] horse. The next morning, at the crack of dawn, the first person to depart from Margilan's Qoqan Gates was Hasan Ali.

15

TASHKENT UNDER SIEGE

The day marked the fifty-first of Tashkent's blockade. The cold weather turned a bit mild as the sun crossed a clear blue sky.

The earth began its thaw; mud abounded throughout the length and breadth of the land, and white frost covered the clusters of towers while wisps of steam rose into the air.

At dawn, an attack from the Qoqan contingent against Tashkent's Samarqand Gates[136] handed the aggressors a bloody defeat. Sepahi[137] fighting on behalf of Qoqan had retired to their yurts to mend their wounds and rest up for the next attack on the battlements. The sight of the battle was too grim to gaze upon and subdued the witnesses to silence. No one wished to recall the scene.

The span between the Kamolon[138] and Samarqand Gates, under the fortress walls, an area of approximately five hundred paces, was full of the dead—headless, stripped to the waist, and coated in thick black blood.

Tashkent's defenders, exhausted and warming themselves in the sun, sat on the battlements in turbans or peaked fur hats while observing with great pleasure the open cemetery stretching out before them. There were two human conditions represented between the two gates: Those under the battlements, spread about, headless, smeared with congealing blood, bereft of clothing in a hellish display, and those others manning the walls, who swam in an ocean of worldly pleasure, reveling in their recent victory.

One of the gallant soldiers on the fortress battlements laughed when he retold the tale of how he had shot a Qipchaq officer with his rifle: "When I shot the coward, damn his father, he rose three meters above his horse and crumpled to the ground!"

Another singled out a body from the corpses and said, "You see that one? Look at him! That Qipchaq was suffering from a gunshot wound, moaning aloud in pain. I cut off his head with my sword and claimed his gold belt and gilded robe for myself."

Everyone bragged about the day's courageous acts and how they heroically obtained trophies of gold belts, ruby rings, otter skin jackets, and swords sheathed in silver, among other spoils.

Suddenly a voice sang out from the top of the fortress:

Let your reign be a golden age.
Let our dear Bek remain safe.
Let you deny him a cure for his pain, my friend.
Let your fate be to burn Normat alive![139]

If we pass by the fortress, making our way through the stench of corpses and moving a bit farther along, we come to a stop at the Samarqand Gates. They are built six meters high, five meters thick, and flanked by two battlement walls that are eight meters thick and face the setting sun. Since we fear the enemy suddenly attacking from any direction, we will knock on the gate, impatient to enter.

"Bek-aka, open it, please! Be quick, please."

100

The gate guards continue to sit, ignoring us. After we plead for fifteen excruciating minutes, one of the bored guardsmen slowly rises to the top of the gate tower and cautiously looks down to survey our predicament. If we convince him that we are truly from Tashkent, he opens the lock the size of a camel's head and unravels the chain with great difficulty.

After we enter, the guard murmurs all that decorum permits him and starts to close the gates. Finally, we can view the soldier's appearance: he wears a tanned sheepskin jacket, a cheap fabric belt from which dangles about half a meter of keys, and a Turcoman[140] fur cap.

After noting his features, we walk to the right of the gate. Fifteen paces closer to the gates, there are more guards sitting at a fire and smoking a chilim[141] under an awning. As we proceed into the fortress, we can survey the defenders from inside: wearing all makes and sizes of clothing, some holding swords, some rifles. The defenders sit on the roofs of the fortress, leaning against the tower walls and warming their heads in the sun. The battlements up to the Kamolon Gates are also full of defenders, offering us a new perspective. Under the walls of the fortress, one bek with a gilded robe, a glorious turban, and a silver belt displaying a sword is speaking to a young soldier. He is pointing to a mound. If we take another fifty or sixty steps we will reach the place where the beks are conversing. The horrible gristmill we saw outside would pale in comparison to the scene before us: our eyes fall upon a gruesome mound that will sink us into oblivion for hours on end. A hill of three to four hundred heads! There are beards of a pious hand's length, their thin hair mingled with blood, and pale, waxen faces with, instead of black pupils, milky-white eye sockets dotted with blood, half open as if damning the world of the living.

One particular head stands out, its owner not even twenty. Beardless under thick, dark, blood-caked brows, his eyes are half-open, seeking someone in his moment of death... His white teeth, visible in his mouth, are frozen in horror, clenching his tongue, damning himself for his birth into such a frivolous land and life.

The fortress commander, lingering in front of the mound of heads, shows a nearby soldier a head of one of the slain and informs him that it was indeed once owned by one of the beks he knew well. At that moment, three armed horsemen appear at the

Kamolon Gates, riding forward, and a commotion begins among the fortress's defenders. "Hudaychi,[142] Sulayman Hudaychi!" they shout. Sulayman Hudaychi rode to the fortress commander and informed him of Azizbek's impending visit, then turned his horse's head, trotting back to his retinue.

The news spread to all the soldiers, and the fortress commander, worked into a frenzy, ran back and forth as if he had a worm in his boot.

"Fellow warriors, those of you manning the fortress! Ready yourselves, straighten your lines! Bek is coming! Husseinbek, hurry to the gatekeepers, tell them to prepare themselves! Ganibek, put your soldiers in order! Sergeant of the guards, assemble your men!"

Those standing on the top of the fortress, as well as those on guard below, started moving. They descended to the ring of assembly points, making a uniform line. During the racket, the fortress commander rode from one side of the wall to the next. "Be prepared, men! Put yourselves in order. Be ready to greet Azizbek!" he shouted.

The heroes of the day stood in line, holding rifles, swords, halberds, scimitars, and pikes. A green banner flew from the middle of the line. In this manner everyone readied themselves for the audience of Aziz Parvanchi, according to the honor and ceremony due to him.

16

AZIZBEK

After three or four minutes, Azizbek arrived at the Kamolon Gates with a retinue of one hundred soldiers and military and civilian staff. Azizbek was a man about fifty years old who rode on a black stallion with gilt trappings glimmering in the sunlight. He wore a gold brocade robe, an Algerian sword in a silver sheath hung on his golden belt, and a silk turban wound around his head.

His lean legs were decorated with silver stirrups. He had thin eyebrows balanced by a wheat-colored pointed beard.

Following him on a black horse was a man who wore a blue-green broadcloth robe lined in fur, a sword hanging from a silver belt on his right side, a pistol on his left, and a sheepskin qalpak on his head. He was browless, as if his eyebrows had been plucked by jinn[143] themselves. On his dark face he had a sparse black beard lining his jaws, thin wispy hairs on his chin, and deep-seated bloodshot eyes. He was the commander of the army and Azizbek's right-hand man, Rayimbek Dadkhwah.[144]

Next to him was another person on a smaller horse wearing a striped robe from Bukhara, but instead of a belt binding his robe, it fell loose. A large turban wound around his head and, as he leaned forward in his saddle, one could see his full wise face, with expansive, round yellow- brown eyes, and the long gray beard of a mullah. In keeping with his tradition, he was unarmed.

After the two horsemen riding behind Azizbek, a troop of personal guards followed, wearing knee-length short tunics of blue sukno[145] and red rough-woven trousers with leather boots on their feet. Their turbans resembled those of Rayimbek Dadkhwah, but they were covered in red velvet. White belts held their swords on the right side and pistols on the left and they marched in groups of four by four. Despite their well-worn equipage, their appearance was in good order.

The warriors lining the battlements clenched their hands to their chests and bowed all in unison, their heads almost touching the ground. Riding past the contingents with his gilded whip on his breast, Azizbek greeted his men in return, bowing his head. At this moment the fortress commander near the pyramid of heads descended from his horse. A span of forty or fifty horse-lengths remained between the mound of heads and Azizbek. The cheering of the troops seemed to distract Azizbek, who stared at the carnage. The retinue accompanying Azizbek also looked at the horrific display and now sat uncomfortably in their saddles as Azizbek and his troop stopped near the heads. For some time, Azizbek took in the sight, finally smiling at the fortress commander and then saluting him.

"Thank you. Bless you for your courage," said Azizbek. "This day you welcomed the Qipchaqs like Rustam,[146] killing them like dogs. Many thanks to the citizens who displayed true courage. May they live to the end of time!"

After Azizbek's concluding remarks, the Hudaychi relayed to the army his sincere praises, which resounded over the fortress walls.

"Our honorable Bek gives thanks to you all for your courage. You have displayed great bravery reminiscent of Rustam, and he wishes you long life! He performs prayers on your behalf!"

The defenders responded as if they were bringing the apocalypse: "Our praises to you and Your Honor! Let Your Honor also live until the end of time. May the blessings of his shadow cover our heads for eternity!"

Placing his whip to his chest, Azizbek saluted the defenders and gave an order to the Hudaychi: "Give a gilded robe to the commander of the fortress. Silk robes to the yuz boshis, three silver *tenga*[147] for soldiers with meritorious service."

At this, the defenders replied, "May his wealth and power multiply!"

The treasurers, leading two horses through the soldiers, made their way to the Hudaychi. One horse was loaded with Chopans and the other bore two saddlebags filled to their brims with coins. The Hudaychi first took a gilded robe from its horse and awarded it to the head of the fortress. Putting on the brocade robe, the fortress commander prayed on Azizbek's behalf, excessively singing his praises to God. Afterward the herald and the fortress commander, along with a soldier bearing robes and another with the coins, moved toward the troops. The commander doled out three coins to those worthiest and silk robes to the others.

Circling the mound of heads on his horse, Azizbek pointed out to Rayim and the person in the striped Bukharan robe the heads of significant Qoqan leaders known to him. He relayed what functions they had performed while alive and their various offences against the Black Robes.

Although Rayim listened attentively, the man in the striped Bukharan robe only replied with "Taksir," his head turned away in disgust, staring at his saddle. After half an hour, the awards ceremony for the assembled soldiers concluded. The Hudaychi walking toward Azizbek with his empty saddlebag, bowing in salute.

Standing at attention, Azizbek asked the fortress commander, "Well, did all the deserving receive their awards?"

"Under the shade of your power, Taksir."

"At what time did the attack of the Qipchaqs begin?"

"At dawn they started an artillery bombardment from the direction of Oq-Teppa,"[148] said the commander. "After fifteen minutes, Qipchaq cavalry appeared, riding toward the Samarqand Gates. To prepare against such an attack, under the shadow of your benevolence, I placed sharpshooters between the two gates. Initially, I ordered them to shoot from the Samarqand Gates. For fifteen minutes, the sharpshooters gave withering fire. The Qipchaq cavalry could not withstand the volleys from the Samarqand Gates and withdrew to the Kamolon Gates, whose emplacements also delivered fire to the cavalry. After a one-hour engagement, the enemy retreated, leaving behind three to four hundred dead between the two gates. There were only five dead and nine wounded on our side."

Azizbek enjoyed the account immensely. Once again giving his thanks, he asked, "Was Nur Muhammad, the Qipchaq commander, spotted?"

"No, Your Honor. He did not approach the fortress. If he had..."

"We must be ready for him."

"With the assistance of your power, our aim is clear!"

Azizbek shouted to the defenders, "I am satisfied with your actions!" and under the exultant prayers of the defenders, rode on toward the Samarqand Gates with his retinue.

On that day, in the spirit of the victorious mood felt throughout the city, Azizbek made the rounds to inspect the defenses. Passing through the Samarqand Gates, they moved toward the Chaqar Fortress.[149] The fortifications lay above the southern banks of the Bozu Su River's deep beds, with its fast-moving waters at the base of the battlements making further fortifications unnecessary. Furthermore, with the Kokcha Stream to the west, the two waterways formed a natural peninsula and barrier discouraging the enemy from attack. Several defense positions had been built on top of the hill by the soldiers, with a total of three artillery: one faced southwest, one faced west, and the other toward the northwest. These positions were constantly manned by artillery detachments and foot soldiers.

With his soldiers, Azizbek descended to the bottom of the hill. They traversed the water facing the mound of skulls. The artillerymen and guards were reviewed and awarded with several coins. After that Azizbek and his soldiers mounted the eastern side of the hill. Because the other side of the hill measured the height of several poplar trees, in order to get to the Kokcha Gates, one had to pass through the Suzuk Ota Cemetery[150] and cross the Kokcha Stream. At that point, one would arrive at the Kokcha Gates.

There were not as many defenders at the Kokcha end of the fortress. The Hudaychi led Azizbek, warning the guards of his arrival. The defenders, both young and old, welcomed him. After hearing Azizbek's blessings to the citizenry, they felt great joy. In this manner the retinue passed through the Kokcha, Chigatay, Sagbon, Qoraserai, Takhtapul, and Labzak Gates.[151] Finally, they arrived at the Kashgar Gates.[152] Since the Kashgar Gates were near the orda, many soldiers had congregated nearby.

While Azizbek was showered with greetings as he reached the Kashgar Gates, his reverie was interrupted by some unknown intruder urgently banging at the gate, making a din that rang out in all directions. His horse started forward a couple of paces because of the racket and attempted to bolt from Azizbek's control. His followers also jolted in fear as Azizbek shouted at the gate guards, who were still holding their hands to their chest in salute:

"Why are you still staring at me? Go to the gates. Who is that cur?"

The sergeant of the guard fled to the fortress walls.

"Taksir, there is an old man!"

"Open the gates and bring him in," said Azizbek.

The gates opened. Entering from the outside was Hasan Ali, leading Qutidor's Saman Yo'rg'a horse. Nervous that he was intruding on the ceremony, he greeted Azizbek meekly.

17

YUSUFBEK HAJJI

Alongside Rayim Bek Dadkhwah, a man in a striped Bukharan robe straightened in his saddle upon seeing Hasan Ali.

"Oh yes! Ha! It is our very own Hasan Ali," he said. "Come here, Hasan. Otabek is in good health?"

Hasan Ali descended to where Yusufbek Hajji was standing. They greeted each other, and then Yusufbek Hajji turned to Azizbek, saying, "This is our man, Your Honor, just now arriving from Margilan."

Azizbek bit his lower lip. He would have liked to pass a capital sentence upon Hasan Ali and thrown him into the hands of the executioner for daring to spook his horse by pounding on the gate. Not responding to Yusufbek Hajji, he continued on his path. Yusufbek Hajji followed Azizbek, while Hasan Ali fell in behind the detachment of soldiers winding their way toward the orda. Upon reaching the fortress gates, the orda begi[153] offered his arm to Azizbek, helping him dismount from his horse.

As Azizbek entered the fortress, Yusufbek Hajji dismounted his own horse and requested his leave: "May I take my leave, Bek?"

Azizbek glanced at Hajji. "You have my permission—attend breakfast in the orda tomorrow."

"Very well, Your Honor."

One of the soldiers assisted Yusufbek Hajji in mounting his horse, which then trotted over to Hasan Ali, who up until that point had waited apart from the others. The cavalry then filed into the orda, leading the horses behind them.

Yusufbek Hajji fretted over Hasan Ali's sudden arrival without Otabek at his side and was convinced some evil had transpired.

"Why have you come earlier than planned? Is Otabek all right?" he asked, blurting out the question before he had even reached Hasan Ali. Hasan Ali either didn't hear the question or pretended he hadn't heard it; either way, he made no reply.

"Why do you remain silent?"

"Otabek is in good health."

"Then why did you arrive early? Where is Otabek?"

Hasan Ali struggled to give him the news of Otabek's arrest. Finally, drying tears from his eyes, he admitted, "Otabek has been detained by the hakim of Margilan."

"Why, why?" asked Hajji, looking as if he would fall from his horse.

"For what reasons?"

"The reasons are still unclear."

"Astaghfurallah!"[154] exclaimed Hajji, before remaining silent for some time.

Hasan Ali relayed to him the details of the recent events, from Otabek's visit to Margilan up until the moment he was arrested. Yusufbek Hajji, stunned into complete confusion, did not even pay the slightest heed to Bek's recent marriage but focused only on his arrest.

"Certain that I would be ineffective in rendering aid to him in Margilan, I then fled to Tashkent," said Hasan Ali, concluding his account of the scandal. Hajji, deep in thought, took in the recent events, oblivious to the people of Tashkent who greeted him as he passed. They were from all walks of life, both young and old, and they rose to their feet to acknowledge his renown. But Hajji did not respond. It was if they did not even register to him. After ambling along for quite some time, lost in his thoughts, he turned his horse's head back to Hasan Ali, who was following behind, and asked, "How many did you say were arrested along with Otabek?"

"Three people: the first, Mirza Qutidor, the second, Ziyo Shohichi, and the third, Rahmat."

"All right. Did you attend the party with all four persons?"

"Yes, I did."

"What did they talk about? Did Otabek say anything derogatory about the Qipchaqs?"

"He didn't. The others also did not utter a single criticism."

"Were you absent during any of these assemblies?"

"I was present for all of their parties."

"Where were these gatherings held?"

"First, we were in Ziyo-aka's house, second—"

"Hold on, how many guests were in Ziyo-aka's house?"

"There was Qutidor, Otabek, Akram Hajji from Andijon, myself, and Ziyo Shohichi's brother-in-law, someone by the name of Hamid. Along with Ziyo-aka and his son, there were seven altogether."

Combing his horse's mane with his riding crop, Yusufbek Hajji thought for several moments, then asked, "Where did the second party take place?"

"The second party took place in Qutidor's house, two days after Ziyo-aka's get-together. Those same persons mentioned also attended, with only Hamid absent."

"Where did you meet with him again?"

"We did not meet with him again. Twenty days later, a wedding took place. A wedding is certainly not an appropriate venue in which to speak against the Qipchaqs."

"Who did you say, Hamid? Why was he absent from your second party?"

"I don't know why he was absent. Possibly he was not invited by Qutidor."

"Those arrested were Otabek, Qutidor, Ziyo-aka, and Rahmat, are you certain?"

"That is it, Hajji."

"You were also sought for imprisonment by the qorboshi's soldiers?"

"Yes, they searched for me as well."

"Akram Hajji went to Andijon, and for that reason they couldn't find him. Is that correct?"

"Yes, it is."

"What about Hamid?"

"It seems to me they were not looking for him. I think I saw him for a moment somewhere after Otabek was arrested..."

"Didn't you say that a very beautiful woman is now our daughter- in-law?"

"May God protect Otabek. She is indeed worthy of all the love in the world."

"If the bride is of such great beauty, her charm must be renowned all over Margilan?"

"Yes, she is indeed held in great acclaim. Her beauty is a legend on the tongues of men."

"Do you know if Hamid is married?"

"He is married. We heard from his own mouth when he visited our room in the serai that he has two wives."

"Why did Hamid come to your room in the serai?" asked Hajji. "Why didn't you say this before?"

"I forgot to mention it," Hasan Ali said, apologizing. "He came along with Rahmat, who planned to invite Otabek to Ziyo-aka's house. We welcomed them with plov and tea, but they did not say anything to cause alarm at the time. They visited and then left."

"What kind of person is Hamid?"

"His speech was vulgar. He seems to me a person with a black soul," said Hasan Ali, and after a while he asked, "Do you think Otabek is in deep trouble?" Hajji made no reply. Even he feared arriving at that inevitable conclusion. In his view, this was a delicate matter, since the prisoner held in Margilan's jail was the son of Azizbek's spiritual adviser, thought to be the enemy of all Qipchaqs. While rebellion reigned in Tashkent, Otabek's confinement in Margilan, whatever the crime, was really a terrible predicament. For the sake of his son's freedom, Hajji entertained every possibility, but he could not come to a resolution and only became more hopeless. His mind faltered as a result. Finally, the full weight of the threat to his son left him unable to imagine a solution to this disaster. His brain shut down and he sobbed aloud, "Dear God, please do not visit my later years with tragedy," washing his beard with his tears.

"Hasan Ali, by no means let his mother know her son is in jail."

"Certainly."

After this exchange, they arrived, dismounted, and entered the yard, leading their horses behind them.

18

ANNOUNCEMENT[155]

At noon on the appointed day, a town crier proclaimed that Otabek and Qutidor were due to be hanged for treason; subsequently, rumors surrounding the two were on the tongues of the whole populace.

The qorboshi dismissed the mirshab[156] who led Hamid into the room and invited him to sit.

It seemed the qorboshi meant to relay some new piece of information, yet for some reason his tongue hesitated; he seemed irresolute, not knowing how to broach the subject. Finally, the qorboshi girded himself: "Our fathers tell us the world is full of shortcomings; we are always short two pennies to make a nickel. This proverb holds true: We whip ourselves in a hundred ways, but we always fall short of achieving an adequate livelihood."

Paying close heed to his words, Hamid divined the qorboshi's true purpose. "You are right, Your Honor," he said. "In this world we always fall short. Fed up with disappointment, sometimes a person desires to step outside the normal order of things and perish from the earth. However, in this world there are also those who are our friends; if we did not have such allies, we would indeed perish from the earth.

"For that reason, I care very much for my friends. When I see them in need, no matter what, I make all attempts to help them, even at risk to myself."

Shifting his sword to one side and resting on his knees, the qorboshi made a small gesture.

"Thank you, thank you, Mullah Hamid. If only I had friends like those," he said and cleared his throat, then scratched his neck.

"In the days to come, I have to sponsor my son's circumcision[157]—no small affair— according to the Sunnah of our Prophet. I have already acquired most of the necessities for the ceremony but find that I have still come up short. I was just pondering my situation when you arrived."

"Bek-aka," said Hamid, his face beaming a false smile, "even if this pains you, I am going to say it, 'The swords of our exalted beks will be raised in solidarity with the common classes—especially yourself. The weight of your position requires you maintain your distance from us, while in your head you struggle with a great dilemma. Why don't you tell me about it?"

Appreciating Hamid's perceptiveness, the qorboshi smiled. "No, no, Mullah Hamid," he said. "Here is my dilemma. If you serve the government, you must take a hundred angles into consideration."

"Fine, Bek-aka, but my friendship with you is an exception," said Hamid, taking out his purse and beginning to count out gold coins from one hand to the next. The qorboshi's eyes played upon these gold coins, and he imagined his son's circumcision ceremony being augmented with the help of this gold and how his own esteem among the Margilan beks would increase because of its lavishness. When twenty gold coins had finally been doled out, he felt as if he was seeing a mirage, not believing the quantity of gold coins.

Hamid handed him the gold coins. "Here you go, Bek-aka! The quantity of the coins is irrelevant. It is just a symbol of our natural friendship, making our bond even tighter. If you should encounter further shortcomings, I am here for you."

Hands shaking, the qorboshi placed the coins in his change purse.

Hamid was pleased he took the money.

"Well, Mullah Hamid, let us discuss the topic of the day," said the bek. "It is a terrible thing that your brothers-in-law and nephew have become ensnared in this matter."

In response to these words, an anxious expression crept over Hamid's face, and he paid close heed to the words that came from the qorboshi's lips. The qorboshi continued: "The reason for their involvement is that bastard who implicated those two innocents. Otherwise, Qushbegi would not have ordered them to be detained alongside the others. Your testimony to Qushbegi will jail Otabek and his father-in-law, leading to their death, and at the same time, will give little tangible evidence against your brother-in-law and nephew. Under these circumstances, I hope that I will be able to rescue your relatives before their verdict is delivered—I will go today. I hope that your relatives will not be severely punished. Have you heard that yesterday I ordered the town crier to announce that the only ones to be hanged today will be Otabek and Mirza Karim Qutidor?"

"Thank you for your benevolence," said Hamid. "But I am still worried about my relatives. Is it possible to find another way out for them?"

The gold coins recently exchanged made the qorboshi's brain work overtime. After thinking for a while, at last he said, "Yesterday, how did you lay blame on Otabek to Qushbegi? Let me hear it again and I will formulate a plan."

"I relayed the following to Qushbegi: Otabek had stated that the people of Tashkent 'had become fed up with Qipchaq oppression and their weak leadership. The first steps to shake off the yoke of the Qipchaq oppression of Tashkent were Azizbek's and my father's preparations for rebellion. To that end, they have sent me here to incite my friends from Margilan against the Qipchaqs.' Furthermore, he also asked, 'For how long shall we be downtrodden under the Qipchaqs and subjected to rule by nomads?'[158] Qutidor and Akram Hajji joined Otabek in these sentiments, even offering assistance. As for me, I opposed these ideas wholeheartedly, saying 'Your views are misguided and uninformed. During three years of Uttaboi Qushbegi's leadership, no harm has befallen us. Therefore, any action we take against the government will be like stepping on bread, like biting the hand that feeds us.'

"Otabek then made an egregious attack against my character. My brother-in-law and nephew took my side, but out of respect toward a guest in their home did not argue with him. They could not openly speak against him. After this gathering, not wishing a bloody reprisal toward Otabek and his cohort, I kept my silence for some time, but when Azizbek and Yusufbek Hajji's rebellion broke out, I realized my silence was treasonous and I informed our honored qorboshi. As a reward for my faithful service, my one humble request was that nobody, especially those rebellious bastards, should know that I was the informer. This was my testimony laying blame upon Otabek and the justification for the defense of my relatives."

"Bless you," said the qorboshi. "It is evident that your words were spoken honestly and without reservation. I am sure Ziyo-aka and Rahmat will be freed."

"On what basis can you make this assurance?" asked Hamid.

"We already know what our arguments will be," said the qorboshi. "Your words convinced Qushbegi to hang Otabek and Qutidor; why would they not deliver your brother-in-law and nephew to freedom?"

"Do you recall what my brother-in-law and nephew testified during their interrogation yesterday?"

"Their responses did not contradict your testimony, since they denied spreading rebellion during the gathering. This means that, while still respecting their guests in their house, they did not support them either; again, in harmony with your testimony."

Hamid drifted off, deep in thought and clearly worried. Taking note of this change of mood in him, the qorboshi sought to reassure him, "Worry yourself no more, Mullah Hamid. Nothing threatens them."

Hamid looked as if he was about to say something but thought better of it. He tried to get out the words but failed in the attempt. The qorboshi sensed the issue at hand: "Speak, speak. There are no outsiders here."

With the qorboshi's prompting, Hamid finally dared to speak. "What will happen if my brother-in-law and nephew misspeak while responding during the interrogation today?"

"Why would they make a mistake? They will only relay what they know. When the likelihood of death is in sight, the principle of respecting guests such as Otabek will be washed from their conscience; they will be forced to speak the truth and the verdict rendered will be in the spirit of your testimony—blame will be placed accordingly."

Hamid again felt uncomfortable, damning the qorboshi in his mind for not comprehending his hidden intentions.

"Let us for a moment put aside the idea of blame and consider the core of the issue, Qorboshi-aka," he said.

The eyes of the betrayer and bribe-taker met and for several moments an unspoken agreement passed between them. A silence lingered for some time.

Until that moment, the qorboshi had not fully realized what Hamid's secret motives were. He had only understood the gold coins passed to him as incentives, meant for freeing Hamid's relatives. But now that he sensed that the gold was the price of Otabek's and Qutidor's blood, his integrity was shaken, making him hesitate. The qorboshi's clearly fading resolve placed Hamid at a crucial fork in the road, wracking him with indecision in the face of such perilous choices. Before him, in the hands of the bek, was, all on a whim, the fate of either being cast into hell or gaining safety. He dared not take his eyes off of the qorboshi. To relieve the tension, his eyes promised to pay out even more gold. Reading these hints of increased lucre from Hamid's face, the qorboshi gave no heed to his conscience, which remonstrated, "This is blood money for two human beings!"

"How do you plan on achieving your ends?"

Sensing the beginnings of tacit support for his endeavor, Hamid said hurriedly, "I think that the testimony I gave to Qushbegi, placing blame on Otabek and Qutidor and exonerating my brother-in-law and nephew, should be explained to them."

"Yes, it would be best to warn them," said Qorboshi.

"Thank you, Bek. If this is so, we must not lose any more time. Can you go down to them and relay the information before the time of the verdict?"

"I can. But it would be better if you did it yourself."

Hamid shook his head in disagreement. "Not just Otabek and Qutidor, but even my brother-in-law and nephew should not know of my participation in these matters."

"All right, yet one factor may work against your scheme. What will happen if Qushbegi calls upon you during the verdict? What if at that time they learn of the hand you had in concocting this plot?"

This consideration bode ill for Hamid. He wanted to appear as pure as an angel, and if his secret were to be revealed and the veil torn aside, exposing his role, he would be forced to come face to face with his prey.

"Can you arrange for my absence at the delivery of the verdict?"

"That would be difficult to arrange," said the qorboshi, shaking his head. "Though perhaps it is possible, since Qushbegi rarely revisits evidence once he is already convinced."

Hamid took no heed, and a cold expression came over his face. "All right, I am ready—even if I have to challenge them face to face," he said, and, with this resolution, they parted ways.

19

THE VERDICT

The executioner, with a sharp, bloodthirsty knife hanging from his waist and an ax shouldered at ready, waited for Qushbegi's verdict. To the right of Qushbegi was the qorboshi and then the city authorities sitting in a row; the accused—Otabek, Qutidor, Ziyo Shohichi, and his son Rahmat—stood before the assembly, and soldiers guarded them from behind. Since Otabek and Qutidor had been accused of capital offenses, they remained shackled. Ziyo-aka and Rahmat were left unshackled. Qutidor's face looked like that of a corpse, pale and lifeless. Otabek seemed like he was in shock, but the others kept their wits about them. With the written verdict in his hand, Qushbegi prepared to read it aloud. All were silent, staring at the ground.

"I, the hakim of Margilan, Uttaboi Qushbegi, will hereby render my verdict on behalf of our sacred khan of khans, our honored Khudayar Khan."

On hearing the name Khudayar Khan, the authorities all rose and then sat down, demonstrating their obeisance. Qushbegi began to read the verdict.

"According to evidence provided by a reliable witness, the son of Yusufbek Hajji from Tashkent, Otabek, under the aegis of Azizbek Parvanchi and his father, who have incited rebellion against our khan, came to Margilan in order to, in turn, mobilize the local population against our honored khan. These efforts by Otabek have demonstrated beyond a doubt that he is indeed an insurgent against the great Amir Khan. Hence, Otabek, son of

Yusufbek Hajji, should be executed by hanging. Secondly, a citizen of Margilan, Mirza Karim Qutidor, who has aided Otabek in his treasonous endeavor, should also be punished with death.

"As for Ziyo Shohichi and his son Rahmat, for not revealing their knowledge of the conspiracy to overthrow the government, they are each sentenced to a year of imprisonment."

"An unjust sentence," said Otabek, grimacing. As for Qutidor, he blanched even more.

Ziyo-aka and his son were escorted to prison, while Otabek and Qutidor were handed over to the executioner. This meant that the sentencing was final. After ten minutes, the qorboshi, who had waited for Qushbegi to finalize his instructions to the city authorities, could remain silent no longer and stood up.

"May I attend the execution at the gallows?" he asked. He had not finished his request when a fortress guard named Pirmat suddenly appeared, bowing to Qushbegi.

"A lady has arrived, asking about submitting a petition. May she enter?"

After Qushbegi motioned for the qorboshi to leave, he said to Pirmat, "Let her in."

The sudden arrival of a lady bearing a petition caused the qorboshi to become suspicious. Though he was eager to know the purpose of the strange lady's petition, he had to leave the chancellery since Qushbegi has already given him permission to go.

As the qorboshi exited into the corridor, a lady in an old paranji[159] passed him and made her way through the doorway toward Qushbegi, bowing to him as she entered. The supplicant seemed on edge and overly anxious, which only doubled the qorboshi's suspicions. Concealing himself from Qushbegi, he edged behind the door. The woman slipped her *kuvash*[160] off in the doorway and began to search for something inside her paranji.

Perplexed by the lady's actions, Qushbegi said, "Enter and bring your petition here, sister."

Finally, the lady entered the room, approached Qushbegi, handed him a paper folded three or four times, hurried back to the doorway, and waited there. Qushbegi began to open the petition slowly.

"Please be quick, for God's sake," said the lady. "Otherwise you will drown two innocent men in blood."

Hearing the lady's plea, the authorities present exchanged glances. Qushbegi quickly opened the letter. He read the petition written in broad pencil strokes. Again, the lady became impatient, this time at how long it took him to read the letter. When he reached the end of the letter, Qushbegi suddenly stopped reading and called out, "Pirmat, Pirmat! Come here quickly."

Pirmat rushed into the room. "Yes, Your Honor?"

Qushbegi's voice, taking on a strange, hitherto unfamiliar tone, filled the room.

"Ride quickly to those recently sentenced to death. Even if they are standing in the gallows, have them released! Give my order to the qorboshi. He will accomplish it."

Pirmat bowed and nodded toward the corridor: "The qorboshi is still here."

"Call him in!"

The qorboshi entered from the corridor, bowed, and asked, "What can I do for you, Your Honor?"

"It is fortunate that you had not left yet," said Qushbegi. "Go quickly with Pirmat and retrieve the two men sentenced to death. Bring them back to me."

The qorboshi's suspicions were finally justified. He glanced at the lady standing nearby. "For what reason, Your Honor?"

"This is no time to question me. I said run!"

Bowing, the qorboshi left with Pirmat. Qushbegi swore at his back, "Damn your father." The lady's tension seemed to ease a bit as Qushbegi again started to read the letter in his hands. The city authorities looked both at the letter that had had such an impact on Qushbegi and at the lady who had delivered it. Qushbegi looked up at the lady.

"Sit down, sister," he said.

As she sat down, the lady's silk dress and delicate white hands could be glimpsed underneath the paranji. Qushbegi observed her closely and checked the letter for signs of fraudulence. The letter was crumpled.

"What is your relationship to Qutidor and Otabek, my sister?" he asked her.

"I am the daughter of Qutidor and I am also the wife of Otabek," she replied. Upon hearing her response, the city authorities again exchanged glances.

"Why did you not bring this earlier?"

Qushbegi's question alarmed Kumush. She seemed to understand it to mean that it was too late now. And so she asked in a shivering voice, "Is it still of any use?"

"No, no, my daughter," said Qushbegi. "I only meant why didn't you bring it yesterday or even the day before?"

Kumush Bibi started to sigh, but caught herself and said, "I myself saw this letter only today."

"You never saw this letter before? Where was it found?"

"It was found inside Otabek's old shirt."

Qushbegi then passed the letter to the Azim Ponsadboshi, who was sitting next to him, saying, "Ponsad, read this letter." He asked Kumush, "Did you also read it?"

"Yes, I did."

"Were you aware of your husband's actions against the government?"

"What kind of actions?"

"The various actions for which we were going to hang your husband and father?"

"Unjustly! Wrongly!"

"Who told you that your husband and father could be freed by this letter?"

"I understood that on my own."

"In that case, you knew about your husband's plans, correct?"

"No, Your Honor," said Kumush. Now she fully understood Qushbegi's line of questioning. "We, my mother and I, were not aware of my husband and father's supposed transgressions and were very upset regarding these accusations. Only today we learned that you accused him of being a provocateur from Tashkent. Today I found this letter almost as if by a miracle and ran to you for assistance..." Kumush could not finish her words. Pirmat came in from the corridor, panting from running, and bowed to the Qushbegi.

"They have returned, out from under the very noose around their necks!"

Kumush Bibi almost jumped out of her skin and looked toward Pirmat, taking a long breath. Ponsadboshi, who had been reading the letter this whole time, showed that he was favorably impressed by it. Passing the letter to the official next to him, he informed Qushbegi of his conclusions: "This letter completely changes my views on Yusufbek Hajji from Tashkent, Your Honor! Rumors abound that he is on Azizbek's side; however, one can never really know what he believes in his heart. Only God knows what one really believes!"

As with all situations where "When cowards flee, the brave bear the brunt of battle," the city authorities understood the underlying issue and started to discuss them among themselves.

"It is a relief that the poor man's blood was not spilt needlessly. God transforms injustice into justice."

"It is impossible to even fathom how such a docile lamb such as Qutidor could have a hand in such violence."

These words illuminated Kumush's previously fading lights once again. It seemed that the stars under her sky of lost hope had returned. The darkness all around receded from the resurgence of the stars' light.

The echo of footsteps was heard coming from the corridor and the qorboshi appeared in the doorway.

"They've returned. Can they enter?"

Instead of responding, Qushbegi warned Kumush under her paranji, "If you speak at the meeting without my permission, it will result in their death. Do you understand?"

After Kumush agreed, Qushbegi told the qorboshi to let them in. Though Kumush had seen them proceeding to the orda, she had continued to run, horrified, to the fortress in order to deliver the letter, hoping against all odds to save them. After hearing the command, "Let them enter," her heart began to race. Although she stood there crying, wanting to hang onto their necks, the "monsters" guarding them forbade it. Suddenly Otabek and Qutidor entered in front of the soldiers, with their hands shackled.

"Men, leave us. Qorboshi, remove the shackles from their hands!" ordered Qushbegi.

Seeing himself descending into a valley of tragedies, the qorboshi put his key first in Qutidor's shackles. His hands shook as he turned the key in the lock. He felt that he would soon be sacrificed for the sake of Hamid's hidden treachery. Certain that his role in the affair had been revealed, the qorboshi waited to be delivered into the hands of the executioner.

After a thousand difficulties, Qutidor's hands were freed and the qorboshi then turned to Otabek. Qorboshi's hands shook even more feverishly as he unshackled Otabek, a known enemy. Though freedom remained an uncertain prospect, to gauge the qorboshi's complicity, Otabek gathered all the wrath and loss he felt from his period of incarceration into an unrelenting stare and challenged the qorboshi with his accusing eyes. The fury he could see in Otabek's scrutiny overwhelmed the qorboshi, forcing him to stare at the ground guiltily.

His reaction confirmed Otabek's suspicions. At Qushbegi's command, the two accused men knelt. Looking like a beggar who had lost his begging cup, the qorboshi sat to the left of Qushbegi and next to Kumush. Though Otabek and Qutidor's eyes fell on Kumush, they paid no attention to her, not wondering why a woman in a paranji would visit the hakim. Their sudden release from the gallows and the removal of their shackles surprised them. They looked to Qushbegi's lips for a reason for their freedom.

Qushbegi sat thoughtfully, saying nothing. Nervousness over his long silence reigned over those assembled, all of whom had their ears turned to hear him speak. The qorboshi, however, hoped this situation would persist not for days, but years.

"Otabek," began Qushbegi. "The day you were arrested, you testified to me about the character of your father, yourself, and details regarding your profession. We cannot, however, accept your testimony without factual evidence. Our request for a temporary reprieve is to delay the execution of the verdict so that you can provide evidence for your testimony or show us that the accusations are groundless. Can you produce evidence for us to support your testimony?"

"My testimony today revealed personal, secret information known only to my father and me," said Bek. "No doubt we would not be able to find a witness. Even if my father were to come and confirm my views, you would still consider them biased, still believe my detractors, and still execute your verdict."

Qushbegi spoke as if struck by lightning.

"So, you do not have any documentation to support your testimony?"

"I have nothing other than my honesty."

"Have you received any correspondence from Tashkent?"

"What do you mean?"

"For example, a letter?"

Otabek did not take long to react. He cried heartily, "I have, I have! I have a testimony as well..."

The city leaders pitied his predicament and wept for him.

Otabek continued, "If you provide a messenger, I will retrieve my witness!"

"Calm down, Otabek," said Qushbegi and, with these words, Otabek relaxed a bit. "What do you have as proof?"

"A letter."

"From whom?" asked Qushbegi.

"My father."

"When was it delivered?"

"Before the rebellion began in Tashkent."

"And then what did you receive?"

"I have received nothing since then."

"What was the topic of your father's letter?"

"It stated that the people of Tashkent do not understand Azizbek's deception, and finally," he said, his hesitation and fear ebbing, "he warned me of getting embroiled in this very situation. Foreseeing its possibility, he advised me on a course of action."

After Otabek's response, ponsadboshi looked at Qushbegi as if to say, Maybe this is sufficient. As for the qorboshi, he said nothing since he knew there would be more to Otabek's questioning. Removing the letter from under his blanket, Qushbegi showed it to Otabek.

"Do you recognize this letter? Do you know its contents?"

Otabek looked at it in disbelief. "I recognize it," he said. "This is the very letter from my father that I just told you about! Incredible! Who brought you this letter, Your Honor?"

With a wry smile, Qushbegi pointed toward Kumush.

"A guardian angel," he said. Both Qutidor and Otabek looked quickly at Kumush, who now could not restrain herself.

"Father, it is me, your daughter."

Her familiar voice, reaching Otabek's ears, touched a tender spot in his heart.

Not looking at his father-in-law, losing his composure, he asked, "Is it you, Kumush?"

"It is. It is."

With this exchange, all their pain and anguish became known to each other. The joining of their voices held an unspoken and inexplicable meaning.

"Is this you, my daughter?

"Yes, Father."

Remembering another question, Qushbegi interrupted them and asked Otabek, "Why have we not been able to find your slave Hasan Ali until now?"

"I have heard nothing of his status since my arrest, Your Honor," said Otabek, looking at Kumush.

"It has been twelve days since Hasan Ali Ota left for Tashkent. We have not heard from him since," said Kumush.

"For what purpose did he go to Tashkent?" asked Qushbegi. It seemed like an obvious question.

Kumush explained Hasan Ali's reasoning for fleeing, and Qushbegi was satisfied. The conversation turned again toward the letter, and Otabek asked Qushbegi, "Considering the contents of the letter, perhaps we were exonerated?"

Qushbegi nodded in the affirmative, and Otabek continued: "Now, all I request is a just conclusion. Those who instigated this slander against us, those conspirators, those who cast aspersions should be made known to this gathering. Let them make public their testimony, let them demonstrate what despicable acts we have committed, let them state aloud what they have heard or seen. If their testimony be true, let us again go under the noose. If their words are found to be false, let them suffer the same pitiful fate meant for us. This is our only demand from your just rule," he said, looking at the qorboshi. Then he saw the signs of fear and panic in the qorboshi's face.

"Your demands are fair," said Qushbegi, "but we have many concerns other than bringing your enemies to this gathering. However, I promise to catch them and will assemble everyone here to decide upon the final verdict."

He then turned toward Kumush Bibi. "My daughter, your father and husband should praise your cleverness and your courage. They should appreciate that they owe the rest of their lives to your blessing and grace. As for myself, because of your assistance, I will free your husband and father. Otabek, however, should guarantee that he will not leave our jurisdiction before this matter has been settled." Qutidor agreed to be Otabek's guarantor and pledged all his property for this purpose. Praying for the prosperity of Qushbegi, all three left the chancellery together.

"Set free Ziyo-aka and his son Rahmat only after you have caught the offender!" Qushbegi commanded.

Upon receiving his orders, the qorboshi left the room. In this manner, the day's sentencing was finished. The city authorities left for home, mystified and amazed at what had transpired.

20

LANGUISHING FOR FREEDOM

Nur Mohammad retreated empty handed after seventy days of the blockade; his army of three thousand had been reduced to fifteen hundred men; half of the souls in his force had been sacrificed under the walls of Tashkent.

During the blockade, the people of Tashkent had showed their faithfulness to Azizbek's rule through demonstrating great self-sacrifice, serving him with all their hearts, and exhibiting great heroism. Repulsing their attacks, they stripped the Qipchaqs of hope and forced them into an inglorious withdrawal back to Qoqan. However, the people of Tashkent's success weakened them dangerously.[161]

The seventy days of battle meant they had had no connection to the outside world, even the villages, turning Tashkent into a wasteland. The city could not supply itself with grain, and the unharvested crops were destroyed by the enemy. Subsequently, trade came to a complete halt and the traders went bankrupt. Craftsmen and ordinary citizens were in peril: they were without bread, without grain, without clothing, without water, without other bare essentials. They only just survived the calamity of the blockade. The population consoled themselves for their seventy days of hardship and suffering with their victory over the Qipchaqs. At last, the city's residents began to think about bread, crops, and their everyday lives again.

Turning now to Azizbek, the independent ruler of Tashkent, our Azizbek! He is joyous about his victory over the Qipchaqs. Now he is no longer burdened with speculation and questions over what would happen if the Qipchaqs retook Tashkent.

Now Azizbek was the all-powerful ruler of Tashkent, perhaps even his own khanate, with all its surrounding area. Now he would no longer be satisfied with sitting on velvet and silk, but would instead build a throne and wear a crown worthy of his might and honor. Now, no longer content with his old *mahram*,[162] he would find a new dancer or singer—a beautiful boy whose fame would be known in Bukhara and throughout Turkistan! Azizbek was at peace. He assumed that the Qipchaqs would not make another attempt at his throne for a hundred years after his conquest. Only one factor troubled his heart, darkening the rosy world that surrounded him. Those sweet dreams of crowns and thrones all seemed still out of reach, no doubt due to the fact that the seventy days of conflict with the Qipchaqs had swept away the treasure he had amassed through his endless machinations. The treasury was depleted, and the budget was spent on gifts and food distributed to families whose relatives had given their lives fighting the Qipchaqs. Generosity was an affront that cast a pall over Azizbek's sight!

Azizbek sent a soldier to summon Yusufbek Hajji. He did not intend to ask Yusufbek Hajji for advice on finances; he sent for his counselor so he could implement a new policy he had in mind.

After half an hour, Yusufbek Hajji appeared in the doorway. Azizbek displayed an unusually high degree of respect by motioning for Hajji to take a place of honor above his own. Hajji was in no frame of mind to evaluate the motives behind this extraordinary munificence. His heartsickness for his lost son weighed upon his thoughts. What has happened to Otabek, the fruit of my loins? Maybe he has been cast into a dank, dark prison buried beneath the earth, suffering from hunger, thirst, and cold, only to die with his dear breast to the earth? Has he perished

125

among the brutality of the beks, with their bloodthirsty hakims, merciless executioners and their terrible nooses, who lord over their submissive subjects, unable to see his old father and mother again? Maybe he has left this world? Yusufbek Hajji was so deep in thought that he forgot that Azizbek stood before him.

As for Azizbek, he was fantasizing about crowns inlaid with precious stones, golden thrones, beautiful maidens, and a famous mahram.

"Hajji," Azizbek began. "You do not know the reason I called you to the Orda."

Yusufbek Hajji woke up from his thoughts. "Your Honor, no doubt you summoned me for the benefit of our citizens' peace, our people's relief, and our government's stability."

Hajji's words struck Azizbek like a thunderbolt. His eyes darkened; his innermost dreams and aspirations were concealed yet again under a dark cloud. Confusion took hold of him and, not knowing what to say, he hesitated. "Yes, it is for this reason I called you," he finally muttered and then thought for a bit. "These past seventy days have depleted our treasury. We are in dire financial straits and unable to feed the soldiers. I called you to advise me on these matters."

"As you wish, Taksir."

"But I have already made a decision on this matter," Azizbek said.

"Blessings on your decision."

"I have decided that, starting tomorrow, you will tax each citizen thirty-two tengas."

At this, Yusufbek Hajji grew even more nervous over both the people's inevitable discontent with Azizbek's policy and his son's predicament. He trembled, appalled at Azizbek's craven decision. At first, he thought to offer an honest opinion, but then he collected himself, realizing to whom he was speaking and what the repercussions of such an offence would be.

"Your Honor, I have no qualms about implementing your order. One should take heed, however, that the people survived a siege over the past seventy days, enduring a baptism of fire, of hunger, and of death. In my opinion, it is hard to collect thirty-two copper pieces, not to mention thirty-two tengas, even for me.[163]

The people should be allowed to recover from their losses for ten or fifteen days..."

Hajji was not allowed to finish his thoughts. Azizbek could no longer stand to hear a counterargument and screamed savagely, "What are you saying?"

Hajji had not anticipated matters taking a turn for the worse. At this point, his fate was in Azizbek's hands, and if he did not appease him, Azizbek would call for an executioner.

"Taksir, if you order it, I will do it not tomorrow but today. We will order the people to pay the required taxes. I only need you to say the word." These words had a magical effect on Azizbek. Just a moment before he had been ready to call for one of the soldiers to execute Hajji, but now instead he said the words that would in the near future play an important role in Hajji's fate: "Tell the orda begi to present a gilded robe to Hajji."

*****

Yusufbek Hajji left the orda in a gilded robe. In response to the functionaries' congratulations on his new attire, he answered with a crooked smile. Walking across the drawbridge of the orda, his lips spread in a toothy grin, he kept saying to himself over and over, like a madman, "He orders me to collect thirty-two tengas in taxes from each citizen and have the money ready in less than a week. I have been ordered to beat with a mace anyone who protests the collection or to perform a public hanging if necessary... As if he would turn Yusufbek into a bloodthirsty tyrant like himself... I did not perform the hajj, an injunction from Allah, to become a bloody tyrant... I have a son... I am honest... I have a conscience, a sense of truth, a faith that calls me to task when I place the sons of our people under the lash. May the earth swallow our people whole. For seventy days the people sold themselves for Azizbek's fox-like craftiness, forgetting in the end his brutality. In turn their service has been repaid by a tax of thirty-two tengas, a tax called a 'gift of allegiance'! You will end by giving Azizbek your last piece of bread!"

21

Revolution

Yusufbek Hajji reached Zanjirli mahalla in Shayhontahur[164] district, wearing his newly awarded robe. He called out to the people as they rose from their places to greet him and finally settled into the *guzar*, the crossroads:

"Your home is under attack, fellow Muslims! Azizbek, on whose behalf you risked your lives, believing him to be a benevolent ruler, on this day will reward your loyalty with a tax of thirty-two tengas. We are now at a fork in the road: you must decide whether you should sell your sons and daughters into slavery for thirty-two tengas in order to enrich Azizbek's treasury or whether to remove Azizbek from power while we still have time... Your homes are in peril, my fellow Muslims! Thirty-two tengas!"

Yusufbek Hajji, beloved of the people and commanding complete respect, represented the voice of restraint in a time of chaos. Because of this, the people would act at his behest, following him to the ends of the earth. Hearing that they were going to be burdened with a tax of thirty-two tengas quickened their hearts in anger, and the people assembled in the guzar revolted.

The uprising began with the denizens of Zanjirlik,[165] who constructed barricades and prepared to resist Azizbek's decree with street battles. Yusufbek Hajji's declaration of indignation reached every level of society, including the commoners in the street, and made its way even to the mahalla of Eski Juva.[166] In this last neighborhood he called for a protest, displaying his embroidered robe and stating sarcastically, "As you can see, it is in my best interest to levy the taxes since your obedience brings me wonderful robes such as this one."

The crowd's agitation sparked like a flame set to a dry forest. As it was later recounted, both the wet and the dry, the young and the old, raged and started to burn.

"He has forgotten our service—the ungrateful bastard! We will reward him with more than thirty-two tengas! Not even a month has passed—shameless!"

As rumors spread, three messengers were sent to the Sebzor, Kokcha, and Besh-Yoghoch[167] districts to announce the rebellion. The Oqsoqols[168] swore aloud and read out a fatwa, proclaiming that either Azizbek would be deposed or the rebels would die fighting. Not one hour passed before shop owners shuttered their storefronts and the streets of Tashkent filled with barricades. Everyone was armed and ready to go to war. The din from the city's unrest reached even the orda.

Azizbek, ambivalent about the matter, sent Rayimbek Dadkhwah into the city with fifty soldiers for reconnaissance. When the soldiers reached Zanjirlik[169] mahalla, they began to understand the extent of the agitation: the streets teemed with barricades manned by crowds of civilians bearing swords, rifles, knives, and pikes, prepared to fight. Nobody heeded Rayimbek's attempts at quelling the crowd, "Clear the barricades and go home!" When the Dadkhwah finally resorted to threats, someone in the crowd fired their rifle, killing two soldiers. Close to late afternoon, just before prayers, a street battle between the general population and the government soldiers began.

After thirty minutes of pitched battle, the soldiers forced the Zanjirlik militia to retreat to the Baland[170] mosque barricades. Growing angry, Azizbek left a handful of soldiers to protect the orda and, with a unit of soldiers, hurried to Rayimbek's aid. Finally reinforced, the soldiers pushed the civilian combatants to Hadra. With the threat of taxation looming, the populace sent more fighters from Besh Yogach, Sebzar, and Kokcha to join the fight.

That night Tashkent drowned in blood. Men associated with the present leadership, known in their own mahalla, were nevertheless executed by the people. Houses were set alight and properties looted. Bold young local men ran toward the Hadra barricade,[171] while the timid and old built fires from tree stumps throughout the guzars and mahallas—all angry over the taxation and sending cheers of victory to the fighters. At half past midnight the civilian combatants were forced to retreat from Hadra to the Eski Miskarlik[172] neighborhood. This unexpected setback worried Yusufbek Hajji.

Taking the reports seriously, he dispatched couriers to seek assistance from Nur Mohammad Qushbegi—currently on his way to Qoqan after his defeat in Tashkent. In the vicinity of Eski Miskarlik[173] neighborhood, the two factions made camp for the night, and the fighting ceased until dawn. In the morning the bloody engagements renewed, with Azizbek's soldiers unable to advance farther, withdrawing from the fray, as every minute new reinforcements funneled in from all sections of the city. The local population committed themselves fully in opposition to the regime's troops and sought to eliminate them at all costs.

Ultimately frustrated by the stalemate and wishing to break the impasse, Rayimbek Dadkhwah unsheathed his sword. Wielding his blade, he rode to the front lines and motioned for his men to advance toward the crowd. His initiative was only rewarded with his own death—he fell from a chest wound delivered by the rifle of marksman Usta Muminjon.

Rayimbek Dadkhwah had been a bulwark of Azizbek's government. With his death the troops' spirits fell. They disregarded Azizbek's orders and withdrew in a disorderly mob.

In the end, Azizbek withdrew with his retinue of fifty faithful servants, blockading himself in the orda. Victorious under Yusufbek Hajji's leadership, the elated population surrounded the orda. As Azizbek had yet to surrender, thousands of people remained in place and even began to prepare meals.

An unexpected turn of events brought Azizbek to the ground—while preparing to flee the orda, he was betrayed by his own men and detained. What could he do with no wings to take flight and flee? On the second day of his imprisonment, he ascended to the roof of the orda. He would gamble for his last miserable chance at life, this so-called khan. He greeted the citizens in a crushed and trembling voice, and attempted to exonerate himself before them:

"I repent my foul deeds. I failed to remember your faithful service to me... by your spiritedness, you have put my arrogance in its place, returning me to my prior humility. For this I thank you, my citizens... Please excuse my failings, I repent my foul deeds!"

His audience did not heed his words, since the time for reconciliation had passed—a piece was missing that could no longer be returned.

"Have you gotten wise, you thief? If you had taken time to consider it beforehand, you could have avoided your fate. Off with your head. The terrible deeds you have inflicted on us! Every day hanging the innocent by the noose, beheading people, making orphans out of our children, our mothers crying over the blood spilled. While threatening us with death from your dagger, you covered the mahallas with taxes, poisoning people with a scorpion's venom. Die, you swine! Our days of sorrow have passed," the people cried out. "Accept your fate."

The citizens shouted at him from all sides, their curses assailing him. Azizbek kept pleading. "Accept my apologies, let these matters pass, citizens. My dear citizens, your shortsightedness will have you chopping off your hands to spite your feet. You will become vassals of the Qipchaqs! Please accept my apologies for your own sakes."

At Azizbek's words, the crowd's anger flared and their words carried to the heavens. "We will not be painted red twice.[174] It would be better to be ruled by the Qipchaqs than by a dog like you..." Their words echoed the pain in their hearts. At this point Azizbek was overcome by hopelessness and, grief-stricken, he descended from the roof.

Yusufbek Hajji's courier reached Nur Mohammad Qushbegi near Kirovchi. He accompanied Qushbegi with his troops back to Tashkent. The vengeful Qushbegi received this information gladly. Flying along the roads, he arrived in Tashkent on the third day of Azizbek's imprisonment, his arrival declared with the trumpeting of qarnai[175] and surnai. Once the Qipchaq soldiers joined the mob outside, both groups stormed the orda, seizing Azizbek.

The capture and transportation of Azizbek, the individual who had shed the blood of one thousand people and forced them into a seventy- day march, to Qoqan satisfied Nur Mohammad Qushbegi's honor.

Sitting cross-legged in the orda, Qushbegi thanked Yusufbek Hajji profusely, for Yusufbek Hajji had been the main instrument in the capture of Azizbek, his greatest enemy. Qushbegi continued to promise him that he would relay his great service to the khan and Musulmanqul, recommending that he be elevated in rank. No doubt these declarations meant nothing to Yusufbek Hajji. For him, positions and respect were worldly issues; news of his son's health and promises of his release from prison in Margilan were the only things that mattered to him.

Dismissing Qushbegi's promises, he said, "Thank you for your respect and confidence in me, Qushbegi. These days I find that I am but an old man passing from this world. Further high-ranking positions do not interest me. If my service warrants these displays of respect, I would rather have a few wishes fulfilled by His Highness the khan."

"Please ask them, Hajji. Even if the khan refuses your wishes, I will fulfil them for you on his behalf."

"My first wish is on behalf of the oppressed population here. From this day forward, no more of these contemptible bastards should be appointed hakim of Tashkent."

"You share the same objectives as His Highness the khan. We, too, are as frustrated as the people with the likes of Azizbek," said Qushbegi.

After a long discussion concluding with an agreement about Tashkent's future leadership, Yusufbek Hajji finally confronted his deepest wound. Knowing Nur Mohammad Qushbegi to be an understanding person, he displayed his hidden pain to him. While he spilled forth his inner heart, he shivered from the terrible implications of his fears, and his tongue hesitated in the telling. He feared that his request was delivered too late, like a bullet shot after a bird has flown. He feared that by now it was a moot point.

"If my service is worthy of His Highness the khan's respect," said Hajji, "the greatest reward for me would be the release of my son. To a father who will soon wash his hands of the world's scandals, to such an old man, the highest reward is to not grieve for his own son." There were tears in his eyes as he said this.

Deeply impressed with this display of emotion, Qushbegi soothed the despondent Yusufbek Hajji: "Fear not, Hajji," he said, "the hakim of Margilan does not take innocent blood lightly. My first task on my return to Qoqan will be your son's release. Fear not, my sad Hajji."

"My sincerest thanks, Qushbegi. If you undertake this task, I will be obligated to you for the rest of my life. I fear it may be too late by the time you reach Qoqan however..."

Qushbegi considered this and, afraid that Yusufbek Hajji's concerns were correct, the two decided to send a courier posthaste to Qoqan bearing a letter. Since Hasan Ali fit the job, he was chosen as courier. He had been waiting for this assignment for fifteen days and he turned his horse's head toward Qoqan, instantly disappearing before everyone's eyes. After a day, Nur Mohammad Qushbegi prepared for his departure to Qoqan, leaving some soldiers in Tashkent as a garrison. Azizbek was bound to a horse's harness and, when the army started their march toward Qoqan, people collected near the Qoqan gates, cheering and watching Azizbek being dragged in shame and humiliation under the horse's hooves.

22

One Poor Miserable Wretch

Qoqan's original orda had been built by the khan during his second reign; now we find ourselves standing on its foundations, which constitute the Khoda Bazar.[176] We have already described the Margilan orda in the thirteenth chapter of this novel, and the Qoqan Orda was its exact duplicate, with a perimeter resembling the Kuragan's palace;[177] to describe this again would be a chore, not to mention a waste of paper. The gates leading into the fortifications, the guard posts that flank the entryway, the width and length of the courtyard, are all the same as in the previous structure, with the only exception being that figures stand at attention inside the four corners of towers.

However, after entering through the gates of the orda, the interior structures differ considerably from the structure previously mentioned in Margilan. For this reason, we must better familiarize ourselves with the layout.

The buildings lining the right and left walls of the courtyard were intended for military purposes. In that clearing, the guards, dressed just like the Askari witnessed previously in Tashkent and under the command of the ponsadboshi, engage in small groups. A wall dotted with arches bisects the orda diagonally from north to east, with gates leading into the khan's palace, hence the main structure.

Though this gate seemed a touch darkened by age, the delicate carvings and colorful shades of paint made the viewer pause to wonder over the finely chiseled ornamentation and the craftsmanship applied to create such beauty, amazing passersby.

Especially marvelous were the bouquets of flowers rendered in the Ugar Margul[178] style. On both of the outward-facing doors of the gate and the alabaster sculpture in relief standing on the arches, the carved flowers took on a vividness both delicate and refined. The rays of the sun shone on the gilded crescents on top of each bouquet, promising bountifulness. The gates were guarded by two sentries who stood on raised platforms in niches, flanking the entryway. Passing between the guards was a narrow-arched passage leading to the entrance of a divan khana on the right.[179] The khan's reception room stood to the left, also heavily guarded as in the previous orda. As we saw in Margilan's fortress there was an antechamber, the artisanship on its walls—again intricately carved ornamentation—surpassing Margilan's in skill and beauty. Despite age having darkened the finest of details, the sublime inspiration that brought such art into being refused to be diminished.

Passing through the corridor of this waiting area, a larger painted chamber, also lavishly decorated, awaits. Working through the ancillary rooms, an expansive hall beckons with two sides of the room lined with the khan's Shighavulboshi,[180] armed Yasavulboshi,[181] attendants of various ranks, the khan's Oftobboshi, night watchmen, Parvanchi,[182] along with sundry other advisers, government employees, nobles, ministers, and state officials.

From the hall's third small window, a thin, meticulously carved screen set a smaller ceremonial space off from the larger area—its only entrance was a wide opening in the middle.

In this manner, the two sections were offset against each other. On both sides of the entryway were niches and in each of them stood an executioner holding a halberd. Passing the two executioners into the remaining third of the room, a white marble throne half a meter in height raised slightly off the ground, and upon it sat a young man of eighteen with an oval face of olive complexion. He was dressed in a red velvet coat, wrapped in a silk *bilbak*.[183] On his head sat a silvery *chalma*;[184] on his knees lay a gold-handled sword. This individual was none other than Khudayar Khan.

The gold chair on the left of the khan was empty; in the one to his right, near the small door, sat a flat-faced middle-aged Kyrgyz. He had narrow eyes, wheat-colored skin, and a flat nose barely visible between two full cheeks and a small beard; he wore a *chikming*[185] from Ura Teppe[186] tied with leather belt and simple sword on his left. His head bore a white *kalpak*.[187] Here was Musulmanqul himself, reading applications and letters that had just been delivered to him by their Hudaychi. Presently he reviewed one of the many complaints received. Perhaps it was unimportant, as he tore it into pieces and threw it under his legs, opening the second letter. This letter was written by the governor of Osh.[188]

Let it be known to our Bulwark of the Government, Father-in-Law of the Blessed Khan Himself, Musulmanqul Bahadur,[189] with this blessed letter, that his gifts were divided among the poorest Kyrgyz[190] students raised in the Madrassas of Osh, all according to their scholastic achievements. Kyrgyz mullahs, who until now were forced to spend their days satisfied with only the roughest of food and living in poverty... upon receiving assistance from the Father-in-Law of the King of Kings, his munificence and his dignity impressed the recipients and tears flowed freely from their eyes. They pray to Allah, again with tears in their eyes, to grant a life as long as Zol's,[191] the Khan's Father-in-Law, victory over his enemies, and glories to rival those of Amir Timur Kuragan.[192]

In the end, we should not withhold from His Highness, indeed we should relay with an open heart, that our cities and their outlying settlements are safe under the protection of his powerful reign and exist without any present danger. Concluding our letter, your faithful servants wish that the young Khan of the Khans, His Highness the Sultan of the Sultans under the protection of the Father-in-Law of the King of Kings will have long years of prosperity, health, and peace...

While describing the situation in Osh[193] to the khan, Musulmanqul opened a third letter, a note that appeared to be from a private person since it was free of a seal, markers of diplomatic correspondence or signatures:

To the service of Musulmanqul Qipchaq, ever vigilant with his sword of justice against the cries of the oppressed people, the long wails of the unduly oppressed... As my pencil composes these words, my eyes fill with tears from oppression; my heart shivers in fear of the government's treachery. As a faithful servant to the government, a man devoted entirely to its triumph, I must reveal one who seeks to sunder its rule to the core, who, through the auspices of his father, sought again to agitate the people who were once peaceful and obedient to the authorities and the laws of the city. Instead of the authorities rewarding and heaping praises upon the faithful slave who attempted to render justice, by way of a noose around the conspirator's neck, and through the painstaking application of truthful testimony and reliable witnesses, those same leaders seek to arrest and fetter him...

Paying no heed to the warrior, His Highness Musulmanqul, they make glad his enemies and mournful his friends.

Musulmanqul, not fully comprehending the underlying meaning of the initial section of the letter, scanned to the final paragraph:

Maybe until now you have not understood my meaning, which has been obscured by my excitement and sadness. Please don't be angry with me and accept your faithful servant's excuse.

It has transpired that Yusufbek Hajji, one of the instigators of the Tashkent rebellion through the prodding of Azizbek, has dispatched his son here in order to agitate the

136

*people of Margilan against Your Highness. Your wretched
faithful slave once unwittingly participated in a gathering
where the said insurgent was surrounded by his
coconspirators who sat plotting. Needless to say, I became
alarmed after discovering his purpose for traveling to
Margilan. His words meant the elimination of the Qipchaqs,
and that power would be delivered into the hands of the city's
common citizenry.*

*Unable to contain this secret in my heart, fully
sympathetic to the Qipchaqs, I duly informed, at peril to
myself, the hakim of Margilan—Uttaboi. Uttaboi Qushbegi
managed to catch Otabek, who is the son of Yusufbek Hajji,
and his supporter as well as father-in-law, a person who goes
by the name Mirza Karim Qutidor, and imprisoned them.*

*When summoned by Qushbegi, I was fully prepared for
his decision, at once relaying to him in full detail all that I
had heard from Otabek's own mouth. After my unbiased
testimony was given, Qushbegi sentenced Otabek and his
father-in-law, Mirza Karim, to hang from the noose, yet a
bag of gold coins from Mirza Karim's family found their way
into the treacherous pockets of Uttaboi Qushbegi and, as a
result, he freed the rebels right from under the gallows.
Instead he intends to imprison and hang your faithful
servant, all because he fears that your most loyal slave would
complain of the treachery. Except through the protection of
your power, through the assistance of the loyal Margilan's
Qorboshi, I would never have gained my freedom and been
released from the shackles of Uttaboi...*

On reaching this point in the letter, Musulmanqul raised his
head, his lashless, slanted eyes now all aflame. He cried,
"Chilim!"[194]

*So, in this manner, Uttaboi, your own man, shows extreme
lack of gratitude[195] and, all for the sake of a bag of gold, goes
over to the side of the enemy. Yet I, one of your most
sympathetic slaves, was forced to escape to Qoqan, seeking
shelter in your distinguished lands. I, your faithful slave, feel
no regret for being awarded in such a manner for my faithful*

service to you, but I am only concerned that traitors of such ilk as Uttaboi and Otabek grow stronger and intend to wreak havoc upon your honored rule. This letter stands as proof of a devoted slave's unswerving faithfulness. Perhaps through this small gesture I have fulfilled my sacred obligation and taken the burden on my shoulders. Perhaps I will be the instrument through which we topple the enemies of the government. I expect no recognition from my efforts; whatever pains I have taken upon myself for the sake of Your Highness, I consider my sacred duty. For that reason, I remain anonymous.

Wishing peace and glory upon our young khan and death to traitors of the state,
One Poor Miserable Wretch

Musulmanqul raged... His anger spewed forth through his hookah as he pulled on it, threatening to break it to pieces—the water pipe's coal stand responded with a long, burning shrrrrrrrr.

Exhaling streams of smoke from his mouth, he relayed the contents of the letter to Khudayar Khan. For Musulmanqul—already under a pall of deep depression over dispatches informing him of Nur Mohammad Qushbegi's ignominious retreat from Tashkent, his troops greatly reduced—this new correspondence spread salt in an already raw wound, only increasing the sting of defeat farther.

"Hudaychi."

"Yes, Your Honor."

"Call the Mirza,"[196] said Musulmanqul and, after folding the letter, he addressed Khudayar Khan: "Are you aware, my son, what Azizbek, with the aid of Yusufbek Hajji, intends to commit against us? Uttaboi, whom we thought to be a reliable and faithful individual, also seeks to join our enemies... Fine, let them do their best, in the near future we will have prepared the best measures to counteract those traitors."

Khudayar Khan displayed no sign of distress at the news that a plot would weaken his reign; he only sat as before—immutable and unconcerned. Wishing, however, to not appear ambivalent to Musulmanqul's burning excitement, he replied in a cool, dry, noncommittal voice, "Yes, it appears so, especially in regard to

Uttaboi. In the end, he shows himself to be a complete bastard. If he has no respect for me, at least he could respect you."

"As it turns out, we cannot expect goodness in return from one we created out of the goodness of our own hearts," said Musulmanqul. "Take, for example, Azizbek. He grew by our own hands. We appointed him hakim of Tashkent, removing Salimsoqbek Bek. Yet, in complete disregard to our kindness, he becomes our enemy. Fine, let it be so. Not satisfied with Tashkent, he seeks to move against Margilan as well? Fine, we will see."

The Mirzaboshi,[197] upon entering, paid obeisance to the khan, then looked toward Musulmanqul and gave him a deep bow, his hands folded in front of him. Musulmanqul again yearned to smoke his pipe.

"Chilim!" he cried again, raising his voice so it could be heard outside the room. He then said to Mirzaboshi, "Immediately, write a dispatch to the hakim of Margilan, Uttaboi Qushbegi, immediately, and send it by courier. As soon as he receives the message, order him to detain Otabek, son of Yusufbek Hajji, and deliver him to our presence."

Mirzaboshi, paying his respects, walked backward so as to not show his back to the khan.

23

MUSULMANQUL

The whole of the khan's court began to gather. Khudayar Khan sat on his throne, yet Musulmanqul, though not of royal lineage, commanded such great political sway that in reality he held more power than the khan. Initiating the proceedings, the otalik entered and greeted the khan. He delivered a long prayer on his behalf and then departed. After the main adviser to the khan took his place, other branches of the government entered, each consecutively reciting a prayer. Finally, after the last prayer, the Hudaychi appeared and, once he had paid his respects and delivered his own blessings, he turned his attention to Musulmanqul: "The hakim of

Margilan, Uttaboi, requests your permission for an audience!" he announced. Uttaboi had commanded Musulmanqul's complete attention since he had received the news of Uttaboi's complicity in treason, and so Musulmanqul took a deep breath, snapping at the Hudaychi: "Is he alone? Or are there others with him?"

The Hudaychi bowed in affirmation. "He is accompanied by twelve armed soldiers."

"Anyone else?"

"An unarmed young man."

"Allow only Uttaboi, unescorted, into our audience," said Musulmanqul. Stopping the Hudaychi who, at that moment, moved to make his exit after paying obeisance, Musulmanqul then asked, "Is Uttaboi's escort outside or inside the fortress?"

"Your Honor, they are inside."

"After Qushbegi enters, our soldiers should be on guard against his detachment."

The Hudaychi again paid his respects and finally departed. In a victorious tone, Musulmanqul said to the khan, "The instrument of the usurpers has fallen into a trap. We have not one, but two plotters in our grasp! This is fortunate."

Qushbegi entered, bowing twice to the khan so deeply that his head reached below his waist. He approached and kissed his hands. Musulmanqul rose from his place to greet Uttaboi, hugging him and pretending nothing was amiss. Musulmanqul motioned for Uttaboi to sit in the chair to the left of the khan. After Musulmanqul's seemingly sincere gestures, Uttaboi's fearful heart calmed itself. Out of respect, Uttaboi again rose, returning Musulmanqul's respect with another show of obeisance by bowing before returning to his place of honor. Musulmanqul observed Qushbegi with suspicion, asking him, "Are your regions peaceful? Are you in good health?"

"Al-Hamdulillahi,[198] under the khan's powerful shadow and through his support, our country is at peace. The citizenry continually pray for the health and happiness of the khan."

Khudayar Khan acknowledged him with a slight nod. In response, Qushbegi again stood and bowed in respect for the khan's gesture. Stroking his beard, Musulmanqul considered something for several moments while Khudayar Khan and Qushbegi waited for his mouth to move.

"You may or may not know that we received unfavorable intelligence from Nur Mohammad Qushbegi, who was dispatched to quell Tashkent," said Musulmanqul turning to Uttaboi.

Perceiving his unresponsiveness as indifference, he continued to divulge the new information, "With three thousand soldiers, Nur Mohammad Qushbegi blockaded Tashkent for seventy days. Unsuccessful, he and his soldiers at last retreated. Azizbek and Yusufbek Hajji's bold defense forced our contingent to flee with empty hands. In the future we should attempt to achieve success through other means. Yesterday we heard from someone... that Otabek, Yusufbek Hajji's son, was reportedly in Margilan. We believe that we should use him in our future efforts against Tashkent. For that purpose, we called you here to confer with us..."

At that moment Qushbegi stopped Musulmanqul, smiled, and said, looking at the khan, "There have been some scandals surrounding Otabek. It is a long story. Let us hear Mingboshi's opinion now..."

"Is Otabek here with you? Please continue," said Musulmanqul.

Receiving confirmation, he continued his calm pursuit.

"As I just mentioned, we have no options for eliminating Azizbek other than Otabek. I believe that no one else but Otabek can help in our future plans. His return to Tashkent will mean that he will be in close vicinity to Azizbek since he is the son of his main adviser. Poisoning Azizbek, or assassinating him through some other method, is the best option. If pain desires succor, the healer will arrive soon to render aid,[199] as they say. Hearing that Otabek was in Margilan made the khan and myself overjoyed... This was our purpose in calling you. If you have any advice, we would like to hear it."

Uttaboi was completely deceived by Musulmanqul's subterfuge. Khudayar Khan, on the other hand, who knew of Musulmanqul's plan beforehand, became confused. Musulmanqul's intention was to mislead everyone.

"I agree with your plan," said Qushbegi, "but there is one consideration. It all rests on whether Otabek will stick his neck out for this mission or not. Previously I suspected Otabek's supposed allegiance to Azizbek to be warranted. After investigating allegations made by the qorboshi twenty-five days ago that Otabek had come to Margilan on Azizbek's order to raise a rebellion, I imprisoned him with other members of the plot. I believed the accusations completely since he was the son of Yusufbek Hajji.

"Again accepting the veracity of the witness who informed on Otabek to the qorboshi, a testimony that confirmed my suspicions, five days ago I sentenced him and his father-in-law, an individual from Margilan named Mirza Karim, to death. A few moments later, as the sentenced were being taken to the gallows, a lady appeared in the chancellery and handed me a letter. When I read it, it became clear that it was a letter written by Yusufbek Hajji to his son Otabek. The letter's timeline showed that it had been written at the moment when Azizbek sought to attempt a rebellion against Qoqan. I was relieved because this letter was proof that Yusufbek Hajji was aligned against Azizbek. I ordered that the two sentenced men be returned from the gallows. Not yet satisfied as to the validity of this letter, I did not release the accused until I could interrogate them further.

"Otabek's testimony coincided completely with the letter's contents. Still, I only freed Mirza Karim, making Otabek collateral until the end of the investigation. I considered the possibility that perhaps the witness who had informed on Otabek created these rumors for his own revenge. I intended to implicate Hamidboi by bringing them all together. For some unknown reason, this person has evaded our attempts and so far it has been impossible to locate him. His flight has demonstrated conclusively that he was motivated by personal revenge, yet I am still holding on to Otabek. Finally, I recently received a summons from His Highness.

"Immediately, I took Otabek, with my soldiers, to the palace of Our Highness. In conclusion, this is the nature of the scandal surrounding Otabek in Margilan. As for me, since there is a continuing investigation into Otabek, I wonder how we can task him to conduct such a sensitive mission..."

Qushbegi's impartial delivery forced Musulmanqul's cunning deception to come apart at the seams. His ire toward Uttaboi slackened. Musulmanqul instead redirected his all-encompassing rage against his two main opponents, with the consequence that he intended to make Otabek the hapless victim. He would revenge the blood of his soldiers martyred under Tashkent's fortress wall with the son of the person who was Azizbek's right hand.

"Do you have Yusufbek Hajji's letter on you?" he asked.

"Yes, Your Honor," said Qushbegi, taking out the letter and handing it to Musulmanqul. Glancing momentarily at the letter, Musulmanqul gave Uttaboi a sarcastic smile.

"Maybe there is no one in Margilan who can divine the machinations of Yusufbek Hajji. That fox sent his son to Margilan in order to incite rebellion and supplied him with this letter to protect him in case of detection. If the simpletons in Margilan do not understand this, we can see it clearly!" he said, beamingly proudly at Khudayar Khan.

Qushbegi was forced to swallow this insult. If he uttered one ill- considered word, he would be implicated in the same plot as Otabek.

He understood the matter completely and kept silent. "Bring me the Hudaychi!"

"Your servant is here, Your Honor!"

"Prepare a reception for Qushbegi's young companion," Musulmanqul demanded, his fearful visage now apparent for all to see. Khudayar Khan, sitting on his throne, appeared as emotionless and immovable as a statue. Uttaboi had entirely lost his previous composure and did not know whether he would live through this moment or not. Otabek arrived, following the Hudaychi. He bowed to the khan yet stayed his hand in acknowledging the others at the dais, only showing respect to his liege. Though Otabek knew Musulmanqul by name and by his savage reputation, he did not recognize the "Shah-an-Shah" himself, sitting near the khan. His lack of respect swayed Musulmanqul's opinion against him irrevocably. Musulmanqul's anger mounted and crested, yet on the surface he offered only an ironic grin and a kindly voice.

"Young Bek, give me your attention," he said. Then, when Otabek turned toward him, Musulmanqul asked, with a predatory smile, "And what is your name?"

"My name is Otabek."

"There are all sorts of 'Otabeks' in the world. Who are your kin?"

"I am Otabek, son of Yusufbek Hajji."

"So you say... That very Yusufbek Hajji from Tashkent who is a coconspirator with Azizbek. You are the very son of that holy figure."

Otabek now recognized Musulmanqul as an effete old functionary[200] and recognized the designs behind his predatory insults and how they led to his present situation. He preferred to remain silent and hold his tongue in response to these biased questions. The ensuing silence seemed to express to Musulmanqul Otabek's intent. Musulmanqul became infuriated at this unvoiced insult. Fuming, he screamed at Otabek, "Why don't you respond?"

"I am the son of Yusufbek Hajji. You already recognize me as the son of my esteemed father," said Bek. "Though my father and I have been depicted to you and Qushbegi in a negative light, we are the sort of people who stand by their honesty and live with integrity. In the end, choose your verdict for whatever role you imagine for us and give your orders."

The rage in Musulmanqul's face diminished and his expression changed to one of appreciation for the acts of a brave man. Observing Otabek, he smiled.

"You have a courageous heart, young man... It is a pity you carry guilt around your neck," he said and called out, "Executioners!"

Men wielding axes near the door stepped forward for the order: "Our axes are ready for blood!"

At that very moment, the Hudaychi, pushing his way in front of the executioners, announced to the khan, "There is a courier from Tashkent. He is asking your permission for an audience."

Khudayar Khan looked to Musulmanqul who, for the moment, refrained from passing Otabek into the hands of the executioners.

"Let him come in," said Musulmanqul. Then, to the executioners waiting on his word, "Wait for my command," he said, motioning for them to leave.

The courier from Tashkent introduced a new element into the present matter; therefore, Musulmanqul would wait to deliver Otabek's death sentence and see how things played out. Perhaps the arrival of the courier would provide the legal basis for his verdict of death, and at least once in Musulmanqul's lifetime, he would spill a man's blood justly.

Otabek slouched against the wall. The sacred ideas of the throne, the crown, the khan, and the class of beks began to seem as corrupt to him as a counterfeit coin...

Indeed, he was disoriented, feeling empty and numb. Nevertheless, though he felt like a sacrificial sheep, bound and tied, with its throat ready for the sharp blade, he remained fearless. His life, the government's power, endless darkness... he was indifferent. His calmness ebbed and flowed. Resigned to death, he wore a blank expression... Only one person could not be bled from his heart and remained difficult for him to let go of... for a moment it seemed as if he had unchained himself from that final anguish, but... to the last breath, he longed to be united with that one person, even as the knife sank into his throat... he wished that, as his eyes dimmed ever more, he might gaze upon her image... All his thoughts at that moment revolved around this deep reverie.

The Hudaychi led in the courier, who presented the letter while kneeling. As he backed out of the room, his eyes fell upon an individual with a blank expression, leaning against the wall...

Instantly he forgot that he was in the presence of the khan and threw himself at Otabek. The Tashkent courier's sudden movement startled the khan, as well as Musulmanqul, Qushbegi, Hudaychi, and the entire assemblage of the main hall. Even though Otabek tried to calm him, Hasan Ali could not help himself from loudly shedding tears.

"Where is your etiquette?" shouted Musulmanqul while clenching his fists and looking about. "Whose courier are you?"

"I am assigned to Nur Muhammad Qushbegi."

"From what region?"

"From Tashkent, Taksir."

Astonished, Musulmanqul took the letter passed to him by Khudayar Khan and opened it. He read in a loud voice:

To our young khan, and his father-in-law, Musulmanqul, King of Kings, a hero's greetings. Our young khan's future happiness and fortune brought us a new spirit and once again gave resolute hope to our sad hearts. Four days ago, your devoted slave retreated from Tashkent with his soldiers, hopeless and in defeat. I had previously sent a dispatch to your court concerning these events. Retreating in this

145

manner, our contingent had gained Kirovchi when a courier reached our rear flank and gave us a letter from Yusufbek Hajji, stating that a rebellion against Azizbek was underway. He requested that we return in order to relieve Tashkent.

As soon as I received this intelligence, I ordered the soldiers to advance on Tashkent, which we reached on the second day. Upon entering the city, we saw that a mob, led by Yusufbek Hajji, had blockaded Azizbek into his citadel. The crowd, and especially Yusufbek Hajji, gave us a warm welcome.

We then breached the doors of the fortress and captured Azizbek. Initially I thought that Yusufbek Hajji would ask for the governorship of Tashkent for himself. However, once he had put under my guardianship the entire fortress, the treasury, and the armory, my doubts were left unfounded. It seems that Yusufbek Hajji has no political ambitions and is solely concerned with the welfare of the people. Our previous suspicions toward him were misplaced. The reason for the rebellion against Azizbek was due to his raising taxes to thirty-two tengas on the starving population just two days after our withdrawal from Tashkent. The people were duped by Azizbek and beg pity as our erstwhile enemies. They are overjoyed to be free of their oppressors.

I attempted to assure Yusufbek Hajji that due to his heroic service he would receive a position from our great khan. He refused, asking forgiveness and saying that he only wished that an honest person would become bek of Tashkent. He hopes for a small blessing from the greatness of the khan. It has come to his attention that his only son was detained in Margilan by Uttaboi Qushbegi for reasons not yet revealed.

If the great khan deems it appropriate to demonstrate appreciation for his service, then his reward would be the release of his imprisoned son.

In your humble slave's opinion, Yusufbek Hajji's actions have been a godsend to our government. Therefore, if his son is still sentenced to death, then if the great khan's blessing would release him, it would be of great significance to us soldiers. I appointed Qosh Dadkhwah[201] as the bek of Tashkent and have garrisoned some soldiers with him. As for *my own situation, I have Azizbek under my care and will soon be in your presence.*

Nur Muhammad Qushbegi.

Musulmanqul finished the letter, smiling shamelessly at Otabek. He ordered the Hudaychi, "Bring two gilded robes!"

Uttaboi grabbed at his own collar in surprise, not believing that he was witnessing Otabek's magical release yet again. Khudayar Khan smiled upon Otabek, as if to congratulate him on his release from the shackles of his savage father-in-law.

Musulmanqul half-heartedly placed a gilded robe on Otabek's shoulders.

"Due to your father's deeds, you are freed from a death sentence and have managed to gain a gilded robe as well," he exclaimed, his hypocrisy again knowing no bounds.

After several days, Otabek went to Margilan. Hasan Ali traveled to Tashkent to calm Yusufbek Hajji's fears.

Thus Ends Volume One

VOLUME TWO

UZR[202]

The novel presently in your hands, this innovation birthed into our world, has encountered some unfortunate obstacles: For five years we were not able to publish it. Ultimately we met with success, but it seems three or four of our editors committed orthographic errors along the way, turning the book from something wonderful into something ragged. Our experts' carelessness seemed to stem from technical aspects, as if the ears were not listening to what the eyes were seeing. For these reasons, I alone made the decision to hold off on publication. It is now necessary to say that this was due to my own ignorance; indeed I did not see the situation clearly. I only ask my teachers for forgiveness.

I am not able to promise that the novel's second volume is without mistakes, but it has fulfilled its destiny in being published, in my being able to inform you of its publication and by placing it in your hands.

Meanwhile, with Azizbek expelled from Tashkent, his replacement, Nur Muhammad Qushbegi, left Qoqan and was appointed as his replacement.

By overthrowing Azizbek, Yusufbek Hajji's credibility rose in the eyes of the Qipchaqs. But he did not accept any high positions offered for his services and for that reason he was still known, as before, as Yusufbek Hajji. However, he now held the same position with Nur Muhammad Qushbegi as he had with Azizbek, and gained more authority. His every wish represented a legal obligation in the eyes of Nur Muhammad Qushbegi. Injustice, summary executions, unjust taxes, exorbitant fortress budgets, unfair prohibitions, and extravagant ceremonies were reviewed and deemed unsatisfactory and wasteful by the current administration.

Now the people of Tashkent, who had suffered from three years of Azizbek's oppression, took a breath of freedom: trade, business, agriculture, all flourished again.

The people became renewed and expressed their sentiments through a popular song:

The time, the time, the time of blessings,
let Nur Muhammad Qushbegi Tura[203]
remain in a good health forever!

1

The Aspirations Of Parents

Uzbek Oyim was a lady approximately fifty-five years of age. Although she would fit the description we often apply to wives as *Chaladumbul Tabiyatchilik*[204]—a bit narrow minded and unworldly—her renown for having a headstrong and willful nature toward her husband preceded her. The wives of Tashkent also felt the brunt of her overbearing nature. They even greeted her shadow, always reserving the most respected place of honor for her in their homes during weddings, performance of the *azar*,[205] and funerals. Planning any occasion without Uzbek Oyim's council was unthinkable. She oversaw matchmaking on behalf of sons or daughters, circumcisions, and various other sundry rituals. Every wife sought to have their family's occasions planned with Uzbek Oyim's guidance, dreaming of commanding their husbands to implement her advice on niceties and decorum without delay, quashing any subsequent protest with this irrevocable statement: "Uzbek Oyim has ordered it thus."

Her word carried the weight of law. Ceremonies began and ended at her behest. Even the husbands conceded her unassailable position in society. Uzbek Oyim took great pains to discern which wedding or funeral merited her attendance, saying, "Don't take shoes to the street to only wear them down in vain."[206] Due to her strongly held scruples, anyone who could boast of Uzbek Oyim's attendance, who was even privileged enough to have her play a role in the planning of her ceremony, well, that woman would consider herself one of the most fortunate wives in the city, constantly declaring to others while beaming with pride, "My wedding was attended by none other than Uzbek Oyim and she had a hand in assuring the success of our occasion." Uzbek Oyim's authority did not limit itself to social engagements, either. She had the respect of the ladies—the Orda Khanums—who referred to her as "Ona Hon."[207] At times the Orda Yasavul would ride directly to the doors of Yusufbek Hajji's home, announcing "Orda Begi Oyim[208] has extended an invitation for you to attend." And then, they would consequently be forced to wait for Uzbek Oyim to dress appropriately. During social gatherings, Uzbek Oyim would create a stir among the wives, sniffing, "Orda Begi Oyim sent a carriage, but I was not in the mood to socialize so I sent it back. Never mind if it was the Orda Bek Oyim, I am my own person." Or, "Yesterday I was in the orda. Their ladies forced me to spend the night at their residence through their constant pleading and begging... So, I slept the night there..." and then she proceeded to tease them further with juicy pieces of gossip. The wives felt privileged that a lady of such high standing deigned to confide in them, and their estimation of Oyim increased further.

When at home, she usually wore a silk atlas shirt under an *adras* overcoat, accompanied by a white silk turban as worn by ladies, with amber prayer beads in her hands. Uzbek Oyim reclined on a fur pillow near a sandal during the winter months. The summer months were spent under the shade of the veranda, from where she gave directions to Oibadak, wife of Hasan Ali, and the slave girl Hanifa. Uzbek Oyim was preoccupied with teaching Hanifa her household duties—such as how not to spoil the dough or burn the bottom of the plov.

If Otabek's marriage in Margilan raised no objections from his father, we could not say the same for his mother. One could only imagine her thoughts on her son's wedding, an event that crushed so many of her hopes and dreams. Since her son's circumcision, she had begun to painstakingly assess the qualities of eligible Tashkent girls, dreaming of the day she would plan and witness her son's marriage. She would appraise the various female candidates with unforgiving criteria—"Though his daughter is kindhearted, I found their house to be lacking; though his house warrants no rebuke, the daughter proves disagreeable. As for this girl's house, it is *zotapast*,[209] being of lowly birth." Through systematically checking a girl's pedigree by tracing her lineage, by mapping out previous marriages of sons to daughters, she would arrive at a final decision.[210] As someone so consumed with evaluating a potential mate's household, place of birth, family genealogies, and the social positions of family members, clearly Uzbek Oyim viewed Otabek's marriage as a catastrophe that annulled all her efforts to arrange his future union. Her only baby boy married in a distant land called Margilan, through the wiles of strangers, now bound to a strange woman of unknown social origins—Uzbek Oyim, who had patiently nurtured her son for the moment when he found nuptial bliss, was now left standing alone, appearing a complete fool... When Hasan Ali announced the news of his marriage, she exploded in anger.

She cried inconsolably, calling down the heavens, weeping bitter tears, displaying for all the entire weight of the pain and suffering bearing down on her head. "I wish I had thrown all the white of my milk to the blue skies above. He is forbidden to return to Tashkent. He married without any consideration for his parent's wishes. No, that egotistical malcontent shall never return to Tashkent!" Fifteen days passed before Otabek arrived home from Margilan. Instead of hugging her son, who she had not seen for three months, Uzbek Oyim turned her face from him, not asking how he fared, if he was well, and remaining stone silent in reply to his greetings. She seemed like a hen ruffling her feathers in contempt. Otabek immediately divined that his mother's reticence was due to his recent marriage in Margilan. He attempted to apologize once or twice, but could not come to grips with Uzbek Oyim's unbending nature. Her stubbornness forced him to abandon attempts at compromise and resort to acting as if nothing had happened. Furthermore, it became clear that Otabek could not remain there long without traveling back to Margilan. After a couple of weeks had passed, he concocted some sort of excuse to leave, made some preparations, and, without giving notice to his mother, left for Margilan.

The smoke from Uzbek Oyim's rage billowed into the heavens. In retaliation for her son's blasphemous behavior, she vented her awe- inspiring wrath on her husband: "You have become old and senile! Giving your son to a Margilani! Yet you still walk among people oblivious, a complete laughingstock."

Yusufbek Hajji possessed a rare trait: not only in dealing with his wife, but with all members of his house, he never made rash decisions, regardless of the dilemma at hand. Whether it was Otabek, his wife, or Hasan Ali. No matter who, if they had a problem or needed advice, they would approach Hajji and relay their worries, eyes downcast, not daring to meet his gaze. He would stare off into space, as if expecting to arrive at a resolution at any moment, yet seemingly an eternity would pass denying a final judgment. If Hajji finally agreed to a proposal, he would simply mutter, "Yes." If he did not completely understand the matter at hand, he would deliver an open-ended, "Well, all right." If he disagreed, he would give a "Not good." If the matter were disagreeable in some way he would satisfy himself with just a slight grin, and then add nothing.

Members of his household steered their various problems through his strange method of reaching a resolution. In the midst of the familial upheaval over Otabek's marriage, he invited his son into his guest room in an attempt to resolve the current impasse. During this period, Uzbek Oyim harangued Yusufbek Hajji relentlessly, with her husband's only reply being that slight grin peculiar to him—she understood the futility of her attempts to scold him. So, for thirty days she resorted to slandering the Margilani.

Upon his return to Tashkent, Otabek thought, "Perhaps we will have some peace. Perhaps the hurt between us has dissipated." With these hopes in his heart he paid respect to his mother. Yet Uzbek Oyim's ire toward her son only multiplied; she looked blankly at the individual greeting her, replying only, "My son, your good wishes are meaningless. Why would you give salaams to me? Go receive blessings from that Margilani mother of yours." At this she turned her face away from her son. Otabek dismissed his mother's ranting and bitter words with a scoff, fanning her anger further. Spending fifteen more days among his family, at last he concocted another feeble excuse to depart and, without his mother's permission, left for Margilan. Again, Uzbek Oyim's blood boiled in her veins as she broke dishes, plov cups, and a ladle used for drinking tea.

The whole house would hear her weeping: "Are you a father or not? Can't you put a stop to your son's behavior? Do you even consider his future? Something is happening to your son. The Margilani cast a spell on him. Curse your persistent scatterbrained ambling about. The loss of your son is close at hand, fool. He is destined to lie like a mat under the door of the Margilani, a slave..."

Yusufbek Hajji bided his time, paying no heed to his wife's warnings. His only reply was, "Let him be, wife, as long as he is in good health. Someday he will come to his senses."

This time around Otabek spent another month and a half in Margilan before once again returning to Tashkent.

The same anger festered between mother and son. And again, more anger. Fifteen days later, Otabek was leaving for Andijon, and again Uzbek Oyim's smoke rose to the sky. She wished death to the Witch of Margilan, cursing her:[211] "As she separated mother from son, so let fate separate her from her beloved."

Finally, after a year, during which his visits to Margilan increased seven- or eightfold, a change of heart could even be discerned in Yusufbek Hajji, perhaps as a result of Uzbek Oyim's frequent scolding.

In response to his wife's criticisms, he told her, "You failed in raising your son," and asked, "what shall I do now?"

"If we do not marry Otabek to someone from Tashkent, giving him roots here, we cannot prevent his constant flights to Margilan. If he marries someone from Tashkent, he will be as still as water, and perhaps even forget the tragedy he committed in Margilan," explained Uzbek Oyim. Through this means, she took advantage of the moment to further the secret machinations that had festered in her heart and soul for some time.

"Let's wait for our son's return then..."

The words of Uzbek Oyim's husband made her fly into a rage, her shouts contorting her mouth into a snarl. "You did raise your son as a son, or a man as a man; you have created an egoist. You have forgone your fatherly prerogative to guide your son, instead relinquishing to him the right to choose... One should not bring up a son in this manner. Whatever his wishes, you should have molded them to his best interests. Your only solution was to repeat over and over, 'Your son will find the one,' and meanwhile you gave up many outstanding potential brides for him, finally leading to the Margilani calamity. Now I have made my decision: We will make an engagement between him and a suitable girl before he arrives."

"All right, fine, but let's wait," Yusufbek Hajji said wearily.

Hajji, finally giving into her demands, gave Uzbek Oyim wings of hope, reinvigorating her every move. The next day, she ordered Hasan Ali to prepare a cart and then departed to all four corners of the city in search of a bride worthy of her son. She had heard Hasan Ali brag many times about the bride from Margilan possessing beauty of great renown. In order to cool Otabek's heart toward that maiden, she searched for an even greater beauty in her city. She rejected many girls, knocking on countless doors in Tashkent. On the seventh day, she discovered the daughter of an army commander named Olim Ponsad and, upon receiving satisfactory results, duly informed Hajji.

At first Hajji laughed at this news from his wife. Then he said to her, "Wait for your son's arrival."

Uzbek Oyim had anticipated this response, and her protests grew stronger.

"Do what you want but keep in mind that, if your son will not agree to it, I will not force him," Hajji finally said.

Uzbek Oyim started to plead with her husband. "Don't pontificate, husband. She is from the highest levels of society. Can you at least promise to ask your son?"

"All right, I will speak to him, but you should not count on his engagement quite yet."

"I won't, but we will tell our son that he is already engaged... all right?"

"All right, I accept."

After their conversation, Uzbek Oyim livened up, and the next day she again took a cart to Olim Ponsad's house. During their second meeting the members of Olim Ponsad's family lavished attention on her, dignifying her position as *quda*[212] to the renowned Yusufbek Hajji with the utmost displays of deference and respect. As they say, a mouth treated to good food greases the tongue for kind words. Accordingly, Uzbek Oyim behaved as if they were already relatives, assuring her future in-laws: "Bek-aka and myself have agreed upon everything and are only waiting for Otabek to arrive." That evening when she returned home, an admission of her indiscretion slipped out to Hajji, but of course she left out the most incriminating pieces of information about how the negotiations might have already been resolved. Hajji bit his lips, finally showing anger, and said to her, "You will never be clever."

After a month of delays, Bek returned to be struck with the reality that his arrival not only meant an announcement of his pending betrothal to a second wife, but also the even more painful truth that he must accept this engagement. He sensed his doom immediately upon dismounting from his horse, as his mother's previous bitter harangues had sweetened into adoring words of welcome.

"Are you still in good health, my son?"

Wishing to avoid the moment when his parents would inform him of what his heart and soul did not desire, he attempted to evade them, an endeavor destined to fail.

Finally, one day when father and son were chatting in the guest room, Uzbek Oyim slipped in unheeded and winked at Hajji, signaling for him to begin. Even though Otabek didn't notice his mother's signal, he sensed the inexorable arrival of what would prove to be a nasty conversation, yet he could not concoct a plausible excuse to leave. The moment Uzbek Oyim entered, Yusufbek Hajji began to rack his brain for a tactful opening for the looming discussion; meanwhile, Uzbek Oyim persisted in casting clumsy glances toward her husband. Moments of silence passed as Hajji sat, and then finally, with a measured, judicious delivery, he said: "My son, have you heard yet? We arranged something on your behalf."

Otabek certainly knew what "they had arranged on his behalf." Nevertheless, he baited his father: "Of course, a clever person would never willingly commit to something harmful to their son's best interests."

Yusufbek Hajji stared at the ground, not knowing how to proceed. He looked up at his wife with a wry grin and again an unbridgeable stillness widened between the three of them. Uzbek Oyim remained oblivious to the underlying tensions leading to these strained lulls in the conversation. Her heart consumed with burning intent, she lost her patience and blurted out:

"We have engaged you to the daughter of Olim Ponsad Boshi. Now we are going to discuss the wedding arrangements."

Not saying a word to his mother, Otabek gave his father a look of reproach. Hajji, abashed, confirmed the news: "Yes, it's true."

"But I am already married... no matter how much it grieves you... and now?"

"How can we be upset with your marriage?" said Hajji, smiling. "And if you are not dismayed by my first marriage, then why a second?" Hajji squirmed and fidgeted in his place, finally straightening his back. "This is not about anger. This is about necessity."

"What sort of necessity?"

"From Hasan Ali's own mouth, we hear that your father-in-law will never agree to send your wife to Tashkent. Your mother, who raised her son with her own hands, wishes to have a daughter-in-law present..."

Otabek looked at his mother.

"You have survived until now without a daughter-in-law; you can survive without one in the future," he said.

Uzbek Oyim fell into a blind rage at her son who had married a spell-weaving Margilani. All the anger that had gathered within her over the past year finally spilled out.

"I had no intention of bringing you up in this manner. Instead of raising a new generation to carry on our legacy, you ground it into the earth, ruining it. We had no idea that you would be so dependent on this Margilani villager. You ignoramus! Considering this Margilani as a suitable wife, shame on you!"

Otabek returned her anger: "What is she then, if not a suitable wife?"

"She is an *andi*[213] who bats her eyelashes at you."

"What do you mean by andi?"

Instead of forcing his son into a corner, Yusufbek Hajji only gave his wife a wry grin, compelling her to offer a rebuttal to his silent mockery. Uzbek Oyim wanted to humiliate this woman who had stolen her son by lowering her to the status of an andi, yet she could only stutter a half-reasoned response.

"A seer, a seer... it's usually a Chinese man, a calamity of sorts... It originates from the Kalmyk[214]... If it is too complicated for you to understand... simply put, they are a sort of gypsy."[215]

Yusufbek Hajji burst out laughing at this strange attempt at an explanation; on seeing his father's reaction, Otabek could no longer restrain his own amusement. Wiping tears from his eyes as his wife sheepishly picked the dirt from under her fingernail, Yusufbek Hajji had at last had his fill of her bumbling defence and finally said to his son in a serious tone:

"My son, you must not be angry at your mother's stance, she alone speaks against your marriage in Margilan. As for me, I have nothing against either our Tashkent quda or Margilani bride; on the contrary, I consider them both worthy of the title quda and give you my thanks, son. Those parents who are not glad at their progeny's personal success and well-being cannot call themselves parents. Believe me when I say that you need not follow all our wishes—you have that right—but, on the other hand, do not deny us our rights as parents. My son, our only hope in life is in your happiness. All our dreams and aspirations are on your behalf. We give thanks to Allah over and over a thousand times that you have matured into a wise and sober-minded man, like the other sons in our land.

"If decorum forbids us from openly displaying our pride in you, deep within us, in our heart of hearts, we have always held onto the belief that you would not disappoint our hopes for you. Your mother, who raised you, who cared for you, also nourished her own hopes for you. Today your mother prostrated herself on her knees before you, and, in effect, so do I, since her one request only grows from a mother's heartfelt appeal. You married once according to your own desires—congratulations on your bride. Your parents wish you nothing but happiness. Meanwhile the one person responsible for your creation wants to see one of her own dreams manifested through her son. Whether you will help her realize her dream or not depends on you."

Uzbek Oyim reveled in her husband Hajji's sage words, while Otabek stared at the ground, ashamed. Hajji, more talkative than usual, concluded the dispensing of his wisdom with these words: "As the saying goes, 'Those with wisdom find words, the thoughtless will bite first then speak'.[216] Your mother really intended to relay the softer version just provided you. Her purpose was only to defend her rights as a mother, yet unfortunately she could only utter bitter words. You know better than I do."

Otabek remained silent. Uzbek Oyim continued to nod her head in affirmation, "This is so." Yusufbek Hajji had eloquently exemplified the tradition and spirit of his generation in his well-measured argument. Effortlessly, he had elevated his argument through the immutable truths of time-honored tradition and the modes of deportment canonized throughout the civilized world.

Otabek took these words to heart, as he too was a product of his generation. Honestly, he had no argument against traditions sanctified by time, and he stood powerless against the truisms espoused by his father. On the one hand, he wanted to honor his parents, who had raised their son for the sole purpose of fulfilling their dreams of arranging his marriage and enjoying the subsequent grandchildren. He did not want to sully his parents' reputation, for they had already given their word to Olim Ponsad. Yet those imploring eyes imprisoned his heart, reproaching him: "You are unfaithful... with a false heart..."

Those eyes remained the only real obstacle to capitulating to his parents' wishes. Her gaze was etched indelibly in his mind, exerting an unrelenting pull seemingly impossible to resist. Although on one level, acquiescing to his parents' plan would not spell disaster when measured against his sublime devotion to his beloved—he truly believed no harm could come from such a superficial act—yet he hesitated, and his conscience gnawed at his heart.

Otabek struggled for some moments to arrive at a compromise. Those waiting for his answer became impatient.

"Don't make us wait too long, my son," said Hajji.

Otabek looked up at his father, defeat in his eyes, pleading, "I am always willing to follow your wishes if doing so brings you happiness. You will be thrilled to hear that I accept, but, regarding the bride's inevitable suffering..."

Hajji did not immediately understand the meaning behind his son's response. "You mean your wife?"

"No, your proposed wife. Though it seems as if your son's only concern is to go along with your plans, you should understand that I will forever be a lifeless monument to your chosen bride."

Yusufbek Hajji glanced at his wife with considerable apprehension.

Uzbek Oyim, confident in the allure of the future bride, answered without due consideration.

"Fine, son. This is of no concern to you, not yet anyway," she said. Otabek spoke not one word in reply. Yusufbek Hajji interjected, keenly aware of the weight behind his son's candor and its shadowy portents, yet choosing to ignore the full implications of this dark horizon.

"You are quite right, my son. I too must bite my tongue in the face of your mother's ill-chosen words. However, I am still forced to maintain my position," he said. "We must face the fact that we are slaves to our wives' agreements, your mother gave them her word of honor, not I. I cannot abide people thinking of us as dishonest, our family the very paragon of rancor and discord."

Otabek relented to his father's will, appearing, as he put it himself, a lifeless monument. As a condition of his agreement, he insisted on going to Margilan before the wedding to inform his wife and in-laws. Ironically, the mother who previously would not condone her son's journeys to Margilan asked him to depart forthwith, glad that matters had been resolved so easily, and eager to plan a wedding.

2

WILL YOU NOT FORGET ME?

His preparations for traveling to Margilan weighed heavy on his heart, robbing him of the prior joy he'd felt about being on the open road, traveling toward his love. He understood that this time the elation in Kumush's eyes upon seeing him would turn to grief, then irreconcilable sadness. Instead of the beautiful gifts he brought each time he traveled to Margilan, he would present her with a vessel full of poison, of fatal insult. This time he would present her with... a new *kundosh*,[217] and with it the potential for calamity, something inconceivable. Maybe her parents would refuse this odious gift; maybe they would inform him that his new offering was unsuitable for their only daughter, throwing their reply in his face: "We do not need such 'donations' as these, just as we don't need you." These apprehensions oppressed him and, for the first time, made him irresolute in his preparations. Despite his pain, he had to grant his mother's wishes, and against his will he started his journey, carrying his base gift for the Margilani.

He let his horse have the reins and move at his own pace, not wishing to urge him on to his destination. Haunted by the hundreds of premonitions that separated him from the living world, he rode meek and powerless, as if he were a piece of bread soaked in water.

It was springtime. The deep, freshly green rolling hills, the mountains frozen in the distance, with overflowing rivers now rumbling from that timeless horizon. The valley was adorned with flowers in shades of blue, red, white, yellow, green, violet, purple— colors overwhelming the senses. They gave new life, new hope. All winged creatures who had spent the winter in whatever shelter available now sped and tumbled about: sparrows, thrushes, starlings, hummingbirds, songbirds gurgling *"visher-visher."*[218] Singing out in a cacophony of laughter, they kissed the surface of the flowery carpet that enveloped the earth and rose into the clouds... Far off, a cuckoo bird made a passionate application to all around to tell them of his existence: "Cuckoo-cuckoo!"

The array of flowers, stretching off into the distance and fading away into the endless far hills, their ever-present aroma dazzling the nose, the blooming spring earth could breathe happiness into anyone. These garlanded hills beckoned to Otabek, who fled, cleaving through an ocean of flowers. Though dark thoughts clung to him, his eyes soaked in the renewed life of the flowers, his nose inhaled their perfume, his ears were enraptured by the songs of the birds, all the while observing the all-encompassing display of spring that lay about him. Gradually he resolved that he would seize his portion from this panorama and hold it in the recesses of his memory. "There's a swallow," he thought, "racing in a beeline like a bullet on its trajectory, free from worries, hurrying toward his true love. It sings a song that relays the joy of meeting with its true love. A content swallow...

"Perhaps he bears no terrible gift; his parents entertain no aspirations. The laws birds abide by are simple. They choose for themselves their loved ones, and afterward, they take flight into the mountains, along the earth, toward the horizon. I wish I could be that swallow soaring along with its love, only a song in its heart, on my way to beloved Kumush."

Otabek's wings had been clipped by his parents' "gift" of a new wife. He had lost his will and even his freedom. His horse, however, had not lost its wings and it continued at an aimless, plodding canter, trotting past the hills, the mountains, the waterways, willing itself straight toward the city of the past seven or eight trips. When he had passed through this area during his previous travels he had felt great joy and urgency to conclude the journey and arrive at his destination, but now he felt only dread. In a corner of his mind, he wondered if he had the will to turn back without completing his trip.

In the distance, one could hear a young ploughman tilling the earth and singing aloud: "Fate separates two loving hearts!"

The spirit of the song emerged deep from within his powerful chest, resonating out to the world around him and affecting Otabek to his core. The "gift" he bore brought bad omens for the future. The truth of the verse rose to Otabek's own lips, echoing around him. Another thought stirred in Otabek's heart: "It is not fate that separates two lovers, but the cruel wish of the parents."

The verse's sublime meaning prophesized Otabek's future grieving. Tears streamed down his cheeks, dropped to the pommel of his saddle, the mane of his horse. Drops fell freely.

His journeys to Margilan usually took four overnight legs, but now he drew it out to six. He arrived when the muezzin was just calling the evening prayers. He dismounted from his horse and led it by the reins through the passage to Qutidor's home, butterflies rising in his stomach. He was ten days later than usual. He thought that perhaps she was waiting for him. As he proceeded through the entryway to the main yard of the guesthouse, the butterflies grew stronger, forcing him to stop and lean against the neck of his horse.

In fact, she stood in front of the veranda, lost deep in thought, not noticing Otabek's sudden appearance. Finally, she looked up, disapproval in her wide, doe-like eyes as she turned her back on him and, without uttering a word, moved into the courtyard. Otabek already understood the implications of her behavior— punishment duly meted out for his late arrival and for making her wait too long. If this was the maiden's reaction to his tardiness, it was easy to imagine her rage when she found out he was meant to take a second wife.

Otabek felt adrift. He tied his horse to the stable post and, carrying his saddlebags bursting with gifts, he at last entered the house. Upon seeing the beloved bridegroom enter the hall, Oftob Oyim stopped what she was doing and ran toward Otabek. She graced him with a thousand blessings, all the while bursting out with remonstrances over his late arrival and relaying the nightmares she had suffered as a result. Toibeka, appearing from nowhere, also ran to him, but felt too shy to greet him openly. She only took the saddlebag from the handsome young man's hands.

Oftob Oyim franticly fussed about, arranging *korpacha* and inviting her son-in-law to lie back, completely doting over him. But Otabek's guilt weighed upon his heart, knowing full well that, if not today, then tomorrow he would inform them of his "parents' dream"—and the respect he had previously enjoyed would dissipate.

Unaware of what he was doing, he sat down and raised his hands in a short prayer as Oftob Oyim then asked God's blessings, knowing that curses from the same beneficent protector were soon to follow.

Was Otabek afraid? Muttering some final words of supplication, Oftob Oyim eagerly offered a cup of yogurt to her son-in-law. "Please drink, it gives strength after a long trip." Otabek declined.

Ordering Toibeka to boil water for tea, she then started to ask after everyone's health:

"Are your parents in good health?"

"They are, thanks to God, and they send you their regards."

"Is father Hasan Ali all right? Why did he not come with you?"

"Thanks, he is well. He was busy with some tasks and could not come."

As he replied he thought, Why are you lying to her? Isn't Hasan Ali busy with wedding plans...?

Some time had passed since Otabek's arrival, yet Kumush remained sequestered in her room. Obviously she harbored some grievance. Oftob Oyim noticed concern in Otabek's face and naturally thought his worries were connected to Kumush's anger.

"Kumush, your soulmate has come! Don't you know you should come out and greet him?"

Though Oftob Oyim called out to her three or four times, Kumush feigned distraction with some menial task, as if oblivious to her calls. Looking again into Otabek's careworn face, Oftob Oyim's suspicions increased further. She finally got up and entered her daughter's room, scolding her. "You are losing your mind, Daughter. Your husband has come to you from Tashkent. You are ignoring him and not greeting him. Stand up, go out and greet him. What will you do if he leaves angry?"

These last words really made Kumush reconsider her behavior. "Indeed, what would I do if he left?"

She took these words to heart and, pretending she needed something on the veranda, left her room. She glanced at Otabek with a slight, hopeful smile, removed a plate from the shelf, and reentered her room. Kumush's demeanor gave credence to Uzbek Oyim's accusation that she practiced witchcraft, as her smile transformed Otabek completely. He felt a timeless exuberance bursting in his soul, provoked by the spell of a slight smile, which released him from the grip of an oppressive dream. An endless ponderous mountain finally loosened its grip upon him as he broke free, as free as a bird in flight. All the dreams, wishes, and machinations of parents, the profane traditions of this world, and the people who perpetuate them dissolved in the face of Kumush's one passing twinkle!

His moment of revelation sealed a sense of finality and resolve in his heart. "I will not inform them of my parents' wishes, and will never return to Tashkent again."

His decision stood stark before him. The dilemma that had tied his heart in knots for days suddenly untangled through the magic of one slight smile, which in turn bound him to live forever in Margilan. An ease of mind descended upon him, revitalizing his soul, bringing him a sense of new life, new beginnings. Looking at the home around him, serenity and acceptance of his place in the world made his eyes squint as they misted over. That very moment, an "angel who delivers the pain of love to all those around her" graced Otabek with another bewitching glance, lips upturned, lording her power over him.

Fifteen days passed and Kumush asked him many times, "Is it true?"

"Yes, it's true. I will never return to Tashkent," he reassured her time and again. Kumush wondered, half-believing him, if it was God's honest truth, since pure contentment seemed to have arrived from out of nowhere.

On the twentieth day of his stay in Margilan, Otabek was off and about somewhere. Against his habit, Qutidor returned from the bazaar early, around three p.m., asked for Otabek, and, on learning of his absence, led his wife to the guest room.

"Are you all right?" asked Oftob Oyim.

His reply seemed like a black hole bereft of joy or hope. "Everything is fine."

The husband and wife sat together in their guest room. The long pregnant silence between them made Oftob Oyim uneasy.

"Have you heard from Otabek?" asked Qutidor.

"He says many things and I only listen. What exactly do you want to know?"

"Has he mentioned anything about Tashkent?"

"Has something new happened in Tashkent?"

"Nothing about Tashkent itself," said Qutidor. "I meant something else. Have you heard anything new from your daughter?"

"Nothing," said Oftob Oyim. "Ah... although... she said something about her husband never returning to Tashkent again."

Qutidor's eyes danced from side to side, considering this clue. Then he asked, "So, he will never return to Tashkent, ever?"

"I do not know whether it is true or not, however, I heard it from your daughter. What happened? Did he quarrel with his parents before his trip here?"

"Not at all," said Qutidor, as he took something from his pocket and continued. "Today I received an interesting letter from Tashkent."

"From whom?"

"From your in-laws," said Qutidor and opened the letter. "I am going to read it to you."

"What is happening?" asked Oftob Oyim.

"You will know when you hear." Here is the text of the letter:

Let it be known as you read this that we pray five times a day for the health of our in-laws Mirza Karim Qutidor and Lady Oftob Oyim. You are most respected and honored. We are also in good health.

It should not be a secret to you that your son-in-law was sent to serve you in Margilan. God willing, he arrived in good health. Respectfully, no doubt you know that Otabek, as our only son, is all that will remain after we depart from this earth; and our only hopes are for Otabek.

We are grateful that you received our only child with open arms, but are saddened that you do not send our

167

daughter-in-law to Tashkent. This shortcoming fails to fully honor our son. But the fault does not all rest on your shoulders, because the issue of an only child is true in your family as well. However, Otabek is spending most of his time in Margilan and this unsettles us.

Dear Brother, please do not become upset with our words because as I write them they are only a small issue. This world is full of dreams and desires. As we mentioned above, your in-law's only hope in this world is that she wishes to fulfill only her own dreams through her son's betrothal. We did not know whether your honor would find our efforts agreeable or not, but without your consent, our dearest friends, we have decided to give him roots here and sought Otabek's engagement to a second wife in Tashkent; we even began the preparations for his engagement. Initially, your son-in-law protested against our wishes, but eventually relented to his mother's constant pleadings. His primary purpose during this trip was to approach you with this issue, receive your agreement, and then return with your reply. This endeavor depends on the blessings from you, our respected peers. Our purpose in this letter is to discover whether Otabek, again not willing to accept the second engagement, has decided to keep you in the dark, leaving us in confusion.

My dear friend, you are a person of the world. Please consider his mother's demand. More will depend on your decision than your son-in-law's. Please make an effort to have him reconsider. It would be best if you did not yet inform our daughter-in-law regarding the second engagement. You, we hope for the sake of our happiness, will come with Otabek to Tashkent and participate in the wedding preparations so that you see the sincerity in which we propose it.

Yusufbek Hajji and his wife 17th of May 1265 Hijra 1848

Finishing the letter, Qutidor looked at his wife. Oftob Oyim shivered from the contents of the letter as if she had been doused in ice-cold water, freezing her in place. Perhaps these sorts of communications are run of the mill to fathers of households, but one knows all too well the effect they have on wives. Oftob Oyim believed that this measure reflected negatively on her daughter in her role as wife, as if her daughter possessed some irreconcilable flaw. Kumush seemed to be dismissed, thrown away like a useless rag. Still it seemed the letter deceived Oftob Oyim's ears.

"Can you please read it again?"

Qutidor laughed at his wife's response. "There is no use reading it again. You understand the meaning of the letter."

Oftob Oyim's head sank as if she were a snake, having its head crushed. "A second wife above my daughter?"

Qutidor attempted to calm his wife, who fluttered like a bird caught in a box.

"Do not overexcite yourself. Arrive at the truth of the matter."

"What truth of the matter?"

"There is truth in this."

"What truth would that be?"

"If it was a matter of your son-in-law's desire to marry a second wife, neither you nor I could calmly countenance such an affront to our daughter, but we do not feel our son-in-law has participated in this decision and for that reason I remain calm. Did you not say that he had promised our daughter not to go to Tashkent again?"

"Was that a lie or the truth..." Oftob Oyim considered, hesitating. "It seems I heard him mention this quite clearly."

"Since you think you heard him mention it yourself, it may very well be true," said Qutidor. "We can arrive at this conclusion through the content of the letter and see clearly that Otabek vehemently opposed this second marriage. The second marriage is only through your in-laws' initiative. For that reason, we cannot fairly call your son-in-law's second marriage a matter of placing another woman above your daughter."

Completely unanticipated by Oftob Oyim, Qutidor seemed to be defending a view sympathetic to Otabek's second marriage. By doing so, he angered Oftob Oyim even more.

"If Otabek agreed to a second marriage, first of all, he would not come to Margilan to ask for permission," he continued.

"Wait. Please just wait," said Oftob Oyim, surprised. "Are you talking to yourself now? Have you lost your mind?"

"I am speaking about Otabek's not agreeing to a second marriage."

"If your son-in-law does not accept it, God bless him! Then there is nothing to talk about."

"That's not the point," said Qutidor, laughing.

"What is it then?" said Oftob Oyim, her anxiety increasing further. "It sounds like you are going to place the calamity of a second wife on the shoulders of your own daughter with your own two hands!"

Qutidor laughed coldly. "You do not understand, my wife."

"I understand completely."

"If you understood, then how you would respond to this letter?" asked Qutidor.

"Tell them that we do not agree."

"That is an insufficient response. We must at least give a reason!"

"You can find a reason."

Qutidor scratched his head, looking at his wife, who was beside herself with anger.

"They made it clear in the letter that their reasons for the second marriage were that you would not consent to send your daughter to Tashkent," said Qutidor. "Now if you say that your son-in-law should not marry someone in Tashkent, then we should send Kumush to your in-laws to live. Is that all right with you?"

"Why would I send my only daughter to Tashkent?" asked Oftob Oyim, her eyes mixed with surprise and anger. "In giving our daughter to him, we received a promise that our daughter would not leave Margilan."

"You are correct," said Qutidor. "I am also against sending Kumush to Tashkent. But the matter is this: When did we ever demand from Otabek that he should disregard his parents' wishes and not marry a second time? Did we ever receive that promise?"

"Whether he promised this or not," she replied, barely catching her breath, "if he married out of true love, the words 'second marriage' could not possibly leave his mouth."

"Who said those words left his lips?" asked Qutidor.

"If Otabek himself did not mention those words, then stop being a mediator in this matter. By doing so, you will chop off your feet with your own knife."

" 'Cut yourself first with a knife; and if it does not hurt, then cut the other with it,' " he said, losing his patience. "You should understand better than anyone that Otabek will not marry again without our consent. Imagine our in-laws' predicament, with their only son in another city, married to a foreign girl. Would we stand for a similar fate? Whether our son agreed to it or not, wouldn't we try to marry him to another bride from our city? Wouldn't we wish death and damnation on our in-laws for taking our son away to their city against our wishes?"

These words quieted Oftob Oyim for some time, but still her foot twitched like that of a dying sheep. "And so what are you going to do now?"

"What will I do?" said Qutidor, now that the initiative was in his hands. "Even if it is against Otabek's protestations, I will force his agreement and we will go with him to Tashkent."

"And your poor daughter?"

"Nothing will happen to my daughter. She still retains her dignity and the respect of her husband."

"Let the affairs of the world turn to dust!"

"Then you should agree to send your daughter to Tashkent." Instead of replying, Oftob Oyim burst into tears.

Father-in-law, mother-in-law, son-in-law. The three of them assembled together did not bode well for Otabek. Why would this meeting take place in the guest room? Why was Kumush not invited to the party? Why did his mother-in-law's eyes bore into him, piercing straight through him?

Qutidor posed an unanticipated question. "Otabek, do not take this the wrong way. Answer me honestly: What was your real purpose in leaving Tashkent this time around?"

Otabek was thrown off-balance and mumbled an answer. "Just to see you..."

"Please be honest, Bek," Qutidor said, half-laughing, half-serious, attempting to lighten the mood.

"I have told you the truth!"

"But you have not..."

Cornered into revealing the truth, Otabek was caught off guard by this line of questioning.

"Frankly, the reasons behind my departure from Tashkent will upset you both, and they are difficult for me as well. And, I have made up my mind concerning that situation. Nothing good will come of telling you my motivations," he said.

Oftob Oyim glanced at her husband as Qutidor asked in a calm voice, "Is it that difficult of an issue for you?"

"Not only for me. It would be painful for all of us."

"What if we were to agree?"

Oftob Oyim's face wore an unhappy expression, for she was displeased at her husband's boldness. As for Otabek, he jumped, startled as if he had been woken from a deep sleep, and stuttered, "To what do you agree?"

"Perhaps to that 'reason' for which you journeyed from Tashkent?"

Otabek began to sweat and feel disoriented. "Did you already know the reason for my departure from Tashkent?"

"Yes, we knew already," said Qutidor, laughing. "Who or what forced you into this agreement?"

"Nobody has forced me into this," said Qutidor, smiling. "What compels me to discuss this with you is respect for the wishes of the parents who brought up their only son."

"Let those reasons dry up—I have nothing to say if the only reason for a second wedding is the wishes of my mother and father. When I was in Tashkent I almost agreed to a new wedding, but now I see that it is absolutely impossible."

Oftob Oyim seemed ready to burst in agreement, but Qutidor stopped her with a disapproving glance.

"You are being shortsighted, Otabek," he said. "If your father had not brought this issue up with us, our neutrality would have been the best stance, but now if we take your side, we will be blamed."

"Do not worry yourselves with that."

"Why not? Consider the implications of blame."

"Place all blame on my shoulders in a written reply to them."

Qutidor laughed again and asked, "Did you agree with your father's request when you were in Tashkent?"

"Yes, I did."

"You came to Margilan to get our agreement, then. Didn't you...?"

"Yes, I did."

"All right, thank you. Then once you arrived in Margilan you changed your mind. You went back on your word."

"Yes, I canceled my agreement."

"Now you will go to Tashkent from Margilan and again back out on your word..."

Otabek paused for some moments.

"Now you see my point? In this matter, our name will be sullied because of you backing out on your word. This is not going to happen. You should have thought it through beforehand, and now you have nothing else to do but follow your parents' wishes."

Otabek, too weak to utter a reply, slowly became embarrassed at his own childish behavior. "When did my father write you?" he asked.

"I received it yesterday. Are you telling me that you agree with his letter?"

"I cannot provide an honorable reply right now. I have to think about it."

"You can think all you want, but there is only one answer—to agree." Qutidor's words were firm. They made Otabek think harder. On one hand, the necessity of following his parents' wishes seemed like an easy way out, even though it sucked the joy out of his life and put an unbearable burden on his soul. On the other hand, the issue required a better solution.

"All right," said Otabek. "But if I agree with your line of reasoning, your daughter has the final say in the matter."

Until that moment, Oftob Oyim had sat looking at her husband with a devastated expression. Now she turned her head to Otabek with a look of endless devotion.

"Do not concern yourself with what our daughter thinks, Bek," said Qutidor. "It is better that we not discuss this with her at this time. She will adjust. You have nothing to fear from our side."

"No," said Bek. "If I agree to this, I will not keep it a secret from your daughter."

"Why?"

"Without her agreement, I will not put one foot forward in this matter," reiterated Otabek.

"What if she does not agree?"

"Then I will have to refuse as well."

At this definitive response, Qutidor remained quiet, thinking. As for Oftob Oyim, she felt a boundless love and respect for the young man who raised the value of her daughter to the seventh heaven. She wanted to weep and kiss the face of her son-in-law.

"Fine," said Qutidor. "Will you approach her for her agreement yourself?"

"No, I definitely will not, because if those words were to leave my lips, they would be an insult to your daughter," Otabek said.

Husband and wife exchanged glances. Inexplicably, tears welled up in Otabek's eyes. Perhaps they were the result of his feeling embarrassed by the situation. He stood up and left not because he was embarrassed from this display of emotion, but from the situation that confounded his true desire. After his departure, husband and wife sat quarreling with each other for another half hour.

Once *khuftan* prayers ended, Otabek, seeking solace from the unbearable strain placed upon him, sat by his candle and leafed through the pages of Fuzuli's *Divan*.[219] Though he searched and searched through Fuzuli's flowing verses, he could not find a poem whose tone captured his emotions. The poet's words seemed bland and meaningless as Otabek mechanically turned one page after another.

All at once, he closed the book with a snap and looked toward the veranda, astonished, because an inexplicable stillness had cut short the voices of Kumush and her mother echoing through his door. The silence seemed to have a special significance, as both mother and daughter disappeared from the veranda. Otabek returned to his seat. He sensed that he was on the edge of an inexplicable tragedy looming and threatening to engulf them all. When one encounters such a singular pain and a void within themselves, they forgo reason and follow intuition as a guide. His present anguish finally put Otabek in the mood for Fuzuli.

Suspicions over the situation outside persisted for half an hour, then a whole hour. Otabek read on, fully aware of the inescapable nature of that fatal conversation.

But it would be better if it took place later... One must master Fuzuli completely, so of course he did not raise his head from the heady and graceful lines—his whole conscious being inextricably bound to the book.

He did not notice Kumush enter the room. Silent and gentle as a small bird, not yet revealing her melodic voice, she made her way along the carpet and slowly sat down near the candle, opposite Otabek.

The slight movement of her dress made the light of the candle flutter, as if greeting her with a bow. Otabek, sitting deeply involved in the book, looked up, startled, at a vision. A fairy sat before him, with lashes dark and fluttering, like arrows in flight soaked in tears, cheeks flushed red as ripe apples hanging from a bough, an image that Fuzuli himself might have captured with his quill. She now knew the whole truth, and Otabek hung his head in shame, waiting for Kumush's recriminations. He prepared to prostrate himself before her demands for an explanation and acknowledge the sin his parents' wish required of him. Yet, something else happened.

To his great surprise, Kumush soothed him, releasing him from pain: "Fuzuli is a wonderful poet, I agree. In my loneliness I could not put the book down and often meditated on his lines. Is it the same with you?"

He wanted to say something to this merciful, beautiful woman, but he did not know where to begin the conversation.

"Who made you cry?" asked Otabek. "Was I crying?"

"I can tell from your eyelashes."

"They were like this before."

"Was it me who made you cry?"

"Why did you close the book? Open it and read for me. I would like to listen to you say the words aloud for me."

"Are my parents' will and wishes worth a single teardrop?"

"I agree to the marriage. Everything is fine with me," she answered suddenly, as if afraid of her own words.

"You agreed? But why?" Otabek was stunned and visibly affected. "Because I trust in you... and..." Kumush trailed off.

"And what?"

"And that is why I agreed."

"You have the soul of an angel."

"You do as well."

Two souls, two hearts intertwined in mutual affinity. Both surrendering themselves to the other, caught in the moment, lay in each other's arms.

"Why did you cry then?"

Kumush felt a bit uncomfortable and smiled shyly.

"Just at my own predicament," she said, and then, as if voicing all the inner workings and wishes in her heart at that moment, "will you not forget me?"

He could not find an adequate reply that did not reveal all the secrets of his heart. Instead of answering, he could only murmur, half to himself, "The dreams of parents..."

"I know," she said soothingly. "Do you know my dream too?"

Kumush moved next to Otabek and leaned against him, and with her arms wrapped around his knees, put her head into his lap, comfortable.

That same day, Qutidor announced that he would depart the next day for Tashkent with his son-in-law. Otabek and Kumush stayed up all night, talking around the candle.

3

THE SASH OF MAD THE GOURD

After eating a mean repast of garlic to fill their empty stomachs, the guests in the tearoom were lying about, drinking green tea. Obviously bored, they perked up as Mad the Gourd[220] entered the room and rained down on him a chorus of greetings:

"Hey, hey, come on in, Mad, come on in!"

"Do you have a cup of tea for me, you indolent wretches?"

"We do, we do, Your Highness! You saint among men! If you dance *bacha* for us, just this once, we will give you a whole pot of tea."

The person dubbed Mad the Gourd was a wizened middle-aged man with a wispy beard hanging from his chin, wearing an old hat riddled with holes despite the burning sun and a threadbare quilted robe with cotton stuffing escaping from each tear. A new cotton sash wrapped several times around his waist carried five or six gourds—gourds for water, gourds for tobacco, and gourds used as flutes. His legs seemed to bow under their weight.

This madman was well known to all of Tashkent. He was a favorite topic of discussion among even the most affluent beks, and he had many friends among the city's young and old who thought of him as a holy man or mendicant, famous for his gift of sight. The stories of the miracles he performed were the stuff of legend, known by all, near and far.

Everybody in the city knew him as a friend. Even those skeptical of the miracles he claimed to perform through his strange gestures and the outlandish phrases he mumbled to himself nevertheless held a soft spot in their hearts for him. The public that frequented the present teahouse found great interest in him.

He was presently occupied with gratefully devouring a substantial amount of food from someone's outstretched hand.[221] Now he sought to quench the thirst his meal has caused.

"Who is your bacha? Am I a bacha? My mother did not give birth to me so that I would become a bacha... Give me a cup from your teapot, please."

"Then why else did your mother give birth to you?"

"To hang gourds around my waist. Give me some tea, you thug." Mad could not drink his cup of tea in peace as, in a flash, someone grabbed one of the gourds from around his waist and ran away. Things had gone awry for him. He could not catch the thief. He returned to drink some more of his tea, asking one or two times after his gourd. As this yielded no result, he began to weep for his gourd—"*Khnuger, khnuger.*"

The audience waited for the tears to flow from his eyes and the spittle and mucus to drip from his face. The man who had fled with his gourd climbed onto a rooftop, hung the gourd from a ledge, and then descended, dropping down near the inconsolable, unhinged lunatic.

"Did you catch the thief who stole your gourd, Mad?"

"No, my brother. Let him die festering like my gourd. He got away."

Someone from the crowd said that he had last seen the thief in Eski Juva District, riding a gourd like a horse.

Another said, "It was a great gourd."

A third taunted him: "It's a great pity."

177

Mad the Gourd launched into a series of loud wails as the pranksters taunted him to the point of heartbreak.

"Your gourd was the only one of its kind in this country," someone said.

Mad revealed to all the stolen gourd's life story: "My father was a wine gourd. My mother was a bean gourd. I am a belt gourd," he said. Everybody laughed.

One of his fans pointed to the gourd hanging from the ledge, his eyes widening in dramatic surprise. "Hey, look! Who's the owner of that gourd?"

Overjoyed at discovering the beloved gourd hanging over his head, Mad called out, "Hey, you delinquents and laggards, you're a mindless lot..."

"Dear, dear saint. What will you give me for it?"

"You'll get what you ask for, you dimwit. If you want, you can become the bek of the village Oyim. You'll even mount a horse with golden reins, you fool."

"Managing my home village would be too much for me. You better tell us how you manage your gourds. Who are they?"

Mad agreed to this condition. The gourd was brought down and delivered into Mad's hands in good condition. At last the beloved gourd was tied to his waist, near its partners, with great care and respect.

"All right. Will you start with your story, Mad?"

Displaying one of the curved and misshapen gourds, he said, "This is Musulmanqul the Lame." Pointing to the smaller musical gourd hanging alongside the first one, "This one is Khuday-bacha,[222] Khudayar!" He began to stroke the large gourd. "And this one is Nur Qala—bigheaded Nur.[223] And these two slim gourds are thin-necked tobacco gourds." The pranksters laughed.

As the distraught Mad attempted to take his leave of these gourd pillagers, one of the group cut him off.

"Wait a minute. There is something for you!"

Mad swore out loud but then stopped short.

"Where did you steal that sash around your waist?"

"Eh, let me go! May you die in your youth!"

"Isn't this the sash stolen from you earlier, Karim Qul?" one of the spectators asked his neighbor.

"Yes, that is my stolen sash. We have caught the thief!"

Mad the Gourd grabbed the sash with both hands, afraid that it would be taken from him.

"This is not yours, silly man!"

"No, for certain it is mine. Untie it or I will call the police."

"Hey, you imbecile. Why do you slander me?"

"Tell us the truth, where did you steal it from?"

Mad held the knot of the sash with all his heart, crying, "I tell you, I did not steal it, you lunatic. I received it at Hajji pasha's wedding, imbecile."

"Who is Hajji pasha? Do not lie, thief."

"You do not know Hajji pasha, imbecile?"

"There are many Hajjis in Tashkent!"

"You have gone crazy. You have lost your mind... I am talking about Yusufbek Hajji; there was a wedding, his son got married... Leave me alone. May you die young, fool!"

Mad finally managed to escape from the hands of the pranksters and ran away. One of the *chaikhana's*[224] patrons, a patch hanging over his eye, broke off from the crowd following Mad as they got farther from the teahouse.

"Mad, hey Mad," called his pursuer.

Mad recognized the man with the eye patch moving toward him... but kept up his pace, grasping his gourds even tighter just in case.

"What do you have to say for yourself, Eye Patch?"

"Don't be afraid, Mad," said the man with the patch, quickening his steps.

"What do you want?"

"Wait!"

Mad slowed down. In order not to frighten him, the man stopped at a distance, reaching into his pocket.

"I have something for you."

On hearing these words, Mad moved away. Eye Patch moved closer to him.

"Here, take my gift!" he said, showing Mad some money, but when Mad continued to move away from him, "I say stop!" the man commanded, in a threatening tone.

Mad stopped at a safe distance. "Don't come near, don't come near me, Eye Patch!"

Eye Patch stayed ten steps away. "Who did you say married his son recently?"

"Who married, you ask?" replied Mad.

"You just said it in the teahouse!"

"You just said it in the teahouse..." echoed Mad.

"Where did you get the sash?"

"Your grandmother gave it to me."

"Tell the truth. Did you get it at a wedding?"

"I got it at a wedding..." said Mad.

"At Yusufbek Hajji's house?" asked Eye Patch.

"Yes, Yusufbek Hajji's house."

"What if I wanted to get a sash?"

"Yes," Mad replied. "You have already missed the wedding."

"Which of Yusufbek's sons was married off?"

"How many sons does he have?"

"How many sons does he have!" he exclaimed.

"Only one... Have you come from Qorategan?[225] Is that sister of yours in good health?" mocked Mad.

"She's in good health... when did he get married?"

"Are you married yourself? How many days did the trip from Qorategan take?"

"Five days. When did he marry?"

"On donkey or by foot?"

"By donkey."

"Do you have *nasha*?"[226]

"Yes, I have some."

"Give me a small pinch."

"I will give you some if you tell me when the wedding took place."

"You arrived too late for the wedding, you silly man... As for me, they gave me a big cup of plov."

"Would you like to eat? What if I buy you some plov from the bazaar?"

"When did the smallpox appear on your face?"

The man with the eye patch lost his patience. "I say, when... did... he marry?"

"You came too late to see the wedding. I already told you—a week ago, ten days ago, a month ago. Hey, hey, now *charlar*[227] is going to take place—to charlar. Qorategan!"

"Did he marry off his son to the girl from Tashkent?"

"He, he, he, you moron, of course the girl is from Tashkent. Should she be from Qorategan?"

After this exchange, the man with the eye patch went back to the teahouse.

4

THE HINDU JODUGAR[228]

The new father-in-law seemed struck by a strange malady: he found neither a cure for his ailment, nor release in death, a small mercy meant to set the living free. Instead, he found himself bound for Tashkent, because, according to custom, the newlyweds must visit the bride's parents' home after the wedding. So Otabek could not make his exit without first performing charlar.

"Dearest Mother, consider me for a moment! A poor wretch, Mirza Karim Qutidor, agreed to my second marriage, submitted his daughter to a brutal competition between brides, and even celebrated the wedding ceremony with you just to make you happy. He put his business aside, spending over ten days in Tashkent. You should appreciate the kindness of others…"

Uzbek Oyim had stubbornly recited the same refrain many times over the past week: "There is nothing I can do now, my son. It is a great shame on us to not spend charlar here."

"You are always lecturing about shame, but you do not understand the meaning of the word."

Her son's challenges multiplied Uzbek Oyim's agitation.

"Don't worry, my son. The charlar will be over soon. You will get to see the face of your village girl again…"

"Dear mother," replied Otabek, "I am at a loss for words with which to respond to your venom. Fine! If I am worried, as you state, I am anxious on behalf of my wife and her parents. It nags at me that perhaps they are troubled by my presence here. When I resisted fulfilling your dream and refused to even utter the word

'Tashkent,' these poor people dragged me here against my will to satisfy your wishes. If you yourself have any shame, at least we should take their feelings into consideration. Shouldn't we?"

"If this is the case, don't wait for the charlar, just leave," said Uzbek Oyim. "That Margilani is the night and day of your dreams. That is for sure."

Otabek clenched his teeth in silence, his throat constricting in anger. The envy in her heart opened a deep wound in him. Her aspirations were becoming increasingly delusional day by day. The source of his secret anguish was obvious to her and she appreciated its implications full well. Yet despite this, her most genuine concern was that the Margilani's magic held power over her son. She saw that the veil of enchantments cast over her son were more powerful than she had dared to imagine. She had attempted to free him from his prison by means of a large wedding, but her efforts had given him no release from the spells of the Margilani. Evidently, she mastered great power.

On his wedding day, she had had a spell placed on Otabek's clothes by a Jewish *domla*[229] so that he would ostracize the Margilani and warm up to the Tashkentlik,[230] yet it was clear her efforts had been futile.

Later, the "five main" mullahs[231] brought sacred smoke and mixed *izab ichki*[232] in his tea—more prayers and amulets with no effect... Though Uzbek Oyim knew Margilani mullahs to be powerful, she was surprised on one point: if a Jewish qalandar's[233] magic could be nullified by another Jewish qalandar, then a Muslim mullah's magic should be able to be canceled by another Muslim mullah.

"But why can't the Tashkent mullahs do anything?"

The secret power behind the enchantments escaped Uzbek Oyim. Her thoughts did not linger in this dead-end street for long; soon, the truth almost blinded her.

"The Margilani seer is neither Jewish nor Muslim, but Hindu! He is a satanic Hindu![234] Neither a Muslim mullah nor a Jewish mullah can negate the magic of Satan. We have no way out unless the Hindu that cast the spell counteracts it."

What should she do? There were no Hindu mullahs in Tashkent to counter the spell. Should she consult a sage? Should she go to the Margilan herself? A great calamity had fallen upon her head. She needed to find a way to get rid of it.

Uzbek Oyim saw that the solution to this unhappy situation lay with her.

"If Otabek goes to Margilan, I will send Hasan Ali with him. Hasan Ali will meet with a Hindu mullah and untie the magic knot that binds Otabek... Let the Hindu mullah take whatever amount he wishes. I will sell one of my expensive dresses and pay the money."

Otabek remained silent, sitting opposite his mother. After arriving in her mind at the heart of the matter and its resolution, Uzbek Oyim said to Otabek, "My son... you have earned the title of 'newlywed.' You don't have to sit by me anymore while your poor wife is all by herself in her room."

Otabek glanced up at his mother, making no reply. "Go, my son, go. It does not suit you..."

After her prompting, Uzbek Oyim motioned to Oibadak, his mother's servant, who moved closer and stopped near a small window.

"Milk and tea is ready; shall I bring it?"

"Bring two cups to the bride's room and call Hasan Ali here." As his mother's servant turned to leave, Otabek stopped her. "Bring mine here too," he said.

Oibadak looked at Uzbek Oyim as she turned and glared at her son. Ignoring her disapproving gaze, Otabek made a gesture at Oibadak that indicated "Do as I say."

"Then bring the bride's tea here as well. Call her to us," Uzbek Oyim countered. "And Hasan Ali can drink his tea in his room."

After Oibadak left, she asked her son, "What do you mean by challenging me so openly, my child?"

"It's not a challenge."

"Why would it matter if you drank tea with your bride? It is not right to insult the daughter of honorable parents."

"I did not mean it as an insult. You invited her here yourself. It's fine."

Uzbek Oyim started to reply but Oibadak entered just then with a tablecloth.

"Did you call the bride?"

"I did."

The tablecloth was laid out as lunchtime tea arrived. Dipping bread in her cup, Uzbek Oyim kept her eyes on the door. It was clear that she was waiting for her daughter-in-law. When the girl appeared at the door, Uzbek Oyim motioned to her son as if to say, "Welcome her properly."

The girl was seventeen years old with a round white face of moderate beauty. Zainab, submitting to the authority and desires of her mother- in-law, approached the tablecloth, demurely following the customary standards of etiquette.[235] As she took one measured step after another toward the table, her mother-in-law finally gave her permission, motioning for her to a take a seat beside her, where, without making a noise, Zainab shyly sat down. Meanwhile, Uzbek Oyim closely monitored her son's reaction, though he only sat dipping his bread into his tea. Unable to meet her son's eyes, Uzbek Oyim frowned and had to address him directly.

"Your charlar has not been arranged yet, as tradition demands. Maybe you should not wait till the right day and just go visit your sick father-in-law now."

Zainab stared at her husband.

Otabek replied coolly to his mother, "I can maybe make a quick visit." And then he looked at Zainab with a slight grin.

Zainab smiled in reply. Their momentary exchange calmed Uzbek Oyim a little, but this small hope soon faded as again silence reigned between them.

The mother, completely obsessed with analyzing her son's every move, was taken over by the need to look at him compulsively. Zainab's eyes often fell on Otabek, who only responded by drinking his tea in larger and larger gulps.

Uzbek Oyim continued to eat her insides out, swallowing food now tasteless to her; it seemed as if her disquiet left life with no flavor or meaning. As a final attempt to save the emptiness of an arranged marriage, Uzbek Oyim asked suddenly, "Did you order a gold ring for the bride, Pasha?"

"I did. It will be ready in a few days," replied Otabek shortly, showing no desire to continue the conversation. But his mother struggled to keep it alive.

"What about *sochpopuk*?[236] Do you have any?"

Zainab looked at her husband and answered, a bit embarrassed, "I don't."

"If you do not, then I will buy them for you," said Otabek.

Their exchange lightened Uzbek Oyim's heart and she started to chat about this and that, yet the conversation quickly died out again. The milk and a teapot brimming with tea were brought in. Pouring tea into the first teacup, Zainab stood up and handed it to her mother-in-law with both hands.[237] As she moved to stand again after filling the second cup for her husband, Otabek stopped her.

"There is no need for you to stand again while offering tea," he said, "You can pass it to me while sitting."

The mother-in-law disapproved of this direction, though: "What are you saying, child? Offering tea while standing up is an honorable, graceful, and pleasant duty of a new bride. Isn't this the sole beauty of a marriage?"

"I am not saying that you should not be handed your tea while she stands, but I have no need for social niceties," he replied quickly, emptying the teacup in his hand. He said a prayer as he stood up and repeated, [238] "Certainly you should receive your tea while she is standing..." Then he left the room.

Zainab took these words at face value, unaware of their true meaning. As for Uzbek Oyim, she turned pale. The vision of Hindus bent on malfeasance appeared before her, and she quaked in fear, shivering to her very bones.

An hour after tea, Uzbek Oyim called Hasan Ali, dismissing everyone in the room so that they could speak alone. Hasan Ali did not know the reason for the summons, nor did he suspect his mistress's secret intentions; he thought that perhaps she was calling him so that they could discuss the preparations for the upcoming charlar. Uzbek Oyim sealed the door against interlopers, sat down near Hasan Ali, and whispered urgently.

"You see that the mullahs in Tashkent cannot stand up to this challenge... I believe that the Margilani seer is a Hindu and there is no way to counteract the effect of a Hindu spell—I call upon you for assistance. All I ask is for you to hear me out, to remain sympathetic to my point of view, if you can...

"As you know, instead of forgetting his Margilani wife, Otabek thinks about her every hour of every day. His torment originates from the spells cast by those Hindu seers who cleverly placed a noose around his neck, one that draws him ever closer to his Margilani wife..."

Although Hasan Ali knew of his mistress's dealings with the mystic *Domla Khodja*,[239] he had no clue what she meant by "Hindus pulling him by a noose." He also had great respect for his mistress's volatile temperament. Out of fear of being scolded, he kept his mouth shut, thinking to himself, "Let's see what happens." But instead of giving further explanations, Uzbek Oyim questioned Hasan Ali.

"What do you advise concerning our dilemma?"

"How can I advise you? I would advise you to do whatever you wish," he said.

Hasan Ali's cautious response revealed that he did not fully comprehend her designs behind these strange theories, but his answer pleased Uzbek Oyim.

"Thank you, Hasan Ali, for your wise counsel. You will help me to do what I have planned."

"So be it..."

"We can act tomorrow or the day after tomorrow, after the charlar. No doubt Otabek will travel to Margilan soon afterward. You must find a reason to accompany him to Margilan, find a Hindu magician, and pay him *baksheesh*[240] to counteract the spell cast."

"On whom?"

"On Otabek, of course."

"What spell?"

"Didn't you understand anything?"

"I understood... I simply wanted more details..."

"The Margilani managed to sway Otabek toward her with the help of a Hindu mullah. You must have noticed it yourself?"

"Although I haven't noticed anything, I now see what your intentions are," said Hasan Ali, laughing. "Your wish is to chill Otabek's heart toward his Margilani wife."

"You are right," said Uzbek Oyim. "Not just to chill his heart, but to free Otabek from her claws entirely."

The revelation that his mistress had such malignant designs against the Margilani alarmed Hasan Ali.

"Why so?"

"Because I will not sacrifice my son to the hands of that Margilani. Before, he did not have a Tashkent wife, but now he does. Besides, I will not tolerate that lowly village bride."

"Well, what do you intend to do now?"

"My intentions are clear as daylight," said Uzbek Oyim, and laid out her plan: "As I just said, if we put an end to the spells of the Hindu Mullah, she will be crushed. Otabek will immediately demand *talaq*[241] from that lowborn—"

"Where did you discover that it was a Margilani Hindu magician who contrived to beguile your son?"

Confronted with the voice of reason, Uzbek Oyim hesitated and inner doubts crept in, nagging at her. "Oh, I know," she said.

"Did someone tell you?"

"I came to the truth of the matter of my own accord, through my own intellect."

Hasan Ali could not help but laugh out loud. "Yet concerning this matter, your intellect has erred slightly..."

"How so?"

"No Hindu mullah has bound them together. No Margilani has cast a spell, and Otabek is not under the influence of magic."

"Why then does Otabek after his second marriage still pine for the Margilani?"

"You still don't know the reason why?"

"I know. It's the power of some sort of magic."

"Who is behind this magic?"

"It's his father-in-law, his mother-in-law, and maybe his wife."

"You are mistaken, Mother."

"How am I mistaken? What other purpose do you think could be behind casting this sort of magic? *Qalvak*.[242] They are going to drain the mental faculties of my stupid son and milk him for his money."

"Milk him of his money?" repeated Hasan Ali, laughing. "Compared to the wealth of your Margilani in-laws, we are poverty-stricken. I know for a fact that they will not allow Otabek to spend three coins on household goods. I know this myself and I have heard your son say, several times, 'I feel uncomfortable over them not allowing me to spend money.' You should know that if your spell-casting in-laws were evil, it would not have been so easy to marry your son to someone from Tashkent. No doubt you have heard from Hajji that your son intended to break his promise and never return."

Uzbek Oyim wavered and felt like surrendering her position, but she did not want to do so in front of Hasan Ali. As if this information were not new to her, she replied emphatically, "Now I understand the secret behind all this." She said these words over and over.

Hasan Ali laughed again. "Though you think you have discovered some hidden secret, you understand everything wrong. The secret is not what you have imagined it to be."

"Such as?"

"Your son's anxiousness to go to Margilan is due... well, this time around, mostly."

"What then?"

"To a feeling of shame toward his in-laws. But mainly to the fact that your senior daughter-in-law is your son's first love. He opened his eyes to the world and found Kumush."

"First love?" Uzbek Oyim exclaimed, laughing sarcastically. "Isn't Zainab just as beautiful as that Margilani? Are you saying that she is more beautiful?"

"I don't know. Perhaps your son thinks so."

"You have seen both of them. Tell the truth. Which of them is the most beautiful?"

Hasan Ali hesitated over answering this awkward question. "True love does not depend solely on physical beauty."

"Depend or not depend, I am not asking about love. I am asking which one is more beautiful."

Hasan Ali again felt uneasy and attempted to change the subject. "What should we do now?" he asked.

"Just answer my question, damn you! May the earth swallow you whole!"

"Your question is tricky. I am not sure how to answer it. Shall I tell you the truth?"

"The truth, please!"

"If I told you the real truth," he said, pausing. "Every flower has its own smell."

"I said tell me the truth!"

"Even if Kumush were dead, her corpse would be more beautiful."

"Don't say another word!" screamed Uzbek Oyim. "First of all, you are the reason that the disaster of this Margilani has been visited upon us, and yet you still speak on her behalf! Your beard grew long, but your wit fell short. I am the stupid one for asking for advice from a long-bearded dimwit!"

Hasan Ali's repugnance and alarm at her reaction came from a profound appreciation for Uzbek Oyim's character. She insisted on not seeing any truth that contradicted her wishes, a trait that stood out in her personality.

"You are the one who forced me to tell you the truth and now you are angry with me, mistress?"

Uzbek Oyim became even more aggressive toward him as he protested. "Enough, enough... May God take you. You eat my food, yet now you spit at my feet," she said.

Hasan Ali left the room, giggling under his breath at the thought of his mistress swearing at him.

Though this debate had brought out the worst in Uzbek Oyim's personality, it did not seem to have broken her spirit...

About a week after their argument and on the fifteenth consecutive day of waiting for the charlar, Otabek was searching for a book among the collection on his bookshelf. Hasan Ali entered and stood near him.

"They said the charlar will finally take place on Thursday. Somebody told me."

Otabek picked out one of the books and began to leaf through it casually, murmuring to himself, "They can go to hell. Let them take their charlar! Take it, dry up, and blow away!" He counted down the days in his heart: "If today is Monday, there are only four more days."

"This letter is for you," said Hasan Ali, holding out a folded paper. "Someone passed it to me to give to you." Then Hasan Ali began to hurriedly lay out a prayer rug, as it was getting late for evening prayers. Otabek's eyes opened wide at the heading of the letter. "To Tashkent, meant only for the hands of the son of Yusufbek Hajji, Otabek, who lives in——Mahalla." He immediately knew who the author of this correspondence was, and he put the book back onto the shelf as he quickly opened the sheet to read its contents fully.

It was a long letter, written on a large piece of parchment with flowery, elegant script in violet ink. As his eyes moved along the flowing words, a great change came over his face and his body shivered with emotion. It was unclear whether the letter gave him pain or joy. When the indiscernible ebb and flow of emotions reached a crescendo, he finally took his eyes from the letter, saying aloud in a voice lost and helpless, "She frightens me." After hearing these words, Hasan Ali quickly finished his prayers and turned his head from the carpet toward Otabek.

"What happened?"

"Nothing happened," said Otabek and, with a lost look, faced him. "But something frightens you? Who is the letter from?"

"The letter," he said, gaining some composure, "the letter is from Kumush... She delivered some veiled threats in order to admonish me."

After this reply, he folded up the letter and put it away. Having completed his prayers, Hasan Ali approached Otabek.

"She might have written it out of frustration over your delay," he said. Otabek nodded his head in confirmation.

"Especially during this special time, your long delay has made your poor bride overly concerned." Hasan Ali continued: "Really, it is very difficult for her. They say that the second wife is a death sentence for the first wife. And yet now you only have a few days left for charlar and then you will return to Margilan." Otabek did not reply since he knew Hasan Ali was only trying to console him, but his words about first and second wives meant nothing to him.

Attempting to calm him further, Hasan Ali said with a smile, "If your heart continues to ache, you can write her an equally tough response. The postal courier mentioned that he will again make his rounds through here tomorrow..."

Otabek brightened up a bit at these words. The thought that the letter had been written in jest and shouldn't be taken seriously ran through his head again.

"Is it true that the postal courier will return to pick up the reply?" he asked.

"Yes. He promised to come by tomorrow if you write a letter."

"Good," said Otabek with a smile. "I will prepare a letter for his arrival tomorrow."

As soon as Hasan Ali left the guest room, Otabek gained control over himself and looked through the letter a second time:

To the unfaithful adulterer,

I am writing this letter while weeping bitter tears because at present, not only my tears, but the whole of my existence is like black ink. I will never believe in the word faithfulness again.

I no longer believe in it, because I have seen treachery in a young man in whose trustworthiness I once had faith. I am unable to raise my head out of shame, because now it seems the earth and the sky, the stones and the mountains, and all beings in this world mock me for having been deceived. I pray for death to come to me so that he will free me from these tragic days, but it is as if death hates my wretchedness and wishes to betray me as well.

My dear Bek, though you may become angry, I still insist on saying:

You have no conscience, no pity, no honor towards your promises, no gratitude, and quite simply you are devoid of anything good, devoid even of humanity. On the contrary, you are a sly fox, a bloody-mouthed wolf, a merciless assassin, a shameless young man!

I called you sly:

Do you recollect how you deceived my simple father and poor old mother? I hope you keep these recollections in your memory.

Do you remember the words you said at night by the candle? Promises given to me, tears you shed. Do you remember them? Enough... ! These tricks and these deceptions, who but you are capable of them?

I called you a wolf with a bloody mouth:

Because you are merciless, with your terrible diseased jaws tearing at the breast of simple creatures. You make the flowers that have just bloomed fade before their time; you crush the tulip buds, killing them before they have a chance to open.

I called you shameless:

Knowing that your cruelty makes you unworthy of my love, you now shamelessly enforce your will.

I am surprised at your proclamation:

It turns out that you were ashamed of revealing your intentions to my father when he was your guest in Tashkent, but can you prove to anyone that you have a conscience? At times my mother would repeat a verse to me, "When you find a new love, one should forget about old loves. Consider the old love dead and cover it in a burial shroud."

At that time, I did not understand the meaning of that advice, but now I am a victim of this wisdom and the person to whom it is most relevant. As a last wish of the one cast aside, I request from you:

Do not turn the second wretch into a shameless whore when you find your third love. Do not be surprised at my wish. As the saying goes:

"Cut yourself with the knife before harming others."

Blessings be upon your new beloved, and to me—the fate of the victim of shamelessness.

This letter was not written by Kumush "The Silver One," but by an abandoned wife, covered in mud, 17th of Juva, 1265

5

TREACHERY

Qutidor's return from Tashkent alone made Kumush anxious, but the fact that the charlar had not transpired gave her some small consolation. The endless torment of suspicion and panic eased.

"He did not forget me. His promises were real, his words were truthful... He still loves me..."

Out of habit, she again looked toward the road, expecting him to appear. It was the eighth day after her father's return from Tashkent. That night her dreams seemed to foretell the arrival of Otabek. Waking in the morning, she unbraided her hair and, as she thoroughly combed out the knots over the washbasin, the gentle waves of her long black locks splayed along her back and chest, creating the very image of feminine beauty. Cleansing her hair first with yogurt and then with soap, she asked her mother to braid her hair into two braids. Responding to Oftob Oyim's question, "Why are you not braiding forty?" she laughed. "Your daughter has passed from girlhood into married life. She has entered into a period where she does not need another sovchi other than your son-in-law."

The two braids suited her better than the prior forty braids— they lent her an air of authority and maturity. After preparing her hair, she entered her room and stopped at the shelf where her clothes, at least fifteen or so exquisite silk dresses, were folded and arrayed.

Although she had originally intended to wear her lemon-yellow atlas silk dress, after taking it off the shelf, she changed her mind. Red... blue... pale pink as apple tree blossoms. She couldn't make up her mind. Among all these dresses, all suited her, but which one to put on at this present moment?

Though at that moment she preferred the yellow silk, she put aside her present whim and decided to don the one Otabek preferred. Otabek usually asked her to wear the black silk dress. Putting on a black otter jacket, she wrapped her head in a blue silk scarf, took her small gold earrings with pearls from the box and pinned them in her ears. After dressing in this simple ensemble, she went to the mirror placed on the second shelf. She made herself up in the mirror, arranging her hair. Pleased with the maiden contained in her reflection, she smiled a lopsided, seductive grin, revealing pearly white teeth between ruby lips. She ran her finger along the black beauty mark near her gentle, sloping nose—the focal point of her beauty—as if confirming it was real, natural. She moved away from the mirror and thought, Though the other may be beautiful, my beauty mark is mine alone.

She kept herself busy with preparations for the evening meal. Her dream from the night before still gave her hope that Otabek would arrive soon. She made Toibeka water the yard and she started sweeping the tamped-earth floor of the yard with her own hands, keeping her ear pricked for voices from the outside passage.[243]

Having completed the yard work, she paused near the front of the veranda to tidy herself up. At once, the echo of footsteps from outside the gate met her ears, quickening her heart. The sound of shoes clicking on stone neared, causing her to shiver in excitement. Finally, the voices and footfalls ceased, and before Kumush appeared the unexpected image of a lady in a paranji. Kumush took a long breath in disappointment.

A stunted and misshapen woman, presumably married at some point but now clearly alone, approached Kumush as if she had been coughed up from deep within the bowels of the earth. Upon closer review she seemed a creature whose nose splayed out flat on her face with deep- seated beady eyes resembling holes dug out with a leather awl. Her gaping mouth disproportionate to her face, spread from ear to ear, terrifying those unlucky enough to look upon her horrible visage. The sallow, waxy skin could have belonged to someone bedridden for forty years, stricken with an illness. She seemed to be—but it was anyone's guess—a lady of approximately forty-five years of age.

It was the first time in her life Kumush had seen such an ugly woman. "What is this hungry ghost doing here?" she thought.

From about ten steps away, the woman's face emitted a cold and strange, almost nightmarish, nasal laugh.

"Hee, hee, hee, my dear, my beautiful princess, tell me. Is this Mirza Karimboi's yard?" she asked.

"This is," replied Kumush and reluctantly took two steps toward the woman, extending her arms in greeting with poorly masked disgust.[244] The loathsome being with the body of a tree stump was eager to accept the greeting, but her hands could barely reach the shoulders of the young woman, shoulders as slender and gracious as a gazelle. "Are you in good health, Pasha daughter?" Without taking her paranji off, the woman sat on the edge of the veranda, swayed her body from side to side with a tired sigh, and complained, "It turned out to be a long road. I am really tired. Is this really the house of Mirza Karimboi?"

"Yes, it is."

"What's your relationship to the wealthy Mirza Karimboi?"

"I am his daughter."

"Qeh... qeh... qeh... I can give it to you then," said the woman and took a letter from her purse. "My son conducts business between Tashkent and Margilan. During his last trip from Tashkent, someone gave him this letter and asked him to deliver it to the house of Mirza Karimboi... how nice are you, Pasha girl... qeh... I am not one to boast, but my son and I would kill ourselves for the sake of serving others. Today he arrived from Tashkent during lunchtime in such a hurry that he did not even greet me properly, handed me this letter, and said, 'Dear Mother, I am weary of the road, and, though it is not appropriate, could you please find Mirza Karimboi's house and deliver this. A client requested me to expedite it. He practically begged me.'

"Of course, I was merciful. How kind you are, Pasha girl. Though I have just recovered from an illness and the strength to take an extra step seemed to have eluded me, but, out of kindness, I nevertheless performed my task, wearing myself out attempting to find your house. I almost perished before finally finding it... qeh..." she explained.

Taking the letter from her hand, Kumush thanked her and quickly glanced at the heading of the letter: "To the House of Mirza Karim Qutidor, resident of Margilan."

"Are you sure you're not mistaken, Mother?"

"How could I be mistaken, Pasha girl? As it turns out, everybody in your neighborhood knows of your distinguished residence." The woman attempted to flatter Kumush, taking to her feet again. "Now let me go, my poor son traveled a great distance and is hungry. No doubt he craves hot food, if even just a spoonful."

"Come in. We will boil tea for you."

"Thank you, Pasha girl, we will drink together some other day... qeh. As the proverb goes, 'If you meet someone once, you become acquaintances; meet twice, and you become good friends...' "

Not wishing to give her guest the hope of hospitality, Kumush escorted her up to the passage. On reaching the doorway, the woman stopped and turned toward her.

"In this world, our wealth is through service to others. If your father has letters for Tashkent or Qoqan, my son will deliver them with pleasure. May I see you again if I happen to be in your neighborhood?" she asked.

Kumush could not say no and so answered, "You may do as you like, if it is not too much trouble."

The woman turned toward the narrow passage leading outside. Upon returning to the veranda, Kumush quickly opened the letter. It had been written on a small piece of parchment in a language overly formal and measured.

To Kumush, the daughter of Mirza Karim
From Otabek, the son of Yusufbek Hajji of Tashkent
When your father was in Tashkent, I felt hesitant to talk about my intentions. To be honest, it was extremely uncomfortable for me. As you know, when I married my second wife in Tashkent I found that I could not afford to support two wives—one in Tashkent and the other in Margilan. Therefore, I must release one of my wives from my responsibility. I have made a decision that will take a burden off my life and meet my wishes. I have concluded that I should remain with my wife from Tashkent and divorce you. Upon taking receipt of this letter, you may consider yourself free of any obligations to me and divorced from me. No doubt the judges of the Shariyat court will find my letter seeking divorce legitimate and upon completion of the Idda[245] period you will be granted the right to remarry.
Signed Otabek, the son of Yusufbek Hajji, 13th day of Javzah 1265,[246] Tashkent

With her last drop of strength, she finished reading the letter, cried out in a weak, anguished voice "Shameless!" and dropped to the ground in a dead faint...

As it fell out of her hand, the letter was picked up by the wind and dropped to the ground by her side. The terrible visage previously described peeked out from around the corner of the entryway, snickering with joy, and then disappeared.

Qutidor had just then returned from his work at the bazaar and, upon seeing his unconscious daughter lying on the ground, ran toward her in alarm and lifted her limp body off the cold earth.

"My daughter... Kumush... open your eyes."

Kumush remained unresponsive. His fears for her life increased a hundredfold as he carried Kumush in his arms inside his house; Oftob Oyim and Toibeka wailed, finding her in this state. Though he set Kumush down in the veranda, they remained at a loss about how to help her regain consciousness. They racked their brains, trying to remember what to do. It was Toibeka who, though considered dim-witted, for the first time in her life outsmarted the others. She brought a basin of cold water and sprayed Kumush's forehead and chest with it, shocking her back to consciousness. The poor family, who were almost losing their minds for fear of losing their beloved daughter, began to relax. Kumush lay silent in a cold sweat for several minutes, then moved slowly and opened her eyes.

"What happened, my dear daughter? Has something happened?" Kumush again closed her eyes, sighed heavily, and offered no reply.

Only after they persisted in questioning her did she finally ask her father, "Who found me in the yard?"

"It was me, Daughter," said Qutidor. "Did you see anything there by my side?"

Qutidor thought from this question that she meant someone had attacked her.

"No, Daughter, you were lying there alone."

"Was I, or..." She could not complete her sentence. "Go ahead, Daughter."

"There was a letter near me... It was this letter that caused me to faint," she said, struggling to find the words.

The time for evening *khuftan* prayers approached, making Qutidor impatient to hear from his daughter the cause of her fainting spell. Qutidor took down a lit candle to examine the yard and found a letter on the ground right where his daughter had fallen. He read the letter that had put his daughter in harm's way; the ensuing words froze him stock-still with shock and disbelief. Qutidor himself almost fainted at the string of incomprehensible insults, and the sheer boldness of its claims challenged credulity. "Of all the deceptions, the sheer lack of self-respect... a man who has no honor has no pride," he said aloud. For a few moments he kept repeating, "That bastard knows nothing of decency."

The letter's existence had remained a secret to him until that moment.

He stood there, at a complete loss about how to approach his daughter, not to mention looking her in the eye, as he believed that he was in large part complicit in the tragedy. In a daze, he lumbered over to the veranda, slumping down and placing his head in his hands. This fresh insult—unparalleled in its shamelessness—injured Qutidor's pride. He had now ventured into unknown territory and wondered how to console his egregiously shamed daughter, how to survive these dark times. He obsessed for some time over a solution until his wife became worried over the delay. Oftob Oyim found him in his present condition.

Husband and wife entered their daughter's room, quietly sitting down at her feet.

They looked at each other for a few moments until Oftob Oyim could not swallow the weight of recent events any longer and burst out crying, her tears dropping like rain. Qutidor, as if on cue, drenched his beard with tears. Even with her eyes closed, Kumush knew her parents wept and her tears welled up, running down her cheeks and onto the pillow. Inexplicably, a candle placed on the shelf fluttered and expired... Reflecting the mood of the moment, the house itself seemed to sink into darkness...

Three days passed. Kumush lost weight and her skin yellowed as if her body were wracked by a fatal illness; she faded like an early jasmine bloom poisoned by a treacherous hand. One bent upon evil intent had delivered this poison, supposedly at the behest of the one man she trusted above all others; the instigator had defiled the honored treasure of the enchanted garden, left her bereft of all hope, hardened into a lifeless statue.

Eternal sadness haunted her eyes; her chest rose in shallow breaths, crushed by despair.

Oftob Oyim's offense knew no bounds, yet she buried her emotions to console her daughter, the most immediate concern; she sought to soothe the humiliation and grief brought on by Otabek's letter and harbor the apple of her eye—Kumush—from any illness or harm. Her soft mantra, murmured every other sentence, was "Pay him no attention, Daughter, erase him from your memory! Grieving him will offer no relief."

Despite all of Oftob Oyim's efforts, Kumush stared blankly at her mother's mouth, her eyes drowning in inextinguishable mourning and loss; this only further broke her poor mother's heart, compounding her anxiety.

"Kumush," said Oftob Oyim at afternoon tea, "maybe it would be a good change for us to visit your uncle's house."

"What shall we do at my uncle's?"

"We will play, dance, laugh, throw your sadness into the street."

Unexpectedly, Kumush laughed, agreeing with her mother's idea.

"Get ready, wash up, and let God bring death to your shameless husband."

Kumush looked upon her mother with the affection and devotion of a daughter. She stood up to clean at the washbasin Toibeka prepared for her. They were just about to leave when the lady who had delivered the letter a few days prior appeared from the passage. Though it seemed like an ill omen to Kumush, the lady was glad to see her. Kumush introduced her mother to the newcomer.

"Qeh... qeh... how benevolent the wealthy are... I was just passing through, on the way to visit my daughters. Qeh... qeh... and decided to stop by as promised..." said the woman, fawning on the two to the point of embarrassment. As for the mother and daughter, they were forced to pull aside their paranjis and had to stand in place, holding them in their hands. Once greetings were exchanged with Kumush, the woman inquired:

"Bless you, princess. What has happened to you? You look so thin."

Asking the flat-faced woman to sit, Oftob Oyim answered, "She has been ill for one or two days."

"May God double her blessings," said the woman. "Qeh... it seems I visit at an inconvenient moment. You make your departure. Have a good day, may God protect my sister from the evil eye," she said, putting her hands together in prayer.

"Please, stay. Be our guest," said Oftob Oyim.

"May God bring you happiness, my dear, qeh..." said the woman and, looking to Kumush, she continued. "I stopped here along my way to fulfill my promise. Tomorrow my son leaves for Tashkent. If your father has a letter, or something else to deliver... Qeh..."

Instead of replying, Kumush glanced at her mother. Oftob Oyim, understanding the intent behind her daughter's gesture, answered with "We do not have any letters to send." After this exchange, the flat-faced woman gave Kumush a quick meaningful look.

The girl replied, "My father has nothing to send. I have a letter, however. If you will wait a moment, I will write one quickly for you to deliver."

The flat-faced woman's hidden agenda was to obtain such a letter, so Kumush's request overjoyed her.

"Write it, my blessed princess. I will wait. I may be a little late to where I was heading, but it's worth doing a good deed, qeh," she said, grinning.

Thankful for the woman's services, Kumush entered her room to write the letter.

This letter is the one that Otabek would receive later. And thus they both became victims of an unthinkable treachery. Now we will reveal to the reader the perpetrators and reasons behind this falsehood.

6

BURNING WITH FEVER

Second day of Saraton.[247] A young man on horseback brushed the dust off his riding coat while holding the reins as he dismounted on the main corner of a narrow street that sloped south from the eastern wall of the B Mahalla in the northern district of Margilan. The telltale signs of fine dust covering his eyelashes, brows, and sparse beard revealed him to be a long-distance traveler. About twenty-two years of age, the youth had yellow skin and the round, bulging eyes of an owl, red and inflamed; his flat nose seemed to be slapped onto his face, completely crushed, which in turn contrasted with his large protruding forehead. He resembled a demon from before recorded history. He arrived at high, western-facing double doors built on a corner lot.

The young man took off his skullcap as he opened one of the doors and entered, with his horse trailing behind him, a narrow passage that eventually led into an expansive yard. Old, decrepit buildings and timeworn, crumbling walls comprised the eastern and southern sections of the yard. Rubbish littered the ground as if the bristles of a broom had not graced the area in years. In the middle of the whole complex stood a stark mulberry tree ringed in ashes and sundry discarded pieces of garbage. A small hovel leaned against the western wall of the enclosure, adjacent to the previously described entryway; the hovel, perhaps recently built, with two low-set windows and locked shutters that also served the dubious function of doors, and a small ramshackle veranda complete our tableau of misuse and disrepair.

A cooking stove was in the place of honor in the corner of the veranda. No room warranted being called a kitchen in this home. A foul-smelling soot blackened the construction one could call a veranda, and indeed the area was so pathetic it seemed sorry for its own fate. Filthy unwashed cups, spoons, and bowls lay scattered around the stove. Several chickens pecked around the cast-iron pot, contributing to the overall chaos and degradation. Through the open shutter, we can see a room with bare earth floors and a black ceiling; the place of honor in the corner of the house was decorated with an old white throw covered in lumps of yellow, resinous substance resembling sulphur and worn so thin that its holes were grouped into constellations of stars. An old chest, resting in the wall's *tahman*,[248] was filled with a pile of torn quilts with chunks of cotton filling peeking out.

The other discernible household goods consisted of three or four chipped teacups whose patterns had faded, a dented black teapot on one shelf, and a corroded green copper tray, most likely never cleaned in its lifetime, stacked on top of one another, and a rancid tablecloth hanging on the wall peg.

All items accounted for, we have completed the inventory of the home. If we do not include the mouse sitting in the corner lazily gnawing on a piece of stone-hard stale bread, no other living creature remained in the room. One could discern from the fine workmanship and démodé architectural features of the ruined building—which functioned as the eastern wall of the yard—that, despite the half-sunken roof and the mushrooms growing throughout the rotted wood, at one time people of means had lived here and their fortunes had left them in poverty.

The young man hitched his horse to the mulberry tree and was making his way from the ruins toward his small hovel when a tiny woman appeared from the ramshackle house in the corner and hurried toward him while tidying herself—the same "wicked witch" we met in Qutidor's house. She greeted him warmly and afterward they entered the hovel with its one solitary room. After removing his riding coat, the man threw it into the center of the room and hung his skullcap on a peg.

These actions completed, they both sat down on the throw.

"How are things?" asked the woman. "Is everything all right with your work?"

"Not so bad."

"Your client himself was here earlier. He was deeply troubled about whether you were giving proper attention to his task. He departed just before your arrival."

"He went home?"

"No idea. Maybe he will come back. He is very impatient to see results and visits often. He was here last night too... Qeh..."

"Why is he so worried?"

"He told me that if you do not perform your tasks as he directed, all of his plans will be worth no more than a black coin."

The young man smiled at this response and asked, "So, how is our business going?"

At this question, the woman's face turned into the very mask of hopelessness.

"I do not know who to blame for it, our friends or enemies, but nothing has worked out, even though I went looking for a bride every single day... Qeh... Let the earth swallow our backstabbing neighbors whole. Mamat Rahim Qudim—the fabric maker— seemed sympathetic to my cause, but the neighbors slandered us... as for Hamidboi, he says if I arrange an engagement today, he will pay for a wedding tomorrow... Qeh..."

Upon receiving this news, the young man's eyes widened, sparkling with hope. "Which neighbors are the ones spreading rumors?"

"Bad neighbors, let them all dry up. Everybody did. How should I know which ones in particular?"

"Show me those neighbors, damn them all... I will teach them a lesson!"

Both lost themselves in arguing with each other. Hamidboi, just entering through the passage, saw the familiar horse hobbled to the mulberry tree. He knew that these signs spelled the return of his messenger. Too impatient to enter through the doorway opposite the veranda, he burst in through the window, giving a full hug to his young protégé. Greatly excited, Hamid began flinging questions at him:

"*Hosh!* Now! Sadiq Polvan[249] the Mighty, how are things? Any news from Tashkent?"

"What news could be there? Everything is well in Tashkent. While there, I had an opportunity to explore the city, visit some sights."

"Were you able to locate his house?"

"I was. As you said, everybody in Tashkent knows his house."

"Then did you pass on the letter, too?"

"I did."

"Thank you. Who took the letter from your hands?"

"An old man."

"Was he an old man with a long face and a narrow head?"

"Yes."

"Did you get a return letter?" Hamid asked, eyes glued to Sadiq's mouth, impatient for a response.

"I received a letter of reply as well," he answered proudly, a victorious look on his face.

At this positive response, Hamidboi was beside himself, slapping Sadiq's shoulder, upon which, taking out a letter from his inside pocket, the young assistant relayed to him his trickery:

"I gave a letter to an old man and informed him that I was leaving for Margilan tomorrow. If he were to give me a letter to deliver, it would be my pleasure to take it with me. The old man, after considering for a while, said, 'At this time, we do not have a letter to send. If it's not an inconvenience, could you come by tomorrow to pick up a letter?'

"He then asked where I would stay for the night. I pretended that it would be inconvenient for me to come again tomorrow, but I said, 'All right, though I am staying at a place far from here, I will pass by tomorrow.'

"Content that my machinations were going as planned, I stayed overnight in a teahouse and the next day I returned at the time we had settled upon. Our blessed father—the old man—was waiting for me with a letter. I took the correspondence and spurred my horse yet again, taking off for Margilan."

Taking the folded paper, Hamid again patted Sadiq on the shoulder and said, "Thank you, thank you," adding, "now I owe you, my brother."

He wanted to open the letter casually, as if indifferent to its contents, but joy tinged with obsession and anxiety lit his face.

For my Kumush, the bright star of my hope, the flower in my dreams, the bulwark of my life!

I received your letter filled with poisonous insinuations and hurtful accusations. I can imagine that you wrote it while burning with fever, sailing in the fiery sea of suffering. But if my princess, dealing with the grief that I inflicted upon her against my will, has lost the ability to understand me and trust me, and if she has gotten confused by her own guesswork, then my position is a hundred times more grave. Truthfully, not only could I not understand your letter, which was full of venom, but I found it unworthy of deciphering, because reasonable people never take such words, uttered in fury, seriously.

Yet, I did not understand to what to attribute one point of your letter. You wrote:

"Knowing that your cruelty makes you unworthy of my love, you now shamelessly enforce your will... You were ashamed of revealing your intentions to my father when he was your guest in Tashkent, but can you prove to anyone that you have a conscience?"

What did you mean by this? Are you not feeling well? I admit that I felt ashamed to tell your father for some time that I could not accompany him back to Margilan as I had to attend the charlar. But when your father started to ask permission to travel home, I explained everything to him and through him sent my apologies to you. What is shameless about that? It seems that a fever has struck you down and taken control of your senses...

On reaching this point in the letter, Hamid burst out laughing and said, "Oh you fool, how stupid you are…"

Though both the hatchet-faced woman and Sadiq joined in his laughter, he continued reading, ignoring them:

Now, I am certain you wrote your words in a fever. Therefore, I would be remiss in blaming you for the tone of the letter. You are excused. The circumstances that influenced you to write this uncompromising and venomous letter, calling me a "sly fox," a "bloody-mouthed wolf," a "shameless young man"… along with some other acrimonious appellations known only to you, were no doubt caused by your father telling you what kind of catastrophes kept me here—my new father-in-law's illness that prevented the charlar from taking place on time as the custom instructs.

Ironically, your vicious missive reached me the same moment as the invitation for the charlar. When you read this letter and resolve to grant me amnesty, I will be enroute to Margilan.

The interpretation of the passages your mother prefers to focus on do no justice to my reputation, my self-respect, or my character. In truth, a parent's genuine desire will never replace your love. You are equal to the earth and stars. You said you were not Kumush, not "The Silver One" anymore, but I wanted to call you my "Golden Kumush"!

My whole being is infused with the fire of love for you, your husband, Otabek

26th of Javzah, 1265 Tashkent.[250]

The joy illuminating Hamid's face faded as he progressed to the second half of the letter, and lines of concern overtook his countenance. He once again read the line "When you read this letter and resolve to grant me amnesty, I will be en route to Margilan" and asked Sadiq, "How many days have passed since you left Tashkent?"

"Six days."

Sadiq's answer weighed heavily upon his shoulders. He tilted his head to the side, grabbing his goatee as if putting his head to the earth to discern the changes in the wind. Not comprehending the sudden change in Hamid's mood, the hatchet-faced woman, who had been pretending to organize the blankets on the shelf, sat down near Hamid and asked, with an ugly smile on her face, "How are things, Hamidboi? Are things going according to plan? Are we ready to approach Pasha Nisa[251] to arrange an engagement?"

Shaking his head hopelessly, Hamid answered in a serious tone, "Our plans have not come to fruition just yet, we have only overcome the first barrier between us and the matchmaking."

As we know, the treacherous letter that he himself composed and dictated to the scribe on Otabek's behalf had deeply affected Kumush. Success to Hamid had seemed certain when Kumush's response to Otabek, handled by the aegis of the hatchet-faced woman, prompted him to send Sadiq to Tashkent with the intent of gleaning insight into Otabek's heart and mind before taking further action. As for his protégé Sadiq, he had faithfully delivered the malicious letter to Otabek, received one in reply, and in turn intercepted the letter meant for Kumush.

Alas, Otabek's reply clearly showed that his feelings for Kumush had not changed, and he was not willing to give her up for another. Hamid, once emboldened by his initial success, now hesitated regarding his next move. Today or tomorrow, Otabek would seek out and find Kumush. He would prove to her that the treacherous correspondence was not written by his hand, in turn delaying or destroying entirely Hamid's ambitions. This scenario was not some vague speculation on his part, but a reality as clear as day, and it drove Hamid to distraction as he racked his brain over how to play his next hand.

However, Hamid relegated his indecision to a mere distraction; resolution and conviction drove him to bold action. He asked the hatchet-faced woman, "Now, Jannat[252] opa, could you prepare me a pipe?"

As Jannat opa stood up to fill a fresh water pipe, Hamid said to Sadiq, "Oh, my brother Sadiq, our work has not ripened yet."

With his bloodshot, owl-like eyes suddenly alert, Sadiq answered, "Do not let your worries eat you alive, brother. If our work has not yet ripened, we will do anything to expedite it—if we do not die first."

Sadiq's firm response cheered Hamid's soul, making him take off his skullcap, throw it on the blanket, and say with gratitude, "No doubt it will come to fruition if you and my Jannat opa endure." He took the water pipe from Jannat opa's hands, drawing quick initial puffs, then feverishly sucking in long, forceful pulls from the pipe as the water gurgled and threatened to shatter the glass. Smoke rings flowed from his lips as he passed the water pipe to Sadiq and said to Jannat opa, "Auntie, you will have to bring one more letter, one more time to Qutidor's house..."

"Qeh... Bless my soul. Is that the letter Sadiq brought?"

Hamid laughed. "Oh no, Auntie. If you take this letter, then all of our diligent efforts will turn into a black, worthless coin. I will have to concoct another message, one that will work in our favor."

"Qeh... he-he... bless you... how could I ever fathom your plans, Hamid dear."

"Of course, they are beyond you, yet be mindful that if you make even the smallest error, all of our work will be blown to the four winds, and after that—"

Suddenly one mistake struck Hamid. When he had composed his very first letter from Otabek to Kumush, he had not considered the handwriting and all that time had been afraid that Qutidor or Kumush Bibi would notice this flaw. The letter he held in his hands now was written by Otabek himself, and Hamid decided that the scribe should make the next letter as faithful to the original as possible. He lost himself in his thoughts for quite a while before finally saying to Sadiq, "My brother Sadiqboi[253], there is yet again another task for you to perform."

"I am not the sort of pupil who runs from serving a noble man."

Hamid feigned disbelief toward the sincerity of Sadiq and Jannat opa, asking, "Aren't you?" and, upon receiving sincere affirmations and protestations that allayed his suspicions, he dipped his hand into his pocket to retrieve his coin purse.

"Jannat opa," he said. "It seems that Sadiq is hungry and tired from his long voyage. I, too, have eaten nothing since this morning. While we sit discussing our venture, could you go to the bazaar on the corner, purchase some meat, and make us a soup? Here are some coins."

Taking up her paranji, Jannat opa went to purchase some meat as directed. After she had left, Hamid asked Sadiq again, "So you stated that you would not mind rendering me another service."

Hamid, it seemed, doubted Sadiq's capabilities, even though the latter assured him repeatedly that he was not a man to shirk serious business.

"Stop challenging me. Tell me at once what you need me to do."

After some moments, Hamid said, "What if what I require of you is of quite a different nature and poses a greater challenge than what I have required of you so far?"

Sadiq immediately understood Hamid's insinuation, asking directly, "Should I kill someone for you?"

Hamid looked at Sadiq with distrust for a moment, then, after looking around, asked scornfully, "What if someone did ask you to kill?"

"As of today, I have buried two people. What does it matter if I bury a third?" said Sadiq, laughing proudly. Hamid gave a sigh of relief, as if a great weight had left his shoulders.

"I am not someone who forgets a service rendered," he said. "I am a man to any man who does right by me, but a blackguard to those who mean me harm. I give you my word of honor that I will uphold my end of the bargain...[254] On the condition that you take full responsibility for this deed, I give you my word of honor that half of my wealth will be yours."

Sadiq extended his hand to Hamid and asked him, "Are you certain you will not back out?"

Taking Sadiq's hand in his, Hamid answered, "There is only one word and one God."

They agreed to start out early the next day. Sadiq intended to lie in wait near Qutidor's front door for the moment Otabek arrived. When Otabek entered the dark passageway, he would creep up behind and finish him. Sadiq thought that the front gates would offer the best point of attack. But Hamid dismissed this plan, preferring the long dark passage as an ideal place to initiate an ambuscade.

To Sadiq's question of "When do you think he will arrive?" Hamid responded, "The city gates open every morning and close in the evening. Therefore, according to my reckoning, if he leaves

Qoqan in the morning, he will enter Margilan's gates by evening prayer." After this answer, he again reiterated their agreement, advising Sadiq yet again, "Be careful. Consider your actions carefully, the world will bear witness. If you are caught, attach the blame to your neck. Do not involve me."

"Do not worry. The man you know as Sadiq will never succumb to cowardliness—even at the hands of the executioner, even before God."

"Another condition: this secret remains between us. My sending Jannat opa out for meat was meant to assure that this matter remains only between ourselves and no one else."

"Fill your heart with confidence in me, brother—do not worry. But remember you promised to give me your Afghan knife."

"I will bring it by the time the soup is ready," said Hamid, stepping out.

7

QUTIDOR EXPELS OTABEK FROM HIS DOORS

For three days Sadiq maintained his observation of Qutidor's front door, loitering nearby. On the third day, as it was approaching seven in the evening, he concluded Otabek would not arrive that day either. He decided that in the next few minutes he would depart for home, yet he kept to his post in case the expected rider should appear in the distance.

Meanwhile, Hamid passed by on his horse, casting covert sidelong glances at Sadiq, evidently intending to take stock of their machinations. He gave Sadiq a probing look; Sadiq responded by shaking his head in the negative. Finally, Qutidor returned from the bazaar and, as usual, entered his house. As closing time approached for the denizens of the streets, the shops open until evening now closed their doors and passersby were increasingly rare. "I waited for so long; let me wait ten minutes longer," thought Sadiq, who continued to mill around.

At the end of the street, to the east of the shoe district, a group of young men made their way toward him. He became uncomfortable as it was increasingly clear that the unruly group nearing him were friends of his. Attempting to hide, he stepped into Qutidor's passage, yet one of the young men called out, "What is Sadiq doing here?"

Another person joined in, "Sadiqboi, hey Sadiqboi!"

Sadiq was forced to greet them and turn his back on the passage. "Sadiq, why are you out here, sitting and shivering like an out-of-work mill donkey?" yelled one of the young men. The others laughed at this insult. Sadiq laughed too and approached them.

"I have a meeting with a client and am waiting for his arrival."

"Sadiq, hey Sadiq," said the same man. "Is that your nose or a baker's glove?" The men again burst out in raucous laughter, practically shaking the whole street.

"How about you come to the wedding party with us?"

"Which party is this?" asked Sadiq.

"To Shamshodbek's get-together. You didn't hear about Shamshodbek's wedding? Let's go, my nephew Sadiq. Is that your face or cow-shit patties beaten down by a hailstorm?"

In a halting voice, he said, "I will go later on."

"Eh, simpleton," responded one of the group, who then jumped across the small canal lining the street and approached Sadiq. "Just think, Qaimoq Khan, a *kizikchi* from Andijon, will be present tonight.[255] It promises to be legendary, a veritable Jamshid's[256] feast, so let's go." The individual started pulling Sadiq along with the others, nudging him jovially, but he still hesitated even though his friends continued to insist. On the other hand, he was almost sure that the one he'd been waiting for would not arrive that day and, after ten or fifteen steps in the direction of the party, he no longer needed nudging from his friends but walked of his own accord. They moved along the southern street.

As they crossed the intersection, Sadiq saw, from far away, a man riding on a horse toward them and then stopping in the middle of the street. The leader of the group gave Sadiq a push on the chest with his large hands, and all his friends at once shouted at him, "Go, go, bitch. Have you lost your mind?"

He started to push back but the others joined in, shoving him in a circle like mynah birds pecking at seed. In this manner, poor

Sadiq was forced against his will farther up the street. About thirty or forty steps from the main thoroughfare, the horseman, on what now appeared to be a black horse, turned from a small side street onto the main boulevard from which Sadiq's acquaintances had arrived. Walking away, Sadiq looked back at the horseman. He recognized the familiar black horse he had first noted at the stable when he passed on the fake letter to Hasan Ali. He attempted to free himself from the clutches of the young man holding him fast, to no avail, crying out as he resisted, "Bastards, sons of bitches!" His eyes bugged out with a savage glare as living shackles bound his arms.

A crystal-clear voice rang out, resonating throughout the surrounding neighborhood with the call to evening prayers. The horseman reined in his horse near Qutidor's front gates, taking his right foot from the stirrup. At that same moment, Qutidor hurriedly stepped out of the passage in order not to be late for evening observances. Qutidor stopped in his tracks, visibly shaken. He seemed to forget where he was headed when he saw his son-in-law, who, so eager to greet his father-in-law, left his horse loose in the middle of the street. Refusing to shake Otabek's hand, Qutidor stepped back toward his gates. At this, Otabek stood stock-still, like a peg nailed into place. He did not know whether he should move toward Qutidor or what he should say.

"What does this mean, Father?"

Qutidor replied in a quavering voice, "We have no room for shameless men in my house, as we have no wish to speak to a shameless liar! Go away! Never stop at my door again!" And he went back through the gate, locking the chain noisily.

When Otabek at last slowly regained consciousness, evening prayers were over and people were making their way home. Like an automaton, he climbed into his saddle and gave his horse a "shoo," yet it remained unmoved by the command. He started prodding his horse with his whip, and only when the bridle tore itself in half did he realize that somebody had tied his horse to a poplar tree. "Shoo," he repeated, and the horse moved toward the east side of the street.

It was unclear whether Otabek was conscious of his reasons for urging his horse in that direction. Perhaps he just wanted his horse to move in some direction, anywhere. When his horse finally reached a fork in the road, it stopped as if to ask, "Where do we go now?" His owner again gave a "shoo" and his horse turned north. After walking for some time along the road, the companions arrived in Mahalla B, and again the horse stopped, not knowing its destination. Again, an insistent "shoo" moved it to the east side of the road. They ended up at the two northerly corner doors already familiar to the reader, and then turned into a narrow side street.

The night had advanced to *khuftan* prayer, with darkness engulfing the city. The horse now ignored the constant "shoo, shoo" from its owner and stayed obstinately rooted to its spot. Otabek was finally forced to survey the area for his exact location. Suddenly aware that he and his horse had stopped in a narrow dead-end street, he took stock of recent events. He vaguely remembered arriving at his in-laws' home and tethering his horse in front of it, yet he could not recall the rest. He had no idea how he had ended up in a blind alley in the suburbs of Margilan near two large gates. He seemed at a loss as to whether he should turn his horse's head around out of the narrow road or not. As he sat on his horse, hesitating and irresolute, the sounds of two men parting ways for the night could be heard echoing through the outer gate. The noise of footsteps neared the gates and, so as not to interfere with the person making his departure, Otabek turned his horse to the other side of the road. Otabek stopped in a square with buildings on all four sides enveloping him in darkness. He could faintly see the white turban of the person walking through the gate. The person started upon seeing a horseman.

"Who brings me a rider on horseback?"

"It is I on the horse," said Otabek, eking out an answer that made no sense coming from a stranger. He stuttered further, attempting to provide an adequate response.

Again, the stranger from the house asked, "Who are you?"

"Me... just a poor stranger. I arrived in Margilan in the evening and lost my way to my destination."

"Then let me take you to our guesthouse."

Despite the friendly tone of the stranger's voice, Otabek wanted to decline the offer.

"Thank you, brother, but I shouldn't," he said and understood again that his words made no sense.

"You just said you lost your way! Where would you go?"

"If it's not too difficult for you."

"It is no inconvenience at all, let's go in," the man said, leading the way to the house. "Gharib,[257] I am also a poor wanderer like you."

Without saying a word, Otabek followed the stranger back to the main road. After walking for some time, the man leading his horse finally said, "There is a place for your horse, too."

Otabek gave no response. In this manner they reached the bend in the road without one word passing between them. The man motioned for Otabek to stop and started patting his pockets, looking for a key to open the gate—the one next to the gate of Jannat Opa's house. After opening the door, the stranger said, "Please dismount from your horse, my guest," and, taking the reins from Otabek's hands, added, "take your saddlebags and enter through the passage straight to the inside."

Carrying his saddlebags, Otabek went through a covered passage to a large yard and placed his saddlebags in the middle of the yard. After hitching his horse near a trough, his host approached him and picked up the saddlebags. "Welcome, let's go to the veranda," he said, moving away. He provided Otabek with a place to sit and took a ceramic cup, dishes, and a stone from the shelf. Striking the stone, he lit a fire and then a candle.

The man was about forty years old, of lanky build, with a pale bloodless face lined with a thin beard, and brown sheeplike eyes[258] weary from long study in the madrassa. Though his belongings lying along the carpet on the veranda were not of high value, they were kept clean and orderly, as if a testimony to the owner's delicate and careful nature. To the left of the veranda there was a door leading to a small room that resembled a monk's cell.[259]

The owner of the house, eyeing Otabek closely, said, "You must be hungry, my guest."

Not waiting for a reply from Otabek, he decided for the both of them. "Of course you are hungry from the road. I have already sliced the carrots, onion, and meat, now all I have to do is make a fire in the stove. I myself have not had anything to eat yet, but I will not make a big plov—only a couple of bowls."

Disregarding Otabek's polite refusals, he began to prepare the plov. As for Otabek, he attempted to review his situation. He could only process events five seconds at a time. He felt uncertain about what in fact had occurred and what might be a trick of the mind. Yet his in- law's crushing words pursued him. "We have no room for shameless men in our house... Go away! Never stop at my door again!" echoed in his ears, and profound offence and anger filled his soul. The present slamming of the gate with a chain rattling in place seemed to give voice to the truth of the egregious insult and hurt delivered. At that very instant, the venomous words in Kumush's letter passed before his eyes. Assorted oddly phrased points in the letter came to him like poison to his heart, but any sort of conclusion evaded him since he remained barely lucid, almost in a fever. He seemed incapable of tying the disparate ideas together, but the most striking phrase was, "Go away. Never stop at my door again."

Accustomed to the tender greeting of his black-eyed gazelle, he had never thought he would be facing such humiliation. Otabek, a man with a strong sense of pride, born and nurtured in love and care, and having only heard honeyed words, acutely felt the heavy blow of the offence. The sensation overcame him as if a satchel containing his innermost private heart, meant only for Kumush, lay torn to pieces, defiled under his feet; as if precious pearls carefully wrapped in a scarf had been snatched from their owner, who was left lost and despondent over their brutal theft.

Placing thin carrot slices in the plov, the owner of the house approached Otabek, who for a moment forgot his worries and attempted to look cheerful. His host sat down near Otabek and asked him, "Where are you from, guest?"

"I am from Tashkent, mullah-aka."

"What's your name?"

Otabek, after scratching his forehead, answered him, "I am Shokirbek..."

"Is this your first visit to Margilan?"

"It is my first visit..."

"I suppose you have come to trade." His guest's appearance and clothing reminded the host of a tradesman of sorts.

"No... originally I was heading to Qoqan, but one of my father's friends who owes us some money lives in Margilan, so I traveled through here." Uncomfortable at his own lies, Otabek laughed unexpectedly. "Having recently arrived, I did not know exactly where our contact lived and, since I had no other friends in Margilan and evening had fallen, I lost my way..."

The owner of the house laughed. "You cannot run from fate, Shokirbek. Today it seems you were destined to be my guest. What is the name of the person you are going to meet?"

"He is Kamilboi..."

The owner of the house thought for a while. "No one by that name lives near here. Perhaps he is in the next district," he said, getting up and again attending to his plov.

Otabek was ashamed of his lie and even blushed. But he was forced to conceal the truth, because his name, previous imprisonment with Qutidor, death sentence, and salvation were known to all of Margilan, and if he revealed his real name he would have to reveal other secrets. When his host moved over to the pot, Otabek got up from his place and descended to the yard. Going around the veranda, past the passage leading to the east, he crossed a small open space... and happened upon a small fruit garden.

In a night black as ink, a swathe of impenetrable darkness permeated the garden, which was in turn subsumed under a dense canopy of trees; an unsettling allegory for Otabek's own forlorn and mournful bent. His soul weighed heavy at the day's grim turn of events—an aching burden like this orchard replete in gloom, a void of light so complete that he could not distinguish the variety of trees, the shapes of their leaves, and the quality of their bark. Sinking deeper and deeper into the pitch, nearly merging with it, he walked into the heart of the garden. Finally, Otabek sat down under the tree whose branches bowed under the heaviness of its fruit, remaining frozen for some moments in this pose.

After some minutes spent in this manner, he let out a long breath— "Ooofff"—as if a bubble had burst and tension had been expelled upon its release. Standing up, he walked back through the west-facing section of the orchard, past the half-ruined buildings.

When Otabek returned to the veranda, the owner of the house, having tamped down the plov, was waiting for him.

"I gave your horse some corn."

"Thank you, mullah-aka," said Otabek.

The owner of the house wanted to ask something but changed his mind and just kept watching Otabek closely.

"My profession is that of a weaver, Shokirbek," said the owner suddenly. Otabek looked at him inquisitively, realizing that his host had something else to say.

"Since my work constantly exposes me to the damp, or maybe due to some other weakness in my constitution, I have a chronic illness," he continued. "At times my chest also aches. Recently I have visited a Tabib who told me I had anemia and advised me to drink wine made from grapes or *qimiz*[260] before eating. Following this consultation, I fortified myself for three or four days with qimiz or wine. The results have appeared to be positive. The reason for this long story is to see if you would mind if I drink one or two cups of wine before our dinner?"

He smiled shyly.[261]

"How can I protest? You are welcome to, and your health necessitates it."

The owner stepped into his room, still grinning, took down from the shelf a wine jug with a cup, and sat down near Otabek. Noisily pouring wine into the cup, he sheepishly looked at Otabek and grinned again.

"Have you ever tried any?"

"No."

In fact, Otabek had a strong revulsion to alcohol and never touched it. The host drank down a cup full of wine, shivered just a bit, attempting to disguise its effects, and repeated his question: "Really, you have never tried it before?" Otabek only shook his head in response. "If there are no firm reasons to do it, it is better not to drink," the host continued, pouring out a second cup. "However, sometimes it's good for your health, and helps you forget life's sorrows and pain. I have been plagued with such sorrows and disasters that only death could give me respite. Especially in the last few years, desperate to find relief, I finally got to the point where only this bitter liquid gives me consolation," he added and, sighing deeply, put another cup of wine in front of himself. For some time, both remained silent. After downing the second cup, the host looked closely at Otabek.

"If I am not mistaken, you too look a little bit sad, my dear guest.

Would you like a cup of wine?"

"Thank you, mullah-aka," said Otabek, feeling an urge to ease his grief with wine. Indeed, he had many good reasons to have a drink. His host must have noticed this or just wanted to try his guest one more time, so he poured the third cup of wine and handed it to Otabek.

"Don't refuse my hand, guest. It seems we both share the same need."

Giving further excuses, Otabek continued his stubborn refusal, but his host persisted, continuing to hand the cup to Otabek and saying, "I prepare the wine in complete accordance with the Shariyat. A few days ago, even the *akhunds* of the mahalla[262] certified it as halal."

Otabek was pressed to take the cup ordinarily meant for chai. The grapes were indeed prepared brilliantly, and the drink was as clear as a well-brewed green chai. Otabek did not waste time admiring its qualities, but instead drank it in one gulp. The strong alcohol burned quickly in his empty stomach, and the heat of it rose to his throat. After getting Otabek drunk on the first cup, the owner of the house went to serve the plov.

8

HAPPINESS AND UNHAPPINESS

Before serving the guest plov, the host again took the wine jug from the shelf, poured a cup, and handed it to Otabek.

"Drink another one and then we will eat plov," he said.[263] With this round, there was no need to plead for long. The first cup had made Otabek's eyesight grow blurry. He felt light-headed and his body became almost weightless. The second cup seemed to whisper to him, "If you drink me, you will find even greater relief." After Otabek's second cup, they sat down to plov.

It seemed inconceivable prior to his drunken repast that one grain of rice would gain entry to his stomach, yet now he gulped down one handful of plov after another—he refused nothing. Never in his lifetime had he known this sort of appetite. Between bites he answered his host's questions enthusiastically, at times going into superfluous detail. A volubility overtook him, at times overly so, and his gloominess and silence vanished.

After their meal, Otabek's bloodshot, drunken eyes saw his host in a new light, as he began to collect the various scattered cups and the tablecloth. His gratitude and appreciation toward the owner of the house showed in his expression. This man, a mere stranger, who had given him a place of solace, expecting nothing more than genuine company in return, made a profound impact on Otabek. His host then laid out two pillows near Otabek, taking one for himself.

"Lean back, relax, Bek," he said, reclining on the pillows. Otabek followed suit. A candle glowed between them, casting warm light about them and flickering with the breeze. Both of them stared at the solitary flame as their minds wandered off to the different refuges of their memory. Some moments later, the owner took his eyes from the candle, stole a glance at Otabek, and asked, "Are you married, Bek?"

Whether Otabek felt sluggish from the alcohol or had not completely heard him, he did not answer at first.

At last he responded: "I am married."

The questioner waited for a while, then asked, "Do you love your wife?"

Otabek lay silent, lost in the face of the question's weight, and then finally, unconsciously, he sighed a long "Offff."

"No... I do not love her."

"That is for the best," said the owner of the house. Not understanding his meaning, Otabek looked at him inquisitively.

"You seem to be surprised by my words."

"No," said Otabek, yet the owner of the house could still read surprise on Otabek's face.

"Maybe love is good, but only for those who can know happiness. For those who are lost, such as myself, love is misery. As you say, if you are genuinely devoid of any feelings of love toward your wife, you yourself can testify to my words—when you are at home, you feel married, but as soon as you cross the threshold of your house, your wife seems to disappear and you disregard any feelings you have toward her. Is it not so?"

"Yes, it is," said Otabek. These words of wisdom regarding the nature of love brought a soft glow to his drunken eyes.

The owner of the house continued. "Of course, I am not speaking from my own experience, and perhaps I am mistaken," he said, taking a long breath, and then asked: "when you married, was it out of love or through the guidance of a matchmaker?"

Otabek did not immediately understand his interlocutor's agenda. "To satisfy my mother's wishes."

"That was smart!" said the owner of the house. "In my opinion all problems in marriage arise from marrying out of love." Silence then intruded on the conversation.

Otabek understood at that moment that the man before him was seasoned by the years, had worn more shirts than he, and clearly had lived through the hot and cold of the world. His reminiscences reflected the events of his own life, and perhaps they shared the same fate—perhaps he too had been turned away from his father-in-law's doorstep.

So Otabek asked about something that had been occupying his own mind.

"Did your beloved leave you?"

The host shook his head in the negative.

"Indeed, she left me, but not by her own will."

From his response, Otabek concluded his in-laws too had made him grieve.

"May the faces of the wicked wither away," he swore, an invective that puzzled the owner of the house.

"I risk becoming a boorish host, but I wish to tell you the narrative of my life with all its trials and tribulations," he said.

Otabek felt a deep affection forming within him for his host, compelling him to listen to his tale.

"Had you not volunteered it yourself, I'd have asked you to share your story with me."

"My life's challenges are more mundane than you would expect, but I will attempt to relay them faithfully," he said, pressing his pillow against his chest and beginning his story.

"Originally I am from Qoqan. An orphan at an early age, separated from my loving parents. I was initially brought up by the tender hands of my maternal uncle. When I reached seventeen or eighteen, I struck out on my own. On the advice of a friend, approximately twenty years ago I moved to Margilan and trained as a weaver under the guidance of a well-known master, the father of the textile mill's current owner.[264] After four years I worked as the right hand to the master himself. Unlike other young men, I lived modestly, did not squander money, and in a short time was even able to save a few gold coins. I put a great deal of my heart into my job. My weavings were well regarded, sold competitively, and I became known to all my customers as 'little Usta Alim.' As you may know, it is mostly women who come to the weavers to buy new fabrics. My newly spun weavings dazzled everyone with their vibrant colors and were enjoyed by all—especially by women and girls who would gather in front of our workshop throughout the day.

"One day, a pretty girl, approximately thirteen or fourteen, not quite ready for the paranji,[265] approached me, inquiring about a new silk pattern I was currently weaving. The variant to which she referred had already been sold and I duly informed her of this. The girl's clear bright eyes pleaded with me to weave one more for her.

"Meeting the girl's eyes, I replied, 'There is no sense, sister, in weaving and dying a piece of silk fabric for just one dress.'

"The girl persisted in beguiling me with her charms; she wanted me to weave the exact same fabric for her, nothing else would do. One of the part-time trainees sitting near me nodded to the girl and said, 'So weave it, Master. Do not upset our sister.'

"Looking a third time at the girl, attraction crept into my heart and my gaze lingered for some moments on her. To weave yet another bolt of fabric was no doubt irrational, yet the girl possessed a mysterious hold over me. Finally, I relented and promised the girl a special weave just for her. Upon receiving my word of honor, she left, though I felt a nagging regret that my promise had been made in haste. Perhaps when she returned I would concoct an excuse to not deliver. Yet those brilliant, dark, playful eyes offset with apple-red blushing cheeks remained frozen in my mind, her words 'Could you weave it just for me?' ringing in my ears.

"For several days I was wracked with indecision, but, finally, pushed by some hidden hand, I began to fulfill my promise. Dying a large piece of silk meant for just one dress seemed the easiest of tasks—in truth, I could have made enough for thirty such dresses at that moment. All the difficulties of dying the silk, stretching the warp threads on the loom and preparing the weft of the yarn, seemed trivial. Two days before our agreed-upon day of completion, the bolt of silk lay prepared for her arrival, but, alas, the day came and went without her gracing my presence.

"I must say that those met in passing, these encounters throughout our day, never linger long in one's memory, but, as for this girl, my impressions of her left an indelible mark on me: haunted by her eyebrows, her eyes, her lithesome form, it seemed as if I had known her for a lifetime. Though the sound of her voice did not have a strong hold on me, the words 'Could you weave it just for me?' still seemed fresh in my ears.

"Three or four days passed from the date set for our meeting, yet there was still no sign of her. The days spent waiting caused a slight change in my disposition. I became rude and heavy-handed with the trainees and apprentices, taking my frustration out on them.

"Finally, the girl arrived on the fifth day. Upon seeing her, I felt at a loss and for some time struggled with finding the right words to say to her. The girl did not request the silk from me but only gave me a long look. Just her gratitude alone seemed as if I was overcharging for the work done.

" 'Why did you not come on the promised day?' I asked finally.

"She became visibly uncomfortable and guiltily looked down at the ground.

" 'Have you already sold all the silk?'

"I placed the wrapped cloth in front of her. She inspected the silk fabric lovingly, saying, 'You have woven it well,' and glanced up at me again with a hopeless look in her eyes. Returning the silk, she tossed some small coins in front of me. 'How much does it cost?'

"Instead of quoting a price, I counted the coins. With the exception of a sixty-tengas piece, the rest were small copper coins, green with patina, that seemed to have been saved for a long time. I told her that the money she had given me would barely cover half the price of the silk.

" 'How much more do you need?' she asked.

" 'Three tengas,' I replied.

"Disappointment overcame the girl. I observed in her pretty face a sort of maturity that is often only seen in older girls, and then I understood the reason why she had not come on the promised day. My heart could not bear seeing this young fairy suffering in this state and I asked, 'When could you bring the remaining balance?' She did not answer immediately and in her silence, I read an unspoken plea. 'Will you pay me when you come across some money?' I added and, not waiting for her reply, handed the silk to her. The girl stood there in disbelief.

" 'You trust me?'

"I did not answer but asked instead, 'Where is your house?'

" 'In Ch Mahalla.'

" 'Whose daughter are you?'

" 'I am the daughter of Sharif the rifle master.'

" 'Is your father elderly?'

" 'He is dead. Only my mother remains.'

" 'You don't have an older brother?'

" 'No. I have only one little brother.'

" 'What is your name?'

" 'Saodat.'[266]

"After this, I sent Saodat off with the silk.

"She left in disbelief, not quite grasping the meaning behind my actions. Trainers and apprentices all exclaimed, 'You have done well, Master,' taunting me with their sarcasm. But as for me, I was prepared to endure any jokes for the sake of Saodat..."

Usta Alim, for it was now clear that it was he who was the owner of the house, stopped at this point in the story and asked Otabek, "Is my story too long? Has it become boring?"

Otabek, who'd been listening with rapt attention under the influence of the wine, responded, "Proceed, please proceed."

Usta Alim continued with his narrative.

"Three tengas meant nothing to me, but because they connected me to Saodat, those three tengas were worth a thousand. After three days I visited Saodat's house for the purpose of collecting the three coins. Saodat was not home, she was out visiting an aunt, but I introduced myself to her mother and we spoke at length across the mud wall.

"Saodat's mother lamented her fate. After her husband's death, there were no men remaining in the house, so she eked out a living spinning thread. She lamented that her daughter had ordered the silk without consulting her first and pleaded to postpone the payment for another week. I was afraid that as soon as they paid me our communication would end, so I came up with another plan and proposed, 'If you make a living only by spinning thread, it will be hard for you to save three tengas for payment; even three copper coins sounds like a lot of money. But I have an idea... You live in this house without a man, and I, an orphan myself, live alone. I often find it difficult that I have no one to wash and mend my clothes. What would you say if I asked you to help me sometimes with these chores to pay off the debt? Of course, if you don't mind...'

"The old woman, happy to accept my offer, promised to send Saodat the next day to pick up my clothes for washing. In this manner I assured our future interaction and returned back to my shop. The next day Saodat came and took my clothes. After three days, she delivered clean clothes to me and sat near my loom, watching me work for some time. I had appointed Thursday of each week as her delivery day. Each passing day, I felt increasingly attached to Saodat. I waited for her Thursday visits as if they were the feast of Qurban Hayit.[267] Three or four weeks later, I even decided to hand her some money, no more than twenty or thirty coins, instructing her to give it to her mother. On the fourth month of our acquaintance, Qurban Hayit in fact arrived. Following the tradition of giving Fitr Uraza alms[268] to the orphans and the poor during the month of Ramazan,[269] I prepared a cut of the best dress silk for Saodat and some unbleached calico to make clothes for her mother and little brother. I took these gifts to their house myself, calling upon Saodat.

"Saodat welcomed me at the entryway and casually took my hand, leading me into the courtyard.

"I told her, 'Saodat, have you lost your mind? Shouldn't your mother have a moment to cover her face from me?'

"Upon which she replied, still leading the way, 'My mother herself instructed me to bring you here, saying, "If your brother the master weaver visits us, we will not hide from him."'

"I entered the women's half of the house, following Saodat's lead. Saodat's mother sat at the front of a veranda, spinning yarn in a spindle. She was surprised to see her daughter holding the hand of a young stranger. Leaving me in the center of the yard, Saodat ran to her mother and said, 'He is my brother the master weaver, can't you see him before you?'

"Her mother straightened the scarf wrapped loosely around her head and stood up in a greeting. We greeted each other and asked about each other's health. Saodat laid a blanket for me to sit on, and, as I sat, I took out the contents of my pocket and put them on the blanket in front of them. After they had delivered the customary thanksgiving, we all fell silent, no one daring to speak first. Finally, the old woman picked up the conversation from where Saodat had left off, saying, 'Saodat feels a sisterly attachment to you. It turns out you recently gave her thirty coins to buy scented soap. After her purchase she brought it home, sleepless from praise and blessings for your generosity. She wishes you a long life and happiness, Master; she has prayed from night until dawn.'

"I lowered my eyes as the woman revealed these truths, and I stole a stealthy glance at Saodat. She flushed bright red in embarrassment, turning her face away from mine. The old woman continued, 'As you are providing great assistance to us in our poor condition, I hold you in my prayers five times a day. I think about you week after week and the blessings you place upon us. God is merciful to his slaves, easing our condition by giving us this kind young man. Whatever thoughts you have in your head, they are known by God as well. If you care for orphans, God will care for you.'

"Then the old woman took a long breath and said, 'My child, the fate lines on my forehead show nothing but salt and sorrow.[270] Saodat once had an older brother named Qayumjon. When he was seven years old, just as his blessed father was preparing his circumcision celebrations, he fell ill and died of measles.[271] To make matters worse, his father also succumbed to the illness, leaving Saodat and I in bitter circumstances. Sometimes I think that if my boy had survived, we would not be in such dire straits.' Drying her tears, she finished her story, 'My child, all that is left for the slaves of God such as myself are tears and sighs.'[272]

"I tried to console her. 'Though they are young, you have both a daughter and a son left to you. You will live to see brighter days, Mother,' I said, presenting the items I had brought for the old woman. "I have brought a modest gift for Saodat and her little brother for Hayit. I hope you will not be angry with my presumptuousness.'

" 'How can I repay you for your kindness,' said the old woman, who began a prayer of thanks, the words flowing freely from her mouth. Saodat, who was timid at first while her mother prayed, now moved shyly closer to us and slowly opened the paper wrapping and took out the silk.

" 'Is it for me?' Not waiting for my answer, she took out the striped cotton fabric and said, 'This is for Safi.'[273]

"And upon discovering another piece of simple cotton fabric, she added, 'This is for my mother.'

"Saodat sorted through these gifts and talked about them as if she had known I would bring them. After lovingly examining the silk, she seemed about to tell me something but chose not to—I guessed at what she wanted to say. As I began to discuss the difficulties of life with the old woman, she approached us, interrupting.

" 'Usta-aka, are you keeping your fast?'

" 'Yes, I am fasting."

" 'If you were not keeping the fast, I would have boiled water for tea,' she said. Her mother smiled.

" 'You can make me tea when I come for the Hayit holiday when the fast is over,' I replied.

" 'If you come on Hayit, I will prepare plov too,' Saodat said and looked at her mother.

" 'Your brother is worth anything, my daughter,' said the old woman as tears filled her eyes. I could barely hold back my own tears.

" 'Why don't you stay with us tonight to break the day's fast with an *iftor*?'[274]

"Saodat's mother agreed to this idea. I used business as an excuse not to stay, but in reality, I wanted with all my heart to sit together with Saodat to make iftor. I did not want to leave this house and could not help feasting my eyes on Saodat and her childish charms. Saodat felt completely at ease with me and made me and her mother laugh as she held the silk up to her full, maturing breasts, saying over and over, 'Ah, I would give anything for silk like this!' As for me, a euphoria overcame me, as if she were caressing me, not the silk.

"Finally, I began saying my goodbyes to the old woman and preparing for my departure. While showing me to the door, Saodat asked 'Shall I come on Thursday?'

"I walked back toward the old woman and said, 'Your Saodat has grown older, maybe it would better if from now on you send Safi to me when he is out of school. And when I am free, I will come to visit you myself.'

"The old woman seemed to have expected these words from me and praised my cleverness and concern for the honor of her family.

" 'Look, have you heard your brother the master's words?' She turned to her daughter. 'From now on, you should not go out alone into the street so freely.'

"While taking my leave, I turned to take one last look at Saodat, who was clearly upset with me. My restrictions on her movements were justified. The lascivious eyes of my trainees passing over her had already come to my attention. From that day forward, Saodat's brother picked up my clothes, returning them clean later in the day, so in time we struck up a friendship. Saodat's mother stopped covering herself in my presence, bringing me great joy that the bonds of familiarity between us had grown. Euphoria from my success and anxiety overwhelmed me as if soon, very soon, if not that day, then tomorrow, Saodat would be my bride.

"Soon, I took on the responsibilities of the head of Saodat's family: I cared for them and would do anything to further their well-being. On Fridays I brought ingredients for plov to Saodat and would eat it from her own hands, returning to my home late. Saodat matured day by day, her beauty blossoming, as did my devotion. In this manner two years passed and Saodat reached her sixteenth year. An awareness of the underlying meaning of my loving glances grew and she ceased addressing me as 'brother.' Over those two years I considered hiring a matchmaker to speak with the old woman, but for some reason marrying Saodat had always seemed like an unobtainable happiness, always out of reach. I only hoped that Saodat's mother would see me as a suitable husband and either approach me herself or send her own matchmaker. I myself was wracked with shyness and could not force myself to send a matchmaker, or, rather, hesitated to do so due to an intangible fear that defied explanation.

"One day, as was my habit, I went to Saodat's house. After eating plov and finishing with tea, the old woman dismissed Saodat to perform her usual duties at the stove, looked up at me, and said with a smile, 'A suitable bridegroom from a good family appeared the other day for Saodat. Yesterday we were to arrange an engagement, but I turned away the matchmaker to seek your counsel first.'

"How could she even venture such a proposal? I sat stock-still, as if doused with cold water, completely tongue-tied. Immobile as a mound of earth, I willed myself to respond, hardly believing my own words:

" 'If he is from a suitable family, we should consider it...'

"When she went on to describe the boy's lineage and his profession, my patience faded and I said bitterly, 'In that case, it is unfortunate that you turned away the matchmakers.'

"The old woman did not catch my sarcasm and continued, 'Both the suitor and his family are to my liking. The only thing I am waiting for is your advice. Though you are not Saodat's maker, you have done much more for her than a real father could. Please help me arrange Saodat's marriage and settle her life.'

"At this point, as the saying goes, she continued beating a dead horse. I could hardly listen to the old lady's well-meaning explanations—they stung like poison from a scorpion. Telling her that I needed to think until tomorrow, I got up and left her sitting there.

"Leaving the house, my steps took me in all four directions and I was consumed with passion. My thoughts sped past, reflecting my erratic changes in direction. Completely addled, I sought the company of a confidant of mine who knew of my secret love to discuss my dilemma. Without pausing for a second he promised to approach the old woman the very next day on my behalf as a matchmaker. That whole night, sleep did not find my eyes. Pain wracked me as if I lay on needles, and I damned myself for my indecision..."

Usta Alim paused, trimmed the wick of the candle, and after asking Otabek, who sat rapt, listening to him, if the story was boring him, continued:

"After sending the matchmaker, I was unable to reach any sort of peace. My hands were unable to work, yet they moved unceasingly. I would get up to stand and then immediately sit down elsewhere. Madness crept in as I was bombarded with a thousand different thoughts. My messenger still had not returned and once or twice I even walked to Saodat's gate. My mind aching, I had sat down under the shadow of a walnut tree near Saodat's house, when, finally, my matchmaker appeared. My heart pounded with fear! I sought to avoid my friend by walking some distance away from him, worried that the possibility of being rejected would overwhelm me.

" 'Wait, wait, don't run off, don't run off. Hey, bridegroom, stop running away,' said the matchmaker. Since this friend of mine was a well-known prankster, I believed that my cause was lost and he was only mocking me by calling me 'bridegroom.' This kept me walking. He pursued me and caught up with me: 'Take off your robe,' he said and proceeded to pull off my robe jokingly.

" 'It is customary to pay for a job well done.'

" 'Please don't joke with me—my heart will break,' I pleaded, but his words were no joke.

"It then dawned on me that he spoke the truth and I kissed him on his lips, not ashamed of the tears filling my eyes. On the way home, my matchmaker relayed to me his conversation with the old woman in great detail. It turned out that almost for an entire year, matchmakers had arrived daily to negotiate for Saodat's hand, but the old woman refused them all, saying that Saodat was already engaged. All the while she waited for me to send my own representative or request an engagement myself. Finally, she decided to inform me of this last visit to divine my intentions. In short, the old woman gave her reply: 'If I had not one daughter, but one hundred daughters, I would give them all to Usta Alim.'

"I could barely contain myself. Finally, two years of heartsickness was healed. For a few days, shyness kept me from going to the old woman's house. She finally invited me to visit through her young son. I went, but I do not have the words to explain the myriad of feelings I had during my visit. Passing through the entrance, a dreamy haze drifted over me—Saodat was hanging out laundry. Upon seeing me, she blushed and hid behind the drying clothes, but I could discern the light of joy in her comely eyes.

"Negotiating with the old woman about the wedding preparations felt somewhat uncomfortable. Though the old woman forbade me to plan elaborate ceremonies, I insisted on a large feast to please Saodat. When we had set a date for the wedding, I took my leave. Saodat had hidden herself upon entering, so my eagerness to whisper a few words with her nagged at me. She stood washing a kettle near the stove as I headed right to her. Whether she truly did not sense my presence, or she was just pretending not to notice me, she busied herself with her duties with her back turned to me. Her long black hair woven into one thick braid swayed from side to side, every graceful motion giving it a life of its own. I stood behind her for some moments, observing her movements.

" 'Saodat,' I whispered. She turned to face me. Maybe it was from the fierce heat of the stove's fire, or from shyness, but her face flushed like a bright red apple. She rose and stood right in front of me with the wash towel still in her hands.

" 'Have you heard the news?' I asked.

"She looked at the ground. To ease her shyness, I turned toward the door and asked on my way out, 'Do you agree with the arrangement?'

"Instead of answering, she said, 'Are you leaving without eating plov?'

"An unspoken agreement had been struck. No, it was more than an agreement, it was tenderness, like the tenderness a woman shows for her husband of forty years. As I passed through the gate, I was drunk with joy and under the spell of her sweet words, 'Are you leaving without eating plov?' "

As Usta Alim told of this intimacy, Otabek furrowed his eyebrows, sympathetic to the elation and the subsequent agony of losing it forever.

Usta Alim continued with his story.

"Over the next ten days, we finished our preparations and celebrated the wedding. In the end, Saodat became mine, and my happiest days unfolded before me. Since by now you understand the extent of my love for Saodat, you can fathom the great joy I felt during that period.

"Saodat, my wife, indeed made me happy. That year my profits multiplied and I was so focused on work that I recovered all my wedding expenses. As we prospered, Saodat's house could no longer accommodate all of us and I succeeded in purchasing this yard—" Usta Alim pointed to Jannat opa's residence—"from our present neighbor. All of us moved to the new expanded hovli[275] and lived in harmony.

"As my love for Saodat grew stronger each day, my craft became more profitable. The second year of marriage, I purchased the small garden you just saw from our neighbor. During the third year, Saodat became pregnant. I as husband, she as wife were thrilled, thinking that any day one of us would be a father, the other a mother. Each night we were sleepless from excitement. Finally, Saodat's third term of pregnancy came to an end..."

After taking a deep, ragged breath, Usta Alim continued, "And my days of eternal suffering and dark hours of unhappiness began..." he said and fell silent.

"Please proceed," said Otabek.

Taking another long breath, Usta Alim continued, "For three days, Saodat was exhausted by labor pains, and she died during the fourth day, along with the child."

Upon hearing her fate, Otabek drifted out of his drunken stupor. His eyes widening in shock, he sat up from his pillow and asked, "Died?"

Usta Alim wiped away a tear.

"Died," he said. "I lost the only happiness I have had since I was brought into this world. I met with a terrible blow that took the joy out of my life. I cried for months, tears pouring like an autumn rain. Because I remained inconsolable, my mother-in-law finally forced me to marry a second wife a year after Saodat's death. She could never be Saodat. My happiness—her name was Saodat for a reason—was buried with her body. My mother-in-law weakened each year, and twenty months later she too died, leaving me her eleven-year-old son. After my mother-in-law's death, my second wife became the mistress of the house and wasted our money on frivolities. She began to funnel money to her gambler brothers, who secreted away our savings. As time passed they became more and more brazen in their endeavors. My business began to fail, declining day after day. Success and well-being left my home as soon as the bad wife took everything in her hands. I realized that all my earnings and the blessings of my life had left this world with Saodat, so I divorced my second wife and kicked her out of the house. Now I am entering my third year of living alone, wifeless, with no thoughts of marriage. The blessed memories of my days spent with Saodat haunt me, making me cry bitter tears, yet those memories also fill me with joy. To my friends who push me toward another marriage, I always say, 'I am a person who has passed from the world. I am a moth that seeks death in the flame of a candle, to lie on the grave of my beloved.'[276]

"Now I think only of finding a wife for my brother-in-law and then entering into the embrace of my Saodat with a clear conscience and the sense that I have fulfilled my obligations," he said, dropping languidly onto his pillow.

Usta Alim's story moved Otabek so deeply that his cheeks once again shone with teardrops.

Both kept their silence for some time. Otabek's past sadness seemed forgotten. His eyes were focused on the man lying in front of him, a monument to true love and melancholy. Usta's narrative struck a deep chord within his own heart, both in terms of the love it demonstrated and in the deep embrace of a life as an outcast. The future had disappeared for Usta Alim, leaving only emptiness. Otabek envisioned his own horizon as the same vast void, leading nowhere. The only disparity, the only pale sliver that kept Otabek from becoming Alim's mirror image in grief, was that single word— "died." But no. Even if he were to hear of Kumush's departure from this world, he would still refuse to share in Usta Alim's fate. Otabek had fallen victim to the intolerable affront of Kumush casting him from her home.

Saodat had not cast off her husband and had offered him no insult. Though her young life ended before its time, and regardless of whether or not it was Usta Alim's fault, he had not been evicted like an animal by his father-in-law... no traps had been laid in his path to tear him from Saodat. The devil had played no part in the deal; there was no reward in it, no darkness.

Otabek's sudden understanding of the hidden machinations against him came from an unanticipated inspiration: the fact that Qutidor had agreed to his marriage in Tashkent, had even helped to arrange the wedding with his own hands, as if laying well beforehand the trap to ensnare him. He could find no other explanation. When his thoughts reached their logical conclusion, he could not resign himself to the same path as Usta Alim.

Lying in a bed prepared by Usta Alim, he murmured to himself, "Otabek, you were expelled and insulted. How can you relegate yourself to a simple unhappiness like Usta Alim's?"

As he faded into sleep, his heart stood empty like a nest abandoned by a mockingbird that had taken flight with her young...

Waking for morning prayers, Otabek saw Safi sleeping in contentment, having returned in the early morning from Shamshodbek's celebration. The exceptional beauty of this fifteen-year-old boy was a testimony to the stark beauty of his sister, Saodat. After drinking a half cup of tea, Otabek bade farewell to Usta Alim.

9

WHAT TO DO FOR ONE WHO CANNOT FORGET

Otabek's sudden arrival from Margilan thrilled Uzbek Oyim, as she believed that the Jewish prayers made at her behest had finally overtaken the magic performed by the mysterious Hindustani. Yet Otabek spent all of his time in the men's quarters and did not visit his second wife. Suspicion grew in Uzbek Oyim's mind over this behavior. She considered visiting another magician to divine the reasons for his standoffishness.

As for Yusufbek Hajji, he did not have the time to involve himself with these frivolous matters. When he was not attending to Nur Muhammad Qushbegi, he was spending his time on the council and in gatherings at the homes of various beks. But even he noticed that Otabek no longer criticized the poorly planned policies and the ignorance of the leadership, for the most part keeping silent. During that period, Hasan Ali remained the closest person to Otabek. Because Otabek spent his days in the guest room, Hasan Ali resided with him and maintained communication. Though he witnessed Otabek's gloom, Hasan Ali dared not speak to him of his sleepless nights and the precipitous change in his mood. Quizzing him would have yielded no results anyway. Hasan Ali suspected that Bek's second marriage was to blame—an immovable barrier to his love for Kumush.

Uzbek Oyim's irritation over Otabek's indifference toward his "perfect dream bride" increased daily. At last her anger boiled over and she entered the guest room while Otabek was preparing for bed, rumpled his sheets, and screamed, her voice reaching a crescendo, "Why do you insist on sleeping in the guest room? Sleep in the main house with your wife!" But she no longer saw the obedient son she had once. He ignored his mother's entreaties and continued making the bed. Uzbek Oyim's anger flared again.

"Are you listening to a word I speak, deaf man?"

Otabek answered coolly. "I can hear, but in the face of your offer, I am deaf and blind. Don't worry your head about this now, do not waste your energy in vain!"

"Shameless, unjust!"

Otabek's voice dripped with sarcasm. "Remember what I told you at the very beginning of all of this?"

"And what was that?"

"Wasn't it I who said that your handpicked bride will never see goodness from me? My father and you committed to this arrangement and you cannot deny it."

"So now you are saying that with your mother and father's permission, you can torture your wonderful wife."

"If you do not want me to hurt your daughter-in-law, and if you have a conscience, then... there is one very easy solution..." said Otabek, stopping short of supplying his mother with the solution.

Uzbek Oyim only bit her lip and shook her head, encouraging him to continue.

"If you will not say it, I will. If you genuinely wish no harm to come to your bride, arrange a divorce and do not inflict pain on this wretch in this manner!" He paused for a moment then went on: "I have a conscience and a sense of justice. It pains me to think about the injuries she suffers, all for the sake of bringing you pleasure. If you sacrifice your dream, you should know that you will alleviate the pain of not one, but two lives, Mother."

Uzbek Oyim had not anticipated such firm resistance from her son. For the first time, she was speechless in the face of Otabek's resolve. Whether at a loss for words or afraid that this argument would create a public scandal, she remained silent, giving him a stone-cold look of contempt.

"You have lost your mind, my son," she said, leaving the room.

This last exchange precipitated a change in Otabek, who no longer seemed satisfied with sleep and the solitude of the guest room. He took a dark turn and began to disappear at night, frequenting the seedier areas of the city—only to reappear on occasion completely inebriated— leaving Hasan Ali at a loss for words. He did not know what course to take: to speak with Otabek himself, or to inform his parents.

One night, Otabek left the house according to his new habit. Foreboding gripped Hasan Ali's heart. To keep Otabek from sneaking back into the guest room, he prepared his own bed there and locked the front gate with a chain. The old man resolved to show Otabek that he would not abide his continued late-night drunken ramblings brought to their doorstep. He waited for some time, yet Otabek did not return at the usual hour of eleven or even midnight. Finally, after sitting hour upon hour, drowsiness crept over the old man, as the desire for the warmth of his own bed made eyelash join eyelash, and sleep crept over him without so much as a word of warning.

After an untold amount of time, he was startled from his slumber by a knocking at the gate and ran to the front entryway. Searching in the darkness for the chain on the gate, he asked, "Who is there?"

In response, he heard a slurred voice: "It... is... me."

Hasan Ali's heart skipped a beat at this ill-defined, drunken voice, and he thought bitterly, "Today is like all the other days."

As he loosened the chain and opened one side of the gate, Otabek, who was leaning against the door, fell at Hasan Ali's feet. Hasan Ali understood immediately that Otabek was drunk and senseless, as nausea welled up in him from the sour smell and the alcohol filling the entryway. Escorting Otabek to the guest room, he kept his eyes fixed on the doors of the Ich Kari, fearing in his heart that Yusufbek Hajji, in his midnight wanderings, might walk out into the yard. While undressing Otabek in the guest room, Hasan Ali said in a reproachful voice, "My son, why do you need to deal in the devil's poison?"

Otabek laughed drunkenly. "Who needs it if not me?"

"At any rate, I do not approve of your behavior," said Hasan Ali, waiting in trepidation for a response. Otabek, lying down on his bed, only let out a powerful "Ooofff." Hasan Ali waited for a rebuttal, yet after some moments he heard only snoring...

Though no explanation for Otabek's sudden destructive behavior presented itself, Hasan Ali suspected that being forced into his second marriage was the root cause. For two months, he had heard no mention of Margilan, which made him suspicious: "Perhaps some conflict arose between them?" He spent hours ruminating over the issue. In the morning, he ignored a pot of tea prepared by Oibadak and waited for Otabek to wake up. When Otabek did appear toward midday, Hasan Ali himself prepared the tea. Otabek sat sheepishly near Hasan Ali, waiting for him to lay the tablecloth. Perhaps he recollected the previous night's events and could not look at Hasan Ali or say a word to him. Otabek's demeanor softened Hasan Ali's big heart and he soon forgot all the intended lectures on morality; his only thought was to save Begzoda[277] from his present condition.

"Old people say youth is without reason," said Hasan Ali, laughing. "I only worried that someone from inside the house would notice you... Mercifully, nobody noticed."

Otabek looked toward Hasan Ali with gratitude on his face, taking a long breath in relief and nodding in acceptance of his bad behavior. Hasan Ali did make attempts to get Otabek to talk but received only half- hearted answers. However, the old man found a chance to ask casually, "Are you delaying your departure to Margilan this time around?"

Dear reader: We mentioned before that Otabek had never given a reason for his sudden return from Margilan—not to Yusufbek Hajji, Uzbek Oyim, or even Hasan Ali. Nor had he revealed to them that all ties with Margilan had been severed.

Granted, nobody asked him any questions, so he kept silent, drowning his sorrows in wine.

Over the past two months, Hasan Ali hadn't pressed for a reason regarding Otabek's absence from Margilan, and this moment seemed a suitable time to finally reveal the secret. But his answer was totally unexpected and would surprise anyone who was aware of the true state of affairs:

"I leave today," he said.

And so Hasan Ali's suspicions regarding a possible tiff turned out to be groundless. Drinking his tea, Otabek concealed his genuine intent by gaining his father's permission to leave and prepared to strike out on the road after midday. As nobody knew his secret, nobody bothered to ask, "What are you going to do in Margilan?" Otabek too avoided posing this question. He readied himself for Margilan as if nothing were wrong...

After approximately twenty days, he returned from Margilan, but it was unclear what had been accomplished during that time. The reader will learn from the following chapters the events surrounding his journeys.

He stayed in Tashkent for about a week and then, taking Hasan Ali with him as a traveling companion, he went to the city of Oq Masjid.[278] There, he sought to revive his trading company, which had remained dormant for two years...

10

WHO CRIES THE MOST AMONG US; OR, IN THE GRIP OF SUFFERING

Six months had passed since the counterfeit divorce declarations changed hands. Men, both married and unmarried, lost sleep over Kumush's beauty. Applying the maxim "There is no harm in trying," they procured the services of the *orzumand*[279] who flocked to Qutidor's house like spring birds. It goes without saying that the swallow leading this flock was the matchmaker sent by Hamid, who knew about the upcoming divorce before Kumush herself—even before Otabek, for that matter. Not satisfied with one visit, Hamid's matchmaker shamelessly applied to Qutidor three, even four times, reiterating Hamid's wish to become his new son-in-law. Only one answer met the matchmaker's entreaties: "We see no barriers to making Hamidboi our son-in-law, but our daughter remains firm in her decision never to marry again. Hamidboi should accept our sincerest apologies." All other matchmakers received the same response. Qutidor and Oftob Oyim disagreed with this decision, but it indeed reflected Kumush's deepest wishes.

They did not place much value in Kumush Bibi's severe response of "I am finished with attempts at marriage. I do not need a spouse anymore," since they considered this decision a childish whim. Privately, they planned on her remarrying if an honorable arrangement arose. So, they found it convenient to refer to Kumush's will when rejecting the matchmakers; meanwhile, they searched for a more suitable groom.

One day, a matchmaker unexpectedly presented herself on behalf of Salim Sharbatdor's[280] son Kamilbek—widely regarded as the most moneyed and influential member of the city's elite. All parents dream and hope for such a princely bridegroom, so his matchmakers were met warmly, with an array of soups and plov. The lavish display indicated to the guests that not only did their hosts intend to deliberate seriously over any offer, but would also provide a positive response upon their second visit.[281] They thought over the matter for moments only—this matter demanded decisiveness—and Qutidor and his wife resolved to accept the conditions forwarded by the matchmakers upon their return. Surely, they anticipated that Kumush would refuse, yet, as her parents, they believed they understood what was best for her—to disregard their wisdom would be to ignore the earth beneath her feet.

The last days of autumn faded into the first days of winter. Falling yellow leaves covered the earth's surface with a dappled gold brocade, clothing it for winter. Even the cherry trees, sheltered behind mud walls from the biting wind, that had held on to their precious leaves until they could no longer resist the stark cold of late autumn nights, shook off their foliage with a soft rustle at the slightest touch of a breeze. Brilliant clear skies promised a sun high on the horizon yet brought no warmth. The cold air robbed the sun's rays of their energy.

Kumush Bibi appeared at a central door. Her former voluptuousness had faded, yet this detracted nothing from her beauty. On the contrary, her allure only rose to new heights. Her bow-shaped brows arched farther, outlining seductive eyes that had sunk a bit but bore a dark luminescence. The collar of the otter fur jacket she wore against the chill of the past two days enveloped her gentle neck, provoking envy from all around her.

But an inexplicable change marked her appearance: her seductive eyes had lost their prior playfulness, and the sparkles of joy in them seemed to have faded—her gaze was stern and devoid of emotion. This seriousness lent her a sort of noble sublimity. She went out to the veranda, sat on its edge, and watched the last leaves of summer fall, one by one off the trees, her cold eyes following each of them to the earth. It seemed that Kumush saw her own destiny foretold in each fallen leaf—she couldn't help comparing her fate with this dry foliage, torn from the tree's branches and ready to turn into dust. She couldn't help thinking about her life as something doomed like the autumn leaves.

Her gentle breasts lifted four or five fingers high as she sighed, eyes finally filling with tears. Raising both her hands, which were hidden in the long sleeves of the jacket, she silently wiped her tears as Oftob Oyim came out from the inner yard. For some moments, she surveyed her daughter out of the corner of her eye. She was about to open the doors of the guest room, when Oysha Buvi, who had followed Oftob Oyim, approached Kumush, asking, "What are you doing here, outside?"

"Nothing... in particular," said Kumush, frowning and arching her eyebrows as she turned her face away.

"If you would enter the guest room with us, we would like to have a couple words with you."

"What sort of words do you have prepared for me?"

"First enter, my child, then we talk," said the old woman, wrapping her arms around Kumush's shoulders to get her to stand.

The mother and the grandmother had come to gain Kumush's word of agreement, leaving the matchmakers waiting inside for the final answer. As for Kumush, she intentionally left the inner yard to make it clear to the matchmakers that she would never agree to this arrangement. Entering the guest room, she shuffled about, feigning indifference and avoiding conversation by pretending to search for something on the shelves.

"What you are looking for is not on those shelves. Come and sit with us," said Oftob Oyim.

"My sitting with you will bring you no profit. Give my reply to the matchmakers as I have given to all the ones who preceded them."

Oysha Buvi exchanged glances with her daughter. "My child, you should consider a couple of words from us before you decide," she said.

"My daughter, what purpose does your opposition serve?" said Oftob Oyim, her anger already welling up at her daughter's flippancy.

"I have told you and Father repeatedly, I do not wish to marry again."

"You wish to pass from this earth single?"

"Whether I pass single or not is the will of Allah."

"I know that your heart is still bound to that shameless husband of yours. You are still hoping for something, but these hopes are childish. You should accept that your father will never give room again in our home to that miserable liar, who has left you for good anyway. If you do not trust my words, read this," Oftob Oyim demanded and passed her a note, continuing, "we received this in reply to the letter you wrote him, but hid it from you, thinking that the letter of divorce was more than enough for you. As you still cling to hope, I intend to reveal the contents of this letter to you."

Kumush took the letter from her mother, which read:

To my former wife, Kumush Bibi:

My first letter's intent was to put an end to your childish games with me. It turns out you did not or would not understand its contents and you still attempted to play coyly with me. They say that "there is no sin in wishing," so, for the sake of our old intimacy, I forgive you your reproachful attacks that went beyond all limits. I wish for you to find a new husband, who is not a trickster and a liar like myself.

239

The letter opened all her old wounds, making Kumush's heart bleed. Her tears flowed freely along her cheeks. She placed the letter back in its envelope, hid it in the folds of her clothes, and told her grandmother and mother, who waited for her answer, "I have no hope of reaching a compromise with this savage; at the same time, I will not accept another husband."

"Why?" asked her mother.

"Why?" Kumush bawled. "If my husband, whom I loved so much, whom I trusted so much, put me through this pain and humiliation, then other men cannot be any better. For me it is better to pass from this world single, alone and in peace, so do not mention the word 'husband' to your daughter, do not make her shiver in horror again, like the leaves on the trees outside!"

These words melted Oftob Oyim's heart, the heart of a mother. She could not even find a reasonable answer for the matchmakers waiting outside.

"Don't cry," she said simply and exited the room with Oysha Buvi, leaving Kumush alone.

The house of Salim Sharbatdor was very much to Qutidor's liking. Therefore, without asking either the wife or the daughter, he arrived at an agreement with one of the male matchmakers who had come to his shop, informing his wife when she returned home, "Today I made an arrangement with the matchmakers and we recited the Fatiha. You must convince your daughter to agree to a marriage by 'any means possible,' " he said.

This news struck Oftob Oyim dumb, for she had no strength left to persuade her daughter, who would again start shivering and crying at the mere mention of marriage. When she promised to gain her daughter's word of honor, the stark image of being caught between a double-edged blade appeared before her: whatever move she considered would result in irreparable wounds. From that day forward, the poor mother's life turned dark. She did not know how to fulfill her promise to her husband and dared not speak to her daughter about marriage. The first words out of her husband's mouth when he came back from the bazaar every evening were "Did you make her agree?" At night she had to bear his scolding, and during the day she suffered from even looking at Kumush, dreading fulfilling her promise.

After several days, Qutidor himself understood his mistake. Day after day he had to give various excuses to the messenger who arrived on behalf of Salim Sharbatdor, asking for the date of the wedding. He even considered closing his workshop. One day, he returned angry from his work and delivered one of the worst rants of Oftob Oyim's life.

"I am a pariah in this town, not daring to hold my head high, and all because of your stubborn daughter. It is so embarrassing that if you do not get her to agree, I will have to flee this city."

The next day the beleaguered mother had to broach the subject with her daughter. She sat down next to the girl, but instead of speaking, she burst into tears. Kumush, who secretly knew of the circumstances that were making her mother weep, did not ask why she cried but instead joined her, washing her face with her own tears. Mother and daughter sobbed for a long time until their tears ran dry.

"These days I would rather not remain in this world any longer. It would be better to perish than to live like this," said Oftob Oyim finally.

"You are mistaken, my dear mother," said Kumush. "You are a worthy inhabitant of this world, but I am the reason for your weariness and bitter tears. If I—the desolate one—had not come into this world, you would not be visited by such sadness and calamity. For that reason, you should pray to God to destroy me, to take your wretched daughter and to give you peace instead. I cannot stand to see you in such a miserable state, sacrificing everything, and all for the sake of my selfish desires. Who is she, your discarded daughter—a toy, passing from hand to hand—to make her loving mother cry? She is not worth one drop of your tears. Go and inform my father that I agree to everything. Our father does not have to endure people's rebukes any longer, all because of his ill-fated daughter. Pay no heed to my grief-stricken visage, announce my agreement without further worry!" So she said, and smoothing her disheveled hair, added, "If you truly pity me, state that one of my terms of agreement is postponing the wedding till next autumn. Tell my father that whether he agrees or not to the sole wish of his unhappy daughter, it is not worth one tear from my dear mother. Your ill-fated daughter agrees to undergo any hardship to give her dear mother peace and joy!"

Unable to stand Kumush's words, Oftob Oyim took her daughter in her arms; mother and daughter again washed themselves in a torrent of tears...

Through Oftob Oyim's strict adherence to Kumush's wishes, Qutidor relented to his daughter's one condition. The bridegroom agreed to wait until the next autumn. And so it was settled that the following autumn, Qutidor would gain a new in-law in Salim Sharbatdor, and Kumush Bibi, the former wife of Otabek, would be given away to Kamilbek.

11

NAVO; OR, MELODY OF THE NOVEL

Although our people have proclaimed that those years were a period of Musulmanabad,[283] we cannot say that infractions contrary to this lofty appellation disturbed those blessed times. The khan was a Muslim, the beks were Muslim, the people were Muslim, and all lived as faithful Muslims under legal verdicts delivered according to the Shariyat. Thieves had their hands cut off or were hung from nooses. *Zoni* and *zoniya*,[284] prostitutes and adulteresses alike, were thrown to their deaths from high arches. Drunkards were given forty lashes. The *rais afandi*,[285] who enforced morality, and their minions conducted searches and interrogated suspects, whip in hand. Those who did not attend prayers or who were ignorant of the Shariyat canon also received lashes as punishment. Even the rais afandi, in pursuit of an Islamic domestic tranquility, handed out beatings to his servants, checked whether they prayed or not, and flogged those deemed in violation of the Shariyat.

Though city administrations adhered strictly to these tenets, it was business as usual for thieves. They bore holes through the back walls of the houses of ordinary people and took off with their life savings. A plentiful supply of female prostitutes abounded, even though the law commanded that they be tied up in bags and thrown off tall towers. Many citizens never once in their lifetimes touched their foreheads to *sagda*, the floors of mosques, and did not like to bow during prayers[286] yet could recite by heart the first four or five sentences of the Quran, popular prayers, or simple incantations. In many houses, people were busy fermenting wine in jugs and distilling spirits from grains, and, as a result, there was no shortage of those who openly engaged in the alcohol trade. Plenty of *boza*[287] houses were opened by the Kazakhs in the village of Chukar, a settlement near Tashkent, and were always full of well-to-do, respected customers.

Upon returning home, Otabek, who had been away on business for five months in Oq Masjid, began to frequent one of these boza houses.[288] Though he rarely dared to visit during daylight hours, there were few evenings he did not in fact frequent these locations. The owner of the boza house knew whose son he was, and so Otabek got the best treatment: he did not sit among the ordinary drinkers but instead was ushered to sit in a special room and served the finest quality boza, not the cloudy sort everyone else drank.

At present, he sat finishing his third jar and calling for a fourth. The proprietor entered.

"Shall I give you another jar of boza, Bek-aka?" he asked.

"Give it to me," Otabek said, "and invite your musician in here too!"

It was past midnight. The other clients, who had been drinking since noon, slowly drifted away to their houses, calling out and jeering at each other. Peace now descended over the establishment. A musician, fatigued from a day of playing, entered Otabek's room despite the late hour, hoping for a generous reward. Having drunk boza from Otabek's weaving hand, the musician strummed his dutar and asked:

"What melody should I play for you, Bek-aka?"

With a slurred voice but absolute conviction, Otabek said, "If you know any, play a melody of separation.[289] Play a melody of divorce."

The musician was surprised.

"This is the first time I have heard of such melodies, Bek-aka."

243

"You think that there are no such melodies in the world? I have heard them for sure. Well, if you don't know any, play whatever you do know..."

The musician, still tuning his dutar to warm the strings, asked again, "These melodies you are talking about must be new compositions?"

"Yes, they are new."

"Where did you hear them?"

Otabek looked at the musician with eyes slowly turning sober.

"I heard these melodies in Margilan and Ferghana..." he said.

The musician, who up to that point had only played a simple tune to warm up his dutar, suddenly started in with the first chords of the "Navo."[290] At the very first chords of the melody, Otabek winced, quickly emptied the cup placed in front of him, and gave himself over to the spell of a sad tune. The dutar spoke to him of his own aching disquiet, relating its sadness not just in the language of music, but in the voice that resonated in Otabek's own soul... Memories of *o'tkan kunlar*[291]—bygone days—passed by Otabek, one by one, especially those last, most recent, woeful days. No, they had not passed by... brought back to life in his vision, they froze there indelibly, lingering...

The dutar that breathed life into those memories could not withstand the tragic implications of their meaning, and the strings wept. They cried bitter tears that rippled throughout the universe, quivering inside heavy hearts... Otabek could bear it no longer and burst into sobs, hiding his eyes behind a handkerchief... His will was crushed by the weeping of the dutar, by the sadness of its song. The young man's soul needed this music, for it expressed all the longing and pain overflowing his heart. Otabek cried and cried, letting out his grief in those tears...

At last, the sad melody of the "Navo" that had made Otabek cry, that complained of the fickleness of fate, that revealed the sufferings of man, suddenly changed, and the music broke into the joyful Savt[292] melody. The unexpected transition from the Navo into Savt brought gaiety, dried Otabek's tears, and eased his mind. In the flower garden of his hopes, newly blossomed flowers appeared, nurtured by the melody of Navo.

After that night, he did not enter a boza house for a month. But when he returned again from Margilan, he picked up his old habits.

All the following trips to Margilan were fruitless and brought no good news. Each time, Otabek would stay at Usta Alim's house, but he still kept his secret, providing Usta Alim with the alibi that he was on his way to or from Andijon. Usta Alim was very grateful for his company, although Otabek never lingered in Margilan for long. He usually would stay only one day, never more than two or three days, and at times would make an overnight pilgrimage to the shrine of Khodja Ma'oz.[293] The reader will see below whether ten days' travel to and from Margilan, combined with the travails of the road that Otabek inflicted upon himself, were worth it or not.

Returning to Tashkent after another pointless trip to Margilan, Otabek would forget about Kumush, preoccupying himself with trivial matters for three or four days. But after a week or so, his thoughts would inevitably wander toward Margilan. Unable to find a distraction, an escape from his thoughts, and unable to beat the pain, he would go back to Chukar to find relief. He would again drink himself into a near stupor for ten or fifteen days, still unable to reconcile with his past. At this point, some kind of premonition would stir in his soul; it seemed to him that if he went to Margilan right away, something would be made clear to him, change something, but if he did not follow the imperative to go, he would irrevocably lose something precious and regret it until the end of his days.

Girded with resolve, he suddenly found himself on the way to Margilan and, during the trip, he imagined a particular someone impatiently waiting for him and spurred on his horse as if every hour mattered. Upon entering Margilan's gates, his resolve wavered, his heart pounding in his chest, the unbearable pain reaching a crescendo as he neared the familiar line of shoe shops. Nervous from traveling along that street so familiar to him, Otabek was driven to indecision, so, seeing the shoe stalls, he nudged his horse's head to the left, almost hearing the echo in his ears, "Go away, never stop at my door, you shameless..."

He began to second-guess himself. "Perhaps I am in fact shameless!" he said aloud, and with these words all his hopes turned to dust, and his resolve was in vain. With his head clear of empty dreams, he decided to abandon his plan to summon his father-in-law and wife to the Shariyat court to protest the divorce, which would in turn incriminate them. "But if I do so, I will have to meet face to face with this sly fox in the judge's office. Let his face dry and drop off!" he said to himself and turned his horse's head straight toward Usta Alim's.

Otabek valued Usta Alim's companionship a great deal and was completely at ease in his presence. He took delight in hearing over and over Usta Alim's epic story of love found and lost—an epic Otabek cherished in his heart for ten years and would take with him to the grave.

As for Usta Alim, he enjoyed reminiscing about his deceased wife, Saodat. At the end of the long narrative, he would always say, "It turns out that the fate is indeed written on our foreheads. Since the beginning of time our threads were meant to diverge, as she died young and I remain chained to the world." At these words Otabek's heart would grow cold, and he would think to himself, "My own beloved has also perished from my world, even if not by dying." He would spend two or three days at Usta Alim's house, then ride around Margilan, looking at the town with a wistful parting glance, revisiting all the familiar places, and finally taking the first road out of Margilan. On the way back, he would not spur his horse and would spend a day or two in Qoqan, three or four days in Kerovchi, a few days in Kura Qurama, Telob, and other villages, until yet again he would finally reach the town of Tashkent[294]...

This was the story of Otabek's travels to Margilan. Since no one knew his secret, no one asked for explanations or laughed at him. He was only accountable to himself, and he only listened to the voice of his own heart. His days and months passed in this unseemly, restless state.

12

Horrifying News And A Terrible Night

If our accounting of time is accurate, during his seventh rambling trip to Margilan—in the autumn of 1267,[295] eighteen or nineteen months after the above-described events, an event of great significance occurred.

After a morning spent drinking tea, Usta Alim and his brother-in-law were busy dying silk in his newly built workshop attached to an adjoining kitchen. Otabek stood leaning against a column in the workshop, preoccupied with his thoughts, and answered Usta's questions about Tashkent with a simple "yes," "no," "of course," or "certainly."

After standing like that for about half an hour, he turned to go without saying a word. Lifting his eyes up from his work area, Usta Alim asked, "Yol-bolsin.[296] Where are you going, Shokirbek?"

"I am going to take a walk around town," Otabek answered from the passage leading to the gate.

"Good idea," said Usta. "Don't stay out past noon. I will prepare plov and wait for you. All right?"

"All right," said Otabek, passing through the entryway onto the street.

At that very moment, Sadiq came straight toward Otabek from the house next to Usta Alim's. Passing him with an attempt at an indifferent glance, Sadiq hurried onward to a narrow alleyway on the right as Otabek continued making his way straight along the wide street. It was a cloudy day, but these clouds, white and fluffy, easily let the light through, and the sun gazed at the earth like a bride from under her veil. A gentle breeze, pushed by the smooth sailing of the clouds, brought a slight nip to one's face. Though this frosty air was not uncomfortable, the smell of overheated flaxseed oil brought in by the breeze was nearly nauseating.

Otabek stopped at a fork in the road. His hesitant expression was understandable, as one road led to the cobblers' district and the other to the main boulevard. He finally took his first bold step toward the cobblers' lane. This street plunged him into a storm of memories, making his face flush, then go pale, but he continued taking firm steps forward. For the first time since the infamous events, he summoned up the courage to go to the place where, as our mothers say, he "was bitten by a snake." Although his footsteps slowed at the turn in the road, he continued moving forward. Qutidor's mythical gate could be seen in the distance. There stood the dreaded teak tree, the fatal witness to Otabek's humiliation. Summoning all his will, Otabek looked at the gate.

The days long gone rushed through his memory, and he let out a heavy, bitter sigh, suddenly shivering. Under those cherry trees, standing right there behind the gates, somebody used to wait for him. "What about now? Who does she meet under those trees now?" This question, like a sharp knife, sliced through his brain. He still believed that Kumush loved him and that she had fallen victim to her father's oppression. He imagined Kumush's face, yellowed and pale like the faded leaves of the autumn cherry tree, and his heart burned, broke into a thousand pieces from the pain, but not for himself—for Kumush. He felt on the verge of performing some unexpected act of courage. He thought, "Maybe I should force my way into the house and talk to her?" But... the ominous tree opposite the gate seemed to look at him mockingly, and laughed, repeating, "There is no place for shamelessness in this house! Go away, do not stand at my door!" He was almost at the gate when something startled him. Suddenly afraid that one of the two men who had walked out of the gates might be his father-in-law, he turned around the corner. The chilling insult caused by the word *shameless* had already cooled his desire to enter Qutidor's house, but he felt compelled to hear any news at all about his beloved. He thought that perhaps the two men who had just left the house would give him some news, even if it was just about Qutidor's dog, so he quickened his pace to catch up with them, until he was barely three steps away from them. Unfortunately, they continued to walk in silence. Finally, after a hundred paces, he succeeded in catching a couple of words between them.

One said to the other, "We made a good decision by planning *nikah*[297] and wedding celebrations for the same day."

"Why should we set a separate engagement date for a divorced woman? She is not a virgin anymore. Only first-time brides have separate engagement and wedding celebrations. I am surprised the father insisted on celebrating them separately."

"But Qutidor is well respected in this town."

On hearing this news, Otabek froze in place, as if nailed to the ground. He remained stock-still, in midstep, as if he had been doused in boiling water—his whole skin separating from his body, falling to his feet...

After several minutes of stupor, he suddenly moved mechanically forward... "Take away one's wife without official divorce papers and then the next day marry her off," he said out loud and laughed like a lunatic. He rambled along the streets of Margilan, sometimes speeding up into a run, and talked to himself. The heartbreaking visage he presented is impossible to put down in words...

Although it was already mid-month, the overcast night sky hid the unspoken truth of the moon. Night fell, a true dark autumn night. The orchard surrounding Khodja Ma'oz's cemetery had thrived for several hundred years, only multiplying in size, and seemed to be the sole source of this darkness. The wind grew stronger; it was now blowing from all directions as if trying to carry everything it could pick up to a certain place. A crazed individual, fearsome and unshaven, with matted hair, walked around a smouldering tree stump, poking it with a stick in an attempt to kindle a fire in one dark corner of the orchard. The wind grew more and more powerful; the trees shook from side to side with great force, flinging off their last leaves with a shivering racket. Crows and jackdaws,[298] rudely disturbed from their sleep, showed their anger at the wind by circling the orchard and, calling out "ghaw-whoo!" The wind gained even more strength, it roared and wailed, breaking tree branches that could no longer resist its might with a loud crack. The old trees creaked mournfully over the cemetery, and the terrifying impenetrable darkness wrapped the surroundings in its heavy shroud. Fear penetrated everything.

Finally, completely enraged, the wind howled with a force intended to flatten all earthly beings. It brought down one of the huge plane trees, making the earth shake, then picked up the fire tended by the lunatic and threw it into the thickets, filling the orchard with sparks. The whole cemetery took on a fiery cast, as if the orchard had been born from the flames.

Suddenly the wind slowed down, calmed its temper, as if it had gotten out all its rage with this conflagration, and the wails and roars of a hungry lion gave way to mercy. The crows and jackdaws, which had flown around for half an hour in great consternation, informed each other of the dying wind and started to land in their old nests with the call of "ghaw-whoo."

The black clouds covering the sky began to part. The moon half- revealed its face through its black veil, beaming at the earth. Owls,[299] which had hidden somewhere from the wrath of the wind, filled the dry branches of two old skeletal plane trees growing opposite the cupola. The moon continued to play hide and seek beneath the black clouds. Its peeking out at the earth could not bring light to the dark mass of the cemetery's orchard; it only emphasised the eternal silence of the marble tombstones resting on the grave mounds. A separate veranda for pilgrims had been built opposite the cupola, under the two old plane trees that housed the owls. Although the moonlight streamed fully into the cemetery, the reception area remained pitch black. The branches of the plane trees were filled with rows of owls arrayed like prayer beads. They were not thrilled by the smiling moon, and every time it shone from under the clouds, they hid their heads under their wings and shrank into tight balls.

When the moon was concealed, they livened up, peeked their heads out from under their wings, and hooted to each other "Kikiki." A low moan, barely discernible, rumbled beneath the chorus of the owls.

The night retreated. A sad call to morning prayer spread from the tower of the mosque, covering the surrounding area in a pall, filling the air with the life-giving force of spiritual purity, and the natural world echoed the sentiment. At the final refrain of "Allah Akbar," Otabek descended from the darkness of the veranda's reception area, sat near the stream running through the cemetery, and performed his *toharat*...[300]

13

An Unsmiling Happiness

With all hope decimated, his heart was still in flames. As if bitten by a snake, he anxiously surveyed the surroundings with the dancing eyes of a madman. In a state of utter confusion, he kept telling himself, "Finally her father has succeeded in his aims. He has satisfied himself by pawning his daughter off on a new groom." And last night she... but that, the nuptial union that had to have been consummated the night before, he rejected as poison, trying not to think about it, looking around restlessly, searching for distraction.

His travels to Margilan were over now, and the city seemed to beckon to him, saying, "What hope could you have expected from me?" He bid goodbye to Khodja Ma'oz and walked straight to Usta Alim's house, to take his horse and depart from Margilan forever. Yet he still had the feeling that somebody dear was reaching out to him, pleading for help, trying to break the embrace of a stranger.

He had almost arrived at the doors of Usta Alim's house. Totally consumed with grief, head bowed, the flame in his heart a red-hot coal, he moved along, rocking from side to side, paying no attention to those who passed him. Thus, he did not notice a man who had just walked out of the house next to Usta Alim's and glanced at Otabek without recognizing him, though his features vaguely reminded him of something long forgotten. Just as Otabek entered Usta Alim's house, Hamid—for it was he who had come out through Sadiq's door—froze in the middle of the road, following Otabek with his gaze.

Usta Alim had been worrying about Shokirbek's absence since the morning before, and upon seeing him in the passage, he bombarded him with questions:

"Thank God you showed up, Shokirbek! Where have you been? I worried myself to death... What happened to you, how could you have become so pale and thin in just one day?"

In fact, Otabek's transformation, his withdrawn features, made him almost unrecognizable. His eyelids were sunken as if he

251

had been stricken by the plague. He willed himself to make his baggy eyes smile.

"I have been to Hajji Ma'oz's tomb."

"Why?"

"Just for an overnight stay."

Usta Alim surveyed him once again, with a look of surprise. "Did you really stay there overnight?"

Otabek sat at the edge of the veranda and answered, to dispel Usta Alim's suspicions, "I had been intending to make an overnight stay there for some time."

"So, you had some wishes to convey to the holy man?" said Usta Alim, smiling. At that moment, the echo of footsteps through the passage neared, and they turned and saw a young man, thin and pale, in an awkwardly wrapped turban.

Usta Alim rose to welcome him.

"Hello, Usta Farfi. You are welcome here. Is it really you? Come in, come in," he said.

Usta Farfi greeted Usta Alim with salaams and shook his hand. Otabek and the visitor exchanged salutations and shook hands in greeting, saying, "Are you in good health, my guest?"[301]

All sat on the veranda as a prayer was read. Then Usta Alim said, in a friendly, sarcastic way, "Finally, I have been blessed with a visit from you, Usta Farfi."

The newcomer looked at the newly built workshop and asked, "Are you working on a big project, Usta? You have built a workshop, too."

"It's been fifteen days now. I waited for you to come and bless it, but you have just now arrived."

"Of all people, you should know the reason, Usta," replied Usta Farfi. "Once you promise to do something, you can't leave work. Only on Fridays is it possible to visit friends and those close to you, otherwise I do not have the time. I think you have been in my shoes before."

"No, I haven't," said Usta Alim with a laugh. "I am not a hen like you, sitting around all day in the workshop, keeping his eggs warm. I would believe you if you just told me honestly that you did not want to lose good money!"

"Now you are correct," replied Usta Farfi with a giggle. "But what can I do? Children are like chickens—they grow and multiply

252

each year. If I don't put food on the table, there will be an unavoidable scandal."

When Usta Alim went to retrieve a tablecloth from his room, Usta Farfi turned to Otabek. "Where are you from, guest?"

"From Tashkent."

"Fine, fine indeed. Please take the place of honored guest," he said.

Thanking him for his kindness, Otabek remained in his spot. Usta Farfi looked at him again and then made himself comfortable in his seat, crossing his legs. The tablecloth was laid out and breakfast tea served. Although Usta Alim had asked Shokirbek to take the place reserved for guests, he remained where he was, without removing his kuvash.[302] They began to sip their tea and discuss various issues of the day. It became clear from Usta Alim and Usta Farfi's conversation that they had both served under the same master twenty years before. Usta Alim had had some sort of falling-out with his master, and after that he had built his own workshop attached to his house and had been working on his own for some time. When Usta Farfi asked what had caused the falling-out, their host only said, "What a total swine, what an evil individual he turned out to be." At that, Otabek emptied the cup of tea in his hand and said to Usta Alim, "Now if you will permit me, I need to take to the road, Usta."

Usta Alim looked up at him, surprised, and asked, "Why do you want to leave again? You said you were going to stay three or four days."

"My work in Margilan has concluded and I have become anxious to go back. Besides... Hoja."

"Let's finish our tea and then you are free to go," said Usta Alim and filled his cup again. Interrupted by Otabek's announcement, Usta Farfi now continued with his questioning.

"Tell me the truth, Usta. Why did you quarrel with our master?"

"He never told you?"

"He did not. When I asked, he immediately changed the subject."

"He felt the unholy shame of revealing the truth," said Usta Alim, frowning and looking off to the side in disgust.

253

"And when I persisted in uncovering the reason for your quarrel, he continued to change the topic."

Usta Alim emptied his cup in one gulp, and then finally revealed the origins of his anger towards his master.

"I had noticed for some time that Hamid had been glancing lasciviously at my brother-in-law... The morning of our dispute, I sent Safi to work a little early, as I had met with some delay. As I entered through the front gates of the workshop, I heard someone weeping and pleading for help. Startled, I opened the door to see that bastard Hamid trying to rape my brother-in-law. Interrupting his efforts, he became frightened and freed Safi from his grasp, looking into my eyes. I was speechless, my indignation rising. That swine tried to slink out of the workshop, but I said, 'I served you and your father faithfully for twenty years, and this is the thanks I receive from you?' He left, not saying a word. Evidently, that morning neither you nor Karim and Ortikboi had come to work at the workshop, and that swine had used that opportunity to assault Safi. After that, I left with Safi, not wishing to see anyone again, and started my own workshop. So now you know what happened between us."

Usta Farfi felt a great revulsion at the master's behavior.

"Damn him! So that's what he was doing, bastard! And this is not the worst thing he has done!" he said, lowering his voice, and continued, "It turns out that that bastard has done unbelievable things before without our knowledge."

Otabek, who had listened to Usta Alim's revelation with great interest, respect, and empathy, asked, "Which Hamid was it? Is it a dark man with a pockmarked face? Hold on! I think I just saw him leaving your neighbor's house."

Usta Alim looked at Otabek in surprise. "Indeed, he is that same person. How do you know him?"

"I once met him at a gathering."

Usta Farfi, amused at Otabek's revelation, laughed, saying, "Then you must have loved his foul words." Now Otabek smiled appreciatively. At this point in their conversation, Safi entered with something wrapped in a scarf. After greeting Usta Farfi with a kiss, he said to Otabek, "Yesterday we waited for you so long, our plov turned cold, Bek Aka."

"I thought that was today's plov," joked Otabek.

Safi seemed anxious and was eager to say something.

"By the way, last night someone was murdered in a shed by the hammam."[303]

"Who was it?" asked Usta Alim. "I don't know who was killed."

Usta Farfi answered for him, "I know. While on my way here, soldiers under Qorboshi's command were loading the body onto a cart. The one murdered was the son of Salim Sharbatdor, poor Kamilbek."

"Oh my!" said Usta and asked, "Has the murderer been caught?"

"Forget about catching him. Just finding the dead body was a miracle.

After a considerable search, they found it just before midnight," said Farfi.

Otabek listened to the news of the murder indifferently and was about to get up and leave to read the evening prayer.

"Are there any suspects?" asked Usta Alim.

"No firm suspects, but it is strange that the poor man's death happened that particular night," said Usta Farfi and went on: "Yesterday, Kamilbek and Mirza Karim-aka's daughter were to be engaged. The victim went with his friend to the hammam just two hours before the ceremony and vanished into thin air. Even the person accompanying him did not notice his disappearance. Everyone in the bride's household was ready for the celebrations and the guests had arrived. Kamilbek's father, the Qadi, and his staff hired to perform the ceremony, were waiting for the groom. At that moment, the person who had gone with the groom to the hammam hurried to the girl's house. Those waiting for the groom asked him where he was, but the companion himself did not know the groom's whereabouts and told them about how he had disappeared from the hammam, leaving all his clothes behind.

"Abandoning the plov, everyone left to search for the bridegroom. Finally, at midnight, they found him lying in his own blood in the farthest corner of the cow barn adjoining the hammam, near the washroom. Evidently, when the wretch entered the washroom to make ablution, someone stabbed him to death without making a sound and threw his body under the trough in the barn... What a strange incident! Who murdered him and what were their motivations, nobody knows," Usta Farfi concluded his story.

Otabek entered a state of odd stupor. He did not know whether he should be happy with this news, for, even though the rival's death revived his lost hopes, he was exceedingly worried. As for Usta Alim, he was stunned by this tragedy and kept saying "Poor man, poor man."

"He must have had some kind of enemy?" Otabek asked cautiously. "No doubt he did!" said Usta Farfi, looking back at Otabek. This look made Otabek's heart sink.

Usta Farfi continued, "There are all sorts of people in this world. Some of them spit at other people's lives, not considering the Day of Judgment." Again, he looked at Otabek... Otabek was on pins and needles, feeling Usta Farfi's glances on his skin... Usta Alim also noticed Usta Farfi's looks, but, thinking that he knew something and hesitated to reveal it in front of Otabek out of mistrust, encouraged him:

"Go ahead, Farfiboi, say it, he is one of us."

"What should I say?"

"What you know about Kamilbek's enemies."

"Did I say I knew something?" said Usta Farfi with a smirk, looking at Otabek. "Look how subtly you are fishing for information..."

At these words, Otabek relaxed a bit. "Since you kept stealing looks at me, Usta thought you were nervous about my presence," he said.

"Be honest, you know more than you are telling us, but you are afraid to say it in front of Shokirbek," added Usta Alim.

"These accusations are all erroneous," denied Usta Farfi.

"They are not, not at all," said Usta Alim. "You should know that Shokirbek is not the type of person you should suspect of something like that, so speak your mind. Have mercy!"

"*Astaghfurallah.*"[304] Usta Farfi laughed aloud and, having thought for a while, said, "Is this incident really any of our business, Usta?"

"If you do not want to discuss it, then do not make insinuations. But if a word slipped your tongue, you should speak the whole truth—even if it is none of our business!" insisted Usta Alim.

Otabek was becoming even more impatient than Usta Alim. He forgot the issues surrounding his whole life now, since it was crucial to learn the details of his rival's murder. Usta Farfi realized that he couldn't shake this conversation off and looked at Safi apprehensively.

"Nephew, you are young still. You have yet to learn to keep your mouth shut and earn trust," he said. "Though you will be upset with me, I will ask you to go spend some time in the workshop."

Usta Alim motioned for his brother-in-law to leave and asked him to take carrots from the storage room and chop them for plov. After the boy's departure, Usta Farfi said in a hushed voice, "If my suspicions are correct, Kamilbek's murderer is no other than Hamid."

This revelation surprised Otabek, but it made Usta Alim sick. "Hamid, you say?" asked Usta Alim.

"Hamid!" repeated Usta Farfi and asked Usta Alim in a low voice, "No doubt you know that Umarbek was close friends with Hamid?"

"Of course, I do," said Usta Alim. "They were together day and night."

"So then," said Usta Farfi. "This very Umarbek had a falling-out with him recently, and ten days ago Umarbek relayed to me a horrible savagery that Hamid committed. Though I did not witness Kamilbek's murder, based on the secret revealed to me, I have to conclude that Hamid is Kamilbek's murderer. Do you remember, about three years ago, a certain Otabek, a young man from Tashkent, who married the daughter of Mirza Karim and settled in Margilan and then was arrested together with his father-in-law? They were sentenced to hang but saved at the last moment right out from under the noose... You must remember it—we were drinking tea in Sariboi's shop at the time... ?"

"I do seem to remember now," said Usta Alim, asking Otabek, "maybe you know the son of Yusufbek Hajji, a luminary of Tashkent?"

"I know him," said Otabek, amazed that he was the one being talked about and that the story, which had begun so far away, now concerned his own self. He could not take his eyes off of Usta Farfi, who continued in a low voice, "The wife of that same young man was renowned for her beauty, but our Hamid also wished to claim her for himself. After Otabek married the girl, our Hamid, in his rage, plotted to destroy Otabek and Mirza Karim by creating slanderous statements and succeeded in having the noose put around their necks..."

At this point Otabek sighed heavily.

Usta Farfi continued, "Under the shadow of God, who reigns justly, they were spared, saved by some kind of letter delivered at the last second. When the truth was revealed, the authorities intended to arrest Hamid, but, with Qorboshi's help, he escaped to Qoqan, saving his own hide. But even there he did not give up, he petitioned Musulmanqul the Lame, accusing Uttaboi Qushbegi of bribery."

Pausing at that point, Usta Farfi asked Usta Alim, "You must remember it too—when Hamid disappeared overnight and fled for three months, completely off the map, as the soldiers of Qorboshi searched for him."

Usta Alim nodded in confirmation. "I remember. Go ahead," he said.

Otabek could not believe his ears—the terrible revelation threatened to overwhelm him, and he struggled to control his temper.

Usta Farfi lowered his voice to barely above a whisper. "After Hamid's false testimony to Musulmanqul the Lame, Otabek and Uttaboi Qushbegi were again summoned to Qoqan and, following interrogation, they were exonerated.

"Hamid was unable to enter Margilan for three months, but with the help of the same Qorboshi, he managed to return to the city again. Still, he remained ill at ease, thinking of the moment when he could put his foul plans into action and claim Qutidor's daughter as his own. And that moment finally presented itself, much to this swine's joy, who then came up with a new dirty trick. Having learned of Otabek's second marriage in Tashkent, he wrote a counterfeit letter on Otabek's behalf, requesting a divorce, which was delivered to Mirza Karim-aka."

No matter how hard he struggled to contain his temper, emotions overtook Otabek and he jumped to his feet, screaming, "Scoundrel, dishonest swine!"

Usta Alim could not conceal his indignation either. "Faithless bastard!" he said.

The sudden eruption from Otabek raised vague suspicions in Usta Farfi, but the fact that Usta Alim shared this emotion made him discount them. When Otabek, calming down, took his place, Usta Farfi went on: "Otabek's countermeasures concerning this fake letter of divorce were not known even to Hamid himself, but everything worked according to his plan and, three or four months later, rumors arose that the daughter of Mirza Karim Qutidor would be divorced. Our Hamid waited for a few months and sent a matchmaker to Karim's house, but Mirza Karim sent the matchmaker away with no result.

"Some time later, his daughter was promised to Kamilbek, but for some unknown reason their wedding was delayed for a period of a year. Yesterday was meant to be the engagement party, yet, as you know, we heard news of Kamilbek's murder in the hammam. Because of all of this, I believe that Hamid is the one who murdered Kamilbek," he concluded.

Usta Alim nodded his head in agreement.

"Without any doubt, Hamid is the murderer," he stated, as if speaking to himself. "Oh, fellow Muslim, what kind of shameless bastard lusts after the lawful wife of another man while having two of his own... all the while spilling the blood of innocent people, knowing he would never achieve his aim of possessing this young woman? No, he is not a man—he is a child of Satan!"

"He is like a scabby dog," said Usta Farfi. "Unable to eat food stored on the roof, he keeps it from others as well."

At last Otabek knew the name of the bastard who was the source of all the tragedy in his life. He swallowed limitless hatred toward his enemy so that he would not reveal his secrets to the others, yet his strong emotions boiled inside him, taking shape in his expression, his eyes flashing with fire, his face flushed.

During the pause in the conversation, Usta Farfi said, "I am surprised that we were unaware all along that Hamid had committed such cowardly deeds."

"There is no reason to be surprised," said Usta Alim. "You started to work with him recently, but as for me, though I worked with Hamid in his house for twenty years, I was never able to see his true self. He always seemed like a terrible person to me, a deep dark abyss." He paused for a moment and then went on, after discovering some new truth, "Although Hamid is the main instigator in these dealings, no doubt he has someone aiding him. Do you remember a young man with bulging eyes who used to visit our workshop asking for Hamid?"

"He is still in close contact with Hamid. His name is Sadiq. Isn't he your neighbor?"

"You are right! Of course, this young man and his mother are likely Hamid's secret helpers in these dealings, as over the past two years he has often visited my neighbors. Sadiq's family used to live in poverty, always scraping for food, year by year, little by little, slowly selling me pieces of their property. This was their sole source of income. It has been a year since they suddenly began to live well, and Sadiq even got married recently. I only thought that the young man had finally found his path in life, but now I understand that Hamid married him off!" said Usta Alim and then asked Otabek, "Weren't you just saying that you saw Hamid leaving my neighbor's yard?"

Otabek nodded in confirmation and took a long nervous breath. In fact, Usta Alim's last question had caused him great agitation. He searched for an appropriate response to this vicious enemy who had poisoned all his past days and tainted his happiness. This question of Usta Alim's reminded him of his prior meetings with Hamid, and he cursed his fate, which had revealed the name of his archenemy so late. Otabek understood that his life was still in great peril and that what was to come might be even more dangerous than what he had already been through.

Usta Alim was going into the kitchen to cook plov when he saw Otabek preparing to leave.

"Wait, Bek, you have already spent so much time with us, stay for another half hour and start your trip with a full stomach," he said.

Remaining where he stood in the middle of the yard, Otabek excused himself. "Thank you, Usta, but I have to depart immediately to catch up with my goods, which were shipped out this morning."

"I will be offended if you leave without trying my plov. They say if you can manage forty minutes, you can take on the forty-first."

"Please sit, please sit, guest," Usta Farfi chimed in. "If the carrots are in the plov, it means that it is almost ready."

"I have eaten Usta Alim's plov many times. If my trade continues to do well, I will be here once every fifteen days and Usta Alim will be tired of me," said Otabek and made his way toward the orchard where his horse was tied.

Usta Alim was busy by the stove.

"I will not insist, but if you become hungry on the road, blame yourself," he said.

Otabek entered the orchard, cleaned his horse, and started putting a saddle on it; meanwhile somebody was watching his every move, peeking out from behind the half-ruined wall of the neighboring yard. Whether Otabek was aware of this secret observer or not, he continued adjusting the saddle without looking in that direction. When he led his horse by its reins toward the gate, the head of the watching person disappeared behind the wall.

Otabek left his horse in the middle of the yard, took his saddlebag and fur coat from the veranda, and parted from Usta Farfi. As Safi led the horse through the gate, Usta Alim saw Otabek off to the street and helped him mount the horse with a friendly reproach: "Remember, Bek, that you are leaving without trying my plov."

Otabek asked, making himself comfortable in the saddle, "Are you really offended?"

"Why would I be offended? I sympathize with you because you will get hungry on the road."

"I understand I will be famished on the road, Usta," said Otabek, "but I promised the camel drivers that I would meet them in Andijon today. If I do not reach them and pay them for their travel expenses, I will have knowingly forced five people to go hungry, all for the pleasure of plov."

Releasing the reins of Otabek's horse from his grasp, Usta Alim asked, "Will you give me your word that you will visit when you pass through Andijon again?"

"Certainly," said Otabek. "Prepare for me within these fifteen days at least two reams of your best silk. And please don't forget!"

"I will remember. Don't worry."

"All right, goodbye. Be safe, Safi!"

The black horse took to the road at the urgent double snap of the riding crop on its hindquarters, disappearing from sight in a flash. As Usta Alim entered his house after making his farewells to Otabek, the door of Jannat opa's house opened, quietly letting out Sadiq with a horse led by the reins. He quickly mounted the horse and Hamid, who remained on the other side of the gates, ordered, "Hurry up!"

Sadiq set his horse on Otabek's trail...

Meanwile, Usta Alim sat down at the edge of his veranda. "Our guest has an interesting character," he said.

Usta Farfi asked, "What is your relationship with your guest?"

"Do you remember I told you that, a year and a half ago, a young man lost his way in the city at night and I met him at Hamid's front gates? And that I invited him to be a guest in my home and to stay overnight?"

"Yes, yes—is that the same young man?"

"Yes, the very same. Since then, whenever he comes to Margilan, or while passing on his way to Andijon, he stays at my house. He is a very serious and especially clever young man. With some interesting character traits," he said.

"In which way, interesting?" asked Usta Farfi.

"Very interesting, very unusual," said Usta Alim, relaying the events of the previous night. "Yesterday, for example, he went out for a walk in town and had promised to return by lunchtime. I had dumplings and plov waiting for him at the agreed upon time, but he never showed up! Finally he arrived, just before you did. When I asked him where he had been, he said he had stayed overnight in the Khodja Ma'oz's cemetery. His eyes were sunken, he looked exhausted after a sleepless night... very interesting man, indeed!"

"He seems like a nice young man," said Usta Farfi.

As they finished eating their plov, the sound of the *azan*[305] calling for Friday prayers echoed from all directions. That left them with no time to drink their tea. Usta Farfi left earlier for Friday prayers than Usta Alim did, and, as he left Usta Alim's yard, he met with Hamid, who by coincidence crossed his path.

"Oh, Farfi Ota, what business brings you here?" asked Hamid.

"I have been visiting with Usta Alim."

"Then you must have had a lavish table!"

"In fact, it was!" answered Usta Farfi, smiling. "Usta Alim finished building a workshop in his house, and I came to bless it for him so that it did not lean to the side."

"Is that so?" said Hamid, and they continued to walk together.

"So, you say that Usta Alim built a loom in his own house?"

"He has built a workshop worthy of a *ziyofat*."[306]

"Without first providing blessings to the spirit of craftsmen?"

"He will do so in the winter," said Usta Farfi. There was a long pause in their conversation.

"He must have made plov?"

"Certainly."

"Was there another guest too?" asked Hamid.

Usta Farfi then remembered that Otabek had met Hamid before. "There was one guest who is a trader from Tashkent," he said.

They were close to the mosque. Thinking again, Hamid was going to ask something else, but Usta Farfi hurriedly turned toward the mosque's entrance.

14

ON THE TRAIL OF THE ENEMY

The crescent moon barely peeked through the clouds, sparkling and shining. The streets were dead quiet—everyone was in the mosque, offering up the last prayer of the day, *khuftan*. The silence itself seemed to be an ally of the stranger who stopped by the gates of Usta Alim's house. The stranger hid in the shadows of the rooftop and, remaining unseen, waited for some time, then gently opened the door and eased himself through the passageway. Again, he remained still on the inside of the doorway and, with the same gentleness with which he had opened the door, he closed it.

The slanted cone of the moonlight falling on the passageway illuminated only part of it. The stranger walked on tiptoes, avoiding the lit area and peeking into the yard. A candle shone in the niche of the veranda, casting its light on Safi, who was busy laying out beds for the evening. The stranger, keeping to the shadows of the passageway, stared at Safi, not taking his eyes off him. Once Safi had completed making the beds, he picked up the tablecloth and the serving plate from the edge of the veranda and entered the room. The person hiding in the passageway waited for this moment and, again on tiptoe, made his way into the yard...

The leaves had fallen already and the bare trees of the orchard were bathed in misty moonlight. The intruder's face emerged from the shadows as he clung closely to the ruined house. It was easy to recognize the same young man who had fallen prey to treachery and cruelty and who now prepared for the last great struggle...

Standing near the wall of the ruined house, Otabek put his ear against the wall and listened, focusing all his senses on the stirrings in the next yard. One could discern the sounds of wood being chopped, the crackling of the burning flames, and, at times, the sound of a female voice. Once or twice, Otabek moved along the wall, looking for the right spot to jump over it and into the neighbor's yard. He found a break in the middle of the wall through which he could enter. And stopped next to it, leaning forward, as he suddenly heard approaching footsteps, which forced him to nearly lie down on the ground. The sound of the footsteps died down. He recognized the voice of Usta Alim and concluded that the master had returned from evening prayers and, since there was a possibility that Usta Alim might come to the yard, Otabek continued to lie there, unmoving.

The moments ground slowly past as he counted his heartbeats. Autumn's harsh wind penetrated his lungs, making him want to cough. Otabek lay on his back, pressing a handkerchief to his mouth, and looked up at the sky, as if waiting for help from above.

An hour and a half passed in this manner. Somewhere, roosters made their first calls and, at that moment, the sounds of several footsteps were heard from the side of the ruined yard, making Otabek rise a little to hear them. Indistinct voices that seemed to come from the direction of the gates were replaced by the creaking of doors and then they faded away completely.

Still clinging to the wall, Otabek carefully raised himself up. Through the break in the wall, he could see the veranda on the opposite side of the yard and a fire burning in the stove. The voices of several people speaking in the house could now be clearly heard.

Carefully, so as not to topple the half-ruined wall, he climbed on top of it and easily slid inside the dilapidated construction. Since the roof of the house had caved in and, in some places, had come down altogether, the open space in front of it was rather wide. He took three or four cautious steps, stooped near the sunken doors, and carefully looked into the yard. Both of the shutters on the windows in the house across the yard were closed, but candlelight crept out through a cracked door, and one could hear soft murmurings. After fifteen minutes, the voice became louder. At that moment, a small woman holding a serving platter in her hand stepped out of the house and started ladling something onto a plate. When the woman returned to the house with a full plate, Otabek took a knife out from under his clothes, looked at its sharpness in the moonlight, put his knife hand behind his back, and continued to listen to the sounds coming from the house. The woman came out again, ladled food into bowls, took them back into the house, and returned to the stove once more. Finally, she finished her business, went back into the house, and closed the door behind her.

Otabek stepped into the middle of the yard, near the mulberry tree, and looked about to see if anyone was in the southern corner. Satisfied that he was alone, he quietly sneaked up to a window by the passageway and carefully squatted under it.

The smell of alcohol mixed with soup wafted out. Now he could not only hear the conversation of the inhabitants of the house but even discerned the smacking of their lips as they ate. Somebody spoke through the noise of munching: "I have had enough, Sadiq, pour some wine for Mutal the Mighty!"

Otabek knew the owner of this voice.

"Why do you keep filling my cup all the time? Give at least every other one to Jannat opa, too! Ha ha ha!"

"If you give it to our old woman, she will never refuse and drink it all!"

"If they pour, I will drink, Qeh... Qeh! Though I am just a woman, I can outdrink ten Mutal Palvons,[307] qeh..."

After her boasting, everyone burst out laughing and the uproar reached even Otabek outside the room. When the laughter calmed down, the talking continued.

"Now you will drink this one, Hamid-aka."

"No, Sadiqboi, my brother. I have had enough. It appears to be a very strongly made brew."

"Oh no, I will not leave you alone until you drink it up."

"Give it to Mutal Palvon. Please take it and drink it!"

"So, you refuse to drink? Even if it's to the health of my Kumush opa?"

On hearing these words, Otabek reflexively leaped up. Jannat Opa's wicked laughter could be heard.

"He-he-he."

"Had you not mentioned her beautiful name, I would not drink, as God is my witness. But to me the health and wellness of your sister Kumush is the most precious thing in the world. Pour me a cup!"

"Ha ha ha, did I hit on a delicate topic?"

Otabek, hearing this exchange, could barely stop himself from breaking down the small door and attacking the revelers. They talked some more about different trifles, and then a loud sigh was heard.

"What is it again, Hamid-aka?"

"Today's news worried me a great deal, Sadiqboi."

"Why don't you believe me? I told you a hundred times that I saw that bastard leave from the gates today. I followed him for some distance, waited for him to join the caravan, and then returned. At his pace, he will have reached Qoqan by nightfall."

"Heh, you don't know, my brother."

"From my point of view, we have nothing to worry about. He is probably acquainted with Usta Alim and stayed at his house as a guest. If he is a trader, maybe he went to Margilan on business—you heard with your own ears what he said before he left!"

"Your observations are valid, but it is hard to let go of the fact that he was a guest in the house of a man who I had a falling-out with—not to mention a neighbor of yours..."

"If Usta Alim were aware of your secret, then your fears would be justified, but, in my opinion, that bastard Otabek has forgotten that he even had a wife from Margilan."

"Nobody except you knows my secrets. I had some misunderstandings with Umarbek a little while ago, but, thank heavens, no problems remain between us."

"If that's so, why are you afraid again?"

"I fear that his departure to Tashkent is only a ruse to pull the wool over our eyes."

"All right, let's say he has not departed. In that case, I will go to Salim Sharbatdor tomorrow, as we agreed, and explain that the former Tashkentlik son-in-law of Mirza Karim murdered his son and I saw it with my own eyes. He can eat the earth, lamenting his loss! If he had known your secret machinations already, he would have run away from Margilan with his tail between his legs."

"Qeh... Sadiq's words make sense," said Jannat opa. Otabek shivered with horror at these words.

Sadiq continued, "Now we should give our attention to the matters at hand. Upon witnessing your cowardliness, even Mutal Palvon has dozed off."

"I am not sleeping, you impudent fool. Pour me some more of your potion!"

"Mutalboi, my friend," said Hamid. "We are not the sort who forget someone's kindness. Your friend Sadiqboi was on my side and I returned the favor, so now, with God's help first and mine second, he is married... If I become friends with someone, I take him to heart and sacrifice my life for him."

Sadiq chimed in, "Mutalboi knows you very well, Hamid-aka! He knows what kind of service he has to do for you... but he has something to ask of you too..."

Hamid's voice: "What sort of request do you have for me, Mutalboi?"

Mutal's drunken voice stretched out the words: "I n-e-e-e-d to repay a loan of three or four tengas I bo-o-o-rrowed from someone, Ha-a- a-mid-aka."

Hamid's voice: "Our friendship will not falter on only three or four tengas, Mutalboi. As I said to you before, I will sacrifice my life for friendship. If you need, you can ask for thirty or forty as well!"

Jannat Opa put in a word. "Let Hamidboi be successful in his deeds with God's help, qeh. He will sacrifice the whole world for the sake of his friends!"

For some time, the clinking of coins could be heard. Then Hamid's voice rang out: "Here, take this for now, Mutal Palvon. Though it is not much, your services will be generously compensated."

The drunken voice replied, "Th-th-thank you, H-Hamid-a-aka. If you sacrifice your life for me, I will give my head to save you, I swear by Jamshed the Bold!"[308]

"Our Mutalboi is a worthy young man as well!" said Sadiq. "Will you clear the tablecloth, Jannat opa?" interrupted Hamid.

The sound of cups and plates clinking was heard and, without a sound, Otabek made his way to the passageway leading to the gates. Jannat opa appeared at the stove, clattered tableware for a minute, then walked down into the yard, shook the tablecloth under the mulberry tree, and returned to the room.

But as soon as Otabek took his post at the window again, he heard Hamid say, "Will you check the chain on the door? Bless you, Jannat opa!"

Sadiq said, "You are overly afraid, Hamid-aka. I set the chain on the door myself."

"You are still young, my brother Sadiqboi," answered Hamid. "Please go out and check, Jannat opa!"

It was a terrible moment for Otabek. He did not have time to hide in the ruined house—Jannat opa would notice him.

Yet if he fled through the gates, all his present suffering would have been in vain and he wouldn't find out what his enemies had planned against him. Taking short gasps, he looked around and his eyes fell on a wheelbarrow leaning against the wall shared with Usta Alim's yard, a little farther up the passage. Though it was a dangerous gambit to hide under the upturned wheelbarrow, it was far more dangerous to leave without divining the full nature of their conversation. If discovered, he decided he would be ready to fight three enemies at once. As soon as he hid himself under the wheelbarrow, the door to the outside opened. Though he balled himself up the best he could, it would not have been difficult to see a grown man in such a confined space. With knife in hand, he crouched down, like a cat ready to spring on a mouse.

Jannat opa came forward to check the chain, completely unaware of the man under the wheelbarrow. It was clear to her at a distance in the moonlight that the chain was in place. For that reason, she only went halfway down the passage and turned back. Suddenly the cries of herons[309] flying rang out in the sky above. Jannat opa looked up into the dark sky and, watching the birds fly past, straight as an arrow, toward the northeast, she walked past the wheelbarrow and back to the house. When she reached the veranda, the wheelbarrow was a hand's width above the ground—it was Otabek putting it back in place. As soon as she opened the door to enter the house, he carefully approached the window with closed shutters. His heart was still racing in his chest; he was prepared to defend himself if necessary. Upon hearing Jannat opa say, "The door is chained," he calmed down and settled under the window.

Hamid's voice resounded: "Then let it be on Monday night."

Sadiq answered, "We are ready to act on whatever day you decide."

"As for me, I am ready right now," replied Mutal.

Hamid said, "It is better on Monday. No earlier, no later, as we need one or two days for preparations."

"What else is there to prepare for?" asked Sadiq.

Hamid replied, "After kidnapping her, it will be impossible to hide her in Margilan. We should send her to one of the villages until she gets used to her situation. It's also impossible to tell in advance the right time to seize her on Monday. If we do not take her out of Margilan immediately, it will be very dangerous to attempt it during the day. We all know that Margilan closes its gates at night. For that reason, we should bribe one of the gate guards. No doubt we need to...!"

"Good thinking," said Sadiq. "How will we infiltrate Qutidor's house?"

Hamid answered, "We still have to think about this part of the operation."

Sadiq said, "The best way is to enter through the gates."

Mutal replied, "If it is impossible to enter through the gates, we will go in over the roof!"

Sadiq laughed. "Ha ha ha, what an idea, Mutal my boss!"

Mutal answered, "Do not mock me, you impudent *Abdikarim!*[310] What have you experienced in this world? And yet you laugh! And my poor head has experienced a lot in this world! You think your brother has just now embarked upon a life of crime? He-he, your brother Mutal has done much more serious business! We are all Muslims but not all without sin, isn't that true, Hamid-aka, ha ha ha! There is a saying: A true Muslim remains faithful even to his father's ghost. So, hear me out! One day, Jon

Kildiboi confessed to me that he had fallen in love with the son of Khotan Tura, so much so that he had lost his mind and could not take his eyes off the boy. I was with Qalandar Palvon at the time. I said to Jon Kildi, 'Give us ten tengas and we, along with Qalandar, will bring your beloved to you, still warm.'

"Jon Kildi was dying for the boy, so he immediately took out the money and said 'Agreed!' Together with Qalandar we waited until night, then came to the house of Khotan Tura. We racked our brains trying to figure out how to get in. The walls were made of stone and too tall to climb over. Assessing the situation, Qalandar ranted, as if he were breaking a watermelon on the ground. 'It is indeed a pity to give back five tengas.'

"Being a little drunk, I took my dagger from its sheath and banged on the gate of Khotan Tura's house. Qalandar's soul dropped into his feet—he went crazy from fear—and he started pulling me away, saying, 'Hey, Mutal, what is the matter with you?'

"And I kept banging and calling out to Khotun Tura, saying to Qalandar only, 'Silence, you cowardly bitch!' Qalandar became unhinged and fled in fear. Finally, from behind the gates, Khotan Tura called out, 'Who's there?' I gave an urgent tone to my voice. 'It's me, open up, open up, hurry!' Imagine it, this simpleton Tura opened the gate. I rushed in, seized his hand, and dragged him through the yard. The wretch finally recognized me and realized there was trouble. I put a knife to his throat and said, 'Do you want to live, you dishonest scoundrel?'

"That unfit Humza's[311] tongue swelled from the shock. He could barely mumble, 'I do, I do!' I said to him, 'Now here's the deal, while you have a good night's sleep here next to your son, a poor young man pines with love for him, rolling on bare earth... Now, where is your son, show me the place where he lies, warm and snug!'

"Khotan Tura quaked in horror. His knees buckled to such a degree that I had to help him to the veranda myself and make him show me where his son was. I had just dressed the boy for the road, sleep still in his eyes, when his mother started to wail. Baring my knife to her, I screamed out, 'Shut your mouth, you stupid donkey! I am not escorting your son to his death. He will only drink one cup of tea and then return!'

"In short, I initially visited them with terror, then consoled them with honeyed words and convinced them I meant no harm. I then gave the boy into the loving arms of Jon Kildi... Fortunately, that night I had no run-ins with the police. Hey, Sadiq-cha, what do you think now? You think you cut one or two people like weeds and that means you have become a man? Ugh, I have gone on for too long and my good mood has drifted away! Pour me some more cups!"

Hamid said, "I sit in admiration of your exploits, Mutal Palvon. As I am fully aware of your prowess, that's why I called upon you and brought you here!"

Mutal answered, "If you know this, that's enough. Let me run this job."

"I don't want to enter through the gates as Sadiq suggests, because that place is often patrolled by police," said Hamid.

"Then we'll have to get in through the backyard!"

"Is there a yard behind Qutidor's house?"

Jannat joined in: "Qeh... that... damn his name... that's the yard of Malikboi!"

"That's advantageous. Would a ladder reach the roof?" asked Hamid. "Qeh, it's too high."

"If it is high, that is no matter. The easiest way is to make a hole in the outside wall, that's all we need!" said Mutal.

"Would it not be too difficult?" Hamid asked.

"The easiest way of all is to dig a hole. We just need to dig the right path."

"Can we make a hole in one or two hours?"

"And what is there? An empty yard?" asked Mutal.

"Qeh, it is an empty yard..."

Mutal asked, "Are there people nearby?"

"No, qeh."

Mutal concluded: "Very well. In that case, say the word and I will start digging tomorrow."

"You are brave. Thank you, Palvon," both Sadiq and Hamid replied.

When the conversation reached this conclusion, Otabek moved from his place over to the gates. Already reaching out to remove the chain, he paused in consideration and went back. Through the half-ruined wall, he climbed into Usta Alim's yard, walked past the veranda where Usta and Safi were sleeping, made sure they were snoring peacefully, tiptoed across the yard, opened the gate, and walked out into the street.

As we heard from his own mouth, Sadiq, following Hamid's directions, had spotted Otabek leaving the city through the Qoqan Gates and had pursued him until he joined the caravan.

Otabek, instinctively aware of his pursuer, had moved on to another caravanserai when Sadiq seemed to have given up the chase, and then turned around and reentered Margilan through the Toshlok Gates.

On hearing the terrible stories relayed to him by Usta Farfi about Hamid's crimes, instead of remaining in Margilan to clear up the misunderstanding with his father-in-law, Otabek created the illusion that he had made a hasty departure from Margilan, which was the right decision. To remain within eyesight of Hamid after Kamilbek had been murdered would be like signing his own death sentence. Even worse than digging his own grave, he would lose all semblance of honor, get labeled as a murderer and held in derision by the local population. Hamid would not only slander him but would be able to logically prove his accusations in a court of law.

Otabek understood this danger and initially fled Margilan to avoid it. He had realized he was being followed earlier when he noticed a person peeking his head over the wall while he was putting a saddle on his horse. The shadow of a man standing behind the neighbor's gates when Otabek bid farewell to Usta Alim confirmed his suspicions.

Arriving at the second caravan station from Margilan, he had emptied a couple pots of tea so that he had time to consider returning to the city, even though it meant a possible threat to his life. Otabek could not reconcile himself with the idea that Hamid would achieve his victory, and he resolved to remain hidden in Margilan in order to learn Hamid's future plans and adapt his tactics to those machinations. Therefore, he stole into Margilan at twilight, between evening prayers and nightfall, settled in at the caravanserai where he had stayed during his first visit to Margilan, and decided to begin his pursuit immediately. Since Otabek was convinced that the den where Hamid had made his devilish plans was in Alim's neighbor's house, he made his way directly to Sadiq's house.

Once he had left Usta Alim's yard, he had listened a little to a loud conversation in Sadiq's yard and then slowly took a route back to the caravanserai.

He was content with the day's success and, since the final day of reckoning with his enemy was settled, his mind focused only on Monday night. He considered the upcoming struggle with not one but three enemies. The issue of these unfavorable odds made him consider his tactics carefully. He thought of hiring mercenaries, of informing the government, or even of making the plot known to Qutidor, but his honor rebelled against these cowardly options. He abandoned these thoughts as quickly as they arrived.

Fighting his enemies alone behind his beloved's house, destroying his rival and even dying almost at his love's feet seemed to him a more poetic and fitting end. Entering the caravanserai, he said to himself, half-aloud, "If I die, it will be a sweet death."

Although he had not slept well in Khodja Ma'oz's cemetery the night before, he lay awake for a long while, turning over again and again in his mind the words he had overheard that day. As he drifted to sleep, he dreamed of himself simultaneously lying in a pool of his own spilled blood, and in Kumush's arms, loving her forever.

15

MONDAY NIGHT

That day's dark night embraced in its black arms the balance of Otabek's and Hamid's lives and deaths. Which one of them had reached his last hours remained as impenetrable as the night that surrounded them. If Otabek's imagination was filled with battle scenes and he was preparing himself accordingly, Hamid's thoughts were of partaking of the sweet smells of the delicate flower, anticipating a stroll in the blossoming garden...

A narrow, perhaps half a yard in width but infinitely long side street ended at a small gate. Between evening and night prayers on Monday, our main character arrived at the beginning of the side street, stopping to stealthily survey the area. Nobody walked the streets at that hour, no footsteps could be heard. Still, Otabek took his time to observe the neighboring gates, the surrounding rooftops, the cracks in the walls, and, satisfied with the situation, slowly, slowly he stole along the narrow alleyway. Reaching the halfway point of the alley, suddenly he spun around to look behind him... He moved out of habit—not suspecting anything in particular, but to confirm that no one was following him.

Reaching the small gates, he checked behind him with the same nervous movement, stopped to consider the situation, and lifted himself over a gap in the mud wall to look over the yard. Although the door was not locked or chained, he did not dare enter through it, instead choosing to hoist himself over the wall. The night was in full reign after the last prayers, but the moon was already high and the yard had no trees growing in it, making it easy to discern even the sharp silhouette of a twig. Confident there was no one there, he slowly lowered himself down from the wall and walked into the yard.

The width of the square yard was about two *tanob*.[312] The southern section consisted of Qutidor's property and the back of his neighbor's house, and the other three walls were also backed by buildings. Something had been planted that summer in the clearing's soil. Deep rows had been dug for seedlings and the earthen mounds had become soaked with rain, making it impossible to walk freely; a mass of mud clung to Otabek's feet with each step. With great difficulty, he moved to the southern section of the square.

On the left side of the southern wall, a break the size of a prayer rug formed a hole in stark contrast to the stucco wall. Since he had already seen the tunnel from his surveillance the night before, he did not care to review the work, but it was impossible to remain indifferent as he passed by it. There, behind the bored-out opening, was Kumush's private room. Bek's memory still held sweet recollections of the most joyous days he had spent there. And at this very moment, the light of his life—Kumush Bibi—was lying there. Eyes widening, Otabek took in the building, as if expressing a final farewell to his angel. Having stared at the building for some time, he took out a letter from his pocket, read it dreamily, and tucked it under his arm again.

He looked at the house one final time, then walked about five steps from the tunnel toward the western section of the yard, where a mudhole, a quarry to provide mud for the repair of a roof, had been dug out. During his last visit, he had decided upon this as his hiding place. He crawled into the hole and lay down, with his hand propping up the back of his head. The tunnel and the ditch where Otabek lay were very close to each other, but the pitch-blackness of the night and the shadows of buildings cast by the moonlight made it impossible to see someone hiding in the muddy ditch.

*****

It was midnight and everyone lay sleeping soundly in their beds.

The gate to the narrow alleyway opened and, one by one, two shadows entered. Noticing the interlopers, Otabek unsheathed his knife and, while holding it fast, lay facedown in the earth... Silently, the two shadows crept forward and halted near the building with the dug-out tunnel. One of the unwelcome guests was Sadiq and the other, Mutal. Otabek observed them like a crouched cat stalking its prey.

When they stopped, Sadiq whispered, "Is the hole almost finished?"

"I reckon a small amount remains to be dug out. We removed approximately one meter."

Mutal spoke in a normal voice, as if they were out on the street. For that reason, Sadiq hushed him, "Speak quieter, fool!"

Mutal took a trowel from his belt, saying, "Does even this scare you?

Perhaps I will sing a song!"

"Don't be insane, Mutal-aka! Shall I remain nearby?"

"Whether you stay or not is up to you."

Mutal, climbing into the tunnel, started to dig. "Don't dig too hard with the trowel," said Sadiq. "Don't lecture me. I know what I am doing."

Sadiq seemed concerned about Mutal's carelessness. He watched Mutal work for some moments, then said, "I will go stand near the gate... As soon as you have breached the wall, whistle to me as a signal."

"Fine! Where is the bridegroom Hamid?"

"He must be waiting at the entrance to the alleyway. Shall I call him when I hear your whistle?"

"Call him!" said Mutal, and lumps of earth erupted from the tunnel.

When Sadiq walked through the doorway, Otabek raised his head and slowly, gradually crawled along the earth toward Mutal. As for Mutal, he remained oblivious and was busy dropping rocks from the tunnel onto the wet earth... The moment he rotated to pick up another rock, arms reached around him, squeezing his throat. Mutal struggled fiercely, but Otabek was more powerful than him. Mutal attempted to free the hand from his throat, but all went to waste as a short blade sunk into the left side of his back with the sound of "Gracha..."

Mutal kept up the fight and continued to try to free himself from the overwhelmingly powerful hand that crushed his windpipe. After a short struggle, Mutal slackened, ceased resisting, shivered one or two times, and gave up his life. Otabek's eyes remained fixed on the gate as he dragged Mutal toward the mud ditch where he had hidden himself previously and, cautiously taking his hand from around his victim's throat, he pushed him down. Mutal's head dropped heavily to the muddy ground, and he did not move, having drifted off to eternal sleep...

Otabek moved back to the tunnel and whistled. Hearing the corresponding whistle from the gate he hid in the dark hole and crouched down, poised for violence. At the end of the tunnel a small hole was now visible from Mutal's digging and the soft cooing of someone sleeping met his ears... Sadiq approached but remained a little removed from the entrance and whispered, "Did you make the breach, Mutal?"

"Yes, I did. Come here."

Still nearer, Sadiq bowed to enter the narrow opening to the tunnel and as he did so, a hand shot out, grasping his throat as a knife sank into his stomach...

Still alive, Sadiq swung his own knife in a wide arc a couple of times. The low wall shielded his attacker. Otabek sprung up and out of the hole and with all his power pinned Sadiq to the ground...

All his weight pressing him down, it seemed that a distant pain appeared somewhere on Otabek's body. His left hand was on Sadiq's throat; his right hand, holding the knife, was held in check by Sadiq's opposite hand, which held its own blade...

Gathering all his power, he squeezed the throat with all his might. Sadiq gasped but refused to drop his knife. From the doorway Hamid appeared... The air hung heavy with tension... time stood still...

Turning Sadiq to the side, Otabek freed up his right hand and stabbed Sadiq in the chest. Sadiq's knife responded by attempting to lash out once or twice, to no effect, and its attacks became weaker and weaker. Upon the second strike, Sadiq lay limp and the knife dropped from his hand.

"You made a great sacrifice for your brother Hamid, Sadiq!" said Otabek. "You gave your whole life for him."

Sadiq only murmured in a dead, flat voice.

"Who is that over there?" asked Hamid, moving closer.

"Come quicker, quicker, Hamid-aka. We killed Otabek!" said Otabek urgently, in a muffled voice.

"Aha!" said Hamid, moving more quickly toward Otabek. Otabek left Sadiq behind and caught Hamid by his knife hand.

"Mutal is dead. Sadiq is on the edge of death as well. Now only you and I remain!"

Hamid attempted to free his hand, but Otabek held him fast, saying to him with a menacing calm, "Hurry no more, Hamidboi. I will let go of your knife hand. But first, I have a couple of words to say to you."

Hamid still struggled to free his hand. "Don't struggle, Hamidboi."

"If you are a man, little boy, let go of my hand!"

"Don't rush. I will let it go when I am ready," said Otabek. At that moment, Sadiq, who lay at their feet, began to convulse. Otabek guided Hamid a little farther from Sadiq. Hamid resisted, but, pointing his knife to the mouth of the tunnel, Otabek started to question him.

"Indeed, you, better than me, know that the person sleeping in this house has put you through great difficulty. That person deceived you into enacting limitless trickery, made you spend endless gold coins, and brought you to this moment of final failure.

"If the declaration of divorce—supposedly written on my behalf—is proven false, the person sleeping in that room is still my legal wife. For two years, I have been driven mad with love for her. Therefore, our struggle is really about this person. Until this moment, you won victory after victory over me: had me placed under the noose, had me labeled a black robe, had me handed into the clutches of Musulmanqul. Yet when these efforts were all in vain, you wrote a declaration of divorce on my behalf and succeeded in separating me from my wife for two years. Meanwhile, you murdered an innocent man. Finally, you have taken the road of a kidnapper. And you produced two dead men, slain by my own hands... Can you answer me now? Were you in the right to conduct these evil acts?"

"I was right!" said Hamidboi, as he pulled his knife hand free of Otabek's grasp and stumbled onto his back. Seizing the moment, Otabek flung himself on Hamid, dealing him a decisive wound. As Hamid lay, life ebbing from his body, Otabek stood five paces from him, observing his death. And at last he asked, in a voice flowing with sarcasm:

"Were you right?"

Struggling for life, Hamid replied "I was right!" and he flung his knife at Otabek, though it only fell ineffectually at his feet...

As Otabek moved from the scene of slaughter toward the alleyway, a slow moan could be heard from where Sadiq lay, five or six footsteps from Hamid. Otabek stepped out of the small yard, his heart wracked with guilt.

16

RECOGNISING HIMSELF

Throughout the whole next morning and well into the day, the events that had occurred in Malikboi's square were on everyone's lips:

"Mutal and Sadiq dug a tunnel and attempted a kidnapping. Perhaps they intended to burrow left into Qutidor house... but

Hamid is well known as one of the city's wealthiest traders, why would he... Fine, let's relegate Hamid to the role of a thief, but who killed them? This is most peculiar."

As for Qutidor, once he woke in the morning, he understood the source of the previous night's events immediately. The clock struck noon and Otabek finally made his way out from the caravanserai. His left hand was bound in a white bandage and his arm was in a sling. The night before, when Hamid's knife hand twitched in pain, he had cut a deep gash between this thumb and forefinger, down to the bone. Otabek walked with a slight limp as well.

Some distance from the serai, he saw Rahmat, who approached from the opposite direction, forcing Otabek to greet him.

"Hello, Mullah Rahmat, are you all right?"

Rahmat seemed pleased to see him.

"When did you return, Bek-aka?"

"I have been here for a couple of days. Why do you look so glum, Mullah Rahmat?"

Rahmat took a long, pained breath.

"Eh, Bek-aka, I would not wish the horrible events from last night on my enemy!"

Otabek feigned surprise, asking, "What happened? Are you in good health, is everyone in your family all right?"

"You know that my father passed away last year. Today, death has visited our family once again. Someone stabbed my uncle Hamid, leaving severe wounds. He is on the edge of death."

Otabek's eyes widened in surprise. "Are his wounds fatal?"

Rahmat did not dare tell the whole story and where it had happened.

"His wounds are grievous. He murmurs and fades in and out of consciousness. We attempted to suture his stomach, but the surgeon found it impossible."

"Did he say who stabbed him?"

"He would if he could communicate," said Rahmat. "There were two other corpses where he fell... I think maybe they killed him."

"May God grant him health!" said Otabek. At that, they parted company.

When Otabek turned onto Usta Alim's street, he became a bit worried at the sight of three or four men with waists wrapped in black belboq at Sadiq's door, preparing a litter for the dead. He heard the wailing and sobs of Jannat opa and another woman...

Usta Alim, preparing his ablution for Ja'noza[313] with a water pitcher, was surprised to see Shokirbek, who had so suddenly left for Tashkent three or four days ago.

"Shokirbek, weren't you in Tashkent?"

Otabek chuckled as he sat down on the veranda. "I have gone to and returned from Tashkent..."

Usta Alim appreciated the joke and, while cleaning himself, told Otabek of the recent events.

"If you had not left Margilan, you would have heard, Shokirbek, that Hamid, Sadiq, and an infamous villain named Mutal were murdered behind the yard of Mirza Karim-aka. Looks like the evildoers have met with their final judgment."

"I heard already," said Otabek, laughing again.

Oblivious to his laughter, Usta Alim asked him his views: "Who do you think murdered them?"

"Who do you think?" Otabek countered with a smile.

"As for me," said Usta Alim, "no doubt it is Mirza Karim's former son-in-law, Otabek... I admire his bravery, he committed a just act. I thank him from my heart and give thanks that Uttaboi Qushbegi granted him his freedom. He is a man among men!"

Otabek felt bashful at the compliments.

Usta Alim dried his eyes and face with a clean towel and, when he turned to shake Otabek's hand in greeting, his eyes fell on the bandage.

"What happened to your hand, Shokirbek?"

"It was cut by a knife..."

"It's a serious cut."

Usta Alim sat down near Otabek.

"Why did not you leave for Tashkent? Did an issue arise?" he asked.

"There was a problem."

"Of what kind?" said Usta Alim

"The issue?" said Otabek, grinning slightly. "I have done you a great disservice... On my way there, I felt burdened with the guilt and I turned back at Qoqan to ask you for forgiveness... If you do not relieve me of my guilt, I will return right this moment to Tashkent."

Usta Alim looked at Otabek, alarmed. "You are joking..."

"I am not joking. If you promise to forgive me, I will admit my wrongdoing right now."

Usta Alim asked, smiling, "Will you please admit your crime now?"

"First promise me that you will forgive."

"If it is truly up to me, you cannot possibly be guilty of anything in my eyes... If it is some unknown slight, I forgive you unconditionally..."

"Thank you," said Otabek and asked, "who am I?"

"You are Shokirbek, of course!"

Otabek laughed, a bit embarrassed, and said, "Usta, this is in fact my great disservice to you: that until this day you have only known me as Shokirbek!"

"Then who are you?"

"You have forgiven me my slight? Still?"

"I have."

"I am not the person you know as Shokirbek. I am Otabek, the son of Yusufbek Hajji from Tashkent and the son-in-law of Mirza Karim Aka from Margilan."

Usta Alim jumped back and rubbed his eyes. "Are you indeed?"

He walked closer and gave Otabek a bear hug... Safi, who did not understand what had transpired, kept looking out from the workshop and had ceased to work entirely. With grateful tears, Usta Alim kissed Otabek on each cheek and then lay out a blanket on the veranda.

"What are you doing, Usta?" asked Otabek.

"I am preparing for my new guest a place to sit," answered Usta Alim with a laugh.

"I have sat on your blanket many times. There is no need for you to pay me any further respect."

"You are right, Otabek. This whole time, a young man named Shokirbek has sat on my blanket. Now I intend to show newly acquired respect for my guest Otabek... Well, Otabek, take your place on the blanket."

Otabek laughed at Usta Alim's lightheartedness and sat on the blanket. At that moment, Jannat opa's sobbing could be heard. "My child died as a *shahid*!"[314] Otabek looked at Usta Alim with a guilt-stricken face and Usta Alim, in turn, understood the feelings behind such an expression.

"You have committed an honorable act, Otabek," said Usta. "This is how evil should be punished... Did you have your people with you?"

"No."

Usta Alim looked at Otabek for some time, not comprehending, and asked, "You stood alone against three enemies?"

"I was alone. One is enough if God wishes to punish the wicked."

Usta Alim was astonished.

"Sub-han-ollah—oh my God—it turns out you have a pure, brave heart, Otabek. Do you have any other wounds?"

"Not really. The tip of the knife just barely pierced my chest, though that is unimportant."

"Thanks be to God. Otabek, does your father-in-law know of your deeds?"

"No, he does not. Until this moment, only God and I knew. And now you are the third to know my secret."

"Astaghfurallah—unbelievable!" exclaimed Usta Alim. "Did you discover that Hamid was your true enemy from Usta Farfi's tale?"

"For the very first time, I finally understood the source of my travails," said Otabek, letting out a breath. "I have no words to express my thankfulness for your friendship. You helped me understand."

"My heart is astonished at your unbelievable courage! Otabek, how did you learn of Hamid's final plans?"

Otabek laughed.

"Many thanks to God who sent me Hamid's secret or all my suffering would have been in vain. Shall I tell you my story from the beginning or only how I knew of Hamid's plan?"

"From the beginning, from the beginning, Otabek!" Usta Alim exclaimed and ordered Safi to chop carrots instead of weaving.

When he saw that Usta Alim had settled in, Otabek said, "Perhaps you forgot the purpose of your ablution."

"I have not forgotten, Otabek. It seems more fitting to hear the tale of a good man's acts than to attend the funeral of a rotten man... So, tell me the story then!"

Otabek burst out with a stream of words relaying to his best friend the whole story, starting with his first visit to Margilan. All the adventures over the past three years took only an hour to tell and he finished the voyage with his encounter with Rahmat just as Safi brought the plov. Usta Alim patted him on the shoulder and said, "You have a courageous heart, my friend. Your heart will never fail you, never cause you distress, but I cannot blame you for not revealing your name to me. I am only upset that you entered my yard while on Hamid's trail without informing me of your intentions—what would have happened if some unforeseen disaster had befallen you? God bless and protect you."

Usta Alim recited a prayer after they had eaten plov: "May your enemies always fall. May you live long and happily with your beloved."

Otabek thanked him and they drank some tea together. Then Otabek took two letters out of his satchel and said, "If it wouldn't be a bother to you, I am going to ask you for a favor, Usta!"

"Order it!"

Otabek gave him the letter in his hand. "I have to leave this very hour to return to Tashkent. Can you please deliver these letters to my father-in-law with your own hands?"

Usta Alim did not understand the request.

"Why are you leaving for Tashkent? Why can't you yourself..."

"It is impossible to deliver them myself because... it is uncomfortable for both sides. I have to go right now, maybe you can understand."

"I understand," said Usta. "So, you will come back when the rumors quiet down a bit?"

"Perhaps..." said Otabek, stopping. "One of the letters is addressed to my father-in-law, the second one is for her."

"All right."

"What I wrote my father-in-law is to the point. Maybe you can explain more to him and pass on what you have heard from me?

And as soon as you finish with Qutidor, please give her this letter. Can you do that?"

"I accept."

"You would make me most grateful to you if you would write me a letter telling me how the meeting went."

"With pleasure."

After this they parted, giving each other warm hugs and saying farewell. When Otabek stepped outside, the people who had buried Sadiq were just spreading out to their own houses, murmuring passages from the Quran.

17

THE SYMPATHETIC MURDERER

Qutidor was detained and taken to the police station for questioning by the qorboshi's representatives. When he appeared in the passageway, Oftob Oyim and Kumush were revitalized, having sat stewing in a thousand worries. Kumush ran to her father, spreading her arms for a hug like a bird spreading its wings. Stroking his beard, she asked, "Did they harm you in any way, dear Father?"

"No, my daughter."

On hearing her husband's words, Oftob Oyim gave the seven tengas she had been saving for a *waqf* donation[315] to the shrine of Khodja Bauhaddin to Toibeka and sent her to the Ishon's[316] house. Then she asked her husband, "They did not blame you for the murder?"

"Thank God, I was exonerated," said Qutidor. "Why on earth would I be accused? We only learned of the scandal after waking up. Though the tunnel was dug through the foundation of our house, the fact that it was not large enough for me to pass through proved my innocence. Even if it had been big enough for a man, those guilty cowards who dug the hole showed evil intentions. They intended to take our property and life. Even if they did find me guilty of murdering those burglars, I would have been justified.

For defending my life and property, I would have been blameless. Anyway, this tragedy marked us with no real harm so we must be thankful to God," he said.

Making himself comfortable near the tancha, he asked Kumush, "Has your grandmother arrived yet?"

Oftob Oyim answered, "She fell ill," and then asked, "do you know who murdered them?"

Qutidor looked at his wife, surprised.

"You ask a bizarre question!" he said. "The whole city has been caught off guard by this insanity. Investigators who can split a hair into forty pieces cannot reach a conclusion... My heart tells me that the original interlopers were five or six men with evil intentions toward our property; while they were digging the tunnel, a disagreement arose between them and they went for one another's throats."

Kumush disagreed with this theory.

"You are not being entirely truthful with us."

"Why do you say that I am not being truthful?"

"Because having turned on one another, they would not have fled, would not have left us alone."

"Maybe it was near morning and they were fatigued from their efforts," said Qutidor in reply.

"What part would Hamid have in this, then? Wasn't he rich enough?" asked Oftob Oyim. Kumush cast a slight glance at her mother.

"Hamid was a dissolute young man," Qutidor replied. "Perhaps all his wealth came from theft. It is difficult to judge someone's character by their wealth alone."

"Thank God," said Kumush, both relieved and terrified, "God has punished evil with his own hand. What would have happened to me if the thieves had succeeded in breaching a hole into my room? Oh, dear Father, I would have died five days before the time of death prescribed to me by God.[317] You would have been separated from your daughter forever... I would have been in a deep sleep, and they would have cut the hole near where my head lay. I would not have noticed a thing."

Oftob Oyim said, shaking her head, "That is my point exactly, my daughter!"

285

Qutidor answered, "God has been visiting bloody events upon us during these past days and nights. When we agreed on a date for your engagement to Kamilbek, he was murdered at the bathhouse."

A spark of recognition appeared on Kumush Bibi's face.

"Yesterday, behind our house, not one, but three people were killed. Let God's blessings end with this act..."

"Inshallah. The conclusion of these deeds would be a blessing, dear Father," said Kumush. "The defeat of the tunnellers behind our house— with their evil wishes and their dark eyes focused on our property—is a blessing for your future, dear Father!"

"You have spoken wisely, my daughter," said Qutidor.

Kumush continued to rattle on breathlessly: "But, who are those left murdered behind our house, why did they wish us ill will? Not to mention, who defeated them, mixed them with the earth, who is the murderer who wanted to keep us safe, or were they just killers...? Who is the person that watched over us? Let God award his good deeds!"

Qutidor agreed fully with his daughter's observations.

"If they intended us ill, God punished them accordingly. Perhaps he will award those who are sympathetic to us as well," he said.

Kumush decided that she could no longer live in her room. Oftob Oyim ordered Toibeka to move Kumush's belongings to the next room. As for Qutidor, he was busy all day with visitors and close friends, who all asked about his health and wealth.

After evening prayers, Qutidor freed himself from his guests and entered his house. Toibeka, who was cleaning the guest room, came to him and said, "Somebody is calling for you."

"Who is it? Do you recognize him?"

"No, I do not recognize him."

Qutidor went out slowly and coldly greeted the unfamiliar person sitting in his guest room: "What can I do for you?"

Usta Alim smiled at Qutidor.

"I beg your pardon for entering your guest room without warning you in advance," he said.

"You are not to blame, Mullah," said Qutidor, as they sat opposite each other.

"Congratulations on your escape from the blades of your enemies."

"Let's give thanks to God," said Qutidor.

As the inside of the room dimmed, he called to Toibeka, who was nearby, cleaning the yard, "Toibeka, please light a candle for us." Usta Alim sat with a bowed head as he waited for the candle to be lit. Qutidor looked at him with a questioning glance as if to say again, "What can I do for you?" He was amused by this strange man who sat as if he were listening to the Quran. Finally, after the candle stood on the shelf, casting its light, Usta Alim raised his head as if from deep meditation and looked at Qutidor.

"My sudden appearance must be off-putting," he said, taking one of the letters from inside his robe and passing it to Qutidor. "Perhaps this letter will surprise you even more."

Qutidor looked at the heading of the letter, cracked the seal, and then opened it with a look of alarm, as Usta Alim had predicted. Having finished reading the letter, he turned still as a stone column, simultaneously horrified and stunned.

If Usta Alim had not been sitting next to him, he would have been transported to unknown times and places.

"The bastard who was the enemy of your life and family has now received his punishment for his deeds. My friend Otabek meted out his punishment properly," said Usta Alim and then continued, "By this deed, the most terrible and tragic periods of your great family have passed away and now peaceful times are upon you again. You must take joy from this letter, not horror; you must thank God your enemies lie facedown before you."

Qutidor slowly collected his wits and let out a long, relieved breath, asking excitedly, "Was it Hamid who had Otabek and me arrested, placing the noose around our necks?"

"It was Hamid."

"Otabek did not write the declaration of divorce?"

"Otabek was completely unaware of the letter, without a doubt. That bastard Hamid wrote the letter in his name."

Qutidor then got up, ran halfway inside, and cried out to Oftob Oyim, while Kumush remained at the tancha.

"I have discovered the secret!"

Both women turned to look at Qutidor and asked, "What? What secret?"

Qutidor did not return to the tancha, but instead remained at the edge of the veranda and reread the letter in his hand, this time aloud:

To you, my respected father-in-law!

Finally, after two years of fruitless roaming, I have succeeded in coming down to earth. A swine of a man named Hamid and his minions buried you and me in the pit of a dark prison and placed the noose around our necks. Yet after his vile plans did not meet with success, he had a letter writer near the gates write a false declaration of divorce, supposedly from my own hand, and murdered an innocent man...

No doubt the violence that transpired near your honored yard has put you and the loved ones in your home under great duress. I assure you I had no other option; those villains intended to kidnap my wife, compelling me to perform these acts. I hope you will excuse me. The resulting hassles and rumormongering will no doubt inconvenience you—though I think that no grievous harm has been done.

Asking you to forgive my transgressions, your exiled son, Otabek, son of Yusufbek Hajji

As Qutidor read the letter aloud, he skipped the word "exiled." When the letter was relayed to them, Oftob Oyim, and especially Kumush, felt the same feelings of horror and loss that Qutidor had. Kumush shivered, became pale, and squirmed in her place... Tears spilled from her eyes, making clear to everyone her most heartrending turmoil.

Qutidor, too, expressed his own emotions at that moment. "It was that coward Hamid who put me and Otabek under the noose, divided us from one another through a fake letter of divorce, murdered that poor Kamilbek, and intended to kidnap Kumush by digging a tunnel into our foundation. Yet Otabek ground that bastard into the ground along with his minions?"

Oftob Oyim agreed in a quaking voice. "Shameless Hamid," she said.

"My poor Bek," Kumush Bibi said.

The three of them were silent so long, it was as if they meant to stop their hearts from beating.

"Is he in any way harmed?" asked Kumush finally.

"As his letter states, he is healthy," said Qutidor.

Oftob Oyim asked, "Where does he keep himself? Who delivered the letter to you?"

This question made Qutidor remember Usta Alim, sitting in the guest room. He stood up at once and, not saying another word to his wife, went out and sat down opposite Usta Alim. Oftob Oyim and Kumush placed themselves near a small door to the guest room so as to overhear the words of the strange deliverer of the letter.

Qutidor begged his pardon: "I'm so very sorry, the weight of the news you brought us made me almost forget you were here."

"I noticed," replied Usta Alim, laughing. "Hamid's devilish tricks were unleashed upon your family, not to mention what he did to your person, but our lionhearted Otabek defeated that bastard. Not many people can make that claim."

"How many people assisted Otabek in slaying the thieves?"

Usta Alim laughed. "Otabek was alone!" he said.

"Alone against three people?" Qutidor could not believe his ears.

"The solitary giant!" Usta Alim said.

"Astaghfurallah... Why didn't he let me know?"

"He considered it unmanly to inform you of his plans. He didn't even tell me. When I scolded him for this mistake, he told me, 'I decided to struggle alone with my cowardly enemy, either he would take my life or I would take his. For that reason, I decided to not make it known to anyone.' On the one hand, I was horrified, but on the other hand, I was in complete amazement at Otabek's brave heartedness."

"Was he wounded?" asked Qutidor.

"He received wounds to his hand and chest, but they are not life- threatening."

Usta Alim, causing considerable discomfort to his host, relayed to him Otabek's wanderings, his travels to and from Margilan—seven or eight times, no less—his arrival at Usta Alim's house, and how they became close friends; then, the way Otabek had withheld his true name from Usta Alim until the day he learned from Usta Farfi the true identity of his enemy, and how, finally, he had told Usta Alim his true name.

"As for his letter of divorce, it turns out to be false," said Qutidor. "Why didn't he come back after he left? Why didn't he come to us once this was revealed?"

"According to him, he was expelled with great insult from your gates," commented Usta. "He thought that perhaps his second marriage in Tashkent was a ploy executed by your own hand to force a divorce from your daughter, so he didn't dare put one foot on your doorstep. He even had the idea of summoning his wife to court to avoid meeting you, but you nullified this idea too. Therefore, since she is your daughter, he decided to leave his beloved wife behind."

Qutidor still did not understand Otabek's logic. "If I offended him, why didn't he send a representative to us?"

"That would have been impossible," said Usta Alim, amused at Qutidor's naivety. "When I asked him this same question, he responded, 'A person who believes I am a liar would not believe a person who speaks on my behalf.' One can arrive at some conclusions as to the nature of your son-in-law from this reply. As it turns out, his mother and father were also completely unaware of these tragic events."

"A strange young man," said Qutidor. "But a great deal of the blame for dull-wittedness lies in me as well."

"All matters in life are simply twists of fate, Uncle. None of this depends on either of us."

"Certainly not," said Qutidor and asked, "is he lodging with you?"

"He left this afternoon for Tashkent."

Qutidor did not understand. "Why, why?" he asked.

"I don't understand the reason either."

"Did he perhaps give you the date when he will return?"

"When I asked, he gave me a vague response," Usta Alim said, uttering a prayer and standing up to leave.

At that moment Oftob Oyim entered the room, leading Kumush and asking, "Did you know that the flat-faced woman who delivered Hamid's evils to us has also been touched by the same fate—one of the murdered young men turned out to be her son."

"What good does Sadiq's death do me?" asked Kumush.

Oftob Oyim was surprised with her daughter.

"Indeed, the benefits are clear."

"The benefit is that Otabek left for Tashkent?"

"He will be back again soon."

"He will not come back," Kumush protested, full of hurt. "It seems all his efforts were only to take revenge on his enemy."

"Who said this to you?"

"I found it out from the person who delivered our letter." Oftob Oyim laughed.

"Your husband will not leave you. Don't be afraid, my daughter," she said. "Otabek, who vanquished the calamity that hung over your head, and almost sacrificed his own sweet life, will never forget you. Let's read what he wrote you first. Your father has the letter."

Widening her tear-soaked, puffy eyes, Kumush Bibi asked, "Did he write me a letter?"

"Didn't you hear from your father that he wrote you a letter too?"

She had in fact heard something regarding a letter mentioned from among Usta Alim's prior statements and thought: "How could I forget that there was a letter for me?"

Kumush yearned deeply to hear the letter Otabek had written for her to be read aloud; years had passed and his image had never left her mind, she had never forgotten Otabek's face.

As soon as her father came in through the doorway, her gentle breasts heaved with a sigh, raising and lowering, and her heart began beating fiercely. Qutidor sat at the tancha and passed the letter to Kumush.

"A letter for you."

Putting aside all shyness and not asking who it was from, Kumush Bibi neared the candle and at once started to open the letter. Her alluring tearstained eyes illuminated by the candlelight, her eyelashes soaked with tears, her arched dark eyebrows, and her tousled hair all gave her a timeless beauty as she read the letter.

To my moonfaced, sun-browed companion, Kumush Khanum!

The fires of hatred that threatened to consume me— through a false letter of divorce written by the master devil

291

Hamid— are fading now. No doubt your thoughts turned toward me, resulting in tears upon receiving this letter... My heart has filled with love for you as I write this letter —my heart that shivered when the possibility of losing you presented itself, shivered like a leaf cast loose, cast loose, unable to express its pains or the crimes suffered... I tell you openly, my beautiful and charming companion:

It seems to me that, while spilling longing mournful tears for Kamilbek, breathing hot longing gasps for him, you are no longer interested in the complaints of a cast-aside old heart, incinerating it in the fire of the long-passed lover. Although you have no doubt by now read the letter of divorce, you burn it in the flames of the deceased—this makes no difference to me. You ask why I say this? It is because you are my legitimate wife—I will proclaim this through both the good and the bad.

Please excuse my misadventures, the bloodshed created by me behind your house... I performed this brutality unwillingly. These acts were all justified by preserving your life, retaining your honor... I believe that you will be grateful for my good deeds, but I do not consider myself worthy of gratitude for killing one of my enemies. As I understood the situation, after killing one of them, I would in turn lose my life to the second one, losing my life at your side...

At that moment nothing could have been sweeter to me than to lay down my life at your feet, something I had longed to do for many years. So that I would perish near you, I nearly met with death in order to breathe in your sweet smell, I crawled through the hole already dug out by our enemies, I entered, took in your aroma, heard the gentle voice of your breath as you slumbered, full of charm. Subhonallah...[318] At that very moment an unanticipated fierceness rose in me, a power that lent me strength against not one enemy, but even against two hundred opponents...

I found the source of my inner strength, and that source that transformed me was my beloved sleeping in the next room... It was you!

Reaching this point in the letter, Kumush Bibi blushed ever so slightly, paused for a moment, and then continued.

I remained in the hole until my second enemy, Hamid, the main architect of our tragedy, lay supine in my claws, like a mouse with a cat. I joyously drove my point home.

Do you remember that you gave me a new life— removing the noose from around my neck? Last night you again saved me from a second death, yet again you gave me new life! So, in the end, it should be me, not you, who is grateful.

I have no issue with you, but with your father: he did not confirm whether the false declaration of divorce was counterfeit or not. I suspect that you were never shown the letter. If you had seen it, you would have suspected the truth of the matter... Anyway, what use are our actions when fate conspires to play games with us. As far I am concerned, I have my own shortcomings. Meaning, after the first letter you wrote me, I made drastic decisions, made no inquiries, and gave the letter courier a hastily written letter in reply. Making this mistake put both of us in Hamid's clutches.

Circumstances worked against us, forcing us apart. For the first time in my life, I resisted the pull of my heart, all due to a dark thorn that rose between you and me, all due to my actions. From this time forward, you are forever mine. I must live and work in Tashkent, but your image will always be in my mind! Can I hope that you will allow me to think of you?

Your husband, Otabek

Kumush Bibi rushed into the room after reading the letter. Qutidor and Oftob Oyim looked at each other in alarm. Kumush had with her one of the original letters and compared the handwriting of the two letters in the candlelight. One letter was the original divorce document commissioned by Hamid, written in Otabek's style. It was clear from the very beginning that they had been written by two different people. Kumush showed her father the two letters.

"Look at them, Father. It turns out we were completely blind," she said.

Understanding his daughter's meaning immediately, Qutidor saw that the handwriting on the two letters was completely different.

"Deceitful devil. Bastard. Unbelieving kafir," he said.

Kumush Bibi folded Otabek's letter and put it in her pocket. Setting fire to the false document, she asked her father, "Did your son-in-law arrive shortly after you had received the letter of divorce?"

"Yes, he came shortly thereafter, Daughter."

"Why did you send that poor man into exile without at least informing my mother or me that he came to speak with you?"

"I struggled to find the words to explain his arrival to you. In the end, I decided not to tell anyone..."

"Did it not seem strange to you that the man who divorced your daughter would travel straight from Tashkent to your doorstep?" asked Kumush.

Greatly ashamed, Qutidor replied, "When brutality arrives, wisdom flees, my daughter."

Oftob Oyim and Qutidor reached new heights of amazement at Hamid's devilish deeds, saying "Tavba!" but called down blessings on Otabek's extraordinarily courageous heart. Kumush Bibi had entirely different concerns. As the narration of recent events by the husband and wife reached Otabek's sudden departure for Tashkent, Oftob Oyim asked Kumush, "Did he say when he would return to you?"

Kumush looked at both of them with disbelief and derision and gave a sharply worded answer, "No, he did not."

Husband and wife exchanged meaningful glances, which Kumush Bibi followed. Both women looked toward Qutidor, as if he would provide the answer to the question.

"This is the best we can ask from him for now," said Qutidor finally. "If he does not arrive soon, we will go ourselves to Tashkent—indeed, we will," he said, looking at his wife. Oftob Oyim did not receive this decision well, turning her face to one side in disapproval, but Kumush seemed to agree with her father's idea and then appealed to her mother.

"Let your daughter live where she is most happy," Qutidor said to his wife. "It seems to me that it is better to give her to her husband's household and have them be both without peril and in our prayers."

"Is there the peril of a *kundosh*[319] waiting on your daughter in doing so?" said Oftob Oyim, clearly angry.

Qutidor smiled at his wife.

"What peril could there be in a kundosh if her husband is righteous?"

"Though her husband is a righteous man a hundred times over, a kundosh will act like a kundosh. There is a reason why old people warn against the kundosh."

Qutidor laughed, looking at his daughter to say something to calm his wife.

"Don't be afraid, it won't last forever."

"If it were up to me, it would not be for even one day. Even a day of life shared with a kundosh is no life at all."

"Have you forgotten your son-in-law's bravery already?"

"How could I have forgotten?" said Oftob Oyim. "Let him come here. He is welcome. I will have two children, not one. The fact is I would rather fight tooth and nail than send my daughter near a kundosh."

"Even for five or six days?"

"For how many days?"

"If it were up to me, I would rather have her stay until she had one or two children. If you do not agree, let's agree to one or two months at least. What happened is a great shame. We have a young man who, for the sake of your daughter, wandered the earth for two years for no reason at all, and now you want to keep them away from each other all because of a kundosh. That is beyond frustrating."

Kumush Bibi reddened from embarrassment when Qutidor said the words "one or two children." Oftob Oyim finally weakened in the face of her husband's last point.

"I will not agree to any more than a month. I only do this for the sake of my son-in-law," she said.

"You can go with her yourself, wife."

"It goes without saying that I can go myself, or not. My position is unassailable; her mother must accompany her."

"Certainly. You will go together. You have the right to be recognized as quda."[320]

"Will you send us out now?" asked Oftob Oyim.

Qutidor thought for a while and then answered, looking toward Kumush Bibi. "It seems to me that it is improper for us to be running after Otabek hither and thither. Additionally, traveling by cart in the dead of winter is very uncomfortable. Therefore, we will leave after three months, once winter has passed," he said.

Kumush Bibi's face took on a downfallen expression when she heard the words "three months."

"Perhaps he will return in a month," concluded Qutidor, attempting to reassure her.

Thus Ends Volume Two

VOLUME THREE

1

MUSULMANQUL'S TYRANNY FINDS ITS END

Musulmanqul's[321] cruelty, despotism, and oppression grew insufferable to the population of Qoqan. Mercifully the other cities remained untouched by his tyranny, but it weighed most heavily upon the fair denizens of the capital city of Qoqan, singular in lamenting the full weight of his wrath. The egregious taxation piled upon the city's inhabitants was a mere reflection of a capriciousness shifting with the vicissitudes of Musulmanqul's mercurial cunning. The seemingly sole purpose one could discern in these erratic levies that changed not month to month but upon the arrival of each new week was a flaying of the skin off of his citizenry.

The genuine depth of his degenerating mental faculties took stark form with his casual penchant for hangings and beheadings—depending on the mood of the day and for the slightest blunder—of the Qora Chopan beks who resided within city limits; these murderous whims perturbed even his closest advisors into disbelief and horror. Being khan only in name, Khudayar Khan, even he in his naivety, grasped that as long as the power belonged to Musulmanqul, who executed and pardoned at his own discretion, he, Khudayar Khan, was only a marionette in the hands of a despot. Deep in the recesses of his heart, he schemed and enumerated possible solutions to this impasse but found nothing but distemper and dead ends. The beks of Qoqan, his last redoubt of patronage, one by one met their end either under the noose or the axe, all guided by the dread hand of Musulmanqul and his Qipchaq minions. The rousing voices of opposition faded into oblivion one by one, as did the moment for a secret denouement. Beks from the nearby cities and *kishlaks* were mainly Qipchaqs themselves and supporters of Musulmanqul, so no support could be expected from them.

Every stratum of the city's population had to swallow some sort of insult from Musulmanqul, yet the Ulama, the supreme clergy, sided with the despot, creating a second bulwark of support for Musulmanqul behind the Qipchaqs, as they added a credibility that only the religious elite could provide. They further legitimized Musulmanqul's extrajudicial executions and levies under the guise of their[322] legal rulings. Our despot made sure to engineer arbitrary rulings and orders during the ensuing disorder so that he could quietly eliminate those who represented a threat to his reign through the aegis of the Ulama and their issuing of fatwas. Meanwhile all these dark machinations appeared under the guidance of the Shah-an-Shah.[323] The rewards garnered by the Ulama for their favors in supporting Musulmanqul's tyranny took on the enduring gleam of gold, the timeless color whose currency augurs the grave intent of the ruling. Musulmanqul commissioned the building of madrassas in the cities of Qoqan and Andijon, and appointed his favorites as *mudarris*.[324] Yet remnants of the Ulama deemed not sufficiently knowledgeable or half-literate did not bring enough credibility to warrant Musulmanqul's favors and "blessings" and found themselves distanced from their benefactor.

Khudayar dreamed of achieving a monarchy unsullied by the devastation of corruption and tyranny, so he sought to extract himself from the clutches of Musulmanqul's bloody patronage by finally gathering around his throne the last remnant of estranged Ulama to aid him in his struggle against his father-in-law. With subsequent gifts, blessings, and blood oaths regarding their own positions, which would be awarded after gaining freedom from the travesty of Musulmanqul's reign, this last vestige of Qoqan's "righteous" mullahs began their maneuvers.

The Ulama behind Musulmanqul had previously argued that his policies held a firm basis in the Shariyat. Now they met a fresh challenge from those aligned with the khan, who countered those claims with well-reasoned arguments delegitimizing Musulmanqul's rulings, also citing passages from the Shariyat. This cabal initially worked secretly "under the sleeve" of Khudayar Khan, the progenitor of the resistance.

To begin with, covert correspondence was sent to the Ulama and beks of Tashkent, Andijon, and Margilan, among other cities, asking them to join in the liberation from Musulmanqul's despotism. These promulgations declared that Musulmanqul's policies contradicted the Shariyat and were therefore unlawful; the facts chronicling his oppression and brutality toward the people of

Qoqan were revealed to all. Furthermore, they stated that the khan himself had as of late lost patience with and was the victim of these mercenary acts, concluding finally that if the Ulama and authorities of the other cities would come to his aid, the khan was finally prepared to act against Musulmanqul. Finally, rumors spread against Musulmanqul's followers made their way to non-Qipchaq forces within the army, inciting them to pursue bloody work.

The cities of Andijon, Margilan, and Namangan, among others, gave only dry promises in noncommittal language such as "If the khan wishes it so, we are ready to help, we are ready to support him." But from Yusufbek Hajji's group in Tashkent, a letter of concrete measures was penned:

We received your secret dispatch from the respected Ulama and elders of Qoqan, who rightly weep because of Musulmanqul's bloodshed and actions, seen as unjust within the Shariyat. The Tashkent Ulama and authorities—Domla Solihbek Akhund; Mullah Yusufbek Hajji; commanders of the army of Tashkent, from the group's leadership we have Qasim and Niyaz Qushbegi; Karimqul and Mohamed Rajab Qushbegi and Qambar Sharbatdor[325]—have consulted at length about the events concerning the citizenry of Qoqan, as well as the citizens of other cities and villages, and the considerable suffering they are enduring under Musulmanqul's oppression and degradation. We, your humble slaves, agree that Musulmanqul's actions are not in compliance with the Shariyat, are harmful to the citizenry, and are not conducive to peace and prosperity.

In this regard, concerning the future of your Amir Al-Mu'minin, Musulmanqul, if our khan of khans is disposed to be sympathetic to our ideas, we believe it would be for the greater good that the shameless exploiter be exiled from the throne; and, again, on behalf of the people of Tashkent, we give our blood oath that we stand on the side of truth and justice.

If you, noble people of Qoqan, are firm in your decision to fight the tyrant and strip him of the title Mingboshi, here is what we humbly offer for your consideration: that Tashkent will feign once again to turn its face from Qoqan's government and proclaim independence. Certainly, the tyrant Musulmanqul will send troops to Tashkent to quell the rebellion and punish it for insubordination. These troops should have as many of your people as you can muster as well as the khan himself joining the campaign.

When his troops reach Tashkent, we will seize Musulmanqul with our joint forces. We will attack from the outside, you attack from the inside, thus destroying Musulmanqul. We have thought long and hard concerning our proposed plan and we, your humble slaves, have decided upon this course. Nevertheless, it is up to you what our next move will be.

Simply put, we believe that our plan will help avoid the most bloodshed. Let it also be known to you that the current ruler of Tashkent is not to be feared—this man selflessly cares about the peace and prosperity of his own people. He will adhere to any decision we compel him to honor and, God willing, so will your sacred people. Please apprise His Highness of our intentions, gain his views on the matter, and write a letter in reply on behalf of His Highness informing us of his decision.

We hold sincere conviction that unflinching resolve will assure victory in our endeavors.

Upon gracing the hands of Khudayar Khan, the letter and the plan outlined therein seemed amenable to his designs, and he immediately dispatched a courier stating his concurrence and further directives. The inner circle of Tashkent nobility, inspired by the khan's approval, in turn gathered privately and called upon their ruler, Nur Muhammad Qushbegi, to attend their enclave. They read to those attending Khudayar Khan's edict, all developed in consultation with the Ulama and aligned with his interests. Since Yusufbek Hajji and Domla Shihbek Akhund were recognized by the ruler of Tashkent as his spiritual leaders imbued with the greatest gravitas, Qushbegi agreed to foment a rebellion against Qoqan so that the path toward peace and prosperity among the khanate's peoples could flourish unabated. One could conclude that even Nur Muhammad Qushbegi, one of Musulmanqul's favorites, considered the policies of his patron tribe and benefactor to be against the interests of the country.

Without delay Nur Muhammad Qushbegi declared independence, absent of any fear that genuine repercussions would arrive from Qoqan, and hence Yusufbek Hajji's designs began to take shape. Recalcitrant Tashkent, again raising its head in dissent, caused the hairs on Musulmanqul's head to rise in anger; and, with every intention of meting out punishment, he picked up his saddlebags. Khudayar, feigning an equal measure of outrage toward the population of Tashkent and their seemingly limitless taste for insurrections, also assembled his equipage for war. Together with Musulmanqul, he departed for the city on the brink of destruction. Meanwhile, on the road, Khudayar Khan communicated in secret with his allies, who vigilantly maintained their measures of deception.

When the vanguard of Musulmanqul's army reached the banks of the Chirchik River,[326] soldiers from the Army of Tashkent, led by Qushbegi, lined the opposite banks of the river, waiting for them. By afternoon, both armies were arrayed for battle, facing each other. Yet as soon as the soldiers of Qoqan's army arrived at their assigned rallying point, Tashkent's soldiers opened fire with rifle volleys, not allowing the soldiers of Qoqan to regroup or rest. Suddenly, to Musulmanqul's great surprise and consternation, sections of his troops turned on his personal Qipchaq guard and command staff, while the other half of his army raised their hands in surrender to the Tashkent contingent. The Qipchaqs panicked and could not decide whether they should defend Musulmanqul or flee. Musulmanqul immediately ascertained that he lacked the numbers to resist Tashkent. Meanwhile, his traitorous Qoqan troops flew toward him like clouds of sparrows, barely allowing him to run away with a whip in his hand and a horse between his legs.

Pursuit continued for a considerable distance while the Hudaychi proclaimed to the young Qipchaq soldiers still loyal and retreating with their leader, "Brother Qipchaqs! We place all the blame upon the shoulders of Musulmanqul. As you were formerly in the service of the khan, you will remain in your positions. Yet if anyone wishes to swear allegiance to Musulmanqul himself, let them separate from the troops peacefully!"

The young Qipchaqs gathered together and appointed a spokesperson of their own. "We do not recognize Musulmanqul—our leader is Khudayar Khan."

After this impasse both Qipchaqs and Uzbeks[327] formed together, greeting each other with handshakes and hugs, with all enmity flowing away with Musulmanqul. Ten thousand men once again made obeisance toward Khudayar Khan, who regained his rightful place as ruler.

The population of Tashkent, with great reverence toward the khan and his army, welcomed them into the city for a three-day celebration. During the feast, people ruminated at length upon the principle of unity, weighing the benefits it holds for all, as opposed to the perils of its absence.

In agreement with the suggestions made by both Qushbegi and Yusufbek Hajji, Uttaboi Qushbegi—mayor of Margilan—was appointed mingboshi as a replacement to Musulmanqul. On the fourth day, Khudayar returned to Qoqan with his troops.

*****

Late winter's diurnal course passed not quite twenty days after the events surrounding Musulmanqul's downfall. Yusufbek Hajji, two or three times harried by a courier carrying summons to the house of Mohamed Rajab Qorboshi,[328] finally relented to the demands of decorum and begrudgingly accepted the invitation.

Among those attending the subsequent gathering were Muhammad Niyoz Qushbegi, Qassim Mingboshi, Qambar Sharbatdor, Karimqul Ponsad, and approximately fifteen other notables among the Tashkent elite.

The guests enjoyed fruits and sorbets followed by a rich repast. During the meal Niyaz Qushbegi took the floor, acquainting the guests with the purpose of the gathering.

"My dear brothers! It would appear that if our brotherhood unites into one determined force, one entity with steely resolve, shaking off the depredations of the Qipchaqs will prove effortless. Consider our position only one month ago. Musulmanqul's pitiless blade lay sharpened and hungry at the throats of our brothers. May God grant our dear Hajji- aka and his kin a long life with concord, free from disquiet as a small recompense for his wise counsel. It was no small achievement to unify us brothers and shake off the yolk of Musulmanqul's despotic rule. Yet a genuine solution for freedom eludes us still. You might question my wisdom, but consider for a moment that although the white dogs no longer pursue us, the black dogs persist in stealing the silver settings from our table. We still contend with the desert dwellers, the Qipchaq tribes.[329] If it were not Musulmanqul, then some Alimqul would no doubt put the yoke on our heads," said Qushbegi, pausing to eat a handful of raisins from the tablecloth before again continuing. "Although power rests in our hands under Nur Muhammad, the appointment of Uttaboi as mingboshi... was not quite what we had in mind. This was one of our greatest miscalculations.

"I, for one, experienced great frustration from the earliest days of Uttaboi's administration: Couldn't we find among our own people someone we could appoint as Boshi besides that mongrel of Musulmanqul's? I say to you all, let us not wait any longer, brothers. Let us strike the iron while it is still hot! How much longer will our lands be weakened by these desert dogs? Our best policy is to carve out a lasting peace for our people and once and for all rid ourselves of these headaches.

"We arrived at a common consensus while consulting among our brothers—can we expect Hajji-aka to acquiesce with our plans? Even the khan might accede to a demand of this magnitude. The brothers from Qoqan, Margilan, Andijon, and Osh, among other localities, will not turn their heads away in indifference to such a proposition. Why, you ask? Know this: these blackguards, these Qipchaqs, have long ago poisoned the world with their falsehoods." He paused again, shaking his tobacco gourd, placing a pinch of nosvoy beneath his tongue.

During this speech, Yusufbek Hajji was deep in thought, silently swirling a cup of tea in his hand. All eyes were trained upon his face once Qushbegi finished speaking. Since Hajji gave no words in response, Qambar Sharbatdor delivered shrill words in support of Qushbegi's opinion.

"You are completely in the right, Qushbegi," he said. "Two options present themselves to us. We either exterminate the Qipchaqs, or we remain in the grip of servitude."

Yusufbek Hajji raised his head almost imperceptibly toward Qambar Sharbatdor, surveyed the reactions of those attending, and kept his silence. In an attempt to elicit a response from Hajji, Karimqul Ponsad stated, "Efforts planned through a common consensus will be met with success."[330]

"Let's allow Hajji-aka a moment to consider, then have him state his views," Karimqul Ponsad said.

"I don't know..." said Hajji finally, "if the true purpose behind the dreadful act you are considering still eludes me, and I have not been fully apprised of all the facts, or I grasped the meaning of your intentions, which is alien to me and makes me only wonder."

Niyoz Qushbegi scratched his head and asked, "What makes you wonder, Hajji?"

"Your whole purpose as Qambar Bek stated is the extermination of the Qipchaqs. Is that right?"[331]

Qushbegi without hesitation gave his response: "Total annihilation."[332]

"Who on earth," said Hajji with a sarcastic laugh, "is forcing you to commit such an act?"

Qushbegi looked around at his companions.

"Your question is an interesting one," he said. "The reason must be more evident to you than to us."

"You are right," said Hajji, taking his turban from around his head. "We had to banish Musulmanqul, we singled him out as the progenitor of the evil in our lands, we allied ourselves with our Qipchaq brothers, and the ancient enmity between us and the Qipchaqs faded... Enough, do we need to go through this again?"

Those gathered met each other's glances upon receiving Yusufbek Hajji's rebuttal, but Qushbegi, not wishing to lose momentum, laughed out loud.

"Do you think Musulmanqul will lie still now? Bring us peace?"

"Of course I do not think he will remain passive, but I do not believe that, because of Musulmanqul's recalcitrance, we should exterminate the Qipchaqs—it flies in the face of wisdom. Ask yourself: From whom, up to this very moment, have the evils of this world flown? From the Qipchaq people, or from a few ill-placed individuals?"

"In truth, we suffered interminable defamation and insults from the mouths of all Qipchaqs."

"Your words are misguided, Qushbegi. In truth, only through the evil intent of a few individuals do we now see the seeds of hate spread throughout our society... If you would heed my judgment on this matter, peace and concord would prosper. Now, due to the acts of four bastards, you will attack a multitude, a whole people?"[333]

"Not only four bastards, Hajji! Each and every Qipchaq who has now come from the desert seeks only to ride on our shoulders and poke their noses in our cups. It seems to me you are overly sympathetic to their cause, Hajji-aka!"

Qasim Mingboshi added, "Our Hajji only speaks from the voice of mercy. But should we not consider that the Qipchaqs heartlessly spilled our brothers' blood? At one point Rajab Bek and I calculated that seventy-eight Beks met their end in Qoqan over a two-year period. And these numbers do not include the lowborn."

"I do not dispute these facts, Mingboshi. I say injury given for injury suffered achieves nothing; we should remain at the center of wisdom and justice..."

Somebody from the middle of the group interrupted Hajji. "We are fed up with wisdom and justice."

Hajji held his tongue. He fully understood that Qushbegi's sentiments held sway and that his were falling upon deaf ears. He could also surmise Qushbegi's hidden agenda—Uttaboi's appointment to a superior position as the mingboshi had driven him to envy.

"The proposition to exterminate Qipchaqs was born from Niyaz's personal grievance: Why would a Qipchaq be selected as mingboshi when I could be the one!"

The malefactor's own lips confirmed Yusufbek Hajji's suspicions. He relegated the others to the realm of the bored and inconsequential, or to the meek, too fearful, eager to squabble, whose personal gains were more important than the interests of the people. Hajji's instinct told him that silence in the face of these self-serving and corrupt beks would not do.

"My dear beks," he began. "My thoughts are solely for the benefit of our khanate, our nation. I never forget that soulless bastards acting only in their own self-interest can be found not only among the Qipchaqs, but among us as well. And perhaps, while Qipchaqs have dozens of them, we have hundreds of the

307

same sort. For the first time in my life I witnessed, though we knew him to be a coldhearted dog, the Qipchaq Nur Muhammad[334] engage in fruitful work on behalf of our nation, as a mayor of Tashkent.

"These inconvenient truths are what you dimwits refuse to acknowledge. Enough. Guilt does not reside solely with the Qipchaqs, a people used only as a means to an end for the personal gain of their leaders; nor does guilt lie with the Qora Chopans, as the Qipchaqs are led to believe. We can place three-quarters of the blame on the beks' ineffectual leadership and greed!

"Brothers, the Russians[335] lie in wait at our very gates, ready to attack because of such internal conflicts, a struggle whose origins rise from within our community. A nightmare will envelop us if we cripple ourselves by our own hands. We must hold our strength in reserve against the real enemy instead of drawing blades to our own throats, all for the sake of your nonsense. Has anyone here considered this threat? Can we consider for a moment that someday we will be ruled by the infidels who at this very moment conspire against us? How do you intend to oppose them—or do you prefer to neglect this issue?"

Hajji lost his composure and tears flowed freely down his white beard as he continued.

"Now hear me, brothers. While you dig a grave for your own people—the Qipchaqs—the Russians will prepare for you all your own funeral pyres against Islamic tradition. While you raise your swords against the Qipchaqs, the Russians will bring cannon fire against you. The only enemy you see in this world are the Qipchaqs, yet I see a greater enemy, increasing in strength moment by moment, approaching ever nearer!" he said, drying his tears with his handkerchief while rising from his place.

"If you lend your ears to the advice of an old man whose days in this world are coming to their end, turn your back on plots for revenge. *Illah*! If not, consider Yusufbek Hajji as having passed from the earth and not partaking in this evil act!" he said and left, ignoring pleas from the other attendees to sit and remain at the meeting.

Hajji had yet to pass through the gate when Qushbegi's laughter rang out.

"Vai, vai,[336] may your disquietude and hysterics dry you up, Hajji! It seems he partook of some opium today!"

The leader's jeers invited the others to place their own barbs.

"I don't think so," said Qambar Sharbatdor. "It appears senility has consumed Hajji-aka, turning his heart infantile and weak."

"Vai, vai! Hajji the opium eater," said Niyaz Qushbegi. "No longer interested in the hunt before him, only sees the prey at a distance!"

"Indeed, it is so, it is so!"

Mohamed Rajab Qushbegi nodded his head in agreement, looking at Niyoz Qushbegi. "I wanted to mention," he said, "that you can convince Hajji to do anything, except to agree to our plans."

"I guessed so myself since he ignored our summons and made us wait so long."

"Yesterday he seemed suspicious," stated Karim Qul Ponsad.

"We have some cracks in our designs," said Mohamed Rajab Qorboshi.

"What cracks?" asked Qushbegi.

"Our secrets are exposed. He will not rest now."

"Our plans remain hidden, still," Qushbegi objected with complete confidence. "If we brothers remain true to our vows of fealty, our secrets may once again mask our intentions."

"What do you suggest?" asked Qambar Sharbatdor.

"Does our word of honor still hold? Does unity still mean unity?"

The assembly affirmed their allegiance with a collective nod. "It does, it does!" they shouted.

"If we speak with one voice," Qushbegi enjoined, "Hajji's dissent will prove easily remedied. We must all agree that a messenger sympathetic to our cause but credible to Hajji will convey to him our acquiescence to his wise counsel; that we are mistaken. Hajji, being gullible, will trust our capitulation to his august personage and maintain his discretion regarding our previous conversation. As for us, let us initiate our preparations in complete silence if that is agreeable to you all."

"Well said. Excellent counsel! We gird our belts for our task."

"That is all good," said Qushbegi. "So are we ready to proceed with our plans?"

"We are! We are!"

"You must all take great pride in yourselves!" said Qushbegi. "It is clear to me we all speak from the same heart. Now, for another point of interest."

"Does the khan lend his support?" asked Qasim Mingboshi.

Qushbegi gave a smug laugh. "We can rest at ease that the khan agrees," he replied.

The assembly did not catch the meaning of his words and exchanged confused glances.

"Please explain, Qushbegi."

Qushbegi gave a diplomatic response. "Before seeing the khan off from Tashkent, I had the opportunity to run my plan by him away from prying ears. It appears that the khan is amenable to my designs. He gave considerable thought to my stated intent and said, 'Fine, first outline your plans in writing, and I will take them into consideration.' As far as I know, the khan is restless, not sleeping at night, waiting for news from us concerning this issue. Our primary task is to devise an agency with which to instigate our program and still assuage the khan's fears."

"The khan seems ready," said Qambar Sharbatdor, grinning. "Turns out he is!" the group joined in.

At that moment the group began their machinations on the best means to an end. They racked their brains, each person making a suggestion of his own, and finally they wrote the following letter to the khan.

We, your most humble servants, faithful slaves, entreat you, the Crown of Muslims, Khan of Khans, the youthful Shah of Shahs, the joyous crown of your content citizens, Our Highness, to take heed of our persistent fear of the Qipchaqs; a fear interminable, with trepidation that if these wretched desert peoples are not wiped off the face of the earth, Your Highness's peace and security, as your humble slaves attest, remain in great peril. After some consideration, we, your humble Tashkent slaves, gathered together and debated at length with the hope that the Shah of Shahs will honor us as a shade over our heads.

We understand that our faithfulness to you is just a drop in the ocean of your concerns. That said, we believe that all

Qipchaq males between the ages of fifteen and seventy should be slaughtered without mercy.

Our leaning toward extermination should be kept secret until the day of the execution arrives. Let the Crown settle upon a providential time and send secret dispatches to all cities, villages, and settlements that are ruled under Our Highness's guidance, to the people most faithful and firm in heart. What does it mean? The Army of Tashkent should be informed of the destruction of these bitches. Even in a paradise like Qoqan a plenitude of insurgents abounds, seemingly without number. We, your soldiers in Tashkent, could assist you in their elimination, and you can absolutely count upon our faithfulness. When the time arrives, Shah of Shahs, appoint to us the victorious hour, send us a message, as we have the sufficient strength to act. Each of us attending will draw up two hundred to five hundred soldiers, creating the illusion to the population that our intent is to only congratulate Your Highness on your victory over your recent turmoil with Musulmanqul, your newly unfettered crown; you will see as evidence in our attack our complete fealty for, as soon as we enter through the gates, we will suddenly draw our swords against the Qipchaq dogs assembled, massacring them all.

If it pleases Your Highness, please inform us of your private thoughts concerning the Qipchaq Nur Muhammad, who now holds the position of Bek of Tashkent. If you so order we will eagerly rid ourselves of this issue that so confounds our doubts. Please understand that the above missive results from much consideration and reflection. If you believe us recalcitrant, please send us your refusal— relaying in the affirmative or negative—of our plans through our private courier.

Please grace us with your own enlightened view, demonstrate to us our shortcomings, reveal our errors as your lowly, humble, but faithful servants who wield their swords in your defence, or make us abound in joy through asking us to gird our belts in service to Our blessed and merciful Highness— may Allah protect us!

Your faithful soldiers gathered in obeisance to you—
signatures appended.

They all agreed that their appeal should be dispatched the very next day. They relegated the mission to a trusted agent. Fears still existed that Yusufbek Hajji would reveal his misguided views to the public, so Mohamed Niyoz Qushbegi personally decided to meet with him right away. The meeting concluded with those attending taking their own paths from the house.

2

DARK DAYS

Ten days after Otabek returned from Margilan, he received a letter from Usta Alim, who relayed the details of his meeting with Qutidor.

Just as you felt aggrieved with your father-in-law until you found out about the treachery, so he felt aggrieved with you. It appeared to him that you made a mockery of both him and his daughter and he felt he could never forgive you this insult.

When I was finally allowed to get to the heart of the matter with him, he sank into distress and lost his composure for some moments.

Though I cannot divine the emotional state of his home's inner sanctum, I do believe the feelings there mirror those of your father-in-law. As for him, he swung between being speechless in light of the trials you have met over the past two years and praising the defeat of your enemies to the skies. In any case, no doubt that grievances and misunderstandings will disappear now together with your rival.

The letter concerning Qutidor continued:

He asked where you were. I told him what I knew. When he asked about when you would return, I gave him the same uncertain answer I got from you. I think, however, that if not in the winter, then sometime in the spring they themselves will travel to Tashkent.

Toward the end of the letter Usta Alim added a final note:

The day after you left here, Hamid died.

Thank God, he passed away like a pig, not uttering a word. I feared that he would betray your role in his demise on his deathbed. Qutidor was not charged with a crime, as the relatives of the deceased could provide no proof against him.

Investigators stopped their queries, as they had exhausted all avenues.

In my opinion, only the mother of the slain Sadiq suspects something, but she says nothing, only replying to those who ask that "It is God's will." Fearing that this evil housewife could commit almost any intolerable act, I finally advised your father-in-law not to let unfamiliar women into his house and never eat food brought in from outside. He must remain vigilant against those sorts of evils...

Written by your friend, Usta Alim

For two months no further news arrived from Margilan. So Otabek's days flowed past as the sun set and rose in a haze, with the nights' hours transforming him into an astonishing shade of himself, portending a darker fate. One found it hard to discern the animus behind his ever ebbing and uncertain sentiments. One moment hope seemed to embrace and transport him; other moments he seemed adrift in a stygian nightmare. During those hopeful moments he froze in a dreamy embrace: It seemed to him like the moon, peeping from behind the rooftops, the one and only, would enter through the gates any day now, wearing a yellow or black silk dress with a paranji covering her body, a *chimmat*[337] in her hand, and a silent reproof in her eyes.

In another vision a voice whispered to him: "So, you traveled to Margilan only to get rid of your enemies, and as soon as the deed was done, you disappeared? Well, if a good young man comes along, maybe I should marry Kumush off to save her from a life of loneliness."

The conflicting visions smoldered within him as doubts weighed him down further. I have traveled back and forth for two years and now that I have finally got what I want, why do I sit here like a fool? he thought and was about to leave for Margilan, but inexplicably he hesitated. But I've left, why would I go back? What would I say? I was waiting for you to bring your daughter to Tashkent! But you haven't—and here I am, come on my own. Is this what I am going to tell him?

In this manner Otabek's days drifted by in bittersweet torment.

Uzbek Oyim was overjoyed with her son's change in behavior. The one who used to travel to Margilan two or three times a month had now been at home for a three-month stretch.

"It appears that my light-and-dark enchantments have finally produced their desired effect. The word *Margilan* no longer leaves his lips. If I can only warm his heart toward his wife and get him to stop sleeping in the guest room... anyway... Let's continue on with our *dua*."[338] She resolved then to send Zainab to another domla.

As of late Otabek had halted trading, leaving Hasan Ali unengaged, with long, dull days passed at home. He asked Hajji for a small loan and opened a food stall in the *guzar*.[339] Otabek spent most of his days reading books from the library in his guest room. When tired of reading, he would help Hasan Ali in the guzar, but soon lost interest. At times he meanders to the banks of the Salar,[340] at times he lazes about the Chukar Kishlok,[341] where he no longer got excessively drunk but limited himself to several—no more than four—cups of *boza*[342] to satiate his desire. Eyes half-closed in a slight stupor from the drink, he would come home, but even in his *kaif* he could not conceal his inner turmoil from the perceptive Hasan Ali.[343]

One day he departed from Chukar Kishlok, entering the guzar sometime late in the afternoon, heady in a drunken stupor and sitting down in Hasan Ali's stall. He barely registered the horsemen passing the stall from all directions, so sunk was he in the depths of inebriation, eyelids barely able to raise themselves.

Hasan Ali, looking him over a couple of times, asked, "Why haven't you been to Margilan in so long?"

The question sobered him, his eyes opening wide like split peas. "I don't have the will to go there..." he slurred.

"If your father-in-law is amenable, wouldn't it be best for you to take back the one who belongs to you, even move back..."

"I don't know. Who knows?"

Previously, it had been hard for him to lie when he was asked about Kumush. He wanted to pour his heart out and complain, "You were the one who arranged my marriage, but now they have separated me from her." Now he wasn't embarrassed or upset but thought suddenly that if he himself did not want to go, he could send Hasan Ali to Margilan and finally find the time to tell him everything.

A moment of sobriety appeared as this idea revolved around in his head. After helping to closing the shop for the day, he walked along with Hasan Ali. Sitting down with him for plov, the thought completely consumed him as he leaned to eat over the tablecloth. Indecision wracked him as his *kaif* faded moment by moment and his imagination produced barrier after barrier.

"Who knows what goes on in Margilan? Have they changed their minds again? Is it advisable to travel there without knowing the situation?"

That next day the sun ascended through a wide and open sky, the surface of its shining sphere smiling upon the earth. The spring clouds, fatigued from two days of covering the sun's face, finally relinquished their life-giving showers and spread out to the four corners. Sparrows emerging from the cover of their nests sang their songs while doves joined in the chorus. A pair of birds considering building a common nest in a nearby poplar tree held council. Upon hearing the call of the shepherd, a white-headed calf offered a reply while following its mother, who longed to join the pasture. A pigeon blowing out its throat circled its enemy in a challenge to gain the love of the female in waiting. The demeanor of early morning announced to the world its dreams and offered respite and joy.

The enchanted spring morning had imbued Otabek with the same elation over the past two days. Finishing his tea just after Hasan Ali, he went to the bazaar to join him. Upon arriving, he found Hasan Ali and his neighbor Ali opening the boards of their shops. As soon as Ali saw Otabek he paused.

"Are you free today, Aka?"

"I am free."

"If you are, we could ride to Ming O'rik[344] to drink some fresh *qimiz*,"[345] said Ali. "Kazak Tula[346] has just brought his horses from pasture."

"What about your shop?"

Ali closed the shutter he had just opened.

"Can we ever finish the world's work, Bek-aka? If you say so, I will close the shop."

Otabek looked at the beautiful, bright sun. "Close it, then," he said.

During his frequent visits to Hasan Ali's shop, Otabek had recently made Ali's acquaintance. He was still a young man who seemed straightforward enough and gave a pure hearted laugh. They seemed to be old friends who had known each other for years. Ali's proposition gladdened Otabek, because the fields beckoned him to spend the day in the country. They bought some meat and began to walk toward Ming O'rik.

The name Ming O'rik speaks for itself—a thousand acres of apricot trees standing row by row, end on end, beginning from the waters of Shibli until the Salar[347] watercourse. On the Salar side of the vast Ming O'rik orchard are unending steppes, carpeted with green grass, at that time freshly grown. On the banks of the Salar at the other end of Ming O'rik, three or four Kazak yurts were camped. Reaching the water's edge, they gave their meat to the wife of Kazak Tula to prepare soup.

Taking a Qigiz rug[348] from the yurt, Ali laid it on the Salar's banks. The young bride placed pillows and a blanket for their comfort. Otabek spread his legs out to relax.

The sun warmed them but did not threaten to get too hot. A slight breeze brought the fragrance of the plains; a few swallows circled along the stream of the Salar, singing in their flight as if reciting a *surah* from the Quran. The monotone green of the grass, the high and low of the green waves of the foothills made it difficult to discern the horizon, as if a living fog descended in one embracing color, invading the senses. The different rhythms of the birdsongs and the cadences of locusts performed a natural staccato of pulse and measure, stirring man's timeless expressions of passion and remorse.

Otabek, enraptured by the charming interlude provided by nature, lay for some time, thinking, If only she was here. A long sigh escaped him.

Ali also could not remain indifferent to the beauty of the day, bursting with excitement: "What a remarkable day we have!"

Otabek let slip the pain hidden deep in his heart, stealing from him complete enjoyment of the beauty surrounding him: "If only one was not robbed of the strength to appreciate these days by unresolved issues..."

"What sort of issues could you have?" Ali said, smiling at Otabek's dark mood.

"You think I am without conflict? You think my life is devoid of shortcomings?"

"I know you do not have the same disappointments others have."

"For example?" Otabek asked.

"For example," Ali answered with a laugh. "Qushbegi does not have the same prestige as you and your father enjoy. As for wealth, you are nowhere near hungry... two of your wives sit like birds of paradise all day long, preening for Otabek. Bek-aka, what else could you wish for?"

Ali's superficial judgment of what constituted happiness seemed to Otabek naive, forcing him to laugh.

"You spoke wisely!"

"One should thank the heavens, Bek-aka," said Ali, who then began to complain about his own lot in life, the unhappiness that comes from not being able to save enough money to scratch out a living, not to mention marry. Otabek took his complaints to heart, understanding that each one of us suffers blows in life according to his own position in society, without exception.

"This is the way of the world, Mullah Ali," he said, trying to soothe his pain. Both remained silent for some time.

"Have you had a child with your Margilani wife?"

"No..."

"You have been married for several years now. Did they perish young?"

"That's right, they passed away."

Ali then surmised the source of Otabek's angst grew from an absence of children.

"One should not hold onto anger over being childless. You are still young, Bek-aka."

Otabek did not answer.

The qimiz arrived in a large wooden bowl with several small painted maple cups. After drinking down one or two cups, Bek lay back and looked at the sky. Ali sung in a strong voice:

My eyes search about,
My beloved has yet to come to me.
The whole world seems
Black before my eyes.
What bandit stole from me my soul mate?
A desolate young man sits nearby,
Longing for her along the way...

"Will you join me in song, Bek-aka?"

"You were singing quite well all alone. Please don't stop."

Ali sung with all his skill, making his way toward the end of the ghazal.349

"Did you like it, Bek-aka?"

"You are a skilled singer! Indeed, you are!"

"If so, drink this cup in my honor," Ali said with a laugh, handing Otabek another cup of qimiz.

Otabek emptied the cup in one gulp. Sighing, looking toward the far hills, the previous verses echoed on his lips:

My eyes search about,
My beloved has yet to come to me.
The whole world seems
Black before my eyes.
What bandit stole from me my soul mate?
A desolate young man sits nearby,
Longing for her along the way...

"Have you heard news of the army dispatched to Qoqan?" Otabek, emerging from his daydream, looked at Ali.

"I haven't heard anything."

"My brother marched with them... let them be as happy as the moon on their march. Let them come back unharmed!"

"Is your brother a soldier?"

"You know, he was an excellent marksman who joined his friends assigned to march to Qoqan. We quarrelled when I urged him not to go. Are there any rumors about the war? Are they only at the behest of Khudayar Khan's blessing?"

"Who knows..." said Otabek, and after some consideration, "There should be no war."

The qimiz in the big wooden bowl was finished. The soup was also consumed. After reading a prayer wishing the bride who had prepared their tablecloth to have a son, they gave her thirty coins for her *surma*,[350] got up, and walked into the hills to pick *binafshah*.[351]

3

THE MASSACRE OF THE QIPCHAQS[352]

At about four p.m. that afternoon they entered through the Qoymas Gates. At once they were met by the beheaded bodies of three people not ten steps from the gates. Otabek was aghast— those who were found guilty of a crime were normally hung by a noose at an old place of prayer known as Namozgah[353]—so he called out to one of the gate guards from his post and asked, "What were these men found guilty of?"

The man immediately recognized Otabek, folding his hand on his chest.[354]

"Your Honor, they are Qipchaqs."

"That's apparent, but what crime did they commit?"

The guard looked at the bodies lying nearby and came closer to Otabek. "Master, you know it yourself... I don't dare to say anything, master!"

"So, what are they guilty of?"

"They are Qipchaqs, my master." Otabek became agitated.

"I have clearly discovered that they are Qipchaqs, but what I am asking you is what their crimes were."

The gate guard, still holding his hands, looked at Otabek in surprise. "Taksir is uninformed of the circumstances?" he asked.

"Yes."

"Taksir! Today they executed every Qipchaq they could find. Guilt was not a consideration, Taksir," he said, leaving his post and nearing the corpses, providing commentary. "They took this one from his house and killed him on the spot. The other one worked with me as a guard. He attempted to hide behind me. God bless them both. As for this other one, I do not recognize him, but he must be a Qipchaq."

Otabek turned to Ali, who stood near him, completely aghast at the display. He could only stare at the lifeless corpses and bite his lips.

"Who killed them?" Otabek asked the gate guard in horror.

"There were approximately twenty of them, some of the young men from Tashkent, others from Qoqan; they searched for Qipchaqs everywhere as if separating out life with a flour sifter. Taksir... it seems like their orders came from either the beks who recently went to Qoqan or from the khan himself, Taksir... anyway. We are only here to serve... what could we possibly understand about this?"

Otabek finally understood the matter at hand and went on his way with Ali, sickened, with a pit in his stomach. Another thirty steps and they encountered two more corpses, and with each subsequent ten steps, ten more lifeless bodies... Ali finally asked, losing control of himself, "God save us—what is the meaning of this, Bek-aka?"

"Don't ask, you don't want to know!"

"Oh no..." said Ali. "Are they all really guilty of something?"

"They are obviously guilty!" said Otabek sarcastically. "Certainly, you have heard of the famous Musulmanqul?"

"Of course I have. I saw him fleeing from here two months ago..."

"If you witnessed those events, then it seems these people have been slain due to his guilt!"

"Is that so? Oh my God!"

With every step, they met another corpse. Ali counted until reaching the bazaar—the number of people slain was seventy. Yet that only took into account those killed on the main street. If one were to enumerate on a greater scale to include the other streets in Tashkent, one would arrive at an unmitigated tragedy. As they entered the bazaar they saw before them approximately forty corpses carefully laid out in a row...

The day had passed from afternoon into evening, so only three or four shops in the bazaar remained open, including Hasan Ali's, which was half-open, with Hasan Ali sitting in front.

"You come in health, Bek? We worried a hundred times over about you," said Hasan Ali.

Otabek's thoughts were far off. Without hearing the question, he asked Hasan Ali, "Where has my father been today?"

"After you left he went to the Orda. After an hour he rushed down here, frantically asking where you were. From here I don't know where he went."

"When did they start killing the Qipchaqs?"

"As soon as your father arrived here," said Hasan Ali, who then frantically retold the tragedy he had witnessed.

"Ah...! Bek, sheer brutality and mayhem descended upon us... all of this transpired like a nightmare! What possible crime could these poor wretches be found guilty of? They stabbed to death those who were only sitting in their houses, performing honest work... heh, poor wretches. What were they guilty of? Young men continued to drag them here while executioners cut off their heads. The poor wretches went mad as this sudden calamity fell on them, crying out... especially one painter... they had just come near his shop while he still had one hand in a vessel, mixing a color... 'Oh God no,' he cried out, 'What am I guilty of?' The scene too horrific to bear witness to, I shut the windows of my shop and fled, many ran with me as well... if once again..."

"Enough..." said Otabek.

Hasan Ali halted his tale as it was clear that Bek's heart was destroyed; Ali ran away with no parting words to Otabek... On reaching home, Otabek did not eat dinner and refused to meet with his father, as if to hide himself from a world of savages. Even though some daylight remained, he wrapped himself in a blanket.

The inhabitants of the house understood the source of his mood and therefore left him alone...

In the morning, Yusufbek Hajji went to take tea with Otabek in the guest room. Otabek, frowning, sat down for tea without greeting his father. He viewed his father as one of the main architects of the Qipchaq massacre.

The tea had almost reached halfway toward the bottom of the pot. Not one word had been spoken between them. Finally, attempting to lighten his son's burden, Hajji started to speak.

"Do not be so angry, my son."

"Like you, then?" Otabek said bitterly. "Should I be glad?"

Hajji at that moment divined his son's thoughts and the hostility shown toward him.

"You are mistaken in your judgment of me, my son."

"During Rajab Bek's meeting," Otabek continued with the same derision in his voice. "Who was the main instigator of this savagery?"

Hajji sighed heavily and replied, "So, you know of the meeting at Rajab Bek's?"

"I know of it."

"If you know," said Hajji, "then shame on you, child, for placing the blame for this betrayal on my shoulders!"

"Didn't this council take place at Rajab Bek's?"

"It in fact did."

"Then how can you claim innocence?" Yusufbek Hajji smiled as if Otabek were a child.

"Some of your simpleminded conclusions resemble those of your mother's, Otabek," he said. "If you are aware of the meeting, then you should know the opinions each of us held, correct?"

"No, I do not," said Otabek.

"And the primary point under discussion during the meeting?" asked Yusufbek Hajji.

"I don't know what you were discussing, but it was perfectly clear yesterday that the agenda was to instigate the massacre of the Qipchaqs. You must ask yourself why the participants, other than yourself, of course, assemble army contingents to march on Qoqan, only to bring terror upon reaching the city?"

"Your reasoning is sound but including your own father among these animals is where you go wrong," Yusufbek Hajji said

322

as tears welled up in his eyes. "Think for yourself, Son. What purpose does this serve our country, the extermination of our own people by our own hands? And how could I possibly benefit from being a part of this act of terror? If I were ever seeking for power and wealth, wouldn't you be the first one to know about it? Why does your perceptive mind suddenly fail when you come to this conclusion? Why are you pouring oil on fire when my heart is already aflame?"

These words and Hajji's voice quivering in excitement made Otabek reject his accusations as unfair. He realized he was wrong in his suspicions—Hajji's heart was already heavy with this evil day and did not need his son's reproach... Otabek felt as if he had struck a gratuitous blow with an unjust sword.

Recovering himself, Yusufbek Hajji divulged to his son the narrative of the meeting, his ineffectual protestations, the fruitless attempt to convince the others of the error of their ways, and his subsequent departure from the meeting in complete disgust, finally saying, "An hour later, Niyoz Qushbegi came for a visit to offer his apologies and to assuage my fears, telling me that the group had abandoned the plan, in short, they admitted their error in judgment and understood the great harm they would cause through their actions. My relief clearly evidenced in my expression, Niyoz Qushbegi made his farewells, adding, 'Hajji- aka, I plead that our discussion stays confined within the four walls of that room. We would be greatly ashamed if someone were to become aware of our ignorance—our group only asks this small favor from you.'

"I was completely deceived by his diabolical cunning. I didn't mention a word to you nor to Nur Muhammad Qushbegi, oblivious to the ill designs of the contingent of soldiers dispatched to Qoqan supposedly for the khan's blessing... Oh, those devils!"

Hajji, with a catch in his throat, paused for a moment before finally continuing, "Yesterday morning I left for the Orda. I saw a cohort of three to four hundred men at attention in the courtyard waiting for orders; I did not pay much attention to them and entered Qushbegi's chancellery. Qaiyum Ponsad, with three or four soldiers, clearly having just arrived from Qoqan, stood in front of Qushbegi, who sat stricken in his chair with a dispatch held loosely in his hand. Recognizing me in the doorway he nodded his head, handing me the paper, stunned into silence. Not yet able to absorb the situation, I took a seat to read the document handed to me. Then having read the contents, I too felt caught in the same paroxysm of panic as Qushbegi, my head reeling from disbelief. The communication in question was a declaration by Khudayar Khan that went along these lines:

" 'We hereby declare that the Qipchaq tribes are henceforth enemies of the Qoqan Khanate and Khan of Turkestan. We order all beks, hakims, qorboshi, and dakh boshi in our territories to immediately put under the sword without mercy all Qipchaqs between the ages of fifteen and seventy upon receiving this order. Those found derelict in performing this duty will be considered insubordinate and subject to our most egregious punishment. Our khan blesses the hakim of Tashkent, Nur Muhammad Qushbegi, who will execute this order; though you yourself are a Qipchaq, you have demonstrated unwavering loyalty to us during the casting of Musulmanqul into exile, therefore you are exempt from the above punishment and we absolutely hold no suspicions of your faithfulness in performing your duty!'

"I looked up at Qushbegi, who just stared at my mouth, waiting for me to reply.

" 'When did you receive this order?' I asked.

"Instead of answering he only nodded toward Qaiyum Ponsad.

" 'I just now delivered it,' said Qaiyum Ponsad.

" 'Did you deliver it from Qoqan?' I asked."

"Because you knew it was impossible to make a round trip to Qoqan in five or six days," Otabek added.

" 'We were on our way to Qoqan with the beks,' said Qaiyum, 'when we received this proclamation, which came to us directly from the khan. Niyoz Qushbegi assigned to me a cohort of soldiers, dispatching me to fulfill the mandate outlined in the letter.'

"These words revealed their devilish plans and I realized I was deceived: 'What if we execute the order tomorrow?' I appealed to Qushbegi.

" 'I also have considered this option...' said Qushbegi, looking at me.

"Qaiyum's master had already anticipated our attempts to hinder the order. 'An abeyance until tomorrow is unacceptable!' Qaiyum retorted.

" 'Why?' I asked.

" 'The Qipchaqs will anticipate our intent and flee if we wait until the morrow.'

"Ignoring Qaiyum's response, I pleaded with Qushbegi that we adjourn until we could assemble a council the next day to deliberate. Overcome with anger and becoming increasingly impatient with our dissembling, Qaiyum sat facing me. 'Don't bother, Hajji-aka."

"I found his manner aggressive and offensive.

" 'We do not need to take part in this deed!' I stated.

" 'You do not have an obligation to act, but I am compelled to obey orders!' said Qaiyum.

" 'To whom is the order addressed?' I asked.

" 'To Qushbegi!'

" 'There you go then. We raise our hoe only when he orders. Otherwise we do nothing,' I said.

"Qaiyum slowly slid his hand beneath his robe with a grin dripping with poison and withdrew a second dispatch, handing it to me. 'Read it!' he demanded.

"I read the order.

" 'Fine. If you have received your own orders, why are you waiting for Qushbegi to act?' I asked, burning with anger.

" 'Decorum demands I demonstrate the appropriate respect afforded our great leader...' scoffed Qaiyum.

" 'Well done! You act like a faithful dog. Go ahead. Follow the will of your masters!'

" 'Don't be offended, Hajji-aka,' said Qaiyum, taking back the letter, then asking Qushbegi, 'Well, what say you, Bek?'

" 'If you want my advice, let's start in the morning,' replied Qushbegi.

" 'There is absolutely no way out of this, Qushbegi! It was ordered that all cities and settlements execute the order today, without delay!' said Qaiyum.

"Qushbegi and I felt buried beneath a mountain of immutable terror, crushing us into silence. Qaiyum, too, at that moment seemed entrenched, impatiently waiting for Qushbegi's word. Several moments passed until finally, Qushbegi motioned for Qaiyum to step outside.

" 'Do as you wish,' he said.

"Qaiyum left the chancellery with his contingent. Now that he was gone, I asked Qushbegi, 'What should we do?'

" 'What can we do?'

" 'Should we stand by and do nothing? Time is short! We must order our soldiers to detain the conspirators!'

" 'Let them do it, Hajji!'

" 'Why should poor innocents be slain?'

" 'Let it be so!' was all Qushbegi said.

"I remained nailed to my spot in complete disbelief as he sat, moribund, caught between interminable sobs and gasping attempts to explain his reasons.

" 'If killing every single Qipchaq means we maintain peace, let them all be cut down! If the flowing of Qipchaq blood means the flourishing of the khanate, let them all be slain! If our salvation is in the drying up of Qipchaq seeds, let them hang me as well! I disdain any mercy shown by these cowards!'

"I attempted to help him recover his calm, quietly showing him the shortsightedness of his decision. A decision made in an irrational and emotional state; one that must be reversed if we were to save the day. Obdurate and inconsolable, I left him to his thoughts, stepping out of the room alone but resolute in warning the Qipchaqs to flee with their lives.

"I attempted to direct people away from the troops as best I could, but what can one man do against the might of four hundred executioners? Those bastards succeeded in wasting the lives of many wretched individuals. Here, Otabek, is the truth—one should never accuse someone of betraying their people without due cause."

Otabek cast his eyes about in embarrassment for having rushed to conclusions, the irrefutable narration giving him pause to consider. After thinking for a while, he asked, "What possible purpose will these savages achieve from the massacre?"

"Their goal could not be clearer," said Hajji. "One will acquire the rank of mingboshi, the second will replace Nur Muhammad, and the third will gain some other city as vassalage. As for the khan, he is venting his rage over Musulmanqul by massacring the Qipchaqs. I believe they have no other goals, my son," he said, pausing, and then continued, "my whole life has been dedicated to the interests of peace and harmony among our citizens, only to be rewarded with weariness and disillusionment. I cannot imagine people being happy living in Turkistan as long as these bastards who incite peoples against one another— ambitious, gluttonous, an insouciant pursuit of eating and drinking one another alive—will not vanish from the soil of our beloved Turkistan; I cannot comprehend the painful truth that we have become such men.

"If we continue on this path of ceaseless internecine conflict, just over our horizon, Russian oppression will trample us with impure feet and sully the sacred soil of Turkistan.[355] We will place a yoke around our future generations' necks with our own hands. God will visit damnation and judgment upon the blind and ignorant fathers who passed the next generation into the hands of the infidel, relegating their children as slaves before they are even born, my son. We dogs who condemned Turkistan, the land where the sacred bodies of our grandfathers are interred, to a pigsty will without doubt meet with Tengri's wrath![356] This land that begat luminaries such as Timur Kurgan,[357] Mirza Babur;[358] scientists such as Al-Farabi, Mirza Ulugbek, as Ibn Sina, all of whom grew and flourished in our land only to find a bitter betrayal by our coevals—indeed those men are worthy of our Almighty's wrath, my son! These malefactors cut our throats and cast our children's futures into the abyss. May their damnation be met as food for worms and birds as grass grows upon the earth above them."

4

IT IS IMPOSSIBLE TO HIDE THE MOON WITH AN APRON; OR, MURDER WILL OUT

Upon finishing his tea, Otabek recited a short prayer and made to get up from his spot.

"Stay a moment."

Yusufbek Hajji's commanding tone insisted that Otabek take his seat again. He looked at his father as if to ask, What else is there to discuss? Without saying a word, Yusufbek Hajji unrolled the turban from around his head, set the cloth on his knees, scratched his head, and wound the turban back into its usual place. Otabek surmised that this gesture augured some sort of serious inquisition. Girding himself, he again looked at his father expectantly.

Yet the traces of litigiousness and grief drained from Hajji's face as the custodial concerns of every "Eastern"[359] father emerged.

"What exactly did you do in Margilan?"

This unexpected question caught Otabek off guard and left him mute. Instead of answering, he attempted to disentangle himself from the uncomfortable subject, casting his eyes about the room.

"I am asking you a straightforward question, Otabek."

"Perhaps your informants have already told you of my actions there..."

"So you, a member of a noble family, simply killed like a common scoundrel!"

At that moment Hajji could discern a slight smile on Otabek's face.

"I am not nobility; I turn out to be among those who are forced to act in that manner."

Hajji did not grasp his son's irony.

"Who pushed you to kill a man?"

"You still don't know?"

"No, I don't understand," said Hajji. "As they say, no one forces you to kill a man. You make that decision yourself."

"They forced me to do so—that is beyond a doubt, Father," Otabek said with a poisonous smile. "You should know that your son usually considers killing others a dishonorable act, bringing shame and disgrace."

"Really? Who was it that pushed you, then?"

"You and my mother!"

"Have you lost your mind, young man?"

"I am perfectly lucid and mean what I say," said his son. "All for the sake of fulfilling your dreams and wishes, you forced me to fulfill your will against my wishes. By compelling me to do so, you threw open the window of opportunity for my enemies, forcing me to behave as an animal—quite beyond my will, to defend my honor," said Otabek.

"Is that so?" asked Hajji, understanding his own complicity and guilt in recent events for the first time. "If that is true, please accept my profound apologies, my son."

"It is not my place to accuse you or relieve you of guilt, Father, yet as an innocent in these crimes, I must simply defend myself. Even now the shade of undeserved suspicions is cast upon me."

Hajji bit his lip and nodded.

"In the end, we all are just mortals—children of God,[360] suckling on mother's milk, prone to make mistakes," he said. "All right, maybe at the bottom of it all you are justified to lay blame on our heads... but if evil people were standing in your way, why didn't you inform me until now? Did someone force you to remain silent?"

"Nobody forced me to remain silent," Otabek said. "But it seemed pointless to request aid from those who first brought me to this pass..."

Hajji's head bowed in shame. His son's riposte dug deep... What could he do now? Otabek was in the right...

"Indeed, it is true that we insisted on the Tashkent marriage," said Hajji finally. "We never intended to separate you from your first wife, though. If you hid this incident from us all for the sake of our misguided dream, you have erred greatly, my child."

Otabek did not protest. He was inured to any reproach now that he had spilled out his grievances and everything that burdened his soul. His heart, however, was racing impatiently—he wanted to know what had prompted his father to broach the conversation.

Hajji went on. "When we face calamity, we usually seek the aid or counsel of those close to ourselves immediately. It seems lunacy that a young man claiming to be my son would keep a secret this egregious from his parents. Well, your father-in-law wrote me a letter. I have read it over and over again; the contents left me in disbelief and shaken. All this time I thought every month my son traveled between here and Margilan. I reread the letter three times over. At first, I thought this letter had been written in error... but then I realized what had happened. According to Mirza Karim Qutidor, he was somehow unkind to you, but it was nothing compared to your childish behavior... Thank God, your stupidity has fallen upon other heads... Tell me, if you had only dropped a single word about this awful situation, would I not have immediately written a letter to your father-in-law? If I had sent Hasan Ali and revealed the truth, would it still have been necessary to kill a man?"

Otabek paid no heed to his father's words, sitting tortured at not yet being able discover what truly troubled him the most.

"Having now achieved your end, why didn't you at least meet with your wife or your father-in-law to reconcile with him?"

"No opportunity availed itself until now."

"When will you go to Margilan then? Now?"

Otabek mentally struggled to resolve in his head this question of "when" versus whether he should go at all. Having considered it for some time; he said, "I don't know."

That very moment Otabek's heart wished to take wings and fly to Margilan, but something inexplicable, more powerful than his heart, tried to reconcile the desire to go with his head telling him maybe he shouldn't.

"As it turns out, your father-in-law, accompanied by your bride, intended to set out on the road this very week," said Hajji. "According to my reckoning, ten days have passed since the letter was written. Maybe we should prepare for their arrival, say tomorrow or the day after tomorrow, by clearing the main room and laying out some rugs..."

Upon receiving this news, Otabek suddenly felt unbelievably relieved, as if shrouded in tender warmth, and he exhaled deeply. "Finally."

A far-off image of a love long lost emerged and passed before him, making him swoon. Yearning and impatience blurred his attempts at uttering a response. His eyes were subsumed by a disquietude, leaving his words incoherent and him unable to respond to his father, who sat waiting with a sardonic expression on his face of, What do you say to this? Yusufbek Hajji interpreted his son's silence in his own way. He was afraid that Otabek could somehow disrespect Mirza Karim Qutidor, who at that very moment carried with him his daughter from Margilan despite the fact that he, being Otabek's senior, was making the first step toward reconciliation. Perhaps his assumption had led Hajji to resort to his usual pedantic nature as he attempted to give admonitions to Otabek, who found his father's advice ridiculous.

"My son," Hajji began. "Respect must be measured in kind. Even if in your eyes they have lost your esteem, to us they are highly regarded. Qutidor represents to us an in-law whom we have known from our earliest days. As for your wife, she is our first daughter-in-law.

"If you still consider me your father, please attempt to make room for them in your heart. Anger must not enter your heart due to the small matter of your father-in-law exiling you from your home—surely a demon held sway over that poor wretch. Anyway, show them respect. Their whole purpose in coming here is due to the fact that you will not show your face in Margilan."

Otabek sat squirming over another unbidden piece of his father's wisdom, all outlining his future role in the drama.

"If we knew the exact arrival date," said Hajji, "you could meet them on the road."

Otabek remained silent.

"Regardless, they might arrive anytime now. Though you refuse, at least let Hasan Ali meet them on the road."

"Fine, let him go," responded Otabek.

5

THE LETTER

Satisfied at their reconciliation, Yusufbek Hajji, after taking his last sips of tea, recited a prayer, and as he made to take his leave, absentmindedly took a letter from his robe and handed it to Otabek.

"The handwriting appears to be your bride's; it must be for you," he said.

Otabek took the letter and waited for his father to depart. The parchment was folded into eight and tied neatly with a red silk string with a dedication to Otabek. His father now out of eyesight, Otabek's heart beat furiously, like that of a horse faltering and stricken with death. Unbinding the knots of silk he opened the letter, his eyes eager to read the words within.

In the name of Zulaikha, who was made for the love of Yusuf;[361] *in the name of Layla, who wept tears of love for Majnun: I give to you limitless greetings; as numerous as the hairs in my braids, fathomless guilt is placed upon me. Please forgive me for all I have done to you. Let us please forget past events. For me, to remember those dark days that passed before me for two years is like living through them again. You may do as you wish—forget or hold on to them, but I would rather forget. I want to begin this letter from a memory of my own past where I once smelled the sweetness of real lasting happiness.*

You are a refugee. You hurriedly wrote me a few lines and ran away. Finally, after two years, I found out the reason you secretly traveled to Margilan. As it turns out, all your movements have been to seek revenge against your enemies, otherwise you would have come to me.

Even if you do not want to see me, let me see you, let me feast my eyes on you... It does not surprise me then that a sullen and capricious woman such as myself tired you out and made you want to flee... Indeed, you still attempt to evade me, but over these past days I have tightened my belt and set out in pursuit of a certain refugee: Accompanied by my father and mother, sometime soon I will arrive to be your slave, to serve your every need. At last, I will find out what I am worth compared to my rival, your favorite wife... You are a noble man; for the sake of our old love, you will mercifully smile upon me... or at least, you will deliver me from my present unhappiness, filling me with joy. But... I greatly fear your beautiful young wife's scolding. For the love of God, as soon as you receive this letter and have your first happy moment along with her, please make her promise not to insult me—assure her that she has no enemy in my arrival. My only purpose is to be you and your beloved's slave, which will give me the opportunity to see my Otabek...

I have made my peace, and with these last thoughts end my letter: All this while I fear in my heart the danger of your parents taking revenge on your other wife, and I too being exiled and thrown into the street. If God blesses me, and I am given a place in your household, I would like to know what my future holds and what you would have me do. I long to see the road before my eyes, and I know in my heart that my path will always lead to you for as long as I live.

Third of Hamal, Margilan; written by your Kumush Bibi

Joy welled in Otabek as a broad smile beamed across his face. Reading the letter over again, certain that the scenes from yesterday portended today's events—a presentiment that now sundered the maleficent branch from the tree of life that only yesterday had held so much sway over this future. Carefully folding the letter back to its original state, crease upon crease, as a keepsake from his beloved now sacred and precious to him, he secreted the letter in one of the folds of his robe. Standing up, he made his departure...

He lingered in the courtyard for some moments. The weight of those visions held for so long, those dark and terrible thoughts, seemed to lift from him as the letter's contents pervaded his soul. Leaning against the guest room's small door, he weighed the words that most struck a chord in his heart. Again, reciting the letter aloud, the same ebullition that had so overwhelmed him before now escaped him. Those same words boded an ill omen, a eulogy for the deceased in yesterday's massacre:

"But... I greatly fear your beautiful young wife's scolding."

He was surprised by this unexpected joy appearing before him. These words harbored such yearning that their meaning gave no reason for joy. This phrase was an omen of future upheaval and bitterness, still vague and hard to define but still in the realm of the possible.

Though Otabek did not seriously fear conflict between the two kundosh, in other words Kumush and Zainab, his heart only shivered at the thought of his mother, the incurable illness that poisoned the most fruitful days of his life, for two years infecting him with a malignant disease that had exiled him to travel aimlessly along treacherous roads and even resort to murder. Was it not the very same selfish wish of his mother that had opened an inroad to his enemies?

Wasn't it she who had turned the whole city upside down looking for a second bride that suited her idea of charm and beauty? Finally, having found a singularly beautiful and clever girl, had she not unceremoniously plunked this unsuspecting woman into his lap even before the ardor of his first wedding had cooled? She had rudely presented this girl in the form of her dreams and wishes as if defiantly challenging him: "This is what a wife should be." He cringed, considering how she would ill-treat his Margilan *pari*. How she would imagine Kumush's arrival to signify a sort of challenge against the cherished bride of Uzbek Oyim. Kumush feared insult from her kundosh. Yet Otabek felt mad with dread over how his mother's transgressions toward Kumush would leave in the shade any petty fears Kumush might hold.

6

CAPRICIOUS UZBEK OYIM; ZAINAB'S SORROW

Yusufbek Hajji's appreciation of his wife's volatile nature and narrow-mindedness made him take a cautious approach in revealing Otabek's secrets. He knew better than Otabek his wife's hostility toward the Margilani and listened to her constant complaints about their son's marriage to "Not a Margilani but a calamity." He also knew about her frequent visits to mystical domlas and Khodjas in the hope of warding off their son's first wife by using magic spells. Knowing all this, he resolved to guide Uzbek Oyim toward appropriate behavior, sparing them both opprobrium and shame.

Hajji was used to the fact that every time they were alone, as soon as Uzbek Oyim opened her mouth, endless complaints about the Margilani "simpleton" and their dissolute son would pour out. She seemed obsessed with that single issue alone.

If earlier he had dismissed the old woman's wailing and remonstrance with a bemused silence, now he patiently waited for Uzbek Oyim to wind up her old song whenever she had a chance.

As the saying goes, "A hungry chicken dreams about millet," or "Mouse's only concern is a bushel of wheat." Uzbek Oyim's concerns were surrounding her son's consumption of fermented camel's milk. One word spoken birthed another word, and finally, as Hajji patiently waited, the inevitable complaints surrounding her son began.

"It seems that your simpleton son has regained some of his senses," said Uzbek Oyim. "Thank heavens that over the past three months he seems to have forgotten about Margilan."

Hajji laughed.

"Perhaps your spells have hit their target..."

"Possibly... Anyway, it seems as if someone has quenched his flame. Praise Allah the spells have achieved their desired effects."

"Praise God his blessed magic has worked," chortled Hajji.

Uzbek Oyim, noticing the sarcasm in her husband's voice, exploded in rage, her mouth contorting in anger. "Why do you laugh?" she shouted, stomping her foot. "This whole time you have done nothing but laugh, showing nothing but indifference to the fate of your nearly lost son. Why do you even now... Oh, let God forgive me..."

"Useless effort will only break your back."[362]

"Damn your Tajik sayings!"[363] said Uzbek Oyim. "Honestly speaking, you are the source of all these problems, my husband, all you know is laughing and making your jokes! It would be more appropriate if you would just admit that you are illiterate in raising your children!"

Hajji howled again. "Indeed, I am unskilled, dear wife—my Oyim Cha!"[364]

"Be gone, and take your laughter with you! Go! May God bring death to laughter!" said Uzbek Oyim, turning her face to the side, offended.

"Look here, Wife," said Hajji, suddenly growing serious. Uzbek Oyim's eyes met his. "The Tajik saying rings true. 'Useless effort will only break your back.' All your efforts thus far have been in vain. If you persist, you will make me complicit in this failure."

"Then you think all my efforts are for nothing."

"For nothing."

"Why would you say that?"

"Your purpose," said Hajji, "has only been to separate your son from his Margilani wife and force upon him a bride of your choosing. Isn't that so?"

"Certainly, I have sought that."

"They say your machinations are the root of all unseemliness. If you question my premise, let us bring your son before you and ask him 'Which wife do you prefer to be with? If you want neither, let them go.' What would your son say to this offer? You know for a fact he would choose his first wife!"

"I know," said Uzbek Oyim. "The Margilani's domla is powerful. He has maddened my son. He has totally bound his heart to her."

Yusufbek Hajji once more could not restrain his laughter. "Well," he replied. "In fact, for three years you have visited the doors of all the domlas and khodjas of Tashkent, one by one. Fine, but why in the end could you not succeed, even until his last days on earth, to bind your son's heart to Zainab?"

Uzbek Oyim did not seem at all surprised by her husband's question.

"The Margilani domla was an Indian seer. As for me, I could not find here an Indian domla to counter his magic."

Hajji offered no laughter at this response, but only felt profound sorrow and empathy for his wife's superstition. "Wife, let us put aside this foolishness," he said in as kind a tone as possible. "If one does not comport oneself with compassion and wisdom, he or she will be plagued forever with ill fortune. If our thoughts are only for our son's best interests, if we live only for his health and happiness, we should only seek those ends that give him joy. I know that you make these efforts on behalf of your son solely through your love and devotion toward him.

"With this in mind, to place blame only on your shoulders would be unjust... you should take this to heart. While your son's monthly trips angered you, they angered me as well—more so in some respects. Many times, I could barely refrain from scolding him. As for my so- called ignorance and laughter that has so upset you, one proverb is apropos: 'One can only laugh and lay one's face upon the earth since all remedies are in vain.' You persist in misreading my reactions to these dilemmas surrounding our son. You persist in accusing my demeanor as imperturbable and nonchalant, yet I managed to keep your son from wandering off to Margilan, turning him from the road..."

Uzbek Oyim sat with a straight back, nodding her head in agreement. With her husband's last words, she lowered her head to her chest as if blessing him in prayer.

Hajji continued. "The confusion must lie in that you were unaware that I put a stop to his travels. The whole time your heart revolved around prayers from domlas and khodjas, meanwhile, my laughter toward your superstitions, to tell the truth, meant only my awareness that I was their main architect..."

Uzbek Oyim at this point pleaded with her husband: "Why didn't you just tell me?"

"Of this I feel guilty," responded Hajji. "We hold the same purpose. Once I was done with scolding Otabek, without consulting you, I wrote a letter to your in-laws asking them to bring his wife to Tashkent. Thank heavens they have relented and granted my request.

"Today I received a most blessed letter of reply from our in-law. He is a just and worthy man, God give him health. This is what he wrote:

" 'Up until now we have hesitated to visit you without an invitation. Having read your letter, we felt uncomfortable, as your daughter-in- law—Kumush—has forever blushed in shame at the thought of how she could possibly show her face to Uzbek Oyim. We are confident that you will not reveal our daughter's naivety to your wife.' The letter's contents follow along these lines..."

Uzbek Oyim looked to her husband, mouth wide open. Hajji's cunning ploy left this shortsighted woman totally confused. Not waiting for his wife to respond, Hajji proceeded to finish her off by reinforcing the layers of the proverbial roof he had skilfully fashioned.

"Which house do you think we should prepare for them?" he asked, and again, not waiting for a response: "You are already well-versed in the proper manner in which to greet your in-laws. They are most honorable. Among the quality of society who are not easily impressed, even if you sacrificed a camel in their honor," he concluded.

Perhaps Uzbek Oyim's mind has weakened or the Indian seer had now gained influence over her. Either way, everything turned upside down in her head. Three years of rancor flew out the window and all complaints gave place to a single jubilant thought: "I will have two daughters-in-law!" The silken whispers of mothers everywhere murmured in her ear: "Ah! Uzbek Oyim's Margilani daughter-in-law has graced our presence. She appears as beautiful as the hatchling of two birds of paradise. We must go pay our respects: we must go feast our eyes on her." If up until that day Zainab had been the only individual Uzbek Oyim could order around, now a vision of two daughters-in-law serving her every need and bowing at her feet emerged.

"Since they are such refined people," concluded Oyim, "we ought to greet them with the respect they merit. Should we offer them our room?"

"I defer to your knowledge on the proper etiquette."

"We can move to the room at the end of the hallway. No doubt their sensitive tastes expect more in the way of lodgings..."

In a moment, she was filled with the utmost kindness and care. She would not even have blushed if someone had reminded her that three minutes earlier she had been overflowing with three years' worth of hostility—but then, *shameless* was not a word with which she was overly familiar. From that time forward she once again held herself up as the grand doyenne, far superior to Hajji in the matters of etiquette and child rearing. As for Yusufbek Hajji, this farcical change in his wife did not at all surprise him; nor did he laugh at her, as he had been wedded to this wife and her peculiar nature for thirty-five years.

Having achieved his designs of calming Uzbek Oyim, he asked her: "Shouldn't we break the news to Zainab gently?"

"What does Zainab have to do with it, if it was our decision to make?" asked Uzbek Oyim. She had completely lost interest in Zainab, for whom she had cared greatly not even three minutes ago.

"The problem does not lie in Zainab," objected Hajji. "When two wives of one husband live under the same roof, we should make sure they get along. The kundosh's role is an especially arduous one. If quarrels arise in the women's half of the house and cups smash on cups, life will be tortuous for your son, not just us."

"So you think we should call her?"

"Call her."

Uzbek Oyim was surprised to come upon Zainab talking to Otabek, full of smiles and laughter.

"Is this a council meeting of husband and wife?"

Otabek only smiled and looked at Zainab. As for Zainab, she stood up, smoothing out her dress and motioning for her mother-in-law to sit in her place.

"You almost guessed it, Mother. Today is a good day for a husband- wife get-together," she said and looked at Otabek, smiling.

Uzbek Oyim did not sit, blurting out instead, "Buy for them identical dresses. Show no preferences; don't be stingy with one or the other. Behave as if this is your wife and the other is your wife as well... Zainab, could you please come with me? Your father-in-law is calling for you."

For a moment the instructions confused them and seemed to portend disaster, as if the roof had caved in upon them.

Otabek suddenly grasped the implications of the strange instructions. He understood that although his mother held no love for the Margilani, he had managed to escape from the clutches of his powerful enemy. He also understood why Zainab had been summoned. As for Zainab, she trailed behind her mother-in-law, completely unsuspecting.

When mother-in-law and daughter-in-law took their places in front of him, Hajji looked at Zainab affectionately.

"My child, Zainab," he said. "We have decided to bring your Margilani sister here to live. What is your opinion concerning this?"

Zainab turned to look at her mother-in-law, startled. She now comprehended the meaning behind Uzbek Oyim's recent request. She sighed imperceptibly, coming to terms with the idea of a rival.

"What can I say..."

"The matter at hand does not depend on what you say or don't say, Zainab." remonstrated Hajji. "Could you become a sister to her when she arrives? This is what I ask of you."

"I guess, I could..."

"Would you become like sisters?" her father-in-law persisted.

"I don't know," said Zainab.

"Why don't you know?"

Zainab sat, considering the situation for some time.

"It takes two hands to clap," she finally said. "What does it serve to give my word now to remain congenial, when my sister could prove to own a bad nature?"

"Well spoken. We will ask of her what we ask of you." Zainab kept her silence.

"Zainab is not what you would call a wife one should be careful of or afraid of," said Uzbek Oyim. "Thank God she has a good head on her shoulders."

"Take not the vicious words of others to heart, Daughter. We make no distinction between you and the wife from Margilan. You both are our children—indeed, you are our daughter!"

Zainab responded only with a nod of her head. Upon Yusufbek Hajji's recitation of a prayer, Zainab returned to Otabek's room.

Otabek knew the moment he saw the sad expression on Zainab's face. For a few minutes they sat facing one another, lost in their own worries, not a word spoken between them out of fear of upsetting the other.

"Why did they call you?" Otabek finally asked, agitation in his voice. "You ask a question you already know the answer to?" asked Zainab with a forced smile.

"What do I know?"

"That a certain someone is arriving from Margilan."

In his embarrassment, Otabek only managed to mutter, "This is not my will... everything is according to my father."

"It may be your father's will, but it is your desire."

"What is my desire?"

"To be reunited with your beloved. Of course, this is what your heart seeks."

"You think I love her?"

"Certainly you love her."

Otabek attempted to keep his calm. "You are mistaken!" he said.

"I am nothing of the sort," said Zainab. "You married her out of love. As for me... I was married to fulfill the wishes of your parents," she said, her eyes filling with tears.

Otabek had arrived at a great moral dilemma in the face of the undeniable truth; to again deny her point, hence to continue to speak lies, seemed most unseemly and disrespectful to her. Despite his misgivings, there was nothing to do but to tell a white lie.

"In the beginning... I married her out of love, as you say; this is in fact true, but this is not the situation now," he said.

"I do not believe you."

"Why don't you believe me?"

After surveying him for a time, Zainab said, "I have my reasons for remaining skeptical."

Otabek became alarmed. "You must tell me your reasons."

"How long has it been since you married me?"

"Two years..."

"During these two years your relationship to me has not changed a bit. You do not consider me your wife!"

"That is nonsense."

"My argument makes perfect sense, my dear," said Zainab, becoming flustered. "You cannot deny that since you returned from Margilan, you have slept in the guest room every night. You did not even consider that I could tie my life with yours with the hope of spending many happy years with you. The reason you have completely disregarded me is that you hold on to the same hope that one day, she will put her head on your pillow..."

Zainab could not finish her statement, as she began to cry, looking sideways to avoid his eyes. Otabek felt crushed beneath a mountain of shame.

"You completely misunderstand..."

"Why then is this issue even under discussion?"

"The reasons are clear," said Otabek, not sure himself what the reasons were.

"So then will you tell me?"

"I think you already know."

"I know nothing."

"You must know!"

"For the love of God, I have no idea."

"If in fact you don't know," said Otabek, "it is better you don't. I am ashamed to explain the reasons from my own lips..."

"You feel ashamed to speak the truth in front of your own wife?"

"Shouldn't I be ashamed?"

"Don't be."

"Then I have to confess... I am weak... I lack what we could call manly resolve in this matter..."[365]

341

Zainab looked at him in disbelief, not entirely trusting his words. "You are not being truthful with me..."

"Believe it or not, this is the reason I have distanced myself from you."

"Even if I believed you, it is not a good enough reason to sleep separately... Your sleeping in the guest room is not the reason I am so hurt..." she said, looking at Otabek with full, longing eyes. "I don't need your so-called 'manly resolve'... I need you..." Tears streaming down her face, she threw herself into Otabek's arms. For the first time Otabek realized the extent of Zainab's heartache. Poor Zainab had profoundly demeaned herself by pleading to and kissing a lifeless monument.

7

Meeting Of The In-Laws

A trader who had arrived the day prior informed them that their in-laws would arrive in two days. Hasan Ali rode ahead to greet them. Yusufbek Hajji himself managed all preparations and ordered Oibadak to clean the outside yard. As for the Ich Kari, Uzbek Oyim asked for assistance from several neighboring wives to Hashar.[366] For everything they found a place, and the surface of the yard was swept so clean one could have licked butter off the ground. During the previous three days, Uzbek Oyim had made ready her own room for the guests, placing sumptuous rugs on its floor, and had prepared all the food proper for the eagerly anticipated celebration in honor of the in-laws. A fat sheep was bound to a column in the stable, ready to be slaughtered once the in-laws passed through her door.

The khan atlas dresses tailored especially for both Zainab and Kumush did not meet Uzbek Oyim's standards. She decided that the local wife had enough clothes, and since the other one was a guest of high standing, she bought Chinese silk and made another dress for her Margilani. In this manner she also ordered a couple extra shirts for the Margilani.

Deeming one Chinese velvet robe insufficient in number, she added her own priceless gold-embroidered overcoat; and, not satisfied with two scarves, she added the wedding *qalmaki*[367] she had not unwrapped since the early years of her marriage.

Zainab showed no signs of sadness. She attended to her mother-in-law's guidance as before, preparing the tablecloth for the anticipated guests.

Uzbek Oyim ordered one of the Hashar wives to prepare a fire in the *tandir*.[368] After that she approached Zainab. "Did you finish laying the tablecloth, my child?" she asked.

"I did, some time ago. It seems to me that there is not enough honey for the guests' Ich Kari dasturkhon."

"Take what you need from storage. After that, since Oibadak is too busy, look to the dough, it has already risen." Uzbek Oyim finished as she had begun, standing from her spot, peering through the small window at the tablecloths spread outside. "Your tablecloth is nice. Don't forget about the Varaqi."[369] Upon spotting Yusufbek Hajji in the yard, she gestured him to come over. Yusufbek Hajji, wearing a silk-blend robe and white skullcap, slowly approached his wife.

"What is it?"

"Did you have a look at our tables?"

Hajji looked at the splendid food indifferently. "It's fine as long as you like it."

"Have you asked for the butcher yet? We should not be in a rush when they arrive."

"The butcher is ready. Should we slaughter the lamb now?"

"No," said Uzbek Oyim. "Meat is tastier when it is cooked in front of the guests. By the way, have you sent for our local in-laws?"

Zainab, who had been hurrying about to retrieve the honey, stopped for a moment to hear from her father-in-law's own mouth his response.

"I have," said Hajji. "It turns out that Alimbek has gone to his fields.[370] It seems that only the mother-in-law will come to visit."

Zainab left to get the honey. Hajji leaned closer to Uzbek Oyim and quietly asked, "Does Zainab seem sad?"

"Why should she be sad?"

"Well, I am asking you."

343

"She is well enough," said Uzbek Oyim. "Has Oibadak freed herself from cleaning the outer yard?"

"She just finished. I invited three or four persons from the Mahalla as well. We have to make more plov."

"Will do."

Hajji looked about and asked, "Where is your son?"

"He was just in the men's half."

"It seemed that before, he was on his way here."

"Maybe he is off to the guzar or somewhere else," replied Uzbek Oyim.

Oibadak, having finished her task in the outside yard, entered through the door. Hajji left to search the guest room for Otabek. Following Uzbek Oyim's orders, Oibadak, Zainab, and the Hashar wives sat down to form small loaves of bread.

The sun progressed just past noon and everything was tidied up. Uzbek Oyim made herself up as if she were about to attend a wedding. She had on a simple khan atlas shirt, a white silk scarf on her head, and she outlined her eyebrows with surma.

After she said to Zainab, "One must not say that we overwork our daughter-in-law. Make yourself up too," Zainab swam in an ocean of silk; she was the very image of a newly married bride.

Mohira Oyim, Zainab's mother, Khushroibibi, her sister, and Hanifa Nisoz, her sister-in-law, also attended. Karima Otin, Sharofat the seamstress, and Mahina Bonuz, who were favorite neighbors of Uzbek Oyim's, also arrived, dressed to meet the occasion. Altogether, eight wives sat around the small tablecloth quickly put together in the inner yard. Uzbek Oyim relayed to the gathering that her Margilani in-laws were well-bred and had no qualms about Otabek marrying a woman in Tashkent; that they would arrive in Tashkent soon to witness the Toi; and how the husband was a wealthy and prosperous authority in his city.

"It seems fated that she is their only child and now she is our daughter-in-law. Holding a powerful paternal love toward Otabek, his father-in-law forever enthuses that he is better than his own child. 'If I had a son, Otabek would fit the description. I will bequeath all of my earthly belongings to him when I perish from this earth. May God grant him a long life."

344

Mohira Oyim, clearly squirming from the puffery, replied, "Yes, my dear in-law, 'clapping is made by two hands,' they say... 'If the calf is obedient it may suckle on two mothers...' "

Oibadak, who was splashing the water around the yard to keep the dust from rising under the heat of the sun, heard the clip-clopping hooves of an entourage over the wall. Frantically hurrying to where the guests were sitting, she announced, "It appears they have arrived."

Uzbek Oyim halted halfway into her litany of embellishments and stood up from her place with the guests following her in tow. Zainab turned pale and ran into her room. Uzbek Oyim, sovereign among the wives, descended into the yard. Whispering something into the ears of her daughter, Khushroi, Mohira Oyim snickered softly. Just as Uzbek Oyim neared the middle doors dividing the two yards, a neighbor child entered in, running to her.

"Give me *suyinchi*,[371] Grandmother Bek. Your in-laws have arrived!"

Uzbek Oyim took a handful of coins out of her pocket and gave them to the child. Behind the child, Hasan Ali appeared.

"Well then, Mother, you should give me *kormana*,[372] right? I brought you your lost daughter-in-law!" he said, looking toward the passage. "Wait, wait, let me earn my suyinchi!"

Oftob Oyim appeared from the passage. She had a paranji over her head, with her veil still in her hands. Hasan Ali introduced her to Uzbek Oyim: "We have your in-law, Oftob Oyim."

Uzbek Oyim and Oftob Oyim exchanged a flurry of greetings, embracing each other.[373] The other wives welcomed her next. Everyone looked about as if searching for something that had gotten away. They seemed to be looking for Kumush, who had yet to enter. Uzbek Oyim's eyes were glued to the passage, and Hasan Ali was winking mysteriously, looking at Uzbek Oyim and the gate though which Kumush would enter. Oftob Oyim, who stood to the side, greeting the other wives, finally moved closer to her in-law.

"Perhaps she feels a bit shy," she said with a smile.

Uzbek Oyim, beaming toward the passage, said, "Hey, Pasha Kilin![374] We have waited for you long enough. Don't be shy, my child. And the present for Hasan Ali is ready."

Hasan Ali beckoned to her, looking into the passage... Finally, blushing beet red, Kumush stepped out of the entryway, holding her paranji in her hands, a black atlas shirt under a robe of a rich blues and greens, a white scarf wrapped around her head, her bewitching eyes cast about shyly, and her crow's-feet wrinkled with her slight smile.

Hasan Ali made introductions. "This is your mother-in-law, Beg Oyim."[375]

Kumush greeted her with a salaam, dropped her paranji to the earth, and rushed forward into the arms of Uzbek Oyim.

Uzbek Oyim returned her embrace, taking her in her arms, kissing her cheeks, blessing her over and over again, and finally gazing into her eyes, crying... The guest wives, Mohira Oyim, Khushroi, and Hanifa, upon seeing Kumush, exchanged glances charged with meaning, biting their lips...

The greetings between the mother-in-law and her new bride took a whole minute to complete. After Kumush greeted each of the other women, Uzbek Oyim introduced her by name to each wife. Zainab appeared at last. Uzbek Oyim smiled at Kumush and pointed to Zainab.

"Well, do you know who this might be?"

Kumush seemed not at all flustered... looking at Zainab, also covered in luxurious silk, she took one step toward her.

"Zainab, my sister!" she said.

Zainab reciprocated the greeting while moving to Kumush, a smile beaming from her face... The two kundosh exchanged the obligatory "Are you in good health?" and "How are things?" Gentle hands laced, arms akimbo onto each other's shoulders in an embrace, offering each other a warm welcome.[376] Imposing himself amid these greetings, Yusufbek Hajji appeared from the passage. Female guests, observing the tradition of retreating from unfamiliar males,[377] modestly moved aside and turned their faces away. In the presence of Hajji, Oftob Oyim gave a momentary greeting and covered her face with a scarf wrapped around her neck.[378]

Hajji greeted his in-law with a smile.

"*Barakalar*,[379] my sister! Has your trip made you tired? I am sorry. I feel like I have put you through some trouble," he said apologetically, putting the embarrassed Oftob Oyim at ease.

"Well, our dear Bek, give me the *kormana*!" said Uzbek Oyim, motioning to Kumush.

Kumush, still quite reticent, could only muster soft greetings as she neared Hajji and bowed her head in supplication. Hajji gave Kumush's shoulder a fatherly pat and kissed his hand, with which he then touched Kumush's forehead.

"We have such a lovely Margilani bride among us, yet we knew nothing of her until now." He delivered his compliments with a broad smile, looked about, and opened his hands in prayer.

"Your arrival renders deep respect to my family. If we cannot return such goodness in kind, let Allah give it on our behalf. Let Allah give to the young ones a peaceful and blessed life. Dear God, Allah, Taqabbul,[380] receive all our prayers."

Everyone cupped their hands for the prayer and upon Hajji's finishing it, all ran their hands over their faces, then Yusufbek Hajji turned to Kumush and Zainab.

"It gladdened my heart to see you both in greeting," he said. "I wish you two to be like sisters as well." And then to Uzbek Oyim: "Well, take the guests inside." And at that he turned to leave.

8

UNDERLYING HOSTILITY

Uzbek Oyim led her in-law and Kumush to the inner sanctum of the house, the other guests following, all the while ordering Oibadak, "Quickly, tend to the tea. These poor women must be thirsty from the interminable ride in their wagon." Then she turned to Oftob Oyim and Kumush. "I am extremely offended and displeased with you both."

Oftob Oyim, giving a sidelong glance to Kumush, responded, "You do not have to tell us—we are already burning with shame."

Passing through a hallway into the main hall, Uzbek Oyim invited them to sit in the center of the circle the ladies were forming. "Well, take your places in the seat of honor." While Oftob Oyim took her place, Kumush, bashful in front of the other guests, remained still. Uzbek Oyim now pleaded to her, "Don't be shy, Kumush Khotin. For today and tomorrow you are our guest as our

347

new bride and, three days from now, I will grind even your pretty little head under the millstone!" She laughed.

Oftob Oyim and the rest of the entourage joined in the laughter. "You haven't washed clothes with my soap yet!" Uzbek Oyim said.

This time Kumush also permitted herself a slight smile. Oftob Oyim and Mohira—the female in-laws—had taken the seats of honor; Kumush sat to the left of Oftob Oyim; Khushroi next to Kumush; Hanifa to the right of Mohira Oyim; and after that Karima Otin, Sharofat the seamstress, and Mahina Banu sat in a row by the doors. Uzbek Oyim was the last to take her place. Karima Otin opened her hands in supplication and recited a prayer, then Uzbek Oyim welcomed everyone.[381] After the prayer, as if in silent agreement, all eyes fell on Kumush. Kumush, overwhelmed and feeling bashful, looked to the ground. Silence came over everyone until Mohira Oyim said to Oftob Oyim, "You must be exhausted, traveling so far from Margilan?"

"Actually, we are not as tired as we expected to be," said Oftob Oyim. "The wagon road from Margilan to Tashkent takes about ten days, but we were not in such a rush and made it here in twelve days."

"Was the road muddy?" asked Mahina Banu.

"Not so muddy," said Oftob Oyim. "As it turned out, the road was mostly clear. On both sides were fields of dark green grass. Tulips covered the hills. The time was right to enjoy the journey."

It was now Uzbek Oyim's turn to speak.

"If you had not finally come to visit us, I had decided that I would not allow Otabek to travel anymore," she said. "I said to my son, 'My God, have you not tired of traveling to Margilan every month for the last three years? Shouldn't they come here for once?' In this manner I made up my mind to forbid him from taking to the road."

Upon hearing the name Otabek, Kumush slowly raised herself from her place. Because Oftob Oyim had been made aware by Hasan Ali of the family secrets, she understood Uzbek Oyim's rough manner in dealing with people.

"No need to reproach us. We are ashamed of the situation as it is," she said.

Zainab entered with a *dasturkhon* in her hands, and after welcoming the guests, laid out the tablecloth.[382] Receiving trays of food from Oibadak, handed to her from the hallway, she once or twice took furtive glances at Kumush, their eyes finally meeting. When the trays were laid out on the table, Oibadak brought in a tea service with four teapots on a copper stand. Zainab sat near the service in order to pour tea for the guests. Uzbek Oyim stopped Oibadak, who was making her way out of the room. "Has the butcher arrived?"

"He arrived a while ago. If you were to receive a prayer from Oyim, I would take the sheep out to slaughter."

Uzbek Oyim looked at Oftob Oyim.

"Will you recite the Fatiha, In-Law?"

Oftob Oyim looked at Mohira Oyim.

"Give your blessing instead, Oyi!"

"The sheep is devoted to you," said Mohira Oyim. "It is in your right to give the blessing. As for us, we have already delivered many prayers..."

Uzbek Oyim nodded to Oftob Oyim as if to say, "You should give the blessing." Oftob Oyim quietly recited lines fitting to the occasion. After Oibadak left, they looked to the tablecloth and started to urge one another to help themselves and "Please eat something," enjoining each to partake.[383] As before, all eyes were fixated on Kumush. Uzbek Oyim especially regarded her for some time, pleading with her to eat.

"Help yourself, my child, help yourself! I can't abide it when a person stands on etiquette and won't eat. Or are you offended that I have become too familiar with you since you entered through my doors?"

"I am not at all offended but instead glad," said Kumush, making herself eat something from the tablecloth.

"Your abandoning of formalities with Kumush right away truly shows that you have considered her to be your daughter for three years now. I am most grateful to you for that," said Oftob Oyim.

Karima Otin added, "A person shows familiarity with their own child.

One would not be overly familiar with strangers."

And Zainab chimed in, "She was overly familiar to me starting with the moment I left the *Chimildiq*..."[384]

"I cannot say that I stand on formalities with those who are close to me," Uzbek Oyim said, now praising herself. "Dear Kumush, please have at least some *varaki*, one or two, please. Your heart must be wracked with hunger."

Kumush pardoned herself. "It seems I have become a bit tired. I suddenly lost my appetite."

Uzbek Oyim laughed. "If you have lost your appetite, it is not due to fatigue but longing for your husband."

All of them burst out in laughter. Zainab joined in as well... but Kumush only turned her face to the side. Perhaps deep down she appreciated her mother-in-law's cleverness.

Uzbek Oyim again urged her in-laws Oftob Oyim and Mohira to eat something from the *dasturkhon*. "Help yourselves, In-Laws. You should distance yourselves from the activities of the young ladies. If young men occupy their thoughts, you and I are preoccupied with food."

Again, they all roared. Oftob Oyim too laughed, not able to contain her mirth. Kumush also opened up, appreciating Uzbek Oyim's raucous humor and looking to Zainab, who returned her smile.

Just as their snickering died down, Zainab's sister-in-law asked Kumush, "How long has it been since you have seen your Bek?"

Kumush looked to her mother, terrified. Oftob Oyim answered. "About three months."

A sudden brutality rose in Khusroi's eyes. "Your dear aunt is right then. It is apparent that your appetite is diminished for the reasons mentioned."

"Indeed! Indeed!" said all the wives.

"I know it for a fact myself," said Uzbek Oyim. "That is why I stopped Otabek from traveling for three months."

This revelation pierced straight through Kumush's heart. "No doubt you do," she thought ironically. "You kept him from traveling intentionally."

Oftob Oyim responded, chortling, "Not only my daughter's, but my own appetite has faded..."

The thought of Otabek now entered Uzbek Oyim's mind. "Have you yet seen Otabek?" she asked Oftob Oyim.

"No, I have not."

Uzbek Oyim looked at Zainab. "Maybe he is outside?"

"I have heard nothing of his whereabouts..." said Zainab.

Uzbek Oyim was surprised. "A while ago your father was also asking about his whereabouts..." she said. "Where has that fool gone off to... Didn't he say something to you this morning?"

Kumush looked at Zainab for a response; Zainab looked at her. "He asked me for his robe this morning" she said. "When I gave it to him, I asked him where he intended to go. He said he had something to do somewhere..."

Zainab's response stung Kumush greatly, causing a wave of nausea to come over her. Oftob Oyim also became heavyhearted. Zainab's relatives smirked, raising their eyebrows at one another. Uzbek Oyim noted the conspiratorial conversation, unspoken but full of meaning, passing between them. "Maybe some critical duty arose at the last minute," she said.

At that moment Hasan Ali peeked in through the small door. He held in his hand a leather bag full of qimiz. Standing in the doorway he welcomed the guests and passed the qimiz into the room. He then turned to Oftob Oyim and smiled. "Your son-in-law brought you some qimiz."

Oftob Oyim regained her composure, and Kumush's face flushed. As for those who had smirked at their expense, their mood turned sour and their faces became ashen.

Uzbek Oyim, delighted to have qimiz on hand, asked Hasan Ali, "When did he arrive?"

"Just now."

"Where did that fool get lost to?"

Hasan Ali commented, "Yesterday, Hajji gave him a task to complete. I am not certain but it seems that, being preoccupied, he forgot to complete it. This morning he remembered and thought that he could perform his responsibility before the guests arrived. His destination was a bit far from here. He knew he was late on his return, so, feeling guilty, he bought these two leather bags of qimiz... Giving the qimiz to me, he said, 'Go in and give my apologies. I am ashamed to ask for forgiveness.'"

Karima Otin replied jokingly, "He will not be forgiven. What nonsense is it to bring qimiz!"

Oftob Oyim, looking around at the guests, answered Hasan Ali, beaming, "We arrived parched as if lost in a desert. So we have forgiven him already."

"Thank you. Thank you!" said Hasan Ali. "I will leave now and tell him that he is excused."

"Yes, go out and tell him," said Oftob Oyim.

"What about you?" asked Hasan Ali, turning to Kumush.

Kumush looked at Zainab, who sat motionless like a frog, before shyly answering, "I also excuse him..."

"I knew already you would have excused him two times over," said Hasan Ali as laughter both fullhearted and grudging mixed to fill the four walls of the home.

After it again died down, Uzbek Oyim asked, "Why didn't he come in to say all this himself?"

"He is talking with his father-in-law..."

After Hasan Ali excused himself, Uzbek Oyim ordered Oibadak to serve the qimiz in a copper basin. In the meantime, the sheep's throat was cut and the animal readied for cooking. Uzbek Oyim asked her in-laws for their wishes: "How would you like the meat prepared?'

"Please don't ask me. We are amenable to whatever the other guests prefer."

Uzbek Oyim went out into the yard to make arrangements for the meal. Zainab ladled qimiz from the copper basin Oibadak had poured it in into cups and served the fermented mare's milk to the guests.

9

HAJJI SHAKES THE HEM OF HIS ROBE; IN WHICH HE RENOUNCES WORLDLY AFFAIRS

Qutidor occupied the place reserved for guests; near him sat the imam of the Mahalla, Yunus Mohamed Akhund; a leader within the Mahalla, Pir Nazar the Executioner; and an elder named Sotib Oldi. Otabek sat next to Pir Nazar the Executioner, and Yusufbek Hajji, alongside Sotib Oldi-aka. At the end of the row, near the door, Hasan Ali poured qimiz from one of the bags. The discussion was about the events surrounding the massacre of the Qipchaqs that had taken place four days prior. Yusufbek Hajji led in the depiction of the events.

"I resign myself to the despair of not knowing whether our nation will ever achieve a degree of civility... From infancy, as far as I can remember, my gaining of accolades, further power, or greater titles have shown no meaning—my sole concern in engaging in such work has been toward benefiting the lives of Muslims. All told, all my efforts have shown me to be a naive child manipulated by sycophants chasing the titles qushbegi and mingboshi... That same individual we know as the Shah-an-Shah has lent his ear to the contemptible counsel of these dissolute schemers and disregards the counsel of his own community. Meanwhile, I was one of those people who saved him from the disaster of Musulmanqul. So, there we have it. The council of those who engage in obfuscation is well received. The learned and wise are deceived as if they were small, naive children..."

Yunus Mohamed Akhund interrupted him at that point: "Eh, Hajji," he said. "All conflicts arise from the Shah-an-Shah himself. If our Shah- an-Shah were of a lucid sort, the evil intentions propagated by these shallow bastards would reach no one, and the blood of these innocents would not have flowed without justification. His Greatness the Prophet gave to us in the holy Hadith the following: *'Bismillah, his-Rahman ir, Kollah un*

Nabiyo-Alli-Hissalom'—'When the practice of honoring a trust is lost, expect the Last Day.' " [385]

"Enough. If people's fate is in the hands of incompetent rulers, the future of the people will remain in peril and riddled with uncertainty. And since we have been governed by unworthy people since time immemorial, no wonder all sorts of calamities fall on our heads. Well, I say, may their evil deeds be removed along with their heads."

"*Saddaqta Asulilloh,*" said Hajji, continuing the Hadith, " 'When the government is entrusted to the undeserving, then await the Last Day.' "

Sadness descended upon him, forcing him to take a moment to compose himself. Gathering his thoughts, he continued.[386]

"My whole life's purpose has been to serve the downtrodden, to turn them onto the righteous path. Now my life nears its end," he said, grabbing his beard. "This beard has turned white caring for the well- being of the nation. This heart has been blackened by the machinations of ingrates who worship material gain. I do not remember a time in my sixty-five years I have not sent prayers to Allah and blessed him by pressing my forehead to the earth with eyes wide open. Now Allah has punished me for letting myself be deceived by unworthy scoundrels.

"As for my being deceived, it seems to be a bad omen sent through God's righteousness—ironic for one in service to the unfortunate. The world was created in five days; it seems to me it is more important to shake the hem of my robe from the scandals of the world and prepare myself for my final home."

These observations darkened the mood of the gathering. All remained silent for some time. Hajji's words made a great impression on Pir Nazar-aka. He relayed to the conclave his ideas through the beauty of his oratorical skills.

"Bringing calm to the nation is difficult without cutting off a few heads—through identifying the villains one by one," he said.

Those gathered looked for Hajji to respond, and he in turn after some moments snickered. "You have spoken honestly, Executioner. Perhaps you can call my son sitting next to you for help."

At this everyone guffawed. Qutidor gave a sidelong glance at Otabek, smiling. As for Otabek, his father's wit turned him dark red like a sugar beet. Thank God no one other than Qutidor and Hasan Ali understood the underlining meaning of the joke.

Pir Nazar-aka regarded Otabek with some gravity.

"Otabek could command an army, but not be an executioner like me. If you prayed thus, and Otabek gave the order, I would not refuse the removal of an evildoer's head!" he exclaimed.

"We all, both young and old, think that beheading is the answer to all problems. We believe that with the removal of heads, the world would calm itself and life would continue. Fine. To tell the truth, I am not against the taking of an evildoer's head, but we must consider some of the finer points: We must first gather those individuals dedicated to service, not personal gain, who wish only advancement of the nation. This group must also have a common aim shaped by their convictions. Only in this manner would one be able to sweep away the thorns that plague our footsteps. Only in this manner would the blood spilt be deemed just and honest— seen as legitimate sacrifice. Otherwise the taking of heads will be no different than the massacre we just witnessed." As he took a moment to pause, a look of mercy descended upon him, and one could see a tenderness in his eyes. "Reaching my advanced age, I have yet to meet among us three or four people who are fit to join my proposed group. It is a pity."

The men passed the requisite words among themselves as they rose together to go to the mosque for midday prayers. As Otabek stood to join the group, Hasan Ali stopped him.

"One moment, Otabek," he said as the gathering moved into the main yard. "It would be scandalous for you not to visit the women in the inner yard... As for your being late, I devised some tale—barely credible, hardly believable, to distract them."

Otabek slumped down, resigned to his fate.

"All right, then..." he said.

10

HASAN ALI'S TRICK

We know that when a person succumbs to fear, he freezes in place, struck dumb, paralysed with indecision. No doubt we have all experienced this sort of terror at some point in our lives. In truth, if a savage tiger were to appear before us, we would react as described, accepting that death awaits us. And nothing represents to human beings a more terrifying barricade to life than always waiting, always patient death. In the end we all regard our feelings surrounding death to be natural; but what is most interesting is that even when a world of happiness awaits us, even when portents abound intimating our great fortune, we still react as if death is imminent and our spirit, once graced with hope, descends into the above-mentioned state.

*****

Otabek at present found himself in this very situation. A debilitating mood had gripped him that morning, progressing steadily to culminate in a crescendo of agony and terror. By the time Hasan Ali came to speak to him, he was almost struck dumb with fear.

Hasan Ali attempted to advise him on how to behave when he entered the female half of the room: "Your mother and Zainab know nothing of your scandalous adventures in Margilan. I have warned your mother-in- law and Kumush already. Therefore, when you greet them and exchange words with them, act as if you have not seen them for three months."

Otabek turned pale and sighed. "That is easy compared to..." he said. "What exactly is so difficult."

"You still don't realize?"

Hasan Ali studied Otabek's expression for a few moments... "Are not you a Yigit?[387] He-e, bless you!"

"Being a Yigit does not stop my heart racing..."

Hasan Ali considered his options for a few moments; Otabek's present condition was truly delicate. Hasan Ali several times scratched his head and tugged at his beard, deep in thought. Finally, he laughed out loud. "Stop your worrying," he said. "Let me do you a kindness..."

"What are you going to do?"

"Don't ask. From this moment on pass onto me all your willpower."

Otabek gave a forced laugh. "What do you intend to do?" he asked again.

"Don't ask," repeated Hasan Ali. "Remain calm, take your ablutions, and say your prayers."

Upon speaking these words, Hasan Ali left the guest room. Otabek, as if under a spell, got up for ablutions and, entering the washroom, started his Taravih[388]... A half hour passed, and Hasan Ali walked into the room from the yard while Otabek's forehead was still touching the earth in prayer.

"Haven't you finished yet?" Hasan Ali asked from the doorway. Otabek turned to look at him, forgetting to bow his head to both sides as custom required. Hasan Ali could only laugh at Otabek's nerves.

"Well, come with me."

"Where are we going?"

"To the Ich Kari."

"Again?"

Hasan Ali answered, laughing, "If you enter now we should meet with success. You... from the middle passage slowly enter my room. The women are still praying so nobody will see you once you have entered. I will close the door behind you and, after a while, I will bring your wife to you, all alone... Will that do?"

"Yes! Yes! Of course!"

"Well, quickly, quickly, get up."

Otabek rose, his heart calming as another half an hour remained before their rendezvous. He entered the middle passage. Hasan Ali, leading the way, stopped and showed him the door to his room.

"Go in," he said.

Otabek did as he was told. Hasan Ali all but closed the door to the room, leaving it slightly ajar, and cracked open the shutter just

357

enough so no one from the opposite room could see what was transpiring inside. Chuckling, amused by some hidden joke known only to him, he crept over to where the wives congregated.

Hasan Ali's room had been tidied by Oibadak. It was a simple room with austere decorations common to simple people. The walls were now covered with alabaster, the ceiling painted. Purple flowered camel rugs were spread out on the floor and beautiful blankets woven from gorgeous textiles were draped on the walls, hiding a niche of folded, quilted blankets. Taking off his galoshes, Otabek paced across the room a couple of times and let out a nervous sigh. At that moment the beautiful fabric that covered the niche waved slightly with florid ripples. Otabek did not notice this movement. Then someone lifted the fabric as Otabek jumped, startled... She looked from inside the niche and smiled with a face full of joy and serenity. Otabek shivered with excitement...

After a moment that seemed to hang suspended in time, they cautiously drew closer to each other and embraced without saying a word. Otabek reeled from the sweet musk of her curls; as for Kumush, she throbbed, enveloped in the all-pervading strength of his arms. They stood there for some moments then pulled apart, walked to the end of the room and sat down, knees akimbo. Neither desired conversation, they only gazed into each other's eyes. For some time they remained in silence. Finally tears welled up in Kumush's eyes as quickly as laughter.

"You... are a runaway," she said. "And you..."

"Me what...?"

"You are a persecutor."

"And I have a right to be!" said Kumush, gently slapping her husband on the face.

"On this side too..." he said, turning the other cheek. "Let Zainab slap that side."

"Zainab... does not have the privilege to hand out beatings."

Kumush's eyes danced with a long-lost but newly recovered joy. "Are you telling the truth?"

"I speak the truth."

"Fine, here it is then," said Kumush.

She softly patted Otabek on the other cheek, and they continued with their smiles and endless gazes.

"I have aged looking for a special someone," said Kumush. "Nonsense... That description fits me better," said Otabek. "You!" exclaimed Kumush. "You have only become more mature."

"You lie."

"No, really, I am telling you the truth," she said. "But you..."

"Me?"

"I will talk about it later..."

Kumush protested, "No, tell me now," and she used the magic of her eyes to compel him. Instead of providing the desired answer, Otabek only kissed her face... Kumush, freeing herself from him, got up.

"Please stay here for now."

Otabek looked at her, confused. "What's wrong? Where are you going?"

"To Margilan..."

"It is too late in the day to leave now. Leave tomorrow."

Kumush only chuckled and slapped Otabek's face again. "Our secret meeting," she said. "Nobody knows about this other than my mother and Hasan Ali Ota. It would not be good if your Zainab knew about this rendezvous."

"What if she did?"

"Nothing would happen... it is just not right for us to meet like this," she replied. "After a while, enter and greet my mother. Your tardiness makes your other mothers-in-law kill themselves with glee."

Again, giving him a mischievous look, Kumush left the room. Otabek was now perfectly calm. If his heart was beating faster than usual, it was only because it was filled with love for the one who had just left the room. Sitting alone, an unexpected grin crept over his face and gratitude to Hasan Ali grew within him. The euphoria that swept over him defied description. Otabek forgot about everything and did not even once think about Zainab, as if all the cares of the world were swept from his memory.

Once an adequate amount of time had passed to allow Kumush to take her place in the gathering hall, he left the room he was hiding in and casually entered the room where the guests were assembled.

Zainab, who saw his approach from where she was sitting, quickly got up to follow Otabek as he entered in front of the guests.

Upon seeing Otabek, those sitting got up from their places; only Uzbek Oyim remained seated, ignoring him. Otabek first greeted Oftob Oyim, who gave him a warm hug and kissed both his cheeks as tears welled up in her eyes. After this, he greeted his other mother-in-law, Zainab's sisters, and the remaining guests. Finally, turning to Kumush with a broad smile, he said, "How are you..."

Kumush gave a soft laugh and said, "Thank God."

Now that all greetings had been duly delivered, they all took their seats. Otabek sat near his mother; Zainab sat next to him. Kumush was angered by Zainab's slight and cast dark looks in her direction.

After a prayer was recited, the son-in-law begged his pardon from his mother-in-law: "First of all, I made a fool of myself this morning. I fully intended to return before you arrived. Then, remaining in the guest room, I made a second shameful mistake..."

Oftob Oyim replied, "No blame lies on you. You are as if our own child."

Uzbek Oyim added, "If you had not brought the qimiz and wet your mother's mouth, then you would have had a terrible problem, my child."

Everyone laughed in response. Now Karima Khotin said, "As for Kumush, she was reproaching Zainab for hiding her husband."

Again, everyone chortled. Despite the previous offense Zainab had shown to her, Kumush sat completely at ease. Laughter blossomed in her as she glanced covertly at Otabek; meanwhile Zainab pursued Kumush's every move, every gesture, and every smile.

A momentary silence rose among the guests, and Otabek attempted to dispel the tension by offering a dramatic appraisal of Zainab and Kumush. "I am surprised about one thing," he said.

"What's that?" asked Mohira Oyim. "Why is Zainab fat and Kumush thin?"

Uzbek Oyim attempted a riposte, "You should ask me for the answer, my child," she said. "Kumush resembles you in thoughtfulness; Zainab resembles me in jolliness."

Kumush seemed to enjoy her mother-in-law's comparison of her to Otabek, but Zainab seemed disappointed. Karima Otin took a divergent view.

"You are mistaken, Mother," she said. "Only those who have read the love poem 'Yusuf and Zulaikha'[389] will know the difference... three months is not an insignificant period. Kumush Khanum has thinned, lost in longing for Otabek!"

Karima Otin's literary allusion was as if she had poked someone in the eye while trying to highlight their eyebrows; instead of defusing the perceived insult, she only compounded the hurt.

"Uzbek Oyim is right," said Mohira Oyim. "Zainab is jolly but Kumush Nisa[390] to my eyes has a more serious cast..."

"Indeed," said Khushroi.

Kumush and Oftob Oyim sat in manifest discomfort, countenances clouding, fully aware of the ill-concealed designs passing between them. Kumush looked at Otabek imploringly.

"Will you all please stop," said Otabek finally. "These are all conjectures, none of which approach the truth." All heads turned to him.

"If this is so, please tell us the facts," challenged Sharofat the seamstress. "Why should I when you all remain clueless?" replied Otabek.

"I know what you will say, devil!" exclaimed Karima Otin. "He means to say that the red and the white flower each have their own fragrance!"

All burst out laughing. "Exactly, exactly!" they all said together.

Otabek, clearly amused, rose from his place, saying, "You'll never find out, you'll never find out," and left the room. The hearts of Kumush and Oftob Oyim brimmed with the life-affirming goodness of that simple statement; Zainab and Mohira Oyim also appeared relieved. So, wives and daughters were encouraged by Otabek's words, each side interpreting them to their own advantage. After another exchange of raucous guffaws and banter, the guests were presented with a meal of *quyuk-suyuk*.[391]

11

KUMUSH'S WORD GAME

As evening arrived, the guests finally spread out to their homes. Only Hajji, Qutidor, Hasan Ali, and Otabek remained behind in the guest room. From the inner rooms, Uzbek Oyim bade farewell to her guests as she filled Oftob Oyim's and Kumush's ears with her same melodramatic, perhaps half-serious, complaints.

"I was angry with you both for some time. I had the mind to ball you up with the other scraps of fabric and place you on the shelf. Indeed, for three years you insisted on not coming here yourselves. As for my poor son, each month he traveled about like a seamstress's awl... Here I have my own reputation to consider. I am the wife of Yusufbek Hajji of Tashkent. Even Khudayar Khan visited us as a guest one evening... As for members of Qushbegi's house, they do nothing without obtaining my council... Such prestigious and illustrious personages we have hosted. Why should we be the object of such rudeness and disregard from our in-laws...?

"Day and night, old and young in the city chewed off my ears, burning my brain with constant queries. 'Has your Margilani bride arrived yet?' 'Why did you leave her in Margilan when she is such a renowned beauty?' As for me, I was lost for words. 'It turns out that my bride's mother was ill...' At other times I would say, 'My poor daughter-in-law is so feeble she wouldn't be able to come here on her own...' I would mutter my excuses, embarrassed. Now I can see for myself that all along I had a daughter-in-law straight as a bullet from a rifle and really as a rich purple flower of the Pustighul[392]... now I have given the scamp free rein of my personal quarters. I am so silly." In this manner she went on for some time...

Oftob Oyim and Kumush could now comprehend Uzbek Oyim's simplehearted nature through her rambling exposition; at times they would laugh out loud at her storytelling, other times beg her pardon for their offense. As for Otabek, he did not participate as a member of her audience, so, perhaps, that explained why

Zainab busied herself with personal matters in her room while the guests remained under the wheels of Uzbek Oyim.

Candles now lined niches as evening neared. Otabek entered the room, and upon his arrival Oftob Oyim and Uzbek Oyim thought it impolite to linger about and, conversing with each other, left for the other room. Almost as if she were waiting for the women to depart, Zainab, holding in her hand a teapot, entered and asked Otabek whether he would take tea. When Otabek answered in the negative, Kumush said to her, "I will drink. You may also sit with us."

Zainab did not have to be asked twice. Sitting down, she started to pour tea and pass it to Kumush. Kumush, attempting to start a conversation, asked, "Perhaps our arrival spells disaster for you. Are you offended by our presence?"

Zainab looked up quickly at Otabek. "Why would I be offended?" she asked. "He would have gone to you if you had not come here..."

"He would most certainly not have!" said Kumush. "Until this very moment he has scandalized me..."

Otabek gave a conspiratorial smile to Kumush, who responded in kind.

"Is he the quarrelsome type?" asked Zainab. "I don't ever remember in two years him ever even muttering a word in anger..."

"You are correct," said Kumush. "He is not of that sort. I was the cause of all bickering... This man is without guilt, and the source of all our hostilities was one pig in particular."

"What kind of devil is this?" asked Zainab.

"The most infamous bastard of our city," explained Kumush. Turning to Otabek, she asked, "Did you hear that a bek recently killed him?"

Otabek grinned. "I heard..."

"Since hearing the news, I often offer prayers on behalf of that bek..." Zainab asked, "What issue did he have with you?"

Otabek turned to Kumush as if to say, "What will you say to that?" As for Kumush, she replied, feigning indifference, "The swine continued to send sovchi to my friend in order to arrange a marriage. As for me, I advised my friend against marrying him. My words reached the swine's ears and revealed to him my complicity. Because of this he spread slanderous lies about me to him"—with

363

these words Kumush nodded toward Otabek. "And he was angry with me for mediating between them..."

Otabek laughed at Kumush's elaborate lie. As for Zainab, she only sympathized with her husband. "It appears you are to blame," she said. "Why do you interfere in others' affairs?"

"Indeed, I am at fault," said Kumush, looking at Otabek. "Honestly speaking, the fault is in my aunt's daughter Zainab who has built a wooden wall between us. Isn't that so?" she asked.

Otabek turned to Kumush, shocked by her words. "Why do you speak of Zainab in this manner?"

Kumush laughed, not at all embarrassed. "Don't get excited, Bek," she retorted. "The other day I visited my aunt. She complained about her daughter Zainab and she insinuated that it was her daughter Zainab the Fat who fed all these wicked words to Hamid the Swine's ears. Did you know that?"

Otabek could hardly stop himself from bursting into laughter. "Whatever happened, it was your fault: why did you get involved in that affair?" he said.

"Your interference in the affairs of others does not suit you," Zainab added.

Kumush took a more serious tone. "As you have said, Zainab the Fat is herself without fault. If it were up to me, I would place the blame on Bek Father and Khan Mother," she said. "If it were not for them seeking some elusive dream, they would have married their daughter to a decent man, and none of these sordid affairs would have transpired... Why have those poor wretches been worrying for two years? Do you think the distance between the village of Tashkent and Margilan is a short one?"

Otabek again could hardly keep himself from laughing aloud. "You still take no blame on your shoulders. *Astaghfurallah!*"

Zainab asked Kumush, completely confused, "Who are the Bek Father and Khan Mother you speak of?"

"Those are the parents of my already mentioned friend... in pursuit of their miserable dream, they have aged their poor daughter."

"Why did you convince your friend not to get married when there was the chance?"

"Though very wealthy, his appearance was pitted and full of pockmarks... Those who marry for wealth commit themselves to something shallow and worthless, better to die than marry someone for those reasons..."

"Certainly, that is true," said Zainab.

Otabek became increasingly surprised with Kumush's word game, looking at her as if to say, "Cut it out, you devil!"

And Kumush again could not resist: "Karim Qutidor also is at fault for creating disputes between us," she said.

Otabek played along, asking, "Why would he be at fault? If you had it your way, you would place blame on the whole city for our past issues!"

"Don't get excited, darling," said Kumush. "Why did he exile a young man without considering the consequences—a young man who beat his head on his door in supplication?"

"*Astaghfurallah*, again, Hamid is the cause of his exile, and you were the source of Hamid's anger..."

Zainab tried to ask a question, but Kumush cut her short. "No one is at fault; it is all God's will."

"Now you have finally spoken the truth," said Otabek, and Kumush went on: "God sealed the fate of the flat-faced woman who was chasing her tail, got her ears cut off, and left with nothing!"

Otabek laughed. Not grasping the meaning of it all, Zainab asked for explanations, but Kumush was tired of making up stories and suddenly changed the topic of their discussion.

"How old are you, sister Zainab?"

"About nineteen years old."

"You are still a child," Kumush said.

"How about yourself?"

"Don't ask, I have become ancient..."

Zainab looked at her enviously, and quietly said, "Yet you look very youthful..."

"How old do you think I am?"

Zainab looked at Kumush's possession of a yet still nubile figure and the dewy youth of her visage—the face of her rival. Though Kumush seemed eternally frozen at what must be the illusory age of sixteen, Zainab dared not follow this line of inquiry as it would reveal her hidden animosity. Zainab feared that in fact Kumush might be younger than she.

"How would I know?"

"I am now twenty years old."

"It turns out you are only a year ahead of me."

"Of course I am older than you," said Kumush.

Otabek grasped the secret meaning of these words: Not only Kumush's beauty, but her wit and intelligence and all other attributes were unmatched by Zainab.

For several minutes silence reigned between the three of them. Otabek gave sidelong glances to Kumush while Zainab played with a thread of carpet, no doubt occupied with some private thought. As for Kumush, she didn't meet anyone's eyes. She sat as if in a daydream. Seeing Kumush in this state, Otabek felt sorrow in his heart.

"You look tired from your travels, Kumush."

Zainab stopped toying with the thread as Kumush seemed to wake from her torpor, startled by the sympathetic words...

"I don't know..."

"We can leave and you can get some rest," said Otabek.

"It's all right... It looks like I will not be able to do the evening prayer."

"That's all right," he said. "Aren't you afraid of being alone...? Should Zainab sleep in the same room with you?"

"Zainab should sleep with you. I am used to loneliness..."

"Should we call your mother for you?"

"Thanks."

"If you mother hears about you sleeping alone..."

"If you and Zainab tell no one about my sleeping alone, no one will know... Is that my bed?"

Zainab suddenly became almost euphoric and, maybe for that reason, not letting Kumush lie down, placed a down blanket on the floor for her. Still drowsy, Kumush thanked Zainab and took her place in the corner of the room. In the doorway, unable to move to her corner, Otabek quietly shook his head in frustration, giving her an ironic smile. Kumush, drifting off to sleep, answered with a winsome smile... After laying out the bed, finally Zainab started to exit the room, but Kumush stopped her.

"Zainab," she said. Zainab looked up at her. "Don't let him sleep away from you, okay?"

"Why?"

"Because my father will suspect ill intentions."

"Okay," said Zainab, looking at her husband with an expression of, "Did you hear that?" and leaving the room with him. Kumush demanded of Otabek in a strong voice, "Now, go to your own room!"

Zainab, more confident, reached her room. "I mean it. Do you hear me?"

Otabek, ignoring her command, approached Kumush. "You..."

"Me?"

"Think you are so perceptive."

"I am not," replied Kumush with a laugh. "I am still conflicted with anger. I am not reconciled with you yet."

"Now what are you going on about? I am dead afraid that our secret will be revealed."

"Why shouldn't it be?" she said. "I wanted to talk to you about past events."

"She entered with intent to discover our secrets. I also could not contain myself and tried to explain the past through other means."

"Did she notice anything?" asked Kumush

"She noticed nothing... no doubt. Nevertheless, I am afraid," declared Otabek.

"You coldheartedly killed three people. I don't believe you," said Kumush, her eyes falling onto the thin line of the knife wound on Otabek's hand. "The knife cut deeply... Did you cut the sparrow in return? Now, get out. I am going to sleep."

"Go ahead, sleep," said Otabek. "Should I disrobe now?"

"If you are shy, I will turn my face," he said, turning away.

"Don't look," she replied, taking off her clothes. "Not finished yet, not finished yet..." she teased five or six times, and finally sliding underneath the blankets, she chuckled mischievously, "Not finished yet, not finished yet."

Otabek, tiring of these games, looked at her. "You are a liar."

"These are not lies... I am not lying. I will teach you to wait for me, you escape artist."

"Aren't you afraid of being alone?"

"Why should I be afraid? Two years of sleeping alone, I have become used to it... Perhaps you are the one who is afraid of being alone."

"You are being sarcastic..."

"Not sarcasm, but the truth," said Kumush. "I am not alone either..."

"What do you mean by that?" asked Otabek.

"It means that I have a companion. In short, don't worry your head about me."

Otabek again remained lost... "Your companion..."

"My companion?" challenged Kumush. "My companion is the dream of my beloved. That sacred someone lingering, remaining in my thoughts every moment. Enough. Is there any greater friend than this? Sometimes this companion is sweeter than sleep."

Otabek understood now what she meant and laid a kiss on her face. "I don't believe you."

"Why not?"

"Why, you know why... these days you are without companionship... you sleep as if dead..."

Kumush rested her head on Otabek's shoulder. "These long days I have slept without a companion," she said. "My hope absolutely cut off from the world of the living. My dream companion only brought me hopelessness, further compounding my fears. Sleep was my only sweet escape. I could only find my beloved in my dreams, so all I sought was slumber. Even now, my dreams are my constant companions... What do you say to that?"

"I will say no more. But you are not the Kumush of two years ago."

Kumush hid beneath the blanket.

"Leave... I want to sleep."

Otabek was rooted in place... he willed himself to stand. After he distanced himself, Kumush slowly lowered the blanket from her face and with weary eyes looked up at Otabek. Otabek heard the tread of footsteps approaching from the yard and extinguished the three candles burning in the niche. Zainab appeared in the small doorway.

"You are still here. I thought you meant to follow..." she said. Otabek, not responding, extinguished the other candles. Upon hearing

Zainab, Kumush's eyes widened... Otabek stepped out, closing the door behind him.

12

A KUNDOSH WILL ALWAYS BE A KUNDOSH

Within three or four days Kumush endeared herself to both her mother- and father-in-law through her charm and careful consideration of their standing. Yusufbek Hajji repeated over and over, "She is not a worldly child, but an angel"—though never in the presence of Zainab. As for Uzbek Oyim, she dispatched all her former hostilities and animosities into the other world. She began to treat even more snobbishly the coterie of wives who visited to see for themselves the Margilani bride. To each laudatory exclamation of, "Such a bride!" aimed at Kumush, she replied with a "It turns out my true bride was a Margilani!" At times, when especially overcome with Kumush's charm and attention, she would meet with Hajji alone and say, "Oh dear, look at the marvel that is your son's wife." As for Hajji, he would reply, "It seems that the Indian seer has had his effect on your head as well..."

Smiling, Uzbek Oyim only replied, "Yes, really, this young bride has attributes other than beauty!" She laughed.

As a response to the high praises directed toward Kumush by the visiting wives, as soon as they left, Uzbek Oyim would immediately direct Oibadak to covertly make amulets against the evil eye as well as burn sage, spreading its smoke on Kumush. And then, so as not to anger Zainab, she would direct it on her as well, and if Otabek appeared he would receive some as well.

"If someone respects the owner, his dog should also be thrown a bone"—according to this folk saying, Qutidor and Oftob Oyim were also held in great esteem. Since his arrival, Qutidor was not idle one hour, as each day he was hosted at one of his many friends' homes and enjoyed the company of Yusufbek Hajji.

As for Oftob Oyim, Uzbek Oyim gave up her seat of honor. Instead of the title Quda, she addressed her as "my sister," and a meal was not served without first consulting her wishes.

For the fifteen days since Kumush's arrival, the family spent all hours in receiving the wives of the city's authorities and local notables. Oftob Oyim became acquainted with Tashkent society through meetings with Yuz Boshi Oyim of Tashkent, then Ponsad Boshi, on to Qorboshi, until finally Orda Oyims visited, each bestowing upon her special esteem. A countless number of invitations arrived, all saying, "You should not leave without being a guest in our home," so Uzbek Oyim was forced to pick the ten most worthy among them, with the very first visit to be paid to the house of Sorabek Oyim, the wife of Nur Muhammad Qushbegi—so their first visit would be at the Orda.

On the sixteenth day, guests became increasingly rare and Uzbek Oyim sent a courier to the house of Sorabek Oyim regarding their planned visit, ordering Hasan Ali to prepare a cart. Since Kumush had never before witnessed the lifestyle of Orda Oyims, she also wanted to join them. During that morning's tea, when the name Zainab was mentioned, Kumush asked, "Is your Zainab going too?"

Uzbek Oyim replied, "Zainab has been once."

"What about me?"

"You will not go today."

For some time Kumush sat sulking in silence, to which Uzbek Oyim responded, "You are the daughter-in-law of Yusufbek Hajji of Tashkent, my child. You are above the shame of your shoes alone in the street outside an uninvited place."[393]

Otabek had left for somewhere on horseback. Yusufbek Hajji and Qutidor were guests in the Hujra of Solihbek Akhund in Kokiltosh Madrassa.[394] Those who remained at home that day were only Kumush, Zainab, and Oibadak.

Uzbek Oyim said to Kumush and Zainab, who were seeing them off as they climbed into the litter, "Two kundosh find themselves alone in the same house—don't fight with each other! Oibadak, take heed around the kundosh!"

Oftob Oyim, stepping aboard the carriage, added, "God protect them, Mother! Thanks to God that both are clever enough and have their heads on their shoulders!"

"These two are not kundosh! These are in truth sisters!" said Hasan Ali, holding the reins of the horses.

"On whom should I place blame other than Zainab for not being allowed to come," said Kumush, laughing while undoing the chain to the front gate.

"Should we argue now?" she asked Zainab. Zainab remained silent.

Uzbek Oyim, after giving some instructions to Oibadak, said to the brides, "Do not go long without a nice hot meal for lunch!"

And, at that, the carriage lurched forward.

First Zainab and then Kumush turned back into the yard. Contemplating the nature of the kundosh in silence, Oibadak stood for a few moments in the yard and then also turned to enter her room.

Day by day Kumush could now see that a silent gulf between them spread as Zainab grew more and more distant, treating her in an increasingly coarse manner. Even just today her attempts at humor with Zainab, meant only in play, were met with dead silence, further increasing her concern. With foreboding in her heart, she sat down near her door. She did not know what to do and was incredulous that Otabek's advice for her to patiently attempt to assuage Zainab's jealousy had borne no fruit, and that she was now struggling to build a bond with her. The fear nagged at her that if relations with Zainab were strained after only fifteen days, where would they be in a month's time? If this situation persisted, she would not remain in this house for long. However, the thought of leaving her new home unnerved her, as it meant that she would pass Otabek into the hands of Zainab for one- to two-month stretches, her own jealousy rising... Her thoughts turned over as she remembered a particular day when Otabek laughed with Zainab as if sharing a secret, Zainab exhibiting the beauty of the moon, full of charm. From this apparition she jumped up from her place, took a mirror from its shelf, and examined her image...

It is well known to all that one who looks at his or her own image in a mirror discovers only their deepest insecurities and shortcomings, as now happened to Kumush, who instantly found fault in her appearance. Seductive doe eyes, full eyelashes, arched eyebrows as if arrows in flight, and a singular beauty mark, among other charms, did not satisfy her... She found herself dull and childish compared to Zainab...

Placing the mirror back on the shelf, full of envy toward Zainab, she returned to her place and sat down. Caught for some time in a torrent of doubt, a feeling crept into her heart.

"I am not for him. If he really loved me..." Without anger or remorse she resigned herself to the truth that her life as the beloved would meet its end in just a few months as Zainab's beautiful visage, redolent as the moon, would bring the demise of her and Otabek's love within five to ten days. Now compelled to reassess the vision of Zainab, to genuinely surrender to the overwhelming truth of her allure, she rose from her place...

When Kumush entered, Zainab was embroidering a skullcap near the small door.

"Just as my mother foretold," said Kumush, laughing manically. "I came to fight with you."

Putting the skullcap to the side, Zainab stood.

"I was almost ready to come to see you..."

Kumush scoffed, dripping with sarcasm.

"Yet you are sewing a skullcap. How then would you have had the time to see me? Thanks."

Unable to furnish an excuse, Zainab remained in her place with the expression of a confused child sealed on her face. Wishing to alleviate her disarray and bring her to her senses, Kumush picked up the skullcap and pretended to check the stitches.

"You sew nicely. Who are you making this for?"

"I am not preparing it for anyone in particular. Someone will wear it... Take a seat."

The two kundosh sat opposite each other. Kumush kept a determined stare; Zainab remained confused, and her face blushed crimson as her gaze awkwardly fixed on some point on the floor. Deathly silence reigned between them for two minutes.

"You are not taking my not coming to see you to heart?" Zainab finally said.

"Taking it to heart? Am I a child?" Kumush retorted. "It is only that fifteen days after my arrival, you began to distance yourself from me... I thought we would become like sisters..."

"What will become of us... if you let this nonsense into your heart..."

"Is it really nonsense," retorted Kumush, "when I know that we are the only two at home, yet you remove yourself from me at the first opportunity? It is clear that you do not want to see my face."

"You don't mean that it appears that you are the sort who needlessly takes things to heart..."

"I am nothing of the sort..."

What began as seemingly amicable banter between them shifted to a parlay with a much deadlier intent. Kumush exploded, releasing all the pent-up anger and emotion held in check over the prior fifteen days.

"If I take something to heart, it will be for something of value," she said.

"How can you possibly say I hold myself at a distance from you? How can you say I dare not face you? You cannot know what is truly in my heart."

Zainab's extreme agitation could not compare to that of Kumush's: "As for knowing your inner thoughts your manners alone have revealed to me your true nature."

"What do you mean, manners?"

"Don't ask..."

"If I am remiss in some area, please inform me."

"If I tell you, your anger will only increase..."

"If it is the truth, I will not become angry..."

So that Oibadak, who was performing her daily chores nearby, could not hear, Kumush said in a low voice, "If you assure me you will not become angry, then I will tell you. When your husband comes near me, without any apparent regard or reason to do so, you spring up out of nowhere and sit near us. But when I am alone, you are nowhere to be found. Why is that?"

"I expected you to say something along these lines," said Zainab. "If you truly take my being reserved around you to heart, let me remain away from you forever."

"You said if I spoke the truth you would not become angry. Where did that go?"

"I am only saying that I will not enter your room again while you are sitting alone with your husband."

"Don't interpret my feelings so literally, Zainab," said Kumush. "I did not give this example so that you would leave my husband and me alone. I meant it only to illustrate the rude manner you show toward me..."

Silence again rose between the two. Oibadak appeared in the small doorway.

"It is lunchtime. What should I prepare for you?"

Kumush looked at Zainab:

"What food should we order?"

"You are asking..."

"Prepare whatever Zainab likes," said Kumush.

"Shall I prepare *laghman*?" said Oibadak, looking at Zainab.

"I don't have an appetite right now, make whatever is easy."

Oibadak left. Zainab breathed an "Oh my."

"Don't just say 'oh my,' Zainab... though this is not just about us. My intent was to show you have isolated me with little regard for my feelings... I have never been to your house in my whole life... I only came here to visit for three or four days to meet my mother- and father-in-law, but all for the sake of a miserable misunderstanding, we ignore each other. This hostility is hard to bear."

Kumush's statement that she had only intended to stay three or four days seemed to delight Zainab.

"Oh, I should wither and die, sister Kumush," said Zainab weakly. "It seems to me that you have taken all of my actions too much to heart—I should die this very morning."

Kumush laughed inside at Zainab, who attempted to placate her once she heard the magical word "three to four days"; she in turn deep inside meant ill intent toward Zainab with the thought "I would not return home even if I died."

Silence again rose between them. Kumush sat deep in thought, her arms wrapped around her knees; as for Zainab, she began outlining long lines to embroider on the skullcap. Sewing for some time, Zainab slowly raised her gaze at her archenemy with hostile intent. Moments passed, then she took a deep breath and again started out on three more lines of stitching...

"You have nothing to fear."

Kumush remained still for a long time without answering and then moved toward the wall and leaned against it.

"What would I have to be afraid of?"

"Indeed... All I am saying is that you don't have to be so greedy for..."

"For whom am I greedy?"

"You surely know for whom."

"Shame on you, Zainab!"

"Shame on you as well!"

Again, the two kundosh strained toward each other like two cocks preparing to fight.

"How have I acted shamefully?" asked Kumush.

"It is shameful to order me to not approach you when you are sitting with your husband."

"First of all, I made this statement to depict your previous behavior—if you believe anything I tell you. Let me ask you honestly: Have I ever entered your room while you sat with your husband?"

Zainab was at a loss for words as she attempted to arrive at an answer, for she could not recollect a time when Kumush intruded on Otabek and Zainab when they were together.

"If you had entered, I would not have pushed you away," she said finally. "You are jealous and seeing yourself in me, that is why you never enter when we are together."

"Stop casting lies, Zainab. You are not a blacksmith who can just link together deceptions as if forging some chain."

"God save me from resembling a blacksmith. My parents have never known the work of a blacksmith," responded Zainab.

"Who said that they were blacksmiths?"

"That is what came out of your mouth..."

"Oh my," said Kumush, laughing. "You misunderstood. At one time you say that I am jealous of you; another that I am seeing myself in you. And then you make up some other aspersion as if sticking a needle in me by saying I shouldn't worry... this is what casting lies like a loose- tongued blacksmith is."

"But I am telling you the truth. You have no reason to worry..."

"Go on with it."

"But..."

Zainab said nothing more. As for Kumush, she pursued her attempts at gaining a confession.

"I understood your meaning," she said. "You meant to say that I have nothing to fear because my husband loves me."

Zainab paused momentarily in her stitchwork as she looked at Kumush, the color ebbing from her countenance... Struggling to recover from her mistake, she remained addled.

"Indeed... as with me he has cursed you with his assurances."

"What did he assure you with?"

"Perhaps... he also said to you that he could not live without you..."

"Never."

"If not you... he spoke these words to me a hundred times... I thought he said the same sweet words to you as well..." mumbled Zainab.

Her struggle to arrive at the proper rebuttal bred still more lies, astounding even her. Yet they took on a life of their own. These inspirations of questionable veracity defeated Kumush in her pyrrhic victory. The self-doubt that plagued her in the mirror materialized, and the words she used for battle abandoned her.

She believed at that moment that Zainab spoke the truth. "If he in truth loved her why did he wait so long to arrange my travel to Tashkent...?" she asked herself.

Zainab, fearing the effects of her obfuscation, hid in her work, flustered and upset. Kumush surrendered to lassitude as if deprived of the will to live. The lunch, previously served and laid out between the two kundosh by Oibadak, was left cold for some time. Zainab timidly offered, "Help yourself, Sister."

The two parties pretended to enjoy the food, perfunctorily taking a serving from the bowl. In turn each one wiped their hands on the edge of the *dasturkhon*...

An hour later Otabek returned and was immediately welcomed by Zainab. Disrobing, he handed her his *chopan* while standing in the yard, hesitating while trying to decide which room to enter. If he entered Zainab's room, who presently fluttered around him like a pest, he considered Kumush's reaction; if he entered Kumush's room, he thought of Zainab.

Kumush did not appear to be in Zainab's room so he thought maybe she was asleep. He chose the latter room and entered with her. Zainab, overly obsequious, had her husband sit upon a plush four-layered blanket and placed near him three down pillows for him to rest upon. Cleaning her husband's shoes, she asked permission to fan him; Otabek deferred, becoming a bit concerned over her excessive kindness—even though he had just ridden through the noonday heat on horseback and was thirsty for a cup of tea.

As soon as he mentioned tea, Zainab rushed outside toward the stove, and as she did so, she glanced at Kumush's room.

Though both the outer and inner door were open, no one was visible inside.

From the moment of Kumush's arrival, Otabek day by day felt his soul healing, as it was enveloped in ever deeper levels of intimacy. He was judicious in his decisions to seek advice from no one, as if a bird with a special morsel taking one quick bite and then looking about in all eight directions. Yet a disquiet lingered within him... His past considerations and relationship with Kumush in Margilan were unknown to Zainab. He wanted to show regard and respect to Zainab, but that was becoming increasingly impossible. If he smiled at Kumush, he must do the same to Zainab; whatever considerations made to that, he had to make to this. The first wife was an act of the heart, but as for the second one... So as to not bore our readers, we will not ask them to revisit those events described in previous pages. Because Otabek and Kumush's love was authentic, a transcendent, unspoken poetry passed between them; considering the second dilemma of Zainab, and taking stock of it and calling it what it is, we find nothing in Otabek other than cold obligation.

If we were to discover some new revelation regarding the above, the reader would find it mundane and uninteresting— though our esteemed readers can already appreciate the reasons for our hero's "obligation"— anyway, we will revisit them and offer our perspective.

Our religion mandates that we defer to our parents' wishes and show them the respect they deserve. Compelled through the strictures of this most powerful and time-honored injunction, Otabek endured the burning tears shed by Zainab as she opened her heart to him, all to no end. Her latest breakdown furthered Otabek's desperation, as he knew this heartache well. He had drank fully of both the sweetness and the agony of separation from his beloved for three years, so he bore this heaviness out of sympathy for Zainab...

Zainab, after forcing three cups of tea on him, asked, "We did not lay out a meal for you, thinking you would return later, Bek. Though the food is a bit cold, I left you a little bit just in case... Will you eat?"

Otabek felt a bit of a hunger pang. "All right, I'll have some." Upon those words, the unfinished *laghman* was served to Otabek.

When he saw that the *laghman* had hardly been touched, Otabek asked, "Didn't you eat yourselves?"

"We ate. Sister Kumush was also here... it turns out she does not like *laghman*. She didn't eat much... Since she only picked at it, I felt uncomfortable eating in front of her."

"If you didn't eat, help yourself," said Otabek.

Zainab, not shy around her husband, joined him.

During the meal, Otabek learned from Zainab that Kumush was sleeping. After finishing his meal, Otabek also lay down to take a nap. As his eyes closed and he drifted off to sleep, Zainab, waiting for that moment, sat near the pillow with a fan in her hands. As her husband dozed off, she began to fan him... Passing the feathers to and fro, Zainab's eyes moved toward Kumush's room... Zainab intended to demonstrate her success in pleasing her husband to her fellow kundosh, thus validating the truth of her prior claim.

In this manner Zainab fawned over her husband for some time, her efforts resulting in success when her kundosh emerged from her doorway. Kumush, departing her room for some purpose, glanced at Zainab's room in passing and saw her squatting near Otabek's pillow with a fan in her hand. An hour later Otabek woke up and Zainab had to stop the windmill that flowered in the heart of the kundosh.

When Otabek made his way into her room, Kumush had fallen back to sleep, her tousled hair covering her pillow. Otabek gazed at her for some time while she slumbered, but not wanting to disturb her, he slowly backed out of the room.

While taking one last look from the doorway... the sleeping eyes were now open.

"Please continue to rest. I will go."

Instead of returning to sleep, Kumush raised her head from the pillow and, picking up a scarf from the floor, wrapped it around her head and sat up. Her eyes were bloodshot, as if she had not been sleeping at all. Otabek entered the room again.

"Why are you getting up? Get some sleep," he said. Kumush did not answer. Her eyes were angry. "Your eyes are bloodshot. Couldn't you sleep?"

"I don't feel well..."

"God protect you," said Otabek, sitting down near Kumush to inspect her. "Where does it hurt?"

"I don't know," she answered. Her eyes fixated on some object on the shelf.

Otabek realized that she was again making a bad joke, laughed, and stroked Kumush's forehead.

"Why don't you know?"

"Take your hand off."

"Why should I?"

"I am contagious and you need to protect yourself from me..."

"I don't need protection from you..."

Tears barely traceable appeared at the corner of Kumush's eyes. "What about Zainab?" she asked.

Taken completely off-guard, Otabek's eyes cast about to the yard, looking for an answer. "As for Zainab... you know better than me..."

Otabek's evasiveness seemed to affirm the veracity of Zainab's prior claim. Kumush's disappointment manifest, she appeared a disheveled mess, as if she had put her robe on backward, and turning her face to one side, she said, "Don't be so duplicitous."

Otabek still sat uncomprehending. Kumush's eyes now welled with tears, stirring in him an all-consuming passion. He gave her a smile. "You got up on the wrong side of the bed," he said.

"Because I do not have someone who makes me get up on the right side..."

"Is this the reason for your hostility?" asked Otabek, laughing.

Kumush wiped her eyes dry. "Yes, for that reason alone."

"If so, it's all for nothing..."

Kumush grew irritated. "Is your two-sided face and forked tongue also for nothing?"

"I don't understand."

"Of course you do not understand and do not want to understand."

Although he laughed, he was furious with Kumush for her rough words. For the first time, various vicious insults heaped upon him reemerged from his memory.

"Did Zainab insult you in some way?"

"She said, she also said that you told her... 'I can't live without you.' "

From that he came to understand that harsh words had passed between the two kundosh. Zainab had managed to kindle a fire in

Kumush's heart through some subterfuge, but, so as to not diminish the passion now pervading his heart, he asked, "Did you believe Zainab?"

"Is it not half-true?

"Fine, if I did say these words to her, your anger toward me is most ironic. Especially from what you just told me..."

Kumush remained silent. Otabek, catching in his hand the nape of her neck, now lay with her on the floor. "Now tell me. Did you exchange words?"

"Yes, we did," said Kumush, who smiled, looking to the side, embarrassed.

"And it hasn't even been sixteen days?"

"Any other wife than I would have been hostile to your Zainab from day one..."

"God bless you..."

"Don't be sarcastic with me."

"If I hold my tongue, will you speak freely? Please."

The fire of competition was stirred within Kumush and now burned with great intensity. She spilled all the tension built up for the past three or four days. Otabek dismissed these incidences as inconsequential. Zainab's latest honeyed words and affected subservience, as seen through her ludicrous fan, made everything clear in his mind. Once he comprehended the seriousness of the tension, Otabek's nonchalant treatment faded. Instead, a pensiveness struck him dumb for a few moments until finally he looked at Kumush and chuckled as she waited for his response.

"Why do you laugh?"

"Because what you said is not worth crying over."

Kumush arched her brows. "I can no longer suffer from your Zainab's actions."

"Let's put your sufferings aside for a moment," said Otabek. "Most of all, I ask you now: Do you believe in me?"

"Yes and no," said Kumush, who finally smiled again. "Zainab's machinations can make anyone suspect."

"There were some special letters exchanged between us that should relieve you of your suspicions."

Kumush shyly turned her face to the side. Otabek in a low voice continued: "Over the past few days I have asked you whether you are going to stay in Tashkent. That was also me asking you to dismiss such insinuations and verbal barbs aimed at you. If you are so depressed, in my opinion, you should not stay in Tashkent, because I can't stand to see you suffer like this."

"Unless you expel me, I will not go to Margilan."

Otabek laughed. "If you keep abusing me with these ridiculous words, I will no doubt expel you."

Kumush, taking umbrage, answered, "Can I even believe you?"

"What does your heart tell you?"

"My heart... my heart tells me not to believe you."

"Then that is not your heart."

"It is certainly heartfelt."

"Is there any practical reason for your heart to say not to believe in me?"

"Yes, there is."

"Please explain."

"My heart asks who benefits from this expulsion... now you give me an answer from your heart."

Otabek now understood her intended meaning and became flustered, unable to arrive at an answer. Really, Kumush had touched upon a tender nerve.

Not waiting for an answer from Otabek, she continued, "Though I cannot truly know the heart of another, my heart cannot be filled with two objects of affection."

"You mean your heart cannot be devoted to two objects."

"I would not say that, entirely," said Kumush, "because that option is not available to me."

Kumush meant to further clarify her words. Otabek was surprised by the drastic change in her character; her resoluteness, even the extent of the metamorphosis evident in one day, seemed not a physical but a most interesting psychological transformation.

"I understand your meaning well," he said finally. "You are right in every way, but until then... my hope is you feel that yourself..."

Kumush gave no reply. Perhaps she only needed to hear from her husband his reassurances regarding the conflict from earlier that day...

13

WE WILL SEE EACH OTHER IN BETTER TIMES

Upon the twentieth day since their arrival, Qutidor began to consider his return to Margilan, despite Yusufbek Hajji and Otabek pleading with him to stay longer. His departure was unavoidable, and he gave the requisite apologies: "The house is vacant with only Toibeka and Oysha opa present; what could their condition be? How they are faring all alone is unknown to us. On the other hand, my affairs are also unattended. We have become such pampered guests. Enough. Thank you for honoring us and paying us such great attention," he said.

Hajji answered, "It turns out we have decided against sending our daughter-in-law back."

Qutidor only laughed in response. "She is not my child, but yours. Here or there she has a home. Whatever our respected guest prefers, I agree," he said.

Hajji attempted to steer the conversation. "Despite all that has been said between us, we would never force her to remain here and leave the three of you empty of one another's embrace. I would like to offer the opinion that, if my gentle reminder of tradition does not pose such a heavy burden on you, she should stay for a year in Tashkent and then afterward, if she could, return to Margilan."

Qutidor gave his enthusiastic support. "Your reasoning is quite sound, she is obliged to stay here for one year!"

Kumush's father evinced a complete disregard for her staying in Tashkent. He did not think it necessary to take into consideration Oftob Oyim's view or gain her agreement. He didn't even examine his own heart for the wisdom of his rash decision... Even though Qutidor agreed again and again to Oftob Oyim's injunction that Kumush must not leave Margilan to reside in Tashkent.

There is no need to belabor the point.

"Our respected spouse's regard for Oftob Oyim was brushed aside."

News of their departure reached the ears of Oftob Oyim, and she immediately met with her daughter. She knew full well that matters rested with her daughter, not her husband. As soon as she learned the news from Hasan Ali, she went to Kumush, saying with a broad smile, "Your father said we are leaving soon."

Kumush's hands were busy stitching. She did not lift her eyes from her work. "Farewell, if you are leaving."

Poor mother, these casual words of dismissal made her bend double, suddenly frail, unable to find her seat. "What are you saying?"

Kumush smiled at her mother and returned to her sewing.

"If you are leaving, I say goodbye to you."

"What about you?"

"I'll stay here."

In disbelief, Oftob Oyim fixed her eyes on her daughter for some moments. Without returning her look, Kumush continued to stitch the cloth.

"Don't make fun of me."

"It is no joke. I am telling you the truth."

"Aren't you ashamed?"

Kumush laughed.

"Why should I be ashamed?"

"Please stop it!"

"If I were to stay here, it would be in my husband's house," said Kumush. "I am not in a strange house and have no reason to be ashamed..."

Oftob Oyim tensed as if lit on fire.

"You will stay under your own freewill, with no one compelling you to do so?"

Putting her work to the side, Kumush looked up at her mother. "First of all, as far as my staying here, only you voice resistance.

Perhaps Zainab would take your side, but I don't care about her wishes."

"Have you lost your mind, child?"

"My wits are about me," she said, laughing. "I am your daughter, Kumush. Now I sit in my husband's home in Tashkent."

"Are you denying the mother who gave birth to you her will, all for the sake of your husband's—shamelessness?"

"No, I am denying your will for a short time. I will long for you the whole time."

Hearing these words, Oftob Oyim burst into tears.

"Your mother cannot keep pace with her longing," she said. "I cannot believe you will live in the same house as a kundosh."

"If I have one kundosh, I have eight friends." Oftob Oyim dried her tears.

"Don't play games with a kundosh, my daughter." Kumush, as if to lash out against Zainab, flared up.

"If she is a kundosh, don't I also hold the title of kundosh?"

"In this lifetime," said her mother. "You could never be a genuine kundosh. Why? Because your husband takes your side. Zainab is now the exemplary kundosh, with all her venom and hostility."

Kumush, with a slight grin, whispered into her mother's ear, "Don't concern yourself with these problems."

"Why shouldn't I worry?"

"If Zainab continues in her 'kundosh' machinations against me, your son-in-law will cast her out... Therefore, my remaining here is necessary."

"If he makes her go away then it will be easier for you to return..."

"If I leave," said Kumush, "he will never let Zainab go."

"Why do you say that?"

"Because my presence here will deter him from needing a young bride at his side. If I stay here, she will bite her lips in envy."

Oftob Oyim still dragged her feet. She pleaded with her daughter. "You are still my baby girl. Do not wish ill of others. Return with me. Let them do whatever they like. Zainab lays her head down in hope for the same pillow as yours."

"You don't understand," said Kumush, and hearing footsteps approaching, paused.

Uzbek Oyim entered, asking, "Why do you scurry off? Does some enemy pursue you? Please stay at least one month more... you came from the distant land of Margilan with a long caravan of horses and camels in tow, yet you leave without staying a full month."

Oftob Oyim and Kumush rose from their places as a show of respect.

Taking her own place, Uzbek Oyim asked, "Have you heard?"

"Yes, we did, and we were in the middle of arguing about it," said Oftob Oyim.

"We are completely scandalized by this turn of events."

Oftob Oyim apologized: "Our home is unattended. We have inconvenienced you enough and would not dream of staying for twenty more days... We have felt completely at home thanks to you. Many new friends fill a place in our hearts. The honor and respect you have shown us leave us speechless... Now it is your turn to visit our city."

"Nonsense," said Uzbek Oyim. "We have yet to demonstrate proper respect to our in-laws. Our reputation is at stake if we show you off in this manner... I am approaching you, my dear in-law, to say that if you wish to sully our reputation, go home tomorrow."

Oftob Oyim reiterated her apologies: "If you wish to shame us... Please take our needs into consideration, please do not force us to stay." Turning to Kumush, she said, "We have stayed long enough. Now our mother-in-law should take Zainab with her to visit our house..."

Once Kumush's name and departure were brought into the discussion, it was Uzbek Oyim's turn to ask, "Is Kumush departing as well?"

Kumush gave a wry grin to her mother. Oftob Oyim again asked her pardon.

"Thank God you have Zainab with you. As for me, my wings only have strength through Kumush. It's inconceivable you would not acquiesce to Kumush departing with me, my mother."

Uzbek Oyim glared at Kumush. "No, no, Oftob Oyim" she said. "Although I permit you to leave, not so for Kumush."

"You must give permission now. My request is from me to you."

"Your supplications fall on deaf ears, Oftob Oyim. You should be a little embarrassed of your request," Uzbek Oyim said and turned to look at Kumush. "Aren't you a little ashamed yourself, daughter-in-law? You only came yesterday to render us respect, and today you wish to leave."

"The matter is not up to me, dear Mother..." said Kumush. "Whatever your preference—it's all the same to me."

An unspoken agreement passed between daughter-in-law and mother- in-law, all made with a slight nod of the head. As for Uzbek Oyim, she gave a definitive "Thank you."

Oftob Oyim glared at her daughter in return.

"What say does Kumush have in any of this?" she asked. "Kumush does nothing for my sake. She would not leave here, anyway, even if I begged."

Uzbek Oyim persisted: "Abandoning us now would be shameful. Otabek traveled to and fro for three years. What would only one year in Tashkent mean?" she said emphatically.

Finding herself at a dead end, Oftob Oyim took another tact. She ordered Kumush from the room. Kumush duly left. From there, she said, "You must not think I am overly possessive of my daughter, my mother. We must consider other aspects of our impasse..."

"Name them."

"What I mean to say is..." continued the poor mother. "Kumush's character is quite familiar to me, as she is an only child—her forked tongue cannot abide the 'machinations of the kundosh.' I say she will make your life intolerable with constant backbiting... Eventually, you will meet with disappointment and call into question my shortcomings as a mother... As the folk saying goes, 'The cow that births a defective calf takes the blame.' I epitomize this piece of wisdom... One sees in her great hostility and a dark heart..."

Her descent into rambling insecurities produced compassion in Uzbek Oyim's face.

"Without doubt we are all guilty of these traits," she said. "Thanks be to God that your father, Hajji, and I are still breathing. We will not allow this behavior under our roof. As for Zainab, she is a child of God: She does not know hostility or the meaning of rancor."

"You seem to have an appreciation for Zainab's character; I cannot say the same for Kumush."

"For the first time in my life," laughed Uzbek Oyim, "someone who denigrates her own child. Am I right in saying that you do not believe in your own child?"

"I have only relayed to you what I have heard from her own mouth."

"Nevertheless, you do not have my permission to take Kumush with you."

"Fine, let her stay," said Oftob Oyim. She squirmed in her seat, becoming agitated. "Do not complain to me when Kumush shows her dark side."

"If you do not instigate evil deeds through your daughter, no complaint will be forthcoming."

As the two in-laws entered the yard, Kumush was seen pacing about in the clearing. Without delay they entered Zainab's room. Zainab welcomed them, asking them to sit and saying in a sorrowful voice to Oftob Oyim, "I heard that you will return home soon. It seems you decided to not spend the month."

"We have stayed long enough, Zainab," said Oftob Oyim. "Now it is your turn to visit us."

Uzbek Oyim contradicted her response.

"We talked at length already. Convincing them to stay was futile—it's as if enemies are nipping at their heels. If your guest were left to her own wishes, she would spirit your sister Kumush away with her."

Zainab issued half-hearted protestations.

Oftob Oyim leveled irritation at her in-law. "In the best of all worlds she ought to depart with me, Zainab. Yet your family provides her a clever, calculating ally to assist her; I have no one other than your sister, Kumush. Fine, she must stay. But understand that I will die without Kumush. Your mother-in-law does not seem to appreciate my perspective."

Zainab's embarrassed glance at her mother-in-law furthered Uzbek Oyim's irritation with her in-law, who continued with her tirade.

"Enough," she said. "What is five or six days without her daughter?

What could happen?"

"You wouldn't understand... anyway, her own mother knows what's best for her."

"I now appeal to you, Zainab," declared Uzbek Oyim, ignoring her in-law. "It appears your mother-in-law, your guest, seems to direct her comments to you alone. She fears you will antagonize your sister in desperation. I say to this: Zainab is not the daughter-in-law you believe her to be. She is from the very best of society—

her lineage is of the purest line. If she refuses Kumush her esteem, she will respect us. But all this means nothing..."

"Has God damned me?" asked Zainab.

Oftob Oyim's frustration arrived at its end through her in-law's barbs. Though she sympathized with Kumush's desire to remain behind, the fear of Zainab surrendering to the failings of a kundosh haunted her—a constant nagging that delayed her final decision.

"You are mistaken, Mother."

"Whether I am mistaken or not, Kumush will not move from this room."

Oftob Oyim choked, lost in futility, resolving to consult with her husband concerning this issue...

Hasan Ali was appointed to lead the cart all the way to Margilan as the previous driver had been paid and dismissed once he arrived in Tashkent. As the time of departure for the in-laws neared, preparations for the road began in earnest. Uzbek Oyim occupied herself with the frying of sourdough cakes[395] and the kneading and molding into round loaves of bread dough. Oftob Oyim also washed her hands of her husband, who only replied to her supplications with, 'Hajji Afandi stated he wanted her to stay a year. Now we must leave. As for ourselves, putting two feet into one shoe is unseemly."[396]

Qutidor had had his fill of this issue, turning his back in an attempt to ignore her... "Hajji is just in the guest room. I cannot argue with you in the passageway. It is unseemly."

Qutidor's dismissal of her concerns furthered the poor woman's despondency, forcing her to appeal to Otabek with no success, only receiving apologies muttered softly. Otabek agreed with his mother-in-law.

"Please, for my sake, let lie the burden of losing your daughter on your shoulders for the next ten to fifteen days. If I satisfy your wishes now, your daughter will be devastated... I am embarrassed to reveal this to you. My interference in this matter is inappropriate. Your fears regarding the looming conflict between the kundosh are well-founded, yet if matters become too severe, or so I believe... before that happens, I will send Kumush to you posthaste. Don't worry."

In this manner, Oftob Oyim lost all hope, surrendering to the inevitable. Upon seeing Kumush, great sorrow entered her heart as she was stricken with the inconceivable days of separation that lay before her. As for Kumush, she pitied her mother's condition yet kept her distance; the same with Zainab, from whom she also walked one step removed, observing her gloomy countenance with suspicion.

Preparations for the road were completed. Uzbek Oyim made ready embroidered dowry offerings for Oysha Bibi, Oftob Oyim's mother. It was the last day of the guests' visit. Uzbek Oyim consulted late into the night with her in-law. Afterward she departed for her own room to sleep, leaving Oftob Oyim alone with Kumush. When finally alone, Oftob Oyim made her peace with her daughter.

"You feel no hesitation in surrendering your mother to the flames of separation, my daughter?"

"Why flames? Why should you burn?"

"Why shouldn't I? In all truth nothing is sacred to you, my daughter... If I could open my heart to you, I would show you the burning pain I suffer... if only you were in the same city."

Kumush shared in the pain that consumed her mother's heart; estrangement from the woman who had held her in her embrace for twenty years would cause her great distress.

"Five or six months will cause no harm, my mother. We will meet again if we are well and healthy."

Oftob Oyim shed great tears, sobbing out loud. Kumush's previously held convictions softened as she choked down tears.

"If you stay, you stay," said her mother finally. "Serve your mother- and father-in-law, do your best for them, especially wish no harm to your fellow kundosh, whatever their good or bad intentions, let them do it with their own hands, you should never get involved..."

"These affairs don't interest me..."

"Certainly... Nevertheless, yesterday's exchange worries me. Your fellow kundosh seems innocuous, yet holds a secretive and cunning nature. One must be wary of such a person. If hostilities arise between you... seek no revenge... better to apologize to your father-in-law and try to leave the house. I consulted your husband about this. All right?"

"All right."

"Thank God you can write to us if you need anything—please do not leave us without writing to us. You'll only compound our sorrows. Write every fifteen days. Pass the letter only into your husband's hand for delivery."

"Of course. Please do not forget to do so yourself."

Silence lingered between them for some time until Kumush gasped in the realization of what was to come then gave her mother a sad, tender smile.

Irritated, Oftob Oyim said, "You are mocking my current state, aren't you?"

"No, I wanted to tell you for a couple of days," said Kumush

"To tell what?"

"You... Remember you said that you felt nauseous then," said Kumush, blushing.

A smile appeared on Oftob Oyim's face as well. "Is it true?"

"I don't know..." Kumush turned beet red, looking to the ground. "Lately I have felt an unpleasantness in my stomach... the smell of plov, especially, nauseates me... I crave spicy food."

"Congratulations," said Oftob Oyim, laughing. Kumush, uneasy, murmured something to herself.

Oftob Oyim whispered conspiratorially into her ear, "Tell no one beside your husband. One could call your mother-in-law capricious, to say the least. Your fellow kundosh should remain completely unaware of your condition." Kumush nodded in agreement. Mother and child lay down together. Oftob Oyim was for some time unable to sleep, keeping silent vigil, devoting all prayers toward the birth of a grandchild. Eyes open, the thought recurred to her, over and over: "If I can only live to see the days to come."

Rising early, they drank their morning tea. The first prayer was recited, the cart prepared, provisions for their voyage duly loaded. Hasan Ali held the reigns of the horse while Qutidor and Hajji conversed near the cart. The women were gathered near the passage as Oftob Oyim gave her parting farewells to each woman. Taking Kumush in her embrace she openly sobbed with her. The other women, overwhelmed, joined in their lamentations.

"I pass you into God's hands, Kumush. If my final days are near and I pass away without ever seeing you again, remember me well!"

"You too, Mother."

Qutidor entered in from the street and kissed his daughter's forehead. "Farewell, my daughter."

"Farewell, dear Father."

Facing the doorway, Yusufbek Hajji and all assembled raised their hands in prayer. Then Otabek led a brown horse out of the stable, passing the reigns to Qutidor. Oftob Oyim again embraced her daughter, and with the help of Otabek, the whole time crying, took a foothold and passed under the canopy of the cart. Qutidor quietly locked arms with Yusufbek Hajji then bade farewell as Otabek gave him a leg up into his horse's saddle. Otabek also took his spot near Oftob Oyim in the cart, and after a general "*Allahu akbar*," Hasan Ali turned the horse's head to the road.

Kumush, meanwhile, stood near the gate.

"Goodbye, dear Mother! Bring my embraces to Grandmother for me. Say hello to my friends!"

"I pass you to God, dear Kumush. Farewell, my in-laws!"

"Have a pleasant journey, Oftob Oyim!"

"Goodbye, Zainab!"

"Goodbye, Mother!"

The words "Goodbye, good luck, say hello..." continued until the cart faded from sight at a turn in the road, and Kumush disappeared inside, crying. Otabek accompanied the guests for some distance to see them off, intending to make his return shortly thereafter.

14

KHUSHROI BIBI AND ZAINAB

Zainab's elder sister was known as Khushroi Bibi. Mohira Bonu had brought two sons and two daughters into the world, the eldest son being Azimbek, with Khushroi Bibi to follow—as a child, she was called Khushroi. The third child was Karim Bek, and the fourth, our Zainab. Zainab was seven years junior to her sister Khushroi Bibi. Though these sisters came forth from the same belly as if in a race to enter the world, their characters were as different as night and day. Their contrast in temperament was reflected in their divergent facial features and bearing.

Khushroi Bibi was willowy, with olive skin. As for Zainab, she was petite, but a tad pudgy, with fair skin. Khushroi Bibi's movements were mercurial, and similarly, she had a quick tongue. As for Zainab, she seemed timorous, speaking one word to everyone else's ten. Khushroi Bibi's playful eyes darted about in all directions—their attention changing every second. As for her sister, when she spoke to people, she fixated her eyes at some distant point. Always.

During her youth, her household and neighbors gave Khushroi Bibi the appellation "the Capricious One," as she insisted her every wish be fulfilled, no matter by whom. If anything contradicted her wishes, it became standard for her to create a clamor that shook the whole house. Therefore, meals were not prepared without the cook first consulting her; if she was sensitive to an issue, it must not be touched upon; and when she was present, every step she made was taken into serious consideration.

Diametrically opposed to her sister, Zainab earned the nickname "Keeper of Secrets" from those close to her; even her own mother would berate her when she became angry with the invective "you damned secret keeper." The following situation best illustrates the fundamental differences in the characters of the two sisters.

When they were younger, Mohira Oyim was in the habit of requesting her husband to buy new clothes for her children one month before Hayit. If the purchased clothing was not to Khusroi's liking, she would immediately insist that her father pass off the unwanted clothing to the other sibling and would calm only after obtaining her desired apparel. Zainab would at first never complain about the new clothing provided, but when the freshly tailored clothing was presented on the eve of the holiday, she would grow angry, stomp off, and refuse to speak with anyone. Mohira Oyim, noticing her loss of composure, would ask, "You damned secret keeper, what in the hell is wrong now?"

Zainab would only glower in silence. Finally, upon the holiday's arrival, Zainab's peevishness would transform into sobs, making it clear to all concerned the true reason behind her behavior—yet accomplishing nothing in terms of her needs.

If they were leaving to go somewhere as guests, Khushroi asked, "Shall I go too?" Of course, no one dared leave her behind. Then, after a second thought, she would declare, "I am not going." Could anyone force her to take one step if she didn't wish to? Yet Zainab would not say either "I am going" or "I am not going." Whenever her mother and sister prepared for their departure, the folk saying "If the baby does not cry, he will not be suckled on milk" would be on their lips. Upon their return Zainab would be found crying in a corner.

"Why are you crying?"

"Why did you not take me... with you?"

These inadequacies in Zainab did not improve when she grew older and was married. Nothing remains to be revealed to the reader regarding Otabek and Zainab's relationship. She made no signs of protest when her own husband paid her little attention for months, even years, on end. The only person to object against Otabek's ill manners and instruct Zainab again and again was Uzbek Oyim. The reasons must already be clear to a large degree to our esteemed reader. As they say, "The source of the mother's milk determines the character and the life of the child who suckles it." She received Uzbek Oyim's declarations and protestations with equanimity through her obligation as a "bride." For example, she would not stir from her place until her mother-in-law ordered, "Zainab, go to the andi and do such and such," never complaining to her mother, sister, and close associates about the cold regard she received from her husband.

To be fair, it would not be warranted to describe Zainab's predicament as "Her husband is dreadful, paying her little or no attention. Or, even if he did hold her in regard—it would be wasted on her, she seems indifferent." After all, we saw how Zainab threw herself into Otabek's arms upon hearing the news of her kundosh's imminent arrival.

In conclusion, we still see that young Zainab, who wept on the eve of the holiday over clothes sewn the previous month, at present only declared her love for her husband upon the looming arrival of her fellow kundosh.

We have already given a cursory introduction to our readers of Khushroi Bibi, so now let us turn to familiarizing our readers with her family life as well.

Khusroi's marriage reflected her own extraordinary character. Most daughters are obliged to marry in accordance with their mothers' and fathers' preferences and tastes. But quite another situation existed for Khushroi Bibi. When Khushroi Bibi turned eighteen, sovchi began to arrive, inquiring about her. Naturally, both mother and father were afraid, knowing full well Khusroi's character, to proceed without asking her will. Young men preferred by Olim Ponsad Boshi, many famous households favored by Mohira Oyim, all were denied by Khushroi Bibi...

"Is that the son of some so and so?" Khushroi Bibi would ask, not waiting for an answer from her mother... "God cast out that husband from my sight. It would be better for me to marry black earth than that thing!" she would declare. For some time both husband and wife would get upset, attempting to bring about an engagement they found suitable. Khushroi Bibi grasped their ambitions, initially making no protest at their designs. But, when the final prayers were read and matchmakers, in-laws, and wives all arrived at their house as her future relatives, she would approach them boldly, saying to their faces, "I am not yet hungry for your husband. Do not bother with reading the prayer and return to your homes."

Mohira Oyim, anything but nonplussed, wished only to crawl into a hole from this unprecedented display of shamelessness. As for the matchmakers, they were completely scandalized that a daughter would protest in this manner. Of course, both mother and father could do nothing more than scold and abuse her with the inevitable disappointments to follow. Her brother Azizbek at one point raised his hand to beat her, but became irresolute from her one simple, well- laid-out statement: "Why do you want to beat me, am I a prostitute?"

After each infamous event, the matchmakers' Achilles' heel was cut. They would stop in the street to gossip about the time that Khushroi Bibi...

Those same sovchi would then tell everyone they saw about the extraordinary treatment they received at her hands—it soon became a legend. At that point, Mohira Oyim finally opened her mouth to deliver her final verdict on her daughter: "You will now pass from this world without a husband, my daughter!"

Yet Khushroi Bibi would admit no wrong. "Husbands have not dried up. If I wanted to, tomorrow I could marry," she retorted.

Sometime after the above event, matchmakers arrived representing a bek by the name of Nusratbek who was also friends with Azimbek and had already been married. Instead of consulting with her husband beforehand, Mohira Oyim addressed the proposal directly to her daughter, with Khushroi Bibi making no protest. Upon hearing the agreement, her father and brother were delighted, as Nusratbek was the scion of a notable family among the beks, with all the considerable positions found accompanying such a personage. Therefore, the stigma of a prior marriage was disregarded. In the second week of the engagement, the wedding took place. The Yanga attending as witnesses of the consummation heard from Khushroi Bibi's own lips from under the Chimildiq that she and Nusratbek had already engaged in extramarital liaisons.

She had not placed one foot outside the bridal tent before Khushroi volleyed a barrage of sarcastic remarks belittling her kundosh, who was at that moment dutifully performing her responsibilities of serving tea. By the second or third day of that first week she had instigated an altercation with her kundosh; within ten days she had wheedled her husband away from sleeping with his first wife. By the second or third week the kitchen staff was entirely in her hands, and finally, turning her focus on her kundosh and her two children, she started limiting their food intake. As for Nusratbek, held in esteem as a respected bek in the community, he succumbed to Khushroi upon her entering his home. The wretched first wife eventually became downtrodden from Khushroi Bibi's constant barrage while witnessing her own husband subjecting his own children to merciless mistreatment—and she succumbed to utter hopelessness.

By the second month Khushroi Bibi regularly beat and choked her fellow kundosh, feeling no compunction about tearing her hair out like dry grass.

The poor kundosh, fed up with her life, upon reaching the third month asked her husband for a divorce. Nusratbek had no other option but to comply with her wishes, his hand being forced. In desperation and in anguish, the poor wretch intended to leave her two children to her husband, but heard the following from Khushroi Bibi: "Those birthed from a dog cannot be used for sacrifice! If you wish to cut off all hope for your children, leave your puppies in this house!"

These terrible threats from the mouth of Khushroi Bibi wrenched the poor mother's heart. Coming to the conclusion that Khushroi would not deny herself even this revenge, she took her children with her, full of foreboding and anguish for their future.

Khushroi felt satisfied with the victory of pulling the present family up by its roots within the span of three months and with Nusratbek's complete obedience to her every whim.

Now, over the past seven or eight years, she had lived only for her own pleasure. She was pleased with the world around her, but... she was disappointed from not obtaining motherhood.

Two years from now, her husband Nusratbek would mock her... "You have not given me a child. You have left no doctor unvisited. What shall we do now?"

Khushroi divined her husband's purpose. "If this world, deprived of a child, becomes unlivable, first I shall give you some poison and leave some for myself."

This rejoinder compelled Nusratbek never to speak those words again. Really, in truth, to Khushroi, those words were not at all spoken in jest.

15

SHE COMES TO HER SENSES

They say that "scandal visits the houses of kundosh every day." Whoever coined this witticism was no doubt drawing upon personal experience. One could say that if a scandal does not arise on a daily basis, or a disturbance every week to ten days, one cannot deem a woman a genuine kundosh. If you ask why, we all know that families without kundosh—even the most ordinary families—have their dishes and cups broken every three days in battle.

I, the author, though countless times hearing the tales now depicted in *O'tkan Kunlar* from my late father—perhaps ten times over—never became bored by their telling, except for one scene. Today I arrived at the point in our story where picking up my *qalam* to depict the events in *O'tkan Kunlar* fills my heart with dread. Really, who among us does not already know the perils of the kundosh? Whose eyes have not seen for themselves the troubles of kundosh—who, all for the sake of some nonsense, ruin the world around them? Since I value the precious time of our dear readers, I wish to free my pencil of further frivolities. I must be excused, however, in pursuit of a conclusion to our tale. My apologies.

Zainab would seek solace among her family as her frustrations with her lot in life multiplied. Over a three- to four-month period she confided in her sister, Khushroi, on a couple of occasions. She presently arrived for her third consultation.

"Have you been touched by God?" asked Khushroi, welcoming her sister. Despite September's mild weather, Zainab was soaked in perspiration.

"What happened, Zainab, why so pale? Is your homelife satisfactory?

How is your husband?"

"Damn them to hell," said Zainab, wiping tears from her eyes.

Khushroi laughed, absent of any empathy.

397

"Come onto the veranda," she said. "Have you seen Mother yet?"

"No."

"Are you coming from your home?"

"Yes."

Khushroi, forcing her sister to sit, ordered her slave to bring tea. After a quick prayer on behalf of her sister, she asked, "How is my brother- in-law? Is he in good fettle?"

"May your brother-in-law die!" said Zainab, demonstrating great anger. "He has gone to Naymiddinbek's summer house. I have received no news from him—alive or dead, I have no idea."

Over the past three or four months Zainab's situation had distressed her greatly, and her visage had taken a drastic turn for the worst. She seemed to have aged years. Her former plumpness was lost to a shadow of herself. Her eyes took on a strange tic that reigned sovereign over her previous melancholy and now became noticeable with every movement.

Zainab disagreed with her sister's earlier comments on her husband. "How ungrateful you are, Sister!" she said. "It is unsuitable to complain about my brother-in-law. What would you do if God placed upon your head such suffering as mine?"

"If I were Zainab, I would suffer accordingly, never uttering a word," her sister cackled. "To my mind each of us deserves either the bad or the good placed upon their head..."

"Don't say such things, my sister."

"To this day," said Khushroi, "I find it shameful to bow my head in obedience to another human being, and accordingly, I bend everyone to my will..."

"Don't think so highly of yourself."

"Whether I boast or not," continued Khushroi, "my character is well known to everyone. You most of all are familiar with it... Fine, let's change the subject. How are you doing?"

"Don't ask."

"Tell me or don't tell me," said her sister. "It seems your peaceful life has been disrupted."

"May God damn those who ruined my peace."

"Nobody has ruined your peace, Zainab! You bring all this suffering upon yourself."

"You always say that," protested Zainab. "Who wishes suffering upon himself in this world?"

"You and those like you..."

"God will damn..."

"Whether you say it or not, God has already punished them..."

"Did I wish these days upon myself?"

"You did!"

Zainab looked at her sister's face, perplexed. "If I did, tell me..."

"Do you know how I married my husband?"

"I know."

"If you truly know, take the following to heart," said Khushroi. "Now, as for your marriage, you cannot deny that it was arranged without consideration of your will or wishes. Perhaps even then you did not know the meaning of the word *will* or *wish*. Maybe you had dreams and aspirations, but nobody took notice of them. For these reasons your fate was in the hands of your mother and father who, in other words, treated you like a camel load, mindless, to be sold to whoever received you. Do you remember at my wedding I entered the cart laughing and talking freely; as for you, you left the house crying all the way to your husband's bridal tent... It is all good that you found your husband agreeable, but liking your husband was beside the point... Your husband discarded you, yet you did not make a sound, did not consider your future... only when your kundosh appeared from out of the water, you threw up your hands up in protest... But now it is too late, however you protest, faithful to your character, you always arrive at the same conclusion: each day will either be a small death for you, or you will leave your home."

These stark truths delivered in her usual brutal fashion by Khushroi made Zainab weep.

"I did not think it would be like this..."

"Have you ever thought?" scoffed Khushroi. "Someone is dying yet you laugh!"

"If not, I would cry. When people cry, all I want to do is laugh."

"If you were in my place you would do nothing but weep..."

"Do you know what I would do in your place, Zainab?" said Khushroi. "I would turn this world upside down. I would spread a hundred drops of poison for one drop of my tears."

With those last words Zainab's eyes surveyed her sister's face, taken aback by Khusroi's wicked visage.

"Fine," said Zainab in a broken voice. "What would you do if all your friends had become your enemies? If your mother-in-law, who for three years was your companion and consoled you, also joined the enemy camp? Even your parents who gave you life only say, 'Be patient, my child'!... Enough, enough! What could you do in this situation other than cry?"

Khushroi, with her terrible expression still cast across her face, again laughed.

"What does the word *enemy* mean, anyway?" she asked. "I told you this before: a person has no other friend in this world than his own greed! For example, you believed your mother and father were your friends, but what good have they ever done for you? Will your wounds ever heal from their counsel to 'Be patient, my child'? Of course they won't. From the outset your husband ignored you. Yet again you believed in your mother-in-law's promises, among other illusions... think for yourself, a child is brought into this world by its mother; but can the mother force her child to love someone? Of course, that's impossible. You poor thing, you accepted this lie as well. What else can I tell you?

Father forces patience down your throat as your mother-in-law revels in the presence of your kundosh, meanwhile your tears only embrace tears..."

"I did not seek your counsel so that I could consume myself with anguish!" said Zainab, weeping still more. "I have backbiters already in my own home who do so without lifting a finger... don't you, too, burn my soul to cinders. Please, if you can, bring calm to your sister consumed by the flames."

"Calm is impossible for you..."

"Your wit knows no bounds... at the least, you could use it for the sake of your miserable sister, indeed... this calamity has haunted my mind without respite, I came to your door for advice and will leave with no relief—now you too..."

Khushroi surveyed Zainab's face for a while.

"Will you take my advice?" she finally asked.

"Why shouldn't I if it is reasonable?"

"If so," continued Khushroi, "leave your husband."

Zainab burst out in a long wail.

400

"I was waiting for you to say that…"

"Why such advice? Because this is the only cure for your pain."

"How can I divorce my husband?"

"Just as others divorce their husbands, so shall you!"

Zainab did not respond. The slave woman laid out the tablecloth before them and served tea. Khushroi, ordering her to attend to the stove, poured the tea herself.

"Help yourself, Zainab."

"I have lost my appetite."

"If you follow my advice, your appetite will return."

"My husband… how can I part with my husband?"

"If you asked for a divorce," laughed Khushroi, "would your husband be willing to part from you in kind?"

"I don't know."

"Of course you do. Don't you know, deep in your heart, letting go of all illusions, that he would easily part ways with you? But you are stupid. You do not know which end to lay your feet on in bed or how to clap with both hands!"[397]

"Are you suggesting I leave without a fight?"

"There is no alternative for you!"

"I must live my life to the end of my days wronged by others, but my kundosh should live a blessed life—is that what you mean?"

"Aren't you protesting now, and isn't your kundosh already flourishing?"

"Fine, she is," said Zainab, "but each step she takes, I harass her, making her more nervous with each bite."

Khushroi laughed.

"What will you achieve with that?"

"In some way or another, I will not allow this interloper a moment of peace."

"Whether you deny her peace or not," said Khushroi, "the others will certainly deny your peace."

"What do you mean?"

"If you continue to harass her, will her husband allow you to remain there?"

Zainab's mind raced in the face of this simple truth. Khushroi watched her sister mulling the question over with savage eyes and a broad grin on her face. She seemed to be saying "What can you do now?" while grinning even further. Zainab's face broke into a new, until then yet unseen, menacing visage. Inexplicably, her tears, which had until then flowed freely, dried, and her voice took on a sharp tone hitherto unimaginable for Zainab.

"You've made me come to my senses, Sister," she said. "Thank you."

"Don't thank me," said Khushroi. "If you believe this is the path, thank your own heart..."

16

HER DELIVERY DATE NEARS

Kumush's delivery date neared. Though a month remained to build a *beshik*[398] for the baby, Uzbek Oyim, thrilled to see a grandchild on the horizon, engaged in busybodying about, loudly barking orders. Questions of who the midwife should be, how many sheep should be slaughtered for the baby shower, on what date the baby's future marriage would take place, how many men and women should be invited and who should not?—Uzbek Oyim's mind was preoccupied with these sorts of sundry issues. Deriving conclusions drawn from Kumush's bearing, she suspected that her grandchild would be a boy and kept saying: "You will have a son, Kumush. I also carried Otabek light like you." As the last month before Kumush's due date arrived, her duties were transferred to Zainab's care.

As Uzbek Oyim's joy grew over the promise of a grandchild, Otabek's apprehensions multiplied every time he looked at Kumush, as he was haunted by the tale of Usta Alim's tragedy.

Yusufbek Hajji, after suffering through further skullduggery and trickery, washed his hands of his service to the khanate and spent most of his time in the guest room, reading the Kuran and Dalil.[399] When matters between the two kundosh rose to new heights, their invectives echoing throughout the household, he called the two young brides before him, sitting them down next to each other.

First, he castigated Kumush.

"Upon my word, Mother, you are the eldest of the two, Zainab is still young; the elder should be merciful and patient with the youngest, this is most egregious!" he declared and then looked at Zainab. "My child, Zainab, youth and ambition persist in your heart, but do not forget you are my child!" he concluded, and in a gentle voice, prayed for them both, making them hold each other's forearms and bow three times "All right, it must be this way, my charming daughters."

Their gathering drawing to a close, he gave them leave. Of course, upon their departure Uzbek Oyim entered her husband's room, and Hajji mustered as much respect available and said to his wife, "You have not managed your brides well; you have left Zainab languishing in pain. You should take special care of Zainab's heart—Otabek should be instructed to follow suit."

Upon hearing Hajji's invective, Uzbek Oyim defended Kumush. "Goddamn that Zainab—it's all her fault."

Hajji was startled, unable to staunch the torrent issuing from Uzbek Oyim's mouth. "Hush, hush, for shame! A mother-in-law should above all remain impartial. Wasn't Zainab the result of our dream?" Hajji finally understood Uzbek Oyim's underlining anxiety surrounding her grandchild and the ensuing attacks on Zainab, reminding her: "What about Zainab—have you forgotten Zainab? Zainab is your bride of choice!"

Fifteen days later Kumush began a correspondence with her mother.

Since it is pivotal to our story, we have copied it here:

Dear Mother,

What has your son-in-law written to you? I am writing the sixth letter to you including this one. I have received three letters from you and two from my father. Most notably, from the terrible news contained in my father's last letter, the obligations of this world have become irrelevant in my eyes. No one can escape death, but I have anguished over my loss of being able to tend to my grandmother or receive her prayers. Being far from my homeland has had an ill effect on me. My tears bathe my face. Today, on the fifth day of her death, I started to read the Quran on behalf of the ghost of my late grandmother. I will dedicate my reading to her. May

God bless her with prayers; may they give you consolation. For now, you will not perish without prayers from your refugee daughter.

You must know that, Al-Hamdulillahi, your son-in-law, and in-laws are in good health—under their protection, I, your faithful daughter, live in peace. I greatly long to see you and my father; if I were not pregnant, despite the winter weather, I would leave for Margilan. According to your in-laws, especially my mother-in-law, I am due next month. Your in-laws, over the past fifteen days, have not trusted me to the earth or the sky, not even letting me touch cold water. As for her, it's as if she is preparing a wedding, making a cradle and serving out dowries... As for me, I have an intangible fear in my heart... In my previous letters I wrote about it lightheartedly. My relationship with my fellow kundosh has gone sour. In truth our relationship is completely broken. I also am guilty of wearing the robe of scandal common to a kundosh. As for Zainab's endless hostility, it began in earnest the day my pregnancy was announced. Though you are fully aware of the potential for kundosh scandals, you will now know in truth: if they were to let us, we would eat each other alive...

Recalling my behavior over these past days embarrasses me... It is a relief that my father-in-law very rarely heard of our scandals. Nevertheless, these domestic disturbances reached his ears, and we two combatants were summoned before him to receive guidance from him, the two of us feeling most guilty.

Though you will be offended, let me say: I like my father-in- law better than my own father. My love for him is not due to the fact he is the father of your son-in-law, but from his kind countenance, which seems to emanate light; I love his gentle, persuasive, polite voice when he addresses me as "my mother." When he opens his mouth in reprimand, I feel as if I am transcendent and have woken from a pleasant sleep. In the end, arguing with Zainab and the subsequent resolution is a real joy as I get to sit and receive guidance from him, an even greater pleasure. Please do not be angry with my madness. If you wish to find out for yourself the truth in my view, come to Tashkent, listen to my father-in-law's teachings with your own ears, and see the value in what I say.

I fought with Zainab rather shamelessly, fighting like cats and dogs at every turn. Indeed, indeed, we made your son-in-law's world dark. After some time, he said to both of us kundosh, "If you continue in this manner, I will free myself from both of you and cast both of you out of my sight!" I, of course took no heed of his threat, but only feared: "It would be better if Zainab took it as true." In this manner I pretended to take the threat as real so she would flee to her mother's house, offended. She seemed to receive some sort of abuse from members of her mother's household, and after a few days returned cooled down and calm. Now two months have passed since this event, and not one scandal has arisen between us. When I aim some sharp words at her to achieve some effect, she says nothing. Her new manner bodes ill for me. She is going to stand between us for some time.

My heart dreads the next month... Nights looking up at the sky, I wonder to myself whether I will live another month or not. If my grandmother Oysha had not passed away, you could come to Tashkent yourself for this next month. Please consider that you may mourn her at any time, but it would be better to come now for the sake of your daughter's heart. If you relayed my wishes to my father, he would not be against such an idea. Many greetings to my father.

Again, my heart feels great trepidation about the next month... If we do not see each other soon, remember me well and please send my regards to my father and those close to me...

I, Kumush, written from Tashkent, 1st December, 1853[400]

As Kumush had stated in her letter, over the past few days Zainab indeed seemed to settle down—she gave only the shortest of answers and comported herself in a calm, polite manner; in short, she returned to her demeanor of the previous year.

She bore her mother-in-law's directions that, "When it is time for your sister to deliver, you must take the kitchen duties in your own hands!" with equanimity, almost completely freeing Oibadak from kitchen work, even continuing her lesser chores of sweeping the yard, cleaning the house, and so on. Zainab's newly found composure did not limit itself to housework. The same changes were also seen in her interactions with her husband. She seemed completely oblivious to his presence. Her husband, in turn, became increasingly alarmed with Zainab's answers delivered with an abstract, wistful smile.

The new moon ascended; the due date neared. From Margilan the news that Oftob Oyim had taken to the road arrived at the household. But an intangible, unspoken pain developed in Kumush. The first day of this vague malignancy, Kumush informed no one. But on the second day, first Otabek and then Uzbek Oyim took notice. Though Otabek detected imminent danger, he could not muster the resolve to seek assistance in this private matter. Uzbek Oyim, on the other hand, immediately made Hasan Ali run to the midwife who had attended to Kumush over the past six months.

When the woman arrived at the Ich Kari, all the men in attendance were asked to leave. Bit by bit, the pain increased in Kumush while the midwife and Uzbek Oyim tended to her, using all the skill available to them. By evening the pain became overwhelming, taking complete hold of her.

Otabek was nowhere to be found. Hasan Ali paced between the gate and the guest room, rubbing his hands, again and again entering the stable to rub down the brown horse tethered there. As for Hajji, his mood swung between euphoria and anxiety; it was impossible to divine whether he was glad or upset as he read Dalil. Every five minutes, he cocked his ear toward the inner rooms, pausing in his reading, at times calling Hasan Ali through the small door to ask him "Is there any news... ?"

After reading the evening prayer, Oibadak brought dinner for them to take in their room.

Neither Hasan Ali nor Hajji opened their mouths to ask about her condition. Otabek's absence was not noticed during the meal. Not a word passed between them. They pretended to take something to eat from the cup and, after cleaning their hands: "Have they called for Khuftan prayers?" asked Hajji.

"I haven't heard the call yet... we can go out..." said Hasan Ali. At that moment the wrenching, trilling cries of the women echoed forth from the inner rooms. Their ears sharpened to the weeping of the women, looking at each other in horror... from among the lamentations a weak, bawling voice arose... the two smiled at each other, but still they did not exchange a single word. Not a moment had passed between them when Oibadak ran in from the inner rooms and, standing in the small doorway, said, "*Suyinchi.*"[401]

Hajji, digging in his purse, said, "Alhamdulillah," as Hasan Ali, also grinning, began to dig in his pocket.

"Is it a son or a daughter?" he asked his wife.

"Son!"

"Bless you!"

Smiling, Hajji passed to Oibadak three or four silver coins along with a gold one—"Take the silver ones for yourself, give the gold to the midwife!" and after Hasan Ali gave his offering, he opened his hands in prayer: "Let it be so; God gives life to all." Satisfied with the results, they went out for Khuftan prayers.

As Otabek neared the guest room, hearing the cry of a baby, he moved apprehensively into the inner yard, meeting his mother in the passageway. Though it was dark, the joy was apparent in Uzbek Oyim's face.

"Congratulations, my son! My child!"

"Is she all right?"

"She is fine."

"Shall I enter to see her?"

"No," said Uzbek Oyim. "It is not good to enter the house in the evening straight from the street with a newly born baby at hand... If you must enter the house, go straight to Zainab. Is your father here?"

"How is the mother faring?"

"She is fine. Don't worry," said Uzbek Oyim, turning to go back into the rooms. Turning around, Otabek noticed the outline of his father and Hasan Ali coming in through the passage from the outside and stopped worrying. Especially at that moment, it was rather uncomfortable for him to come across his father.

For these reasons he hung back in the dark of the passage, and after they passed, moved toward the inner rooms. Entering Zainab's room, he darted a few glances at the door behind which Kumush was lying.

"Congratulations on your son!" Zainab welcomed her husband, giggling. Otabek also allowed himself a smile. Both sat as Zainab continued with her chuckling for reasons known only to her.

"I would say..." She trailed off as if forgetting her intended statement, only to try to remember with another "I would say..." followed by another pause, as if she were lost in thought. Anyway, she finally let it rest.

Otabek, waiting for her lips to move for some moments, smiled, asking, "Well, what?"

"I would say..."

"And, what next?"

"Damn its name... yes, well, will you eat your plov?"

"I will."

"If it is not yet cold, that is..."

Otabek had not eaten one bite since morning. "Bring it cold or hot," he said.

Though Zainab's face seemed more open and bright, an impalpable shade hovered over her countenance that gave it a serious and preoccupied cast, as if some frantic mania lay beneath her otherwise cheerful face. During his exchange with Zainab, Otabek several times met with the above-mentioned lapses, and was finally compelled to ask, "Why so absentminded?"

Zainab laughed.

"Why do you say absentminded? Right," said Zainab. "I became afraid..."

"Of what?"

"Of giving birth..."

"Was it difficult for her?"

" 'Difficult' is not the right word," said Zainab. "You would not believe it unless you saw it with your own eyes."

"But my mother did not describe it like that. Is it true?"

"She kept you misinformed."

Otabek's heart skipped a beat. This account made him forget he was in the presence of a kundosh—the effect on Otabek defies description. Consumed with fear, he asked Zainab for more details, barely able to stand another rendition of events. His tea half-drunk, his bed having been prepared, he went off to sleep. Zainab put out the candle.

It was still early to go to bed yet when Zainab left the room to join Kumush, her words prevented him from closing his eyes as he shifted from his right, to his left, to his stomach, Zainab's disturbing account echoing in his ears the whole time.

The noise from the women and the occasional wails of the baby traveling from Kumush's room added to his restless sleep. Though their tender voices evoked in him the irresistible connection of fatherhood, he soon surrendered to his darker thoughts. Caught in these bittersweet visions, he finally faded off to sleep. The experiences over the past couple of days in various shades passed through his sleepy mind... waking him in a cold sweat... Only Kumush remained near him... Zainab was not even in his thoughts. With drowsy eyes he listened to the other room and still hearing that voice of hers ringing in his right ear, he buried himself under the blanket, soon sleeping with a peace of mind...

He saw in his dream: Flower blossoms abounded in his garden...[402] he knew the flower garden was his own... yet he could not take his eyes off the colorful blooms as if he instinctually felt the presence of enemies all around... He held his blade ready to defeat the enemy... yet it had fled... among his assailants might have stood his mother and father... when he returned to the flower garden, a cow stood in its midst, trampling the flowers and eating the grass... no, not a cow, but a yellow-haired devil... as if he had suddenly lost all strength, the knife fell from his stricken hand... as if all the world turned dark... He finally woke in a great fright and saw Zainab sleeping near him. His heart beat fiercely from his vision and his body was covered in sweat. Slowly turning on his right side, he lay looking out into the yard. As he turned, Zainab's eyes slowly opened and closed.

Early morning neared as cocks crowed from all corners of the neighborhood. The water mill nearby churned, making a frothy earthquake. Candlelight from the other room barely made a glimmer through the crack under the small door, yet not a sound was heard. He could not fall back asleep. He thought about Kumush's exertions of the day before. The early morning prayer echoed as the dawn brightened, and as the mosque near their house also called out in reply, he rose to perform ablutions.

In order to create some justification to infiltrate Kumush's room, he ate breakfast in Zainab's room. Uzbek Oyim gave him permission to enter. After tea, the midwife left Kumush's room for some moments. At the far end of the room Kumush lay with Uzbek Oyim at her feet holding the newborn baby. When Otabek entered, Kumush smiled at him through her pale face and sunken eyes. Otabek, losing control of himself, cried: "Congratulations!" Instead of answering, Kumush bashfully hid her face under the blanket.

Uzbek Oyim spoke. "Congratulations upon the one who made it. Sit down," she said.

Otabek sat near Kumush's head. Uzbek Oyim prayed. Then, handing the baby to Otabek, she said, "Give dowry for this young foal—his father." Otabek turned red and looked at the child. Kumush again hid her face under the blanket.

"Are you yourself all right?"

"Thank God..."

"I heard that you had difficulties..."

"Is giving birth just a game to you men?" said Uzbek Oyim.

Kumush motioned to Otabek, pointed toward herself, then whispered in his ear: "It's your fault."

"Did you eat... ?"

Uzbek Oyim answered. "Since yesterday she has not eaten anything hot. Let me speak with Zainab. She will make milk porridge."

"Certainly!" said Otabek and, after giving a gold coin to his mother as a *suyinchi*, left the room, satisfied with the situation.

After lunch Otabek was reading a book in the guest room as Hasan Ali was repairing the horse equipage; Hajji was off to the mosque or some other demand of the day.

Oibadak came out of the house and approached Otabek.

"Otabek, you must come to the room, immediately," she said.

Otabek closed the book with a snap. "What is the matter?"

"Everything is fine, of course, but come quickly!"

Otabek entered close behind Oibadak. Zainab at that moment was departing, pale faced, from Kumush's room.

"What's the matter?" Otabek asked her.

"I don't know," she said. "My sister is vomiting with a stomach ache."

When Otabek neared the door, a woman carrying veils exited, and he entered the room.

Uzbek Oyim held a basin while Kumush vomited into it.

"What happened?"

Kumush, completely stricken, could not answer.

"I don't know... she has been vomiting for some time," said Uzbek Oyim. Tired from the constant retching, Kumush weakly lolled her head on her pillow. She momentarily looked up at her husband, her eyes brimming with tears.

"You have given her something spoiled to eat."

"She has not eaten anything rotten or spoiled," said his mother. "Besides, since the porridge, she has not eaten anything. And she only ate a half a cup of that. The remnants are on the shelf..."

Uzbek Oyim had not even finished when Kumush moved toward the basin. Otabek held her hair.

"Shall I call for a doctor?"

"Yes, I also considered this."

Otabek waited for Kumush to finish vomiting, then he ran out of the room. Hasan Ali was still tending to his work.

"Father, could you run down for a doctor?"

Hasan put down his work. "What's happening?"

"Your daughter-in-law has been vomiting for some time..."

Hasan Ali raced for the doctor. Otabek returned to the room. Zainab was holding the baby while Kumush continued to vomit... Kumush weakened further, laid her head on the pillow... A bluish tint grew under her eyes, and she was unable to look at Otabek, who moved nearer to her.

"Are you all right?"

"My heart."

Otabek's body shivered all over. Nevertheless, he held firm.

"Did you try to make her drink sour milk?" he said to his mother.

"No."

"Order some sour milk."

Until Oibadak arrived with the milk, Kumush repeatedly retched over the basin. Gasping once or twice for air through bouts of vomiting, she rinsed her mouth with water cupped in Otabek's hands, and having drunk one or two mouthfuls from the cup of sour milk, threw her head onto the pillow. Her temperature burned; her pulse fluttered. When Otabek pressed his hand to her forehead, it seemed to soothe her a bit. Uzbek Oyim took the baby from Zainab, who until then had sat in the corner coddling the child, and ordered her to clean the basin. Otabek's hand cupped Kumush's forehead as it burned even hotter. Feeling a clamminess on her forehead, Kumush opened her eyes.

"How is your heart?"

Instead of answering, Kumush rose from her pillow. There was no basin. Otabek hurriedly took a Chinese cup from the shelf. Kumush heaved. This time her sick was sour milk mixed with green and yellow bile. After rinsing her mouth, Otabek again offered her more milk but she refused to drink further, her head returning to the pillow...

Hearing that the doctor was on his way, Otabek regained his nerves. Zainab, who stood in the doorway holding the basin, turned back. Uzbek Oyim, the baby swaddled in her arms, left the room. Otabek, forgetting to rise out of respect for the doctor, only sat, his hand pressed on Kumush's forehead. After being apprised of the matter from Otabek and checking Kumush's pulse, the doctor pursed his lips and sniffed the vomit in the cup, looking at it.

"What has she eaten today?"

"Milk porridge."

"Is there something left of that meal?"

"There is!" said Otabek and taking the cup from the place where his mother had indicated, placed it in the doctor's hands. The doctor took a taste from his finger, immediately spitting it out.

"She has consumed poison!"

Otabek leaped up, his face masked in fear...

"What nonsense!"

Otabek's present agitation terrified the doctor...

"I will immediately send for an antidote," he said rising from his place.

"Who delivered the poison?"

The doctor was speechless in shock:

"I... I... can you think of anyone yourself? Let me send for an antidote immediately. She must drink it quickly, do you understand?" he said.

"I know, I know," said poor Otabek, "Zainab, Zainab, Zainab... ! Prostitute! Send for it, send for it immediately, send for it!"

The doctor hurried out while Otabek rushed about like a lunatic, finally settling at Kumush's head. He held her face in his hands, passed his hands along her forehead, and kissed her... Kumush opened her eyes and through an act of will placed her left hand on her husband's shoulder...

Uzbek Oyim entered with the baby in her arms...

"Call Zainab here, Zainab!"

Uzbek Oyim was aware of the doctor's diagnosis.

"Zainab, Zainab."

Zainab rushed into the room. Her face was drawn and dead pale. Otabek, remaining beside Kumush, took the porridge from the floor.

"Eat this, eat, you whore!"

Zainab retreated a couple of steps back... Otabek threw the cup at her... Zainab's clothes were splashed with the porridge. At that moment Yusufbek Hajji appeared from the corridor.

"Away, whore, go away! You are divorced, divorced, divorced!"[403] Having heard the word "divorced" Kumush momentarily opened her eyes and closed them again... The doctor had already informed Hajji of events, so he was calm in the face of this tragic scene.

"Get out, Zainab, get out!" he joined in. "Damn a wife like you!" Zainab stepped back farther out of the room... Hajji sat near Kumush's head. Otabek and his mother were at her feet. Kumush's eyes were closed, her hair matted over her face. With his own hand Hajji arranged her hair, and seeing Kumush's pale, drawn face, pressed his hand on her forehead.

"My mother, my mother!" said Hajji. Opening her eyes, she could barely look at him and then, finally recognizing him... tried to get up.

"Don't move, my mother, don't move!"

Tears formed in the corners of Kumush's eyes... Sobs broke freely from Hajji as he dried Kumush's own tears—she managed to nod her head in thanks.

"God will provide a cure, my child!"

Kumush moved toward the washbasin; Otabek moved from her feet to take her in his arms; Hajji held her hand... This time her vomiting produced blood, several drops fell from her nose... after vomiting, she lay back, her eyes circling about with a look of impatience.

"Mother, Father..." And after that, "My Bek..." Muttering this she moved her husband's face to her face and quietly closed her eyes...

*****

The next day, they held the funeral.[404] People from every Mahalla in Tashkent were in attendance.

Only the deceased's loved ones could not manage to reach the ceremony in time.

Poor mother, poor father!

The third day they arrived... Is it possible to find words to describe their reaction?

On the seventh day a Quranic prayer was recited; plov was served, and on this occasion the baby was given the name Yodgorbek.[405]

Not only Kumush's loved ones, but the young and old of the city who had no connection with the tragedy were waiting for a just punishment to be delivered in Zainab's case. But on the tenth day after the tragedy, rumors circulated stating that Zainab had gone mad, caught walking the streets unveiled, and was duly detained. Shackled by her own brother, when the testimony of Zainab's madness was delivered by both members of the court and doctors, the anticipated punishment in her case was rescinded. In truth, overcome with madness, walking the streets unveiled, and being led off in shackles was no small punishment for Zainab.

On the twentieth day of the tragedy another Quranic prayer for the deceased was recited with the whole city served plov—after which the wretch's parents began the preparations to return to Margilan. Yodgorbek would be placed under the care of Oftob Oyim, with no one protesting this decision.

On the last day, farewells were delivered. Otabek, Qutidor, and Oftob Oyim visited the cemetery and stopped near the newly constructed brick tomb placed between two chinar trees.[406] At the right side of the tomb an engraved stone inscription stood out in plain view:

Kumush Bibi, the child of Mirza Karim Margilani Born 1248
Died 1269 January[407]
This inscription is a memory to the princess of—
From a brokenhearted young man
Here is buried the victim of a tragedy born from kundosh

The poor mother embraced the grave as she wailed aloud in a torrent of feeling.

Otabek, also on his knees in front of the grave, made the earth moist with his tears... Qutidor, also in attendance, grew inconsolable after reading the inscription. For half an hour they remained lost in a state of complete despair.

No one had the power to recite from the Quran. A Qori[408] who was appointed by Yusufbek Hajji in the small building opposite the tomb understood they were completely grief stricken. Slowly he exited the building, sat apart from them, and read a *surah* from the Quran. Though Oftob Oyim's weeping quieted, her tears flowed freely—as did the others'. The prayer delivered, Qutidor and Oftob Oyim gave offerings to the Quran reader. Upon the reader's departure, each of them achieved a level of calm and each devoted their own Quranic *surah* to her. Afterward, all slowly walked along the path, bidding farewell to her grave. Oftob Oyim, still weeping, continually looked over her shoulder as if to hear the sound of Kumush whispering to her mother, "Remember me well, remember me well..."

Otabek left them at home, returned to the tomb, and all night kept vigil there. In the morning, Hasan Ali prepared and loaded some items in the cart. Afterward Oftob Oyim descended into the yard with some of Kumush's clothes, carrying Yodgorbek. Some moments later Yusufbek Hajji and Qutidor appeared. As Qutidor bid everyone goodbye, Otabek entered from the street, grabbed the reigns of Hasan Ali's horse, who was still mounted, and said, "Dismount from the horse, please!" Hasan Ali slid down. Otabek jumped into the saddle and asked Qutidor, "Shall I begin?"

Qutidor and Hajji gave each other a confused look. Uzbek Oyim, standing in the passageway, peered through the gate.

Qutidor said nothing as Otabek spurred the horse according to his own wishes.

"Goodbye!"

"All right, bye!"

Hasan Ali, who also had to go to Margilan, seemed lost in the middle of the street and looked toward Hajji, who turned to Oyim in the passageway... Otabek escorted the cart down the road and never looked back.

After a year Otabek traveled to Tashkent with Usta Alim. Hajji and Uzbek Oyim could not open their mouths in protest or anger toward him. He was like a stranger in their home. He kept a distance from his mother and father, rarely speaking a word to them.

He stayed about a week in Tashkent with Usta Alim, and he spent the last night of their stay alone near Kumush's grave. The night sky was bright under a full moon. The cemetery was stark still. The voice of someone reading the Quran was heard at a distance. Three or four owls perched on one of the chinar trees while Otabek kneeled near it; the solemn grave was in harmony with the heavy tone of his recitation. The timeless words of the Quran flowed with great weight throughout the cemetery. The tears of the young man crouched on his knees streamed along with the words of the *surah*. An hour later, the recitation ceased. Otabek, clearly weakened, rose from his place and, upon seeing the shadowy body of a half-naked person, retreated in horror toward the grave... The shadowed form edged near him as if pleading...

"Who is that?"

"I am Kumush!"

Otabek recognized the owner of this voice. It was Zainab. "Get away from here!"

"I am Kumush," Zainab repeated, but was compelled to leave as one of the most intimate people in her world commanded her to "go away!" Looking, looking over her shoulder, Zainab moved away from Otabek. Otabek did not look at her again and sank to his knees again near the grave...

The next day Uzbek Oyim wept while giving to Otabek clothing sewn particularly for Yodgorbek. Together with Usta Alim, Otabek left for Margilan. After this visit, Otabek never returned to Tashkent. Several times Uzbek Oyim traveled to Margilan herself.

It must have been in the autumn of 1277 AH[409] that Yusufbek Hajji received a letter from Qana'atshah from Avliyo Ata:[410]

Your son Otabek, along with another companion, campaigned along with our troops. These two brave young men in an engagement against the Russians near Alma Ata[411] spearheaded the battle, and fighting heroically, died as Shahids.[412] I buried both of them with my own hands...

Yusufbek Hajji in turn devoted a Quran reading to the fallen and served plov to the whole city. Uzbek Oyim wore black and mourned openly[413].

Thus Ends Volume Three

FROM THE AUTHOR

During my later travels to Margilan, I asked from close friends the fate of Yodgorbek.

Yodgorbek, during the nineteenth and twentieth year of this century, during a great famine, died, leaving behind two sons.[414] One of them was an administrator with considerable responsibilities in Margilan.[415] The second was among the Basmachi in the Ferghana Valley. They say that there is no news whether they are alive or dead.

ENDNOTES

1. The version used as a source for the present translation is from the first 1926 publication transliterated into Cyrillic from the original Arabic script and republished in 1994 after the independence of the Republic of Uzbekistan. It is considered the most faithful, uncensored version of Qodiriy's *O'tkan Kunlar*. In the original text the notes show 1264 AH as corresponding to February 17, 1845 or 1846. Thus the novel begins approximately twenty years before General Cherniaev's conquest of Tashkent in 1865. There seem to be some incongruities on dates presented between the original and in various translations of the novel that place 1264 AH in 1848. We will see that although 1264 AH of the Hijra indeed corresponds to 1848 CE, events depicted in volume 1, namely the Tashkent Rebellion led by Azizbek, occurred earlier, in 1847.

One might consider that, in fact, Qodiriy is not referencing the Hijra Qamari calendar, or the Muslim, Lunar system often used in civil calendars, but instead the Central Asian animal-based calendar, with months based upon astrological figures. Use of the Central Asian calendar harkens back to a time before Islam and is tied closely with folk tradition and agricultural cycles—Qodiriy himself was a small-scale farmer or gardener. Some place the origins of this calendar with the Uighur who then, they argue, influenced the Chinese zodiac calendar. Until the introduction of the solar based Jalali calendar by the Seljuk Malikshah, used in Afghanistan and Persia, the beginning of the year was the 5th of February in Central Asia. The preeminent scholar of Central Asia Yuri Bregel cites the Turkish scholar, Dr. O. Turan, with the following description: "...the cyclical year begins on the conjunction between the sun and the moon in the middle of the zodiacal month of Dalv." The Jalali calendar was not used in Central Asia—with the exception of Bukhara— but its influence did shift the new year to 21st of March, or Nawruz Sultani, which is still today one of the great celebrations throughout the region. One must note that in Qodiriy's time that peasants in certain mountainous regions of Tajikistan began their new year on 19th of February as part of their agricultural cycle. See Munis Khorezmii, Muhammad Riza Mirab Agahi, et al., translated by Yuri Bregel, *Firdaws Al-Iqbal: History of Khorezm* (Islamic History & Civilization) (Brill Academic Pub; annotated edition, (September 1, 1999). Above quote from: Dr. O. Turan, *Oniki Hayvanhli Turk Takvimi* (Dil ve Tarih Cografya Fakultesi Yayinlarindan, Tarikh Serisi, No.3)

This would also explain the use of Dalv as a month, January– February, or Aquarius, and Hasan Ali later making a reference to Otabek being born in the "Year of the Monkey." Throughout the novel I will try to pin dates to actual events in the khanate of Qoqan's history instead of navigating the vagaries of different calendar systems. One might consider the opening sentence as a subtle illustration of a world destined for irrevocable change—a pre-Islamic, zodiacal calendar mingled with the designation of the year of the Hijra showing how elements of disparate cultures intermingled to form the distinct identity Qodiriy wishes to chronicle. Indeed, throughout Central Asian historical texts authors often overlapped the Hijri, zodiacal, and Persian dating systems in response to administrative, religious and cultural requirements. That whole system is destined to be lost forever and Qodiriy begins his novel in that spirit.

Qodiriy begins his novel with a clear depiction of Otabek's socioeconomic standing as a member of the merchant class and of local elites, most notably the religious establishment, or Ulama, through his father—yet remaining a man apart. Merchants represented a major constituency within Central Asian society that often advocated for social and educational reform, at times expressed through patronage of reformers such as the Jadid movement, to which Qodiriy is ascribed. From a cynical point of view, one could say that they advocated for the incorporation of Russian language coursework and the sciences into the school curriculum for financial gain, e.g. to be able to better conduct business in foreign markets, but we also see the merchant class during this period undergoing a profound shift toward a nascent national identity. Their trade offered them greater interaction with the world and its changing ideas, which naturally had an influence on their worldview. As a commercial and financial force, they often sought to place their children into Jadid schools in order to offer them a worldly education, thus advancement. One could say that Otabek, son of Yusufbek Hajji, has ties to a past, represented through his father, but is a new man in a new age. See Hélène Carrère d'Encausse, *Islam and the Russian Empire: Reform and Revolution in Central Asia* (New York: I. B. Tauris, 2009).

2. Adras is a silk-and-cotton-blend fabric. It retains the luster of silk but has a tougher weave to allow for more practical uses—i.e. Korpachalar—heavy quilted mattresses with a cotton filling. Central Asians use them to sit and sleep on. Every spring the ladies of the household will change out the cotton. These futons are part of the bride's dowry gifted by the groom so they can begin a household.

3. Margilan is a city in the Ferghana valley in present-day eastern Uzbekistan known for its silk production and weaving industries. Legend has it that the city was founded by Alexander the Great when he was offered Murg, fowl, and non/ naan, bread. Tales of Alexander permeate Central Asia, but, perhaps, for the translator of this work, that the walnut trees in and around Margilan—and seemingly the rest of the Ferghana Valley—were planted by Alexander the Great when passing through is most memorable. For a direct historical reference to Margilan one should consult the Baburnama: "the pomegranates and apricots are superb; the game in Margilan is good; white deer may be found nearby. The people

are Sarts. They are a feisty people, ready with their fists. The custom of exorcism is widespread throughout Transoxiana, and most of the renowned exorcists of Samarkand and Bukhara are Margilanis." We will see later how the reputation of Margilanis being seers or exorcists will hold great relevance to the narrative in *O'tkan Kunlar*. Regarding Alexander the Great and walnuts, field notes 1995-2018. Zaddridin Babur, translated by Thackston Wheeler, *The Baburnama: Memoirs of Babur, Prince and Emperor* (New York: Modern Library Classics, 2002)

4. Hotinboz is translated as "womanizer": "hotin" means "woman" in Uzbek, and "-bozi" is a stem attached to a noun designating enjoyment beyond moderation of the noun it modifies. Therefore "bacha bozi" means "enjoys the company of bachas, or underage boys or young male dancers"—an issue of concern to Qodiriy. In this case, Hamid is hotinbozi; he enjoys the company of women, is a womanizer. "Bozi" is not often a compliment...

5. Central Asian gatherings are held in circles. The Tor, or place of honor, goes to the most senior guest and faces the door from the other side of the room, an area less exposed to drafts and most secure. Since groups sit in a circle, the host should sit opposite the guest or guests, and a junior member of the household, near the doorway, to receive food, placing it in the center of the circle—most notably plov.

6. Surat al Fatiha- "The Opening" is the first Sura of the Quran. It often holds the role as a prayer for everyday functions—from, in this case, breaking bread with guests, to beginning a common task such as opening a door for the first time, ladling plov from its kazan or blessing someone or something. Islam permeates almost all acts of life in Uzbekistan. Qodiriy provides the reader profound insight into the tensions within that faith between modernity and 'traditional' Islam.

7. Sandal: a Persian-style, low-lying table covered with Korpachalar and holding a small stove underneath to keep those seated warm.

8. What follows is a standard social formula used throughout the Turco-Persian-Indo world. It is considered polite to ask after the well-being of the host, as well as their children, three times. Qodiriy is reminding his community through the quality of his hero, Otabek, the proper comportment of an Uzbek.

9. Bek/beg/bey—literally "nobleman" or "ruler" of a province, or vilayet. Throughout the novel "the Beks" are part of a social strata, not to be confused with Otabek, the name. The name Otabek can be shortened to Bek as a term of endearment or respect, a common usage throughout the novel. The Beks or Begs as a social stratum were appointed by the khan. Beks performed the function of governors of vilayets, e.g. regions within the khanates, and held unchecked power as long as they paid taxes. Additionally, once appointed, the Beks often placed members of their

own tribe or family in positions of power within their administration. Qodiriy has much to say throughout the novel regarding the Beks. See Hélène Carrère d'Encausse, *Islam and the Russian Empire: Reform and Revolution in Central Asia* (New York: I. B. Tauris, 2009).

10. As with the standard social formula above, it is standard to ask after someone's health, circumstances, and their loved ones at least three times.

11. Aka: literally "brother," used as a term of address for older males as a sign of respect. Similar to "Agha" in south Asia. On an informal note, the formal term in modern Uzbek, "Janobi," is used only in official circles. Aka is a more common way of rendering respect to a male.

12. Slavery: Although repugnant, Yusufbek Hajji engaged in an acceptable practice of the time—representing a generational split in values and mores between himself and the reform-minded Otabek. As in the United States, the slave trade was widely practiced throughout Central Asia and Russia up until the nineteenth century. Both the Tsarist empire and the Central Asian khanates facilitated mutual trade of its people for commercial purposes; yet, depending on the vicissitudes of commercial, diplomatic, and military engagement, Russia often protested the enslavement of its people, who were often used as collateral to achieve political ends. See Edward Allworth, Central Asia: *130 Years of Russian Dominance—A Historical Overview*, 3rd ed. (Durham, NC: Duke University Press, 1999). Hélène Carrère d'Encausse provides more details, stating that in "Bukhara and Samarqand on the eve of Russian conquest 20,000 and 10,000 slaves respectively inhabited those cities. 'Zarkharid' were mostly Iranians captured by the Turkmens, who raided Khurasan and then sold their captives in the market places of Central Asia." Throughout Central Asian history, slaves or former slaves could perform a number of functions ranging from agricultural work to being the progenitors of their own empire. See d'Encausse, *Islam and the Russia Empire*. According to Jeff Eden, "In the 18th and 19th centuries, frequent Turkmen raids into northern Iran resulted in tens of thousands of Iranian Shi'as being captured and funneled into a booming slave trade in Khwarazm and Bukhara." It is interesting to see Dr. Eden's research parallel Qodiriy's depiction of Hasan Ali's circumstances. Is Hasan Ali a Shi'a from Iran? See Jeff Eden, "Slavery in Islamic Central Asia," *Oxford Research Encyclopedia of Asian History* (May 2019).

13. Hajji: one who has made the pilgrimage to Mecca—one of the seven pillars of the Islamic faith.

14. Ota: literally "Father," used here as a term of address for older men as a sign of respect. Consider the name Ataturk: Father of the Turks. Ota Yurt: literally, Father Yurt, or Homeland.

15. Oq Kungli Odam: A white-hearted soul, selfless and true to his young charge.

16. The Chiroq, or lamp, in this scene makes a clear allusion to purity, but also to a reform-minded individual with clarity of thought. The concept of the lamp bringing light to the darkness is common throughout Turco-Persian literature, especially Sufi literature. Bolshevik propaganda campaigns often coopted the image of the "lamp" or "torch" to show progress and reform under Communist ideology. Qodiriy here is evoking the former rather than the latter. Throughout the novel we will see light used to evoke spiritual enlightenment.

17. Margilan: on historical background see above. Due to Margilan's location at the eastern end of the Ferghana valley they were strategically placed to conduct trade into present day Xinjiang, the traditional homeland of the Uighur people in western China. Margilan produces a number of silk products but most notably Khan Atlas, a silk cloth of a thick weave. Today the largest producer of Khan Atlas in Margilan is Yodgorlik factory, established in 1972.

18. Turkistan: literally "Land of the Turks" a geographic area often contingent depending upon historical context or political perspective. Generally, one could take Turkistan to mean for Qodiriy, before the Russian conquest of Central Asia, the Turkic-language-speaking lands from Mongolia to Xinjiang, northern Afghanistan to Azerbaijan or even modern-day Turkey—today we refer to this region as inner Asia. Russian Turkistan after Russian conquest from an administrative standpoint meant the Zerafshan valley, Syr Dariya and Amu Dariya Rivers, and the Ferghana valley, including the sedentary, oasis cities south of the Kazakh steppe, most notable the Syr Dariya, but not including the Protectorates of Bukhara and Khiva. The events in the novel take place in the Qoqan Khanate, the lands comprising the area of Russian Turkistan described above. During the Khanate period, a line of demarcation between the Qoqan Khanate's main rival, the Emirate of Bukhara, around Ura-Teppe and Shahrisabz fluctuated between the two, with parts of present-day Tajikistan, and at times Qoqan itself, changing hands. The Jadids often evoked Turkistan as a homeland of the Muslim Turkic peoples as a postcolonial concept envisioning a modern territorial delimitation. Their philosophy was heavily influenced by the idea of Turkism: Turks/Turcs of the world possessing a common identity and heritage. As Adeeb Khalid correctly states, this belief is not to be confused with Pan-Turkism, a political belief in the unified efforts of Turkic peoples to achieve a unified political state. See Adeeb Khalid, *Making Uzbekistan: Nation, Empire, and Revolution in the Early USSR* (Ithaca, NY: Cornell University Press, 2016).

19. Dasturkhon: a tablecloth one could consider the symbolic center of the household. Laying of the Dasturkhon is an important part of Central

Asian hospitality. It is changed throughout the meal to keep the eating area clean.

20. Shinni is a sugary syrup made from grapes or mulberries.

21. Interestingly, the zodiac is still common today in Uzbekistan, featured primarily through folk art, most notably the beautifully embroidered suzani, and is considered a holdover from the zodiacal calendar mentioned above. This influence comes no doubt through the centuries of Silk Road trade between Europe and China—with one of the hubs of that activity in present day Uzbekistan. The Qoqan Khanate itself enjoyed considerable diplomatic relations and trade with China well into the late-nineteenth century, most notably through opium and the Heavenly Horses of Ferghana supplied to Chinese rulers for military purposes. When visiting Khudayar Khan's palace in Qoqan, one can find Ming vases and Chinese cannons on display demonstrating that China, not Russia, was the Qoqan Khanate's primary diplomatic concern until the nineteenth century. See L. J. Newby, *The Empire and the Khanate: A Political History of Qing Relations with Khoqand c. 1760–1860* (Leiden, Netherlands: Brill Publishers, 2005).

22. Marriage reform was one of the primary linchpins of Jadid reform efforts in Central Asia. Perhaps here the author is projecting his reformist agenda into a nineteenth-century setting. Ideas such as considering a woman's wishes in selecting a husband and criticisms of polygamy, among others, are prevalent throughout the novel.

23. Shariyat/Shariyat: Qodiriy is well known for his biting sarcasm. Throughout the novel we will often see "The Shariyat says..." as the author pokes fun at common daily practices or customs, orf-odat, erroneously associated with Islamic piety or Islamic law. Qodiriy makes these criticisms as a madrassa-trained, devout Muslim who was proficient in Persian, Turkic, and Arabic, yet cast within the cultural milieu of a Central Asia just years after the Bolshevik Revolution. A common argument, if we are permitted a general summary, follows that the Jadids followed a long tradition within Islamic jurisprudence that attempted to use ijtihad, e.g. independent reasoning, to wrest credibility from religious establishments who insisted on the use of taqlid—or strict adherence to standards within Islamic schools of law. In short, through challenging the basis that formed Islamic institutions through their agenda, the Jadids hoped to bring modernity to a backward Central Asia. A great deal of new scholarship has forcefully argued that, if anything, the general assumptions we make regarding modernism, reformists, etc. during this time period cannot be boiled down to simple constructs and we must avoid generalities. In this case we should avoid a binary explanation of Ijtihad versus Taqlid or Jadid versus Ulama. Yet, despite the current debate, one must consider whatever the importance the Jadids held

during their own period, the importance they hold for Uzbeks today, especially among Uzbek intellectual circles, is undeniable.

The level of negotiation and leeway allowed to prospective spouses really depends on a number of socioeconomic circumstances—or the general temperament of the family. *Qur'an, Sura 4 (An-Nisa), Ayah 3* is the common basis for polygamy or polygany in Islam: "If ye fear that ye shall not be able to deal justly with the orphans, Marry women of your choice, Two or three or four; but if ye fear that ye shall not be able to deal justly (with them), then only one, or (a captive) that your right hands possess, that will be more suitable, to prevent you from doing injustice." Essentially, this statement is carried into a broader, contemporary context to mean that a man may marry only the number of women he is able to support economically and spiritually. Today arranged marriages are too complicated a subject to safely make any generalities. It is now not uncommon for the son or daughter to negotiate with their parents over a future spouse, or the parents present the choices to their child.

24. Known to us as pilaf—a tasty national dish with rice, lamb, and assorted vegetables and fruits prepared in a large Kazan.

25. Qutidor: Refers to Mirza Karim's profession as a tax collector for the khan, specifically related to the taxation of the merchants who set up "Quti," e.g. stalls, in the bazaar. Each stall is taxed an amount determined by location, seniority, and type of wares sold. The merchant class had a disproportionate interest in the Jadid movement as reforms meant that modernized business practices, including tax reform, would mean easier and more profitable commerce throughout Central Asia.

26. Amaki: paternal uncle. Used as a sign of respect. Compare to Tog'a, maternal uncle.

27. Akamiz: Our brother, another term used as a sign of respect.

28. Azizbek / Azizbek Parvonchi: Placed as hakim of Tashkent in 1846 and enjoyed Qipchaq support through Musulmanqul, regent of Khudayar Khan. The above events account for the Tashkent rebellion of 1847 against Qipchaq influence in the khan's court and the onerous taxes visited on Tashkent's population. Many thanks to Uzbek author Hamid Ismailov for his commentary on Azizbek. See Shodman Vohidov and Rahbar Khalikova's work on *Khulosat Ul-Akhval* or "Circumstances of Life" by Abu Ubaidullah Tashkenti in *Moziydan Sado*, 2009 2.42. Text taken from the Institute of Oriental Studies, Academy of Sciences, no 2084.

29. In this case a "Bacha" is a dancing boy. Bachaboz/Javanboz was a major Jadid criticisms of Turkistani society where Jadids depicted those who engaged in Bachabozi as pederasts. Qodiriy wrote the short story "Javanboz" ("The pederast") in 1915 as a criticism of such practices and the destruction visited on those individuals. Bachabozi often occurs on a

Thursday night before Friday prayers. During the Soviet period, the Soviets often replaced practices they saw as morally questionable with acceptable modes of behavior. Today, Thursday night is the night that the man of the house cleans, cooks plov and enjoys the marital bed. For Qodiriy's views on Bachabozi and theatrical works, see Adeeb Khalid, *The Politics of Muslim Cultural Reform, Jadidism in Central Asia* (Berkeley: University of California Press, 1998) on the existence of Bachabozi, field notes by translator in Central Asia 2002–2019.

30. The Ferghana valley is a geographic area 186 miles long that lies within present-day Kyrgyzstan, Tajikistan, and Uzbekistan, with Uzbekistan holding the lion's share of the region. The valley represented the core of the Qoqan Khanate and was multiethnic by nature, considering its area of rule encompassed both sedentary as well as nomadic areas in present-day Kyrgyzstan and Kazakhstan. Because of the nomads' influence in the valley, they often held pivotal roles in the administration of the Khanate. The historical and political events depicted in this novel primarily focus on Qipchaq influence in court politics, offering unique insight into the relationship between nomadic and sedentary peoples. The best English- language summary of the valley's history during this period can be found in Scott C. Levi, *The Rise and Fall of Khoqand, 1709–1876: Central Asia in the Global Age* (Pittsburgh: University of Pittsburgh Press, 2017).

31. Ancient city of Chach now known as Tashkent, city of stone, capital of Uzbekistan.

32. Yusufbek Hajii: An interesting figure as represented in Vohidov's and Khalikova's work cited above. We see in *O'tkan Kunlar* perhaps the conflation of two figures: Muhammad Yusufbek Hajji "Parchabaf," or the Brocade Weaver, and Mohammad Yunus ibn Azimjan from Osh, present-day Kyrghyzstan. The former was in fact the adviser, or "Dirbar," to Nur Mohammad Qushbegi, the military figure who deposed Azizbek in 1847 through the help of Yusufbek Hajji, and the latter was the adviser to Azizbek and called Azimjan Sillik, or the Polished. Poets contemporary to the events depicted in volume 1 in fact refer to an Azimjan and a compatriot, Karimkul Mekhtar, as "Destroyers of Qoqan," clearly making a separation between the two figures. Qodiriy, perhaps for expediency and poetic license, conflates the two figures to streamline the narrative. See Shodman Vohidov and Rahbar Khalikova's work on *Khulosat Ul-Akhval* or "Circumstances of Life" by Abu Ubaidullah Tashkenti in *Moziydan Sado*, 2009 2.42. Text taken from the Institute of Oriental Studies, Academy of Sciences, no 2084.

33. Oling, Oling, Olinglar: literally means "Take, take everyone," but it is a common enjoinder by the host to his guests to eat their fill—again, usually repeated three times.

34. The city of Shamai is also referred to as present-day Semei or Semipalatinsk in the Kazakh area of Siberia. Now famous for nuclear testing during the Soviet period resulting in severe environmental degradation. During Otabek's time it would have been a major trading hub between nomads and Russians bringing goods from Central Asia via river systems—in the case of the Qoqan Khanate, they were known for the production of rhubarb and opium. See Newby, *The Empire and the Khanate*.

35. Russians: Throughout the three volumes of O'tkan Kunlar we see Abdullah Qodiriy wrestle with the nature of the Russian presence in Turkistan through Otabek and Yusufbek Hajji. From volume 1, chapter 2 and volume 3, chapters 1 and 2, we gain insight not just into Qodiriy's view on "the beginning of the end" for Central Asian peoples in the mid-nineteenth century, but his increasing alienation and bitterness toward events in his own time. One could say that the Russian presence in Central Asia started in earnest in the early eighteenth century with trade and diplomatic relations. Through the vicissitudes of the politics of empire, most notably the Great Game with Britain, through Tsar Alexander II's famous liberation of the serfs that led to a mass settlement of landless Russians into present-day Kazakhstan, and through sheer economic greed and exploitation, the nineteenth century proved a pivotal moment for Central Asia and Russian conquest. A common narrative today is that the Jadids initially attempted to reform what they saw as the decaying khanates of Qoqan and Khiva, as well as the emirate of Bukhara, from within, but met with great resistance from calcified elites within those states as well as benign neglect from Tsarist administrators wishing to not stir the pot among the local population, especially with the Ulama. Disillusioned by those efforts, the Jadids saw the great promise of the Bolshevik Revolution, only to again meet with disillusionment by the mid-1920s as it became clear that the Russian elite among the Soviets— who were themselves largely local Russian settlers who held animosity toward the local population—had no intention of allowing self-rule among their newly inherited Central Asian populations.

Yet, we should hesitate to call *O'tkan Kunlar* an anti-Russian novel, per se—perhaps anti-colonial is more apropos. We should be even more hesitant to apply such a general narrative to a cultural phenomenon such as the Jadids— or to the Khanates and the Ulama for that matter—we should see them as a spectrum of activity not one coherent movement. Abdullah Qodiriy himself lived in Russia from 1924 to 1925, studying journalism at the Briusov Institute of Journalism. He was familiar with world literature, having translated Gogol's *Marriage* and Chekhov's *The Cherry Orchard* into Uzbek—both plays that dealt with marriage reform and the feelings associated with the memory and loss of the dying old order in Russia, and both perhaps great influences on Qodiriy's novel. His fellow Jadids held Russians as friends and, in the case of Cholpan, he even married a Russian woman in Moscow. Western methods of governance, modern teaching methodology, curriculum development, and social reform had a profound impact on the Jadids, many of whom traveled abroad, most notably, in the Bukharan Jadid Abdul Rauf Fitrat's case, to Istanbul. Yet the Jadids did not wish to sacrifice their own Muslim identities to Western culture—hence their place in postcolonial literature. In order to construct a national identity, Qodiriy evokes throughout the novel a collective memory of when Central Asia was in its ascendency as a center of scientific discovery subsequently adopted by the West, not the state of decay it found itself in the nineteenth-century khanates.

In this present passage we see Qodiriy's admiration through Otabek— it is often stated that the novel's hero closely reflected his own views—for what Russia offered Central Asia, with its potential for reform and modernity. We must keep in mind that Qodiriy began writing the first volume around 1920, when the author might have still held onto hope for reform. Throughout the subsequent five to six years it took to produce the final novel, circumstances in Qodiriy's life changed considerably, and we can see his growing cynicism throughout the narrative. We will see at the end of the novel Qodiriy's inevitable message and conclusions regarding Russian influence in Turkistan. Regarding the Jadids, see Khalid, *The Politics of Muslim Cultural Reform*.

36. Qodiriy reveals a bit of his agenda here—the language is distinctly that of a twentieth-century Muslim reformist projecting their philosophy of a greater Turkistan into a mid-nineteenth-century social milieu. The concept of the nation state existed in the mid-nineteenth century in Central Asia, but the language itself has a distinct twentieth-century ring to it. "Fathers of Turkistan" would have more likely been a term used during the politically charged period of the 1920s and reflects the "emerging geographic imagination" of those proposing an Uzbek state by placing the concept in the longue durée of Central Asian history. On geographic imagination see Khalid, *Making Uzbekistan*.

37. Umar Khan ruled the Qoqan Khanate from 1810 to 1822. He is credited with the efflorescence of the arts, engineering, and agriculture within the khanate. His military achievements allowed expansion of the khanate along the Syr Dariya river, the conquest of the Kazakh Great Confederation and the Middle Horde as well as expansion into present-day Kyrgyzstan. The Khanate enjoyed over a century of trade with Qing China, with Umar assuring continuous trade. Umar's first wife, Mahlar Ayim, under the pen name Nodira, was a prolific poetess who wrote in both Chaghatay and Persian. In fact, the tribal influences in Qoqandian society, layered with Muslim tradition, allowed considerable leeway and freedom for women to express themselves. Perhaps the strong role that women played in the court of Qoqan, coupled with the Hanafi Madhab and the influence of nomadic culture, partly accounts for the tradition of

the female Oi Mullah, who can lead prayer among women. It was the Oi Mullahs of Qoqan in the early 1990s who attempted to build a women's mosque to be led by the female Qoqandian religious elite. On Umar Khan see Susanna S. Nettleton, "Ruler, Patron, Poet: 'Umar Khan and the Blossoming of the Khanate of Qoqan, 1800–1820," *International Journal of Turkish Studies* 2, no. 2 (1981–1982): 127–140 and Levi, *The Rise and Fall of Khoqand*. On women and Islam in Qoqan translator notes, 1995-1997 and 2002-2003, Qoqan, Uzbekistan.

38. Infighting among Central Asian peoples is a central Jadid criticism of Central Asian society and this novel. The Jadids believed that warfare between the various khanates, inter-tribal warfare within the khanates, and the divisive internal policies of the khans weakened the khanates' ability to resist Russian conquest. Much of the later infighting within the Qoqan Khanate led various disgruntled Central Asian military leaders to assist Cherniev in his capture of Tashkent. See Timur K. Beisembiev, ed. and trans., *The Life of 'Alimqul: A Native Chronicle of Nineteenth Century Central Asia* (New York: Routledge, 2003).

39. Qora Chopans / Qipchaqs: Qora Chopans, faction within Tashkent resisting Qipchaq influence in the Qoqan Khanate. The Qipchaqs in the Ferghana valley originated from the migrations of the Qipchaq tribal confederation, most notably the Kazakh Middle Horde, pushed south into the Ferghana valley by Oirat tribesmen, and concentrated around present-day Andijon and Namangan. They mainly settled with Khirghiz tribal groups but without rights to pastures, eventually becoming seminomadic. See Paul Georg Geiss, *Pre-Tsarist and Tsarist Central Asia* (London: Routledge, 2003): 44–45. By 1926, the Qipchaqs numbered 33,502 and, along with "Turks" and Qurama and other Turkic tribal groups, were during the Soviet period absorbed under the ethnic designation of Uzbek—if one can accept the dated data taken from Soviet sources. See Elizabeth E. Bacon, *Central Asians under Russian Rule: A Study in Culture Change* (Ithaca, NY: Cornell University Press, 1966). Qodiriy again attempts to show the multiethnic makeup of the Qoqan Khanate as well as factions within Khudayar Khan's court.

40. Musulmanqul: Musulmanqul Mingboshi (b. ca. 1794, d. 2 November 1852) played an integral role in installing Khudayar Khan on the throne. He belonged to the Qipchaq clan Qulan from Yaylaq, Sahrikhan Ferghana—a village northeast of Qoqan and north of Margilan. He rose to power in 1842 by helping to expel the Bukharan Emirate from the Qoqan Khanate. Upon completion of the conflict, Musulmanqul capitalized on ethnic tensions between Qipchaq and Kyrgyz tribes in the valley to overthrow Sher Ali Khan, thus gaining the most powerful military position in the Khanate as Mingboshi for the Qipchaqs in 1844. Musulmanqul could perhaps be seen as the most disruptive figure in the khanate's history. After the death of Sher Ali Khan and his usurper Murad Khan, he placed Sayyid Muhammad Khudayar on the throne and married

the newly risen khan to his daughter. He ruled through Khudayar until he was finally deposed by his young protégé and hung in 1852 in Qoqan after an anti-Qipchaq revolt. See Beisembiev, *The Life of 'Alimqul; Levi, The Rise and Fall of Khoqand*. In the opening remarks of *Otamdan Hotira* (Tashkent: 2005), Habibullah Qodiriy explains that these individuals were well known to his father's father and often featured in tales from that period.

41. Sher Ali Khan (ruled 1842–1845): Replaced Madali Khan (1823–1842), son of Umar Khan (1811–1822), placed into power by nomadic leaders after Madali Khan was betrayed by factions within his own court and defeated by the armies of Bukhara. Initially both nomadic and sedentary protest revolved around onerous taxes placed on the population. Madali Khan also lost the support of the Ulama after marrying Khan Pasha, his father's widow. Aggrieved parties in Qoqan sent a letter to the Bukharan Emir, who intervened on their behalf. After Madali's execution by the Bukharans, the people of Qoqan retook their khanate and installed an exile who lived among the Kyrgyz, Sher Ali Khan. The nomadic forces that placed Sher Ali into power soon lost their position in court to a sedentary Hakim of Margilan who was declared Mingboshi, a Tajik. As mentioned above, Qipchaqs took the position for themselves after the machinations of Musulmanqul. In turn, sedentary political forces led a coup against Sher Ali, murdering him and placing Murad Khan onto the throne—he lived for ten days with Musulmanqul's return and recapturing of the throne. See Geiss, *Pre-Tsarist and Tsarist Central Asia*, 44, and Levi, *The Rise and Fall of Khoqand*.

42. Murad Khan: Sher Ali's son, soon deposed after his allegiance to Qoqan was called into question. He reigned eleven days into 1845.

43. Salimsoqbek: Interestingly, the name of the Hakim at the time was in fact Sarimsoqbek—according to academic sources yet Qodiriy used Salimsoqbek. Sarimsoqbek was older brother to Khudayar. See Levi and R.N. Nabiev, *Iz istorii Kokandskogo Khanstava* (Tashkent, Fan, 1973)

44. Mingboshi: Literally "commander of one thousand troops." Highest military rank in the khanate.

45. Khudayar Khan: Sayyid Muhammad Khudayar Khan (1812–1881) ruled the Qoqan Khanate from 1845 to 1875 on three occasions. In 1845 he was placed on the throne by Musulmanqul upon marrying Musulmanqul's daughter, then led a pro-Qipchaq faction and ruled until 1852. His second reign was after the Qipchaq factions were purged from the Khanate, 1853–1858—where he then took an anti- Qipchaq position. He lost his throne to his brother but regained the khanate in 1862–1865 after it changed hands a couple times through the aegis of the Emir of Bukhara. Finally, after Russian conquest in 1866, he ruled during an interregnum period, with the khanate becoming a vassal state to Russia in 1868. Khudayar Khan was essentially a puppet of the Russians in the

1870s, when he finally fled Qoqan during a Bukharan-backed rebellion in 1876. He died in Orenburg as an exile in 1881. Throughout the novel we will see how Khudayar Khan was beset, as all Khans in the Shahrukhid dynasty (1709–1876) were, with contending ethnic tensions exacerbated by an increasingly globalized world. For perhaps the best historical account of this period see Levi, *The Rise and Fall of Khoqand.*

One theory holds that the Jadids—normally depicted as members of the class of traders, businessmen, etcetera—were not the only word on reform in Central Asia; members of the khans's court, administration, and Ulama also saw the need for reform—most notably Islam Khoja, a senior member of the court in Khiva, seen as a more right-leaning member of the Jadid movement. If one considers the close ties between Amanullah Khan, the reform minded sovereign of Afghanistan from 1919 to 1926—the approximate years over which *O'tkan Kunlar* was written— and the descendants of Khudayar Khan, we can see potential for this argument. Islambek Khudayar, son of Sayyid Mukhammad Aminbek and grandson of Khudayar Khan, worked at the Afghan Embassy in Paris during the period of Amanullah Khan's reign. Amanullah is well known for both the Third Afghan War and attempts at modernization in Afghanistan—many of those initiatives resembling those of the Jadids and other reformers. Is it possible that a son of Khudayar held modernist beliefs?

We can see the descendants of Khudayar Khan today around the world engaged in legal, medical, and academic pursuits, all activities befitting a family that has set aside monarchial concerns for intellectual endeavors. Many thanks to Anvar Nazir for his opinions on the Jadids, most notably here on Islam Khoja of Khiva. On an extensive history of the genealogy of Khudayar Khan, see Shohrukhbek Umarov's *Khudayar Khan Avolodlari Tarikhi* (in Uzbek). For general histories, see Mikhail Volodarsky, *The Soviet Union and Its Southern Neighbors: Iran and Afghanistan 1917– 1933* (New York: Routledge, 1994) and M. Waseem Raja, Modernization, *Regression and Resistance: Amir Amanullah Khan's Afghanistan* (Saarbrücken, Germany: LAMBERT Academic Publishing, 2011). For important, alternative views of the Jadid's role in nineteenth century Central Asia see: Paolo Sartori, Moving Beyond Modernism: Rethinking Cultural Change in Muslim Eurasia (19th-20th Centuries), *Journal of the Economic and Social History of the Orient* 59/1-2 (2016). Devin DeWeese, It was a Dark and Stagnant Night ('til the Jadids Brought the Light): Clichés, Biases, and False Dichotomies in the Intellectual History of Central Asia, *Journal of the Economic and Social History of the Orient* 59/1-2 (2016).

46. Tashkent Madrassa: Located in the Isski Juva square, present-day Chorsu Bazaar, made from the bricks of Kukeltash Madrassa, which was built in 1570 by the Shaybanid Dynasty. Abdullah Qodiriy studied both at Beklarbegi and Abdul Qasim Madrassas, Abul Qasim located near the

present-day Oily Majlis or parliament building on Halklar Dustligi Street. Beklarbegi and Kukeltash, later rebuilt, were eventually turned into museums of atheism in the twentieth century.

47. Mullah Hamid: There is a great deal of irony employed in these responses. Using "mullah" in front of someone's name could be considered a compliment or an insult depending on the context and tone of the exchange.

48. Chopan: A Chopan is a quilted robe worn by many Uzbek males. They range from simple designs showing regional affiliation with cotton cloth and filling to elaborate affairs made of silk or velvet with gold embroidery, a design common in Samarqand and Bukhara. Chopans are often handed out as gifts and as signs of patronage.

49. Tavba: Exclamation made upon encountering the devil or an unpleasant surprise. Also, an insult implying stupidity.

50. This is the first time Qodiriy uses the word "Uzbek" in O'tkan Kunlar: Otabek's mother. Many have claimed that Uzbek Oyim is the only time Qodiriy invokes "Uzbek" in the novel, but we will see that it is used later on in Volume 3—perhaps given the timeframe in which Qodiriy wrote his novel his concept of what it means to be Uzbek changed over time.

51. The Bukharan Emirate: The main rival to the Qoqan Khanate and often referred to as the "Second Golden Dome of Islam," or Bukhara Al-Sharif, as it was the center of the Hanafi School of Law and the progenitor of some of the world's greatest Islamic intellectuals. The Samanids, perhaps the greatest empire to hold Bukhara as its capital, represented the efflorescence of Persianate culture in the ninth and tenth centuries. World-renowned scholars including Ferdowsi, Rudaki, and Avicenna enjoyed Samanid patronage. Upon the departure of the Samanids into history, subsequent Turkic groups, most notably the Ghaznavids—former Ghulam, or slaves, within the Samanid Empire who had risen to lead their own empire—and the Karakhanids wrested control of former Bukharan holdings. Subsequent empires included the Shaybanid, the Janid dynasty, and Nader Shah, until the Manghit dynasty, wrested control of Emirate. Because of the city's strong Islamic heritage, the Manghits named themselves emirs instead of khans—hence the Bukharan Emirate versus the use of the designation Khanate in the case of Qoqan or Khiva. It is also this association with high Persian court culture and the Manghit dynasty's decline and failure to modernize in the nineteenth century that drove calls for reform. What most vexed the Young Bukharans, modeled after the Ottoman Empire's Young Turks movement, and the broader Jadid movement, was what they saw a decisive decline in the very values that made their imagined Turkistan ascendant after the fall of the Samanids.

Among the various reformist groups, there was not one movement but a series of factions across the political spectrum, ranging from the avant-garde to the more centrist. But, one common element is that they advocated for the reintroduction of Turkic culture and modern languages into the administration, mainly viewing Persian as the court language of the corrupt. Bukhara would then become its own independent, modern nation state while retaining its redacted Muslim identity. The Bukharan People's Soviet Republic was established immediately after the Bolshevik Revolution with the demise of the Emirate of Bukhara. In 1924 the Bukharan Socialist Soviet Republic was established, shortly thereafter becoming part of Uzbekistan after the national delimitation in 1924. See Khalid, *Making Uzbekistan.*

In terms of the Jadid movement itself, Bukhara was the epicenter of early reform efforts due to its importance in the region and to its pivotal role in the development of Islam. Many of the Jadids suffered torture under the Emirs of Bukhara as political winds shifted in favor of the reactionary Ulama, who lobbied against the reform-minded Jadids, who often, early on at least, enjoyed Russian support. One must note however that although common narratives create an US against THEM mentality of the Jadids versus the Ulama, the movement itself often had religious leaders as participants in reform—along the same lines as those in the Ottoman Empire, Afghanistan, and India. It was the Young Bukharan Fitrat who called Bukhara the "corpse of the world," often citing the emirate's inability to provide modern educational, medical, and public sanitary reforms for the city's population. After the emir's infamous quashing of Jadid protest, many Bukharan reformists made their way to Tashkent, in Turkistan.

In Qodiriy's lifetime he was no doubt aware of the torture Bukharan Jadids, most notably Fitrat and the father of Tajik literature, Saddridin Ayni, received under the emir, and is evoking its unseemly reputation in this narration—one also finds the same sort of language in Western colonial criticisms of Bukhara. For further reading on Bukharan history, see R. N. Frye, *Bukhara: The Medieval Achievement* (Norman, OK: University of Oklahoma Press, 1965) and *History of Civilizations of Central Asia*, vol. 5 (UNESCO Publishing, 2003). For Jadid activities in Bukhara see d'Encausse, *Islam and the Russian Empire*; Edward A. Allworth, *Evading Reality: The Devices of 'Abdalrauf Fitrat, Modern Central Asian Reformist* (Boston: Brill, 2002); Denis Sokol, *The Revolt of 1916 in Russian Central Asia* (Baltimore: The Johns Hopkins Press, 1954), and Khalid, *Making Uzbekistan.*

52. Mehmon Khana: Translated as "guesthouse." Common terminology is used throughout the Turco-Persian-Indo world. In the context of the novel, "Mehmon Khana" means the outer area of a housing complex reserved for guests, especially men. In our contemporary usage, "Mehmon Khana" would mean "hotel."

53. Ich Kari: Inner yards, the actual family living area. The deeper into the housing complex one ventured, the more intimate the setting, e.g. the

women holding the innermost sanctum of a man's home. As a general guide, the outer walls of a man's home would be tall enough so that a man on horseback could not look into the residence.

54. Atlas: Common in an Ikat design. Central Asia, especially Uzbekistan, is home to a wide array of silk production, Margilan being one of the great centers of silk weaving. Atlas is used for Korpacha, women's clothing, and Chopans.

55. Khan atlas: A higher grade of Atlas silk. The silk has many origin stories— most notably the one in which a poor weaver created the weave to assuage the khan's desire for his daughter. Khan atlas holds a more complex weave and was used only by the elite of Central Asia.

56. Tabib: A traditional healer who uses folk remedies, much ridiculed by the Jadid reformists. The necessity for modern medical services was a major theme of Jadid reform, many singling out Bukhara as "the corpse of the world" for its lack of sanitation and medical services. The irony is that Ibn Sina, or our Avicenna, one of the world's greatest physicians, hailed from a town outside of Bukhara. See Edward A. Allworth, *The Personal History of a Bukharan Intellectual: The Diary of Muhammad Sharif-I Sadr-I Ziya* (Boston: Brill, 2003).

57. See above: Thin Central Asian Atlas silk or cotton "futons" made every spring by the women in the household and presented to a newly wedded woman.

58. Fried meat pie.

59. Vai, Vai, Vai, or Vai-woo: A common Uzbek exclamation demonstrating surprise, shock, or irony.

60. As mentioned above, the Tashkent Rebellion of 1847 was instigated by Azizbek, ostensibly as a reaction to over taxation of the local population by Qipchaq factions within the khanate's court. See Khulosat Ul-Akhval or "Circumstances of Life" by Abu Ubaidullah Tashkenti in Moziydan Sado, 2009 2.42. Text taken from the Institute of Oriental Studies, Academy of Sciences, no 2084. Haraj and Zakat: The tax on cattle or merchandise, one fortieth of their value. See d'Encausse, *Islam and the Russian Empire*.

61. Nur Muhammad Qushbegi: (d. August 1864) a dignitary, a Qipchaq from Ferghana, and the governor of Qurama from 1845. He started his career in the ranks of the Ferghana Qipchaqs who seized power in the Qoqan Khanate in 1844. Having become the opponent of one of the Qipchaq leaders, Musulmanqul, he eventually went over to the side of the sedentary nobility. He repressed the Tashkent uprising on 1847 and the anti-Qipchaq revolt in 1852. From 1847–1852 he was the governor of Tashkent with the rank of Qushbegi. In February 1862 he was the head of the conspiracy against Malla Khan which resulted in the murder of the latter. From Beisembiev, *The Life of 'Alimqul*. In addition to Dr. Jeff

Sahadeo, Professors Shodman Vohidov and Rahbar Khalikova provide an excellent source through their translation of Abu Ubaidullah Tashkenti's "Circumstances of Life" or "Khulosat Ul-Akhval," which provides an inside view of the conflicts riddling the Qoqan Khanate and Nur Muhammad's career. See Jeff Sahadeo, *Russian Colonial Society in Tashkent*, 1865–1923 (Bloomington, IN: Indiana University Press, 2007) and *Khulosat Ul-Akhval*.

62. Buzukboshi: Low-level, irregular fighter.

63. Oftobboshi: "Oftob" means "well." But in the case of courtly positions, it is one who handles the water, basin and pitcher for ritual handwashing. The same tradition exists today in more wealthy homes for big events where the men of the house assist guests in washing their hands before entering their home. One must wring one's hands over a copper basin, not flick one's hands, which would be showing disrespect. The importance of the Oftobboshi depends upon whose hands he is washing, but it is generally considered a low-level position. See Beisembiev. Regarding day-to-day ritual, field notes, Qoqan, 1995.

64. Nation: Clearly the local population did not consider themselves part of a modern nation state. This is Qodiriy projecting his own philosophy of cultural change and the conception of the Uzbek nation à la 1920–1926 into an earlier historical epoch through Otabek. As Adeeb Khalid and Adrienne Lynn Edgar so successfully illustrate, the year 1917 morphed Jadid activities from a movement for cultural change into more radical effort to create a Muslim nation state based upon the Turkic peoples of the region. Khalid is quick to point out that he does not view the Jadids as nationalists, per se, but rather an intellectual movement that attempted to conceptualize the nation through a creative impulse and actualize those ideas among the local populations. Indeed, when reading this novel, one could see a postcolonial slant to Qodiriy's writing, but we must consider that Qodiriy himself was criticizing internal forces within his own society as much as the growing Russian influence. See arguments articulating Qodiriy's view of "the Russians" above. See Khalid, *Making Uzbekistan* and Adrienne Lynn Edgar, *Tribal Nation: The Making of Soviet Turkmenistan* (Princeton, NJ: Princeton University Press, , 2006) for a comparison to the creation of Uzbekistan.

65. "Qalam" translates here as "pencil," a sign of literacy.

66. "Mullah" here is a compliment toward a learned person, not actually a mullah.

67. Orda: Refers to camp or in this case, fortress. "Orda" also forms the basis for the Urdu language: the language developed by multiethnic armies that encamped together while on campaign and developed a mutually intelligible language of the camp—or Urdu.

68. Kerovchi: One farsakh or four miles from Tashkent. Located in the present-day Qurama mountain range in an area entering the Ferghana valley. Administrative center for Qurama. Qurama itself means "Patchwork" or "Assemblage" for the various tribes that inhabited that region. Strategically Qurama resides in a chokepoint into the Ferghana Valley itself, thus of great value to both Tashkent and Ferghana depending on your viewpoint.

69. Qipchaqs: Concepts of ethnic identity were contested and in flux in 1920s Central Asia. Qipchaqs, Kirghiz, and Qipchaq-Kirghiz are all variants of nomadic and semi-nomadic peoples largely settled in the northern Ferghana valley. The homogenization of Central Asian ethnic identity is the hallmark of Soviet policies aimed toward consolidation of administrative units within Soviet republics. The ethnic dimension above is widely recognized as a reaction to Qipchaq influence in Khudayar Khan's court; we can also view this conflict as a tension between nomadic and sedentary peoples. The Qipchaqs depicted in this novel were by the nineteenth century a semi-nomadic group from the northern Ferghana valley who played a role in reversing Bukharan advances on the Qoqan Khanate and placing Khudayar Khan in a regency protected by the Qipchaq Musulmanqul, a primary mover in resistance to the Bukharans. See Beisembiev, *The Life of 'Alimqul*. On the development of the Qipchaqs in the Ferghana valley, see Geiss, *Pre-Tsarist and Tsarist Central Asia*.

70. Qora Chopans: Literally "black robes."

71. Taksir: Literally translates as "sir" or "master." Nodir Zakirov notes that it is derived from the Arabic and translates as "I am belittled in front of you." Qodiriy uses many formulaic responses during his dialogue, so for the sake of variety I have translated some responses as "master" and others as "Taksir" to lend a traditional flavor to the dialogue and historical setting.

72. See above endnote on challenges faced with dates and calendars.

73. *Baburnama: The Memoirs of Babur* was written in the Chaghatay language, a predecessor to Uzbek, by Zahriddin Babur (1483–1530) throughout his adult life up until his death. The founder of the Moghul Empire, but originally from Andijon, Uzbekistan, Babur is credited with writing the first autobiography in Islamic literature. Babur relays his adventures in Afghanistan, Pakistan, and northern India with a sort of bitterness at the loss of his original Timurid homeland. Along with the Timurid philosopher Alisher Navoi in his *The Judgment of Two Languages*, Babur defended Chaghatay as not just a Turkic language of the steppes, e.g. warfare, but as a literary language just as sophisticated as the Persian language, the traditional language of the court, bureaucracy, and literature. Despite his use of Chaghatay or Turki as a language for his poetry and memoirs, he still relied on Persian literary conventions for his

work. See Stephen Dale, *The Gardens of the Eight Paradises: Babur and the Culture of Empire in Central Asia, Afghanistan and India* (Boston: Brill, 2004)

Referencing a Chaghatay text in this novel is a clear agenda by Qodiriy to stake a claim for Uzbek, a modern Turkic language descending from Chaghatay, as a language capable of prose and literary beauty.

Here Qodiriy shows his hero as well versed in the Chaghatay classic, reflecting his own participation in the literary circle, the Chaghatay Gurungi. Gurungi translates from Chaghatay as "discussion"—an older version of the current usage of Gap, or discussion, from the verb gapirmoq, to speak. The Chaghatay Gurungi's ideological bent was the development of an Uzbek language based upon Chaghatay but stripped of its Persian and Arabic loan words. Khalid uses the term "Chagatayism" to describe the Jadid use of Chaghatay during the period of national delimitation in 1924 to appropriate all of Turkistan's sedentary peoples as Uzbek. See Edward A. Allworth, *Uzbek Literary Politics* (London: Mouton and Co., 1964) and Khalid, *Making Uzbekistan.*

During the Soviet period the use of the term "Chaghatay" was discouraged as a throwback to monarchist tendencies—a charge used against the Jadids by Soviet ideologues. The repression of the Jadids for the ideas they espoused regarding their vision of an Uzbek nation carries great emotional weight in Uzbekistan today. Qodiriy, martyred in 1938, was the first author to be rehabilitated in 1956 during the twentieth Congress of the CPSU by First Secretary of the Central Committee Nuritdin Muhidinov, with redacted versions of his books published a couple of years later. Abdullaziz Muhammadkarim, former director of Abdul Qasim Madrassa, where Qodiriy studied for a short period and which now houses an artists' union, was a young man working in the primary bookstore in 1958 when the book was republished for the first time since 1938. People wishing to purchase the book circled the block and waited for days to make their purchase. Abdullaziz Aka passed away in 2012 and is remembered here as a testimony to his generous spirit and genuine love of Uzbek arts. See Edward A. Allworth, *The Modern Uzbeks* (Stanford, CA: Hoover Institution Press, 1990).

After Uzbekistan's independence, one could hear in President Karimov's speeches, prepared at the time by Abdullah Oripov, the distinct use of common Chaghatay grammatical features, specifically the direct object stem *-ney*. Regardless of one's position on the vagaries of Uzbek identity, the free use and expression of an idea once repressed carried great weight to Uzbeks post-1991. Notes taken in 1994 in Samarqand during President Karimov's speech celebrating Babur's birthday. Insights provided by Professor Ilsa Cirtautas, NELC, U of W.

74. Mullahnamos: mullahs who are able to recite passages from the Koran, according to the Jadids, largely through rote memorization. Qodiriy is criticizing, like most modernists at the time, the low level of

439

Islamic education among mullahs in Central Asia. One could consider them at times shock troops, guided by the more established Ulama, protesting reforms—especially as tools of violence against the Jadids, as in the case in Bukhara in 1917 when the Emir of Bukhara overturned reforms to the detriment, and physical well-being, of the Jadids—most notably Sadriddin Ainy, the father of Tajik literature, and Abdul Rauf Fitrat. Mullahnamos mainly received income through performing life cycle rituals such as burials and circumcision. On the traditionalists' resistance to reform see d'Encausse, *Islam and the Russian Empire*.

Of course, some Jadids held positions within the Ulama, or at one point, as in Qodiriy's case, were educated in the Madrassa system. Modernization of the curriculum, through Usul al-Jadid, literally the New Method, meant loosening the hold of the Islamic establishment over revenues generated by the Madrassas and their control over the canon required to produce mullahs that would adhere to their vision. It is important to note that many Jadids considered themselves devout Muslims, but they followed the call for *tarraqa*, or progress, and *ijtihad*, independent reasoning, commonly made throughout the Muslim world at the time in the face of European hegemony. The tensions between reform-minded Muslims and those wishing to maintain the status quo, or re-create an imagined "status quo ante," is an evergreen issue seen through the Taliban's rote memorization of the Quran and innovators such as Asra Nomani at Georgetown University and her call for reform in Islam through *ijtihad*—among many others. See Habibullah Qoddiry, *Otamdan Hotira* (Tashkent: 2005); Daniel Brower, *Turkestan and the Fate of the Russian Empire* (New York: Routledge, 2003); and Allworth, *The Modern Uzbeks*.

75. Qodiriy, as with the candle from the opening scene, portrays Ziyo Shohichi as a pure practitioner of the Islamic faith through the symbol of a clean-burning candle. This scene is in stark contrast to the above scene of Bacha Bozi. Again, Qodiriy's main criticism of Central Asian society is largely focused on the Ulama, a society atrophied by poor knowledge of Islam and the Islamic world. Despite early optimism brought by the Bolshevik Revolution, Qodiriy was no Communist, rather a Muslim modernist hoping to take advantage of the impetus of a new order to effect change in his society. A great deal of debate persists over the exact relationship between the Jadids and Islam, not to mention the ideas espoused by the Bolsheviks. I argue that the novel demonstrates Qodiriy attempting to navigate a new world while maintaining adherence to his faith. It is difficult to make generalizations about any movement. Perhaps we can conclude that in terms of the faith, ideology etc, of any person, not to mention a group of people, the full spectrum of belief exists, defying generalizations. With scant documentation or journals extant from the Jadids, we can look to their literary contributions for answers.

76. Nomaz: Muslim prayer

77. Tancha: wood- or coal-burning stove.

78. Bey/Bek: Another form of address complimenting the subject the title is conferred upon. Although Ziyo is probably of the class of Beys/Beks, this is meant as a compliment toward his character, not his status.

79. Musafir/far: Foreigner, outsider, or nonlocal and often considered a pejorative. One must be careful when establishing hard paradigms to describe ethnic identities. Identity fluctuates depending on many circumstances. Central Asian identity, even today, usually begins with the family, the mahalla, or the city the person belongs to, so someone from another city could be considered a foreigner. A great deal of focus over the past few years has been on clan or tribal affiliation. That might be a good jumping-off point in understanding Uzbek social structures, but it tends to be overused and in an oversimplified manner, often belying the West's shallow understanding of Central Asia. In fact the concept of a "clan system" can be applied to almost any society across the globe, and the concept is not monopolized by those living in the "Stans," to deploy another overused term. Many other factors, such as business interests, school classmates, and military service, as well as changing social dynamics, both internally and externally, are often more important but more difficult to understand than just breaking society down into tribes or clans. The historical setting predates the wide acceptance of the concept of a nation state in Central Asia among the general population—someone from Tashkent or Margilan would be considered of a different people.

80. Sovchi: Matchmaker.

81. Offering of chai and bread is the first act of hospitality at the Dasturkhon. Qodiriy intends a bit of comic relief here. One must never cut Uzbek non, rather tear it into pieces and hand those pieces to others. Old non or crumbs are always left for birds to eat and never, ever thrown out. The origins of this custom are attributed to different origins, from the practice of "Mehmon Dust" or "Adab," courtly manners, to periods of famine in Central Asia. Perhaps Ziyo is offering sacred bread as an offering to Qutidor's injured pride?

82. Hasan Ota is of course Hasan Ali, but Ota is used here to designate Father.

83. Chokmon: Long wool robe worn by men.

84. Qodiriy returns to the tension between traditional Central Asian society's view on marriage and the reformist view that a woman should have the right to choose her husband. Today the various views on marriage really depend on a number of cultural, socioeconomic, and political circumstances.

85. The title "Toi, Kizlar Majlisi" translates directly as "Wedding, Bridal Shower." This chapter demonstrates a great deal of cultural depth, with

Qodiriy presenting to readers a view of a world open only to women. The title itself presents the comma as a break in the chapter to another scene: Qodiriy does present some incongruities in this chapter over style and grammar. In the first four paragraphs and the final paragraph he writes in present continuous and then shifts to past tense. I believe he was experimenting with narrative voice and perspective. For the reader's sake we edited the chapter to conform with a uniform tense.

86. Suyuq Osh: A type of watery osh quickly prepared

87. Nishaldah: Fresh marshmallow. Used either during lavish celebrations or during Ramazan.

88. Dutars, tanburs, rababs, and nays: The author describes a four-piece ensemble. A dutar is a two-stringed instrument with a pear-shaped resonator and sounding board; strings are plucked. A tanbur is a long-necked lute with a deep pear body with a number of frets and three to four strings often plucked with fingers or plectrum. The strings are made of metal, silk, in the novel's setting, and at times played upright with a bow, called a sato. The Rubab has five strings, and the main body is made of wood and skin. The nay is a Central Asian flute. For an excellent survey of Central Asian music, see Theodore Levin, *Hundred Thousand Fools of God: The Musical Travels in Central Asia (and Queens New York)* (Bloomington, IN: Indiana University Press, 1999).

89. Yor-yor/yar-yar: The traditional Central Asia wedding song. The song first praises the prophet Mohammad and his creation of mankind. The song then wishes the child of the union be of kingly bearing and the family have an open road before them. The song ends with the line "the scissors on the shelf begin to rust as the bride is anxious for the wedding." Perhaps this is an allusion to a woman growing her hair then weaving the required forty braids for her wedding.

90. Sarpah or Bosh-Oyog: A full accoutrement of clothes for special occasions. Literally "head to toe."

91. Pari: Translated as "angel" or "fairy."

92. Yanga: Translated as "sister-in-law" or "wife of an elder brother," but here we could consider them also witnesses to the consummation of the marriage and protectors of tradition and values. They escort the bride throughout the betrothal process but also produce proof of consummation of the marriage—blood displayed on a suzani, an embroidered sheet that each generation passes on to the next with additional panels added to account for marriages and births. The artwork in the embroidery is complex and highly symbolic, each suzani design representing a different regional identity.

93. Black braids: Referred to as Qirq kokil or Jamalak. Forty braids designate a young woman as a fiancée, and she wears them during her wedding as well as one year after the marriage. Forty is a sacred number

of Near Eastern origin. Sufis engage in solitary meditation for forty days known as Chillah. The forty coldest days of winter and hottest days of summer are also referred to as Chillah, Chihil meaning forty in Persian, as well as numerous other associations with the sacred number. So here "The scissors become rusted from lack of use"—e.g. growing the hair long enough for braiding. Kumush has had her hair braided into Qirq kokil for her wedding.

94. Paranji: A Central Asian paranji is basically a long-armed, thin robe placed over the head with a cloth or horsehair screen, or *chachvan*, held up by the hands to hide the face.

95. Bridal robes: It is customary to congratulate someone on their new clothing to mark a new occasion or a coming of age.

96. Doira or Childirma: Both round, skin-covered, tambourine-type instruments with rings around the edge of the frame. Often musicians will heat the skin over the fire for better play.

97. Ortaklar: Friends or companions.

98. Alif wa Laylah: Known to us as the classic *Thousand and One Arabian Nights*—a collection of tales gathered throughout ecumenical Turco-Persian-Indo- Arab world. The fairies mentioned in the series are entities that at times come to the assistance of the Caliph offering supernatural aid.

99. Ifor/Efor: Traditional Central Asian folksong dealing with passion in love.

100. Yigilarman: Translated as "I am crying/weeping."

101. *O'tkan Kunlar* has many literary allusions that are parallel to Turco-Persian literature. *Laila and Majnun, Alif Laylah wa Laylah*, poems by Fuzuli, are all referenced by Qodiriy, placing the novel in the longue durée of Turco-Persian literature. With numerous mentions of "The Beloved," Qodiriy clearly evokes the parallel between the novel's love story and the loss and memory of Central Asia before the Russian invasion—as seen through the more political and historical statements made during the novel's narration. The renowned Persian language translator Dick Davis states that "The addressee of a Ghazal can be a beloved/lover, patron or God." Although we are reading a modern novel, Qodiriy makes the same allusions evocative of Sufistic love or reunion with God. Walter G. Andrews and Memet Kalpakli, *The Age of the Beloveds: Love and the Beloved in Early-Modern Ottoman and European Culture and Society* (Durham, NC: Duke University Press, 2005).

102. Opa: Translated as sister.

103. Lapar: A vocal duet with alternating male and female parts. During bridal showers, one singer plays the male part and the other the female part.

104. Toikhana: wedding chamber.

105. Qodiriy again presents a complicated chapter, with all the nuances of the rituals of nineteenth-century Central Asia. Throughout the novel he presents the perspective that Central Asia was a multilayered society with beliefs and ritual overlapping in ways difficult for us to decipher in our present period. On a technical note, Qodiriy changes tense throughout this chapter between present continuous and past in order to depict events and to narrate directly to the reader the action of the wedding and the unexpected happiness. I've kept these incongruities to maintain the spirit of *O'tkan Kunlar* as Qodiriy's grand experiment.

106. Here Qodiriy depicts his view of marriage as seen through a Jadid's eyes. Central Asia is famous as the progenitor of the Hanafi Madhab, or Hanafi school of Islamic Law, so the process depicted above follows this reference point. "All the major schools of jurisprudence concur that marriage is performed by the recital of the marriage contract... A mere agreement without the recital of the contract does not amount to marriage... The Hanafi say that a marriage contract is valid if recited by any word conveying the intention of marriage... provided these words indicate their being used for the purpose of marriage... The passage goes on to say that words that do not convey the meaning of perpetuity and continuity do not finalize the contract." Laleh Bakhtiyar and Kevin Reinhart, *Encyclopaedia of Islamic Law: A Compendium of the Major Schools* (Chicago: ABC International Group, 1996).

107. Chalma turban: This reference could be to a turban from Chalma-Kazan in present-day Sinjiang, an area of influence for the Qoqan Khanate, or Chalma, the embroidered tape around the edge of a doppi, or Central Asian skullcap. Perhaps the turban has been embroidered in a similar style.

108. Bilboq: A traditional embroidered sash stitched by the bride for her husband on their wedding day. Worn over their Chopan, or robe, in ceremonial events.

109. Mahalla: A traditional Muslim neighborhood seen throughout the Muslim world and the basic construct of a person's identity.

110. Roof: Many Western readers find this element of the wedding interesting. Guests sat on the rooftops because of the limited space within the main yards as well as the ideal vantage point the rooftop provided. The novel predates the use of Western-style chairs so the main guests sat on raised platforms, further limiting space. Large tois, or weddings, were criticized by the Jadids as wasteful displays of patronage among the elite. During the Soviet period, the size of weddings was often based upon

444

historical circumstances. Present-day Central Asian rulers have at times limited the size of weddings as a means of controlling influence gained through lavish events.

111. Wild rue: Burned in places of worship and public spaces usually by Multani asking for alms. Many believe it has a purifying role.

112. Mahr: Translated as "bride price." A sum set aside for the bride should her husband die or divorce her. Again, Islamic Law states that the bride and her witnesses, the Yangas, must affirm the marriage contract with "I gave in marriage," with the groom and his witnesses replying: "I have accepted." This chapter posed some complications for the translator and editors. The first half of the chapter occurs in present continuous, abruptly switching to past tense halfway through the narration. Further discussion is warranted here, but this switch could mean that since Qodiriy was attempting to depict a customary wedding in a way that would be credible to Central Asians, he used precepts within Islamic Law as part of the narration style. A great deal of energy is spent within circles of practice and study of Islamic Law discussing which tense to use during a wedding ceremony—although the Hanafi Madhab is more lenient on this issues, Qodiriy was madrassa trained and understood the intricacies of the legal process. Perhaps this is an overly complicated assessment and the author simply wished to experiment with narrative styles, as expressed during his opening statement. Bakhtiyar and Reinhart, *Encyclopaedia of Islamic Law*.

113. Khutba in Persian: Traditional sermon delivered by a mullah at Friday prayers or a special ceremony. Usually the ruler is acknowledged in the Khutba, therefore it becomes a benchmark of power. "He read the Khutba in his name" shows a definitive acknowledgment of a ruler's legitimacy—along with striking coins in his image. Persian, of course, was the common language used in the court and administrations of Central Asia. This part of the wedding ceremony would be referred to as the Nikoh—the actual acceptance by the husband of his new bride.

114. Salawat: A series of phrases praising the Prophet Mohammad.

115. Quran Farsi: In regard to the reference of the Koran read in Farsi, I believe it follows the legal reasoning among all schools of law to mean "All the schools concur that the contract can be recited in any language when it is impossible to recite it in Arabic..." *O'tkan Kunlar* was written between 1920 and 1926, during the years before and after the territorial delimitation of 1924 that created present- day Uzbekistan and then later Tajikistan.

As the Soviets gained greater control of Central Asia after the end of the Russian Civil War, they began the process of crystallising identities for administrative purposes. Adeeb Khalid posits that the local intelligentsia had a greater influence on the process of homogenising Uzbekistan into a Turkic state than Russian administrators or ethnographers themselves. Before this process occurred, the peoples of Central Asia often lived in a symbiotic relationship where bilingualism was common. Khalid makes the distinction that Tajik, Farsi, and Persian held different sociocultural meanings for those living in Turkistan. He also points out that language was not considered "a node of identity," meaning that there were other, greater considerations when delineating communities—namely sectarian and confessional groupings. We will see later in the novel other symbiotic relationships depicted, such as the sedentary versus the non-sedentary, and, finally, Yusufbek Hajji's use of "Tajik sayings." The novel was written over a six-year period. Perhaps the use of the word *Tajik* appears later in the novel due to the historical changes occurring around Qodiriy as he wrote the novel. Tajik was also known as the "language of the mountains of Eastern Emirate of Bukhara/ Qoqan Khanate" or present-day Tajikistan. See Bakhtiyar and Reinhart, *Encyclopaedia of Islamic Law* and Khalid, *Making Uzbekistan*.

116. Al-Hamdulillahi: Praise to God. It is here in the text that the tense switches from past to present. There is a liveliness and change in tone, from a serious yet comical exchange to a celebration.

117. Khuftan prayer: Late evening prayers.

118. Perhaps Qodiriy is attempting to experiment with the narrative voice by switching from present progressive to past tense. Throughout the novel he speaks directly to the reader as well. So we see Qodiriy fulfilling his promise at the beginning of the novel to experiment with a new form.

119. Forty braids: See note 93

120. Kundosh: A kundosh is part of a presumably wealthy man's bevy of brides. The literal translation is "day companion"—"Kun" meaning day, "dosh" meaning someone who shares a status or situation with you. Yuldosh, "yul" meaning road, meanings traveling companion. The trope of the kundosh not getting along with and hating the husband is a common theme throughout Jadid literature, and here we are offered a comic tableau for the reader. Qodiriy also strikes upon an important aspect of modernist Islam: A Muslim man may not take more brides than he can "deal with Justly" (Koran, Sura 4 [An-Nisa]. Ayah 3). E.g., he couches his arguments for reform against common Islamic practices within Islam itself—not through erroneous, common beliefs or Soviet ideology.

121. Qorboshi: Originally designated as the arsenal master or custodian of arms; later the chief of police for domestic police, or mishab, with the job of protecting the peace and keeping order. Night guards were called Qorov. See d'Encausse, *Islam and the Russian Empire* and Beisembiev, *The Life of 'Alimqul*.

122. Opium: Naskh or Koknur

123. Shah-an-Shah / King of Kings: a common formulaic praise of a ruler used in Turco-Persian literature.

124. Bahadur/dir: Hero, champion, brave, courageous.

125. Reference to the ruling class, not the name of a person.

126. Orda: Fortress, historically headquarters, residence, or seat of power.

127. Yormazar: This possibly refers to the period under Alim Khan, the Khan of Qoqan who conquered Tashkent and placed it under his rule. In the 1830s the city walls were extended after the destruction of Yunus Khan's fortress with a subsequent newly constructed orda. This area of Tashkent is possibly located in the Shahontahur Daha.

128. Galcha: Translated as mottled, patterned, or vari-colored (with white dominant)—most likely from present-day Tajikistan.

129. Hakim: Mayor or Governor.

130. Utambay/Uttaboi/Uttamboy Qushbegi Qipchaq: (d. 1862) Leader among Qipchaqs. He originated from and at one time led the Iltan clan. In 1842 he had a hand in installing Sher Ali Khan—and in the defeat and expulsion of the Bukharan military forces. In 1844 to 1852 he figured prominently in control of the throne, holding considerable power. He eventually became the Hakim of Qurama after the departure of Nur Muhammad Qushbegi in 1847. During the events of the novel he held the position of Hakim of Margilan where he exerted considerable patronage, most notably the installation of Qipchaq tombs around the Hajji Ma'oz complex, still extant today. He held the position of Mingboshi for two months in 1852 after the defeat of Musulmanqul. Khudayar Khan later in the novel will save Uttaboi from the purge of Qipchaq forces from his court. During Malla Khan's reign, after usurping the throne from Khudayar Khan, he was Hakim of Tashkent, 1858, and Margilan, 1860. He was later executed by the court in Bukhara during a diplomatic mission. One son died fighting the Russians, the other son fled to eastern Turkistan, or present-day Xinjiang. Along with Nur Muhammad Qushbegi, he was one of the few Qipchaks spared by Khudayar Khan during his purge. See Beisembiev, *The Life of 'Alimqul*.

131. "The very white and black of her eyes": The idea behind this phrase is that her daughter is an integral part of her being.

132. Jonkuyar: Devotee. Perhaps the term refers to a person possessed by the love of God or devoted to God who engages in Sufistic practices.

133. Khujand: Established by Alexander the Great. In the nineteenth century it was part of the Qoqan Khanate. Khujand became a major northern city in Tajikistan after the 1924 border delimitation.

134. Family, clan ties: In Central Asia, male family ties are crucial for survival. Having no male family members to represent your interests means limited access to the judicial and financial systems. Oftob Oyim and Kumush are very vulnerable in this scene. Much has been made regarding Muslim customs surrounding the necessity for women to be accompanied by male relatives—a woman bereft or unaccompanied by male companions is seen as truly desperate in those societies. Perhaps Qodiriy wishes to show both the reality of women's' position in Central Asian society as well as the strength of the female characters wishing to help Otabek.

135. Saman Yo'rg'a: A well-known breed of horse in the Turkic world. Known for their hardiness and ability to travel great distances. Chestnut colored.

136. Samarqand Gate: Set near Qodiriy's home. The author based many of his characters on people he knew in his neighborhood or on historical figures relayed to him by his father.

137. Sepahi: Cavalry.

138. Kamolon Gate: Southern gate of Tashkent.

139. Normat: A familiar variation of Nor Muhammad Qushbegi, overly familiar and rude here.

140. Turcoman: Large sheepskin hat with outward-facing fur. A big and bushy hat also worn in Khorezm.

141. Chilim: Traditional form of hookah.

142. Hudaychi: Midlevel and part of the Shighavul's chancellery—known as a standard bearer and distributor of diplomatic gifts. See Beisembiev, The Life of 'Alimqul and Levi, *The Rise and Fall of Khoqand.*

143. Jinn: Evil spirits seen throughout Turco-Persia as well as Arabic literature, most notably *Thousand and One Arabian Nights.*

144. Rayimbek Dadkhwah: Son of Rahan Kazakh Bibi who lived in Besh-Yoghoch district in the mahalla Lakh-Lak-Kon. Little else is known of this individual. As a Dadkhwah he would have been a Tashkent notable and head of one of the four main administrative units, Lakh-Lak-Kon. See Beisembiev, *The Life of 'Alimqul.*

145. Blue Sukno: Cotton cloth.

146. Rustam: A reference to the great hero of the Iranian epic poem, the *Shahnameh*. Since Transoxiana, Marwannahr, or Turkistan was home to both Turkic and Persian peoples, it is interesting that a Jadid engaged in creating a modern Muslim nation-state based upon Turkic identity would quote from the *Shahnameh*— especially since Turkistan was seen as Turan in the poem, the traditional region antagonistic to Persian Kings. Qodiriy was well-schooled in Turkic, Persian, and Arabic, and the use of

Persian poetry demonstrates the symbiotic relationship mentioned by Adeeb Khalid above. Dick Davis's magisterial translation represents the best translation of the *Shahnameh* to date.

147. Robes and tenga: Often distributed as a sign of patronage. Robes are still a standard gift for notable achievements. "Yuz Boshi" means a commander of one hundred troops.

148. Oq-Teppa: Southwest Tashkent near Qodiriy's home — near the Samarqand Gate and present-day Chilanzar district.

149. Chakar: The origins of the term "Chakar" remain obscure. If we follow Zahriddin Babur, Chakar means an elevated plateau surrounded by deep ravines with corresponding deep-running streams—zharlik chuqur. Fortifications were built on these raised areas so we can refer to them as holding Tash Kurgan—fortresses made of stone, or Tash. The Bozsu stream and the Chukar kuprik Ariq—perhaps this was the Kokcha stream mentioned above. "Kuprik" means bridge so perhaps the exact translation of the bridge to the Chukar or fortress—lay southwest of the Chorsu district and bazaar and would have been part of Qodiriy's daily life. Interestingly, the term "Jar/Zhar," meaning *proclamation, announcement* or *ravine* or *canyon* is the name of the land east of the Chakar site that goes by the same name, perhaps the descriptive term for a geographical feature being now used to name a neighborhood.

150. Suzuk Ota cemetery: Located between the Chukarkuprik Ariq and Bozsu/ Bozsu rivers. Most likely the present day Suzuk Ata Mosque is the location of the cemetery. The site of Suzuk mosque was also the area holding the above-described Chakar. After Russian conquest and especially after Soviet control of Tashkent, new buildings, roads and eventually the Tashkent metro system were built on top of old fortifications and walls.

151. Kokcha, Chigatay, Sagbon, Qoraserai, Takhtapul, and Labzak gates: The gates mentioned were part of twelve gates that comprised a radial design of the city walls prior to Russian conquest. Each gate has a corresponding road that denotes either the direction of the road, the tribe associated with the maintenance of the gate (e.g. there were fifteen tribes that settled Tashkent and drew taxes from travelers entering through their gate), or the function of the community surrounding the gate, as in the case of the Sagbon, who were widely regarded as shepherds or Sagboni. All of these roads led to Chorsu Bazaar. Here Azizbek's retinue moves clockwise through the various gates surrounding the city to finally arrive at the eastern gate, Kashgar Gate, just north of the Qoqan Gate. Prior to Tashkent's annexation by the Qoqan Khanate in 1808, Alim Khan expanded the fortifications, increasing the number of city gates. By 1865, the main walls of the city incorporated the western gate, Kukcha, the northwest gates, Samarqand Darboza, the northern gates Sagbon, Karaserai, Teshlik kopcha, and Takhtapul; the southern gate Kamolon

and Beshagach; the eastern gates before the channel Anhor where the streets Labzak and Shayhontahur were made into a fortified wall, with Labzak becoming gate north-east of the city walls. Koimas, which means "impassable gate" was the last to be made into a gate due to the sparse population.

152. Kashgar Gates: Gate leading to Kashgar, or the eastern-facing section of town, which would be the gate facing the Ferghana valley, or Qoqan. Azizbek is clearly making his rounds throughout the circumference of the city. As mentioned above, at times gates were named after the inhabitants of that Mahalla—as in the case of Uighurs from Eastern Turkestan who named the entry point under their control the Kashgar Gates. Takhtapul in the northern section of the city received its name because a large ramp ("pul" meaning ramp or bridge in Farsi), led to the gate.

153. Orda begi: One could generally consider this position that of a commander of a garrison/fortress.

154. Astaghfurallah: God forgive me

155. Jar: Uzbek for "announcement" or "proclamation." Also, a canyon or ravine as mentioned above.

156. Mirshab: Keeper of the peace.

157. Qodiriy means this tongue and cheek. In Hanafi Islam, circumcision is highly recommended but not obligatory—Muslim fathers are generally expected to host a circumcision, or *Toi*. A common criticism by both reformist Jadids and current Central Asian governments is that the lavish expense of weddings and circumcisions might develop social networks but they also breed greed and corruption.

158. Nomads: One of the cultural tensions throughout the novel is the often symbiotic yet at times adversarial relationship between settled and nomadic peoples. The khan's court represented the epicenter of sedentary courtly society relying on Turco-Persianate traditions. The novel illustrates the internal tensions of the period between that sedentary society and the Qipchaq tribal groups that became regents for the khans of the Qoqan Khanate, essentially kingmakers.

159. The scene is reminiscent of the campaign to unveil women in Central Asian society referred to as Hujjum, which means "assault", from 1927–1929 and led by the Soviet Zhenotdel, the women's section of the Communist Party. Unveiling campaigns were also led by Modernists throughout the post-colonial world. Amanullah Khan, the sovereign of Afghanistan from 1919 to 1929 has widely been regarded as the first Afghan leader to attempt modernization. He is noteworthy for having attempted to eliminate the burqa or paranji in popular society, even having his wife unveiled for their frequent trips to Europe. Presently, in Qoqan, the paranji is used primarily among older women during life cycle events, most notably funerals. Qodiriy in this scene has Kumush do the

unthinkable—an educated, independent woman who willingly unveils herself to argue on behalf of her husband's and father's lives. Ironically it shows the level of dedication she feels for the two because she is engaging in behavior that was haram at the time, at least among sedentary communities. The Qoqan Khanate was a multiethnic society. As mentioned above, a symbiotic relationship existed between sedentary and nomadic peoples. Nomadic women did not veil themselves, rather wearing scarves to cover their hair. Much has been bandied about regarding the "fundamentalist" Ferghana valley. One should be skeptical of this generalization and perhaps see the Ferghana as culturally conservative with tensions between conservative interpretations and the prevailing "accommodationist" culture. For an excellent overview of Hujjum, see Marianne Kamp, *The New Woman in Uzbekistan* (Seattle: University of Washington, 2006), Gregory J. Massell, *The Surrogate Proletariat* (Princeton, NJ: Princeton University Press, 1974), and Shoshana Keller, *To Moscow, Not Mecca* (London: Praeger, 2001).

160. Kuvash: Slip-ons that go over leather knee-high boots.

161. "However, the people of Tashkent's success weakened them dangerously.": A major historical theme Qodiriy pursues throughout the novel is the infighting among the peoples of Central Asia leading to conquest by the Russians.

162. Mahram: Spouse, lover, ingénue.

163. Tenga/Tengas: Currency used throughout Central Asia, in this case the Qoqan Khanate. Onerous taxes exacted by Central Asian despots was a common casus belli for revolt in Central Asia at the time and a factor that Russian administrators, both Tsarist and Soviet, often played upon to win over local populations. Per the value of the Tengas: "Silver coin worth 15 Soviet Kopeks in Bukhara, 20 kopeks in Tashkent and Ferghana" (Mikhalov Akobirov, *Uzbek-Russian Dictionary*, 1988).

164. Zanjirli: There are two mahallas or neighborhoods named Zanjirli: Zanjirli, just north of Shahontahur, and Zanjirli Illa, just east of Shahontahur. The orda is at the furtherst southeastern corner of Tashkent, so it appears that Hajji is moving from the orda through Zanjirli Illa to Shayhontahur through Baland Mosque toward the center of old Tashkent, cutting north to Eski Juva. Shayhontahur— Southeastern Daha of Tashkent center, Moziydan Sado, *Echoes of History*, Volume 2, serial 42, 2009.

165. Eski Juva: Just northeast of Old Tashkent Center.

166. "including the commoners in the street, and made its way even to the mahalla of Eski Juva.": Qodiriy is essentially saying that the revolt drew from all districts in Tashkent.

167. Besh Yagoch: Central Tashkent, located near the Anhor canal.

168. Oqsoqol: White beards or leaders of the community. Oqsoqols perform a number of functions within Uzbek society. They often hold positions on Mahalla committees.

169. Zanjirli: Ibid.

170. Baland Mosque: There are a few "Baland Mosques" in old Tashkent, but this one was still located in Shayhontahur.

171. Khadra— Southeast of old Tashkent. A barrier in the Khadra area would make sense considering that Azizbek and Rayimbek's troops would have traveled northwest from the orda to meet with the rebellion in old Tashkent.

172. Eski Miskarlik: Coppersmith quarter. Many mahallas were named after the profession of the denizens of that neighborhood. Eski meaning "old," the quarter is literally the Old Coppersmith mahalla. Directly to the west of Khadra was the Timurchi mahalla, or blacksmiths' mahalla, so perhaps Qodiriy is making reference to that area.

173. Eski Miskarlik: Ibid.

174. "We will not be painted red twice.": Made fools of again.

175. Qarnai: Long deep horns that are approximately six feet long. Qarnai, or horn, is associated with folktales surrounding Alexander the Great—Dhul Al Qarnai, two horns.

176. Khoda Bazar: The notes from the 1926 version of *O'tkan Kunlar*, published again in 1929 and 1994, reveal that presently we have no sign of the orda mentioned in this narration. The notes mention that the orda described here was built by Khudayar Khan during his second reign. Throughout most of the world, conquerors often built structures on the foundations of old buildings, mosques on top of churches, churches on top of mosques. Perhaps the khan decided to build on top of an old foundation with an adjacent Khoda that served as a bazaar. Generally, a Khoda, taken from the Arabic, is considered a flat area near a fortification, in this case presumably dating back to the Arab conquest— hence Khoda Bazaar is associated with the location near the orda. Further research is warranted, but the simple answer regarding the Khoda bazaar is that it was located on a flat area near Khudayar Khan's palace. After Russian conquest much of the Khanate's fortifications were greatly reduced, leaving behind only a portion of the spectacular orda associated with the last khan of Qoqan, which was eventually designated a palace. As for the throne room of Khudayar, it was used as a stable for Russian calvary, then as administrative offices, with an icon placed where the khans once sat. In present- day Qoqan some of the original fortifications still exist and are repurposed—most notably the jail across the street toward the rear of Khudayar Khan's palace. Notes taken in Qoqan, 2018, with Mr. Yuldashev as guide.

177. Kuragan: Central Asian term for khan or ruler, most importantly son-in- law of a Mongol khan.

178. Urga Margul: A vignette, border of floral ornamentation with wavy lines, overlapping floral and geometric ornamentation in the middle.

179. Divan Khana: Administrative building.

180. Shighavulboshi: Master of ceremonies and diplomatic protocol. See Beisembiev, *The Life of 'Alimqul*, and Levi, *The Rise and Fall of Khoqand*.

181. Yasavulboshi: General set of responsibilities. In this case personal bodyguard to the khan.

182. Paravanchi: Just below Qushbegi in rank. See Beisembiev, *The Life of 'Alimqul*.

183. Bilboq: Sash around waist.

184. Chalma: Perhaps a silver-embroidered skullcap.

185. Chikming: Scabbard.

186. Ura Teppe: The gateway to northern Tajikistan's Khujand province. In the nineteenth century it passed between the Emirate of Bukhara and the Qoqan Khanate during their periodic disputes over territory to be conquered by Russia in 1886.The city, now in the Sughd Province, is known as Istaravshan. It's home to Kok Gumbaz—a madrassa that hosts a necropolis of respected religious leaders— whose twentieth-century tombs pay homage to Stalin!

187. Kalpak: Fur or wool cap common in the Ferghana valley and among the Kyrgyz.

188. Osh: City on border of Kyrgyzstan and Uzbekistan. The city is roughly divided between Uzbek and Kyrgyz ethnicities and saw interethnic violence in the 1980s, immediately after independence, and most recently in 2010.

189. Bahadur: Seen as a patron of nomadic groups and a defender of Khudayar's throne, Bahadur must have been a hero to many. Schulyar certainly saw him as one, noting Musulmanqul's fierceness against his enemies. Although not a historically accurate account of events—he uses Russian sources—Schyuler's reference does show that the Khanate of Qoqan did register among diplomatic circles in the West. Due to his bias, he depicts Musulmanqul as a martyr and the khan as a despot! Eugene Schyuler, *Turkistan: Notes of a Journey in Russian Turkistan, Khokand, Bukhara and Kuldja* (London: Sampson, Low, Marston, Searle & Riverton, 1876).

190. Kyrgyz: There were generally economic disparities between the nomadic and sedentary peoples of the khanate. Nomads were often victim to the vicissitudes of nature, whereas settled people could acquire capital.

191. Zol: Legendary king from current Baluchistan who boasts a long life in the Shahnameh.

192. Amir Timur Kuragan: Referring to Amir Timur, or Tamerlane in the West—the national hero of Uzbekistan. Timur conquered an area from eastern Turkey to Russia and into western China, where he died in 1403. Today he is buried in the Gur Emir in Samarqand—with a headstone believed to be the largest piece of jade in the world.

193. Osh is a city located in present-day Kyrgyzstan, on the eastern-most end of the Ferghana valley. The population is half Uzbek and half Kyrgyz.

194. Chilim: water pipe used to smoke tobacco and narcotics.

195. Tuz Haqini Unutmoq: To show extreme lack of gratitude.

196. Mirza: Scribe.

197. Mirza: Scribe. Mirzaboshi means the chief of the scribal class.

198. Al-Hamdulillahi: Praise God.

199. Og'rinqning tuzalasi kelsa, emchi o'z oyog'I bilan kelur. (Chagatai) Og'riqning tuzalgisi kelsa, emchi o'z oyog'I bilan keladi. (Modern Uzbek) If pain desires succor, the healer will arrive soon to render aid.

200. Cho'ltoq: Cropped, clipped, docked, truncated, incomplete, or half-done. Said of people who are useless and old.

201. Qosh Dadkhwah: Perhaps this refers to Qosh Paravanchi, who had the title of Dadkhwah as well. He was of Qipchaq origins and a military leader in Qoqan—as the Qoqan Khanate's last governor of Tashkent 1863–1865, he eventually opposed Khudayar and went on to serve under Yaqub Bek in Kashgar. Ironically, he was Nur Muhammad's brother! See Beisembeiv. *Life of 'Alimqul.*

VOLUME TWO

202. Uzr: Apologies. Here Qodiriy attempts to explain some of the obstacles he faced while attempting to produce the the novel—both technical and linguistic. Before 1928, the Yana Imla Arabic script was used, until the adoption of a latinized script, known as Yanalif, was developed. In 1940 Stalin mandated that Uzbek be written in the Cyrillic alphabet. The changes in scripts presented many technical challenges to those dealing with three separate alphabets over a ten- to twelve-year period. Furthermore, much debate surrounded what would constitute a standard orthography for modern Uzbek, so Qodiriy was attempting to print novels in a fluid and politically charged environment where the choice of an alphabet represented a statement of identity.

The first and second volumes were printed in bound editions by 1925, with the third volume produced by 1926. The note above, for Uzr, was written as a postscript for the first volume in 1925. The second volume was again produced in 1926 with the third volume to follow.

The volume used for this translation is a faithful rendering of the original 1925–1926 publications from the Yana Imla script rendered into Cyrillic after the independence of Uzbekistan. Qodiriy originally wrote: "If you read these two volumes" (he is including his other novel, Mehrobdan Chayon) "you will not read them once but five times and thus engage in the study of history, politics, literature and language." Notes taken from field interviews with Khondamir Qodiriy and Dr. Баходир Карим who provided me with his fine article on Qodiriy as follows: «Ўткан кунлар»га к айтиб...Чоп этилган07.02.2016МуаллифZiyouz.uz

203. Tura—senior high official, or descendants of Chinggis Khan. Perhaps we see some dark humor here as the Mongols were a nomadic people who conquered the settled cities of Turkistan. Is this alluding to Nur Muhammad's nomadic roots?

204.Chaladumbul Tabiyatchilik: Narrow minded

205. Azar: Burial, life-cycle ritual of burying the deceased within the Islamic faith.

206. Kasfshim Kucha Kolgan Emas: Literally: "Shoes do not remain in the street", but translated here as "Don't take shoes to the street to only wear them down in vain." given the context of the passage.

207. Ona Hon: A great show of respect to an older female. Ona means "mother." Hon is used mainly in the Ferghana valley and attached to female names to show respect.

208. Orda Begi Oyim: Wife of Orda Begi. Leader of female notables.

209. Zotapast: Housing reflecting low birth.

210. Final decision: In arranged marriages, the mother plays the primary role in the selection of a suitable bride. Socioeconomic background, clan affiliation, potential for increased economic activity through the marriage, and a number of other circumstances come into play.

211. Witch of Margilan: Qodiriy uses the terms ser-judogar for magician, wizard, witch, seer or trickster. Given Margilan's reputation as a center for the mystical arts mentioned by Babur in Volume 1, we will use the term witch or seer interchangeably throughout the translation. The Jadids were highly critical of folk superstition, though often lovingly so, an essential part of Uzbek Oyim's worldview. She represents what the Jadids viewed as the naive adherence to folk beliefs by the local population: mendicants, seers, witches, etcetera. Uzbek Oyim enumerates throughout the rest of the novel her belief that certain ethnicities hold certain qualities of magical ability. Of course, the Jadids as 'modernists' believed science and reform of public services would eliminate the peoples' reliance on magic to fill missing voids in their lives. Babur in his

Baburnama stated that Margilani, people from Margilan, were renowned exorcists in both Samarqand and the court of Bukhara. Is Uzbek Oyim's referring to Kumush as having cast a spell on Otabek part of the belief about Margilani at the time, or coincidence? Qodiriy is clearly linking Uzbek Oyim's critique of Kumush to this reputation of the Margilani, again exhibiting his renowned humor. Edward A. Allworth, *The Personal History of a Bukharan Intellectual* (Boston: Brill, 2003), Zahriddin Muhmmad Babur, trans. by W. M. Thackston, *The Baburnama* (New York: Modern Library, 2002).

212. Sovchi: Literally matchmaker, but here it means the person who is initiating contact to arrange a marriage on behalf of her son.

213. Andi: Translated as "outcast." In South Asia there is the tradition of the Andi Rishta, who are responsible for love spells. Given Uzbek Oyim's reference to spells cast by Kumush the Margilani, we will view Andi as "the Other" and use it to mean witch or seer.

214. Kalmyk: A Branch of the Oirat, Mongols dispersed throughout Kirghizstan, China, Russia, and the Caspian area. They are a nomadic people who worship Buddha. So, Uzbek Oyim believes there is some shamanistic or Buddhist power at play on her son.

215. Gypsy: known in the Former Soviet Union as Lyuili. For recent scholarship rarely covered in Central Asian studies refer to Kamilla Zakirova—New Voices of Central Asia, George Washington University.

216. Bilgan topib suzlar, bilmagan qopib: "Those with wisdom find words, the thoughtless will bite first then speak." Again, Yusufbek Hajji as a local notable and member of the Ulama represents the multivalent world before the 1924 delimination of borders where language was not a node of identity but a tool set used by members of society to navigate the economic, the political, and the cultural concerns encountered throughout their lives. Despite being a member of the Ulama, Hajji is not averse to deploying folk wisdom in either Uzbek, noted here, or in Tajik, as mentioned in volume 1. Qodiriy in his work focused on preserving the authentic language as spoken by Central Asian society, hence Hajji's folk variant above.

217. Kundosh: Again, "kun" translates as "day." A "dosh" is someone who shares something with you. Yuldosh: "Yul" is road, Yuldosh, traveling/ life's companion.

218. The Uzbek language has a wonderful element where units of sound are used as compound verbs, or converbs. The use of compound verbs in the Uzbek language allows for descriptive elements and nuances within the verb system itself. So, mainly in Uzbek literature, an author can catch the sound of, for example, water sloshing around, or birds trilling, a tramvai traveling along on tracks, by putting the sound of the action in front of the root verb, Kilmok. The famous movie title *Mahallada Duv*

Duv Gap is a great example of this usage: The Mahalla, or neighborhood, makes the sound of "Duv Duv"—or nonstop gossip. So here the birds above are captured by the sound "visher-visher," so "visher-visher Kilmok." A rough parallel in English, though not as poetic, would be "the car goes beep- beep." Ilse Cirtautas, University of Washington, lecture notes, 2000.

219. Fuzuli: Pen name for Muhammad Bin Suleiman, 1494–1556, of Azerbaijani origins. He wrote in a wide array of languages, from Azeri to Persian, Arabic, Ottoman, and Chaghatay. His oeuvre revolved around mystical love with Sufistic undertones, and he is well known for his rendering of the story of Majnun and Leyla—"Majnun" meaning "Mad," so the male lover is mad for the love of Leyla. Kumush is reading the Divan of Fuzuli, a collection of poems dealing with the pain of separation from the beloved. Qodiriy depicts here an educated, Muslim woman who is literate and familiar with the great poets of Islamic belle lettres. Bernard Lewis, *Music of a Distant Drum* (Princeton, NJ: Princeton University Press, 2002).

220. Mad the gourd: One of the reasons for the novel's popularity is that Qodiriy often depicted people either known to him or from stories told to him by his father. In an attempt to capture the essence of the "real Uzbek language," he often traveled to rural villages to gain an understanding of authentic language. Mad the Gourd is clearly seen as a "Fool of God" whose unusual behavior, which is perhaps due to mental illness, is either an insight into the mystical aspects of Islam or just a view of the vacuous behavior of street mendicants... The references to drug use might be an indictment of the low nature of Chai Khanas. The Soviets created the Red Chai Khana as a means to spread Marxist ideology to not a great result.

221. Eating from someone's hand is a sign of submission and supplication.

222. Khudayar Khan was put onto the throne at an early age through the help of the Qipchaq factions, most notably Musulmanqul, his regent. "Bacha" here means "boy," but might carry a double entendre. Not really the public statement you should make in the khanate. Yet there is a quality of mercy given to those who are perhaps "not of the world" in Central Asia and it is considered Godly to give them smalls sums out of compassion. One sees these acts often in Uzbekistan even today.

223. Bek of Tashkent (Nur Muhammad Qushbegi): "Qala" means "head"—so he is describing Nur Muhammad Qushbegi as having a big head.

224. Chai Khana or teahouse, widely regarded by the Jadids as dens of inequity. During the Soviet period the Bolsheviks attempted to created Red Chai Khanas in an attempt to displace the traditional meeting places, to little or no success. Khalid, The Politics of Muslim Cultural Reform.

225. Qorategan: Present-day northern Tajikistan and home of the Garmi ethnicity. As an independent kingdom, the local monarchy claimed descent from Alexander the Great. The region changed hands between the Qoqan and Bukhara Khanates throughout the nineteenth century. The Rasht valley was the center of Basmachi activity throughout the 1920s. Throughout this dialogue we have a sort of oblique series of insults from Mad, so perhaps Qorategan was associated with unscrupulous trade, etcetera. Of course, the insult to his sister is time honored and needs no explanation of its cross-cultural nuances..

226. Nasha: Hashish.

227. Charlar: As with all ritual, regional variations exist, but the Charlar is derived from the verb "Chorlamoq," to invite, where the in-laws of the groom, Kuyov, or of the bride, Kelin, meet for the first time after the Nikoh, or wedding, ceremony. In Qoqan the term used is "Kuyov Chaqiriq," or inviting the son-in-law. The time between Nikoh and when Charlar occurs also varies depending on the region and circumstances. In the Kashkadariya region the time is forty days, in other locations it can be as short as four. The significance of the sacred number forty throughout both the Near East and Central Asia must again be noted. Within the Central Asian context, forty is known as "Chilla"; the hottest forty days of summer and the coldest forty days of winter are also known as Chilla. A Sufi might engage in solitary contemplation for forty days. Many thanks to Nodir Zakirov and Mir Jahon Turdiev for their insight into Charlar.

228. Jodugar: See note above. The term magician creates a 'Rabbit out of the hat" image. In Ozbek Oyim's world, a Jodugar would have been a seer or witch— something more seductive with ill-intent.

229. The placing of spells or sacred passages on clothing is a time-honored ritual for protection in Central Asia, especially with Qoranic passages. Uzbek Oyim here is referring to a malevolent spell placed in Otabek's clothing. Today both in Russian and Central Asian culture, family members will guard a deceased family member so a curse toward another is not placed in the corpse's clothing.

230. Tashkentlik: "-Lik" means "a person from." So "Tashkentlik" means "someone/people from Tashkent."

231. Five main mullahs: Uzbek Oyim's understanding of religious titles is a bit fuzzy here. "Domla" means "teacher." She is using Muslim religious titles for mountebanks of Jewish and Hindu origins. The term of the Five Main Mullahs of Tashkent is unclear here but perhaps she is referring to the major religions in Tashkent at the time. Judaism was of course a major influence in what is now Uzbekistan, where the ancient Bukharan Jewish community thrived and engaged on all levels of society. Uzbek Oyim is not referring to that community but instead to a murky understanding of those claiming it but of dubious origin. What is not

ordinarily recognized is that Qoqan in the Ferghana valley also hosted a very old Jewish community. The Judic Mahalla in Qoqan was located not far from Khudayar Khan's Orda on what was then Oktybrskaya Street near the center of town. Well up until the mid- to late-1990s that community existed in Qoqan, until a vast majority of Jews emigrated to either Israel or New York. Field Note: United States Peace Corps 1995–1996.

232. Izab Ichki: A concoction ground and drank. Prepared by a Tabib or folk healer, a profession maligned by the Jadids.

233. Qalandar: A wandering Sufi or ascetic from Central Asia—also potentially from India but most likely Multani.

234. Hindu: Hindu and Buddhist temples and stupas exist throughout Central Asia, testifying to its millennia-old relationship with the Indian subcontinent. Up until this present period, archaeologists have continued to discover Buddhas in Uzbekistan, Tajikistan, and Kirghizstan that have achieved UNESCO protected status. Of course, one can find the enormous reclining Buddha on display in Dushanbe, Tajikistan's National Museum of Antiquity. These monuments testify to the profound part Central Asia played in the spread of Buddhism, most notably in the Xinjiang region of China. By the nineteenth century, trade between Turkistan and India was thriving, so Uzbek Oyim would be familiar with some of the more unseemly influences brought by traders and traveling mystics. For a full understanding of Hindu culture in Central Asia, see Scott Levi, *Caravans: Indian Merchants on the Silk Road* (New York: Penguin / Allen Lane, 2015) and Scott C. Levi, *The Indian Diaspora in Central Asia and Its Trade, 1550–1900* (Boston: Brill, 2002).

As usual the Jadids were highly critical of the folk beliefs, often erroneously ascribed to Islam, circulating in Central Asian society, but also felt the Moghul Empire to be one of the great achievements of the Turkic peoples, along with the Ottoman Empire and the Timurids. The Jadid writer Abdul Rauf Fitrat, often considered a first among equals, wrote his famous *Tales of an Indian Traveler* as an account of an Indian traveler and his impressions of the Emirate of Bukhara. The traveler's account represents Fitrat's view of Bukharan society and the ills they suffered through the Emirate's misrule. Allworth, *Evading Reality*.

On a more positive note, Babur established the Moghul Empire in India, which led to one among many moments of efflorescence in South Asian culture. Al- Beruni, the Khorezmi-born polymath and scholar, wrote his magisterial Tarikhi al-Hind, considered one of the most comprehensive and objective studies of India yet produced in the Islamic world. These notes cannot possibly capture the enormous contribution these giants made to the development of mankind. For further reading on this topic, see Scott C. Levi and Ron Sela, *Islamic Central Asia: An Anthology of Historical Sources* (Bloomington, IN: Indiana University Press, 2009). For a general overview of Islamic scientific and cultural achievement, see Marshall Hodgsen, *The Venture of Islam: Conscience and History in a World Civilization* (Chicago: University of Chicago Press, 1974).

235. Etiquette requires that the Kelin or daughter-in-law live the first year after a Toi with her in-laws. The new addition to the home must display complete subservience to the mother- and father in-law. There are many elements to this tradition, but most notably the daughter-in-law must not make eye contact with her in-laws, especially while pouring tea. Like any cultural norm, this tradition varies considering the circumstances of the family, especially today.

236. Sochpopuk/ Qapuk: Colored yarn or thread woven at the end of a braid. Could also mean gold ornaments, especially coins, that are woven into a woman's hair, primarily along the forehead.

237. Tea with both hands: Another sign of subservience by the new bride. A revered guest or family member might receive tea in the same manner. During a certain period, the newlywed bride must demonstrate subservience to her in-laws by pouring tea while standing and not making eye contact with the mother- and father-in-law..

238. "Certainly you should receive your tea while she is standing...": Here Qodiriy elucidates a fine point of Jadid philosophy. Otabek adheres to the basic obligations of a devout Muslim, most notably daily prayers, demonstrating that he is a devout Muslim but shows disdain for what would be customs, Urf-Odat, not backed by Islamic legal underpinnings.

239. Domla Khodja: Khodja or Khwaja is an honorific applied to the devout, largely from South Asia. "Domla" means "teacher." In this case we could consider the people referred to here are mountebanks. Qodiriy is being sarcastic.

240. Baksheesh: A Persian term meaning money or, in some cases, bribe.

241. Talaq: Divorce in Islam takes on a number of manifestations depending on the historical period or Islamic school of law. Generally it can take two forms: Talaq, or repudiation of the marriage by the husband, and Khul' or Khula, which would be initiated by the wife.

242. Qalvak: Trickster, swindler, fraud, pilferer, cheat.

243. "She made Toibeka water the yard and she started sweeping the tamped- earth floor of the yard with her own hands": Sweeping the courtyard and watering it in the morning is the first task of the younger women of the household. Wetting down the courtyard of a home is done throughout the day to reduce dust..

244. "extending her arms in greeting with poorly masked disgust.": Central Asian women often approach each other in greeting with arms extended. While approaching each other, they question each other over their health and the wellness of each other's family. The two women often

conclude with clutching each other's arms, offering greetings and then kissing each other's cheeks.

245. Iddah: According the Shariyat law, the waiting period of three menstrual periods after divorce through Khul' or four months and ten days in the event of a husband's death during which a woman cannot remarry. It is generally agreed that these waiting periods are meant to preserve lineage so no questions may arise over the parentage of a child.

246. Date: 13th day of Javzah 1265/1848/1849. Tashkent.

247. Saraton: Summer

248. Tahman: Niches carved into walls, often with ornamentation framing the borders, and used as shelves.

249. Hosh!: Translated as "now" or "so!" Polvan: Hero, Champion.

250. 26th of Javzah, 1265 Tashkent:June 16,1849.

251. Pasha Nisa: The Sovchi sent to arrange a marriage with Kumush. Jannat:

252. Translates as "heaven." Qodiriy is demonstrating his renowned humor here.

253. Boi: Indicates wealth. Clearly Hamid is using the ending "-boi" to flatter both Sadiq and Mutal so that they may do his bidding, for gold.

254. Ogil bola uchun ogil bola gim, yamon uchun yamonligim bor: Literally, "I am a man to a man and a bad person to a bad person." I have polished the meaning above for readability: "I am a man to any man who does right by me, but a blackguard to those who do me wrong." Many thanks to Umida Hashimova for her insight into this phrase.

255. Qiziqchi or Hazelkash: Comedian. Used at weddings and other celebrations.

256. Jamshid: Hero from the Shahnameh—fourth king of the world.

257. Gharib: The stem refers to alien, different, other, counter.

258. "Brown sheeplike eyes" is reminiscent of Tolstoy's description of Hajji Murad. The soulfulness of the eyes is a common literary allusion to one who is a beloved of God. Later these descriptions would be used by Europeans to infer a sort of simplemindedness in the peoples of Central Asia and the Caucasus. Here Qodiriy shows a man of singular belief.

259. "to a small room that resembled a monk's cell.": An ascetic lifestyle reminiscent of the Sufistic practice of Chilla, forty days of solitude as mentioned above, or one engaged in spiritually minded pursuits.

260. Qimiz: Fermented horse milk prepared by nomadic peoples.

261. Wine drinking: A common justification for drinking in Muslim countries— often attributed to Sufism with all its allusions to wine and

majnun—and a practice most common in Turco-Persian literature—the idea that one becomes drunk with the love of God. Babur in The Baburnama rationalized his habit through the reasoning that drinking wine made of grapes is an acceptable practice. One often hears other rationales such as: if someone drinks under a roof God cannot see the infraction, etcetera. Wine drinking was and is prevalent today to such a degree the Taliban, especially in the Uzbek north of Afghanistan, cut down grape vines on farms with the belief the farmers were making wine—not entirely wrong. Another interesting practice is for devout Muslims, when at table with those drinking wine, to touch the rim of the glass to their lips out of respect for the host—an elegant response to maintain one's adherence to one's beliefs while still honoring the host, another sign of piety.

262. Akhund: Member of the religious class. Many contacts have stated that the term "Akhund" was rarely used in Central Asia but primarily in Azerbaijan and Iran among the Shi'a. Perhaps Qodiriy is making light of what many considered to be mountebanks who were willing to certify the sanctity of practices that went against the main tenets of Islam. Again, the rationalization continues. There is an element to our new friend Usta Alim that is reminiscent of Sufism. The idea of drinking wine to forget a beloved, being mast, or drunk with the love of God, were common tropes deployed by Sufi poets. Many associations in Turco-Persian literature between Sufis and wine drinking exist. Qodiriy, as we will see, is sympathetic to this character and perhaps wishes to, through a bit of sharp humor, introduce to his audience someone who might be uncomfortably familiar to their own thoughts and practices.

263. Kaif: Means a genuine satisfaction or contentment over an excellent meal, a great poetic work, or other pleasurable activity—as if to be transported by a mystical experience. It is often used when drinking alcohol before eating plov, a nice state of being while enjoying food.

264. Sufi orders are often associated with certain professions. Weavers among the Naqshbandi in particular with their looms representing eternity and the circle of life are common literary allusions to Sufism or mystical belief.

265. The age a young woman takes the paranji often coincides with puberty.

266. Saodat: Happiness, bliss, peace of mind

267. Qurban Hayit: Marking the end of the Eid Al Adha, which honors the willingness of Abraham to sacrifice his son. Celebrated seventy days after Ramazan Hayit. The day before, Arafa, Uzbeks prepare special sweets and pastries. The morning of Hayit begins with prayer and then the passing of plov between families. Sacrifice of a sheep is made with a portion given to the needy. Gifts are given to children and families visit their loved ones.

Guests also visit families with Kelin, or newlywedded wives. For Usta Alim, seeing Saodat is as if enjoying a feast.

268. Fitr Uraza Alms: Eid Al Fitr marking the end of Ramazan. As with Qurban Hayit, alms are often given to the poor. The merciful are seen as beloved by God.

269. Ramazan: Ramadan. Central Asians pronounce the Muslim observance with a Z.

270. Taqdir or Khikmat translated as Fate: Muslims believe that your fate is written on your forehead. Peshhonada yozgan: literally meaning to be written on the forehead, or meaning it was fate.

271. Qodiriy here shows the concerns the Jadids had for the state of Central Asia's health systems, or lack thereof. They understood that Central Asia was far behind Western countries in terms of understanding of medicine and public health. Many of the Jadid writings criticize the health conditions of the major cities of Central Asia. This critique is also common among other Modernists throughout the Muslim world.

272. Slave of God: (Abeed) Submission before Allah is a basic premise of Islam. As with the Christian Servants of the Lord, the idea is that we humans on earth have as our primary purpose the service to our maker. All strength, all struggle, all hardships, all joy are through his aegis.

273. Safi: Translated as "pure" or "clean."

274. Iftor: Breaking the fast during Ramazan.

275. Hovli: The main courtyard in a standard Central Asian home.

276. The moth before the flame is a classic trope used especially in Sufi poetry— the idea of annihilating oneself before God and one's beloved.

277. Begzoda: A title demonstrating a person of authority. Used throughout the Islamic world in various contexts. Here Hasan Ali is referring to Otabek in a sympathetic tone. The root of the word "Beg" is a variation of "Bek."

278. Oq Masjid: City of Qizil—Orda on the territory of the present-day Kazakhstan.

279. Orzumand: Here Qodiriy uses his infamous humor to refer to matchmakers as "Dream Makers."

280. Sharbatdor: Again, the stem "-Dor" is from the Persian and designates a profession. So, a sharbatdor, "sharbat" meaning sweets, fruit, confectionery, would make our character a merchant of sweets.

281. A family is often approached three times by the matchmakers. Neither side wants to show desperation in making a match. The same applies to invitations: It is considered polite to refuse an invitation three

times to show you are not greedy or desperate. Of course, this cultural sensibility varies based upon circumstances.

282. Jazo 1265: 1848.

283. Musulmanabad: "-Abad" translates as "place of," "land of," as in Islamabad, Pakistan. Affixations of "-Abad" were often politically motivated declarations made by intellectuals and administrators to enforce an identity or idea. Musulmanabad was often used by Modernist Jadids to mean the Muslims of Turkistan. As Khalid puts it, "a territorially limited confessional nation." Jadids took this meaning further to denote the area deliminated as present-day Uzbekistan, by 1924, as the center to Muslim, sedentary communities, cultures, and history. As mentioned previously, the Chaghatay language was used as the basis for the formation of modern Uzbek. Pedagogues engaged in language reform that removed any Persian or Arabic loanwords to arrive at a "pure" Turkic language. Khalid also points out that Muslims of Turkistan, therefore by extension Musulmanabad, was used as a pejorative to critics of this homogenization of Central Asian identity. Not all modernists or Jadids were in complete agreement as to what the final outcome of the national project should be. Qoddiry uses the term here as sarcasm. Khalid, *The Politics of Muslim Cultural Reform and Making Uzbekistan.*

284. Zoni and Zoniya: Prostitute or adulteress.

285. Rais Afandi: Qodiriy depicts here what is commonly known as the Mutaween—or morality police. "Rais" means "director," or "lead." "Afandi" is a Turkic term for "mister" or "sir". The title drips with sarcasm in this passage. Jadids generally wished to show that although the Qadimis or backward religious authorities attempted strict adherence by the population, they were ineffective in their efforts.

286. Sadja/Sadahgay: Prostration in Prayer. "-Gah" means "place for prayer." Qodiriy wishes to show the general ignorance of the population toward Islam. This criticism is common throughout the novel as depicted by Uzbek Oyim and other characters rationalizing their behavior as an act of Muslim purity, e.g. Qoqan Khanate leadership and Usta Alim.

287. Boza: Fermented grain beverage similar to a light beer.

288. The village of Chukar, a settlement near Tashkent: Near present-day Chorsu Bazar

289. Haidalish: Translated as "exiled." "Ajrat": Separated or divorce.

290. Navo: One of the six scales of the Sash maqam: Six Maqams in both Tajik and Uzbek traditions, largely considered developed in Bukhara. It brings together traditions of lyrical and instrumental elements to include poetry and dance. The six Maqams, or scales: Buzruk, Rost, Navo, Dugah, Segoh, Iroq were reduced from the original twelve by the eighteenth

century. The Shashmaqam expressed divine love and the beloved so this is the perfect piece for Otabek to pine over his loss. The Jadids were patrons of the Shashmaqam when it was made illegal during the Soviet period as a "remnant of feudal" systems. It must be noted that there is an Uzbek and a Tajik form of the Shashmaqam that become bifurcated during the period that delimitation of borders occurred in the 1920s. See Allworth, *The Modern Uzbeks*.

291. Of course, the title of the novel.

292. Savt Navo is one of the taronas, or interludes, of the Sash Maqam.

293. Khoja Ma'oz ibn Jabal, or Abu Abdu Rahmon Al Ansari, Al Hazraji, or to locals, Ma'giza (d. 640): Qodiriy refers to the Mausoleum of Khoja Ma'giza. Margilan was part of the earliest settlements to form the Silk Road with anecdotal evidence to suggest that Alexander the Great at one point traveled through Margilan—a not uncommon assertion in Central and South Asia of "Iskandar Aka once visited here." Khoja Ma'giza was one of the earliest personages to bring Islam to the Ferghana Valley, making the site a pilgrimage destination for many within the Khanate. His current tomb was reportedly built in the eighteenth century by the Khans of the newly established Qoqan Khanate, often attributed to Umar Khan mentioned earlier in the novel. Khoja Ma'oz's tomb today is surrounded by an orchard of Khurma and apricots with an adjoining Chillah Khona nearby with both structures under a Chinar tree—see above for the Sufi practice of performing Chillah, or contemplative acts for 40 days. Next to the tomb is also a structure with a veranda for worshippers to rest. Through the orchard one finds an additional tomb for one Mui Mubarak sponsored by Uttamboi Qushbegi mentioned above. He built the tomb as a patron to his Qipchaq tribal group while serving as Hakim of Margilan. (notes taken 2018)

The passage depicted above is perhaps one of the greatest insights the novel provides into Qodiriy's view on Islam. Qodiriy through Otabek takes us on an exploration of the different shades of Islam one could experience in Turkistan at the time—from the pure to the impure. Usta Alim clearly has ties to Sufism in both his comportment and profession. Otabek here finds himself sleeping at the tomb of the one of the earliest bringers of Islam, a Sufi, as he surrenders himself to his beloved. The flames all evoke the common motif of the Moth to the Flame, the annihilation of the ego to Allah, which in turn provides a conduit for Allah to speak through the individual—à la Al Hallaj. Rumi, or Al Ghazali. The symbol of the Owl is one of death in Central Asian culture, perhaps seen as a portent of Otabek's fate. Otabek throughout the novel engages in what Stephen Dale uses to describe the wanderings of Babur—the Kazaklik stage of life where one searches for their Beloved, while drinking deep the cups of Majnun, or madness, and encountering adventure.

Qodiriy here creates an interesting tableau for Otabek during what we could refer to as his "Kazaklik" period, e.g. freedom to search the world for greater meaning in the face of loss, of wandering the world in search of relief for the pain of separation from his Beloved Kumush. As with Babur who engages in similar bouts of displacement and longing, Qodiriy shows both Otabek's surrender to drink and attempts at assuaging his pain and disillusionment by retreating from the world and finding solace in the shrine of an early proponent of Islam in Central Asia. In these passages the world of Persian letters, abandonment to drunkenness, and Islamic purity are conflated to create the unique cultural milieu of the Turco-Persian world that surrounded Qoddiry and was part of his intellectual landscape. It is also interesting to note that he engages in both his drunken peregrinations and prayer in a solitary manner, or, also like Babur, with a companion, a common literary motif, that seems to state that one can know God not through institutions of men but through an honest approach to the All Mighty with humility and supplication. Islam's allowance for humans to approach God as individuals and through their own merits is one of the great practical aspects of Islam—an Imam is often the oldest man among the group who can best recite prayers, one can pray in a 'pure' area even on the ground if the area is squared off and marked with stones, and one can skip prayers in the face of battle or sickness. It seems that Qodiriy takes a similar practical approach. For the mystical aspects of the Beloved refer to the unparalleled remarks of Dick Davis, *From Persia to Napa: Wine at the Persian Table* (Mage Publishers, Washington DC, 2006), Dick Davis, *Faces of Love: Hafez and the Poets of Shiraz* (Penguin Classics Deluxe Edition) (Penguin Classics, New York, August 27, 2013) among many other publications. For further reading on the term Kazaklik refer to Stephen Dale, *The Garden of Eight Paradises, Babur and the Culture of Empire in Central Asia, Afghanistan and India (1483-1530)* (Brill Publishing, Leiden, 2004)

294. Kerovchi, Qurama, Telob: East of Tashkent entering into the Qurama range with Kerovchi as administrative center, around present-day Angren. "Qurama" literally means "patchwork." Scott Levi points out that Qurama referred contemporaneously to the patchwork of tribes that controlled the main pass into the Ferghana valley—a strategically important region. See Scott Levi, *The Rise and Fall of the Khoqand Khanate, Central Asia in the Global Age, 1709–1876* (Pittsburgh, PA: University of Pittsburgh Press, 2017).)

295. Autumn of 1267: 1850 –1851.

296. Oq Yo'l: Loosely translated as "Safe travels, may the road treat you well."

297. Nikah: Muslim wedding ceremony.

298. Crows or jackdaws are common literary devices in Turkish and Persian literature as harbingers of winter. Their black feathers symbolize

the coming of darkness and night. These birds were also known as carrion birds.

299. Owls portend death in Central Asian culture.

300. Toharat: Ritualistic ablution before prayer.

301. Traditionally in Uzbek greetings it is customary to ask after someone's health first.

302. Kuvash/Kalish: Derived from the cognate Galosh/slip-on: I used "kuvash" here to refer to the traditional hard-soled slippers that fit over leather boots—a Ferghana variant of the word. The slippers keep the boots clean so they can be worn inside or in public and private houses.

303. Hammam: Bathhouse.

304. Astaghfurallah: God forgive me

305. Azan: Call to prayer.

306. Ziyofat: Translates as "feast." Usta Alim is a weaver, a common profession among Sufis. Sufi orders were often associated with specific professions. Since Usta Alim has built a new workshop, he is obligated to hold a feast worthy of his profession's guardian, an activity beloved by God.

307. Mutal Palvon: Champions often associated with wrestlers.

308. Jamshid: Hero of the Shahnameh, fourth king of the world.

309. Herons/Mashak: The symbol of birds are used throughout Islamic literature. The timeless motif of the nightingale and the rose as the soul seeking beauty but beset by the thrones of the world and the challenges of the search. In the case of the heron, the most famous example is from Farid ud-Din Attar's Conference of the Birds—a flock of birds symbolizing the faults of humankind seeking enlightenment by a union with the Simorgh, the King of Birds. Only thirty birds reach their end, but the heron, as Annemarie Schimmel points out, is a bird that hunts in dirty water, unable to see its prey whereas the swam or "higher birds" hunt in clear water and are able to see the object of the hunt. Perhaps Qodiriy is making a literary allusion to Otabek hunting in dirty waters, patiently, waiting for an opportunity to strike. Annemarie Schimmel, *The Mystical Aspects of Islam* (Chapel Hill: The University of North Carolina Press, 2011)

310. Abdikarim: Translated as "slave" or "servant of God." Different names denote different meanings and are often historically and culturally contingent. In this context, Mutal Palvon, clearly a roughneck, the name must have meant something along the lines of "callow youth" or being inexperienced or effeminate.

311. Humza: Steadfast or strong and commonly associated with the Prophet Mohammad's uncle Humza Ibn Abd al-Muttalib. So here the character is being depicted as unfit to be called steadfast.

312. Tanob/tanap: A unit of measurement often for agriculture, one-sixth to one-half hectares or the amount of land that can be plowed in one day. Many thanks for Umida Hashimova for tracking down this definition. See Z. M. M'arufov, *Uzbek Tilining Ihlosli Lugati* (Moscow, 1981). The dictionary cited is perhaps one of the greatest resources in translating "Jadid" Uzbek as many of Qodiriy's phrases and vocabulary are explained at great length—an excellent piece of scholarship! Many thanks for Umida Hashimova for helping me track down this definition.

313. Muslim Salah, or prayer, for the dead.

314. Shahid: Martyr.

315. Waqf: Religious, philanthropic, or public benefit endowments meant solely for the purpose under which the Waqf was created. Religious Waqf could be in the form of mosques, madrassas— we will see in volume 3 how this particular endowment is put to use by Musulmanqul—or Waqf lands, which are meant to generate income for religious institutions. Philanthropic Waqf could take the form of medical institutions, scientific research, or public health initiatives that benefit the general population. Family waqf could be held in perpetuity by a family and generate income for their network where surplus profits are gifted to the public. Waqf had a major hand in contributing to the efflorescence of Islamic art, science, and economic development. It could also challenge political leadership since Waqf was seen as an act of piety; it was traditionally seen as sacrosanct and an independent source of income for religious and local elites independent of whoever held the throne. Jadid criticisms of the Waqf system largely centered on the vast amount of power they allowed the Ulama with little or no benefit seen for the local populations they were intended for. Collectivization under the Soviets effectively put an end to Waqf endowments. In this case Oftob Oyim gives up money intended toward Bauhaddin Naqshbandi, the fourteenth-century progenitor of the world's largest Sufi order—a magnificent area of Bukhara. Waqf is a highly complicated topic in Islamic civilization so the above is meant to solely put the above passage into context for the reader. For further reading on Waqf in the Central Asian context see R. D. McChesney, *Waqf in Central Asia: Four Hundred Years in the History of a Muslim Shrine, 1480–1889* (Princeton, NJ: Princeton University Press, 2016), d'Encausse, *Islam and the Russian Empire*. For the influence of the Naqshbandiya on the Timurid court see Jo Ann Gross, Asam Urunbaev, *The Letters of Khwajah 'Ubayd Allah Ahrar and His Associates* (Boston: Brill, 2002), for an excellent overview of Islamic Civilization and the development of Islamic institutions see Marshall Hodgson, *The Venture of Islam, Volume 1: The Classical Age of Islam*

(Chicago: Chicago University Press, 1977), for Waqf during the Tsarist and Soviet period see Edward A Allworth, *Central Asia: One Hundred Thirty Years of Russian Dominance, A Historical Overview* (Durham, NC: Duke University Press, 1995).

316. Ishon: Sufi master, keeper of shrines.

317. Khikmat, Takdir: Again, we see a belief in fate often expressed with "It was written on my forehead." From the belief that God writes your fate on your forehead at birth.

318. Subhonallah: Praise be to God.

319. Kundosh: Again, the classic literary theme of the perils of multiple wives and the wickedness that will ensue.

320. Quda: Mother of the bride.

VOLUME THREE

321. Qodiriy here gives great insight into the clan and patronage systems at play in Central Asia in the nineteenth century. The overarching theme of *O'tkan Kunlar* is that infighting among Central Asian peoples, specifically within Turkistan, led to a weakening of political, social, and economic structures, thus paving the way for the Russian conquest. From another point of view, Musulmanqul, according to our man on the ground, Alimqul (see Beisembiev, *The Life of 'Alimqul*), assured Khudayar Khan's survival during the Emirate of Bukhara's invasion of the Qoqan Khanate in 1842. One could view Musulmanqul's regency of Khudayar as both a saving grace for the monarch's rule but also a challenge to the ruling, sedentary elite, since he was a Qipchaq.

Scott C. Levi points out that rising ethnic tensions was a constant challenge for the Shahrukhid Dynasty, especially by the mid-nineteenth century—and that those tensions were in large part due to, or influenced by, the increased globalization of Central Asia. Indeed, by the time Qodiriy finished this novel in 1926, ethnic violence had taken on a distinct twentieth-century cast. We need not enumerate here the pervasive roles nationalism, ethnic identity, and socioeconomics played in forming the narratives in the late twentieth and early twenty-first centuries. Levi makes a compelling point however that the ethnic violence chronicled in historical sources from that period holds eerie parallels with events in the Ferghana valley in the late twentieth and early twenty-first centuries—notably the Osh riots and violence in Qoqan in 1989. One must hesitate to make any final conclusions that the ethnic violence of mid-nineteenth-century Turkistan is a direct forebear to that of our present era, but it does feel like that narrative still lingers and, perhaps, informs a larger pattern. Qodiriy's *O'tkan Kunlar* provides us with yet another reference point through a literary medium to add to this discussion.

It is hard to know Qodiriy's intent with the forthcoming passages. If one considers that *O'tkan Kunlar* is not just a novel that seeks to remember a world faded into history but a contemporaneous indictment of his own period, in this light, we can see his masterpiece as a warning to his contemporaries of the hard divisions becoming increasingly apparent between Kazak, Kyrgyz, Tajik, and Uzbek—even if his Jadids had a hand in crystallising them. For an in-depth review of the Byzantine politics within the nineteenth-century Qoqan Khanate, see Beisembiev, *The Life of 'Alimqul* and Levi, *The Rise and Fall of the Khoqand Khanate.*

322. Fatwa and Ulama: As a broad generalization, the Ulama were educated in Madrassas and, in the case of Central Asia, under the Hanafi Madhab or school of law. They were entitled to interpret the Quran, Sunnah, and Hadith in order to arrive at religious rulings, or Fatwas. The tensions between political leadership and the Ulama could ebb and flow based upon a complex array of circumstances. In many ways the symbiosis and tension between secular and religious leadership remained as true among Islamic states as it did among their counterparts around the world—to maintain legitimacy in the eyes of the Divine, a ruler must obtain the acquiescence of the religious elite, either willingly or through coercion. Between those two points a vast array of human agency come into play. In the case of the present passage, it is clear that Musulmanqul has chosen coercion and installed his own Ulama into positions of power in order to augment his legitimacy—and revenue. This practice was greatly criticized by the Jadids who sought to challenge the ruling religious elite's hold on the manufacture of legitimacy in Islam. The subjects of their attacks ranged from the corrupt practices expressed above as well as the general decline in the quality of the students produced in the Madrassas. Tsarist administrators generally followed a hands-off policy toward Islam with some notable exceptions such as the case of Governor General Von Kaufmann. The Ulama worked as an intermediary between the governor general and the local population, keeping Muslim groups deemed threatening to the Russian apparatus in check—in fact many of the governor general's policies regarding Islam under their domains centered on not exacerbating religious tensions among the Muslim population, whether real or imagined. Basically, Tsarist administrators utilized the local Ulama to manage potential local challengers to their hegemony, and as that symbiotic relationship grew, the Ulama gained greater control of their overlords by shaping imperial policy to Muslim populations—which proved deadly to their rivals the Jadids. Once Central Asia fell under Soviet control, Joseph Stalin eventually established the Spiritual Administration of the Muslims of Central Asia (SADUM) in 1943 to manage the affairs of their Muslim populations—e.g. the Fatwas and the Ulama were manufactured along Soviet ideological lines. Post-independence Muslim affairs were managed by the spiritual boards of the separate independent republics. We do not

have the space to provide a full discussion of this immensely complex topic here. The following outstanding scholarly works represent a small portion of the many talented intellects engaged in these topics: Joseph Schact's *The Origins of Muhammadan Jurisprudence* remains a classic and a great starting point on the beginnings and development of Shariyat. For the nature of the relationship between the Ulama and Tsarist leadership, see Robert Crews, *For Prophet and Tsar: Islam and Empire in Russia and Central Asia* (Cambridge, MA: Harvard University Press, 2009). For depictions of Islamic law and practice in Tsarist-era Central Asia, see Paulo Sartori, *Visions of Justice: Shariyat and Cultural Change in Russian Central Asia* (Boston: Brill, 2016). For a recent, spectacular take on Soviet Islam, see Eran Tasar, *Soviet and Muslim: The Institutionalization of Islam in Central Asia* (New York: Oxford University Press, 2017). For a take on the modern era, see Stephane Dudoignon, *Intellectuals in the Modern Islamic World: Transmission, Transformation, and Communication* (New York: Routledge, 2006).

323. Shah-an-Shah: Referring to Khudayar Khan, clearly meant as sarcasm.

324. Mudarris: Teacher in a madrassa. One could say this passage provides an excellent portrait of a ruler's—although corrupt—attempt to create at least the illusion of religious credibility through Musulmanqul's patronage of madrassas friendly to his reign. His efforts are illustrative of all historical epochs: the ruler who gains spiritual authority and can sway both the people and the religious elite holds a tighter control of his reign. This passage also lets Khudayar off the hook for any culpability in these practices.

325. The elite mentioned in this passage refer to a group in Tashkent who managed to escape one of Musulmanqul's pogroms in 1266 Hijra who then formed a faction in resistance to his policies and rule. Muhammad Niyaz Qushbegi, Qassim Mingboshi, Qambar Sharbatdor, Karimqul Ponsadboshi. Muhammad Niyaz is an especially interesting character—his father, Tursan Muhammad, was a confidant and supporter of Khudayar Khan, and perhaps his presence at the meeting implies that they had Khudayar Khan's support as mentioned later. Domla Solihbek Akhund will be noted below as a leader of resistance against Russian conquest of Tashkent. See Beisembiev, *The Life of 'Alimqul*.

326. Chirchik River: A tributary of the Syr Dariya River. Now a city established in 1935 hosting a hydroelectric dam and armored tank battalion.

327. Uzbeks: Many scholars have noted that Qodiriy only uses the term *Uzbek* for the character Uzbek Oyim in *O'tkan Kunlar*, but not so. Volumes Two and Three were written after 1925 so by then the term *Uzbek* was in common use among the Jadids as a people tied to a common territory and heritage. The 1924 delimitation of the Uzbek CCP

was a watershed moment in the crystallization of Uzbek national identity and it is clear that Qodiriy wished to use the term to designate a distinct community in Turkistan.

328. Mohamad Rajab Qorboshi: Perhaps this refers to the son of a certain Rustam Dadkwhah of Tashkent who supported anti-Russian engagements against Cherniev in 1865. See Beisembiev, *The Life of 'Alimqul*.

329. Alimqul: We see a direct reference to one of our sources presented to us by Timur Beisembiev. Qodiriy is prognosticating events through Niyaz Qushbegi. Alimqul came to power within the Qoqan Khanate in 1863, two years before the Russian conquest of Tashkent, where he expelled Khudayar Khan and the Bukharan emir, Muzaffar, through a series of tribal alliances. He elevated Malla Khan's son Sultan Sayyid Khan, Malla Khan being Khudayar's brother and enemy, to the throne and acted as regent for the young leader. Alimqul's two-year reign was marked by fierce resistance to Russian conquest of Central Asia, where he lost southern Kazakhstan in 1864. He was killed while defending Tashkent in 1865. Dr. Beisembiev rightly attributes his defeat to the abandonment of his cause by the Qipchaq and Kirghiz tribesmen. Major-General M. G. Cherniev conquered Tashkent approximately one month after his death. Ironically the sedentary factions defeated by Alimqul, namely Khudayar Khan, ruled the khanate until its annexation in 1876 after being installed by the Russians. "Desert Dogs" is a reference to nomadic peoples, namely Qipchaqs, originating from the Dast-i-Qipchaq, a desert area in Kazakhstan. See Beisembiev, *The Life of 'Alimqul*.

330. Ijma: This phrase draws upon the concept conveyed in Islamic theological reasoning—the concept of Ijma, or consensus, among religious scholars. "My ummah will never agree upon an error" is a hadith attributed to the Prophet Mohammad. The idea is that a group of the rightly guided cannot be in error if they arrive at a ruling through deliberation and consensus. In this passage we basically have the use of religion to justify violence against a community. See Bakhtiyar and Reinhart, *Encyclopaedia of Islamic Law*.

331. Kesish: Hajji uses the verb to categorically cut off, cross out, and condemn completely the Qipchaqs.

332. "Total annihilation of": Again the verb *kesish* is used in response to Hajji's question. The verb is used in the sense of carving meat or to condemn/sentence a person or persons.

333. Halq: People, nationality, population. Again, Qodiriy is presenting this as a people in their totality.

334. Beisembiev does provide evidence that Nur Mohammad was a controversial leader, especially in Qurama and as Hakim of Tashkent, and not especially liked. Nur Mohammad in the sources does show a tendency

to shift sides based upon the vicissitudes of conflict. Qodiriy here clearly makes him out to be a hero, perhaps for narrative purposes.

335. Russians: Following the timeline of the novel, we are still in 1852–1853 with the khanate of Qoqan and Tsarist imperial forces engaged in almost constant contact. Between 1844 and 1855, the initial steps in the formation of the Syr-Dariya Line that extended eastward from the Aral Sea along what is now southern Kazakhstan were undertaken. In 1847 a Captain Schultz built two military fortifications known as Raimsk and Kazaklinsk that combined into what was referred to as Aralsk. In 1852, Colonel Blaramburg attempted to take Oq Masjid, established by the Qoqan Khanate in 1817, but was turned back after Qoqan forces flooded the plain leading to their outpost. Finally, in 1853, Russian forces took Oq Masjid after dramatically increasing their forces—they renamed it Fort Perovsky. Soon afterward, in 1854, Vernoye was established and is now known as modern-day Alma Ata, the former capital of Kazakhstan.

Meanwhile a series of forts along the northern border of modern-day Kyrgyzstan were established that held strategic importance for future operations in that these fortifications enjoyed a constant water supply through irrigation canals. In 1859 Russian armies mobilized and marched southeast, taking the town of Julek in 1859 and then Yani Kurgan, Zhanakurgan, fifty miles south. In 1862 General Cherniev took Suzak and his counterpart Veryovkin took the spiritual center Hazrati Turkistan—the center of Yassawi Sufism, where Khawaja Ahmed Yassawi's remains are still interred. Both armies reconnoitered in the area between Hazrati Turkistan and Avliyo Ata to move on Tashkent after conquering Chimkent in 1864. Russian forces under the command of Cherniev arrived at Tashkent in 1864 but were pushed back on a couple of occasions—it was during this action that Alimqul was killed. See note above. Once Cherniev cut off Tashkent's water supply at Niazbek, mentioned earlier in this novel, the Qoqan Khanate appealed to Bukhara for assistance—but before reinforcements could arrive Cherniev stormed Tashkent through the Kamolan Gates, defeated an army of thirty thousand Qoqandian soldiers, and gained Tashkent.

It is interesting to note that the internal instability that wracked the khanate of Qoqan coincided with these events, thus following Qodiriy's main point that internal strife in Turkistan led to the inevitable conquest of Central Asia. See Seymour Becker, *Russia's Protectorates in Central Asia: Bukhara and Khiva, 1865–1924* (New York: Routledge, 2004), Chokan Chingisovich Valikhanov, *The Russians in Central Asia* (London: Edward Stanford,1865).

336. Vai: a common form of exclamation in Uzbek.

337. Chimmat: normally a horsehair screen held in a woman's hands in front of her face while the paranji sits on her head, usually in the shape of a robe covering the body.

338. Dua: Muslim prayer.

339. Guzar: a market.

340. Salar: waterway running through Tashkent.

341. Chukar Kishlok: Kazakh Aul outside Tashkent.

342. Buza or Boza resembles a light beer made with wheat.

343. Kaif: A drunkenness that is said to bring contentment and closeness with God. Kaif is often used in poetry to mean fulfilment and in terms of Sufistic love of God.

344. Ming O'rik: Literally a thousand apricots. A village near Tashkent—now southern Kazakhstan. Highly likely this referred to an orchard that grew apricots.

345. Qimiz: Fermented mare's milk produced by nomadic peoples. Qimiz is often produced in the springtime as that is the time nomadic peoples bring their livestock from mountain pastures to fatten them up for market. Qimiz takes on a subtle flavor from the grass the livestock feed on.

346. Kazak Tula: This scene shows the symbiosis felt between nomadic and sedentary peoples.

347. Shibli and Salar are both tributaries of the Syr-Dariya River.

348. Qigiz rug: Stamped wool felt rugs made by nomadic peoples. Known as the oldest rug-making method in the world.

349. Ghazal: A form of poetry received from the Arab lands in the twelfth century and associated with Sufi poetry and song. The Persians are mainly credited with creating a spectacular efflorescence of the form through famous poets such as Rumi, Hafez, and Fuzuli. The main theme of the form is loss and separation.

350. Surma: A herb ground into a paste and used for eye makeup. It is considered a sign of beauty to have a unibrow. One can find this marker in pictures of women ranging from the Caucasus to central and South Asia, Persia and the Middle East.

351. Binafshah: Violets.

352. The word for the massacre of the Qipchaqs derives from the verb qirgin, to slaughter, butcher, or massacre. Qodiriy depicts an actual historical event that was noted even among Western diplomatic circles, most notably by Eugene Schuyler, who traveled through the region on a diplomatic mission toward the end of the nineteenth century. Scott C. Levi, again, provides the best Western source for the events surrounding the massacre of the Qipchaqs within the Qoqan Khanate. Through largely Central Asian sources, Levi shows how the event described in the novel occurred over several months, with the loss of between five and twenty-

seven thousand Qipchaqs. Interestingly, Edward Dennis Sokol shows that trade with Russia increased from 10.3 million rubles between 1827 to 1837 to 15.7 million rubles between 1840 and 1850, the timeline captured in *O'tkan Kunlar*. From 1857 to 1867, the period of conquest, imports to Russia increased four times. These figures do not capture the full extent of trade with China, which prior to conquest represented the bulk of the Qoqan Khanate's trade. With shifts in demographics, as further explained below, commercial activities took on an existential importance to the various factions within the Khanate of Qoqan that were often driven by ethnic loyalties, e.g. there was real money to be gained through increased land holdings thus trade.

Perhaps no other passage in this novel makes the argument for the universality of *O'tkan Kunlar* better than chapter 3, *The Massacre of the Qipchaqs*. Hajji and Otabek go on to later argue not just a case for the people of Turkistan; their language holds a universality for humankind. Arbitrary arrests, bribes, kidnappings, and murder all permeate the novel, but the protest against the arbitrary extermination of a people based upon ethnic identity makes the case for a possible literary precedent for human rights in an Uzbek novel. See Levi, *The Rise and Fall of the Khoqand Khanate*. For Central Asian sources, see Beisembiev, *The Life of 'Alimqul*; Edward Dennis Sokol, *The Revolt of 1916 in Russian Central Asia* (Baltimore: Johns Hopkins University Press, 1954). Levi provides a more extensive bibliography of academic work surrounding the above event—many thanks for his scholarship.

353. Namozgah: Place of prayer. Namoz means prayer. -gah is derived from the Persian, place of. This means a locality near a mosque.

354. The right hand on the chest is a common form of greeting and deference showing respect towards others.

355. The sacred soil of Turkistan: Edward Dennis Sokol in *The Revolt of 1916 in Russian Central Asia* lays out a compelling argument regarding the elements that led to the unrest and revolt that represented a precursor to the Bolshevik Revolution. As Russian imperial control moved south from the Orenburg Line during the nineteenth century into what is now, roughly, northern Kazkhstan, nomadic lands began to be subjected to policies meant to rob tribal groups of fertile areas suitable for grazing. The tactic is a classic one not unlike those used by the United States toward their Native American population—sedentarization of nomadic peoples and redistribution of their land to settlers and government officials. The category used by Russian imperial administrators, who also personally benefitted greatly through this system, was "Surplus Lands." The Ministries of Agriculture and Foresty basically categorized any land capable of bearing agricultural or raw materials, such as lumber, as Surplus Lands with sparse regions awarded to nomadic peoples for subsistence. This left traditional native groups

bereft of grazing grounds and led to subsequent famine, among other tragedies.

As Tsarist influence moved farther south into what is now southern Kazakhstan, Kyrgyzstan, and Uzbekistan, Russian settlers who were also left bereft of land after the liberation of the serfs in 1863 were encouraged to settle in newly formed farming areas—as with Manifest Destiny, the newly established train system facilitated the movement of these peoples.

Settlers followed conquest. What began as largely skilled labor with major imbalances in standards of living and compensation turned into Russians with few skills escaping Russia for a better life—Tashkent was at one point known as the City of Bread—especially after the emancipation of the serfs. Russian settlers enjoyed greater rights such as gun ownership, access to more fertile farming lands, and favorable trade agreements. Under Governor General Von Kaufmann, Tashkent was divided into a Russian Tashkent and an Old Tashkent that largely housed lower classes with a predominant number of Uzbeks, Tajiks, and other Central Asian people. That stark dividing line between a European-styled Russian Tashkent and Isski Shahr was the Anhor Canal—essentially, Tashkent was segregated.

Wealthy Central Asians would live in Russian Tashkent based upon their influence in society and, notably, what role they played in assisting Tsarist administrators in controlling those who lived on the other side of the canal. In a sense, because the Jadids were multilingual, well traveled, and comprised one of the many groups of intellectuals in Turkistan before the revolution, they in fact played the role of interlocutors between European and Central Asian society. One common narrative of the Jadids espoused by those in Sokol's generation depicts them as a movement that opposed the atrophied, in their view, and corrupt Ulama. The reform minded Jadids proved to be a proper counterbalance to conservative religious institutions—to be played off one another. In recent years that debate has become much more nuanced.

It is widely understood by many Uzbeks interviewed in Uzbekistan that statements regarding the Russians in chapters 1 and 2 sealed the fate of Abdullah Qodiriy. The Jadid phenomena held a vast range of beliefs with their common nexus being societal reform—but what that meant varied among the movement's adherents. We can generally assert, however, that by and large Qodiriy—as with multitudes within the colonial world—feared that his culture or way of life would be subsumed by Russian rule. The hope was to borrow the best elements of the changing world yet resist Russian hegemony through modernization of their society, essentially one centered on Muslim legitimacy. Much has been debated over whether the Jadids were true believers in the Soviet dream and therefore atheists. We have very little in the way of individual Jadids' journals or records, since they were executed in 1938 and their extant writings are tightly controlled. This novel shows that that issue is far more complicated than previously assumed, at least in the case of

Qodiriy. Qodiriy here shows that he did not want to abandon his faith either to a corrupt Ulama or to Soviet cultural hegenomy. As with us all, he witnessed a changing world and sought to find his place in it while holding on to the core beliefs that made him who he was. In this novel we witness Qodiriy's spiritual landscape, with his hero traveling through a Turkistan destined for ruin. Through Otabek he attempts to rationalize his own current political discourse and societal reform. By 1925 national delimitation had already come to pass and the Bolsheviks, who ran similar reforms in tandem with the Jadids, began to alienate the Jadids from society. Hence the Jadids became increasingly disenchanted with Bolshevik promises of societal change, especially that of equality. Qodiriy shows what Adeeb Khalid has argued for in his corpus of work: that there was an increasing radicalization among the Jadids as they met resistance from society at large and betrayal by the Bolsheviks. The Soviets increasingly began to appear as nothing more than an extension of Tsarist rule and heavily biased toward ethnic Russian interests in Central Asia, hence the loss of purity in their sacred homeland. One wonders if Qodiriy was also drawing upon the many ecological issues at the time: the rise of a cotton mono-culture that plagues Uzbekistan today, the canal system robbing farmers of water, the loss of indigenous crops, the persistence of famine, etcetera. See Khalid, *Making Uzbekistan* and Sokol, *The Revolt of 1916 in Russian Central Asia*. For an excellent account of Tashkent during Qodiriy's period see Sahadeo, *Russian Colonial Society in Tashkent, 1865–1923*.

356. Tengri: The traditional pre-Islamic, shamanistic god of the sky to the Turkic peoples. This passage lends fascinating insight into Qodiriy's and the Jadids' worldview and historical orientation toward national identity. To Turkic nationalists, the Amu Dariya River, also known in the ancient world as the Oxus River, is the traditional dividing line between the Irani and the Turani peoples—the Shahnameh being a historical and literary artefact to this belief. The Iranian peoples inhabit areas south of the Amu Dariya and the Turani, or Turkic peoples, north of the Amu Dariya River in an area stretching from present-day Uzbekistan to Mongolia, to Xinjiang China, to Istanbul, Turkey. Tengri is often invoked to appeal to Turkic nationalists as a pre-Islamic faith system harkening back to the millennia before the arrival of Islam, largely through traveling Sufis who brought the new faith with them. Devin DeWeese in his *Islamization and Native Religion in the Golden Horde* discusses the process of Islamization the Golden Horde underwent to convert from shamanistic beliefs to Islam—e.g. the origin story where two faiths grafted onto each other, creating a new quality to Islam that accommodated old belief systems and vice-versa. The vestiges of Shamanism and Zoroastrianism are seen throughout Central Asia today, whether through the use of fire in local practices for weddings and fertility rituals, or the evidence of markers of Zoroastrianism in the brickwork at the necropolis of Chahar

Bakr, Sayyids with pre-Islamic Zoroastrian symbols on their tombs! Perhaps, Qodiriy wishes to show that the core of Central Asian identity is an amalgam of faiths in continual conversation with each other. See Devin DeWeese, *Islamization and Native Religion in the Golden Horde: Baba Tükles and Conversion to Islam in Historical and Epic Tradition* (University Park, PA: Penn State University Press, 1994). Notes from site visits 1994–2018.

357. Timur Kuragan: Present-day national hero of Uzbekistan, Amir Timur was a fifteenth-century conqueror who originated from the steppe area of Shahrisabz. In his lifetime he conquered the Ottoman Empire, pushed back from further conquest by the Mamluks into northern Eastern Europe to Sinjiang. Timur is the progenitor of the Timurid Empire, a group of Turkic rulers who were responsible for the efflorescence of science and art during the Renaissance period. The final stage of that family's epic was Babur's creation of the Mughul Empire in India.

In the Middle Ages, Al-Farobi, born in present-day Kazakhstan, was known as Alpharabius in the West and is a continuation of Aristotelian philosophy, ethics, and logic in the Islamic world. His work, sometimes breaking with Aristotelian and Platonic belief, created a synthesis between Sufism and philosophy. He is also known for his contributions to music therapy, cosmology, and mathematics.

358. Ibn Sina, or Avicenna, born north of Bukhara in 980, brought the Western world his *Canon on Medicine*, a standard medical text in European universities until 1650. He is also known for his work in the sciences, geography, Islamic theology, mathematics, and physics.

Mirza Ulughbek, or Mirza Mohammad Taraghay bin Shahrukh, was the grandson of Timur. His contribution to science was mainly in astronomy, where he built the Ulughbek observatory in Samarqand—the largest in the Islamic world at the time. His measurements were as accurate as those in Europe. He was a patron of the arts and architecture, and the Ulughbek Madrassa in present-day Registan is one of his greatest contributions.

Qodiriy in this passage is attempting to show the reader Central Asia's connection to the greater world and its profound contributions to human knowledge—emphasizing that history was not dead in the fifteenth century but alive and well during the twentieth century in the minds of Central Asians. This heritage stretches back centuries and further shows both Otabek and Hajji's, hence the author's, sense of loss of a tradition that deserves a great deal of pride. One of the common criticisms of the Jadids made by the Bolsheviks, leading to many of them being purged in 1938, was that they were covert monarchists. See the seven-volume UNESCO *History of Civilizations of Central Asia*—a massive accomplishment that spans the full scope of Central Asian history.

359. Qodiriy uses the term Sharq Otaligi to mean Oriental or Eastern father.

360. Children or Slaves of God: This usage means "obedience to God" but is also similar in meaning to "Fools of God," cited by Levin in *Hundred Thousand Fools of God*—those who demonstrate devotion to God through their acts leading to their complete abandonment of worldly concerns. In Levin's work we see a focus on Central Asian music, but there is a mystical quality as seen through Sufism that is vital to the understanding of the phrase. Common names throughout the Islamic world such as Abdallah; Abd, meaning slave; and illillah, meaning Allah, demonstrate such devotion.

361. Yusuf and Zulaikha: Quranic verse related to Yusuf, or the biblical Joseph, and Zulaikha, Potiphar's wife. Qodiriy shows the wonderful ecumenical nature of the Islamic world—a biblical story retold mainly in Persia and South Asia. Layla and Majnun is a thirteenth-century poem written by the Persian poet Nizami Ganjavi, who lived in present-day Azerbaijan.

362. "Zuri Behuda Miyon Shikanad": "Useless effort will only break your back." Again, Qodiriy reveals the multiple layers of language, socioeconomic background, religious affiliation, and cultural mores that make up an individual's identity. If we remember Adeeb Khalid, language was not a node of identity. Hajji being a member of the Ulama, the court, and a learned man would command a number of languages to draw upon in order to capture or articulate a moment in time. Many thanks to Ambassador John Limbert for polishing this phrase on behalf the translator and Yusufbek Hajji. See Adeeb Khalid, *Making Uzbekistan*.

363. Modernization and standardization of Uzbek and Tajik developed in tandem in the 1920s, with Sadriddin Ainiy being the father of Tajik literature and a Jadid. Just as *O'tkan Kunlar* is the author's attempt to standardize a new Uzbek prose and identity for a national enterprise, the same applies to the other Central Asian republics—Kazakh versus Khirghiz, Turkmen, etcetera. Ainiy produced a massive amount of literary work during his lifetime and lived primarily in Samarqand, moving to Dushanbe, the capitol of a new Tajik CCP, just before his death. Considering the entire multivalent cultural influences at play, the term *Tajik* prior to and during Qodiriy's lifetime referred to mountain Persianate peoples who inhabited the eastern end of the Bukharan Emirate or the southern part of the Qoqan Khanate, depending on the vicissitudes of history. As mentioned before, Marshall Hodgsen in *The Venture of Islam* sees the Ecumene within the Islamic lands as the Turco-Persian-Arab world. Turkic being the language of war or the steppes; Persian the language of administration, diplomacy, and literature; and Arabic the language of law. In the Bukharan court or in Turkistan, the court language spoken would have been referred to as Farscha or Farsi

with a strong Persian influence. The tendency to lump Persianate languages into one monolithic group is of course a mistake in that it robs the local languages of their distinct characteristics and cultural milieu. As with the rest of the postcolonial world at the time, Tajik went through a process of de-Turkification to arrive at a national dialect. Uzbek Oyim here is referring to quotes and aphorisms from the mountain Tajiks very much influential in the Qoqan Khanate at the time and not a courtly language used in government and intellectual circles. See Khalid, *Making Uzbekistan* and Allworth, *The Modern Uzbeks and Central Asia*.

364. Oyim Cha: Term of endearment, -cha being diminutive.

365. Otabek is making an allusion to his ability to perform intercourse either physically or emotionally. Either way he has opened the door for divorce, especially since they have not had a child during their first year of marriage. Laleh Bakhtiar, *Encyclopaedia of Islamic Law: A Compendium of the Major Schools* (Chicago: Kazi Publications, 1996).

366. Hashar: Neighborhood effort toward a common effort—e.g. house, garden, wedding, etcetera.

367. Qalmoqi: Thought to be a women's hat in the Qalmoq style.

368. Tandir: We know it as tandoor. A clay and brick oven

369. Varaki: dish with thinly layered bread and meat. Variants of the dish exist throughout Central Asia.

370. Perhaps meant as an interesting innuendo: wealthy men often held land outside the city, where they often maintained an additional wife. The reference here is from Vladimir and Maria Nalivkin, who offer a distinctly Russian, if not Orientalist at times, worldview, but they were deeply engaged in the Central Asian communities and hold great insight into the practices of the times—they were also contemporaries of and knew Abdullah Qodiriy. See Valdimir Nalivkin and Maria Nalivkina, translated by Mariana Markova and Marianne Ruth Kamp, *Muslim Women of the Ferghana Valley: A 19th-Century Ethnography from Central Asia* (Bloomington, IN: University of Indiana, 2017), for an interesting view of this practice.

371. Suyinchi is a gift for being a messenger of good news.

372. Qormana is a gift to see the newly wedded bride or a newborn, often paid by a patriarch.

373. When Central Asian women greet each other, they hold each other's forearms and exchange greetings and questions regarding each other's well being. If they are very close they will exchange kisses on the cheek. Greetings between the matriarchs is most common and a sign of seniority. Field notes.

374. Pasha Kilin: Daughter-in-law, with the Pasha added for regal standing by Uzbek Oyim.

375. Beg Oyim: Beg or Bek, literally meaning "noblemen." Beg Oyim is sort of an optative use of her name to show seniority.

376. See above for female greetings in Central Asian society.

377. Qochadigan xotinlar, "those women who need to run away." Umida Hashimova notes that in conservative places of Uzbekistan, women are still required to make haste, at times run, when confronted by a male not directly related to their family.

378. The directive in Islam that women cover themselves varies culture by culture around the globe. As mentioned previously, the Qoqan Khanate differed from the Emirate of Bukhara and the Emirate of Khiva through the profound influence nomadic groups held in the young court of Qoqan. The common practice today is for women in Ferghana to cover their hair with a scarf and wear a long robe that covers them from shoulders to ankles—with many variations depending on economic circumstances and locality. One must consider that life and culture will often bend religion to fit their needs. In Qoqan it is not uncommon to see women who are wearing Ruhmal, a scarf that covers their hair and head, use the tip of the scarf hanging loose to cover the lower half of their face by placing the loose end over their mouth to avoid exposure to strangers while engaged in labor or other activities that require two hands. The scene above shows the various efforts by the women in the group to maintain decorum, and a practical use of a scarf to maintain modesty by Oftob Oyim in front of Yusufbek Hajji.

379. Barakalar: God bless you all.

380. Taqabbul duo or prayer: An injunction placed at either the beginning or ending of a prayer. Often addressed to other supplicants for "God to hear our prayers." There seems to be some debate as to whether this is Bidah, or an innovation, not directly attributable to practices sanctioned by the Prophet Mohammad.

381. Oi Mullah: Central Asia has the wonderful tradition of Oi Mullahs—female mullahs who can lead women in prayer. Although it is unclear whether Karima is an Oi Mullah, it is customary for one to offer a dua, or prayer, during august occasions.

382. The junior wife, and daughter-in-law of the hostess, is responsible for observing etiquette with the dasturkhon or tablecloth.

383. Oling, Oling!: The common phrase when hosted in a Central Asian home, urging everyone to eat more.

384. Chimildiq: Bridal curtain leading to the bed where the marriage is consummated.

385. From the *Sahih Al-Bukhari*, book 19, hadith 30: Once the Prophet PBH was speaking to us when, a Bedouin came and asked him: "When will the Last Day be? The Messenger of Allah continued in his talk. Some of those present thought that he had heard him but disliked the interruption and the other said that he had not heard him. When the messenger of All concluded his speech he asked, "Where is the one who inquired about the Last Day?" The man replied: "Here I am." The messenger of Allah replied, "When the practice of honoring a trust is lost, expect the Last Day." He asked: "How could it be lost?" He replied, "When the government is entrusted to the under deserving people, then wait for the Last Day."

386. Domla: Teacher, wise person worthy of respect.

387. Yigit: A reference to a "Young Brave," or a person enlisted in the military.

388. Taravih: Additional prayer made during Ramadan.

389. Yusuf and Zulaikha: Islamic variant of Joseph and Potiphar's wife. In Central Asia this is most likely a reference to Jami's *Haft Awrang* or *The Seven Thrones*, written in the fifteenth century. Since Zulaikha attempted to seduce Yusuf, a double entendre exists here—namely is Karima Otin accusing Kumush of being a whore or a whore longing for another man?

390. Nisa: Name of Persian King Mehrdad, literally translated as "Joy" or "Cheerfulness." Again, with Turkic languages, there are a thousand variants to names. Because Kumush is being depicted as serious and more dour, the addition of "Nisa" is an attempt at gentle humor at her expense.

391. Quyuk-Suyuk: A more watery pilov-style dish with rice and mung beans.

392. Pustighul: Pink flower.

393. Shoes in street: Again, Uzbek Oyim uses colorful language to comic effect. It is customary to take off your shoes when entering a home or mosque. Noteworthy guests are often asked to take off their shoes in the entryway, which are then placed inside to keep them warm or closest to the door. Uzbek Oyim is basically saying that "I am not just any guest. My shoes are brought inside."

394. Kokildosh/Kokiltosh/Kukeldash Madrassa: Built near Tashkent's Chorsu bazaar in the sixteenth century under the Shaybanid rulers who deposed the Timurid Zadrridin Babur who subsequently fled to Afghanistan. The complex had many lives: Its bricks in the nineteenth century were used to build the Beklarbegi Madrassa, used as a caravanserai, a fortress. By the twentieth century, under Soviet rule, it was used as a museum to atheism. Currently the madrassa has been

restored and is part of a larger complex. Its location in Tashkent is not far from the Samarqand Gates where Qodiriy lived. Salihbek Akhund Dadwhah (1812–1868): a descendant of a long line of distinguished Ulama. Helped defend Tashkent against the Russians.

395. Bogirsoq: deep-fried tablespoon-size sour dough. Usually shaped roundly.

396. "Two feet into one shoe": In the context of the dialogue, Qutidor is admonishing Oftob Oyim for conspiring to change an agreement or making them unwelcome.

397. In Central Asian culture one should not sleep with their feet facing Mecca— the traditional placement of the body during burial.

398. Traditional wooden crib, very similar to Native American cribs worn on the backs of women. The baby is wrapped tightly in cloth then attached to a wooden platform. A Chimildan, depending on the gender, was then placed over the baby's genitalia so that it could urinate through the hollow wooden device, draining into a pot below. The Beshik was used in a world where women needed to work and move about without worrying their baby would injure themselves. The legend of the Oltin Beshik accounts for the ruling Khans of Qoqan's origins by tying their Ming tribes' recent origins to that of a child produced by Babur just before he fled to Afghanistan from the Uzbek Shaybanid tribal groups. By placing the khanate's origins many centuries in the past through what is basically the story of Moses set in a Central Asian milieu, credibility was given to their origins. See Scott C. Levi, "The Legend of the Golden Cradle: Babur's Legacy and Political Legitimacy in the Khoqand Khanate" in *The History of Central Asia in Modern Medieval Studies: In Memorium of Professor Roziya Mukminova*, ed. D. A. Alimova (Tashkent: Yangi Nashr, 2013), 102–108.

399. Dalil: Proof derived from reasoning through analogy. Generally used to determine proofs of legitimacy for various legal rulings. See Bakhtiyar and Reinhart, *Encyclopaedia of Islamic Law*.

400. November/ December, 1852–1853: Around the same time as Musulmanqul's execution above.

401. Suyinchi: It is proper for the recipient of glad tidings, usually the patriarch or matriarch who sits in waiting, to award the bearer of the news with a small financial gift.

402. Qodiriy was a gardener, so perhaps we see his fixation on flowers here, as well as a common motif in Central Asian literature.

403. Talak: According to Muslim custom, in order to divorce a wife or husband one must say out loud, "Divorce, divorce, divorce" in the presence of the spouse. In some variants the one initiating the divorce must walk around the spouse three times while saying aloud the words.

Earlier in the novel, Qodiriy mentions Mahr, or bride price. Mahr would then be the money allocated to the divorcee so she is not in dire straits. Talak has become somewhat of an issue in our world of technology where Central Asian migrant workers have used cell phone texts to divorce their wives. See Bakhtiyar and Reinhart, *Encyclopaedia of Islamic Law*. Cell phone talak: Field notes, Tajikistan, 2012.

404. It is incumbent to bury a Muslim within three days of death. Central Asian funerals for women stand out as unique within the Islamic world: male relatives carry a sort of litter covered in beautiful atlas robes and cloth sometimes owned by the deceased. The men openly weep and dry their eyes in full view of those attending prayer. Field notes, Qoqan, 1996.

405. Children in traditional households are often not named until after seven days in the belief that their soul is intact after that period. Children's names are often not revealed except among immediate family out of fear of the evil eye. Of course, jewelry to protect the child from the evil eye adorns the baby until they are able to walk.

406. Chinar trees are plane trees considered sacred in Central Asia and are often placed in places of worship or on sacred sites such as the grave of an especially revered individual. Chinar trees also have an association with Sufism.

407. 1248/1269: 1852/1853.

408. Qari: an individual who can recite the Koran from memory.

409. 1860/1861: See timeline above for the Russians. Four to five years before the conquest of Tashkent.

410. Qana'atshah: Although his name is not mentioned earlier in the novel, as governor of the southern Kazakh city of Turkistan—Turkistan being the spiritual soul of the Turkic peoples and home of the Yasavi Sufi order—he was a key player in resistance against Azizbek Parvanchi who led the Tashkent rebellion under Qipchaq patronage. He held numerous positions in both the Qoqan Khanate and the Bukharan Emirate until 1860 when he took control of Qoqan's armies as Amir Lashkar and fought the battle of Uzun Agach against the Russians, subsequently leading resistance to Russian forces around Yangi Qurghan and Turkistan. He died after Khudayar Khan's second reign as ambassador to Bukhara in 1862. See Beisembiev, *The Life of 'Alimqul*.

411. Alma Ata / Almaty: Alma Ata / Ati was the capital of Kazakhstan until the establishment of Astana—now Nur Sultan—as the Kazakh capital. Present-day southern Kazakhstan was hotly contested by the Qoqan Khanate against Russian advances. Avlioyo Ata is outside of Alma Ata, with Azun Agach west of Almaty.

412. Shahid: Martyr for Islam.

413. If one takes a moment to consider, the novel begins with the *Azan*, or call to prayer, in the opening chapter, *Otabek, Son of Yusufbek Hajji*. The Azan is also recited upon the birth of a child. The young soul's family and loved ones celebrate the arrival of their charge and the trust Allah has bestowed upon the family for his or her care. The *Salat al-Janazah* is recited during muslim burial, in this case for Otabek. Thus, as with the life of a devout muslim, the novel begins with the recitation of life to be concluded with the prayer for the dead. Perhaps then, *O'tkan Kunlar* represents a life cycle of a Central Asia doomed to conquest.

414. Famine: Qodiriy's note to the reader brings the novel's timeline full circle, forming a testimony to his own present period. It is hard to narrow down which famine to wrack Central Asia Qodiriy is referring to—famine was a constant threat throughout his life—but we can safely place the moment he cites as around 1919–1922 during the Russian Civil War. The famines during his lifetime were largely due to mismanagement of an increasingly water-dependent cotton economy during collectivization where "white gold" replaced food crops. The newly created Kazakh CCP witnessed a massive famine that led to the sedentarization of the formerly nomadic peoples in 1930–1933. The Uzbek CCP was the only Central Asian republic to have the capacity to produce enough food to feed its own population, but with collectivization, a radical reordering of Central Asian society took place. Even garden patches meant for a farmer's family were lost to the large Soviet-style farms. Famine had a profound effect on the makeup of Central Asian society. Most notably, the sanctity of bread is still paramount. An Uzbek does not throw out bread or wipe the crumbs off a dasturkhon or even throw out old bread, but rather they will place the crumbs and bread scraps on a windowsill for birds to eat, or feed them to the chickens. One never cuts bread, but rather tears it off and passes the pieces to those sitting at the table. For a recent publication on famine in Kazakhstan, see Sarah Cameron, *The Hungry Steppe Famine, Violence, and the Making of Soviet Kazakhstan* (Ithaca, NY: Cornell University Press, 2018).

415. The sons of Yodgorbek: Qodiriy leaves us with an interesting note reflecting on the fate of the two sons of Yodgorbek. The first son was involved in "Ma'sul Ish," which could mean an administrator or just important work of some unknown nature. Some take the phrase to mean "activist" engaged in political activity. Others take it to mean simply someone engaged in important work. The second son became a Basmachi, a resistance fighter in the Ferghana valley. There was not one Basmachi movement but dozens throughout present-day Uzbekistan and Tajikistan during that period, all with different interests but united in their resistance to Russian rule. Enver Pasha even lent a hand to the Basmachi, dying in present-day Tajikistan. The movements lasted well into the late 1920s and 1930s, finally meeting their ends with Stalin and

the outbreak of World War Two. The Russians used the term *Basmachi* in Afghanistan during their occupation from 1979 to 1989.

In this passage Qodiriy arrives full circle from his original address to the reader in volume 1. Thus, his audience becomes a part not just of his experiment of bringing the innovation of the novel to Central Asian readerships, but also of his recounting of the origins of his peoples' memory and loss. The simple act of the reader bearing witness as an objective observer throughout the narrative testifies to Qodiriy's stark warning for their future, but is also testimony to their own survival. By recounting to others the moment before their fall, and its reimagining in the 1920s, he gives a stark warning but also a message of hope. The novel was reissued in 1933 in a heavily redacted version that was quickly repressed. After Khrushchev's thaw, the book was again reissued in 1958 in an almost unrecognizable form, but Uzbeks still celebrated its release— it was theirs, after all. One could say that the reissue of Qodiriy's novel in post-Indepedendence Uzbekistan in an unredacted edition fulfilled Qodiriy's dream—of an Uzbek state ruled on Uzbek terms. His novel remains a guidepost for everyone from the literary-minded to the current President Shavkat Mirziyoyev, and for his attempted reforms. He has even referenced Kundoshlik in some of his speeches!

Qodiriy's story is a painful one. His purge in 1938 was meant to rob a people of their dignity by taking the best and brightest of Turkistan as a constant reminder: You are second class. We define your story, your narrative, your heroes. We will decide what language you will use if and when you are allowed to speak of what we want you to speak. We will decide the songs you sing.

I would argue that since independence, when Uzbeks write odes to Amir Timur, remind us of the importance of Ulughbek, or read passages of the *Baburnama*, they are in fact remembering those who died attempting to remember the names of their forebears. They are, as Whitman wrote, *"Singing a Song of Myself."* Qodiriy's generation, not just the Jadids, fought a desperate battle to define themselves on their own terms. His ideas are controversial and at times inconvenient. Many have noted how his concerns hold relevance today, not just in Uzbekistan but around the world for those interested in justice and reform.

So, perhaps, dear reader, we not only have the origin story of the Uzbek people in our hands; we now have another link to the human condition from a people geographically distant but spiritually close to our own hearts.

BIBLIOGRAPHY

Munis Khorezmii, Muhammad Riza Mirab Agahi, et al., translated by Yuri Bregel, *Firdaws Al-Iqbal: History of Khorezm* (Islamic History & Civilization) (Brill Academic Pub; annotated edition, (September 1, 1999)

Dr. O. Turan, *Oniki Hayvanhli Turk Takvimi* (Dil ve Tarih Cografya Fakultesi Yayinlarindan, Tarikh Serisi, No.3)

Hélène Carrère d'Encausse, *Islam and the Russian Empire: Reform and Revolution in Central Asia* (New York: I. B. Tauris, 2009)

Zaddridin Babur, translated by Thackston Wheeler, *The Baburnama: Memoirs of Babur, Prince and Emperor* (New York: Modern Library Classics, 2002)

Edward Allworth, *Central Asia: 130 Years of Russian Dominance — A Historical Overview*, 3rd ed. (Durham, NC: Duke University Press, 1999)

Jeff Eden, "Slavery in Islamic Central Asia," *Oxford Research Encyclopaedia of Asian History* (May 2019)

Adeeb Khalid, *Making Uzbekistan: Nation, Empire, and Revolution in the Early USSR* (Ithaca, NY: Cornell University Press, 2016)

J. Newby, *The Empire and the Khanate: A Political History of Qing Relations with Khoqand c. 1760–1860* (Leiden, Netherlands: Brill Publishers, 2005)

Shodman Vohidov and Rahbar Khalikova's work on Khulosat Ul-Akhval or "Circumstances of Life" by Abu Ubaidullah Tashkenti in Moziydan Sado, 2009 2.42. Text taken from the Institute of Oriental Studies, Academy of Sciences, no 2084

Adeeb Khalid, *The Politics of Muslim Cultural Reform, Jadidism in Central Asia* (Berkeley: University of California Press, 1998)

Scott C. Levi, *The Rise and Fall of Khoqand, 1709–1876: Central Asia in the Global Age* (Pittsburgh: University of Pittsburgh Press, 2017)

Susanna S. Nettleton, "Ruler, Patron, Poet: 'Umar Khan and the Blossoming of the Khanate of Qoqan, 1800–1820," *International Journal of Turkish Studies 2*, no. 2 (1981–1982): 127–140

Timur K. Beisembiev, ed. and trans., *The Life of 'Alimqul: A Native Chronicle of Nineteenth Century Central Asia* (New York: Routledge, 2003).

Paul Georg Geiss, *Pre-Tsarist and Tsarist Central Asia* (London: Routledge, 2003): 44–45

Elizabeth E. Bacon, *Central Asians under Russian Rule: A Study in Culture Change* (Ithaca, NY: Cornell University Press, 1966)

Habibullah Qodiriy, *Otamdan Hotira* (Tashkent: 2005) (In Uzbek)

Shohrukhbek Umarov, *Khudayar Khan Avolodlari Tarikhi* (Tashkent: 2011) (In Uzbek)

Mikhail Volodarsky, *The Soviet Union and Its Southern Neighbors: Iran and Afghanistan 1917–1933* (New York: Routledge, 1994)

Waseem Raja, *Modernisation, Regression and Resistance: Amir Amanullah Khan's Afghanistan* (Saarbrücken, Germany: LAMBERT Academic Publishing, 2011)

Paolo Sartori, *Moving Beyond Modernism: Rethinking Cultural Change in Muslim Eurasia (19th-20th Centuries), Journal of the Economic and Social History of the Orient 59/1-2* (2016)

Devin DeWeese, *It was a Dark and Stagnant Night ('til the Jadids Brought the Light): Clichés, Biases, and False Dichotomies in the Intellectual History of Central Asia, Journal of the Economic and Social History of the Orient 59/1-2* (2016)

R. N. Frye, *Bukhara: The Medieval Achievement* (Norman, OK: University of Oklahoma Press, 1965)

History of Civilisations of Central Asia, vol. 5 (UNESCO Publishing, 2003)

Edward A. Allworth, *Evading Reality: The Devices of 'Abdalrauf Fitrat, Modern Central Asian Reformist* (Boston: Brill, 2002)

Denis Sokol, *The Revolt of 1916 in Russian Central Asia* (Baltimore: The Johns Hopkins Press, 1954), Edward A. Allworth, *The Personal History of a Bukharan Intellectual: The Diary of Muhammad Sharif-I Sadr-I Ziya* (Boston: Brill, 2003)

Jeff Sahadeo, *Russian Colonial Society in Tashkent, 1865–1923* (Bloomington, IN: Indiana University Press, 2007)

Adrienne Lynn Edgar, *Tribal Nation: The Making of Soviet Turkmenistan* (Princeton, NJ: Princeton University Press, 2006)

Stephen Dale, *The Gardens of the Eight Paradises: Babur and the Culture of Empire in Central Asia, Afghanistan and India* (Boston: Brill, 2004)

Edward A. Allworth, *Uzbek Literary Politics* (London: Mouton and Co., 1964)

Edward A. Allworth, *The Modern Uzbeks* (Stanford, CA: Hoover Institution Press, 1990).

Daniel Brower, *Turkestan and the Fate of the Russian Empire* (New York: Routledge, 2003), Theodore Levin, *Hundred Thousand Fools of God: The Musical Travels in Central Asia (and Queens New York)* (Bloomington, IN: Indiana University Press, 1999)

Walter G. Andrews and Memet Kalpakli, *The Age of the Beloveds: Love and the Beloved in Early-Modern Ottoman and European Culture and Society* (Durham, NC: Duke University Press, 2005)

Laleh Bakhtiyar and Kevin Reinhart, *Encyclopaedia of Islamic Law: A Compendium of the Major Schools* (Chicago: ABC International Group, 1996)

Marianne Kamp, *The New Woman in Uzbekistan* (Jackson School Publications in International Studies, University of Washington, Seattle,2006)

Gregory J. Massell, *The Surrogate Proletariat* (Princeton University Press, Princeton, 1974)

Shoshana Keller, *To Moscow, Not Mecca* (Praeger, Westport, London, 2001)

Dr. Баходир Карим «Ўткан кунлар»га кайтиб...Чоп этилган07.02.2016МуаллифZiyouz.uz

Edward A. Allworth, *The Personal History of a Bukharan Intellectual* (Boston: Brill, 2003)

Zahriddin Muhmmad Babur, trans. by W. M. Thackston, *The Baburnama* (New York: Modern Library, 2002)

Bernard Lewis, *Music of a Distant Drum* (Princeton, NJ: Princeton University Press, 2002)

Scott Levi, *Caravans: Indian Merchants on the Silk Road* (New York: Penguin / Allen Lane, 2015) and Scott C. Levi, *The Indian Diaspora in Central Asia and Its Trade, 1550–1900* (Boston: Brill, 2002)

Scott C. Levi and Ron Sela, *Islamic Central Asia: An Anthology of Historical Sources* (Bloomington, IN: Indiana University Press, 2009)

Marshall Hodgsen, *The Venture of Islam: Conscience and History in a World Civilisation* (Chicago: University of Chicago Press, 1974)

Scott Levi, *The Rise and Fall of the Khoqand Khanate, Central Asia in the Global Age, 1709–1876* (Pittsburgh, PA: University of Pittsburgh Press, 2017)

Annemarie Schimmel, *The Mystical Aspects of Islam* (Chapel Hill: The University of North Carolina Press, 2011)

R. D. McChesney, *Waqf in Central Asia: Four Hundred Years in the History of a Muslim Shrine, 1480–1889* (Princeton, NJ: Princeton University Press, 2016)

Jo Ann Gross, Asam Urunbaev, *The Letters of Khwajah 'Ubayd Allah Ahrar and His Associates* (Boston: Brill, 2002)

Sarah Cameron, *The Hungry Steppe Famine, Violence, and the Making of Soviet Kazakhstan* (Ithaca, NY: Cornell University Press, 2018)

Scott C. Levi, "The Legend of the Golden Cradle: Babur's Legacy and Political Legitimacy in the Khoqand Khanate" in *The History of Central Asia in Modern Medieval Studies: In Memoriam of Professor Roziya Mukminova*, ed. D. A. Alimova (Tashkent: Yangi Nashr, 2013), 102–108

Devin DeWeese, *Islamisation and Native Religion in the Golden Horde: Baba Tükles and Conversion to Islam in Historical and Epic Tradition* (University Park, PA: Penn State University Press, 1994)

Edward Dennis Sokol, *The Revolt of 1916 in Russian Central Asia* (Baltimore: Johns Hopkins University Press, 1954)

Seymour Becker, *Russia's Protectorates in Central Asia: Bukhara and Khiva, 1865–1924* (New York: Routledge, 2004)

Chokan Chingisovich Valikhanov, *The Russians in Central Asia* (London: Edward Stanford,1865)

Stephane Dudoignon, *Intellectuals in the Modern Islamic World: Transmission, Transformation, and Communication* (New York: Routledge, 2006)

Eran Tasar, *Soviet and Muslim: The Institutionalisation of Islam in Central Asia* (New York: Oxford University Press, 2017)

Paulo Sartori, *Visions of Justice: Shariyat and Cultural Change in Russian Central Asia* (Boston: Brill, 2016)

Robert Crews, *For Prophet and Tsar: Islam and Empire in Russia and Central Asia* (Cambridge, MA: Harvard University Press, 2009)

Mariana Markova and Marianne Ruth Kamp, *Muslim Women of the Ferghana Valley: A 19th-Century Ethnography from Central Asia* (Bloomington, IN: University of Indiana, 2017)

Joseph Schact, *The Origins of Muhammadan Jurisprudence* (ACLS Humanities E-Book, 2011)

Abulqasem Ferdowsi, Dick Davis translator, *Shahnameh: The Persian Book of Kings* (Penguin Classics, 2016)

REFERENCE MATERIALS

Z. M. M'arufov, *Uzbek Tilining Ihlosli Lugati* (Moscow, 1981).

Karl A. Kripps, *Uzbek-English Dictionary* (Kensington, MD: Dunwoody Press, 1996)

Allen J. Frank, Jahangir Mamatov, *Dictionary Of Central Asian Islamic Terms* (Kensington, MD: Dunwoody Press, 2002)

Jahangir Mamatov, Michael Horlick, Karamat Kadirova, *Comprehensive Uzbek-English Dictionary* (Kensington, MD: Dunwoody Press, 2011)

SPECIAL THANKS FOR CONTRIBUTIONS

Amaki, Edward Eugene Ricord
Robert Buzan
Berna Diehl
Steven Wrage
Gulnara Ikramova
Bekhzod Khoshimkhujaev
Alexandria Laureys
Robert Buzan
Oybek Botirov
Kent Kuhler
Ibrokhim Karimov
Shokhista Ismailova
Ikromjon Tuhtasunov
Lutfulla Yuldoshev
Azam Kamalov
Abduvosit Ismonov
"GH"
Sevara Nurboeva
Shahrom Rustamov
Nigina O
Farhod Yuldashev
Feruza Ashirova
Humoyunmirzo Abdujabbarov
Botijon Shermatov
Mirakmal Niyazmatov
Nodir Zakirov
Roza Safarova
Nuzkat Islam
Miraziz Zahidov
Umida Khikmatillaeva

Jennifer Murtazashvilli
Daniel Glenn
Jaime
Hamid Ismailov
Asrorbek Toshev
Marianne Kamp
Alexander Morrison
Azamat Tashev
Elzara Turakulova
Sardor Umarov
Shelley Fairweather Vega
Gulnoza
Alikhon Kadirov
Marina Abrams
Sarvar Muminov
Ibragim Atajanov
Johnsie Donaldson
Liubov Kotkova
Otabek Halilov
Ruth
Alon Ja
Katie Putz
Gulnara Rajabova
Mamur
David Hunsicker
Phillip Potocki

www.ingramcontent.com/pod-product-compliance
Lightning Source LLC
Chambersburg PA
CBHW030539020726
47494CB00005B/1434